GW00374175

FORTUNE

FORTUNE

RITCHIE SMITH

Barrie & Jenkins
London

First published in 1990 by
Barrie & Jenkins Ltd, 20 Vauxhall Bridge Road,
London SW1V 2SA

British Library Cataloguing in Publication Data
Smith, Ritchie
Fortune.
I. Title
823'.914 [F]

ISBN: 0–7126–2103–2

Typeset by Selectmove Ltd, London

Printed in Great Britain by
Butler & Tanner Ltd, Frome and London

This book is dedicated to
Barbara Anne Smith,
Henry Smith,
and to the memory of my mother,
Alice Smith (1927–1983).

Prologue:
New York. April, 1954.

The Stantons had come to conquer America.

Everything was possible here. The stock market had been rising for a decade, and now nobody believed it would ever stop. Ideas were turned into fortunes almost overnight. Some mornings both brothers had woken up, almost drunk on money and the endless possibilities of money. . .

Then it all began to go wrong.

Outside, among the crowds of Fifth Avenue, Edward Stanton went up to the second black Cadillac, the one carrying the two boys. Hugh, his own son, was dark, and older than his brother's blond boy. He saw Alex wind down the window.

"Remember, you are both Stantons. In public, never show weakness. If you fight to the finish and still lose, do so without complaint. That is the code men live by. It is my code, too." Then he spoke to the uniformed driver. "Follow when we go."

"Sir."

His wife stepped down elegantly from the hotel entrance. He went to open the first car's door himself, waiting till she was seated inside before he climbed in too, swivelling around with one hand on the spacious back seat. Lady Grace Stanton smiled at him. "You're worried? You expect to – lose?"

"It's my brother's big day today, yes." Edward grunted, settling into the creaking upholstery that smelled of new leather. His expression was momentarily grim. "But I am still the chairman of Stanton Industries."

His wife was tall and angular, with an impressive aristocratic poise, and he noticed she was wearing the grey Dior dress, which matched

1

the pearls that glistened around her throat, pearls looted by a previous buccaneering Stanton from eighteenth-century Ceylon.

"We're going straight to Long Island?" Grace asked.

Edward Stanton nodded, then opened the sliding partition and spoke curtly to the driver. "Take Queensboro Bridge and then follow Queens Boulevard into Long Island. The naval airfield, as planned." The US Navy owed the Stantons some favours, he recalled with satisfaction.

"I don't follow business matters too closely, Edward, but if this flight succeeds – ?"

He slammed the partition shut. Michael Stanton's plane was supposed to break records and land at three, Eastern Seaboard Time – five hours behind the time the clocks of London would be showing. Edward closed his eyes. Michael would walk down the red carpet to a champagne reception, worldwide publicity, and, inevitably, into the leading position in the family firm. He would make Wall Street take notice.

"Then my brother wins everything. I could not hope to hold the Board of Directors, or keep the family and the trustees behind me. A passenger jet crossing the Atlantic faster than sound? It has never been done before . . . and I opposed him. So Stanton Industries will become international, and my position is lost."

"But it was your life. *Is* your life."

Edward spoke with dignity, as he had spoken to the two boys. "It would all be lost."

His wife's voice was unsteady. "I don't want that to happen. Alex would inherit, not Hugh. You must speak to someone."

He shrugged, still not quite knowing what to do, then turned his shoulders from her. Edward Stanton had inherited all the family traits, including courage, had proved it on D-Day morning, though there was more to the centuries-old family business than mere bravery. Profit was as much king now, when the product was the Mach-2 jet, as it had been when the family made steel swords and musket-balls at the time of the Armada.

In 1945, their father had gone missing in the Far East, leaving no obvious successor designate. Family tradition and the legal instruments of inheritance said that the eldest son inherited – Edward. But their father sometimes respected change more than tradition. Edward had never been sure he was the favoured son, and his wife knew it. Even before his father was officially presumed dead,

Edward's wife had made sure the inheritance came to him: she had burned her father-in-law's private papers, which only she and the two heirs knew about, the secret diaries and correspondence, something which looked like notes for a will. And so Edward Stanton was summoned back from his regiment in Normandy and made king of the family firm: shipyards on three great rivers, endless factories, a web of contacts across all the world.

He stared sullenly at the passing crowd. The old doubts had always kept recurring. He had never asked Grace if she had read the old man's papers. He continued to stare from the window until he heard radio jazz, bright and brassy from another car, suddenly overwhelm the rush-hour sounds. Hating my own brother. Is there anything worse?

Fearing him . . .

On the long ride out of New York City his mind went over the past, knowing that today there had to be a final solution to the problem of the succession. There could only ever be one man at the top of Stanton Industries, and he intended to be that man.

But what if Michael was right? Michael, with his charm and energy; Michael, wanting to turn the world upside-down before he rebuilt it; Michael, the qualified pilot. Michael, with Stacey, his wonderful American wife . . .

Long Island was full of graveyards. Even the spring sunshine could not make them cheerful. He looked behind as the Cadillac rocked on and saw the face of his brother's child. Edward Stanton was suddenly very afraid.

Grace uncrossed her legs and turned to him, scowling. "Michael doesn't have your loyalty."

He was adjusting his regimental tie and managed to keep all expression from his face. "Perhaps not."

"You must think of your brother – and his wife – as your enemy." Her voice was icy.

Something twisted in Edward, like a knife. "You can't mean that."

Grace put a hand on his shoulder. He touched it, rubbed the gold of her wedding band. "Edward, his ideas might be good for the company, but they're bad for you. We've earned the right to relax. Why should we change things just to please his mad notions? Look at this plane he's spent millions on, in spite of you opposing it."

"He has been proved right before. That fighter, for instance, the STA-1 that came from Donald Pike's drawing board."

3

"But what does he foresee with this 'STA-C'? Businessmen commuting across the Atlantic? Millions of ordinary people, working people if you please, flying off to the sunshine?"

"Perhaps he's right."

Grace smoothed a fingertip against his taut cheek, mothering him for a moment. "You're afraid he is right, aren't you? But doesn't that make it even more important to stop him?"

"You'll just have to trust me, Grace. I am a Stanton, don't you know."

Now there were fewer buildings. Trees, green fields, the original America. It was suddenly spring here, warm and glorious and blue. He looked around. He was abruptly certain that today, St George's Day, would go well.

The two limousines had to stop at the gates to Long Island Field. News photographers and reporters crowded around the family party: the Stanton airliner not only flew at almost twice the speed of sound, breaking all records for commercial flight, but there were also rumours that the British and American governments were secretly considering the use of its superb Stanton engines in nuclear bombers – and if that deal went through, it would be one of the largest military purchases of all time.

Edward wound down the window. "Let us past, please!"

Flashbulbs dazzled him. "Your brother flying it himself?"

"He's a qualified pilot," Edward said, flinching back.

"The record for the fastest ever crossing of the Atlantic!"

"And the first time it's been done faster than sound."

"If we succeed," Edward said.

"'We'?" There was a spasm of laughter. Michael and his wife were very popular with the press. "Is it true Michael Stanton leads a faction on the Stanton Industries Board of Directors – and that you're losing out to him?"

Edward flushed, hoping the boys could not hear. "There are no factions in our family. Michael is my younger brother and head of the Aviation Division, no more."

"But he's opposed to your traditionalist business methods? He says you're old-fashioned and are letting down the firm? He said when he left London 'I want to restore the old glory of this company and this nation' – comment?"

"Will he take Stanton Industries away from you?"

4

Edward raised his eyes to the sky-blue heaven. The cars swept onwards.

Inside the glass-galleried main terminal building, he found an excellent audience. His brother's staff pointed everybody out. Two US Senators, their father's old friend and link to to the new President, Eisenhower, as well as a young man from Massachusetts with a long Irish name Edward didn't quite catch. Edward shook hands quickly.

"Perhaps we can talk later, Senator – ?"

"Kennedy. I hope so. I'm a good friend of your brother's."

The line of guests was already forming. Five airline vice-presidents to whom he was especially warm; seven other international airlines were also represented.

The French Ambassador was next, and Edward managed a few colloquial phrases before turning to the Minister from 11 Downing Street. Grace stood by his side, equally charming, and he had the exultant sense that Michael, surely, could not match this moment.

Last, as press photographers snapped away, came the high brass from the Pentagon, familiar, uniformed men with stars and famous war records. One air force man paused to whisper. "I hope your brother'll keep us informed about your STA-C fighter. It sounds like the business."

Edward smiled his assurances at the Strategic Air Command general. SI's Aviation designer Donald Pike was a weak and rather unscrupulous character, with debts, but he was also clever; and Edward Stanton liked a man he could dominate.

Then the receiving line disbanded, and Edward could cast an eye over the glass-walled room, at tables with a cold buffet, and waiters in white in attendance.

He took Grace's hand and they stepped onto the open viewing gallery. The sea glinted to the east of them. He inhaled deeply and was pleased to taste the Atlantic's salt.

Then there was a voice behind him. "You tried to stop your brother making a success of his plane, didn't you?"

Edward turned around briskly, confronting a medium-tall man with a military bearing: Senator Davidson, one of Eisenhower's aides during the Normandy landings and the thrust for the Rhine.

He realized that the other man wanted this to be Michael's triumph. He smiled silkily. "In England, our family quarrels are private."

5

The Senator took a coin out of his pocket and idly tossed it in the air. "You may not have noticed the motto on our coinage," he said drily. "*E pluribus unum* . . . Out of the many, we have created one. I was in England in the twenties, you know, a Rhodes Scholar. Your country struck me as being too divided within itself to stand; it's a kind of ongoing family quarrel, isn't it?"

"Family quarrel? I hope that remark is not too pointed, Senator."

"Oh, surely you admit that England is a little like Stanton Industries?" Davidson chuckled, and people had noticed.

"*What the hell do you mean?* That my brother and I can't work together –?" Edward Stanton managed to restrain himself before the notorious family rage could erupt from him, too. He saw the little podium with the microphones at the other end of the crowded room. Michael would give his victory speech from there. Waiters drifted about, offering plates of canapés and more wine. Everybody was smiling. Hugh stood with his back to the wall, arms folded and face polite. Young Alex was examining a massive press camera a newsman, grinning, had handed over. My family, Edward thought. He took no comfort from them. Alex's mother, Stacey, had decided to fly with her husband today which was just as well: he always found her presence disturbing. He turned his back, glad to be outside, in the open. There was a joke going around that Michael's plane was called *Stacey*, after his wife. It was a typical touch.

The voice of air traffic control came booming over the public address speakers.

"The Stanton STA-C is approaching the Long Island coastline and should be appearing in the north-eastern sector of the sky within three to four minutes."

Lady Grace came to stand at his side, a sweet expression on her face and acid in her whisper. "You should have done for your brother years ago."

Edward remained unperturbed, though the news inwardly shocked him. So his brother had made it happen, in spite of everything. There was a mass movement outside on to the balcony overlooking the criss-crossed tarmac runways.

Everybody looked up, so he did too, aware of people pulling binoculars out of shoulder-slung cases and twisting telephoto lenses on expensive cameras. All quarrels and all ambitions had been set aside for this tense moment. Edward, also, searched heaven.

6

There were some feathers of cirrus, over twenty thousand feet high, but nothing moved in that hot blue glare.

"– be visible now in its descent towards us and will begin reducing speed for its landing –"

He saw it. Fast, quicksilvery, high over the sea. It seemed to be heading in much too fast to make a safe landing and there was a murmur of disquiet around him. The STA-C hurtled towards them, terrifyingly, swelling up in the sky.

Edward managed to give a broad smile. "It's perfectly all right! Stand by for a high speed pass over our heads!"

"Doesn't your brother fly?" Senator Kennedy pointed. "I guess he'll –"

Then the huge sleek-winged plane, breaking through the sound barrier and still travelling at Mach-1.5, twisted left.

Wreckage peeled away from one wing. At that speed air has the resistance of something solid; instantly, the airliner broke up into flying fragments . . .

Edward's head jerked back. There was a momentary flash of fire, then a mile-long crooked smear of black smoke. He saw debris begin to flail across the sandy shoreline, the airfield and then all around them.

It was only then that he heard anything – a delayed, earth-shaking boom of tortured air, a sonic boom, followed by the sounds of the disaster itself. It made him think that God was tearing a hole through the sky.

After echoes and re-echoes had rolled away to disturb the unwary several miles off, the silence held sway completely. Each second became an age, and the still air was an oppressive weight.

I don't believe it, Edward thought. The last of the wreckage was still tumbling down. It can't have happened like *this*.

But it had.

He went over quickly to Michael's son, beating the press by a whisker. Alex Stanton was quivering, fists clenched, shifting from foot to foot. He looked devastated and vulnerable. Scalpel-sharp, guilt cut into Edward Stanton, and he put his arms around the boy's shoulders. He had to do something for the boy, say something. He spoke to the bowed, blond head of Michael's son.

"Remember, Alex, you'll always have a family, and that counts more than anything."

7

When Alex looked up there were tears running down his face. "Why wasn't it different? It should have been different!"

Edward stepped back, so powerful was the boy's anguish. He was perspiring as he summoned Lady Grace to take the two boys back to the city.

Then he helped take charge of the disaster, but there were no survivors. None. Of course, that had been clear from the first moment.

It was evening before his own Cadillac left, and he told the driver to take it slowly.

Now, without competition, he could take his wife's advice and relax. But it proved time-consuming to examine his feelings about his brother's death. He sat in the car for a long time when his driver finally parked, staring over the open water at the lit-up ships heading in for the piers along the Hudson. Even a rigorous search had not yet found a body. It was as if, except in memory, Michael Stanton had never been.

Edward got out, and walked to the nearest streetlight. It had all gone well today. Quick, efficient, clean. He had given Donald Pike strict and secret instructions, and he had interfered with Michael's management almost on a daily basis, too – as much as he dared. There had only been one problem. Edward pulled a sheet of paper from an inside pocket. It had been folded and unfolded so many times that it was worn. He had carried it around for weeks, after he had sacked Carrack, the young flight engineer who had written it. Hardly looking at the typed text, he mouthed the words of his own brother's death-warrant, remembering how easy it had been to prey on his chief aviation designer's weaknesses.

". . . producing stresses in the air frame of our 'STA-C' that are cumulative, and after a long flight beyond the speed of sound these stresses may provoke a major component failure; this would lead inevitably to disaster."

Edward Stanton tore the paper into tiny fragments and scattered them over the green, slopping water below – that seemed appropriate. The wind touched his brow with cooling fingers.

From now on, there would only be one head of the family. Stanton Industries would not be changed, and he would be supreme inside it; and after him, Hugh would inherit, with Alex as a subordinate. He would allow nobody to threaten that.

8

Edward found himself breathing heavily, and he was still perspiring. It had all been a terrible strain, and he was not done yet. He looked into his soul. He had saved Stanton Industries from Michael's wild ambitions, but at what cost?

Stanton Industries – the family – was his own domain again. That was ecstasy, even if there had been a price to pay. In him there was guilt and there was certainly sadness – but overriding everything was an exhilarating relief that was all too close to joy.

There was only one thought that troubled him: one little edge of fear.

If the wrong brother had inherited, could Stanton Industries survive?

Book One
1

Tyneside, July 1956

The Queen had come from London in the special royal train. Sir Edward Stanton, recently knighted, was meeting her on the station platform; he stood with the Lord Mayor who wore his gold chain and robes of office, as the top-hatted stationmaster stepped forward. Then Sir Edward personally escorted Queen Elizabeth II from the express through the city's central station, and out towards all the happy faces up to the waiting fleet of cars.

Inside his black Rolls Royce Sir Edward watched as the Queen waved at the lines of cheering people. She was effortlessly courteous: this was *the* great day. The newspapers had predicted that over two hundred thousand spectators would line the route, to see Queen Elizabeth II in the summer heat. Looking at the flag-waving lines, Edward believed it.

It was certainly one of the supreme days of Sir Edward Stanton's life. In the last two years everything had changed – but not at all as his brother had intended. The Stanton Board of Directors was now entirely under his control, he had long since taken charge of the family trusts, he had no brothers, no rivals, and this day would be his, and all the other days to come.

It had all been for Hugh, his son, Edward told himself firmly as he folded his hands on his lap. Everything was under control now, and there was no one to challenge him or argue with Hugh's inheritance.

There was a sudden huge cheer outside the opened gates of the Stanton Industries shipyard.

Inside the unroofed slipway, hidden from the crowd by canvas walls, a powerfully-built man in oil-streaked Stanton overalls looked up at the sound. The new Stanton-built liner, the *Albion*, towered

11

splendidly white in her bright, brand-new paint. But Will Langton, the yard's Chief Foreman, knew he and all the men were still in a race to get her finished.

Building a ship was a long process, from laying down the keel plates and welding them to form the basis of the hull right down to this morning of the launch when the foreman carpenter and his men knocked away the very last of the wooden blocks under the ship, leaving her resting on the greased sliding ways. A long process, Langton thought: hammering and banging, money and brains expended, and sometimes men's lives, to end in all this bloody confusion and haste . . .

Their frantic efforts had begun at dawn the previous day. Everyone had been asked to work three shifts in two days, and not everybody had been able to stand it. He knew even the best of his men were dead on their feet. Now, out of sight of the platform, below and on the far side of the gigantic hull which was still partly supported by gigantic baulks of lubricated timber, he sent his men swarming to get their equipment clear.

"Get those last keel blocks away! Quickly!" he bellowed through cupped hands. "Sir Edward likes to see men in a hurry!"

They were too tired to laugh.

Will had felt anxiety building in the pit of his stomach for the past two weeks as the launch date approached. The Queen's state visit to Sweden had fixed the exact day in July, and suddenly the Stanton Industries divisional managers had realized their ship was still far from ready. Only last night, under the floodlights, had they taken away half of the keel blocks and shores and revealed for the first occasion the graceful lines of the ship.

Langton himself had had a hectic time trying to bring her to launch condition. Last week there had been another problem in the twenty year old compressor house, that noisy building with pipes running from it like arteries up to the air-hammers, which were still used for riveting. So, much earlier this morning, with Sir Edward still in bed in his family mansion up in Northumberland, Langton had gone to search under the hull with a powerful electric torch. For the first time he could see the long lines of rivet heads, as neatly regimented as guardsmen. He remembered the steel plates coming in from the Stanton works, how each plate was shot-blasted clean of rust and impurities, cut to exact shape by a flame torch, rolled to fit the curve of the hull, then laid out and numbered, ready to be fitted into place.

The plates were around him now, and painted; this was a ship above him, with eight boilers driving four sets of Stanton turbines.

Hammering with a mallet, he had found three misaligned plates with two dozen loose rivets. Bloody rivets: the Japs made all-welded ships, he had heard, out of prefabricated sections, which meant the ships were cheaper and easier to build, and went through the water faster. He immediately called in a team with arc welding gear and they had started work in the stuttering glare as he checked the wedges still rammed home under the sliding ways. The whole area stank of diesel oil and fresh paint and, just for today, the fish soap used to grease the skids on the sliding ways.

He had called his chargehands in from their nine o'clock tea-break and spoken angrily. "It's not nearly good enough, lads. Look! She's barely watertight!"

Haddon, his cousin and old friend, had shaken his head anxiously as his young apprentice, Joe, sniffed at the huge drums of fish-smelling soap before grabbing another corned beef sandwich. "It's bloody typical, Will. They had three choices – postpone the launch, pay overtime to get her properly finished, or do a bad job."

"Could we have waited, Mr Langton?" fifteen-year-old Joe asked.

"Postpone? With the Queen coming? Impossible." Will had grabbed his battered mug of tea and emptied it in two convulsive swallows. "The management should have listened to me and arranged overtime last Saturday and Sunday."

"Instead they saved Sir Edward's money."

"Aye, Tom – leaving *us* to save the day."

The rest of them finished their tea quickly and went back to work.

Langton went across to Tom Haddon. "Here, let me give you a hand."

Sweat was trickling from his cousin's face; together, they struggled to pull a hydraulic lifting platform from the hull.

Tom Haddon was nearly fifty, but strong enough for this. "I sent my lad to help with the soaping."

"Young Joe? He's not up to this, not at fifteen."

Even as he heaved, Will remembered how beautiful the liner had looked from the platform built for the Queen. But that view had never been, would never be, for the likes of him.

The Rolls Royce stopped at the foot of the stairs that led up to the launching platform. There was another great roar as the

13

young Queen stepped out, accompanied by Prince Philip and Sir Edward.

In the freshly painted Stanton shipyard, with red, white and blue bunting everywhere, the people pressed forward in a great mass to listen to the speeches as Langton's men laboured on out of sight.

Sir Edward had decided to speak last. The other directors sat around him, though he was closest to the Queen. Lord Montgomery Beauford, SI's merchant banker; Sir George Leslie, head of the Shipbuilding Division since the war. Edward's wife Grace squeezed his hand as he went to the microphones; his son Hugh and young, blond Alex were by him. This would be a great day for them, too, he knew.

The chairman's voice boomed out over the sea of heads, reminding them of history. It was four hundred years since the accession of the first Queen Elizabeth, in whose reign the nation first took to the sea and began to gather its strength.

"There have been difficulties for us more recently. They used to say before the war that 'the sun never sets on the British Empire', and it was true. The war has been won, but that was over a decade ago. Now there is a Commonwealth. So, in this new Elizabethan age, can we still say that our country is Great Britain?"

The speaker paused as if waiting for an answer. The crowd inside the shipyard stirred.

Then, looking at the ship the Queen had come to launch, at the huge crowd, he gave his answer.

"I believe continued greatness *is* possible. Here is the proof; the finest ship in the world."

Sir Edward Stanton heard his words echoing back from the curving white wall of steel that proved his faith: a fifty-seven thousand ton vessel, towering above the guests on the platform. He looked to the river to his right, but the harbourmaster's two launches, one upstream, one down, were flying the special pennants to keep the water clear of sightseers' boats. It was safe to continue.

He saw the turned heads and the expectant faces; he started to finish his speech, his words coming more quickly now as he sensed the excitement and responded to it. This intensely patriotic crowd prepared for their young Queen to complete the traditional ceremony with the traditional royal blessing. Everything today was his responsibility, directly or indirectly. He savoured the moment. Then he stood aside and indicated the cord that would send a jeroboam of vintage champagne swinging down onto the sharp prow of the liner. Queen Elizabeth stepped up to speak into the microphones.

"I name this ship *Albion*. May God bless her and all who sail in her."

She pulled the cord and a great cheer went up. Then it faltered and fell away. The bottle had jerked in its cradle, but it refused to swing towards the *Albion*. On the platform and across the crowd, celebration turned to embarrassment.

Sir Edward took a step back as the recorded music swelled: *Land of Hope and Glory*. Then, suddenly, there was heart-stopping silence.

He felt perspiration beading his brow as he turned to peer at the mechanism. The crowd murmured.

"It seems to be, ah, ma'am, a little problem. I'll get my people to deal with it as soon as –" He turned on his yard manager. "Drummond!"

The manager came forward, and pulled at the cord helplessly. "Perhaps if –"

Then the younger boy, Alex, climbed up from the platform along the mechanism. There was ironic approval from the crowd. He seized the foil-wrapped bottle and pulled it free, then jumped down again. He was beaming.

The Queen was unperturbed, although Prince Philip standing by her side was frowning. She took the cord from the boy's hand. "Thank you."

This time the chairman and chief shareholder of Stanton Industries gritted his teeth and rubbed at his grey moustache, as she began once more to pull the cord. He stepped back again and tried to smile at the cameras. This launch, he reflected, had been a close run thing – and in more ways than one.

This time the bottle jerked free in a glittering arc. It broke, showering sparkling wine and glass fragments everywhere.

Nobody cheered, and suddenly the silence was explosive.

For the ship itself had not moved.

As the first great cheer died away and the speeches began, Langton sent more men under the white curve of the hull to get out the other tradesmen who had gone to weld shut the holes that had been overlooked until his own final inspection. He saw them dragging equipment free, and he hurriedly wheeled a pair of oxygen bottles away from the space under the keel, then waved to tell the other men to get clear. The hull was huge over their heads and for the first time he felt scared of those 57, 000 tons.

"It's only minutes now, lads! But don't start the launch till I say everything's right!"

The launch of a big ship was a bitter-sweet moment for him and the others, the culmination of months of hard work sent crashing spectacularly down the slip in ceremony, afterwards to be tied up at the outfitting quay and finished by other hands. It was perhaps the closest thing to giving birth that a man could know, but building this ship had been a bastard assignment, and he had been cheated of his pure moment of satisfaction in all this last-minute inefficiency and panic.

The relayed order came.

"Launch!"

"No!" Will said. "Everybody has to get clear!"

Men were running about; some fled, some stayed to finish the job. Langton had never seen such chaos, and he jogged to stop the men who would actually send the ship down the slipway. Christ, this is a mess! he thought. There was a hollow ringing as more machinery was pulled clear of the ship's side. Then the crowd up above erupted into applause.

Drummond, the yard manager, appeared under the hull with a loudhailer. "Get this bloody ship into the water or we'll lose the high tide! Launch it immediately!"

Before Langton could countermand the order the chocks were hammered away and the huge, overshadowing hull began to tremble – frighteningly. There was never silence in a shipyard except for times like this, and the silence was eerie. Then fifty-seven thousand tons slid like the beginning of an avalanche.

"You two!" Will roared suddenly. "Leave your gear and get out of it!"

His cousin Tom was fifty yards away with his back to Will, and the boy was still with him. Tom Haddon, thirty years a Stanton worker and made a little deaf by the work, and his fifteen year-old apprentice Joe. Will shouted again. A mass of rusted steel lay heaped six-feet high between them and the side of the slipway – huge drag chains, each link the size of a car tyre, used to brake the ship's momentum as she slid into the river on the first and shortest journey of her life.

They did not hear, because the noise was suddenly tremendous.

Then Drummond was jumping back and Langton's cries were lost in the renewed cheering: the launch had started. Two hundred feet down the slip he heard the last of the chocks driven away. Behind him summer sunlight began flooding across the broad ways.

"For God's sake, jump!"

Will Langton had a choice. Run away, or run down the steep slipway for his men.

He didn't think twice. He ran alongside the drag-chains as the *Albion's* underbelly gathered speed. He saw the lines of chain welded to her flanks suddenly jerk taut and dry rust fly up, showering him with dirt as he tried to beat the weight of metal for speed. He was still shouting his warning. Then he saw Tom turn and try to push the boy to safety, but both men lost their footing as the mass of giant links thundered towards them.

Were they both going under the chains? The noise from that unearthly grinding and the groaning timbers of the slipway filled the air all around. It was terrifying. Langton saw the boy vanish under the mass of rusty chains, ground into the concrete by them.

Langton fekt sick with fear and he crushed himself against one of the slip's concrete supports as more of the flailing iron ran towards him, tons of it.

If there's not enough gap, he thought, I'm a dead man. He did not close his eyes. The chains rushed towards him, clanging. This is it.

Spray leapt up from the luxury liner's stern as it sliced into the water. It seemed to hang there in a perfect arc of foam for a long time; the news photographers were pleased. Further out on the river tugs hooted triumphantly. Then Stanton's time-keeper let off the yards' klaxons, and the Royal Marine band struck up. All heads had turned now to watch the ship crashing endlessly into the glittering water of the Tyne. Then it was done, and the tugs that stood off in the river were swinging her about as she stood high in the water, a white goddess.

Sir Edward Stanton was overjoyed. "Excellent day's work – a day's bonus pay to all the men!"

Then he began to escort the Queen back to the car. His day was almost over and, as far as he was concerned, it had been almost perfect. Luckily, young Alex and Drummond had been there, and

17

helpful, and as usual the Stanton luck had been effective. It was not until half an hour later, as the ambulance was leaving, that he was told there had been an accident, resulting in a death and a serious injury.

Inside the gigantic, sloping valley that was the main slipway, the men had gathered around quickly. The chains had caught up Tom Haddon and scraped him for thirty yards. The boy with him had been smashed to death.

Though his legs felt shaky, Langton was the first to reach Tom. "Joe! Young Joe!" Tom moaned, writhing about.

"Oh, my God!" exclaimed the next man to come up beside him. He turned his face away. Tom Haddon had lost both legs above the knee. There was blood and raw, scraped flesh everywhere.

"He's bleeding to death," someone said.

"Let me." Langton remembered his first aid training from his days in the war. He knelt, pulling off his belt and getting someone else's, and he tied two tourniquets that at least stopped the bleeding. Langton threw a jacket over Tom's lower half. Then he held Tom's iron-hard hand and looked at the twitching mouth, the agonized eyes. "Where's the bloody ambulance?"

The men stood there, their faces shocked grey.

Twenty minutes passed before the ambulance came. The yard's own first aid team were there by then. Incredibly, Haddon was still alive. Will helped the uniformed men strap him to the stretcher and gave a hand to carry it away.

An electrician in faded Stanton overalls came up. "Will he live?"

Langton stared at the river. "Would you want to, without legs?"

Then he wandered away to the end of the slipway, by himself. He lit a cigarette, staring at the white liner in the water and hearing the crowds begin to go home. It had cost men's lives to create that.

Another half hour later, after the departure of Sir Edward, the yard's general manager came back to the slipway.

Dan Drummond shouted down to him from the slip side. "You'd better get your men off the site, Will. I don't suppose there'll be much of a celebration. Poor bloody Joe. And Tom. Still, there's always the next keel to be laid."

Will slung a sledgehammer onto his shoulder in one powerful motion. He had no liking for Drummond, but concealed the fact

18

in front of the men. He looked up, in the shadows now as the sun settled towards dusk.

"You think I'd have it any other way? I remember what it was like to be a bairn in the Depression."

The other consulted his clipboard and gave him a desultory nod. "Keel #142 – a big motor yacht. We start Monday. How does that suit your trade union sensibilities?"

"Sir Edward Stanton's building a new toy for himself, is he?"

The knot of men who had been about to disperse caught the hard, vengeful tone in Will's voice. Drummond came quickly down the rickety wooden stairs to water level, then pointed a finger at him. "I don't know who told you who commissioned the keel, but don't forget who pays your wages, Langton."

"It's not a penny more than we've sweated for now – and fought for, too." Will came up and faced the man, his mouth hardened. "It was Stanton Industries' negligence that crippled Tom Haddon and killed his lad Joe!"

"Negligence? That's slander!"

"Take a look around here. How many of these bloody pre-war machines have safety guards? How many men have hard hats and safety boots?"

"Frightened to take a risk, are you?"

"I know this is man's work!" Will was boiling up inside. He could not forget Tom, and he could not forget young Joe. "But it should be as safe as we can make it! The men here deserve all that and more!"

Drummond licked his lips uneasily and looked around at the hard faces of the men, seeing no vestige of affection and no respect.

Will spat on the ground. "Look at this place! Some of those cutting tools are thirty years old, and the money that ought to be buying us new ones is building Stanton's new pleasure craft."

"That's right," the electrician said.

The manager tried to stare him down, but failed. "Some people have you down as a troublemaker, Langton, because you always seem to think you know better than your superiors."

"If you know better than me, tell it to Tom's wife and daughter, and tell it to Joe's widowed mam!" Will jerked a thumb towards the bloodied patch of ground, then threw his sledgehammer down and walked away in the direction of the mould loft, the huge, well-lit space where the ship's lines were drawn full-scale on the floor and then cut

19

into the templates of wood they used to carve the steel plates of the hull.

Tom Haddon would never work again, even if he lived. Then there would have to be a battle over compensation money. Will promised himself that battle would be won even if he had to get himself elected union branch secretary to do it.

And young Joe, he remembered, dead.

He tapped out another cigarette, his thoughts turning to his own two daughters. There was so much wrong with this world; he wanted them to grow up in a better one.

The mourners had all assembled, and they were trying to cheer the burly man in the black suit, but Will Langton's face was a mask of pain. "Stanton Industries killed him. Everybody knows it."

Tom Haddon had lingered, bedridden and legless, till pneumonia had struck him down.

"It was God's mercy to take him," Bridie Langton said deliberately. "There was no good in all his suffering."

"No," Will admitted, turning up the collar of his coat.

"D'you think there'll be a war in the Middle East, Dad?" Maggie Langton asked her father.

"Unless somebody stops them."

"I will," she said fiercely.

He patted her head. Annie and Maggie, his two daughters, stood dolefully by the cheap wooden coffin as the Irish priest came striding briskly out of the church, his cheeks reddened by the traditional drop of whisky.

The priest began the funeral service: Latin words, ancient, comforting. Langton remembered coming to this church high on a hill in Byker, to marry Bridie. Incense, and the flower odours of the bouquets. He tried to throw off the burden of the past and listen to the funeral while thinking about the future.

Will had no illusions. It was probably too late for him. He had had to make his own way, and it had always been a struggle – and impossible to work and study at the same time. In 1936 he had sacrificed his opportunities to fight in Spain against Franco, and he had been in the front line at Madrid and seen street-fighting in Barcelona; that struggle had been lost, and then the war had come along after the shame of appeasement and he had chosen to fight again, this time for his own country. He had been taken, wounded, off the beaches of Dunkirk. Afterwards, there was a young family to bring up, and so it seemed that his last chance had gone.

His elder daughter, Annie, had missed out too, but his Maggie was still young enough, and bright enough, and he would help her and drive her on; she would go places and do those things that he could not. He folded his hands together and smiled at the daughter he loved above anything else on earth. Tom Haddon had stood godfather for her, in this little Catholic church built when a quarter of the world was Britain's.

Will suddenly felt more determined. These days people had a chance, and he would see to it that Maggie took hers – and in the brave, wonderful world that was struggling to be born, who could tell what might be possible?

He knew he would have to take part in that struggle. The Stantons had killed a workmate, a relative, and the men here remembered young Joe, too, and wanted justice. They were already talking strike, prompted only a little by Langton, even as the earth was shovelled onto the coffin.

Afterwards, the mourners walked away from the dark stones of the church: the air was crisp, the sunlight watery but clear. Bridie and most of the other women left, to cook Sunday dinner for their families.

In the distance rose the huge shipbuilders' cranes, and it was just possible to see the lettering on them – STANTON INDUSTRIES. Langton felt his lips curling. He gathered the men around him and led them into the nearby pub.

"The drinks'll be on me," he said. He beckoned the barmaid over, then turned back to them after he had given his order for the round and met their eyes. "I think it's time we stood up for ourselves."

"Aye, but we need to plan well," one of his workmates suggested.

Light came in through the Victorian stained-glass windows; they showed working scenes, the romance of iron-making, the glow of the forge, the dark shadow of the factory.

Another man, a boilermaker, spoke. "Listen, the regional secretary of our union is retiring next month – idle bastard that he is. Let's make sure you get elected in his stead, Will."

"That's bloody good of you," Will answered, though he had hoped someone would make that suggestion. "I'm willing to stand. But I don't promise an easy time, let's get that said straightaway. It might take me five or ten or twenty years, but the Stantons'll be out – it's

21

action, action, action, until the working man gets what's coming to him!"

The strike began with a walk-out in the Stanton Industries' Ship-building Division, after a mass meeting in one of the Tyne yards, which William Langton had called. He promised the men that, with solid backing, there would be the support of the national union itself, which meant strike pay and political leverage in London, where it counted.

His audience was hundreds strong, but his voice was so big they could all hear, and they wanted to listen. Langton stood under huge lettering that was visible for miles: STANTON INDUSTRIES. But Stantons had left his cousin Tom Haddon a legless cripple, then killed him. Stanton Industries was still one of the largest industrial empires in the country, covering shipbuilding, armaments, and aircraft, but it was also the epitome of everything wrong with the nation.

"Look at this place," he told the hundreds of men. "The firm is old, tired, finished. It has an appalling safety record. It's run by a management nobody could respect, and its owners –" There was jeering. He let it build up then raised his arms dramatically, silencing the crowd. "Its owners are completely out of touch. The Stantons know nothing and they do nothing; they only take. It's time for a change."

It was time for a change. Langton told the men around him again before leading them out. They left cheering.

The Suez crisis had already turned to war. The following day, on October 29th, 1956, the Israeli Army launched a direct attack on Egypt. The British and French governments followed up by issuing a twelve-hour ultimatum that insisted the Israelis withdraw and the Egyptians submit to the occupation of the Canal.

From their bases in Cyprus and Malta, the British and French bombed Egyptian airfields, then landed paratroops in advance of an invasion force headed by six aircraft carriers.

In the British Parliament, there was uproar. The Labour Party condemned the action: they demanded "Law – not War!" but, though their vote of censure was lost, they had made their position clear.

* * *

22

In Paris, Sir Edward abandoned his breakfast with a grim expression. He took the telephone and spoke brimstone into it. "They're demanding *what?*"

Grace winced as he threw down his knife with a clatter.

"A genuine case? Grievances? I'll hold you personally responsible for this, Drummond. I want this Langton to know precisely who's running Stanton Industries! And about that memo he sent me: tell him I have no money for the so-called investment programme he proposes. Just who does he think he is?"

Outside, the grey spire of the Eiffel Tower rose above grey-ribbed rooftops; the trees were beginning to shed their leaves in fiery colours on this autumn day in 1956. Sir Edward looked around the hotel suite as if he expected one of his managers to appear in person, but the *belle epoch* decorations disclosed no one, and his fury focused on the big black telephone on the table.

When he finally slammed the receiver down he was no longer interested in the Ritz's devilled kidneys. Room service cleared the table in double quick time, and brought his English newpaper instead.

"Trouble down at the mill?" Grace asked ironically, combing a stray curl into place.

"They've downed tools on the Tyne because of some damned trouble-maker called William Langton, Labour through and through, no doubt – jealous and treacherous." He picked up his newspaper, studied it, then flung it down. "Gaitskell and the Labour Party are opposing action over Suez," he said venomously. He fell silent, then he became thoughtful.

Grace spent the afternoon shopping. Like Napoleon and Queen Victoria before her, she bought diamonds from the Chaumet brothers' shop on the Place Vendôme, and then returned to the hotel with a bell-boy who carried an impressive pile of cartons labelled Chanel and Dior.

Her husband was on the telephone again. He replaced the receiver as she came into the room, and stood up. A broad grin crossed his face, and he paid her more than usual attention as she held her new dresses up against herself in the mirror and opened her hat boxes.

"I thought this one would be just the thing for Ascot next year."

"Delightful. Such a marvellous shade of shocking pink. You'll quite scandalize the royal enclosure," he told her pleasantly.

"Do you really think so?"

He grinned at her again, and kissed her forehead.

23

"Edward!"

"What's the matter?"

"What's got into you? You're smiling like a Cheshire cat."

Edward preened himself and assumed a look of boyish self-satisfaction. "Nothing, my dear, just doing a little satisfactory business. Making sure that Hugh has something to inherit, don't you know."

Grace unpinned the shocking pink and tried on the cream and powder blue with roses. "There, you see. When I left you this morning you were about to explode. You take those silly deals much too seriously. You really should be more like Monty Beauford – he knows how to enjoy himself."

"I've been speaking with Monty this afternoon, actually. He came up with an idea I'll put to Charles. If his newspaper helps me out with a little something, the strike will be over before we know it."

"Oh, I'm so glad. These disputes take up so much of your time and make you bad tempered – and the *people*."

As they prepared to go out that evening, Sir Edward dawdled in the hotel lobby. He checked his watch as he waited for his wife to come down, and when it was exactly six-thirty he went into the cocktail lounge and ordered a whisky and asked the bartender for a telephone. After a short delay he was put through to an office on Fleet Street.

He kept his voice low. "Hello, Charles? Ah, good, you were expecting me. There's a little something I'd like you to do for me . . ."

He described what he wanted the free press to say, having no doubt that it would be effective: he knew the British workman was almost always red-blooded and patriotic, if properly led in the right direction.

"So: allied to Moscow, and acting against our boys in the Middle East?"

"Exactly," Sir Edward said, vastly pleased.

"How is Hugh, these days?"

"Being groomed for a high place, Charles. He is my son, after all."

There was a faint chuckle over the line. "What happened about your brother's boy? Didn't you adopt him, or something?"

"Of course; he's family."

"But not family enough to inherit, eh?"

24

"He inherits some small percentage of the firm, which is held for him in one of the family trust funds till the boy is twenty-six. Alex has the income as his own, and one day he'll have control of the shares. Seems fair to me; he'll be rich enough, though not, obviously, as well-off as Hugh. We can't all inherit a fortune, you know." He paused. "There's really no problem about the article, I hope?"

"I suppose we have to stand together. This is a crisis, after all. Afraid Eden wasn't a good choice as Prime Minister."

"Oh, we'll win in Suez. Kicking a few wogs has never been difficult."

"Unless President Eisenhower says 'no'."

Edward gave a grunt of amusement at the unlikely notion, downed his whisky and wandered back into the lobby. Grace's delay was beginning to try his patience, but it was another fifteen minutes before she appeared. By then he was in expansive mood again. He had solved the problem on the Tyne, after all. He complimented her on her appearance and she took his arm.

"I'm so looking forward to this. We haven't been to Maxim's for three years."

"Then it's about time we did. I've done myself a favour, and I intend to celebrate."

The strike Will Langton was leading soon became rock-solid through-out the North East. The men at the Stanton Armaments Division had come out in support of the shipyards two days later, and most of the Aircraft Division's factories had shut down, too. Their case was strong. In a week or two, lacking reserves of cash, Stanton Industries would begin to totter, financially.

Through an intermediary, the management tried to offer Langton money, but he refused, and took it as a sign of desperation as well as an insult. He told his strike committee, Robinson and the others, that. The union's national committee was meeting at the end of the week, and gaining their support was a certainty.

But before the pressures could really begin to tell, and on the same day that the engineering workers executive was meeting, a daily newspaper denounced Langton personally:

IS THIS MAN A TRAITOR?

In the parlour of his house in Joicey Street Will paced the carpet, distressed and angry. "Look at it! – 'Communists at his meetings'

25

– it's a bloody free country, do they expect me to put blackshirts at the door to keep out my own union members? 'His extremist speeches against the patriotic action of our troops in Suez' – God, whatever the big corporations do is always bloody patriotic, isn't it! It's all a smear," he told his wife, flinging the paper away, cut to the core. He had never expected this. "The lowest lies I've ever read."

He looked again at the article. *IS THIS MAN A TRAITOR?*

The editor had made it personal, painting a picture of an evil Luddite: Langton, standing in the way of the national interest, paralysing the supply of ships, spare parts and bullets for British guns. The paper even implied his actions had contributed to the late arrival of the Expeditionary Force in Egypt.

Will slapped his hand over the centre spread, pointing a finger at one paragraph in particular. "They're trying to make some connection between us here and the Russian tanks rolling into Budapest. Communist fifth columnists! Traitors! That's what those liars are calling us!"

"And they call themselves British when they can use people's patriotism like that?" Bridie said in disgust.

"I'll not give in to him, Bridie. For the sake of Tom Haddon and Joe and their families, I swear I won't," Will told her, shaking with passion. "All I want is what's right!"

Bridie still held her hand to her mouth. The newspaper was on the table, open at the pages that libelled her husband. "How can they do it? How can people believe it?"

"Old Sir George Leslie at Division headquarters has tried threats and he's tried bribery," Will said bitterly. "But he'd never stoop to this. This is Sir Edward's personal doing. He's the one behind it. His friends own the bloody paper."

Langton looked at his wristwatch, knowing that the union's national committee away in London was already meeting. He knew two of the men who sat on it, good men both. He turned back to the other newspapers. "Let's see what it says in the *Mirror* and on the telly."

He drank two cups of tea, still unable to get the libels out of his mind, then he picked up the telephone and dialled through to London: the union headquarters in King's Cross.

"Oh, Will," the flat Midlands voice said, "I was just composing the letter."

"Ted, can't you just make a straight announcement to the press? Look, with this smear campaign in the bloody press the lads really need your support now, not later."

"Yes, the papers." Ted sighed. "We'll never get fair comment in this country, will we?"

"When socialism comes, we will, but for the moment I'd make do with your fair comment, Ted!" Langton smiled, still expectant.

"I'm sorry, lad. I voted for you."

"What?" He felt sick to his stomach. "You're *not* backing us, because of some bloody journalist's smear!"

"We have to think of our public image, Will. Look, if there's anything we can do, short of making your dispute official –"

"'My' dispute! Why, you –" Will clattered the phone down before he spoke out of turn, his chest heaving.

He stalked into the front room. As he entered, there was the sound of shattering glass and something came flying through the curtains, just missing his wife's face.

"Bridie!"

He leapt to her, and saw the fear in her eyes even though she was unhurt. The half-brick smashed a glass-fronted cabinet on the opposite wall. By the time Will flung open the front door and stormed outside, there was nothing to be seen under the single streetlight except a few parked cars. His big fists clenched, but suddenly he was afraid too, afraid for his wife, and his daughters, and of the public mood.

He had nothing now except the loyalty of his men. The union hierarchy in London had stood aside from the strike. If his men's loyalty changed, Sir Edward might escape him yet.

Things abruptly began to turn. The large meetings called were attended by fewer people; the union's top men in London stepped back even further than before. More of Fleet Street took up the campaign, assassinating Langton's character almost every day. Since neither Will nor the local union could afford libel lawyers, there was nothing he could do. When his daughters came home from school in tears, and when he found his strike committee meetings were no longer welcome at the local pub, it became much harder for Will to stand by his promise.

More bricks came through the windows of his home, and he boarded up the ground floor, but by then even some of his committee had begun to desert him. He couldn't keep the others on his side in the face of the lies Sir Edward had sponsored. To many of Will's men, the label 'traitor' was repugnant.

A vote was arranged for the Tuesday evening, and Langton was still hopeful; Stanton Industries, with virtually all their divisions paralysed, had started to talk, off the record, of concessions.

"I don't know how many of the men will stand by me, though. It certainly won't be unanimous any more."

In the parlour of their boarded-up home, Bridie shook her head. "They still put their patriotic duty above everything, don't they?"

Will gave a shrug of disbelief. "It's no good me saying that it's all a tactic – the members tell me they're being branded cowards and Communists."

His wife laid a hand on his shoulder, and said gently, "People have read it in the newspaper – for some that automatically makes it the truth."

"Bridie, I love you." Suddenly his voice was hoarse and his head was low. "Thank you for standing by me."

"What else would I do for my man?"

He stood up. "As long as I win tonight's vote, I'll win my fight." He closed his eyes and promised his wife fiercely: "I'll get Sir Edward Stanton, Bridie. I'll get him for all this, if it's the last thing I do."

He kissed her, before leaving for the meeting that would make or break the weeks-long agony of the strike. From the back lane behind the house he heard his daughter Maggie and her friend Mary, bouncing balls against the wall and chanting rhythmically. "Temptation, temptation, temptation – Dick Barton went down to the station – Blondie was *there*, all naked and *bare* – temptation, temptation, temptation . . ."

He came back late, after ten, reeling down the street. The stars seemed to be shaking in the clear wintry sky. Either I'm a bit drunk, he thought as he stood looking up, or the stars that look down are.

He couldn't get the voices out of his head. The voices from the meeting.

"D'you think Comrade Robinson –"

He turned to the smooth-faced boy, glared at him, his belly full of beer and anguish. "'Comrade' Robinson? It's 'Mister' to you, lad, till you're time-served."

"It's no use blaming me, Mr Langton. It's them. *Them.*" The youth's thin face screwed up as if in pain. "Them on both sides. The rich standing together, and traitors on our side!"

Langton unbuttoned his collar. "Now listen to me," he said. "Jackie Sutton, you're a fine lad, with a future. So don't go taking this the wrong way. Aye, the rich are strong, because they've got the whole system working for them, but we've always had their measure. Robbo is much too hard-hearted a man for my liking. He draws the wrong conclusions. You see, the real question is – do we have our own measure? Jackie Sutton, don't you worry about that society set above us. They'll be forced to stand aside when we get it all right."

The boy looked at him, worshipping him. "You fought against them, didn't you? In the international army in Spain?"

More memories came back: Spain in the thirties, the gypsy singing, the wine, and the rough-voiced men he was fighting for. "I'll tell you about it some other time. But it wasn't pure, and we weren't all heroes."

"About tonight –"

Langton raised a hand. His big voice boomed out. "Lad, the measure of a man isn't to be found in winning every time. It's in how well you fight. Remember that."

"I will," the boy said, his eyes gleaming. "How well we fight."

Langton went into his house. He did not want the boy to see how upset and defeated he felt.

Bridie was still waiting up in the kitchen. He slammed the front door behind him and slumped against it, his chest heaving. "I don't believe it. Even my own men on the committee turned against me." He shook his head, stunned. "Tuesday, in the evening. I'll remember this day – it'll always be with me. I lost. Eleven votes to three – to *three.* Back to work on Friday, defeated."

Bridie said nothing, but put her arms around him and made him sit down. Then she put a cup of sweet piping-hot tea down by his elbow. He sipped it without noticing how hot it was.

Will sat there in the comfortable armchair, his thoughts in turmoil. The television flickered black and white images that conveyed nothing. He felt a stirring in the pit of his stomach. Lost. *Lost.* How had it happened, when they had such a strong case? He got up and walked backwards and forwards, caged in by the walls of his own house and by the boarded-up windows. Everything had conspired to work for the Stantons. Name, money, social connections; the press, Parliament, even the law itself.

His eyes softened. He had seen retreat at Madrid, at Dunkirk – too much retreat. It had taught him cunning and patience, but there had to be a victory or two sometime.

Then he went to the foot of the stairs.

"Maggie!" he bawled. "Come here!"

She had come down quickly, rubbing her eyes, still in her grammar school uniform. "I was doing my Latin homework – Oh, Dad, you're upset."

"Sit by me," he said grimly, and led her into the boarded-up front parlour. "It's time I taught you about life." He pointed at the smashed windows. "This is our life. It's all about money, and the real power in this nation! Now I want to tell you what that man Sir Edward Stanton and his brood have done to us . . . " It took a while to finish the story. By then Maggie was in tears at the injustice of it all. "Now, girl, will you help me?"

"Of course, Dad!"

"Then," he said grimly, "I want you to go on – go on to university, then to London, and get all the weapons the Stantons have. You're the same age as their younger lad, and your school isn't Eton, but it's bloody good. Will you do it for me?"

"I'll do all that and more," she had promised him, twelve years old, her eyes glittering; this was romance and heroism. "Then I'll help you get your revenge."

It was the summer, in a later year. A slim youth with dark straight hair and sensitive features called at the Langtons' family house at half past eight one morning. A bicycle striped in black and white, the colours of Newcastle United, rested against his hip as he knocked at the door.

He was David Bryant, Maggie's oldest friend, who lived at The Ship, where his father was tenant publican. He was still an apprentice in the drawing office in the Stanton main shipyard.

Already the sky was as blue as a cornflower and the sun, though still low, was giving notice of the summer day it was going to be.

"I'll look after her, Mrs Langton."

Bridie smiled, liking his earnestness. "Not too late."

"Don't worry."

30

"We'll be back long before dark," Maggie said confidently.

Maggie wore her golden-red hair in long plaits, a white shirt with her sleeves rolled up, and a dark blue gym skirt and ankle socks. It was Sunday, so there was hardly any traffic, and they both had racing bicycles.

He followed her down the street, pedalling hard. "Where are we going?"

She looked back, gay on this weekend morning. "Don't spoil my secret, Davey!"

For a long time as they pedalled on he wondered what their destination could be: somewhere north, on the old road to Scotland –

They rode for two hours, perspiring, through the warm summer air. The Northumberland countryside was baking golden-brown in the heat, and the bees were noisily gathering pollen from the blackberry bushes by the roadside. Up ahead, the road turned to pools of shimmering mercury.

Finally, they came to a high stone wall that enclosed a wooded estate. Maggie stopped and hid her bike among the briars; David copied her. Then they climbed over the wall and set off across a green meadow on foot.

"Aren't we trespassing?"

"Yes," she said defiantly. "It's a private estate."

David looked round. "It's huge. It must be the Duke's."

She shook her head. "No."

"A family of princes?"

But she only laughed.

They climbed the hill and ducked under a barbed-wire fence. From the cool shadows of a copse they looked out across an expanse of well-watered grass, to the gardens and the lake set beyond it like a sheet of glass. A huge mottled stone house with columns rose above the water. All around it were Chilean pines and gorgeous lilac-flowered shrubs. It looked to David like Buckingham Palace, only more idyllic.

They crouched quietly together in the shade staring at the house.

"It's beautiful."

"It's called Craigburn."

"Craigburn?" he echoed. "Who lives here?"

Maggie stuck a grass stem in his mouth and looked fiercely back at the mansion. "That's where *he* lives – Sir Edward Stanton. And his family."

31

"What an inheritance," he breathed. "They must be worth a fortune."

"They are. Let me show you something."

She got up and began to run through the glade, her smooth calves gleaming unexpectedly in the light. David ran after her, suddenly desiring her more strongly than he ever had before. Love, a pain stabbing into his chest. They arrived breathless at a collection of little stone houses that had no windows. David looked at them and read the inscription carved within a laurel wreath on the door of the largest; he was impressed. "Sir Samuel Stanton, 1844–1899. It's a mausoleum!"

She nodded. "Look at this one: Albert Edward Stanton, 1874–1945. And here, this seems the newest . . ."

The block of unadorned white marble said that Michael Alexander Stanton had died in New York on St George's Day, 23 April, 1954.

They stood together and stared, not saying anything. David wondered who Michael Stanton had been, and what he might have achieved if he had lived. There was something eerily moving about this plain statement and plainer memorial, and Maggie shivered before she turned away quickly.

No body lay here; there was only the stone.

"Think of it, David. Even a private graveyard."

He led her away quickly. This place seemed haunted and it made him uneasy. There were also fresh flowers on many of the tombs, so the place was visited quite often.

"Even their pets – look!" Maggie knelt by a carefully weeded plot. The small headstone read simply 'Bathsheba'. She looked at him, her face unreadable. "This is the family my father hates above anything else on earth – and we're going to get them, David, you see if we don't!"

David shook his head. "Revenge is a bad thing to devote your life to, Maggie."

Her eyes were glazed, unseeing. "Justice, that's what I want! And all of them in hell!"

"If there was justice . . ." He sighed. "There's enough blood and suffering in the world already."

Now, he saw her tears begin to well up. "Not for them. They've never suffered, never."

"I can't believe that's true." He remembered the memorial stone: the Stanton who had died in his prime on St George's Day, in New

32

York. "Come on, let's find somewhere away from the house and have our picnic."

They walked down to a sunny spot and sat down. She spread a red and white chintz table cloth on the grass.

"It's so good to get away from the town," he said, trying to tear his eyes away from the womanly swell of her breasts. "Fresh air, sunshine. I feel so cooped up all the time at home. In a drawing office all day, and then night school afterwards, or the drama group."

"I'm glad we came here," she said, dreamily.

"Me too."

The sun was high in the sky and Maggie picked daisies to make a chain. Then they lay back, listening to the constant warbling of skylarks.

"You haven't heard about Oxford yet, have you?"

"No," she told him absently. "What about that place you applied to?"

He laughed, shortly. His father had made him leave school at fifteen, and since then he had struggled through evening classes after a day's work. "Oh, I'll be at Oxford, Maggie. Learning to teach at the training college . . . What'll you do if you don't pass? Go to another university?"

Maggie thought about it. She wanted to think she had done well in the exam, but sometimes she felt despondent, feeling that she was doomed only to be ordinary. She did not want to be ordinary. She remembered the music she loved, the harsh beat of rhythm and blues, the sensual, soaring sweep of Maria Callas. Everything should be that intense. There would be men on the moon one day, Kennedy had promised. And there were so many places to go.

"I'll go to Paris," she said carelessly, "and marry Jean-Paul Sartre. Or I'll live in San Francisco and become a beatnik."

She laughed, and David joined in. The future stretched out in front of both of them, a rich, exotic, available new land.

"Oh, I want a fortune, David. A million dollars. Just to be free!"

"But yesterday you were going to join the Committee of 100 to stop wars."

"Yesterday."

"It would be nice to have money," he said.

"I need it to defeat the Stantons. But I don't know whether I want to earn money or marry it."

"Well," he said drily, "you're certainly not going to inherit it."

He rolled over, looking at the play of sun on her face and hair and the daisy chain she had twined in it. She was so relaxed, so fresh, and her face was quite perfect. And he knew that what he hungered for was to look into Maggie's green eyes for ever.

"I love you, Maggie."

His left hand strayed to her knee, then stroked smoothly along her thigh. David's hand was sensitive, sensual, and he felt her muscles throb even as he moved his fingers up towards her secret place. He had never thought before today that he might already know the secrets of giving pleasure to a woman.

She was moaning softly, and her head turned from side to side. Excitement built up in him quickly. His hand, quivering only slightly, moved further up her thigh. She was old enough, he said to himself, and he loved her.

Then she clapped both her knees together. "No. I love you, David. I'll love you for ever! But not like *that*," she added, shaking her head.

"You know what people say about you . . . and me, sometimes."

"I don't care what people say, Davey."

David turned over onto his back. It was very comfortable lying like that, his head pillowed on crushed grass and his own arms. The sky was a luminous blue, like one great jewel. He stared into the sky at a tiny silver point high above them. It moved slowly, trailing a thin vaporous cloud behind it, and he wondered if it might be one of Stanton Industries' planes. In the briars bees hummed busily; he could smell the honeysuckle and the clover. It was a perfect day.

David turned his head to look at her. Maggie had her eyes closed and her mouth open.

He bent over and quickly kissed her. "Maggie," he said.

Inches apart, their eyes met. They held each other's gaze.

"David," she said softly.

"Maggie, I want you to promise that you'll always be on my side. Whatever might happen."

She reached out for his hand.

"I promise you, David."

Maggie returned home at five, to find that her father had come back a little early.

"I found a letter with an Oxford postmark." He looked at her. "Afraid I couldn't wait for you. I opened it."

She felt her blood freeze. "What did it say?"

From his face, it was obvious what the contents must have been.

"You're in," he told her, exhilarated. "And now you know what you have to do."

She threw herself into her father's welcoming arms.

2

The rain had just stopped when Maggie Langton stepped down from the Oxford train. She gripped the handle of the new suitcase her father had bought her, which held a second-hand gown and her best-loved books. She looked around, a little disappointed by the low and functional station buildings – she had expected something else, older and more ornate. Then she brushed back her long red hair and climbed into a taxi, giving the address of her digs just off Iffley Road.

The cab took her across the river into the centre of the city and past a cinema showing *Saturday Night and Sunday Morning*. They turned into St Aldate's and there, suddenly all around her, were old stone college buildings. As the taxi drove down the High, the clouds parted and silver sunlight broke through. It was as though Oxford was enchanted.

Maggie looked up at the mediaeval walls and towers. The people, too, were from another time: here, a curiously-dressed official in a striped waistcoat and bowler hat, there a red sports car crammed with students, and on the corner a group of black-cloaked men walking around quite unselfconsciously. In another city they would have drawn stares and comments, but here they seemed to be regarded as entirely normal. She couldn't quite believe it. It really was like the books said, and she was a part of it.

This, at last, was the town she had imagined, and she looked out greedily until the taxi took her up the main road heading north out of town.

It was a pity there had been no room in the college itself – she had been looking forward to ancient, moss-grown quadrangles, stained glass, palpable history. Still, she would be sharing St Michael's House with six other girls from the university, and Maggie had

36

already decided to use her charm on the landlady and have as riotous a time as possible.

The taxi pulled up in front of one of the large Victorian villas, and Maggie alighted. She carefully counted out her fare in small coins and looked up at the place that would be her home for the coming year. No doubt the landlady would be a homely woman, polite even while listing the expected house rules: in by ten p.m., no food in the rooms, and of course no alcohol or gentleman visitors.

Well, rules were made to be broken, weren't they? Maggie carried her cases through the rank, overgrown front garden up to the front door and hammered the brass knocker. Then she put her hands together and tried her best to look demure and studious: 'Of course I'll behave.'

The door creaked open, and a stooped figure with heavy-framed glasses stepped out slowly as if unaccustomed to the light of day. Maggie's mouth opened, and she took an automatic step back.

The nun gave her a gap-toothed smile.

"And you must be Maggie Langton, my dear. Your mother Bridie wrote to the college about you." She gave a laugh tough and elastic as a piece of gristle. "I said you'd be well looked after here."

The rules, it seemed, were still in place. The house, once she was inside, reeked of cabbage and furniture polish. She was escorted up three flights to her own room. It was surprisingly big, comfortable and dowdy, an attic that contained an armchair and a monstrous rosewood wardrobe and a plain wooden crucifix on the wall.

As soon as she was by herself, she kicked off her shoes and opened the window, despite the autumn cool. The bedsprings creaked under her and the distant peal of college bells came into the room like an acknowledgement.

When she opened her suitcase, she saw an envelope. Inside was a good luck card signed by Annie and her parents. In that moment, she knew that a new life had opened up. There would be opportunities waiting for her here – if only she could grasp them.

In the first days that followed, Oxford turned out to be no city of dreaming spires for Maggie Langton. Even before term started she found the university a surreal place, and its people strange and hard to mix with.

The young men who dominated the student body were from public schools; they seemed to be older and physically bigger than the rest, but their loud, confident voices grated on her, as did their ridiculous pipes, and they seemed forever to be carrying bags with their initials on, stuffed with sports clothes and rackets and other pieces of exotic sporting equipment. She was sure they were making fun of her social inexperience, and that made her prickly and competitive. Still, she had to fight off the men – as one of the most beautiful women in her year that was inevitable, but her truculence and coarse, dismissive wit only made her more attractive and challenging.

Often, too, as she combed her long, red-gold hair in her dressing table mirror, she wondered about the women she was meeting at college. Too many of them seemed to dislike her; she did not know why . . . They talked about life in the country, London, the arts; certainly they cared nothing for the industrial North.

Her subject was PPE – philosophy, politics and economics. It turned out to be less hard than she had feared, but still demanding, and she spent many hours in the library. Unfortunately, though she had an excellent memory and enough force of personality and logic to argue with great effect, she knew she lacked the cultural background of most of the students. She felt left out, disadvantaged.

She talked it through with David, who had driven over from the college of education in the green half-timbered Morris car he had bought, and tried to explain what was happening to her. She had never even been to France, nor to Italy or Greece – though, as she told him, she was determined to go one day.

"Greece." He smiled, as always pleased to see her. "What about America?"

"There as well." She shrugged. There was much more. She had never heard a symphony in a concert hall, and back home no one in the family spoke in intellectual terms, except on political subjects. But as term progressed, she saw that some of her fellow students were more show than substance, and that comforted her, but when David drove them both back to Newcastle for a long weekend she no longer felt at ease there, either.

"It's just a different world," she told her mother.

Bridie Langton looked worriedly at her daughter. "I hope you're not mixing with bad company, our Maggie!"

In the wood-panelled hall inside the ancient stone recesses of Christ Church College, Alex Stanton looked up at magnificent portraits – statesmen, philosophers, theologians, the least of them distinguished, the greatest so impressive that he felt their presence to be an almost tangible influence. In pride of place hung the Holbein portrait of Henry Tudor himself.

Cameron, the young Lord Kintyre, came over to welcome him.

Alex grinned back, pleased to see him. Cameron, delicate, pale-skinned and sandy haired, was one of his close friends. He had come up a day or two earlier, and Alex looked forward to his lively company in the coming term.

"Alex, you're in Canterbury Quad – let me show you."

Alex loped on, carrying most of his own baggage, an athletic nineteen-year-old. His friend followed him into the comfortable room after dismissing a college servant. "So you're reading modern history, too?"

Alex nodded. "Yes, and we're both late for induction."

"Are we? Upper Library, then, and we must jump to it. Then we'll meet again at dinner and afterwards I'll show you the champagne trick."

"Champagne trick?"

"I taught it to de Soutey – you'll see."

They went off in fine mood. After they entered the library, one of the tutors began to acquaint Alex with some of the other idiosyncracies of the House and its glorious history: over the years, eleven governors of India and twelve Prime Ministers had emerged from these portals.

Alex accepted a sherry from the Master of the College and joined the conversation. There was international tension, and even these people in their remote, scholarly world, were worried – the topics ranged quickly from the Red Chinese incursions into Kashmir, to the probability that President Kennedy would impose a blockade on Cuba.

"Then Krushchev will react, won't he? I mean, the man's unstable, and he has the Bomb!"

"Let's hope he doesn't start Armageddon," Alex said, remembering the latest news from the Stantons' connections in Whitehall. "But he'll certainly test Kennedy's nerve to the limit, Master."

"Anyway, the India–Chinese trouble should mean a good opportunity for your father to sell New Delhi all manner of hardware, eh, Stanton?"

"He's not my father," Alex said steadily. Better to get it straight at the very start. "I'm his brother's son. Not the heir to Stanton Industries."

That said, he smoothly continued to talk. Alex knew of Sir Edward's plans to supply the Indians with small arms and a limited amount of

39

armour, but he had the good sense to keep the news to himself. Arms-dealers: that was the popular image of his family, even though they made much of their money from straightforward industrial investment.

Kintyre beckoned another young man forward. "This is James Battersby."

Alex nodded distantly. From their first day together at Eton, he had disliked the man.

"I read a cricket report in the *Telegraph*," Battersby said disdainfully. He was a large, overdressed youth, pink and plump with his own self-importance. "It said you have the style of Attila the Hun."

Cameron was shocked at this dismissal. "Knocked up the runs against Harrow, though – saved the match."

Battersby hitched up his trousers. "You've had some trials for professional sides, Alex?"

"Surrey want him," Kintyre said. "So do Kent. He could play for England."

Alex laughed, a little embarrassed. "I'd like to be on a team playing for England, that's true. But I was thinking of the family team."

Cameron's face fell. "I know Hugh well. They won't let you in, Alex. You're not really one of them, are you?"

"In any case, real English gentlemen aren't professionals – are they, Alex?"

"So many questions." Alex raised an eyebrow and stared straight at Battersby until the other man flushed and looked away. "I might surprise the world yet and be the first. I'm not ashamed of wanting to win."

He looked around. There would be no more de Souteys governing India, or Kintyres holding sway in Edinburgh, but he could speculate on which of his colleagues would become the college's thirteenth British prime minister.

A few days later, Alex was in his rooms, feet up on the austere single bed by the leaded window. He was reading the last volume of Gibbon's *Decline*, listening to the sparrows chattering in the eaves. So hard to believe, such a mighty empire, with such a wonderful language as Latin, with technology and military discipline as well as culture – all fallen.

Then a knock at the door roused him. He shouted coarsely, "Come!"

The door creaked open. His cousin Hugh came in.

Alex threw the heavy book down and stood to give up the armchair. "Hugh. Take a seat. This is a surprise. Abandoning the ship?"

"The captain never does till the very end. Nor does the captain's heir – so father tells me at considerable length." Hugh had always had a premature gravity about him; he refused the comfortable chair and sat down at the desk instead, upright in a formal dark suit in the equally straight-backed chair. His intelligent, rather mournful eyes swept around the room. "Things don't change much, do they?"

"Yes they do," Alex replied tartly, thinking of Gibbon.

"Sporting trophies," Hugh said. "Books on history, as one would expect. But I seem to see books and magazines about business and industry – if I'm not mistaken, even technical manuals for our tanks and planes."

"You're not mistaken. My homework, Hugh."

Hugh seemed strangely ill at ease. Sir Edward had recently put him to work at the company's huge headquarters overlooking the Thames. He had already served briefly in the Shipbuilding Division, then had gone to Bristol where most of the Aircraft Division was based. Alex wondered if there might be a problem over all that.

"Just lost two massive engineering contracts – to the Germans." Hugh sighed, still avoiding his eyes. "I used to be a considerable Greek scholar, you know. Thought of becoming a don at one time . . . Tell me, Alex, did you ever run into Donald Pike, or any of the team that built the 'STA-C' jet?"

"No." This was painful. Alex thought about his dead father Michael and his mother Stacey as little as possible: he would rather appear cold and hard than feel such pain. Also, that terrible disaster off Long Island was all in the past, and he knew far too much of Britain was about obsession with times past. "I don't have the scientific background to follow aeronautical engineering in detail, Hugh – though that jet fighter the STA-1, which I hear my own father had planned, is a brilliant achievement. What I feel completely comfortable with is what the Armaments Division does."

"I see. Killing people, you mean."

"Killing – ? Is something the matter, Hugh?"

"Hmm?" Hugh's gaze came back from the window.

"No. No, just some forebodings. So, I must tell father that you're not considering a sporting career any longer?"

41

Alex shrugged. "Tell him what you want. That's three years away yet."

Hugh leaned forward in the chair. "Why did you go to see the Shah of Persia?"

"I believe they call the place 'Iran', these days. I was invited, don't you remember? Two years back, when we were at the summer palace."

"Father was – curious. The Americans seem determined to take the leading position in Iran."

"Look, have you come to spy on me? Or is something the matter?"

"Spy? No – you're family. But . . . well, things look very different when you're inside, compared with how they look outside. We've had some problems lately, just getting what's in our order-books finished on schedule and at the right price. I wondered if you knew anything."

"Are you asking me if I've sold the family secrets? Certainly bloody not! I'm loyal. I hope the old man didn't send you down here to sound me out. I just like travelling."

"Send me here!" Hugh laughed, abruptly. "Like travelling!" He was certainly in a strange mood. "What in the name of Hugh Trevor-Roper is that?" Hugh pointed at a rough wooden figure lying amid the chaos of Alex's bed.

"It's an old West African fertility symbol. Old juju magic – rub its buttocks and you're sure to grease your pole within the hour."

Hugh regarded the object with new respect. "Left buttock male, right buttock female?"

"Find out for yourself."

Hugh rubbed the idol's backside gingerly. Then the door crashed open and Cameron Kintyre came in, grinning. "Hugh! Unexpected pleasure."

Hugh stood up to shake his hand. "How's business?"

"Kintyre Ross is still making money, far as I know. That's merchant banking for you."

"Were you going out with Alex tonight?" Hugh continued. "I seem to remember there's a place just off Broad Street where the girls from Somerville go. It's cosy and packed to the gills, and dark enough to iron out all the disadvantages of physiognomy."

"Then it must be pitch black!" Alex said.

Kintyre hunched like Quasimodo. "It's the bells . . ."

"I know. I can smell it on your breath."

"My God, you've really got your banter worked out, haven't you?"

"Not banter, Cameron. Wit."

"Just like old times, eh?"

"Just like old times."

Hugh tossed the carving onto Alex's bed, and thrust his hands into his pockets. "Are you still seeing Lord Belton's daughter?"

Alex grimaced. "No!"

"Why ever not? She was frightfully keen on you."

"But I wasn't *frightfully* keen on her. She was like all the others . . . Then there was her brother – always interfering."

"What happened?"

Alex shrugged and threw an arm over the chairback; his shoulders were surprisingly broad. "I had to beat him black and blue. Anyway, now I'm here I'm looking for someone special."

"Special? You bloody snorter!"

"Special," Alex repeated.

In the great world, Maggie had watched with fascinated terror the Cuban missile crisis as it began. On 2 September the official news agency of the USSR, Tass, had announced that Krushchev had signed a security treaty with Fidel Castro's government. Then Washington released U-2 photographs showing the newly-built missile sites in San Cristobal, only minutes from the great cities of the United States. The Home Service brought her President Kennedy's speech as he promised 'a full retaliatory response upon the Soviet Union' if any of those missiles were ever fired. In the Pentagon, the hawks remembered the abortive invasion of the Bay of Pigs, and this time they wanted to go in with everything.

There were demonstrations against the United States and against the USSR, all over the world.

Maggie could not blame the President. The atmosphere of terror that hung over the world could not be his fault, but it was hard to know who to blame. She saw the newspaper maps, and the pictures on every edition of the television news. The Eastern bloc ships came ever closer to the armed naval picket line President Kennedy had thrown around Cuba.

It was beginning to look like total war.

Maggie had friends, not all of them women, who used to cry themselves to sleep.

She sat up late one night with David and told him with blazing fierceness that something had to be done about the merchants of death; the world had to become international and socialist.

Early the next evening, when she went to a left-wing political meeting, she was told that several British defence companies were getting together to bring an exhibition round the universities to recruit more staff at degree level – and the main sponsor was going to be Stanton Industries.

"Next autumn? Thanks, Alan."

She went straight to the college of education and found David directing a rehearsal of *Romeo and Juliet*. She told him of the Stantons' plans, and that, with his help, she wanted to complete her article about the company and its history.

"Let's do it tomorrow, finish it so that it'll be out by the weekend."

"Of course," he said, loving her, willing to do anything to please her. "I'll help you give the Stantons a hammering. Friday is when the university rag goes to press; we'll be good and ready."

"The Stantons make their living out of blood, David. And they're complacent and declining, and I want everybody to know it."

As Alex walked on through the autumnal evening he thought of the article he had just read about his family firm. Was that really true? Stanton Industries was a decaying entity shored up only by avarice and tradition – that it was *dying*, in other words?

He remembered their conclusion. "Like this country . . ." He thought of the great rivers of the north-east, exporting coal and steel and ships, and wondered if there could really be something seriously wrong.

In The Eagle and Child pub, half of Balliol's rugger team had assembled, and he saw Cameron and two or three others were already drinking pints of dark beer. They let Clarence de Soutey buy a round of drinks and slumped in spindle-backed chairs amid the glow of a coal fire that warmed the back room as more students crowded in. Somebody began an obscene rugby song.

De Soutey stood up, swaying. "Let's drink to Comrade Krushchev, and the Bomb – death and destruction!"

Silence fell immediately around their table; people, appalled, peered at them. Alex said immediately, "I'm not drinking to that, Clarence. Have some sense. I'll drink to salvation instead!"

He stood up, raised his glass, swallowed. Several of the others copied him, and the atmosphere was suddenly pleasant again.

They drank on until closing time, moving across the road to the Red Lion, then down St Aldate's to another pub, where de Soutey was refused service. They dragged him away into the night, playing rugger with his blazer. The knot of students re-enacted one of the better tries from that afternoon's varsity match, making whooping cries and shouting until two bowler-hatted university police appeared. Then they fled from the 'bulldogs' down an alley, between high stone walls, back towards their own colleges. Alex and Cameron were breathless as they came upon the statue of Oliver Cromwell.

Cameron grabbed Alex's scarf and threw it up at the bronze figure so that it caught on the upraised arm, then he ran off.

Alex shouted after him, but Cameron had gone, so he hooked a hand around Cromwell's ankle and levered himself up onto the plinth. The bronze was cold and solid, the work of hands long dead and skills lost to the modern world. He looked down at the deserted quadrangle, feeling the beating of his heart and, with sudden, biting lucidity, he knew he had found his destiny. The article by Langton & Bryant, whoever they were, had convinced him.

He inhaled the cold night air. The family, Stanton Industries, the country! They needed salvation; he intended to help provide it.

There was nothing better than the way he felt now – mastery, absolute self-assurance.

Around him the whole of Oxford was spread out like a sleeping giant. Yellow lights twinkled as the distant sound of a clock striking eleven drifted across the grass. How the world had changed since these colleges had been built. This small country had risen to become the greatest power on earth; then, in the dawn of a new century, everything had become suddenly different, as though the fire that had to live in the heart of any nation had guttered and gone out.

The night was still and quiet now, broken only by the sound of his own steady breathing, and it seemed to Alex that it must be the same across all of England. He reached up and took his scarf from the Lord Protector's arm. Cromwell's bronze face, twice life-size, stared out implacable, brooding, over the land he had made his personal domain. Alex was filled exuberantly with a sudden urge to challenge the peace of the sleeping realm. He filled his lungs with cool night air and steadied himself. De Soutey's words came back to him from the beginning of the evening, and his own remembered words rang in his ears.

"Wake up!" he shouted, his words echoing back at him from the walls. "Wake up, England!"

There were footsteps, and in the darkness Alex looked drunkenly down to see the figures of two burly policemen. The silver badges on their hats glittered as the constables regarded him patiently. Between them the smaller figure of Cameron, Lord Kintyre, swayed insensibe.

"Your friends have already woken up most of Oxford, sir," the older policeman said. "So I suggest you come down here before you succeed in your own ambitions."

Tension became unbearable. There was hoarding, supermarkets with emptied shelves; people fled from cities. In the United States people were filmed preparing their own fall-out shelters. Behind her air of poise and her political concern Maggie was terrified. In the Levellers' Club they preached action, direct action, and she knew there was no alternative.

Finally Krushchev backed down. There were rumours the Politburo had refused to back him in his adventurism. The world hadn't exploded; at the end of October the Monday papers spelled out the world's salvation: RUSSIA TO SHIP HOME CUBA MISSILES. But Maggie knew she had to devote her life to changing the world so that mass destruction, mass starvation, would no longer be possible.

A couple of months later, she watched the Queen's formal Christmas address to the nation on television. At Oxford, there were people who actually *knew* royalty; people to whom money meant nothing; people who had been places. She remembered her mother's warning, but dismissed it: how could people like that really be bad company?

The following week, Maggie took the bus into town with her mother to look at the January sales. Northumberland Street was seething with shoppers from all over Tyneside, so they had a cup of tea in Fenwick's before getting down to the serious business of bargain hunting.

In the ladies' clothes department, Bridie looked for an overcoat, and wistfully began to sort through a rack of furs. When she pulled out a mink Maggie's comments were at first approving, but she soon remembered where she was, and whom she was with. She looked at the price tag, and said, "Mam, it's over a hundred guineas."

"I can see that," Bridie said. "But I can dream, can't I?"

On fifteen pounds a week for a household of four, Maggie reflected, the fur was going to stay a dream.

Back in Oxford, Maggie found Hilary term got off to a worrying start. She had begun to lose track of what was important. Who were the people around her? Friends, acquaintances – competitors? What else did the men here want, other than her body?

She could not talk to anybody about that, but she followed the world news in detail as a kind of escapism. Algeria was free, but the U.S. seemed to want to take over the French rôle in Laos and Vietnam. To the surprise of almost everybody, when China and India had gone to war last autumn, the Chinese had come out on top – it seemed as if socialism really was more effective than the left-over Raj.

"That's what I want to cover when I'm a journalist," she told David. "International tension. You know, I bet those Stanton Industries bastards made millions out of their deals with New Delhi."

"It isn't that easy to get rich, Maggie. Look at our own words." He pushed the old student newspaper to her over the wet rings left by beer glasses.

She read out snatches of their article: "Stanton Industries has been severely damaged by the nine-week 'go-slow' of its workers … problems over foreign competition for the Shipbuilding Division, and the lost contracts in Iran and Saudi Arabia, have led to a sharp slump in the share price." She laughed. "To think we wrote that, and it's all true!"

He smiled back at her. "And serve them right."

"I can't wait till they bring their exhibition here. They're dealers in death, David. Death!"

She had felt misplaced both at home and in Oxford all winter, but on this warm, glorious morning after Easter as she walked, with David beside her, down from the Head of the River, she felt more determined; she would defy them all. Maggie sat down and from their bench seat stared across the water to where rowers were readying their boats. She was wearing a long, blue denim coat, her hands thrust deep into its pockets; gold earrings dangled from both ears.

Finally she turned to David and spoke frankly. "Do you still have faith in people? Really?"

He sighed. "What's annoying you, Maggie?"

David certainly could read people; but today she foud insight aggravating. Maggie threw him her hardest look. "You heard about

47

my latest argument. Just because I told that stupid horsey girl I could say 'want to fuck?' in six languages – and she couldn't even say it in English!"

He felt shocked. She saw it on his face. "You think it's unladylike, don't you? What a gentleman you are, David! Well, that'll get you nowhere. I only raise my voice when I'm in the right – and so the moral victory is already mine."

"But doesn't it hurt you to cause a scene? Don't you find yourself worrying what people will think?"

Maggie sighed. "Take a lesson, my dear. It's not that it doesn't hurt. The trick is not minding a damn. You need to learn that."

He put his hands on her shoulders for a moment. Her eyes were a little red and he wondered if she had been overworking – not at her studies, he would guess. "You're so lovely."

She smiled suddenly. "Still working on our charm, are we? You should forget about education and go into politics. As for this acting business . . ." Her nose wrinkled.

"But I like it. Besides, I get to speak better lines than any I could write." He changed the subject. "What's that perfume?"

"Patchouli."

"Very nice." He hesitated. "You know that friend of yours – Livia."

"Oh, God!" Maggie threw her hands up. "Not the handcuffs story! Listen, she's entitled to a life of her own; if you can't be an individual when you're a student here, when can you be?"

"Is it true about her?"

"Men! Why don't you try and sleep with her and find out for yourself!"

He sighed. Maggie knew better than anyone Livia would not be at the top of his private list – and knew who would be. He stroked the nape of her neck until she started smiling again. "There's nothing wrong with making love, David. If it's good enough for the Cabinet, it's good enough for me."

"You'll get a reputation."

"David, I already have a reputation."

"In spite of the nuns?" he asked wickedly.

"Probably because of them! Don't you remember me at school? Sent home twice for too much make-up and too little skirt. I wouldn't change for Danny, why should I change for a few Oxford snobs and gossipmongers?"

They talked at length about the university and its ways as they watched the eights stroking along the river.

Then Maggie reminisced about her mother and her father, who was now regional secretary of his union, and the terraced house where they all lived. "You were lucky," David said sombrely. "You enjoyed your childhood."

"Oh, that was an accident – personal chemistry, whatever," Maggie said. "What's important is the individual, and the future. I hate the looking back everybody does in this country!"

"But we can't get away from that – not everything in life is individual. There's family, religion, class."

Maggie laughed. "Long 'a', darling. When in Rome . . ."

"Now I hope you're not making fun of me," David said humorously. "After all, you're supposed to be on my side."

She stood up, stretching. "Come on. Come back with me."

He followed her quietly.

They bought two bottles of Chablis and then walked back together to the place Maggie had borrowed. The flat occupied the whole ground floor of a big detached Victorian house off the Woodstock Road. David looked around, impressed by this flamboyant abode.

Maggie sat in a high-backed chair, looking inattentively at the wild garden. An expensive book of Dali prints rested in her lap, and in the ashtray on the chair's arm a cigarette smoked, a long worm of ash evidence of neglect. Livia's paintings and sculptures were set among other curious things: a head in Benin bronze, framed fourteenth-century Tarot cards, thousands upon thousands of books and records.

"Impressive," David said, waving a hand.

"Money and taste," Maggie told him, almost dismissively. "But Livia, who owns it, *is* impressive. And different."

He felt drunk enough to be blunt. "Bizarre taste, I reckon."

She shrugged. "The money is real enough." She stood up, reached for a pack of cards and laid them out on the Persian rug, looking carefully at David. The cards were modern, the Tarot. He saw colourful pictures, upside down. Then Maggie sat back on her heels, her mouth distorted.

"Evil. I see there will be evil in your life, David."

Maggie, with her long red hair flying wild about her head, had considerable presence, and David was not too drunk to feel fear. "Evil – you don't mean here?"

49

"No, silly." She touched his arm, and a thrill went up it. "But you must beware. You will meet evil before many months have passed."

"Will I know it?"

"Not at first."

He stood up suddenly, pulled away. "I don't believe in any of that."

"But be careful, anyway." Maggie gathered up the cards, her hands moving with disconcerting speed. "And there is something in it. I'm Aries, a fire sign, and I run true."

David heard jazz playing, cool and remote. The sun had begun to set. He looked up, as huge swathes of gold and red appeared above the rooftops opposite. Then he emptied the last of the Chablis into Maggie's glass, gazing down at her. She was lying on the bright Ethiopian quilt that covered the bed, her shoes kicked off, and her legs inside black seamed nylons were spread wide.

He crossed the floor so drowsily drunk he felt like a swimmer in a warm sea, pulled the curtains closed, then switched on the lamp, which had a red bulb. The light made the room smaller, more intimate. Then eastern music filled the room.

Maggie said she had begun to see things with a blurred focus. David came over to her, holding the little bottle of patchouli oil. His breathy voice was sensual. "Close your eyes. I'll baptize you."

She lay back, feeling quite giggly after the sun and wine.

There was the touch of something cool and oily between her breasts. David's hands soothed the skin of her neck, massaging the aromatic into her flesh.

"Oh, that's good."

Sensual fingers unbuttoned her clothes. It happened so quickly. Maggie arched her back as the massage covered her body, first the long white swathe of her back, then the lines of her ribs, her thighs. It felt very relaxing and good. Everything in the room seemed a million miles away, but there was something telling her that this was not right. Eventually, ten thousand years later, she raised her head. The room was full of a red glow. "No. No."

He kissed her. "I love you, Maggie. Come on. Dare to."

"No." Maggie stood up suddenly, dazed and swaying, realizing she was naked. Nude, her sex glistened. "David, I know I'm on the pill –"

"It's too late to back out."

Soon, she did not want to.

* * *

50

The visit that the articulate young U.S. President made to Birch Grove to see the Prime Minister was the high point of Alex's summer.

He had asked Sir Edward to get him an invitation to one of the informal receptions; his uncle had agreed, and so Alex had been able to shake Kennedy's hand, and be impressed by the intelligence and awesome personal power of Eisenhower's heir, the thirty-fifth of America's Presidents. The handsome man had given his famous wide smile and, before Alex had to pass down the line, made a quick joke.

"The real Mr Stanton – and so we meet again."

Alex puzzled over what the man had meant, standing with the other guests and nibbling and sipping wine and making idle conversation. His eye swept over the Secret Service guards accompanying Kennedy, judging where they had their guns concealed and speculating what they would be; probably police .38s, he guessed. Even expert tailoring could not fool his skilled eye. Later, he saw JFK flown out by helicopter from a clearing amid the heavily laden oaks and beeches around the country house.

It was not till the following day that he came up with the only answer possible. The President must have known his real father. The thought gave Alex a thrill. There had been something familiar about Kennedy's voice, too, but Alex could not place the memory: there was some kind of mental resistance. He wondered if the President had really been implying that the old glory of Stanton Industries should have been inherited by another Stanton entirely. Not Sir Edward, not his son.

He sighed. You could not live on might-have-beens, after all.

After that, Alex flew to Greece for a week, then to Tehran. He was allowed to stay in the Shah's Niavaran Palace. Here Alex met Assadollah Alam, the Shah's first minister; he came from one of the great landowning families in northern Iran. There was much rioting and many deaths, over the arrest of a notorious mullah called Khomeini. Alex, with his fluent French and workable Farsi, was able to follow what was happening. Alam admitted openly he desired Khomeini's execution, but the Shah, under pressure from the Islamic establishment, refused.

"So what will you do?"

"I will do what needs to be done. I tell his majesty, you are the Shah, I am your minister. I will put down these riots any way I can, and take the blame. If I succeed, you have peace. If I fail, you can hang me, and you are still the Shah."

"Amen to that," Alex said stolidly.

Once back in England he spent a little time at the family's London house in Knightsbridge, relaxing and visiting friends, but he took the train north at the beginning of August, arriving in Newcastle in the early afternoon.

Because he was so late, Hugh had driven to the station to meet him. He was taller and thinner than Alex remembered him. His soft voice and affable manner seemed edged with a hardness now that had come to him only recently. Today was Hugh's twenty-sixth birthday and the day of his formal appointment to the Stanton Industries board, to join his father, Lord Beauford, and the others.

"You really didn't have to meet me," Alex said, "now that you're such a busy man – officially heir apparent to our little concern. Though I'm very glad you did."

"Oh, I wanted to. Craigburn is like a madhouse already."

"Better that than a mausoleum."

Hugh settled back. "It isn't just my birthday and everything. Tomorrow, when I'm on the Stanton Board of Directors, father wants me to countersign the Iranian arms contracts."

"Oh?" Alex said, chagrined that Hugh had the honour. "I suppose we should be grateful there's still a Shah on the Peacock Throne, after all that trouble over Khomeini . . . How much are they for?"

"Something like twenty-five million, US. With the oil money, the Shah stands to be very rich. His ambassador is here today. And that chap from Oman."

Alex hoped his cousin wasn't trying to avoid the limelight as he had sometimes done as a child. His birthday celebration had been arranged to coincide with one of the biggest nights Craigburn had seen for many years, a lavish party to mark the start of production of Stanton's new battle tank to which many leading figures of government and industry were invited.

As they came within sight of the estate, Hugh turned to the subject of money.

"What have you done with your share of Great Aunt Lilith's legacy?"

Alex answered only after a moment's consideration.

"I risked it all."

"What? You gambled the whole thirty thousand?"

"Every last penny."

"Good God! On what? Roulette? Blackjack? The horses?"

"None of those, as a matter of fact – the Stock Exchange."

Hugh seemed a little crestfallen. "You mean you spent it all on *shares*?"

"Yes, why not? I happen to know a few people in business, after all, and I thought a little flutter would be in the spirit of Aunt Lilith's bequest. In memory of a grand old lady."

Hugh smiled. "Perhaps you're right. She was never the same since our grandfather was killed, or so father says. Personally, I think she was always that way."

"What do you mean?"

"She was completely off her chump, Alex. You must have realized that."

"I always thought she was rather sweet. Though she did once tell me she thought you were an impossibly smug and self-important little bastard – I think I recall the phrase accurately." Alex grinned, relaxing on the comfortable back seat as the Rolls rocked comfortably on, feeling more like an ocean liner than a car. "Mind you, she was talking about you as an eleven-year-old."

His cousin sighed. "Ah, well, I suppose anyone who still had the good sense to leave us thirty thousand quid apiece couldn't have been completely demented. Anyway, let that be a lesson to you. You're too quick to rush into things. You should be like me and take the sensible middle course. How much did you lose?"

"Lose? I didn't exactly lose . . ." Alex's expression was one of mild amusement. He had bought a red E-type Jaguar with gleaming chrome and a powerful V-12 engine, but that had only been with part of his profit. "I suppose you'd call it beginner's luck."

"At least you won't have to go into business," Hugh said, no longer paying attention. "You should thank God you have your cricket."

"But Hugh, I already told you that I *want* to come into the firm."

Hugh dismissed the question. "There's no question of that for years yet. Besides, it isn't all fancy dinners, you know. Father has put me up against a very abrasive American on this Iranian deal."

"Oh? Doing what?"

"Selling, I'm afraid." Hugh tried to turn it into a joke. "All for filthy lucre."

"You must point him out, this American – *I'll* have a word with him. How will I know him?"

"Oh," Hugh said darkly, "you'll recognize Mr Hacker immediately. But I must warn you, even you may have met your match." He pointed out of his side window. "Marvellous to come home, isn't it?"

The sun was setting over the most beautiful county in England, and Craigburn was lit up like a stone chandelier. They coursed round the last bend of the long driveway towards a stone house which stood amid burgeoning green foliage. Huge trees, exotic species of shrub from all over the temperate world, had been brought here. On such a night the pillared portico of sandstone, the colour of lionskin in the floodlights, and the giant rectangular windows bursting with light, made Craigburn appear one of the most impressive great houses in all England.

Alex saw guests, many in uniform, milling around the extraordinary centrepiece.

"Good God! Look at that!"

"Yes," Hugh said. "Grotesque, isn't it?"

Parked squat and awesomely powerful on the sward between the house and the rose garden was the huge Mark VIII tank that had been brought up from the Elswick factory that morning. It stood like a sentinel beside the east wing, but what made it the centre of attraction was that its entire surface had been chrome plated. From the gun barrel right down to the links that made up its tracks, its armour shone brilliantly in the spotlights.

"Its turret reminds me of General Patton's helmet. What a bizarre, magnificent sight!"

Hugh regarded the tank coolly. "Bizarre, yes."

Their host came across to greet them, grinning and waving his hands like a stage conjurer; his face was florid against the white shirtfront of his dinner jacket, his red cummerbund bulged, and in his hand brandy swirled inside a bulbous glass.

"His Highness's birthday present!" he said, waving at the glistening tank. "For your friend the Shah of Iran, Alex, not for your cousin Hugh – rather appropriate, don't you think?"

Alex rubbed his eyes and looked again at the gleaming, forty-ton killing machine.

"Quite, but haven't you overlooked something?"

"What?"

"A couple of big pink ribbons."

Sir Edward roared with laughter and clapped his nephew on the back. "Better not let the Iranian Ambassador hear you say that. By the way, good show with the cricket, Alex. I'm proud of you – ah, you know Prince Qabus, of course?"

Alex nodded and shook hands with a tall young man in a Sandhurst cadet's dress uniform. His father was the Sultan of a big backward Arabian country with little to offer the world except the finest quality dates – and, so rumour said, oil.

After the Prince had gone, Alex turned to Hugh. "You've been to Oman. What's it like?" he asked.

"Same as in the fifteenth century," Hugh replied, shuddering, "though there has been a massive oil-strike by Shell . . ."

"No rumour?"

"Real oil, Alex. In vast quantities."

By the time they had both showered and changed into evening dress all the guests had arrived. The two Stantons took a glass of sherry each and went inside the great hall. A burst of applause met Hugh from the hundred assembled guests. A bell rang, and the rest crowded in from outside as Sir Edward called peremptorily for silence. Alex stood back against the wall, under a Gainsborough.

A huge, three-tiered cake was wheeled in: pale blue and white with an intricate tank made from icing on top. Around its circumference twenty-six candles burned.

Hugh stood up to deliver a well-rehearsed speech. Alex listened politely, and afterwards Hugh was applauded for his pains. When that finished, a twelve-piece orchestra began to play Strauss, until Sir Edward sent a word that he considered Elgar more appropriate.

Alex looked around the great house, pleased – even though Craigburn would never be his. He felt that the house had come alive tonight as it had not done in his lifetime. It was good to see it functioning properly, and how well it rose to the occasion. Even the acoustics of the great hall, which Alex had always thought cavernous, sounded fine with a couple of hundred people inside.

Later, they all took their places at table, and the first course was offered. Alex cut into the wet, green flesh of his melon, and a big man opposite him introduced himself brusquely. He was an American. The American Hugh mentioned? Alex asked himself.

"I'm Ray," the man drawled, extending a massive hand. "Ray Hacker. Until last month I used to sell airplanes for Lockheed."

The man was wearing neither cowboy boots nor a stetson, but sounded as though he ought to have been. He had a craggy, animated face. Alex nodded, shook his outstretched hand with a notable lack of enthusiasm. "You're on board to sell the new STA-2 to Washington, aren't you? Alex Stanton."

"Stanton? Oh, one of the family?"

Alex smiled circumspectly. "Younger son, you might say."

"I'm from Texas."

"Mr Hacker, you really don't have to apologize."

Hacker frowned. "It's Ray – right? I overheard you earlier quoting Jefferson, and you know, you almost got it right."

"Almost?"

"Yeah, that's 'certain and unalienable', not 'inherent and unalienable'."

Alex regarded his dinner plate thoughtfully. Hugh had been right. "I think you'll find, Mr Hacker, that Jefferson used 'inherent'. It was one of Congress's very first amendments to substitute the word 'certain'."

Hacker grinned, but his eyes were hard like diamonds, and Alex regretted his point-scoring immediately.

"Well now, I work for your Daddy, so I suppose I have to be polite to you. He wants me to sell his STA-2 in the States. I have good connections with the V.P., and Lyndon Johnson's voice in the Pentagon is loud and clear."

Alex eyed the man. "In this country we try not to talk business over the dinner table."

Hacker laughed coldly before he turned away. "If you ask me, in this country you don't know *how* to talk business – or politeness either, come to that."

Alex suddenly felt ashamed; there was something admirable about the man's zest and aggression, so why had he responded with disdain?

"Upbringing," Alex said to himself, suddenly remembering meeting President Kennedy . . .

There was smoked Tweed salmon and Craigburn's own grouse, and case upon case of Veuve Cliquot.

Hugh sat beside his father and mother at the centre of the top table, but Alex had been placed further down, facing the bumptious Mr Hacker and alongside a family relation, a grey-haired Scots baroness whose title had been called out of abeyance in 1921, but whose line dated back to 1309. She told him unstoppably of the days newly gone when debutantes were presented at the Palace, and of her own time as a lady-in-waiting.

Alex chatted with her, liking the company of stately, elderly ladies. The only thing uncultured about her was her pearls. He asked her if she knew the champagne trick.

"The champagne trick? Dear boy, I'm not entirely sure that I do," she said.

Alex regaled her with Cameron's party piece, calling for an unopened bottle of *demi-sec*. "I can drink champagne from this bottle without releasing the cork and without breaking the bottle," he told her.

"How? It's impossible!" she said.

"Mr Hacker?"

The American shrugged his broad shoulders.

A few seconds later Alex turned the bottle upside-down, wiped the cup-like base clean, then poured champagne from his glass into the upturned bottle and sipped at it.

She was delighted. Below the salt, Hacker was less impressed. "One day I'll show you something with a bottle of tequila you will *never* forget," he said, but there was not a single bottle of tequila to be had in all of Craigburn.

After the dinner came the toasts. Sir Edward raised his glass.

"Ladies and gentlemen – the President of the United States."

They drank. Then the U.S. Ambassador stood up to reply.

"Ladies and gentlemen – the Queen."

The guests dispersed while the tables were cleared away. Hugh came over for a moment, looking concerned. His voice was low. "Alex, father has one of his 'games' lined up for me tonight – on my birthday!"

"Oh. Then let's hope you carry it off well.'

"In front of other people, too . . ."

"Have you found out what he has in mind?"

"No." Hugh was still looking at the top table, and he suddenly stiffened. "I'll have to go back, now. I wish I had your good fortune, Alex."

"It's about all I will have till I'm twenty-six too!"

Alex speculated on what his uncle might intend, then left for some air. It was a superbly tropical, star-filled night, and he was surprised to find the Texan smoking a cheroot among the columns of the portico.

He was propped against the balustrade, contemplating the evening, and called out to Alex as he passed.

"Yo! – Stanton! Over here." He displayed a pearly white set of teeth, set in a tanned face. His chin was shadowed and the dinner jacket just didn't look right across his broad shoulders.

Alex breathed deep. "Taking the air, Mr Hacker?"

"Hell no, I'm a regular smog factory." He released a cloud of tobacco smoke. "Some of you British think you're pretty cool, don't you?"

"I believe the term we prefer is *sang-froid*, Mr Hacker."

"See, there you go again. The name's Ray – and nobody in the world likes smart alecs, Alex. So why don't you stick your cold blood bullshit right up your stiff upper lip?"

Alex stared, unable to decide about the man's grin.

"Go on, you sonofabitch, crack a smile. Give me the benefit of the doubt."

"I'll give you this much, Ray, it's a rare kind of charm you have."

"I know it." Hacker grinned again, broader this time, until crow's-feet appeared beside his eyes, then he punched Alex on the shoulder playfully.

"Do you sell many planes on the strength of it?"

"Sure. Enough. How about you? Sold any ships or tanks?"

"I regret to say I'm not a part of the great Stanton family business enterprise."

"Why not?"

"I'm still up at Oxford and, well . . ." Alex stopped. "To be frank, I'm not sure my uncle wants me in the –"

"Kick your way in," Hacker told him seriously. "Ten per cent talent, ninety per cent application. That's what success is made of."

Alex nodded, remembering some of the people around the Shah.

"Listen, I'm very well-paid to make judgements about men."

"Oh?"

"And I can tell you think you're made of the right stuff, Alex. So *prove* it."

"That just isn't done."

"No?" Hacker flicked a plug of ash. "Pity. Pity you didn't meet my old boss – Daniel Jeremiah Haughton: he was a coalminer's boy."

"A pitman's son?"

"Sure. From Alabama. Now he runs Lockheed. I cut my teeth in the business selling his Starfighter to the Germans, then the Japs, Italians, Canadians."

Alex smiled at Hacker, enjoying the man's blend of honesty and front. He combined crass with brash and made it a highly effective blend. "Over two thousand have been sold so far, haven't they?"

"Good," Hacker said. "Checking up? Got anything to suggest? When money talks, I'm all ears."

"You know, I do have some notions about selling our products. I've met many of the important people in the Middle East, and I have the feeling there'll be lots of changes there – and lots of business for our Armaments Division."

"You see! But you have to go for it, Alex."

Alex regarded the other man; Ray was built on a big scale, all right. "So how should I go about getting inside Stanton Industries? Tap on my uncle's study door and ask for a job?"

"Christ, no! That way you'll never be more than the boss's son – like Hugh."

Alex nodded. "You have some ideas, too – don't you?"

"Right. Listen, working for your Stanton big daddy I'm on salary. A good salary, but that's all."

"And you'd like to be rich?"

"Very sincerely, I would, Alex. Wouldn't you?"

That was the one sure way of gaining the respect and envy of Sir Edward and Hugh. Alex nodded.

"So what's your notion, Alex?"

"In the Middle East, in Africa, Asia . . . it can be hard to get to see the right people. But my background gives me access to all that. I can go to the Mid-East, Tehran especially, and talk to the people who count. The people oil has made rich, Mr Hacker."

Ray nodded. "Now I can do that in Korea, Vietnam – and the Pentagon. I'm Head of Sales for the Aircraft Division. The other boys on the board don't want me in, but they know somebody like me is necessary. You ought to do the same in armaments, Alex. I have money to risk. Do you?"

"Yes," Alex said roughly, "I have over thirty-five thousand pounds and the balls to take a chance, too."

"That's good. Buy from the Armaments Division, give yourself ten per cent commission, and sell . . . Can you do that?"

Alex spoke with complete conviction. "Yes."

"Sell everything they make, take a third of their output, a half. Then who will have control? You can go, we can go, up to your uncle's study door and kick it in and do some straight talking!"

Alex laughed, delighted. "First impressions can be misleading, don't you think, Mr Hack – Ray?"

"In your case they're so far out they're coming back again."

"I hope that was a compliment."

"Sure it was. I gave up a good career to work for you people. I don't know whether I'm beginning to regret it." Hacker's teeth champed on his cigar butt. "Looks like your cousin might be."

"You've met Hugh, I understand?"

"Afraid so. We didn't get on, you can bet."

Alex wanted to stay and talk business, but he was called into the house. He realized it was the moment Hugh had been dreading and he gave Ray Hacker his apologies before scribbling down his telephone number. Hacker, of course, had engraved business cards, with three business addresses, and homes in London and New York as well as a ranch in Texas. Things had obviously paid off for him.

The guests stood back as Alex passed, their faces uniformly serious. Cameron raised a glass, then others followed his example. They knew the Stanton traditions: they knew what was happening.

Alex went straight away to the yellow drawing room where he found the pair of shotguns that had been knocked down to him at a Conduit Street auction. He drew out the case and carried it to the billiard room into which the family and their intimates had withdrawn, setting it down on an armchair.

They had all gathered around the green baize table. Lady Grace Stanton was the only woman present. Beside her was the portly figure of Lord Beauford, the merchant banker and member of the Stanton Board.

On the billiard table Alex saw three wrapped boxes. The largest was wrapped in newspaper, and might have contained a small Fortnum's hamper. The middle-sized box, done up in Harrod's green, might have held a Chinese vase, and the smallest, no bigger than a cigarette case, was wrapped in expensive gold paper. They glowed in the pool of light shed by the playing lamps. Sir Edward guarded them broodingly while the rest of the family presented Hugh with their gifts.

60

"I spent some of my ill-gotten gains on these, Hugh. Good hunting."

"Thank you, Alex." Hugh shook his hand without meeting his eyes.

Then Sir Edward banged a silver paperweight down on the edge of the table with the air of a master of ceremonies and raised his voice.

"Tonight, my son and heir is twenty-six. Tomorrow, he will be on the Board of Directors of Stanton Industries – the finest family firm in the world. In short order, I hope he will lead one of our Divisions." He smiled at them, the overhead light making him appear ugly, almost simian. "The world is dangerous, hard. Berlin is under siege. But as that great young man from the United States said, '*Ich bin ein Berliner*'. So, if we stand together, strong and upright, we still have the chance to be great."

He stared around, obviously a little drunk. Alex found the old man's enjoyment rather embarrassing. Hugh, he sensed, felt cowed – and who could blame him? He suddenly felt sympathetic towards his cousin. Perhaps the sheer weight of expectation was not an easy thing to bear.

"But first, the test." Sir Edward was breathing hard. "Before giving any high promotion, Napoleon used to ask the officer under consideration, 'Are you lucky?' He knew that those who truly believe can bend fate to their will."

The assembled guests looked at one another expectantly, and Sir Edward turned to Hugh. It was stiflingly hot in the room. Hugh was perspiring; Lord Beauford's jowelly face was glistening.

"So far as I know, Hugh, he never devised a way to test the truth of their claims, but I intend to go one better than Monsieur Bonaparte. Three boxes are on the table before you. One contains my present to you, and the other two are empty.

"So. Are you a lucky man, Hugh?"

Hugh looked to his mother who smiled at him encouragingly. Then his eyes met Alex's. They were both a little abashed by the theatricality of the dilemma Sir Edward was posing, but both knew Hugh had no alternative but to go along with it. The undisputed ruler of Stanton Industries was capable of creating a terrible scene when defied.

"Isn't this fun?" Hugh said. His nonchalance was paper thin. "Two cheers for father." He put out a hand toward the smallest.

61

"No touching!" Sir Edward swept his hand aside. Alex watched where his own fingertips lingered protectively for an instant as well as the expression on Sir Edward's face. "I asked you if you are lucky?"

Hugh sighed. A dew of perspiration glistened on his upper lip. He knew that his father's game would not be without consequences. "Yes, I'm lucky. I'm very lucky."

Lord Beauford watched Hugh intently. There was silence now as everybody scrutinized the boxes for clues. Hugh found none.

"It isn't fair to put a fellow in such a position on his birthday."

"*Fair?* Who said life is fair? Make your choice."

Hugh drew a breath. "I suspect one really is empty." After pausing between the two lesser parcels he suddenly picked up the bigger of them. "I'll take my chance with this."

"Open it, then!"

Hugh found the box disappointingly light. He quickly tore off the paper to reveal an unmarked carton. Inside it was another. His childhood giggle escaped, betraying him. Inside a third was a fourth, and inside that nothing but a wad of cotton wool. His face fell. "Oh, I . . ."

His mother stepped forward, frowning at this mockery of her son, but his father quickly took the box away from Hugh. Alex watched him thrust a finger in and pull out a shiny key. Then he strode to the curtains and pulled them back.

"*Voilà!*"

Alex followed Hugh to the casement, and there beside the lake stood a red Bugatti roadster.

"Father, how marvellous!" Hugh cried. His nervousness was replaced by genuine delight. "You knew it was what I wanted!"

"Remember, the heart of every matter is buried deep – you must persevere until you succeed. Congratulations, son."

Hugh went down to try out his gift, and Alex followed him. Though he left the drawing room with the others, he lingered a little way beyond the stairs until everyone had gone.

Then he returned to the room and closed the door behind him noiselessly.

He went straight away to the table, carefully picked up the small box and tore it open. Inside he found another key, identical to the one that Hugh had discovered.

In the semi-darkness, a smile passed fleetingly over Alex's face. He had been right! He had read the small signs on Sir Edward's face quite correctly as Hugh's hand had hesitated over the big box. Alex had known it contained the real jackpot.

The newspaper came away easily and he opened the cardboard flaps to reveal an old gold fountain pen on top of a single sheet of vellum. He held the paper up to the lamp.

It was a deed of transfer signed by his father for shares in Stanton Industries – he was avoiding death duties, no doubt, because he retained the voting rights of the shares. Alex admired the scheme, and a moment's calculation allowed him to estimate the value of the intended gift.

Eleven million pounds . . .

Alex whistled.

Then the main roomlights blazed on. "I thought I'd find you here, Alex."

He turned to see his uncle filling the doorway. Sir Edward wore an angry expression, showing his displeasure as he stood four-square in the entrance. He advanced into the room, and accused the son he had adopted after his brother's death, "You couldn't resist it, could you?"

Alex faced him shamelessly. What had he to lose? At the age of twenty-six he would inherit his father's shares, come what may – unless Stanton Industries went bankrupt or something equally unlikely before then. "I was curious. I wanted to know the truth."

"And now you do."

"Yes."

Sir Edward Stanton was not as drunk as he had seemed ten minutes ago. He picked up the deed, folded it very deliberately in half and put it into his jacket pocket.

"All that glisters is not gold?" Alex smiled with self-conscious cleverness. He still had the gold pen as a souvenir.

"Don't banter with me, boy!"

Alex's anger rose. "You forget, I'm a Stanton, too, and I know you better than you think. You had Reid bring the Bugatti round to the front of the house. That in itself is a measure of your confidence that Hugh wouldn't come up to your standards. It was a silly, childish charade and you don't know how much you embarrassed him."

"Are you defying me?" Sir Edward's face had frozen. He picked up a billiard cue, and held it across his chest like a threat. "The test was of Hugh's willingness to take a leap in the dark, to speculate, to see if he possesses the *courage* not to play the safe option. That was always a Stanton trait right back to the first Queen Elizabeth."

"For God's sake, Uncle . . ."

Sir Edward pulled the cue up. He looked along it, checking its true. "You say *nothing* to Hugh about what you found out. Do you understand?"

Alex nodded, slowly. "If you wish. But you can't change people just like that. Hugh is Hugh. He'll never be like you – or what your brother was!"

Sir Edward's eyes flashed rage. "And back to your father, eh? But Michael is dead – and Stanton Industries is to be Hugh's domain! There can only ever be one man at the top. And that man *will* be Hugh!"

Outside, the officially appointed Stanton heir climbed into his new possession. He slapped the side of the car gleefully and smiled. He had been confronted with his father's test – and he had passed it. He gave the Bugatti a trial spin and drove off down one of the tracks that led to the far end of the estate. Its lights twinkled before he passed out of sight.

On the stroke of midnight there were fireworks. The monstrous tank rolled forward under spotlights. As the guests crowded to the windows, and the braver and drunker souls spilled out onto the steps, the turret of the bizarre silver machine turned until its fearsome gun came to bear on the people in front of the great house. A siren began wailing. Then the tank fired a volley of deafening blank rounds to mark the climax of the evening – to welcome with the sound of gunfire, as was traditional, a new generation of Stantons to the business.

3

Maggie did not want to marry David, or anybody – that was the truth. Though she dreamed twice of his soft, sensitive hands caressing her intimate places. They had slept together four more times before she called it off, not by confronting him directly with rejection but by avoiding him.

That was easy enough to do, as she had to work all the hours there were to start her career as well as keep up with her course. She even spent much of her summer commuting between Oxford and London, rather than going home. Maggie had pushed into new activities; she was writing about her time. She began to meet more people with a London base, first journalists, then a photographer, and through his parties models and designers in the fashion business. Things were becoming colourful: there was jazz in Soho, foreign accents abounded – and sometimes drugs.

The atmosphere in all these circles was sometimes full of spite and cynicism, sometimes it was idealistic, and Maggie found herself responding to all the sneers against the Establishment by becoming more and more radical herself. It was not just the Stantons; the ruling class were all a conspiracy, as her new friend Alan Hoyle insisted. He was far Left; some people said he was a Communist and a manipulator, but Maggie admired his energy and good looks – and he encouraged her journalism more than anybody else, even more than David had.

Maggie had begun placing articles in one of the local papers back home – just colour pieces about Oxford, rather than the hard news or celebrity interviews she would have preferred. And besides, she wanted to succeed in London. She had met Peter Cook, one of the backers of the satirical magazine *Private Eye*, and she knew there were opportunities there.

Alan persuaded her to send some work to a weekly called *New Times*, a pleasant forties-style magazine that used to publish Dylan Thomas and now often contained articles by people like Michael Foot as well as the New Left. Alan had told her to get onto the magazine's staff; then it could be radicalized from within.

"Its line on the USSR is embarrassingly wrong and the magazine has a large student readership. We've *got* to have our generation thinking like us, Maggie, so we can turn sons and daughters against the dead generation."

Maggie agreed. Alan Hoyle had a cutting charisma she found rather attractive, and his lips looked good to her even when they had curled into a sneer. He had the power to belittle, and he was a man of his time; the sixties were going to be different.

Then Maggie found her celebrity, just before the start of term. She charmed her way in to a reception held to honour a former Rhodes Scholar and U.S. Senator named Davidson, an old and retired member of Eisenhower's Cabinet. That evening she took him out and asked him leading questions about South Africa, the Freedom Riders, and Vietnam. He was honest with her, and she flattered him judiciously. Maggie had already done her background research, so she wrote up the piece in one twelve-hour stint, and sent it off to London first thing the following morning.

A week later she turned up at the Soho office of *New Times*, excited, full of plans to have her hard-hitting words syndicated abroad.

She sat down, smiling. "I hope you liked the piece. I didn't pull any punches."

The editor looked down solemnly; he had a file with her name on, she saw, opened. Maggie looked quickly around at the crowded office, sure she could smell printer's ink, then turned back to him because he still had not spoken.

Then he did. "I can't run this, Maggie."

"What?"

He gave the article back to her. "Not at all."

Her lower lip was trembling. "What is this – censorship? Why *not*? It's not libellous; what's factual is factual, and my opinions are sincere!"

"This piece is ugly and prejudiced, Maggie." The man closed her file. ". . . 'warmonger' . . . 'racist' . . . 'enemy of peace'. You think

66

I don't recognize Alan Hoyle's house style?" He shook his head, because he liked this talented and passionately sincere girl. "Your opinions will hurt a lot of people, if you're not careful. Including you."

Maggie was very upset that it had all gone wrong. Alan Hoyle was very supportive.

"Listen, Maggie, it isn't over yet. You want to get back at the Stantons? Well, you might have a chance."

She had forgotten about the exhibition. "How?"

He told her.

There were polite ways to kill people – if you believed the Stanton Industries brochures.

Eight days after the new academic year began, the travelling exhibition came to Oxford. It was held in a large central hotel, and when Maggie went to see it she found it more impressive and strangely touching than she had imagined. Vickers, Marconi and Stanton concentrated mostly on up-to-date weapons – tanks in the Sinai Desert, jet aircraft over Korea, guided missiles, and a metallic, silvery model of a British nuclear submarine that would carry ballistic missles – but there were other things, preserved under glass on the Stanton stand. She saw cannonballs from 1588, retrieved from an Armada galleon wrecked off Holy Island. There was the famous, faded letter from George Washington, acknowledging the help of Abraham Stanton in arming his men. Tattered banners from the British assault on Afghanistan in the 1880s were spread above the rifles and Stanton field-guns that had armed them.

There were many students wandering about among the exhibits. None were friends of hers; none seemed likely to be Left, or particularly sympathetic, and she wondered how the bland organizers behind their tables of brochures could be shamed. Everybody knew that NATO was an open anti-Soviet conspiracy, and Alan had assured her that Stanton Industries made napalm that had been used on freedom-fighters in Algeria and Vietnam, and he would not have lied to her.

Two of the students inside the exhibition picked disdainfully through the leaflets as the thin, bespectacled man behind the desk explained. "It's a thing called 'the milk round'. Finding the most promising candidates –"

67

"I don't think much of your salaries," the shorter man said in faintly Scottish tones. "Industry? You pay nothing, compared with the City."

His tall, suntanned companion shook his head. "And you and your brochures keep talking about a 'secure' career. A big business isn't like the civil service. Armaments should give a man the chance to travel, to sell. You could go to Washington, DC one day and to Tehran the next. Why don't you encourage that instead of all this nonsense about the guaranteed retirement pension at sixty? Is that how you attract men with a killer instinct?"

"As they say," his companion added, "profit has to be king."

The man gave an insincere smile. "Are you both students? If you went to the right sort of school –"

"A bloody public school is what you mean! Listen, don't you know the man running Lockheed was a coalminer's son? And that company is expanding a damn sight more quickly than Stanton Industries."

The Stanton Industries representative pursed his thin lips. He pulled his brochures back. "I don't think you two are the sort we need in the firm."

"Why not? I've been to most of the countries Stanton Industries sells to – including Iran. I've even been inside the Pentagon. Doesn't that interest you?"

The recruiter straightened his tie. A few other students, grinning, were eavesdropping.

"Not very much. As for money, if you succeeded in getting onto the 'B' salary scale, then in eleven years –"

"Payment by results. That's what you need," said the Scots voice.

"But –" The man threw up his hands. "You'd spoil the system! You'd get every johnny-come-lately trying to outdo his betters!"

"Of course I'd spoil the system," the tall man said, "because it's so obviously rotten."

"Hummph. I happen to know Sir Edward can't stand loud people who rock the boat."

"Then the more fool him. Ideas are always improved by tough-minded discussion – why else have we got brains to think with, and vocal chords for speech?"

"No future at all," the man said, flushing. He reached for pad and pencil. "Not in our firm. What are your names? I intend to blacklist both of you."

The tall, blond man shrugged and then turned to go. "Alexander Stanton and Cameron Kintyre of Mackinnon."

They went to look again at the letter from George Washington, preserved under glass, and the little pile of gold guineas that accompanied it.

"They say", Cameron mused, "that your ancestor's help was critical, don't they?"

Alex stared at the letter, unable to decipher the eighteenth-century handwriting but impressed by the mere presence of the letter from America. "Yes. Without the Stantons, the War of Independence would have been lost. As it was, it was a damn close-run thing – much closer than most Americans realize."

He suddenly remembered arriving in America himself, the time his father had been killed.

His uncle Edward, the London chairman of Stanton Industries, had brought them over on the *Queen Mary*, first class all the way to New York. It had rained during disembarking and for much of that morning, but that had not mattered to Alex. He would see his father again, for the first time in weeks.

He remembered he had been overwhelmed by his view of Manhattan, the steel and concrete towers. There had even been a faint rainbow over the crested outline of the city. He recalled seeing the Statue of Liberty again, the century-old bronze promise long ago turned green, holding the symbolic torch.

But although his father had been waiting on the crowded pier, his mind had been on business. Though he hugged his son and stood with a hand on his shoulder, Michael Stanton first had to reach an agreement with his brother. He had been in America for four months and he had plans, large-scale plans, which he had begun to describe as soon as he had escorted Edward ashore.

Alex remembered the argument that had raged over his head after his father's brisk greeting. Everything in Stanton Industries, their three-centuries-old family firm, had to be changed. So his father had said.

"It has to be, just has to be, Edward! This is the land of opportunity, and we must take ours."

"The STA-C is only a plane."

"One plane is enough to make a difference! That and the fighters'll get us established here. I'm going to fly to England the old, slow way and then fly back in the STA-C myself. We'll get the record for the

Atlantic crossing. We need the publicity. It's like oxygen for our sales. And we have to do something to get on the map, break out of the old ways and the old traditions, or else we die."

"Everything has to be changed?" Alex remembered his uncle Edward asking, his face grimacing at the rain. "But we have made guns since 1588 and the time of the Armada. Think of the history! What must be changed?"

"*Everything* in the company. We need to reorganize from top to bottom."

"Especially at the top? Meaning me!"

With that single word, Alex realized now, battle had been joined.

What had happened since? Stanton Industries, their company, was still an empire in war industry. It had once been famous for the steel sword and the musket-ball; but now the family produced more modern instruments of conquest. In Korea their STA-1 had been better than the F86, and far ahead of the Soviet MiG-15. Now they produced Mach-2 jet fighters, superb tanks, and their shipyards made some of the very finest fighting vessels in the world. Alex knew there had been recent set-backs, though nobody in the family or company ever talked about them – but there was also the history, the centuries of greatness in the past. Even the US Army and Navy had been proud to use their equipment ever since the end of hostilities in 1783 – though the enemies of their company said that in the Revolutionary War, and in other wars before and since, Stanton Industries had sold arms to both sides. The Stantons knew how to look after themselves and make a profit, and the devil with everybody else.

Alex knew most of those stories were true . . .

Was this gloomy day going to be Stanton Industries' day? Maggie remembered reading about that huge party at Craigburn, held for Hugh Stanton. There had been princes and generals, ministers of the crown and ambassadors, a duke. The Establishment, standing behind the Stanton family. She looked at the letter from George Washington again, standing aside as two upper-class young men had crowded in beside her. What did her family have, in comparison? Nothing at all – except the prospect of justice, and she made the depressing admision that Alan Hoyle was right, and that justice was not nearly enough.

She left the exhibition feeling as grey and downcast as the weather.

In front of the glass doors to the hotel was a little demonstration, a dozen or so people carrying banners that said PEACE COUNTS MORE

THAN MONEY and THE SHAME OF WAR. The few passers-by ignored them, or gave smiles that were close to sneers. A passing bus made a dirty pool of rainwater splash up.

Maggie stopped to chat, annoyed that so little was happening. Alan Hoyle was here, with a little coterie of his followers from the Levellers' Club. She turned up the collar of her long blue denim coat. "Not much happening, Alan."

"We're being what they call 'civilized', you see." He frowned, a tall, athletic man with dark eyes and hair.

Alan was researching for a trade-union sponsored Ph.D, and he had spent time in Italy, France, and both Germanies. In her eyes, as she sheltered in the doorway to belt up her coat, he was a romantic figure. "The more fool us, then."

"I agree." Hoyle extended his hand. Mere weather was irrelevant to his purposeful nature. The day had turned cold, with a thin, occasional drizzle. "Here to see the enemy, Maggie?"

His smile was dazzling as ever.

"I suppose so. They're all warmongers, aren't they?"

"Exactly. I was saying in East Berlin only last month ..." He stopped, and spread his hands. "If only you'd take a more active rôle, Maggie, I could trust you with so much."

"I will," she said, hurt that she had let him down. "I'm still thinking over what you said about me going into journalism or the BBC."

He looked into her eyes. "Maggie, revolutionaries need discipline; you must choose which side you're on."

"I have," she said, as some of the others crowded around, trying to shelter under the eaves. "Now I'm on the student magazine I can get publicity for a bigger demo here in the street, banners and everything."

Hoyle stroked his chin thoughtfully. "That isn't nearly enough."

A badly-dressed girl with him said, 'But Bonnington always says –"

"Forget him," he dismissed her brusquely. Then he smiled at Maggie. "You say your father's an old adversary of the Stantons."

"Cain and Abel."

"That sounds like the Stanton family." He peered at her. "You might get a chance to see your enemy in person."

She raised a wet eyebrow. "What do you mean?"

"One of the sons is an undergraduate here, at Christ Church. I'll point him out, sometime."

She wiped at her eyes, immediately interested. "So that's where . . . But I suppose he'll be another chinless wonder, like all the rest."

The cars hissed through the wet streets as they discussed possibilities; something daring seemed best. They stood talking in the cold, feeling increasingly irrelevant as people strolled in and strolled out. It was obvious to Maggie that Alan resented this with something more than passion, but she could not help thinking about the Stantons, and her father's coveted revenge. She crossed the street again to buy a newspaper.

Hoyle stopped a pair of students as they left the hotel. He waved towards the steamed-up glass doors and the cheerful recruiting posters. "Is that greatness? I say that they're scum. Bloody-handed scum. Aren't they?"

"The Stantons and the rest of them?"

"Exactly."

"I'm sure they aren't saints."

Maggie looked over, seeing turned backs, and Alan's determined face. Then Alan Hoyle jabbed a stiff finger at the man's chest, his followers bunching up behind him. "I know exactly who you are."

It was quite a deep voice, smooth, but with resonance. "And you still insult us with language like that? Cameron . . ." He eased his friend to one side.

Maggie turned away for a moment to reach for a proferred umbrella.

Hoyle showed a fist. "Is this the kind of argument you –"

Then the blond student whirled around too quickly for anybody to stop him and smashed Hoyle in the face with his left hand. Hoyle stumbled backwards two steps, then collapsed into the low hedge. He kicked and sprawled for a moment, groaning.

Alex rubbed his knuckles thoughtfully and glared at the group, wondering if he had actually broken the man's jaw and not caring if he had. There was violence in him. They recognized it, and not one of them dared to confront him. "Nobody else?" He looked around measuringly. "A pity. Let's go, Cameron."

Maggie dodged a hump-back Volkswagen and went over to help. Alan was on his feet by then, wiping the blood from his mouth. His eyes were bright with humiliation and anger, and his lower lip was trembling. "That's the ruling class for you! Violent, violent people!"

"He must be a real bastard, whoever he is."

Hoyle saw her for the first time and his eyes seemed to blaze with rage. *"But I can be a thousand times worse."*

Somehow, she believed him.

That night, there was a fire in the exhibition. Fortunately a late-night reveller had dialled 999 as soon as the flames were visible behind the glass. The fire brigade managed to hold the damage to a minimum. The local paper reported that it was probably arson, and that the lives of hotel guests had been endangered – though only a few exhibits, like the letter from George Washington, had been damaged or destroyed.

On Friday, Maggie stared at the boarded-up ground floor of the hotel, wondering if the fire really had been started deliberately. She sighed, pressing a fingertip on the cold glass. Two post-graduate students passed by; their black roll-neck sweaters and goat beards marked them out as beatniks. Even in this weather they affected open-toed sandals.

It began to rain again, and so she pulled her red mac tightly around her body. Then she realized there was somebody standing beside her. He must have moved very lightly on his feet, because she had not heard him come up.

"Did you see that exhibition?"

"I certainly did."

"They really are killers, aren't they?" She shook her head fiercely. "The Stantons and all those others."

"Oh, worse than that," he told her. "Much worse."

"Are you a student?"

"I am. Very pleased to meet you." He was tall and good-looking. He seemed a little older than she, and somehow familiar. His light hair was drenched and dripped onto the collar of his coat, but his face was tanned as if he had recently come from somewhere warm and sunny, and the rain did not seem to bother him. "I'll tell you what, can't we get out of this rain?"

"Right." She turned her collar up and walked quickly, trying to step over the brown puddles that mottled the path. "I was going to the bookshop, actually."

"Fine." He had a long stride.

By the time she reached Blackwell's, she was soaked, her hair hung down limply from her French beret and her calves were spattered with mud. Inside, the lino was slippery with water and the sales assistants looked peevishly at the unusually large volume of customers. Self-conscious, worried that she looked bedraggled and unattractive, she glanced up at a shelf of history books: von Clausewitz, Winston Churchill, A.J.P. Taylor – so much work to catch up on . . .

Then she missed her footing at the step.

She stumbled against the man who had already turned to catch her. Her red hair swirled, and suddenly her lips were only inches away from his. She flushed.

"Oh, I beg your pardon."

"Quite all right. Here, let me help you."

She had to lean on the wall, her ankle hurting, as he knelt. He handed back her muddy shoe, but pointed to the heel. It had come away from the leather.

"I'm terribly sorry banging into you. It was all my fault."

"No, I'd blame the floor. It's so wet. Not that I minded very much."

She glanced warmly at him. "How's my shoe?"

He showed her the broken heel again. It dangled uselessly. "Well, you can't get far with that. Not in this weather."

"No."

As she looked up, she saw again there was something familiar about him. He smiled suddenly. "The rain it raineth every day, upon the just and unjust fellah, but more upon the just – because the unjust has the just's umbrella!"

She smiled back. "Very good."

"Of course."

"I've seen you somewhere before."

"I don't think so," he said. His expression was warm. "I'm quite sure I would have remembered."

"Perhaps not at Oxford."

"Tyneside, you mean?" He had recognized the accent. "More likely here." He waved at the books. "You're reading history?"

"No."

"So you're not a student?"

She did not answer him directly. "I just wanted to get out of the rain." She brushed a straggle of wet hair from her face. "The weather's terrible, isn't it?"

"I'm enjoying it. Over the summer I was baked in a desert climate for almost a month, and I can tell you, English weather's quite the most unjustly maligned thing in the world."

"How lucky you are," she said with sudden interest. He was from the big world; he had travelled. Their eyes met, kindling. "Where did you go?"

He shrugged. "Iran."

"How wonderful. It must be so exotic!"

"It is, though I had some business out there and they had a curfew running some of the time; I didn't get to see many of the sights."

"Even so –"

"Look," he said quickly. "Why don't I help you to the espresso bar on the corner? I know a place not far from here. They'll fix your shoe in a jiffy. I'll take it down for you."

She looked at him and smiled again. "Would you? That's very kind. My name's Maggie, by the way."

He grinned and helped her hobble towards the exit. "How do you do? I'm Alex. Christ Church."

There was shouting in the street. The door burst open. Everyone looked towards the commotion. A woman stood in the doorway. "He's been shot, he's been shot!" she cried.

"Who's been shot?" Alex caught her shoulders. The woman was hysterical. There was nothing unusual on the street.

"Alex?" Maggie said suddenly. She knew she would have to run, stockinged feet or not. "Alex – Stanton?"

The woman's voice was much louder. "President Kennedy! He's been murdered!"

Later that winter of 1963, David Bryant met James Battersby for the second time, at a theatrical party north of Oxford.

Battersby was a student at one of the oldest colleges; at a backstage reception lavish with cheap red wine and pleasant-faced girls desperate to become actresses he had asked a lot of questions about David's historical knowledge and writing ability, then gone out of his way to impress. David, politely, had allowed himself to be impressed, and accepted Battersby's invitation to a party to be held out of town next evening at the house of a friend.

They were yelling from the back seas. "Party!"

David laughed, steering carefully onto the bend.

Oxford's winter had turned ice-cold, but tonight he didn't mind. Though the east wind had chapped his lips and made his mock-leather car seats brittle, he was in high spirits, and his Morris Traveller insulated them from the worst of the cold. The heater didn't work too well and neither of the doors fitted properly, but tonight no one wanted to complain. A bottle of gin, circulating among his passengers, might have had something to do with that.

Yesterday had been the last of five nights of Brecht's *Mother Courage*, and although it wasn't the OUDS, it had been something of a triumph for their amateur company. As they drove through the dark lanes the talk was of the future.

"Tonight Oxford, tomorrow the Old Vic, the day after Broadway," David said expansively. "And Labour to power in the next election!"

They cheered David, as he drove out of town for fifteen miles, wondering why Battersby had been so insistent on his being here tonight, though he would have appeared anyway; he thought Maggie might show up.

Rolly's farmhouse was surrounded by stands of stark birch trees. Its white walls shone brightly in the moonlight, and the warm orange glow that flooded from its windows welcomed them.

The party was in full swing when they arrived. Flashing lights and loud music created a dynamic atmosphere, and Rolly was already roaring drunk, wearing an outrageous leather suit and grinning inanely at his friends. He had installed a big ten-year-old American juke-box in the corner, and was rattling dimes into it.

Battersby came up, waving a bottle of Scotch and a bottle of French brandy. "David Bryant! The clever man with the memory."

David didn't need total recall to remember him, too. "Hello, James," he said politely. "Did you come in the Jag?"

"No. Still off the road. I had a little bump."

"What'll you do for a lift back?"

Battersby swallowed more Scotch and looked around quickly. "I'll think of somebody." Battersby had a wild sense of fun and was always planning some stunt. Once he had stranded two friends up a church spire. Another night he had emptied a drunken friend's room of furniture, setting it all up in the middle of the college quad with his friend in the bed, and then he had set the blankets on fire. He always knew in advance about the most interesting parties, and he was a prominent member of the Bullingdon.

"Come on, Bryant! Have a drink. Live life a little."

"I'd like to stay sober, actually. I was hoping to meet somebody tonight – Maggie Langton. And I have a car to drive."

"Indeed you do." Battersby clapped him on the back. "Wonderful fellow."

David suddenly felt nervous enough about meeting Maggie to take several swallows of fiery Scotch; he could always get a taxi, after all. Maggie had haunted his thoughts and his dreams even more, after he had slept with her. He wanted to meet her tonight and try to restart their relationship.

Later he tried, haltingly, to explain that to Battersby. By then he had had enough whisky to become confiding.

He told James about the girl from his hometown who he wanted so very badly but who had become so distant. The party had become packed with students, and he was obliged to raise his voice. Maggie was so beautiful. In his memory, she would always be naked that first time in bed, and he remembered her in a wickedly tight red dress. "I don't know what she's doing, and I love her so much, James . . ."

"Isn't it terrible when you can't get the woman of your dreams even to look at you?" James said scathingly. "It's the old problem."

David looked at him. "What do you mean?"

"Women – they're all whores in their hearts. They're only ever interested in money."

"Do you really think so?"

"Of course! I bet this Maggie girl would jump at the chance of a candlelit dinner for two at Mario's – especially if you turned up for her in a white Jaguar."

David had spent most of the money he'd saved from work on his battered Morris Traveller. "Fat chance of that," he began, then he saw James's meaning. He drove a white '61 Jaguar saloon, and it sounded like an offer. "You'd do that for me?"

"Bryant, what are friends for? I knew I'd be able to do you a favour."

"Yes, but –"

"That's settled, then. Now don't look so guilty. Look, if it'll salve your conscience – what do you know about Robert Peel?"

David looked as though he had missed something, then said, "Robert Peel, 1788 to 1850, created the police force, repealed the Corn Laws, broke *and* saved the Conservative party . . ."

Coppling, James's drunken friend, guffawed. "All on his own?"

"So the story was true . . . You have a memory like a filing cabinet, Bryant," James said, and drew out a pound note. "I have an essay to write on Peel by Thursday. If you were to write it –"

"Me?" David swilled down the rest of his drink. It was a strange, not to say immoral, idea, but then he thought of his work being criticized by an Oxford history don. He thought too of the candlelit dinner with Maggie. "I can write the best essay on Peel *you've* ever seen."

James smiled, missing the sarcasm. "Fabulous!" he said, and produced a crumpled paper.

David read the large, spidery writing: "'Forget your principles, stand by your party.' (Disraeli) Discuss this quotation with reference to Sir Robert Peel."

James waved the money enticingly. "By Thursday?"

David's nod was earnest.

"Cash on delivery, then." James stuffed the banknote back into his pocket.

"You're pissed, Bryant," Coppling sniggered.

"And you're bloody ugly as well as stupid, Coppling. But in the morning I shall be sober."

Battersby went on to explain his philosophy; he was the only son of a well-known QC, and he was drinking up his father's money at an impressive rate.

"Like father, like son, eh?"

Battersby squinted at him from behind his glasses. "What do you mean, Bryant?"

"Well, you both spend a good deal of time at the bar."

"Making contacts, Bryant. Not the nonentities your sort associate with, but people of position and consequence! You must clear your mind of all this moralistic nonsense about virtue and hard work!"

David looked at the man, rather wanting to believe in his vision of the world. He made it sound so easy, and clearly he did not spend many nights working till one in the morning.

"Is life actually like that?" he asked. "You think you can *really* take it on and win?"

James was emphatic. "Trust me!"

Then somebody nudged David, and he glanced up in time to see Maggie make her entrance. She was accompanied by a dark-haired man well known in University politics: Alan Hoyle. David swallowed more whisky, remembering Battersby's words. He moved forward purposefully.

Alex put his head back and stared up at the plaster scrolls on the ceiling. He felt restless, unable to concentrate.

Cameron poked him. "What's the matter with you, Alex? You've been a caged tiger ever since Kennedy was murdered."

"I'm thinking, man, thinking."

"Not about the future of the western world, I can tell."

Alex forced a smile. "If you really want to know, it's a woman."

"A *woman*? Good grief – what a tragedy."

Alex's eyes lit up, then just as quickly dulled. "I think I'm in love with her."

Cameron became curiously sharp. "So – who is she?"

"Huh?"

"Her name, man? Where's she from?"

He shook his head. "Does it matter? I don't know anything at all about her. One minute she was leaning on my shoulder, and the next – she'd gone. Vanished. Cameron, I must see her again. I must."

Maggie had been looking sophisticated and attractive in a clinging black dress.

David knew he had ruined everything, everything.

He picked himself up and vomited over Rolly's five-bar gate. His breath came panting, steaming in the cold night air. There was a foul taste in his mouth. Why had Battersby made him drink so much? He remembered running into Maggie there and pawing her. It was so embarrassing even the memory made his cheeks flush.

"Come on, Bryant, I need a lift."

It was Battersby, together with Coppling, who was wobbling unsteadily on his feet.

"I don't feel very well." David looked up at him. The night sky shimmered curiously. James's face was distorted. "Where are my friends?"

James sneered. "Those silly small-timers? I got rid of them, of course. I need your car myself."

"I can't drive. We'll have to walk."

"Walk? It's fifteen miles!"

Almost everyone had already left, and the track was deserted. Battersby lost his temper. He seized David by the jacket and shook him so that David felt his head snap back and forth, then Coppling's hand was digging in his pocket.

"I'll drive," James said curtly. He took the keys from Coppling's hand. David slid to the ground, and James said, "We'd better bring him along – we don't want to be accused of purloining another car. After the last time, my father said he won't hush up any more incidents."

The dark green bonnet was rimed with white frost and the flat, two pane windscreen was milky white.

"Damned thing!"

James pumped at the accelerator pedal as the engine turned over. It sounded rough, like a smoker hawking, then it died. Swearing, he turned off the headlamps and tried again. The heater hissed cold air over them and there was a nauseating smell of unburned petrol before he succeeded in bringing the engine to life.

The Morris's headlights cut swathes through the frozen mist that lay over the road. James changed gear noisily, and the tyres squealed on the road as he followed the gully between high country hedgerows.

"Slow down, James, I feel sick."

"Use the window!"

Coppling began to shift his weight left and right on the back seat like a sidecar racer when the road veered, and started to sing a rugby song. James joined him loudly.

The streetlights of a country town soon began to flicker past like a kaleidoscope. David wanted to be sick again. He saw the speedometer showing seventy-five and told James to slow down again, but Battersby was singing obscenities loudly. David shook his head, and pushed himself back in his seat as the car zig-zagged across the white line. James began rocking the wheel in time to the verses he was singing. Outside was country dark again, a line of brilliant studs flashed in the middle of the road and red-eyed zebra posts reared up at corners, leading them into tunnels of dark winter bushes and trees where trunks rose like columns in a cathedral. He saw a hare's green eye blink at them and disappear.

"I can't find the cigarette lighter," James said irritably. "If you paid thirty pounds for this heap, Bryant, you were robbed."

"It's getting you home!"

"But what a wreck!" James laughed in his face. Now that Battersby was no longer being charming, he was appalling. "Just the sort of heap I'd expect you to own."

As he turned right onto another country road, the gears juddered with the sound of grinding cogs.

"For God's sake, James, you'll ruin the engine."

Battersby laughed. "What difference does it make? You've got ninety thousand miles on the clock ... But I can show you a way to raise your standard of living."

David was sobering up. "What do you mean?"

"Oh, you'll find out. Just trust me."

David swayed as Battersby took another corner, badly, and at high speed. There was nothing worse, he reflected, than being in the hands of a careless driver who thought he was an expert.

Battersby yelled, "Don't you want to listen to more of my philosophy?"

"James, I'm tired – and I want to go to bed."

Coppling took up the words in another song and James echoed him.

David blinked slowly and wondered what Battersby had meant about raising his standard of living.

Alan Hoyle looked round nervously and headed towards the gentlemen's lavatory. Victoria Station was crowded with commuters and people buying tickets to travel home for Christmas. Carol singers chorused behind him: 'God rest ye merry, gentlemen. Let nothing ye dismay . . .'

One last time he checked his watch: five-thirty exactly. Then someone tapped him on the shoulder. He turned round expectantly, but his face quickly became angry. The man in front of him was a shambling ruin: cheeks blasted red, sour alcoholic breath, whiskers and plastered hair. "Spare a tanner for a cup of tea, guvnor?"

Hoyle swore. In an efficient society, human wreckage like this would be disposed of, Christmas or not. He handed the derelict off and plunged into the crowd.

Seconds later he was back.

What if he doesn't come? he thought. Fear made his legs unsteady as he went down the steps to the lavatory. The urinal stalls were all occupied, and as he waited he opened his copy of the *Oxford Mail*, turned it inside out and refolded it. He felt cold under his heavy coat; the ammoniacal smell of the Victorian lavatory disgusted him. As he relieved himself he saw painted on the wall a piece of graffiti that read: *After 100 years of reformist politics still 90% of the nation's wealth is owned by 5% of its population. Revolution now!*

But he was too tense to smile at it.

From behind him someone said, "Excuse me – "

The voice wasn't English. Hoyle turned away and went quickly back up the stairs. Cold air washed over him. Two policemen were standing at the entrance, so he lowered his head and walked on. As he passed W.H. Smith's bookstall he felt someone touch his back. He ignored it.

"I make it five-thirty exactly."

"I always set my watch five minutes fast," he replied, and the man nodded and strolled away.

Hoyle followed him at a distance, keeping his eye on the man's grey raincoat as the hurrying crowd weaved between them, relieved that the contact had finally been made.

They ended up at a Pimlico café. The man looked carefully at him, unable fully to conceal his annoyance. He had a blond crew cut and brown-tinted glasses. "*Never* use the embassy again – do you hear me?"

"I had no choice," Hoyle said. He was worried, but he knew he must seize his chance. "Anyway, you know me well from all those 'conferences' – and your own man Bonnington's been drowned."

The East German took off his glasses and stared at him, light-eyed.

"Not British counter-intelligence?"

"No."

"But not, I think, an accident?"

"Nor that," Hoyle said, knowing he had gambled correctly. "His friends decided they needed a stronger leader. It's a time of changes, Mr Schaller. That's the feeling. Our people are growing out of student politics, you see. They think it's time for action, on the industrial front, against Vietnam, other things. We must move forward."

The East German looked thoughtful. "Active measures, yes?"

"So Bonnington had to go . . . But I made his drowning look like an accident."

Schaller replaced his glasses. "You are competent, it seems. And what is your intention?"

"What do you think?" Hoyle spoke rapidly, urgently. "I know Bonnington was your agent; but I can do far more than be a mere agent of influence. This country is rotten-ripe. It can be taken. I know what you did in Cambridge in the thirties. We can do the same today."

"It is easy to talk, Mr Hoyle."

"Listen to me! We already have a national network publishing a magazine called *Forward*. With your backing I can make use of that network. We can push things inside the Labour Party first; then we will be able to push a future Labour government."

82

Schaller's face had frozen. "You will undertake to enter a Labour government, as our agent?"

"Not myself, no." He shook his head. Better get it said openly. "I want to be the man behind the scenes. I'll place people in parliament, high in the civil service, and the media. They will answer to me; I will answer to you – if you agree to help me now."

"That is a very ambitious undertaking."

"I already have several other alternatives which will pay off quickly."

"In particular?"

Hoyle watched the brown panes of Schaller's glasses. Behind them his eyes were blank, shark-like discs. "You've heard of Stanton Industries – sending guns to Vietnam, making this STA-2 supersonic fighter? I know people there. One especially is very high up. Those people can keep us both well informed."

Quite suddenly, the East German grinned in a way that lit up his face. Once again he seemed fully human. "Already an agent inside Stanton Industries, eh? As you say here – welcome to the club, Mr Hoyle. And be assured, comrade, we look after our own."

Hoyle saw he had succeeded. "That should take the pressure off you, then, Mr Schaller."

Schaller's grin disappeared. "The only pressure you should worry about, Mr Hoyle, is the pressure the British security people would exert on you if they found out what you were doing."

Hoyle leaned back. If there's going to be pressure, he thought, it will be brought to bear by me. And you, Franz Schaller, are going to help me apply it.

This nation is going to be mine.

4

"And so we must believe", said the speaker, "that the Union of Soviet Socialist Republics is leading the struggle for world peace, and we must also believe that in spite of the lies and propaganda coming from capitalism, there is really only one side to choose."

Alan Hoyle sat down to enthusiastic applause.

The Cowley branch of the Levellers' Club met at the Queen's Head on the corner of Temple Road. Here, in a room above the public bar, the most serious and committed Socialists in Oxford gathered on the first and third Fridays of each month, to subject the world to a rigorous Marxist scrutiny.

On such nights a curious mixture could be seen in that shabby but comfortable room: Marxist academics and students, Communist assembly workers from the nearby BMC car plant, and even young Labour careerists who hoped to go as quickly as possible from their Oxford colleges into the House of Commons as MPs – all knew that it did their credibility as radicals much good to be seen lending their support to the Levellers. The Levellers, after all, were the real thing.

David sat at a long table strewn with copies of the *New Left Review* and various strident, duplicate news sheets, including *Forward*, which was produced by the national network of Levellers' Clubs. He threw in a few coins now when a collection was taken up for Bonnington, a founder of the group who had been tragically drowned a few months earlier.

"Everything's changed since '63," a cheerful Northern Ireland girl told him, "since Alan took charge."

"Now we're collecting to help publish the Bonnington essays. He can't, himself."

"Oh?" David looked at her. "Why not?"

"He died."

David was cradling his dimpled beer glass while he half-listened to an old-timer giving a highly personal analysis of the TV series about the Great War that had started on the new BBC 2 channel.

Then Maggie came into the room. She sat on the other side, by the featured speaker, Alan Hoyle. David's heart twisted inside his chest and he had to look away. This was the first time he had seen her since Rolly's party, partly because his embarrassment at the memory of their last meeting was still able to wake him in a cold sweat.

". . . it was cold-blooded murder, pure and simple!"

David opened his eyes, to see Alan Hoyle's face.

The old man's face was reddening. His mouth quivered. "The generals who sent those young lads over the top should've been tried for war crimes! I know – I was there!"

David stood up. He decided to move to where Alan Hoyle was holding court. Only last week Hoyle had returned from a trip behind the Iron Curtain. His speech had been excellent, touching and aggressive by turns, and he had implied that he possessed significant contacts in East Berlin and Moscow, workers' paradises, so-called. David tried to smile, but he was wondering if Hoyle really did believe everything he said he did.

At his elbow David saw Maggie nodding in agreement. He pulled up a chair and sat close behind her. She was arguing with Hoyle with an energy that had been lacking the last time he'd seen her. There was colour in her cheeks, her eyes flashed, and she was as animated and as beautiful as ever. He felt a sudden pang of desire.

"But if you repress counter-revolutionary tendencies by means of *terror* you end up living in a rigid, terror-stricken society," Maggie said.

"You must protect the Revolution ruthlessly, Maggie. It will have its enemies both without and within."

"But then you recreate the very autocracy you're seeking to abolish! You create the machinery that murdered Trotsky."

Several listeners nodded sagely.

"You're too concerned with him," Hoyle said. "Forget Trotsky. He's a distraction, and there are casualties in every revolution."

"Hello, Maggie."

She turned round at the sound of his voice and seemed surprised to see him. "David. Where've you been hiding?"

85

"I've been working. Look, about that party – I want to apologize for being drunk."

She smiled and touched his arm lightly. "Is that all that's bothering you? It's forgotten about."

"I suppose you could tell I had too much to drink and . . ." He let the words run out as Hoyle shifted impatiently and three or four hostile pairs of eyes turned on him. He tried to make it casual. "I'd do anything for you, Maggie."

She smiled again, but this time David felt less warmth in it. He wondered suddenly if she were sleeping with Alan Hoyle. He felt a sudden flare of jealousy and found his fists clenching. He had to turn his gaze away.

The pause grew awkward. Someone blew cigarette smoke across the table. Then Maggie began to turn back to Hoyle, so David quickly produced two tickets and gave them to her. "I know you're fond of Shakespeare. I thought perhaps you'd like to come and see us act. I'm playing the title role in –"

"Thanks." She smiled, her eyes glowing green. "Liked Alan's speech? I hope you enjoy tonight's discussion."

"You can bring a friend."

"I'd like that." She took the tickets.

David cursed inwardly, wondering which friend she meant. Alan Hoyle, or somebody different?

She looked at him for a last moment, her cheekbones flawless and high. She carried her familiar beauty well, but something in him blamed Maggie for leaving him to move to a vacant seat and listen to Hoyle's words by himself.

The man had charisma. David kept up his interest in left-wing politics and had heard him twice before. He was a persuasive speaker who argued very convincingly, and he certainly had the knack of capturing attention.

Hoyle fended off all objections to his beliefs with skill, quoting statistics as well as chapter and verse from the political theorists. His Marxism was solid, and he never budged over principles, though he was able to make those principles seem inevitable. David felt then that he was looking at the kind of man who would take charge if the revolution ever did come. Hoyle was obviously someone to watch out for.

"But how can we do anything?" a quiet, bearded student asked.

"There is one party in this country we can re-make."

David looked up. "You mean –?"

Hoyle shut his eyes. "I have a dream, as Lenin must have dreamed. I see a small, dedicated band of political activists. I see them attending every constituency meeting. I see them dominating Labour organizations. I see them, eventually, selecting MPs – and making them accountable – and then making first the Labour conference, then the Labour government, act exactly as we would wish." Suddenly he was looking at them again. "It can be done."

Hoyle thrilled them with the possibility. The government could be theirs.

David listened to the rest of the evening's discussion and, in spite of himself, found Hoyle rather impressive. Like in him, there was something of the actor in Hoyle. Though David disagreed with Hoyle's lines on the invasion of Hungary and on the U.S.–Soviet struggles over Cuba, he found himself taking part in the heated arguments about Vietnam, and he had to agree with Maggie that the U.S. was in a ruinous military, political and moral quagmire there.

"– and besides," he added, surprised that Hoyle's hungry eyes had stayed on him, "America is sailing to South-East Asia on a tide of newly printed dollars. If it continues, Saigon is going to sink us all because of inflation."

"Inflation – as in the Weimar Republic before Hitler? I'd have to say I never thought of that," Hoyle said. "Economics and history – that's what you're studying? Interesting. I see myself as something of a talent-spotter, you know . . ."

Two people away from David, an attractive, dark-haired girl listened with a disdainful look on her face. She, at least, seemed unimpressed by Hoyle's sharp rhetoric. From time to time she looked at David and he smiled back.

She leaned over to him. "Some people get so carried away. Lenin, indeed."

Though he certainly did not underrate Hoyle, David nodded in agreement. The girl's Welsh accent pleased him.

She looked at him with brown eyes, clearly finding the discussion aggravating. "Actually, I'm none too fond of this intellectual rubbish. In Wales we're a bit more practical about our politics."

"It's like that on Tyneside. We're Socialists by conviction."

She looked up in momentary annoyance as a slop of beer fell to the floor near her shoes. "Instead of Socialists by intoxication," she laughed, and David laughed, too.

87

"I'm David – David Bryant."

"I'm Megan Jones – I'm a student nurse at the Radcliffe."

Hoyle broke away from an impasse by leaning over towards Megan. He said, "What's your opinion, comrade? You haven't contributed much to the debate."

Megan obviously felt that everyone was looking at her.

"Don't you have an opinion?"

"Yes, I have an opinion," she said with annoyance. "Just because I haven't hogged the conversation all evening doesn't mean I don't think."

"Well, come on then, tell us!"

"All right, I will." Megan narrowed her eyes. "Too many people seem to think that being clever and using big words is enough. It never was, Mr Hoyle. You have to *care* to be a Socialist. People can't live on ideas. Bread has to be earned, children looked after, the sick comforted; that's life, the common life we share. You talk all this theory, and somehow the love and caring gets lost between the lines. People aren't ciphers in some five-year plan. You have to put yourself in other people's shoes if you want to understand their suffering."

"Understand people's suffering?" Hoyle smiled charmingly. "That sounds more like Christianity than Socialism."

His words provoked a ripple of laughter.

"So what if it is? What does it matter what name you give to it? It's what's right, and it's what I believe."

Hoyle turned away as if from a schoolgirl, but one of his supporters bristled. "What do *you* know about Socialism? I bet you've never even read *Das Kapital*."

Megan broke away and went to the bar. David shook his head, trying to conceal a contemptuous smile, and followed her. "I think more sense has been spoken in the last minute than I've heard all evening."

"I don't like talking in public," she said. "I say things I shouldn't."

"I thought your sincerity was very impressive, and someone needed to say all that."

"Do you really think so?"

He nodded, and she cast an eye at Maggie who was still deep in discussion. "I couldn't help overhearing – are you really an actor?"

He made light of his ambitions, in the English way. "Just a local theatre group. Actually, I intend to be a teacher . . . . Could I persuade you to come and see us?"

"I . . . " she glanced again at Maggie. "You mean your friend's not going?"

"Maggie and I are – old friends. We're from the same home town."

Megan brightened. "I'd love to see you act. I bet you're very talented."

Their eyes met, and David felt a strange shock of recognition. They began talking, there at the bar and later, privately, at another table, and the sense of recognition grew. She was from Fishguard, a port in west Wales; she was as solidly Labour as he was, and her uncle was the local Member of Parliament. Her directness and sincerity were touching; there was a deep well of moral feeling in her, and he found himself very much drawn to this committed, passionate girl with the sparkling eyes. Suddenly David found himself talking about his own family, his own past, and then they were agreeing he would have to visit Wales.

In a quiet moment later, Hoyle came up to him to say that he had been impressed by David; perhaps they could meet at some future date. "I mean, you're from Tyneside, where the Stantons are."

"The Stantons?" David found his eyes drawn to Maggie. Was this part of some violent scheme of hers?

"I think we might have things to discuss," Hoyle told him. "Maggie tells me you're interested in politics."

David looked from Maggie across to Megan, who was now standing demurely by the bar; he knew what Megan would say about Hoyle. Then he remembered Battersby's advice about getting to know people of present – or future – importance. "I'll be happy to consider it. Maggie knows me well, and in any case my signature and Oxford address are both scrawled in your club's door-book. You could get me any time."

"I'll remember that."

At ten o'clock, Megan and he rose to go together. David went with her down the steps and into the street, still thinking about Maggie.

Megan pointed back upstairs. "Well, that was a waste of time, wasn't it?"

"Oh, I wouldn't say that." She saw him smile honestly. "So can I walk you home?"

She gave him her arm at once. "David's a good Welsh name. Yes, why don't you?"

89

Suddenly he realized that his luck had changed, and when he moved over the solid paving-stones, there was a strange sensation that he was floating.

David Bryant bent over the red-haired girl, the jealousy in him showing raw and poisonous. This was murder, an abortion born out of love.

In heavy disguise here in the garden of Merton College, he was ready to strangle the woman he loved. On this balmy evening, summer stars swarmed over his head.

David flexed his fingers again and snarled. In his black make-up he was grotesque and terrible. The girl lay at his feet, conquered, half-nude, voluptuous. Her long red hair had flown round her head and her eyelids trembled with fear.

The spotlight etched David's face with luminous acid, and his eyes bulged white from his black face. He brandished his silk strangling scarf hideously.

"Out, strumpet! Weepst for him, to my face."

She was on her knees now, by the heaped pillows, her face full of terror.

"O! Banish me, my lord, but kill me not."

Othello, the mercenary, grinned at Desdemona.

There was silence from the wooden tiers disposed around them. The tragic certainty of the play had seized everyone. In the third row of the audience Maggie leaned forward, absorbed by the forceful performance.

"It is – too late –"

Knowing now what jealousy led to, David strangled her horribly, sobbing all the while, and as he stood over the body, his look of terror, madness and guilt transcended the actor's repertoire. What came from him then was no act, and drew gasps from the audience.

At the final curtain, the applause was rapturous. Megan was clapping louder than anyone.

David and the rest of the company bowed. He was exhausted, drained now, with nothing more to give, and yet as he looked over the rows of his audience his eyes strayed to Maggie and he smiled widely. He would always love her, but now he had exorcized her. He had found somebody else to love him.

Maggie clapped enthusiastically, until her hands hurt. David had played the part of the jealous man, the murderer, the madman with

90

such power that she had felt overwhelmed, and she wondered if there was something in his own life he had used in creating the performance.

People were opening bottles of wine and picnic hampers around her, and others began to move off to the public houses of Oxford.

"That was frightening," a deep, reassuring voice said.

She looked at the empty spot on the makeshift stage, where Othello had killed the woman he loved. "It makes you realize how awful jealousy is."

"It makes you realize how powerful love is."

She turned around quickly, covering a gasp. "You!"

He had a wonderful smile that made everything else irrelevant. Then he took her by the shoulders and kissed her, hard, his mouth grinding on hers.

He was a man of decision, and she liked that. Now, a few days after the play, they walked along the river bank, past the houseboats on the Isis, and watched the moon shining like silver on the water.

Maggie was subdued. Alex was becoming more important to her than she dared admit, and the closer they grew, the nearer came the day when she would have to tell her father.

She found him extremely seductive; she suspected she was falling in love with him. As they walked she asked about his family. Alex was reluctant to speak of it, but she badgered him until he told her.

"The Stantons are quite an historic family; 1776 in the States, the wars against France, the Crimea, all the battles of World War I and II – our guns and then our fighting ships and then our planes were there."

Maggie nodded, remembering her own family's legends. "I think you'd find a few Langtons around, too. My father went to Spain in the thirties with the International Brigade; but the Communists put him on their death-list . . . Then he was in the war, and they took him off the beach at Dunkirk after he'd been machinegunned in both legs."

"He sounds like a brave man," Alex said soberly. "And your mother's Irish, you say?"

"That's right," Maggie said, "and *she* spent the war working a Stanton Industries machine in South Shields that made her cough blood!"

Alex pulled his arm away from hers and snapped, "Do you think you have some kind of monopoly on suffering? My grandfather died at the hands of the Japanese after he was shot down north of Australia."

"I'm sorry," she said, instantly contrite; Alex's anger was a little frightening. "I'll go on listening, if you want to talk."

"I still don't know what we were involved in, then. Radar, and I suspect uranium prospecting, maybe even in the Hiroshima and Nagasaki bombs. The family firm is mainly run by trusts, you see, and we don't inherit till we're twenty-six. Usually, power goes to the eldest son –"

Maggie was fascinated. She faced him, her breasts suddenly heaving. "Does that mean it'll all come to Hugh, or to you?"

"Not to me," Alex said. "Never to me. I'm not Sir Edward Stanton's son."

Her eyes opened wide.

"My line goes back through the other brother – the younger brother, Michael, and his American wife – my mother." His throat tightened for a moment; sadness and bitterness. "My father had very different ideas. An office in Washington, DC; more involvement with Europe, more sales to the Middle East – he didn't want to take the risk of Suez. And that's not all. I hear my grandfather was thinking of by-passing the older brother."

"Christ!" she said.

"That's right," Alex said harshly. "I might have inherited control; control of a £120 million company. Instead, I have to wait till I'm twenty-six, then I pick up a couple of percent in the company."

Maggie thought of the inscriptions she had read at the necropolis the day she had cycled to Craigburn with David. The Stantons were some family. One gravestone had said, simply, *God forgive me.*

"And since the war?"

"My uncle has tried to move away from our dependence on the Ministry of Defence, but he hasn't been completely successful. Shipbuilding has problems, and the Aircraft Division is perhaps too small, compared with Boeing and Lockheed."

"So the future could see a shift away from –"

He sighed loudly. "We're walking by the river, there's a full moon, it's June in England and the night is as romantic a night as anyone could wish for. Do we have to talk about my family's business prospects?"

She snapped, "I like serious conversation, I don't like to be patronized."

Alex chuckled but remained charming. "All right."

"Anyway, Alex, I know *you* think about the family business." She held his hand and they walked until she asked if he would show her round one of the Stanton factories.

He laughed. "Maggie, I despair! Most girls come to Oxford looking for a husband so *he* can bother himself about factories."

She looked up at the moon, and it looked back, a pale disc of light a quarter of a million miles away. She knew that, in spite of everything, this was the man for her: and she was conscious of her own certainty and joy, almost as if her emotions were music. "Alex, you already know I'm not 'most girls'."

He grinned, loving her.

"Oh, can't you see? I'm interested in this world, just as you are! I want to make a career in radical journalism. Don't you read any of the student magazines?"

"Of course I do," he said. "That was a very good article about the Beatles. How did you get to interview John Lennon, by the way?"

"Persistence," she said, "and charm. And now that Beatlemania has hit the States I sold the article there, too."

"Is it really a career, though? With money in it? Anyway, as soon as you're married –"

"I'm married to my work. It is me. And as for making it a career, well, there are loads more opportunities now that the BBC has opened a second channel. I want to travel like James Cameron to foreign countries and expose injustice, bring it home to people. Is that so wrong?"

Alex weighed her words seriously. "No, it's not wrong. It's a little romantic and probably quite naïve, and very idealistic."

"You missed out optimistic," she said.

"I can't approve of optimism. After all, I am an Englishman – half of me at least."

She ignored his joke. "The world's changing very quickly, Alex. I want to change and grow with it. One of Alan Hoyle's friends was here last week – a radical student from Berkeley, in California. I have to see all that for myself, Alex. My sister Annie has settled for a life in one of your dreary Stanton factories. Her life hangs on the clock, her future is in a straitjacket. That's not for me."

"But not everyone can break away from dreary factories, Maggie. And I suspect that not everyone wants to."

"Annie has no sense of work satisfaction. She's just a number to the company."

"Maybe you're right," he said softly. "But maybe you're making a mistake supposing that everybody thinks like you. Annie may be happier that you in the end for all her limited horizons."

As she watched him toss a pebble into the river, the smiling faces of Annie and Eric in their wedding pictures came to her. They seemed very contented. She felt a pang of sadness. "Perhaps."

"Of course," he said tentatively, turning back to her, "you could say that there's therefore all the more reason for the non-conformists among us to make our own way."

"What do you want to do, Alex?"

He chuckled, knowing she would never believe him. "I come from a long line of heroes."

"Villians, more like!"

"Well, they're all that little bit larger than life. I'd like to do what the Stantons have always done – even though nobody in the family wants me to." He shifted about. "But they're all the family I've got, Maggie. Their approval would mean a lot to me."

She touched his hand. "I know."

They sat down on a riverside bench and watched the orange glow of a barbeque beyond the water meadow.

"I've never thought of you as a non-conformist, Alex. Is that how you see yourself?

He put an arm across her shoulders. The water lapped, like a cat contentedly licking up milk. "A rebel. I'd sell guns to George Washington. Of course I would."

A wicked smile crossed her face, and she said, "You know, the last time I sat on this bench with someone, an hour later we were in bed together."

Alex frowned at her. "Not your friend, David Bryant? You made it plain what *he* feels about you."

Maggie laughed and folded her hands together in her lap. "I have to keep some secrets from you."

Meeting each other's friends was sometimes a strain. Cameron came out with them one night, together with Livia, a flamboyant lesbian Maggie knew, and a drunken argument coruscated through three pubs and down several streets. Maggie finally sat back from the conversational fireworks and shrugged.

"We live and learn." Alex got up to go.

"I won't try that again," Maggie said, pushing out of the doorway as more undergraduates shouldered in.

"They're enjoying themselves, anyway."

"Two nations," Maggie said.

The next day began well; a quiet Sunday lunchtime in the pub. Maggie was reading the papers, as Alex frowned over some notes.

"I hate that bastard," he said.

"Who?"

He waved a hand over the notes for an essay he had been told to rewrite using approved sources. "Him."

"Oh, the history man."

"Right. I actually dug up some stuff from the family archives about the help we gave to George Washington, and he's scribbled it out! Doesn't believe me," he growled, "just because my facts don't have a stamp of approval from some silly arse of a Ph.D."

She flung back her long red hair and said, a little sharply, "If you had to earn your own living you'd value other people's opinions more."

"A palpable hit." He touched his chest, where his heart was. "But, seriously, you know that nobody could accuse me of a lack of ambition."

"Well, we have that much in common." Her eyes met his, sparkling; he touched her hand. "The fuel for ambition is hard work," she added. Then she stood up, smiling broadly. "Here they are."

He glanced across the bar as the double doors swung shut. A girl with a pretty, serious face, and a medium-sized young man in an unfashionable suit, with dark straight hair hanging over his forehead. Maggie ran through the introductions as they sat down. David Bryant, her old friend, and Megan.

"And my name's Stanton," Alex said. "Alex Stanton."

"Pleased to meet you," David said, putting out his hand. "Obviously I've heard a fair bit about you."

His grip was surprisingly firm. "Likewise," Alex said. "And congratulations on your Othello. Olivier, look out."

"Thanks," David looked around. "Right, another round of drinks." He took their orders and went up to the bar.

The girl considered him a while, then spoke in a soft Welsh voice. "I think I've seen you before."

Alex blinked. "So you have. I took somebody to Casualty at the hospital – de Soutey had an argument with a couple of townies."

"He seemed a bit drunken and violent, your friend."

"Indeed he is," Alex said. "It's in the blood, I suppose. Conquerors of India." He swallowed more beer, realizing he had sounded a touch arrogant.

Maggie came back, with two of the drinks David had paid for.

David took a long swallow, put his dimpled glass down. "You're one of the Stanton Industries people, aren't you?"

"Of course he is, Davey," Maggie said. "I told you that."

"The enemy?" David asked.

"I hope not," Alex said. "Don't hold me responsible for the sins of Stanton Industries."

"Well now," David said, "somebody has to take responsibility."

"Not the Lord Home, I take it?"

David pulled a face. "Not exactly up-to-date, is he? And I was never that impressed with Macmillan's Edwardian country gentleman act."

"Home's a good sort," Alex said automatically, "fourteenth earl or not. He's a friend of the family, actually." He looked David up and down. "You're interested in politics?"

"Certainly."

"You take your man Wilson seriously?"

David imitated the Leader of the Opposition at the Scarborough party conference. "'The Britain that is going to be forged in the white heat of this scientific revolution will be no place for restrictive practices or outdated methods – on either side of industry.'"

Alex laughed. "Very good. Very sensible sentiments, too. But can he make it work?"

"Maybe not," David said regretfully.

"Making Britain work, making capitalism work – that isn't what socialism's about, David!"

Alex cocked an eyebrow at Maggie. "It makes sense to me, though. I mean, the Stantons had a man round about the turn of the century –"

"Albert Edward Stanton, you mean? Your grandfather. Invented the torpedo and sold entire navies to the Czar and the Emperor of Japan. A giant."

"Yes," Alex said, though he had no memory of the man himself. "You're well informed."

"Yes, I am."

The two men exchanged glances.

David lowered his voice. "Actually, I've been researching your family for a play."

96

"Oh? Quite flattering. If there's any help I can give, just ask."

"I probably will. But remember, I was practically raised on Leslie Street in Wallsend, where they build the big ships. In fact, I was in the yard when the Queen came up to launch the *Albion* . . ."

"Were you, now?" Their eyes met again.

"Maggie and I probably know a lot about Stanton Industries you don't. We can see it from the ground up."

"I believe you do." He glanced at Maggie again; she was talking to Megan in a low voice, and she looked very handsome. He felt strangely excited. There was so much he could say now about the company and the family which were his life. He remembered meeting Ray. "First impressions can be misleading, don't you think?"

David lifted his beer glass. "Cheers, Alex."

After they had gone, Alex turned to Maggie. "Well, your friend was quite impressive – in that quiet, English way. Why isn't he here?"

"At university?" She hesitated and, to his amazement, began to blush. "He didn't have very good luck."

"Oh." There was a pause as Alex considered dropping the subject. "Because of you?"

"There's the exam you have to take to get into a good school, a grammar school."

"We've heard of the eleven-plus even at Eton," Alex said crisply.

"His mother was very ill, so they packed David off to relatives. But . . . his mother died just before the exam."

"Terrible. So when they told him, he was so upset he failed the exam? Might have been better if his father had said nothing for a day or two, especially if your man David wasn't at home."

"His father didn't say anything," she said miserably. "But David turned up for the exam – and a schoolfriend told him."

"God, what terrible luck!" Alex said. "Though I always say you make your own luck." Then the realization struck him. "You mean –"

"Yes," she said, upset even after almost a decade. "I told him."

Throughout June and July of 1964, Alex took David and Megan on some of the trips to restaurants and the country he made with Maggie.

Alex was fascinated by Maggie and David; he listened to them talk for hours. It soon became clear that they knew far more about the realities of business at Stanton Industries on Tyneside than his uncle did, let alone Hugh. The three of them began to read the same books, examining the economic miracles in West Germany and Japan, looking at how Americans did things, talking over notions of social justice.

Their arguments were involved and exhilarating. These were the real issues of the day, the exciting issues – all of them missing from the university syllabus.

"David," Alex said once over an Italian meal, "you may love words, but you're not really an actor; you're much too interested in analysis."

Maggie added, drily, "Maybe you should get your uncle to give him a job, then."

"Small chance of that," David said. "Remember, I used to be an apprentice in the drawing office – mainly emptying inkwells and sharpening pencils, would you believe! It's 'public school only' in the Stanton senior management."

"Except for my friend Ray."

They had met Ray, when he came down to spend a weekend with Alex in Oxford.

"Alex," David said firmly, "I guarantee he won't have a job with Stanton Industries the instant somebody at the top thinks they can sell the STA-2 to the Pentagon without him."

"I hope you're wrong, David."

For the first time in his life Alex was in a minority: the privileges he had long taken for granted could not be taken for granted in this company, because both Maggie and David could match him intellectually – but he loved the tough-minded debates. What Alex found most curious were the strangely distorted echoes of the opinions he heard at home in Craigburn. For instance, so many people here felt nothing but contempt for the industry that ultimately gave them all their living, a feeling surpassed only by their contempt for the industry's managers.

"– the owners being *beneath* contempt, I suppose," Alex said, thinking of his own arguments with the family. "So the workers hate the managers; the managers hate the workers and the owners; and the owners despise the others, too!"

"Three sides of industry," David said; "you're quite right. Each hating and despising the others . . . There's no unity, and a fatal lack of purpose."

Idly, Alex reached for the red wine and wondered if it really was different in the United States or Japan.

In September, as soon as the election was announced, David rang Megan at home in Fishguard. He made his proposal, and she agreed immediately.

"I'd love to see you here, especially helping Uncle Frank. I've already told him all about you."

"You have?" He had to speak louder, over the noise coming in from his father's pub. "All lies, I hope!"

"No, David," she said with her disconcerting honesty. "The truth is impressive enough."

David took the train down to Wales the next day, and together they began work. Frank Deacon was Fishguard's MP and on the Privy Council; he had been a Cabinet Minister in 1951. Frank shook David's hand the first time they met, gripping it for a long time and looking into the younger man's eyes. He seemed to find what he was looking for, because he smiled and clapped David on the shoulder. David was staying in the family house, in a spare bed made up in the large ground floor room where the local labour party carried out much of its business. Bronwen, Megan's pretty, but over-made-up, young sister, was asked to help with canvassing for votes too, but usually she made some excuse.

"Oh, she's just obsessed with herself," Megan said disapprovingly, "her make-up and her pop music."

After a week of effort, they were both hungry and footsore. It was early evening; the nights were drawing in.

"Better make these the last few, David."

David wanted to carry on. "Don't you want Labour to win this election?"

He knocked on the door of a big detached house, then he and Megan both took a pace back. A dog began to bark in the hall. A light came on. As the door opened, David, wearing his *Let's Go with Labour* badge, smiled and began for the hundredth time that day: "How do you do, Mr Evans, my name's David Bryant. I wonder if I could take a few minutes of your time?"

The middle-aged man stared back blankly.

"We're calling on behalf of the Fishguard and North Pembroke Labour Party. I want to ask if our candidate can count on your support in the general election."

"You've got the wrong man here, boy," the householder said, the blankness on his face replaced by impatience. "I'm Conservative. This whole ward's Conservative. And it's damned cold in these slippers, so if you don't mind I'll be wishing you good evening."

The door banged shut in David's face. He turned to Megan and shrugged.

David, rubbing his hands together to dispel the unseasonal chill, chuckled, "Some people are good and rude."

"And some people are just rude!"

The next two houses on Pembroke Drive did not answer, but the third showed a glimmer of light round the curtains. David knocked again, and the door opened revealing a tubby man who asked, "What is it?"

"We're from the local Labour Party, Mr Davies –"

"You look like it, too," the man said gruffly as he looked them up and down. "How do you know my name anyway?"

"The electoral rolls," Megan said.

"Well, next time you read them, just pencil a little 'C' by my address. That's 'C' for Conservative."

"I know most of the people round here vote Conservative, but I'd like to put our candidate's case."

"You're wasting your time here."

David stood firm. "I don't think we're wasting our time, Mr Davies. The Conservatives are in decline; don't you know men like Iain Macleod and Enoch Powell have turned their backs on Douglas-Home?"

Davies scratched his nose. "That's so."

David seized his chance. "And locally, our Frank Deacon is a good man – a first-class constituency MP, they tell me."

"That might be true, but why don't you take your ideas down there?" Mr Davies waved a hand down the hill. "That's your patch."

"If you don't mind my saying so, sir, I think preaching to the converted would be a real waste of our time."

Mr Davies laughed. "Well, I can't argue with you there. Deacon was in the war, wasn't he?"

Megan said her uncle had won the Military Cross. Seeing his chance, David went on to put his points across, and when he had done so he offered his hand to the constituent.

"Then we can count on your support at the polls?"

Davies grinned. "I won't quite say that, but I'll certainly consider it. In fact – yes, perhaps you're right."

Later that evening, when they had returned home, they warmed their hands round mugs of coffee in the Jones's kitchen. It had turned into a raw night, but they had an inner glow from their work.

"You're very persuasive," Megan told him.

"Things seemed to go quite well."

"A massive swing to Labour."

"Do you think so?" he said thoughtfully. "A Labour government? The polls still have it neck and neck."

She watched his face a moment and said, "David – have you never thought of going into politics?"

"Politics? Me?" He pondered for a moment.

"You're a good speaker."

"Just an actor's projection."

"And you're brilliant at history."

"I need to be if I plan to teach it."

"See, you have answers for everything." Megan sat back. "But most of all, you care about people."

He stirred aimlessly at his coffee, wondering how much her opinion would change if she got to know him better. "What prompted you to think of me going into politics?"

"Nothing –" she paused. "You promise you won't say anything? It was something that Uncle Frank said about you last night."

"What did he say?"

"He just asked me some questions about you and I could tell he was thinking seriously."

David considered. "It's you who deserves his consideration, Megan. There aren't many girls who'd give up two weeks' holiday for the sake of their uncle's political ambitions."

Megan leaned over and kissed him. "Bronwen and I are his nieces, but really he's been like a father to us. And it's not just for Uncle Frank. I believe in what we're doing, and as long as we're together, David . . ."

Bronwen came in and put a supper plate into the sink. She was in a cotton nightdress, and her calves were bare. "Hello, David."

He smiled. "You'll catch cold."

"Yes, it is a cold night," she spoke conversationally, but her eyes were on David as she tripped back into the living room.

"She's so nosy," Megan said testily.

David had noticed the female underwear from this household of women drying on the line in the back garden; and for a moment he

101

had an unnerving notion of the garments lying along the soft contours of young Bronwen rather than Megan.

Mrs Jones poked her head round the kitchen door. "It's about time you two were in bed," she said with mock severity.

When the door closed they looked at one another and laughed.

"I don't think she meant it like that!"

"What a pity!"

Megan pouted and they kissed, then she drained her coffee cup, said goodnight and followed her mother upstairs.

David sat a while before he opened another history textbook and began making notes. The Labour government of 1945: the Welfare State. Would some of the money spent on that and on private consumption have been better invested in industry? He worked till midnight, sometimes walking around so that the floorboards creaked, then made his way along the passage to the bathroom. Despite the chill he stripped naked and began to wash himself over the hand basin, not wanting to impose on the family so late at night by running a bath. As he lathered his chest and loins he thought of Megan's parting words and felt a thrill.

Sex.

The prospect was delightful, but the Jones' house was hardly the place. The moral tone here was higher than in Westminster Abbey.

A creak at the door made David look up into the mirror, though he did not turn around. He continued to sponge his body, rinsing off the soap. Then he saw an eye watching him through the crack. So, Megan felt the same and had tried to steal five minutes with him.

He felt excitement rising inside.

In a quick movement he reached round the door and grabbed her arm, intending to pull her inside and press the door shut, but as he held her he realized that it was not Megan he had pulled inside.

He let go and covered himself with his sponge. "Good God!"

Bronwen's finger went to her mouth. "Shhh!"

"I . . . I thought . . ."

"You thought I was Megan," she said, her eyes wide, and her mouth curling in a smile. "But I'm not, am I?"

Labour won the 1964 general election; their people were in. Frank Deacon increased his own majority. David celebrated in Fishguard, liking the folk very much. The Labour majority was slender, but even four seats was enough to form a government.

David and Megan went to London to see the new Prime Minister enter 10 Downing Street: "Nice place we've got here," Mr Wilson quipped. Frank was back in the House of Commons.

They took the train to Oxford that night. David had had a good time, all things considered – several new experiences.

Later, Megan asked him why he was smiling. He did not answer.

David was sitting over his history textbooks, very late.

He heard his doorbell ring and he looked up, frowning. It was after midnight, so it would not be Megan. He left his room and walked quickly down the glacial lino to the front door as the bell rang again, impatiently.

When he pulled the door open, the face outside annoyed him. Battersby put a hand on his shoulder. Breath steaming, the other man spoke quickly. "Don't shut the door on good fortune, David. I'm your bloody employer, don't you know!"

David's fists bunched up, but there was some truth in the insult. "What is it you want this time?"

"Now, David, think of what that nurse friend of yours will be expecting – an engagement ring with diamonds, and then a deposit on a chintzy little house somewhere."

Battersby was laughing at the smallness of such ambitions: his contempt stung. "So?"

"So I can give you the chance to earn more money – enough money to do what *you* want. Imagine it, David. London, abroad, anywhere you want. Even acting with your piss-poor friends if that's what you want." Battersby's outline was shadowy, but somehow his eyes gleamed. "Listen to me. Money will make you free. And I have money, don't I?"

David could see it all. His own parents had not had a happy marriage and the thought of such an entanglement frightened him, suddenly, because he knew that Megan was implacable in her wish for respectability. The cold air settled painfully in his lungs. The voice of conscience inside him was screaming, and it was Megan's voice. "What do you want me to do?"

"Another smallish favour, David. Just a little essay – here's the subject." He stuffed a crumpled paper into David's hand. "That's all. Only faintly dishonourable."

What was the alternative? David stood in the doorway. "I don't have much choice, do I? Thank you, sir, I'm so grateful."

Even Battersby could not disregard this sarcasm. "Good, good. So you'll owe me."

"Will I?"

Battersby's eyes narrowed. "Oh yes, you will. And I'll expect you to be grateful. If not today, then tomorrow. One day you'll have something I want, and then you'll see me again. Remember that, David Bryant."

Then he was gone.

When Alex came in, he found Sir Edward pacing distractedly up and down in the yellow drawing room, beating a rolled-up newspaper against his thigh like a riding crop. Hugh stood at the tall windows, watching the wind blowing waves across the iron grey lake while his mother attached baubles to the conifer Reid had brought from a far corner of the estate. Alex heard her sigh twice. The atmosphere, despite the roaring logs on the hearth, was distinctly not that of Christmas.

"Alex," she said politely, reminding him again that, in her eyes, he would never deserve a tenth as much out of life or the family as Hugh. She turned away. "Do sit down, Edward," she said anxiously. "Cameron Kintyre will be here very shortly."

"How can I sit down? Have you seen what the government intends? They're trying to ruin us!"

"Please try to control yourself, Edward."

"Control myself be damned! Socialist government – the first thing they do is give MPs a rise. They're getting £3,250 a year now, and for what? Income tax up sixpence in the pound. £3,000 million borrowed to prop up sterling. The bank rate is up to *seven per cent*, damn it! They even want to abolish the death penalty."

"Look on the bright side, Father," Hugh said. "LBJ's won the election in America. We're bound to sell the STA-2 there now – whatever we do with that awful Hacker."

Alex bridled. "I've kept in close touch with Ray. There's nothing wrong with him."

"That shows how unsound *your* judgement is, Alex."

"If anybody here ever gives me a chance, we'll soon see whether or not my judgement is unsound!"

"I hate these arguments," Grace said loudly, then tried without success to change the subject. "Why don't you tell Hugh about Sir Winston's birthday party, Edward?"

104

His business was threatened, and he spoke savagely about it, ignoring her. "This Plowden Committee wants to nationalize the Aircraft Division – take away our STA-2! They're planning to amputate one of our most profitable sectors and leave us with nothing! We depend on those profits to keep the whole show on the road . . ." His words rolled on.

Hugh looked at his father gloomily. "It's an absolute enormity. I can't imagine what Healey and Callaghan think they're playing at."

Sir Edward shot him a glance. "Nationalization? Politicians and civil servants running companies? It's lunacy! They want to turn the nation into another glorified bloody Russia!"

Grace sighed loudly. "I'm going into the library, Hugh, until your father calms down."

Sir Edward threw the newspaper down, rage twisting his face; he looked distinctly flushed. "They think they can treat us just as they like! But they've got another think coming to them."

He stormed out of the room. Hugh stood up swiftly, always ready to be a calming influence. "I'd better go with him, cool him down."

Grace looked grateful, and it suddenly occurred to Alex that his aunt had been looking distinctly more careworn this past couple of years. "Well, you're always good at that, Hugh. You take after your mother."

Shortly after Hugh went Alex heard the sound of a car sweeping up to Craigburn's great portico. The door was opened, and Cameron appeared.

"How are you, Lady Stanton?" He took her hand and kissed her on the cheek.

"Fine, Cameron, but my husband's in a terrible rage over this Plowden business. He says the Labour government will nationalize aircraft, and you all know how he resents interference."

"They certainly plan to increase government shareholding," Alex said, pouring a whisky for Cameron. "I'd like to discuss that with him."

"Do try not to upset him. Doctor MacDonald is very concerned about his blood pressure."

"I'll be the very epitome of tact and diplomacy."

Hugh reappeared, his smile suddenly becoming much larger. "Cameron, how good to see you!"

"Merry Christmas, Hugh." Cameron and Hugh Stanton embraced and then went together up to the table where Alex was filling glasses with whisky from a decanter.

"Alex," Cameron said warmly, "how are you? You're cutting a fine figure these days."

"You can put that down to Hardy Amies." Alex took off his tailored jacket and slung it on the back of a chair.

The door opened abruptly. Sir Edward stalked in, looking only a little more tractable than before. He went straight to the drinks table. "Ah, Cameron. A dram?"

Alex noticed that his uncle's hand shook as he poured a substantial tumbler of Scotch.

"Do you think you should be joining us, Uncle?"

"I shan't have that old sawbones tell me what to do."

Alex took his glass and set it down. He tried to make conversation, remembering some of the things he had talked about with Maggie. "Well, you see I was right, Uncle. The Chinese have exploded an atom bomb."

Sir Edward grunted.

Hugh said, "You're familiar with the Plowden report, Cameron?"

"Yes. Big changes afoot, eh? A new government flexing its muscles?"

"Good to see you both taking an interest." Sir Edward got up and began to pace once more.

Hugh and Cameron left, talking animatedly. As the gun dogs got up from the fireside and followed his cousin out, Alex watched his uncle, debating whether to broach the subject. Finally he said, "How's the Wallsend order book? I see our quotation's down ten points on the week."

Sir Edward glowered at his nephew. "I expect you've seen the news about the Q4 contract?"

"The new Cunarder's gone to John Brown's in Clydebank. I suspected it would. Are you very disappointed?"

"The last big liner we built was the *Albion* in 1956. Remember?"

"That day with the Queen? How could I forget?"

Sir Edward looked away and sighed. "Perhaps people think we've forgotten how to build them."

"If we couldn't make a competitive bid this time, we'll have to get it right before the next time. The Wallsend yards are a shambles fit only for demolition."

Sir Edward pressed his hands together and leaned over them. "Has somebody been talking? Where did you get your information from?"

Alex remembered those long, detailed conversations with David and Maggie. "From people who know – people on the spot. We ought to spend money on a much larger dry dock and some covered slips, get things moving again. It can be done. In Japan they're doing it."

"Japan!" Sir Edward gave a rough, disbelieving laugh. "So you're a troublemaker who wants to tell me how to use my money?"

"It's necessary to compete, that's all I'm saying. If we look at the current cost rate of profit, which you have to do in an age of inflation, things have been declining here since 1960!"

"But how long do you think the City would support me if I started cutting back on the dividends the shareholders get and began some harebrained investment programme?"

"Then you should tell the City, prove your case, and act."

"And spend money? No, no, we're making an adequate profit; it's foolishness, investing unnecessarily." Sir Edward sat down, calmer now. He regarded his adopted son carefully. "You know, I had been planning to put Hugh in charge of the Aircraft Division from the beginning of the year, but this Socialist government's put it out of the question. Hugh's still not ready for that kind of battle that's going to take place, and it's a battle that has to be won."

For the first time, Alex had the feeling he was talking man to man with the head of his family. "Why don't you give Ray Hacker the job?" he asked. "He ranks third in the Division, now, he's highly competent and full of –"

"Hacker? Dear me, no! He's fine talking with that cowboy in the White House, but he's not a man for the Stanton board. There'll never be room for his kind in the City. He's got no manners, and Hugh doesn't get on with him at all."

"Then who?"

"I'll just have to see it through myself," Sir Edward sighed, and went out of the room.

The following day at three o'clock, the family and their guests gathered round the long oak dining room table, set for Sunday lunch. The room was watched over by glassy-eyed stags' heads and by the pair of gun dogs which lay drowsily by the hearth. Hugh was talking to Cameron, ostensibly about shooting, but he seemed anxious to turn the conversation to the subject of his cousin's girlfriend. Hugh had not met Maggie, but she was a subject on which he had been quizzing Cameron on and off for much of the morning.

"I wonder *why* he hasn't invited her here for Christmas," he asked Cameron loudly, and gave his mother a significant glance.

"You'll have to ask Alex about that."

"Hugh, I told you, I said nothing to her about coming here." There was a weary note of finality in Alex's voice, but Hugh refused to be deterred.

"Admittedly, Craigburn's rather down at heel these days, but I'm sure it's a perfectly adequate substitute for her own circumstances." He turned to Grace. "Mother, I was just hearing from Cameron that Alex's new girlfriend wants to become a journalist."

"Really?" Grace said. A thin smile covered her indifference.

"Oh, yes. Did you know she's from Wallsend?"

"Wallsend?"

Alex's face clouded over, and he kicked at Hugh under the table.

"Yes, near our biggest shipyard. I think her father used to work there – in a *manual* job." Hugh scowled straight at Alex. "Before he became a trade union agitator, that is – our enemy!"

"Alex? Is this true?"

Alex raised his shoulders. "Aunt, I don't see what difference –"

"Alex, you know I disapprove of you slumming."

"Slumming? For goodness' sake! Can't you see what Hugh's trying to do?"

Sir Edward glared. "Well, is it true, or isn't it?"

Alex found he was standing up, a napkin clutched in his hand. "It isn't like that at all!"

Hugh wagged a fork at his brother, then stood up and took a copy of the *New Statesman* from the window-ledge. He tossed it onto the table, clattering the silver.

There was a sudden silence, broken by Hugh's voice.

"Then what's that? Page twenty-one, look for yourself – no, I'll save you the trouble." He picked up the magazine and read aloud. "'Britain's sale of sixteen Buccaneer aircraft to South Africa goes against the spirit of the UN Security Council's June resolution, but South African premier Dr Verwoerd knows that, if the Royal Navy wants to continue using Simonstown naval base, then Harold Wilson must go through with the sale.'"

Alex made a grab for the magazine across the table, but Hugh snatched it away and continued, this time stressing his words carefully.

"'Verwoerd's hand is strengthened because the planes were the subject of a contract that pre-dates the resolution. However no amount of pressure from Stanton Industries can possibly alter Mr Wilson's decision on the twenty embargoed STA-1f fighters *that the company wants to supply secretly through a Middle Eastern intermediary.*' That was written by Alex's girlfriend, wasn't it Alex?"

Sir Edward's hand had shaken as he carved into the succulent flesh of the goose. Now he flung down the knife and looked darkly at his brother's son. "Alex, explain."

"I didn't know about the article, and I don't know how she found out about the aircraft deal. Certainly not from me; I wouldn't betray a family secret." Alex faced Sir Edward. "Look, she wants to be a journalist – and as far as I'm concerned she has the same right to look into Stanton Industries' affairs as anybody else."

"That depends how she goes about it," Hugh accused. "Cameron tells me you took her round the jet engine plant at Filton?"

Cameron looked trapped, Hugh victorious.

"Yes, but . . ."

"There we are! Q.E.D."

"Not at all!"

Sir Edward glowered. "If you ever want to amount to anything in the family business, Alex, you will put this woman behind you."

Alex reddened with embarrassment in front of their half-dozen guests. He could tell Hugh was very annoyed by Maggie's article, and he obviously believed Alex was the source of her information. Sir Edward ate slowly, looking at the three young men from time to time, his expression unreadable. He picked up another forkful of food and swallowed it as Alex spoke again.

"So my 'girlfriend', so called, isn't fit to associate with a Stanton? But you have me wrong, Uncle, Hugh. I have my own life to live *and will live it whatever the cost.*"

Sir Edward made a strangled noise and caught at his throat. At first, it sounded like stifled laughter, as if his uncle was trying to maintain his dignity, but it rapidly became apparent he was choking. The lucheon guests watched in horrified fascination as he tried again and again to dislodge whatever was caught in his windpipe. His arms thrashed and a glass of red wine was knocked from the table. Then Sir Edward was on his feet and bent double. His head and neck had turned purple with effort. Alex jumped up and began to wrestle with him. He hit out powerfully at his uncle's

109

back, but the noises were terrible as Sir Edward tried desperately to draw breath.

"He's having a fit!" someone cried as he sank down to his knees.

"It's a heart attack!"

Sir Edward's hand grasped convulsively at the tablecloth. Knives and forks crashed around him on the parquet floor. Alex was quickly astride his uncle's chest. Sir Edward's lips were cyan, his face cold with greasy sweat, and he seemed to have lost consciousness.

"For Christ's sake, somebody! Fetch Doctor MacDonald!" Hugh shouted.

Alex forced his uncle's forehead back and pulled his mouth open. He thrust a finger to the back of Sir Edward's throat. The obstruction suddenly came free, and Alex threw down for all to see a jagged arc of wishbone.

He looked at his uncle again, wondering if he were really dying.

The front parlour of number twenty-seven was hung with brightly-coloured paper hangings which criss-crossed the ceiling and festooned the chimney breast. A small artificial Christmas tree occupied one corner, and a nativity crib that Maggie had made as a child stood beside it. In his chair by the hearth, Will Langton laughed with pleasure.

"I'd love to see Stanton's face when he sees this!"

"I don't think he's the sort who reads the *New Statesman*," Maggie said, pleased by her father's reaction.

"We'll send him this copy, then. It's really one in the eye for him!"

Maggie knelt down beside her father's armchair. There was no longer any doubt in her mind, but she knew it wasn't the right time to bring up the subject of Alex. She didn't want to spoil Christmas.

Will put an arm round his daughter. "One day you'll change things for the better."

"Make it an issue, Dad, and you can stop anything."

"I believe that. But you must have inside knowledge. You can't do it on your own."

"Investigative journalism is always down to the reporter in the end. You have to build up a network of contacts and then develop a feel for a story."

"Like a private eye following his hunches, eh? But this aircraft deal – it sounds like something they'd want to keep quiet. It beats me where you get your information."

"I have my sources."

Maggie remembered the visit she had made to the Bristol jet engine works, and how she deliberately avoided asking too many questions of Alex. She had no wish to compromise him, and had decided on doing the Stanton piece only because of some information Alan Hoyle had fed to her.

"Well, you can trust your father to keep a secret, my girl."

"Oh, all right. I have a friend called Alan Hoyle, who's running a ginger group to liven up the Labour party. He has lots of contracts in the trade unions –"

Will's heavy brows lowered. "Has he, indeed?"

"Amazing contacts. And money. I really don't know where he gets it from. Anyway, he'd heard about the embargoed planes from somebody at the factory. I went to check, and I confirmed it. So, a scoop, my first big break. Alan says the national press will pick it up; there's not a chance of those planes going to South Africa now."

Bridie came in from the kitchen, a plate of grilled sausages in her hand. Will held up the magazine and pointed to the by-line. "Look. A national magazine. We've a daughter who's a real journalist, and one who doesn't mind ruffling a few feathers!"

"She'll always be my little girl," Bridie said, not giving the article a second glance.

The sound of the evening paper being pushed through the letter box sent Bridie out into the hall. She returned with it, looking at her daughter thoughtfully. "Haven't you thought about getting a job on a Newcastle paper when you finish at university, pet?"

Will wagged a reproving finger at his wife. "I don't want you trying to put ideas into Maggie's head. I know you want her to come back to Tyneside, but she's going right to the top and she can't do it around here."

Maggie hugged her father. "I'll get the truth printed if it kills me."

"If I know the Stantons, it probably will."

Bridie stood silently by, looking at her daughter with a regretful expression. She began to leaf through the paper from the back, then paused before shoving it onto her husband's lap. "Look, Will!" He read the column carefully, then showed it to his daughter.

"Maybe Sir Edward Stanton does read the *New Statesman* after all. He's had a stroke!"

Maggie took the paper. Sir Edward had been rushed to Newcastle General Hospital after choking, and an hour later a blood clot in his brain had been diagnosed.

"Serves the bugger right," her father said.

"Dad, you shouldn't say that. He might die."

"That's what I mean."

Maggie did not share her father's bearish triumph. It was Alex's uncle who was lying in a coma, even if he was the head of the Stanton clan, and she knew how Alex must be feeling, in spite of his estrangement from the rest of the family. She put on her coat.

"Where are you going?"

"Out to make a telephone call," she said, hiding her face.

"What's got into her all of a sudden? Can't she use our wn phone?"

"Don't forget to press button 'B'," her mother called out after her, but Maggie was already halfway down the street.

An extraordinary general meeting was called in March, 1965 at a public hall close to the Victoria Embankment headquarters of Stanton Industries. Alex drove up from Oxford, leaving behind Maggie and his careful revision for his finals. He left his car south of the river and walked across Westminster Bridge, deep in thought.

Then Hugh waved to him from their father's family Rolls. Alex got in, smiling politely. Reid, their driver, stopped outside the hall, and their father's personal secretary received the cousins courteously inside the doors.

"Everything ready, Fowler?"

"Everything's set, Mr Hugh."

The hall was full of shareholders, even though less than thirty per cent of shares were held by what Sir Edward called 'the rabble'. There must have been four hundred people crammed inside.

After they took their places and the meeting came to order Alex felt uneasy. Hugh listened to the proceedings patiently then turned to his cousin. "Such a bore having to sit through it all, don't you find?"

Alex whispered back. "I don't know, I'm quite interested in what becomes of the company."

"A foregone conclusion, old man."

"What do you mean?"

Hugh looked complacent. "Beauford and I worked out the details yesterday."

"That's quite a coup. Can you do that?"

Hugh smiled at his younger cousin's naïveté. "Until father's well again, I'll take over the Aircraft Division – just as the old boy wanted. Temporarily, both Armaments and Shipbuilding will come under Sir George Leslie. And the new main board itself will be reconstructed with some very distinguished people and assume direct reponsibility for Stanton Industries as of today."

"Under Beauford?"

"Of course. Temporary chairman. Then I'll – unless father fully recovers . . ." Hugh recognized Alex's concern. "Alex, Beauford Cleves have been our merchant bankers for half a century. After father, Lord Beauford is our biggest shareholder."

Alex remembered Sir Edward's warning about Hugh's readiness to face down the Plowden Committee's demands, and the company's figures seemed to indicate an enterprise that was stagnant. He was shocked to find that the family's holdings, including the few percent held in the family trust fund for him, had been whittled down to only thirty-one per cent, while in the same period Beauford's and his bank's had increased to seventeen, and it occurred to him that his uncle's recovery had suddenly become a business irrelevance. If the trustees of the family trusts proved willing to back him, then Hugh and his ally Lord Beauford could do as they pleased. He glanced across at LeBlanc, the non-executive director who represented the family trusts: a lawyer from one of the huge City partnerships, clever and decent, but hardly a man who would die for the Stanton family.

Alex listened carefully to the arrangements. First came the auditors' report. Then the three divisions reported individually.

The reports did not satisfy Alex. Shipbuilding was suffering from foreign competition, though the figures concealed this; but Alex knew contracts had been lost to West Germany and Japan, and the switch to huge oil tankers was leaving Stanton Industries behind. In 1963 British shipbuilding output had fallen below one million tons total for the first time since the war, but he was shocked that nobody at the meeting even acknowledged the decline. Only the Armaments Division managed to show a healthy profit, and although new STA-2 should prove to be a bonanza for the Aircraft Division, that was the only major new product they had. Finally, the Board was reshuffled because of Sir Edward's incapacitation.

"What exactly have you got planned?" he asked Lord Beauford after the formal meeting had concluded.

"Alex, you're quite right to be concerned," Beauford told him, his hands folded comfortably across his portly body. The family and directors had met in an anteroom for sherry and a cold buffet. "Many a business empire has fallen while trying to change the baton between generations, but your family's money is safe. Hugh's a first-class chap."

Alex stared back. The banker had made it sound as if his uncle was already dead and buried. Beauford watched Alex's stony reaction closely.

"Alex, you mustn't worry. The firm's in very capable hands."

"I'm sure you're right. I mean, in the past you've been called upon to do nothing in particular, and you've always done it very well."

As Beauford's furious gaze assaulted him, he reflected on the truth of what he had said.

The man's response was cruel: a blade concealed inside impeccable politeness. "We're always there if you need us, Alex. That's the real strength of the company: my own solid financial backing. By the way, how is your dear uncle – or stepfather, should I say? Recovering fast, I trust. Tell him to rest." He beamed. "I'm sure he always listens to your advice."

"I'm afraid he's still unconscious, so anything said by me would be wasted. At present."

"You expect that to change, do you?"

Alex let his expression answer.

Afterwards, he walked away alone, leaving Hugh and one of their cousins to chat with Beauford. Everybody seemed happy enough, but he knew he had been excluded from the family and its business yet again. He wondered what Maggie would think of all this – if he told her.

For the first time, Alex seriously considered the greater implications of his uncle's stroke. Lord Beauford was chairman and increasing his holding in the company. Hugh, inexperienced as he was, was now one of only two people on the Board specifically charged with looking after the Stanton family's interest; only he now would take the long view.

Alex found the prospect frightened him.

5

Alex had rented an apartment in Oxford, in the old quarter called Jericho. There was a glassed-in conservatory on the flat roof of the extension, overlooking the canal, Castle Mill Stream and the Thames, and, beyond, the green barrier of Marley Wood and Wytham Great Wood. He spent many sunny afternoons there, often with Maggie, studying, or reading up on the Stantons' old glory and following the company's present vicissitudes.

He spent many nights with Maggie, too.

The phone rang. She called up from the living room. "Alex, it's that Texan!"

He came downstairs quickly, clad in jeans and a white shirt open at the collar, and picked up the phone.

"I don't have much time, Alex," Hacker said. "I'm calling from home, not the office, and I have to make it fast. Off to Milan tonight."

"I'm listening," Alex said. He knew what it would be about.

"I went down this afternoon to that girl in Archives. Jesus, those files haven't been touched in ages – the dust! Except for some files, that is."

Alex spoke flatly. "Like the 'STA-C' files from the Aviation Division days."

"You're catching on. Anyway, when I came up, the chief archivist suddenly came buzzing around, saying I was supposed to have Hugh's signature to authorize me to look through those old papers. I told him to go screw, naturally, but he seemed pretty upset – too upset, you know? I mean, it's hard to tell with an old woman like that."

Maggie sat down by Alex and turned her expectant face towards him; he put a hand on her shoulder. When he spoke, his voice was rough. "But what about those files?"

"I didn't have time to go through in any detail, you understand. There was the internal report on the crash, Pike's testimony in full, documents from the Federal Aviation Authority, all sorts of stuff. But, sure, there was a lot missing."

"Thanks," Alex said. "I appreciate you looking."

"Looking for what? I found nothing."

"You found a gap," Alex said. "And I'll tell you this for free, they won't like what you did."

"No," Ray said softly. "Something's up in your company. Ever met Lord Beauford?"

"A few times."

"He makes a corkscrew look straight, Alex. Don't you trust him none."

"Thank you, cowboy. I won't."

"Hell, we'll get 'em yet. See you in London."

"Alex, watch out!" Cameron said.

"All right, all right," Alex said grudgingly, and steered the punt away from the thicket. "I've got a lot on my mind."

"What might that be?" Maggie asked, smiling up at him from the silk cushions heaped up in the boat.

"Lord Beauford, for one. He stepped down from the Stanton chairmanship remarkably quickly – and made certain that Hugh inherited overall control." The situation made Alex suspicious and, in thinking about it now, he frowned.

"Ah," Maggie said, understanding him at once, "even though he's by far the youngest and least experienced member of the main board?"

Alex replied by shoving the long pole into the bank, using sheer brute force to get the tiny vessel clear so that the current could catch them again.

Cameron kneeled up. "I hope you're not saying anything against Hugh."

Alex laughed, shortly. "Maybe it's just jealousy. I mean, he was one of us, a student, only seven or eight years ago. In the normal course of events he'd have waited twenty years to run the firm. Now . . . well, it makes me suspicious, that's all. You ought to be interested, too. I suggested to Hugh that your family's bank should be given some of our business. I know Lord Ross is keen on that. But, no, Hugh wouldn't have it. Beauford gets it all."

116

"Hugh's returning a favour."

"Obviously, Maggie – but that really means he's using the family money, my money, to pay off Lord Beauford for a personal debt."

"Or to buy loyalty."

"That's a contradiction in terms."

Cameron said, "Beauford Cleves must be making a fortune out of their commissions on the foreign exchange deals they do for Stanton's. Sterling, the dollar, Deutschmarks, whatever they have in Iran and Japan –"

"In Japan?" Alex asked.

"Oh, I hear things," Cameron said. "I'll be joining the family business, by and by."

Alex was thinking about the new Iran contracts again. Iran had agreed to buy twenty of the new STA-2s right off the drawing board. And Alex, very unofficially, had helped Ray make the deal. The commissions had been good for everybody: that was money, and power – the only things people like Lord Beauford took any notice of.

The punt slid downstream and Alex trimmed its course by trailing the pole. He slowed, grinning wickedly.

"Good grief, those young men are starkers!" Cameron held his hands over Maggie's eyes.

She pushed them away. "Oh, you know I've seen better, Cameron."

At a bend in the river, on the Cherwell's grassy bank, a young man stood with his hands on his hips, and looked out towards them. He was completely naked, his attitude one of calm determination. Others, equally nude, sunbathed or read on the secluded apron reserved for naturists.

Alex propelled the punt deftly forward, listening to the green water gurgling by. "He's standing up for one of Oxford's great traditions."

"Isn't he just?" Cameron was still looking over.

"Upholding his inalienable rights," Maggie said.

Alex spoke jokingly to Kintyre. "You mean to say you've spent almost three years in Oxford and you've never heard of Parson's Pleasure?"

"Oh, perhaps I did. But you or somebody could have told me earlier."

"I didn't want a friend of mine rushing off to become a sun worshipper." Alex saluted the sunbathers with a flourish of his pole. "To all theology students. May their stipends never shrivel."

117

The punt slid on past willow fronds and picnic parties. The day was hot and lazy, and they were soon to be free. The biggest college ball was later this week, but the beginnings of post-examination relief were tempered by the feeling that their small world was coming to an end. There was the future to consider, but it could wait – nothing should be allowed to spoil this glorious afternoon.

Around the bend another punt nosed into view.

"Two points to starboard, Mister Christian," Cameron said, holding an imaginary telescope to his eye.

"Starboard two points, Captain Bligh."

"Isn't it about time you took the helm, Captain?" Maggie said, wanting Alex to sit with her.

"Madam!"

Cameron swept off an imaginary cocked hat and began to rise uncertainly. He climbed over her, swapping places with Alex, who laughed at Cameron's mask of intense concentration as the unlikely gondolier took his pole.

The other punt passed them, Clarence de Soutey lolling in it. As they drew alongside, he produced a water pistol and fired on them. Maggie jumped as water dripped from the brim of her straw hat.

"Death to the French!" Cameron cried, and a look of horror came over his face as a sudden lapse in concentration took away his balance. He jigged comically on the back board, trying desperately to extricate the pole from the muddy river bottom. He was left holding onto the pole as the punt slid away, and with a wail he splashed into the water.

"Oh, look! Kintyre's been doing the Cherwell dance!" de Soutey sniggered. He was refilling his water pistol from a Moët bottle.

"They're loading grapeshot, Captain!" Alex shouted as Cameron splashed at the other boat before swimming breaststroke to the bank. Maggie laughed. She decided to present an open mouth to the broadside, and after the privateers ran out of range she lay back in Alex's arms and they kissed each other.

Life was perfect. If only they could bottle such moments and keep them for ever.

Alex looked into her eyes. "Come with me to Greece."

Maggie's contentment began to evaporate. She put her head on his chest.

"Don't let's talk of the future, Alex. Let's just relax in the here and now."

"I'm not that impatient. As long as you do come."

118

He laced his fingers behind his head and resettled himself comfortably, but for Maggie the spell had been broken.

She had already made arrangements to start her career in freelance journalism. Offers had come her way and she knew she would soon have to make up her mind, but they still hadn't discussed it properly. She was a little reluctant to bring the subject up after the horrible misunderstanding at Christmas.

When she had told him that her sources for the *New Statesman* article were strictly confidential he had respected that – or so he said. That was just as well, because the trade unionists Alan had put her in touch with had been very, very determined to stay anonymous. It was almost, she reflected now, as if they had something to hide.

Alex had been understanding and, strictly off the record, he told her of how Hacker was struggling to change the outmoded outlook of the Aircraft Division, and of his mammoth arguments with Hugh. He had mentioned some plane called 'the Stacey', too; and Maggie remembered from her reading that his mother – Alex never talked about his immediate family – had been called Stacey. Since then, there had been examinations to think about. She had not mentioned her intended career, and neither had he – only telling her once that he wanted to work with Ray.

Maggie's own priorities were to find a place to live in London and start her new life there. For her time was pressing, but for Alex it seemed to be different. He had his uncle to think about. Sir Edward was still paralysed down one side, and at present took no active part in running Stanton Industries. So perhaps it wasn't surprising that Alex seemed even more closely concerned with his family's business interests than he had been.

A cloud passed over the sun; there was a sudden chill and the water's surface lost its silver. The English summer, a maid of fickle mood, had grown capricious and before they had collected Cameron and brought the punt back to Magdalen Bridge a heavy dousing rain had begun to fall.

David found it difficult to tell Megan he did not want to live in Wales – at least, not yet. He had said nothing at all to her about his sexual adventure with her sister, but he knew there was the certainty of excruciating embarrassment if he and Megan and Bronwen ever came together. Bronwen, he had realized, was worse than a troublemaker.

119

It was a hot day. They sat together now on the shadowed steps of the Radcliffe Camera, watching students playing games of croquet and boules.

David faced her. "It's just going to London; just temporary supply teaching over the summer," he said. "I'll regret it for the rest of my life if I don't live in London for a while."

She was surprised and hurt. "But you know I have a hospital post at home. I'm committed. I've got to take the job now."

"I don't see how that's affected."

"But if you're in London and I'm in Fishguard we'll be apart. What about this?" She held out the third finger of her left hand on which a slim engagement ring with a tiny diamond twinkled. "You told me you would become a teacher in Wales. And what about Uncle Frank and his offer? He told us your speech to the Llanelli committee went down ever so well – just what Labour needs, he said!"

David looked at his lap. He was frightened to commit himself, frightened that Bronwen would have a hold over him if he went to Wales while she was still there. "I only want a little time."

"To do what?" Megan sighed. "Acting? Acting isn't for the likes of us, David. It's not a very settled way of life, is it?"

But David felt her opposition waver. "I'll be paid to teach, and I happen to have a hundred pounds in the Post Office. That's enough for a month or two in London. I don't want it spoiled, Megan. You must understand."

She sucked her bottom lip. "*You* don't want things spoiled?"

"Megan, you know I love you. And if you love me you'll understand how much this means to me. Will you wait?"

His voice was pleading. She sighed and gave him a little smile. "You work so hard on your history and everything that I hardly see you."

David looked down, thinking of what he had committed himself to do for Battersby. "Is it all right?"

"If you want to go to London for a while, I won't stop you. But you must come back."

"I will."

"Everybody says that. I hope you mean it."

Maggie waited for Alex to emerge from his last exam. She had completed her own final paper the day before, and once this was over they would both be free.

She waved as he appeared in a tide of short-gowned undergraduates, but as he came up she saw that he was angry with himself. "How was it?"

"A bastard," he told her bluntly. "Much the worst."

"Oh –" She stopped dead. Still, Alex would never starve. "The sting in the tail?"

He pinched his Adam's apple. "I had to sweat all the way through. Ideas, facts! I'm as dry as one of old Roper's lectures."

"Well, let's get a drink, then," she said, looking round as the crowd dispersed.

"The usual place?" he said.

She pointed at the corner. "We could –"

Alex turned back to her as the sentence remained uncompleted. "Mmh?"

"I thought I saw David."

"Quite impossible," he said, feeling for his wallet; after such mental exertion, he had a strong desire for champagne.

She still looked puzzled. "I'm sure it was him. Look, I've known him for twenty years! We got bathed in the same sink!"

"It must have been somebody who looked like him."

"Oh well, I suppose you're right." She dazzled him with her smile. "Thinking you see someone you went to school with is quite common, isn't it?"

"I certainly know the feeling."

"Yes," she said darkly, "but in your case, at this place, it would be entirely reasonable."

David had ducked low and vanished into the buoyant crowd, black gown flapping. In a quiet bar some streets away, he sat down and wiped perspiration from his forehead. That had been a close thing. He shut his eyes for a moment and remembered . . .

He had looked round the ornate hall of the Examination Schools as the papers came round. Just as Battersby had assured him, he had not been asked for identification. As he wrote a carefully imitated 'JPS Battersby' on the cover of the answer book the absurd thought that all the others here were impersonating other people passed through his mind . . .

Tension was devouring him, although it simply made him blend in with the rest of the students.

He shifted about in his chair. Now, he thought, comes the moment of truth. He read the questions for the first time, remembering the essays he had written for Battersby and all the books he had read.

David began to laugh.

Other heads turned; there were frowns and whispers, and he stifled the laughter quickly.

The questions might have been made for him.

I might have been here in my own right, he told himself, then amended the thought. Social justice. *I should have been here.*

A hand on his shoulder brought him instantly out of his reverie. For a moment, he felt fear: fear of discovery, of exposure, of the ignominy of court action. Then he turned his head and saw Battersby's pink, smiling face.

"How did it go, Bryant?"

David had an impulse to annoy the man and say it had gone badly, but he told the truth. "Like a dream. You'll certainly get a good degree – my work, your name."

"But my money," Battersby said. "No objections to taking a cheque, have you, Bryant?"

David's hand came down on the hand that held the pen. "Every objection in the world," he told the man. "I'll take the money in cash. I have a use for it."

He thought of Bronwen's naked, full-breasted body, twisting in passion.

Escape, said a voice inside him as he took the money.

The pub was crowded and noisy, but Alex counted out some coins to make a phone call from it. "I want to see Ray," he explained as he was dialling. "This week, if I can." Then the connection was made. "Switchboard? Mr Hacker, please; tell him it's Alex."

Watching, Maggie saw his expression change and felt momentarily afraid. Alex looked as savage as one of his seventeenth-century ancestors. "What? Since when? Jesus!" He slammed the phone down as the juke-box started to play. "That was the Aircraft Division in company headquarters. Ray has left. Hugh must have sacked him. He's out of the firm!"

She touched his arm in sympathy. "So that means there's only you?"

"Yes," he said brutally, a tone she had never heard him use before. "It means if I went into the firm I'd be on my own."

From the juke-box her friends from home pounded out a song: 'We've Got To Get Out of This Place'.

Sir Edward Stanton sat huddled up in his wheelchair. He gazed down at his shipyard, the summer sky blue and overwhelming above him; there seemed to be little happening – rusting scrap and battered machinery was visible everywhere, and men in dirty overalls strolled about.

"Hope my son is working you all hard."

"Indeed he is, sir." Drummond was now in charge of all the Tyne yards – that meant most of the Shipbuilding Division. He had not seen Hugh Stanton for weeks, though he did occasionally ring up from head office in London. Drummond knew why. Hugh's position, because it was not earned, was not really secure. The young Stanton had to spend much of his time earnestly cultivating the other directors and influential people in the City, many of whom thought he was too inexperienced to run the Stanton empire, and some of whom specifically doubted his judgement.

There had been one notorious case quite recently, which Sir Edward kept worrying at. "Well, the chap had to go."

"From Aircraft? I'm entirely with you, Sir Edward."

"Not that I'm saying he didn't have his uses; fine record with Lockheed, and he's laid the groundwork for us to sell our new fighter to the Americans." He shook his grey-maned head. "But we all have to pull together. Loyalty, absolute, entire. Might try and break in my brother's boy to the sales end . . . See, I have a weather eye on the future, unlike many of my colleagues in industry, and I foresee a problem or two. The boy Alex was telling me those little yellow chaps we smashed in the war have been building more ships than us, as far back as the fifties. Now who else would know that? Terrible, what? In fact I sometimes think we're too complacent by half in this country, Drummond."

"I dare say, chairman," the man said, brushing the lapels on his business suit with his fingernails.

Sir Edward was no longer the chairman of Stanton Industries, merely a non-executive director; but he did not correct Drummond. "I've seen some predictions that amaze me. West Germany's economy due to surpass ours by 1980; the Japanese to do the same by 2000."

"By the year 2000?" Drummond was hoping to leave work before three to get in a round of golf with two of his colleagues. He

123

inclined his head, as always careful not to speak out of turn to Sir Edward or his heir. After all, Hugh Stanton had recently paid off that loud, argumentative and much-travelled American Ray Hacker – and Hacker had usually been in the right, too. "Quite amazing."

Sir Edward glared at what he still saw as his yard, his men. "Britain! I'll tell you what's wrong with this bloody country – it's too full of time-servers and yes-men!"

Drummond kept a straight face. "I have often thought so too, sir."

Maggie would always remember the last ball at Christ Church, and its aftermath. Alex had bought tickets, and they drank champagne together with all the others in evening dress: Cameron Kintyre was at their table, with Alex's cousin Hugh, and David and Megan sat close together at the other end.

"Love," she said to Alex, winking.

He toasted the word with gravity. "It's so good to be here, with my friends – and with you, Maggie, looking so very beautiful."

"Flatterer."

"The truth," he said, "pure and undefiled."

"But isn't there an undercurrent, tonight? Youth's lost yearnings, lost hopes, now that we all have to leave and –"

"And what?" he said, then put on a fashionable Yorkshire accent: "And go down t' bloody pit? What the hell have we got to complain about?"

"You must agree we all have to do our duty, Alex," Hugh put in.

Hug for some reason was frowning, Maggie noted, though the conversations around them were all good-humoured and their table was loaded with good things: the remains of lobster cooked in the shell; boxes of chocolates and Turkish delight; ripe Brie and Camembert; three varieties of superb, sweet grapes; bottles of wine everywhere. She turned to look at Alex. "What's the matter?"

"We've just been talking about my future, Maggie," Alex told her lightly. "A slight disagreement."

She looked at his strong-boned, handsome face, his blond hair cut immaculately short in a style now distinctly out of date. She felt a sudden emotional certainty. "Whatever you choose to do, you'll succeed in it, Alex."

"Thank you." He took her hand and kissed it.

"Thank you, for making this such a perfect evening."

David put in, "You ain't seen nothing yet."

124

Megan looked around, then put her hand protectively over David's. Cameron went to a neighbouring table, swaying drunkenly.

Maggie smiled at them all, then turned back to Alex. "So what are you going to do with your life?"

"Since Stanton Industries have just sacked a friend of mine," he said seriously, "I'm afraid I'm forced to consider my position. Loyalty, you know."

"To something above the family?" Hugh said darkly.

Alex lounged back, looking dangerous. "Luckily, I don't have to decide till the autumn. Ray has business to do till then."

"Oh." Maggie knew how serious all this was to Alex. "So you have the choice of going into the family firm with the family's blessing, or striking out on your own?"

"Exactly," he said.

Later, after even more champagne, Hugh leaned over to her, his face scrupulously polite. "I'm right in thinking your surname is Langton, and you're from Tyneside?"

"Yes."

"Father's name William, as Alex was saying? Used to work for us?"

She would never deny him. "Yes. He's a trade union official now."

Hugh nodded, as if he had now placed her in the social strata.

They continued to drink and dance to the Dixieland jazz band hired for the night, until the eastern sky was touched with pink. Then a black Rolls Royce embellished with the Stanton crest appeared; a dark ghost coming out of the early morning mist, and took half a dozen of them down to Folly Bridge and then right to Donnington Bridge Road.

There was a barbecue, ready prepared, and more to drink. Then Alex took her by the hand. "Come. It's time."

He had hired a hot-air balloon; the burners roared, and as they swayed into the sky he leaned out of the gondola and gave a mock salute. Maggie laughed. Gloriously drunk, the two of them drifted north among the spires of Oxford, among crowds of complaining birds. The Rolls followed them, accelerating quickly back along St Aldate's. It was early, but people were pointing up at them in the pearly morning light. She hung over the side of the basket and waved back as they continued to climb.

She felt dizzy. "This is incredible."

Alex hung onto the rigging, smiling, perfectly poised and perfectly posed. "I want it to be like this all the time."

Though it was cold in the balloon she lay with difficulty on her back, skirt hoisted up so Alex had another view to enjoy. Laughing, she heard the roar of the hot-air burners.

Later, they crash-landed some miles north of Kidlington. He held her tightly from behind, hands on her breasts as the balloon deflated completely. It took David and the others a good twenty minutes to jog over the fields to find them. As they all hauled in the balloon amid much laughter, she knew, finally, that this was love.

She turned around, hugged Alex. "You still want me to go to Greece with you, later on?"

"I want a lot more than that."

"I'll go with you," she told him. "I'll go."

Later in the summer of 1965, David left for London.

He took a cheap bedsittingroom in a large house in Notting Hill and concentrated on building a new life, taking every chance to see the big city. He could live off his savings and what he had earned from Battersby, and postponed taking up his job. London was still new to him, and he enjoyed going about town with old and new friends, putting names to places he had heard about but never seen.

Maggie, who had been loaned a tiny flat in Fulham, came over often, and they went around the big museums, to the Tate and the National Gallery; they took a trip up the shiny new Post Office Tower, and saw a debate in the Houses of Parliament. Afterwards, David peered through the big black railings of Buckingham Palace, watching the guardsmen in their bearskins and bright red tunics marching stiffly across the gravel with all the pomp and circumstance of another age.

"This is wonderful, Maggie."

"Yes." She kissed him. "Are we marrying the right people?"

"Marriage, is it?"

She dug him in the ribs. "It is for you."

They went to as many parties as possible, and he liked to get drunk and tell wild stories and use his talent for mimicry to take off the politicians of the day. Once, an actor who was his idol went to Maggie's party, and there David also rubbed shoulders with models in Mondrian dresses who had eyes like Dusty Springfield's. There was one aristocratic girl, a friend of Maggie's from Oxford, who had a BBC researcher's job and introduced him to some TV people from *That Was The Week That Was* and *Not So Much A Programme, More A Way Of Life*. Although money was short, his own expenses were

126

few, and he always seemed to have a crumpled ten-shilling note in his trouser pocket.

Several times Maggie took him to the bars on Fleet Street and to Aussie parties in Earl's Court. Alex had bought her a brand-new Mini. David enjoyed being with her. He had never felt more capable and alive: *this* was living.

Megan visited him in July and again early in August, just before he was due to start work.

"Look, David, are you sure everything's going all right?" She picked up a three-quarters-empty whisky bottle from beside the sofa, her nose wrinkling in distaste.

He thought of her sister and he was ashamed. "I'm just having fun."

"Fun! Drunk every night," she said scornfully.

He took her along with some theatre friends to dinner at a delightful little bistro in Belgravia and here, trying to impress, he spent the last of his hundred pounds of sacred childhood savings. Now, he suddenly realized, he would have to take up that temporary job, teaching in a boy's home.

"It's very nice," she said, looking around at the fishing nets and artificial lobsters, "but the menu's very expensive."

"No, no. It's fine," he laughed, covering her comments with a joke, but still the other people around them looked disdainful.

Lowering her voice, she asked him how much he had been paid so far.

"There's been a delay with the job, but as soon as I can I'll start saving. Don't worry."

"But I do worry, David. You're seeing an awful lot of that Maggie, aren't you – and frittering away all your money?"

He put his fork down and grew serious. "It was *my* hundred pounds, Megan. Saved from my time at work, saved from what I earned in Oxford. I've sweated for my chance, Megan. When other kids were playing, I was humping beer crates for my father."

"It's because your money was so hard come by that I hate to see you fritter it all away like this."

David shrugged. "It'll turn out fine. You'll see. Why don't you try the gazpacho?"

For the rest of the meal Megan seemed unusually subdued. She was unwilling to join in his drama talk, she had wanted to see a *Carry On* film instead, and as he waved her off from Paddington Station platform at nine o'clock that warm summer evening, he couldn't help feeling that she had changed.

Next weekend Bronwen was coming to town. She hoped to get a job as a BOAC air hostess. She had threatened to tell Megan about their affair unless he let her stay for a day or two after her interview. Like a fool, he had agreed.

The prospect worried him more than it stimulated him. He went out with Maggie the next night and got drunk again, as the last of the wonderful summer night died. The music that came beating out matched the battle in his head: the Rolling Stones demanding 'Satisfaction', the Beatles asking for 'Help'.

"Where's the dear little rich boy, Mags?" He realized he was slurring his speech.

"Alex? Still touring America. Maybe he's planning to be President."

"Then Greece?"

"I must finish the piece on the International Marxist Group first. Another 3,000 words or so." Maggie prodded him as he suddenly slumped over the table. "David, I don't know what you're trying to avoid by drinking, but it's no good. It'll find you out."

He felt cold, knowing he had heard the truth. "You're right."

That night he looked at himself in the bathroom mirror: straight black hair, sensitive features – a poet's face, Maggie used to say as a joke. He peered into his eyes, worrying he would see corruption there. It suddenly came to him that he was hurting Megan who, out of all the people he knew in the world, was the one who deserved it least.

He would ring up about that job tomorrow. Bronwen, if she ever came to London, would have to stay somewhere else.

He slept well.

The Rolls Royce arrived outside the Langtons' house one bright morning at the end of August. Minis and Ford Anglias were parked in the street onto which Reid, one of the Stanton chauffeurs, opened the door. Alex crossed the pavement and knocked on the door of number twenty-seven.

She opened it for him, quickly. She had been waiting.

"Hello Maggie," he said as he stepped inside the narrow hallway.

"Alex, you're late." She was holding over her arm a red plastic mac which glowed against the faded wallpaper, and she looked past him with a nervous glance at both Reid and the car.

128

"Maggie's been wondering what kept you." Will Langton's shirt-sleeves were rolled up on his muscular forearms. He turned to his daughter. "Aren't you going to introduce us?"

Maggie looked to her mother and father, and she seemed to Alex inexplicably inhibited. "Mam and Dad, this is Alex."

The burly man came forward, his hand outstretched. "I understand you're taking our daughter off to Greece, young man."

"With your permission, of course, sir."

Bridie seemed impressed by Alex's demeanour as well as the big car into which her daughter's two brand-new suitcases were being loaded.

"I'm Maggie's mother. Nice to meet you, Alex." Then some of the warmth faded from her words. "Our Maggie will be safe with you, won't she?"

"Mam, it's 1965! I can look after myself!"

"A pleasure, Mrs Langton. I'm sure there's no reason to worry."

Will shaded his eyes against the sun as they moved outside. He examined the black car and the grey-uniformed chauffeur suspiciously.

"That's a funny-looking taxi," he said to his daughter archly.

Maggie kissed her mother and then her father. "I thought you were coming in a taxi," she said to Alex by way of explanation.

"We still don't know your young man's full name."

Alex handed Maggie into the car, and turned. "I'm terribly sorry, my name's Stanton, Alex Stanton."

As the car door closed, Mr and Mrs Langton exchanged a single shocked glance. Will controlled himself manfully.

The car pulled away, and Maggie's hand waved through the back window at them. Then the car rounded the corner and was gone.

"She's kept that very quiet," Bridie said mildly, expecting the worst from her husband.

"I can't believe it," he said, softly. "She knows all about the big strike at Stanton's, and what they did to us! She's watched me preparing for another one all this week. I can't believe what she's done!"

Bridie shook her head. "Do you think he really is the Stanton lad?"

"Of course he is! You saw the car, didn't you? He even looks like his old man used to."

129

"Yes, well, enough said about that," Bridie said sharply. "I hope your daughter'll be all right."

"Associating with the likes of *him?* I doubt it," he said, and went back into the house.

Hugh Stanton stretched and sat back in his comfortable chair. All around him and across the boardroom table the directors shuffled their papers, and he heard talk about Russia's public admission that they were supplying North Vietnam with arms – but then, there was plenty of Stanton hardware being sent south of the DMZ, to help keep the balance. Vietnam, he knew, could be a goldmine for Stanton Industries.

Sir Edward was still absent, and Hugh had discovered with surprise that he enjoyed power. Now Beauford had stepped down, he had control – none of the other directors would oppose a Stanton who commanded Beauford's support – and it would be an anticlimax when he had to relinquish his stewardship of the company. How many more months would it be? Six? Nine? Twelve? Maybe it would be never . . .

He shook himself.

It's not proper to think that way. I have to give my first loyalty to the family – to my father, that means, for now.

His time standing in for his father had so far been quiet. The same could not be said of the next nine months. It already looked as though the shipyard management had got themselves inextricably tied into a quarrel with a particularly awkward union representative – the regional secretary.

Lord Beauford was sitting by the head of the table. Now he leaned forward and tapped at the dossier placed beside Hugh's blotter.

"I think it's time we took care of this man, Hugh."

Hugh tried to look pleasant, but non-commital. Beauford was a powerful man in the City – and, certainly, there had been rumours of impending strikes throughout the past weeks. So far they had not materialized, but this time it looked dangerously as though the peace would be smashed.

"In some ways the unions seem to be talking sense. Safety and efficiency do go hand in hand."

"I think not," Beauford said smoothly, smiling over his half-moon spectacles. "Isn't this William Langton a trouble-maker of long standing?"

Hugh took the point instantly; this was Beauford's test of his own mettle – and Hugh had learned well the lessons his father had taught him.

"Give them an inch and they'll want a yard, my father said many times."

"In his day, an excellent chap," Beauford said, beginning to gather up his own papers. "In his day. Though we, together, today, must make sure the yard they take isn't Stanton's. I think getting to this blue-collar chap Langton is where we start."

Hugh held his breath. The man was offering to become an ally . . . against Hugh's own father, if necessary. Even if the price to be paid was William Langton's humiliation by any underhand means necessary, Hugh knew it would be worth it.

They studied Langton's dossier. The man had shown himself to be a responsible negotiator, but looking further back Hugh found some details of how his father had beaten Langton in '56. William Langton, married to Bridget; two daughters, Ann and, of course, Magdalen. It came back to him suddenly: Maggie, openly confessing that her father was a union agitator. "You know his younger daughter is seeing my cousin Alex?"

"Really? How very interesting." There was a long pause before Beauford spoke again. Somehow he managed to be both avuncular and heartless at the same time. He tapped his thumb on the file. "If this man is going to cause a long and inconvenient strike, it may require something unorthodox to make his influence – disappear."

Hugh was forced to agree. It would be a mistake to antagonize the union, but Lord Beauford was leaving him no alternative. This, now, was his opportunity to show how well he had profited from his father's tutelage, and perhaps to secure further tenure on the Chairman's seat.

He thought about if for most of the morning, and he even considered cancelling his dinner at Claridges in order to go up to Tyneside, but decided that the situation was by no means that urgent. Face-to-face confrontations were usually a bad idea. A plan was already forming in his head, and the more he thought about it the clearer it became.

After all, he happened to know that William Langton had a daughter he loved . . .

He asked to be put through to the offices of a national newspaper, spoke for half an hour, and when he put the phone down he was sure it was what his father would have done.

131

Hugh was able to laugh at the headline they had concocted: UNION LEADER'S DAUGHTER IN SEX ROMP WITH BOSS'S SON. That would make Langton burn with embarrassment, and expose him to the scorn of his members. His own daughter, taking an expensive holiday paid for by Stanton money – as the mistress, the article would make clear, of one of the Stanton family.

Hugh remembered meeting Maggie; her fiery red hair and a temper to match. He had no doubt what her reaction would be: goodbye to any involvement with Alex. A momentary aggravation, no doubt, but Alex would eventually come to understand. If the Langton girl was compromised, that was part of the price that had to be paid to maintain Stanton Industries' position. She had already proved that press freedom was important to her, and she would surely agree that the public ought to know the story of a union leader's daughter holidaying on a yacht which belonged to her father's adversary.

With the right treatment, he would be able to undermine the Langtons' position entirely.

The Rolls touched 100 mph in the fast lane of the motorway, heading south. Maggie snuggled up to Alex, luxuriating in the feel of his body against her own.

"How long has it been?" she asked him.

"Six weeks. God, I've missed you." He put a finger to her chin, pushed it gently up, then kissed her hard on the mouth.

Alex's hair shone like a lion's mane in the autumn light. His clothes were summery and casual, and owing more than usual to current fashion. He had been in America, she knew, meeting Ray and other influential people, and wondering whether or not to go into business for himself or take up some subsidiary rôle in the family firm.

"No women in America went for that crazy English accent?"

"None like you, darling. Anyway, the arms business doesn't run to many women – not during office hours, at least. Ray and I went down to Delaware, then flew to the Cayman Islands. If we ever get the money we plan to get, we might need a chain of companies."

"So what does Ray want from you?"

"Contacts, Maggie – and my name. Last week I went to dinner with the Israeli ambassador in Washington. Last night in London – a greasy little man looking to buy guns for the supporters of Ben Bella." Alex grimaced.

132

"You were in Washington?" She was excited. "What about Vietnam? Now that Nguyen Van Thieu is head of state?"

He shrugged. "The Americans put 20,000 police and National Guard into Watts after the rioting. They'll need to put more into Vietnam, that's for sure."

She considered him carefully. "Do I detect a few American touches in your talk?"

"Why not? I've left home, haven't I?"

"I wish it was so easy for me!"

"Of course it is; it's 1965. And your father didn't try to make a scene, after all," he said. "You were worried over nothing."

"Nothing! Why didn't you come in a taxi, like I asked?"

"Isn't this good enough for you?" He laughed.

"That's not the point at all! What do you think people would say to my dad if they knew you and I were – well, you know."

"You haven't told him who I am, have you? Even after all these months."

"No."

"How silly."

She was annoyed that he belittled her worries. "You don't know my father."

"Well, I wouldn't annoy a man built like that. But he seemed a decent enough chap. A little upright, but it's the first time we've met."

"I wish you hadn't told him who you were."

He looked at her with a puzzled look. "Why ever not?"

"You obviously don't follow the fortunes of your family's firm."

"What do you mean by that?"

She sat up. "Alex, do you remember Suez? And the strike at Stanton's?"

He waved a hand. "The strike? But that was almost ten years ago; I was a child. I spent most of '56 at Eton or with my relatives in America."

"A local union official was dragged through the mud by your uncle. It was a vicious, lying, personal attack, and it resulted in the windows of his house being broken and his being branded a traitor."

Alex frowned. "That does sound despicable. But, God, Uncle Edward's line on trade unions has always been pretty hard."

"I tell people you're not like that, Alex. Are you?"

133

Alex met her eyes, knowing that he would kill for the company – but he would never do anything, anything, to hurt her. "No, of course not."

"Good, because that official was called William Langton. He's my father."

Alex was silent for a moment. When he spoke, it was softly. "I see. But he had to know about me sooner or later – *me*, not the others in the family. And I can't imagine he nurses some kind of hatred for the managers of every industrial enterprise." His blue eyes turned to her. She looked away. "So, if this *is* personal, why is it personal?"

"His cousin was killed."

"Ah." Alex raised a finger. "That comes back to me: 1956, the Queen?"

She nodded. "His name was Thomas Haddon. He was my godfather."

"Maggie, I understand," Alex said with that gentleness which was always so surprising. "But there is always danger in this kind of enterprise: you just have to risk it. Don't you know my own father was killed in a Stanton prototype plane?"

"But how would you feel if his death was no accident!"

"Oh, come on! Listen, I suspect something about my father's death is being covered up – maybe some incompetence on the part of Pike, the chief designer, a terrible, self-indulgent man. Maybe there was some kind of mistake in the launch of the *Albion* back in '56, but these things do happen – without malice, Maggie. And what happened there has nothing to do with me!"

"But what if your family profited from it!"

"From murder?" He shook his head. "I repeat, I was a boy, still at school. That was then, this is now. Surely your father realizes that? And he's met me. Am I really so terrible that you couldn't have told your family about me?"

She looked away. "It's not as easy as that. Mam goes to Mass every Sunday. She hates the idea of me going away alone with a man. Unless we marry . . . And my father is an old-school Socialist. He despises the rich. It's not just that you're a Stanton."

"I'm not rich," Alex said slowly. "Not yet, anyway."

She pulled away from him and pressed a fingernail against the armrest. "It would take *three years* of my father's wages to buy a car like this. That's a difference between you and him that's absolute."

134

"But it's not *my* car," he pointed out. "It belongs to the company. And anyway, I thought Socialists believed in taking people at face value. May I not be judged on my own qualities? Or is that a luxury reserved for the working classes?"

"It's not like that," she said, but sighed instead of trying to make him understand. "Let's not talk politics. Not when there's so much more to talk about."

Alex became thoughtful for a moment, and then said brightly, "How was London?"

"Incredible!" She lit up again. "I'm starting to meet the most amazing people. The parties are wonderful. I even went to David Bailey and Catherine Deneuve's wedding – that's why he took those pictures of me."

He smiled, luxuriating in his own good humour; the Bailey photographs had made her look stunning. "I'm glad to hear it. Mick Jagger was best man, wasn't he?"

"Right. But don't think I spent all my time partying. I've brought my typewriter with me. I intend to work – and I can't afford more than a month away."

He deftly changed the subject again; he was determined they would have much, much more than a month together. "You said on the phone that you've seen David."

"He's still going to all the right places. It sounds marvellous, really, though he's drinking too much. He can be very amusing and charming."

Alex nodded. "Seems to know a good deal about the way people work, too. Not to mention the world economy."

"But I don't think he's got a bean – though he's happy, I suppose. He and Megan are engaged now, you know."

"And you're quite sure he's not in love with you?"

She looked pained for a moment. "David will only ever be a friend to me."

Alex kissed her; her reply satisfied him completely.

"Look what I've brought us." He took a box from beside his feet. In it was a punnet of strawberries and a bottle of her favourite Moët & Chandon. "If it's not too decadent for your Socialist tastes."

"Alex, how thoughtful!" She returned his kiss, and allowed him to feed her the ripest and reddest of them with his fingers. In turn she poured champagne into his mouth until he choked with laughter.

135

"There's at least one advantage to a car like this," he said when the strawberries were gone. "You can pour champagne at a hundred miles per hour with perfect confidence – Rolls Royce confidence, you might say."

An hour later she found one of Stanton Industries' twin-engined planes waiting for them on the apron of a private airstrip in Yorkshire. It was a crisp late summer day; very English and lovely, she thought. After Alex took them through the formalities they boarded and took seats together. The plane's Stanton engines sent them hurtling down the runway.

"Hugh's been very good about all this," Alex said. "Almost too good."

"Oh, it's probably a peace-offering," Maggie answered.

Paradoxically, as soon as they bumped into the air Maggie felt freed from all anxieties. It was the first time she had flown, and maybe it was the champagne, but she was surprised to find the experience pleasurable. Throughout the flight she kept turning to the tiny side window to stare down in wonder, like a child. She saw the English coastline, then they crossed the Channel and flew over Paris. The snowy peaks on the Alps were breathtakingly beautiful, and later the white banks of cloud parted to reveal the Dalmatian islands.

Soon the unbelievable blue of the Aegean was delighting her. They lost height gradually, so the sea became textured with waves and the wakes of ships, and as they circled Santorini, Alex told her that the island had once been a giant volcano. Five thousand years ago it had exploded in an eruption ten times as powerful as the one that had destroyed Krakatoa.

"Are we going there?" she asked apprehensively.

"Yes," he said, smiling. "It's perfectly safe now, and there's nowhere on earth more romantic."

After the plane touched down, an ancient saloon car took them to the crest of the crater, where thousand-foot high cliffs of banded rock fell sheer into a bowl of aquamarine. In the centre of the caldera a heap of black cinders thrust above the sea and smoked ominously. It was, Alex said, the smouldering heart of the volcano.

Along the cliff-top were the tumbled white houses of Thira, a place so unlike anything Maggie had ever seen, it was the stuff of fantasy. Seeing it, she understood how the Greek myths had been created.

Later, they ate chicken salad and drank rough white wine on the verandah of Thira's sleepy taverna until the sun settled into the western sea. The sky was the golden red of Maggie's hair, and as the warmth of the day began to abate, vermilion streamers appeared and the planet Venus, bright beside a crescent moon sharp as an Islamic blade. She shook her head, awed. She had never been so far from home.

"Alex, this is paradise!"

He looked at her again. She was lovely. As if by agreement they spoke little after that, letting smiles and looks serve, and when they went to their tiny room they relaxed among the simple furniture in the pale light cast by a white-lit church. Maggie was trembling as Alex undressed her. In that light her skin was ivory. Moths danced around the lamp.

"I love you, Maggie," he told her. "I want you."

His eyes glittered in the half-light, but she trusted him now, completely. "For now, and for ever?"

He threw his shirt across a chair and turned back to her quickly. "For now, and for ever."

He bent to kiss her nipples, feeling them grow hard against his mouth, and then he carried her effortlessly to the bed. There they made love, and her cries were pure joy.

Maggie awoke first in the early cool and found that Alex had saved a last surprise for the morning. First, he watched her wash in an old basin with a single cold tap and then shrug into her long white cotton gown. Except for flimsy leather sandals, she wore nothing else.

"It's a pity to hide a body like yours," he told her, grinning.

She gave a low laugh. "But what does familiarity breed?"

"Love," he said. "In this case, love."

In the clear morning light he led her by the hand to a pair of rough-haired donkeys, which transported them down a terrifying zig-zag track that was carved into the cliff face.

"Alex! Where are you taking me?"

There was nothing below but a few tiny fishing boats and a small jetty.

"To the *Nereid*," he said.

He would say nothing more until they reached the bottom. There a man in a white shirt, shorts and knee socks met them. He put on his

137

cap and saluted. "Welcome back, sir." He turned to Maggie and gave a slight bow. "Madam."

"Thank you, Carlo. It's good to see you again."

He conducted them to a white tender, and started the engine as they settled into seats behind him. Maggie leaned on Alex's shoulder and whispered, "Did he really salute you, and call *me* 'madam'?"

Alex seemed faintly perplexed. "Naturally. And why not?"

She shook her head. "It just seems so . . . silly."

Maggie perched in the stern and looked back at Alex, turning a lock of hair around a finger. As they began to round the volcanic heart of Santorini she said again, softly, "Where *are* we going?"

"I told you – to the *Nereid*."

"The *Nereid*?" She followed the line of his pointing finger, then immediately looked back at him, because there, anchored in a cove among gigantic black boulders, was a huge white motor yacht, its raked-back funnel painted Stanton black and gold. A red ensign flutterd at the stern.

"Alex! You can't mean . . ." She swept her hair back excitedly.

He nodded.

"But it's a *liner*!"

He laughed. "She berths about thirty, and has a crew of sixteen. Hardly a liner."

"She's beautiful!"

"She used to be used by my uncle, but she's mainly shared by Hugh and myself now."

Alex drew her to him as they came alongside the big varnised nameplate. "Neptune's wife, Amphitrite, was one of the Nereids," he said.

"And Thetis, too."

"Thetis," he told her, "whom Jupiter himself desired."

He caught hold of the ladder and conducted Maggie on deck; once they were aboard the crew made ready. A big engine shuddered to life in the depths of the yacht. She felt the vibration even in the gilded interior of the stateroom, at the big table around which generals and princes had negotiated arms deals.

"You're very quiet," he said later as they stood together on the deck watching Santorini slide slowly below the horizon.

"Am I? Maybe it's because I can't believe I'm here and what's happening to me."

"You'll get used to it."

138

"Do you think so?" Doubt was heavy in her voice. "I'm not sure if I could ever get used to this."

That night, as they rocked naked together in the stateroom's bed, Maggie felt his arms folding around her waist. She knew there was no firm land anywhere near here, and that somebody else was in charge of the itinerary; somebody else was in charge of her . . .

As Alex, half asleep, put a warm hand on her breast, she tried again to untangle her emotions; in the last couple of days there had been so many firsts for her it had all been a shock, and she was uneasy.

She'd seen Stanton wealth at a distance, and considered it as an abstract idea. But it was another thing to find herself sharing in it with Alex. She had never imagined his personal circumstances could be like this. When he had asked her to come to Greece she had been overjoyed, but had expected an ordinary holiday, just the two of them, visiting ruined temples and sunbathing on quiet beaches, normal and right for two people in love. But this was effectively his own yacht, the crew called him 'sir', and her 'madam'. They were never completely alone together now that she was in his world. His wealth enclosed her like a cage. He controlled everything here, the ship, the crew, their journey and their destinations – and maybe he controlled a little of her now.

A shiver passed through her. Alex felt it and held her tighter in his sleep. She had been brought up to believe in equality and independence, but here such thoughts had no place. Already she found it difficult to imagine what her father would say.

The weeks that followed were an idyll. Islands jutted from the blue sea, climbing sheer from the water as they sailed slowly into the west. Dark green pines covered the rocky slopes and, higher up, terraced vineyards and fig trees basked in the sun. Orthodox churches, their domed roofs painted the blue of sea and sky, sat atop naked rock. Maggie exposed roll after roll of film. Wherever they stopped in the Cyclades she saw beauty. Land where the mountains faded into the distance in seven distinct shades of grey, one folded upon another; sea so clear that the colours of small fish could be seen as they swarmed fathoms away round the anchor chain. The salt tang of the sea and the scent of pines drifted across to where they lay on deck sunbathing in the heat.

"I love Greece," she told him. "I love the ocean, and I love the people."

Alex lay on his back, his eyes closed, his skin golden as his hair. His breathing was slow and rhythmic and she saw his heart beating slowly. A copy of the *Wall Street Journal* was by his side, and with it a colour brochure for the new cluster bomb that the Stanton Armaments Division planned to manufacture for the American version of the STA-2.

"And I love you," she whispered. Above them, the mast soared into a featureless void of blue. On the bulkhead was a polished brass maker's plate that shone bright in the sun. It read:

NEREID

STANTON, WALLSEND

1956

Autumn came; the weather became worse. As October turned to November on the Aegean, the yacht put into a small Turkish port – an ugly industrial place, with cranes and what looked like a cement works behind the docks. Alex wouldn't tell her why they were here, and asked her to stay in the cabin after dark.

That night a small boat came alongside. Maggie heard footsteps slap the wooden deck, murmurs and, defying Alex, went outside. There was a big human shape, outlined against the starry sky. She blinked. Turkish speech snapped at her; the big man raised a hand then turned to face her. "Lady, this is no place for you."

"Ray? What are you doing here?"

Alex stepped forward from welcoming two Turks, but her eyes had adjusted to the dark by then.

"I'm not here," Ray Hacker said stolidly. "Do you understand that, Maggie? Not here. This is life and death."

The yacht's captain led the three guests away after a quiet word from Alex, and he came up to her. It was too dark quite to make out his expression, but when he spoke she heard obvious anger in his voice. "Maggie, I asked you to stay inside, and you have to keep out of this or you'll ruin everything."

"But what are you doing?"

His voice was flat and emphatic. "Stay out of my business."

Alex talked with the Texan and two Turks for all the rest of the night. Maggie knew they were discussing arms, dealing in death – and the realization sent her cold. Even worse, and

140

hurtful, was the thought that Alex was excluding her from his life.

Ray was eating a fried English breakfast in the stateroom when Maggie came in next morning. She sat down with a flounce, saying nothing.

Carlo pinned a radio telegram to the notice board:

PENTAGON SEEM ENTHUSIASTIC ABOUT STA-2. IF WHITE HOUSE APPROVES, FORESEE BUMPER XMAS. WE CAN EXPECT ORDER FOR ONE HUNDRED PLANES. $300 MILLION MINIMUM. DONALD PIKE'S TEAM DELIGHTED. HUGH.

Ray glanced over at the print, then at her. "Hugh's little signal to Alex, do you think? Something like: 'Come on into the family, the water's fine.'" He speared a rasher of bacon and snorted. "They don't want your boy and me getting together. Well, the hell with them. And you know it was me made the Pentagon enthusiastic in the first place."

Alex came in, looking tired. He saw Maggie and Ray sitting at the same table and frowned.

"Let her stay," Ray said. "As long as we don't say nothing about our deal, we're all safe, right? That includes you, Maggie."

She made a reluctant noise of agreement. "You're in business together?"

"Makin' deals, makin' money," Ray said. He laughed, his mouth open wide, then pointed a big forefinger at her. Your sort like the PLO, don't you? And the 'Cong over in 'Nam?"

She could not take his politics entirely seriously. "I'm on the side of the poor and dispossessed. That's certainly true."

Ray left that night, under cover of darkness. Maggie was still awake, excited as well as disapproving. But even when he came to bed Alex could not be talked to; he said he had too much to think about. His rejection pained her. The *Nereid* sailed immediately afterwards, and by dawn the next day they were cruising the Sporades once more.

One afteroon when the wind suddenly dropped Alex clapped his hands and called for sport. The crew laughed. The fat French cook threw sealed glass bottles into the sea while, down below, Alex rattled at a heavy metal locker. She stayed on deck, though it had turned cold, and when she saw him again he was cradling a Stanton machine-gun and grinning.

Now the crew were whooping, leaning over the side. Alex handled the machine-gun with easy familiarity, eyeing the three bottles floating fifty yards away. The gun abruptly thundered, making her flinch, and she saw his face as he blew the bottles apart – shooting well, in three short, extremely accurate bursts. He was enjoying himself.

Then one of the crew made it more of a challenge. He was a big man, and he threw bottles one at a time high in the air.

Alex blew them apart. Then two of the uniformed men threw up three glinting, green-glass bottles at the same time.

The machine-gun roared twice, then again. Afterwards, the comparative silence seemed shocking.

"Good," Carlo said. "Excellent shooting, Mr Alex."

There was applause. Alex started to empty the gun of ammunition before packing it away.

Maggie came up to him and spoke in a low voice. "What did Ray want? And those Turks? I heard something about Palestine, didn't I?"

He looked at her for a long time, holding the gun. "Not from me you didn't."

Maggie began to think seriously about what it meant to be a Stanton.

Eight days into December, with an increasing chill in the air, the yacht drew near to a dark, rocky island. They rounded its nearer shore and came to a small harbour. It seemed to Maggie a cruel place.

Alex joined her at the rail. "Hydra," he said. "It was from here the Greek corsairs sailed against the Turks. Of course, it's different now."

She looked at him and he nodded at the welter of yachts that lay within the harbour, so many that their own large craft could not approach. "The crowd have found it out. In the summer it can be as bad as Cannes."

Slowly the *Nereid* manoeuvred round the island; she made her way toward massive rocky bluffs and anchored outside the harbour. They lowered the tender and came in until at last Maggie could see the small, perfect town of Hydra, like a pearl in a shell: all white, square houses with blue and green windows and red-tiled roofs.

She caught her breath. "I've never seen anything like it."

He bent his head for her to kiss him. "It's special, isn't it? That's why I brought you to Hydra. I want you to be here when –" He laughed, suddenly. He was in a good mood.

She looked at him strangely, sensing that he wanted to say more. What was he keeping secret?

He had made his mind up about something, but he was saving it.

Rain beat dismally on the windows of the ward and thunder rumbled in the sky. Last night the clocks had gone back an hour, turning the afternoons dark early. It seemed that the change of time had brought with it wintry weather, and that was a matter of concern to Megan and the other nurses on her ward because the steam heating in the tiny, century-old cottage hospital had broken down again.

Though they had not complained about it, the ward's elderly ladies felt the cold badly, and after Megan emptied a bedpan into the sluice she wiped the sweat from her forehead and tried to shake off her tiredness.

"Nurse?" Old Mrs Rees in the first bed asked her. "Is the heating going to come on soon?"

She sighed and looked down the row of beds which were strewn with extra blankets. Just as well that it was almost time for the night nurse to arrive. Megan went over to the old lady's bed. "Tomorrow morning they think, Mrs Rees. The system's so old, you see. All the pipes are clogged up."

"Just like me," the old lady chuckled. Her white hair brushed the shoulders of her dressing-gown as she tried to lean forward.

Mrs Rees was dying, but she had lost none of her humour.

"We'll get the plumbers to have a look at you as well, if you like."

She laughed wearily. "But it's so cold. My hands are frozen."

Megan sat down on the chair beside the bed. Mrs Rees' snobbish daughter-in-law had visited that morning and left a bag of nuts. Megan had said the old lady would have trouble eating nuts because of her false teeth, but the woman had brushed the comment aside haughtily. She sensed that Megan had a low opinion of her, which was true. After several months' work on the ward she was easily able to spot visitors who were more interested in their elderly relatives' wills than in the old people themselves.

"I'll warm your hands, love," Megan said, and the old lady replied in Welsh, calling her 'daughter'.

Megan stayed by Mrs Rees' bed until long after the new shift came on and the old lady had fallen asleep. She reminded her of her own great grandmother who had lived with the family when Megan was a child. Children and old people seemed to get along so well. Old people so full of memories and the young with their curiosity. Such a shame that the modern world saw people's needs so differently.

Megan took the letter from her pocket and read it again. It was the latest she had received from David, and although it was full of news there was something about its tone that disturbed her. And she had not liked many of the people he knew in London; they seemed agonizingly irresponsible to her – they were from rich families, and could spend everything they had on pleasure, but David had to find the hard cash even to live. He had said nothing about the teaching job he was supposed to start, nothing at all. There was nothing about the offer her Uncle Frank had made, either. Frank Deacon had offered David work, political work. What had David decided about it? She clutched the letter tightly and prayed she wasn't losing him.

Then she laid the sleeping old lady's hands inside the blankets, sincerely sorry that she had forgotten about her patients, even if only for a minute or two.

Megan yawned. She felt the stiffness in her limbs and the hot flushes returning – chills, aching joints, sore feet. It was probably flu coming on. She was desperately tired, but the chair was comfortable and the long walk home was so cold and wet . . .

"Nurse Jones?"

Megan started from her doze to see the ward sister. She looked down sternly. "Megan, your shift finished half an hour ago."

"Yes, sister." Megan stood up quickly, smoothing her starched uniform down. "I'll go now."

The older nurse followed her outside the ward.

"Megan," sister said gently, "you can't be responsible for everything, you know."

"No," she replied, unpinning her uniform cap. "But you have to try, don't you?"

David packed the last of his belongings into his bag and took down the postcard from the mantelpiece. Greek statuary, a dark blue sea. '*Alex and I are still soaking up the sun . . .*'

He did not yet understand what was happening, but he had followed Frank Deacon's instructions, and made contact with Alan Hoyle again.

Hoyle had come over last week. The man's personality had power, David had to admit: he had somehow belittled all David's efforts with working people's children, but he had been very interested in David's

144

link to Frank Deacon, and then he told David how Maggie had turned against her own family . . .

It was still hard to believe, but Hoyle had proved it: the strike had started last week, in November, and on Sunday the cheap papers had been full of Maggie – they had called her a good-time girl, sunning herself on the Stanton yacht as her father led the strike against the owners of the yacht. They had photographs of Maggie in a bikini, Maggie drinking champagne at Oxford. It was shaming, and he burned for her.

'Alex and I are still soaking up the sun . . .'

His fingers seemed to tremble as he put Maggie's card back. Was Alex stooping so low as to use the woman he loved like this? Was that possible?

Alan Hoyle said it was.

In any case, the worse betrayal was Maggie's. Where were her political principles now – or her loyalty to her own flesh and blood! Alan had left him the full sheaf of press cuttings about the strike, making David enraged by Maggie's behaviour and the use the Stantons were making of her . . .

David sat down on the rickety bed. Alex couldn't really be involved: surely nobody could be so despicable? But after listening to Hoyle for hours David did not know what to think any longer.

Outside, the wind was blowing, and the rain slashed down in torrents. It was December and he was alone.

He had loved Maggie once, he remembered; perhaps he still loved her now. But she had sailed out of his life with Alex Stanton, the rich man's son, and he was alone here in a damp and draughty room that smelled of gas.

Still, there was Megan. Loyal, pretty Megan – and some kind of future working for Frank Deacon, presumably in Fishguard. Guilt assaulted him. Megan had been right of course; coming to London, the parties, the theatre set, it had all been crazy, but how he had dreamed! How he had set his heart on living like that in those early days of summer. But now it was December – outside, and in the small bedsit.

"Fishguard," he mouthed bitterly. It was a world away from 'Poste Restante, Hydra'.

David took out the blue airmail paper, knowing he had to write to Maggie and tell her of the trouble that was reported from the Stanton factories on Tyneside, and the plans that her lover's relations were

145

busy fomenting. Alan Hoyle had been to the shipyards and had told David how the dirty tricks were being played, and that Maggie's father and his members were caught up in a web of the Stantons' making once more.

He looked at the rumpled bed, remembering the weekend Bronwen had turned up, and he had refused to let her stay.

Then he took the keys off his key-ring and left them on the counterpane before sneaking out into the street, taking care not to disturb the landlady. He couldn't pay the rent he owed. He promised himself that he would forward it as soon as Frank's first salary cheque arrived, and pulled the door quietly shut behind him.

As he walked to Paddington and felt the rain soaking through his coat, he decided he would have to write to Maggie and tell her exactly what Alan Hoyle had asked him to say.

Alex had become very, very quiet. He found it strange to feel so uncertain; there were so many decisions he had to make, about his career, his family, and Maggie. Decisions that would chart the rest of his life.

Ray had been approached by the Turks to buy arms, probably for the PLO. If Alex could help expedite the paperwork, the deal was on – it would raise a hundred and fifty thousand pounds, Ray had said, and as long as Alex helped export the guns they could double it. Alex was tempted. Arms-dealing seemed much more exciting and profitable than an expedited rise through the Stanton Industries' head office bureaucracy.

They had agreed to do the deal, but Alex did not want to see Stanton arms used for terrorism in the Middle East. He spent many hours trying to think of some means of reconciling their mutual commitment and desire for money with the necessity of preventing terror. One way had occurred to him: it was dangerous, but he was inclined to risk it.

And then there was Maggie, who had grown to mean so much to him. He regretted he could not be more straightforward with her, but that would breach security and possibly even endanger her life.

Two days before Christmas they were in the post office on the corner of Tombazi and the harbour front, a few yards from the hotel where they had decided to stay for a few nights, while Carlo got the *Nereid*'s engines overhauled on Naxos. An old man sat in the corner, passing a cord of bright yellow beads through his fingers one by one, enjoying

146

the cool. Alex collected their letters and flashed a broad smile at the fat postmistress who handed them over in a pile. As the day approached, Maggie had begun, almost reluctantly, to make preparations for her first Christmas away from home. Alex insisted she stay until the New Year. He had been very firm about it. To her surprise, she had begun to long for England and her family. Most days, even now, there were clear skies and sunshine and the perfect blue of the Mediterranean, but it no longer seemed to be perfection to her. The storms had begun, and the weather had turned cold.

She looked forward with special excitement to reading her letters. Except for occasional, week-old copies of *The Times*, they were her only link with home, and the newspaper had lately mentioned her father's name, disapprovingly of course, in connection with a major strike. She was beginning to miss so much – friends, family, even the regular excitement of *Ready, Steady, Go!* Here, she felt like an infant. She spoke no Greek, and always needed Alex to guide her, even through so simple a thing as a menu.

Last night they had had dinner with a man called Anthony Harvey who owned one of the other yachts in the harbour, and he had mentioned he would be sailing to a main island airport soon to fly back to England. The weather would get worse in the Mediterranean, he told them. It was time to go home. Maggie had found herself agreeing.

A howl of Greek made her look up. Alex had provoked the postmistress into girlish laughter. He flirted with her, speaking in idiomatic Greek that Maggie couldn't understand.

"Marvellous; a letter from Cameron, and one from Craigburn! I'm going to do some shopping," Alex told her. "Have a drink, and wait for me back at the hotel."

"Alex, you promised we'd go to –"

"Sorry, must dash – I'll miss the bank." He waved his wallet at her and turned away.

"But I've already been – look, I've still got my passport and the rest of my travellers' cheques."

He said tersely, "I think we'll need a little more money than you can provide, Maggie – unless you *want* to pay for the running of *Nereid?*"

She gave in and nodded her agreement, and he was yards away when she remembered to ask him what time he would meet her.

"Alex!"

147

He waved back, but kept going. Two unopened airmail envelopes flapped in his back pocket.

Maggie stood alone holding her own letters. In that moment her frustration overcame her.

There were times when Alex could be loving and attentive, but he was too much his own man; he liked to get his own way all the time, and he would use his charm like other men used their fists. It infuriated her because afterwards she always felt as though she had been beaten.

"Is a nice man, your husband," the postmistress smiled indulgently.

"No, he's *not* a nice man," she said. "And he's not my husband."

Alex ducked into a side street and watched Maggie head towards a café close by the Hotel Argo on the Quay Mandraki. When she had passed out of sight he purchased a pocket full of change and went back to the post office, and to the yellow-painted booth where he struggled first in Greek and then in English to get himself put through to Craigburn.

Fishing boats bobbed in the harbour and a light breeze wafted across the quay. Something was making the fishermen quit mending their nets and gather in groups to look around them and up at the sky. He hoped the Greek he had told Carlo to take aboard the *Nereid* was able to stomach rough weather at sea.

Clicks echoed on the line, then a distant voice answered. It sounded as if it was coming down an immensely long tunnel.

"Aunt?"

"Grace Stanton."

"It's me, Alex."

Grace's bewildered voice quavered through the static. "Alex? Is that you? What's the matter? What's happened to you?"

"Nothing, Aunt. I'm fine. We're both fine. Listen, I have something important to tell you – I've decided to get married."

"Married?" Grace asked. "To whom?"

Alex ignored the rising tone of his aunt's voice.

"To Maggie, of course!"

There was an appalled silence, then Grace's voice came across the line distorted by distance and emotion. "Maggie? But, Alex – I've never set eyes on the girl. Didn't Hugh tell us her family was from Wallsend? I know young men sow wild oats, but think of her *class* – Alex, don't be so childish."

Alex felt a charge of anger. "Aunt, what does any of that matter?"

148

"It matters a lot, Alex. You know it does. She won't know how to act, how to dress, how to mix socially – it's too much, Alex, it really is."

"Of course she knows how to behave in company, Aunt. She's wonderful, a lovely girl, and I mean to marry her."

"Alex, I won't have it."

Alex gripped the telephone tightly and turned his back to the local people who had gathered to watch the rich Englishman's performance. The old man in the corner had begun counting his worry beads two at a time.

"Aunt, you *will* have it. I intend to marry Maggie. I simply thought you'd like to be kept informed, that's all."

"Don't dismiss me, Alex –"

He cradled the receiver with all the calm he could muster and took a deep breath. Outside the shopkeepers were taking down their wares and clearing the tables of the small cafés. He pushed past the local people and headed towards a small shop where jewellery sparkled in glass cases, but he stopped halfway across the road and looked up at the high dark rags of cloud that were streaming through the sky.

Then Carlo, his Italian chief, ran up with a radio message. It sounded ominous. A depression had swung down the length of Italy and was coming up fast. In the Aegean, violent storms could develop in a matter of minutes. He had spoken with the local fishermen too. A big yacht like the *Nereid* would have to seek the lee side of the island. "And the Greek priest, he says you have offered to take him to Naxos."

"Yes. Give him food, a berth, whatever he wants."

"But, Mr Stanton, he says he must be there in two days, before the *natale*."

Alex made up his mind – he would propose tomorrow, at midnight on Christmas Eve, then the Greek Orthodox clergyman would marry them on board the *Nereid*, and 1966 could begin as he wanted it to.

"Can you do that?"

"So many hundred kilometers – maybe. But the storm. We should leave at once, sir, to outrun it."

Alex chose the ring carefully, looking at intervals to Carlo, who paced the waterfront impatiently. He hoped Maggie had not decided to wander off.

"Sir, I have seen even the *meltemi* make matchsticks of yachts; this storm is much bigger, with a high wind. It could wreck *Nereid* unless we up anchor. We should get aboard and head for a lee shore!"

149

"I've read of Homer's 'wine dark sea', too, Carlo," Alex said calmly. He pointed up at the dark grey breaker of cloud that marked the cold front. It stretched from horizon to horizon and was awesomely dappled where sheets of rain beat into the sea.

Already, in the space of a few minutes, the wind had increased, backing westerly. The harbour was chopping up into whitecaps as the little blue and green fishing boats were brought into its compass. Their tender had very little freeboard. With four people aboard it could well be swamped as they made for the anchorage unless they moved soon. The situation was becoming urgent.

Alex slipped the box containing the ring into his pocket and emerged from the shop. "Get the tender, Carlo. I'll find Miss Langton."

He caught sight of Maggie twenty minutes later as she ran down the steps of the hotel. Her white dress was swirling up and the letters clutched in her hand fluttered madly.

"Quickly, Maggie, we must get out of the harbour –" Alex began, then he saw the expression on her face. Her hand came up and she slapped him on the cheek.

He looked at her dumbfounded. "What the hell –?"

"This!" she shouted. She held up flimsy sheets of blue airmail paper and newsprint and tried to hit him again. "You're part of the plan, aren't you? You knew, you bastard!"

"Knew what?" Alex was rooted to the spot, stunned, unable to make sense of what she said. The wind battered him.

She shook with fury. "Your uncle and your cousin and the filthy cheating lot of you! That's why you didn't want me to leave. God, you must think I'm a whore – but I wouldn't stay with *you* for forty thousand pounds! You were a part of trying to smash him all the time!"

Rage possessed her like a demon. Alex caught her wrist and shouted above the wind. Great fountains of spray crashed up from the harbour wall.

"Look at it! Can't you see we must get aboard?"

Maggie thrust him back from her. She was in tears. "I'm not going anywhere with you!"

"Whatever it is, can't it wait until we're aboard?"

"Damn your boat, Alex Stanton! Damn your money! And damn you!"

Alex's temper broke.

150

Behind him, in the bucking tender, Carlo pleaded. Alex, on the other hand, insisted: "Maggie, you bloody well *have* to come. Immediately!" He looked from her to Carlo. The tender was already shipping water. In another few minutes they would be stranded. "Make it to the island's lee, then send a boat back for me when the storm's blown out."

"But the priest –"

"Just do it!"

He turned around, cut to the quick by her, cursing her stupidity, not knowing at all what had gone wrong. She wasn't there.

Let her run, then – he would still find her and bring her to her senses. There were people here, but they were all trudging away from the wild sea and the quay. He looked back, in time to see the tender just manage to ride a tall wave. Foam splashed everywhere. The big yacht already had its engines going – just as well.

Then there was a flash of lightning so intense it made him flinch, and thunder boomed. The rain that followed came down in drenching sheets. In moments, Alex was soaked to the skin and cold down to the bone. He pushed back against the poor shelter of a stone wall, till the worst of the rain had swept past. Then he asked around for Maggie in the shops overlooking the harbour, but nobody had seen her go by.

Alex trudged back to the hotel, annoyed. The heavy rain still fell, so he sometimes sheltered in doorways. His temper became worse, even though the wind was already dropping. Perhaps it would be best if he didn't find her for a little while, especially if she was sitting off her sulk in a comfortable chair in the hotel bar and sipping ouzo.

He pushed open the door to the motel, glanced around. She wasn't there. He ordered a drink, picked it up and went up to their room. Empty. And she had taken her bags. Alex raced down to the reception desk.

She had checked out of the hotel.

He stared around in frustration, one elbow on the desk. This was ridiculous. What had upset her? Surely nothing could justify this.

The only thing that comforted him was knowing that she could hardly leave the island before he did, even if she had her passport and most of her money. He walked quickly back to the harbour. People were out on the street again, and the rain had stopped: golden sunlight spilled across the steaming cobblestones. The storm was over and gone. On the moored boats the crews were already at work.

Then he saw her.

151

On the dipping stern of Anthony Harvey's yacht, flying before the wind, Maggie stared back, her hair swirling all around her.

"I'm free from you, Alex Stanton! You bastard! I'm free!"

She stood there a long time, looking bitterly back at his stunned, diminishing face, the diminishing island. Still burning with shame and in tears she had run into somebody else who was leaving the hotel; he had offered her passage. Now Anthony's motor yacht, much smaller than the Stanton craft, swung round and began to batter its way through the open sea.

Maggie stepped back from the brink, suddenly exhausted. What had she done?

Then she smiled. She had done it for her father, and she knew she was right. She remembered what he had told her about '56, and the same thing had happened again – except this time the papers had taken it out on another member of his family. Her cheeks still flamed when she remembered the shaming, scurrilous pictures of her, lewd and bare-breasted in a bikini bottom, a self-satisfied grin as she raised the mouth of a champagne bottle to her lips, and the headline itself splashed across three columns: UNION LEADER'S DAUGHTER IN SEX-ROMP WITH BOSS'S SON.

It had been true, but not any more. She was not a whore and had proved it. She had defied Alex Stanton and all his money, and now she had nothing to be ashamed of. Huge, soaking drops of rain started to fall all around her again, but she paid them no heed. This was Greece; she was her own woman, she was young, and she was *free*!

Book Two
1

For some, New Year's Day was no holiday.

A war was grinding on in Vietnam, with Americans and Australians, Koreans, and the North and South Vietnamese clashing in combat. Arthur Goldberg, President Johnson's special envoy, flew to Europe for meetings with the Pope, General de Gaulle and Harold Wilson. Meanwhile, Johnson's other man, Averell Harriman, had been sounding out the non-aligned nations in visits to both Belgrade and New Delhi, but it soon became clear that Ho Chi Minh would ignore the American peace initiative.

In Britain, the Prime Minister had said the war was poisoning East–West relations, and the Americans could not win in Vietnam. Those close to Wilson knew his greatest fear was that his verbal support for the U.S. position would ruin relations with the Labour party's left wing and split the party.

The Prime Minister, some people said, was afraid of the far left – or worse than afraid.

Shivering on the doorstep of 10 Downing Street, David Bryant wondered if any of those rumours were true, although it was already much too late for him to have second thoughts about the work Frank Deacon had recruited him to do.

Deacon, with David Bryant beside him, was asked to wait in the hallway inside Number 10.

David was still tense. "You mean I'm going to be bait." It was not a question.

"A direct line, through me, to the Cabinet Office and Downing Street? That's worth something, David. But please don't overplay your hand; you'll be alone. I don't want my niece's husband-to-be

153

ending up – well . . . "

"Look," David said, "don't you want me to do this job?"

"The thing is," Frank explained quietly, "what we want you to do might be dangerous."

"But you tell me it's my duty – to the country as well as the party."

"Yes. We don't want to make this a police matter, for obvious reasons."

"Embarrassment if anything leaked out?"

"Exactly. As for going to counter-intelligence – look, I hate to say it, because I worked in intelligence myself till '47, but the PM and some of the others don't trust the people in Curzon Street worth a damn."

David kept all expression from his face, though a charge went through his spine. Curzon Street housed the headquarters of MI5.

He pretended to study the wallpaper as he tried to think all this through; the furniture was imitation Georgian, and there were newspapers scattered on the lobby tables – but for all its mundane qualities, this terraced house in SW1 was nevertheless the world's most historically significant dwelling. David knew that for almost two centuries a quarter of the world, most of its wars and *all* of its oceans had been run from here. Surely it was worthwhile to risk almost anything to be connected to this place.

David turned his head to look at the portraits of those great men – Palmerston, Lloyd George, Churchill – who had inhabited *these* rooms. David glanced about and forced himself to relax, savouring the atmosphere of history and subdued power of the place Frank had once called 'the haunted house'.

It was a quarter to ten in the evening when the Prime Minister descended the grand stairs of Number 10, past the portraits of his predecessors, to meet Frank Deacon.

The uniformed doorman looked up and stiffened slightly as the Prime Minister came into view. He was taller than David had imagined he would be, and he greeted Frank with a brisk show of regard, his eyes darting to left and right even in the security of his own residence, a mannerism that made everything he said in his nasal Yorkshire growl sound confidential.

In this case it most definitely was.

Frank turned, thick-set, with a shock of stiff dark hair. Though clean-shaven, his chin was shadowed. His eyebrows, thick and dark, emphasized his eyes. Physically he was far more powerful than the

154

Prime Minister, but his deferential manner left no doubt about who was in charge. Deacon's hand moved to David's arm to present his protégé.

"This is David Bryant, sir, the man I told you about."

David offered his hand self-confidently, and the Prime Minister shook it firmly.

The two politicians moved aside and Deacon spoke in low tones to the Prime Minister. "He's politically reliable. He knows Marxist dialectic, and he's known Alan Hoyle for some years. He's also been an actor. Ideal choice in my opinion."

The PM grunted, and peered at David, who smiled back in embarrassment. "I suppose being engaged to your niece . . ."

"As I said, PM, 'reliable'. I vouch for him."

The man's puffy eyelids hung down over a rather tired, flabby face, and David saw two years of supreme office had taken something out of him.

They went into the PM's private study and sat down on bow-backed Chippendale chairs.

"What do you know about 'entryism'?" the PM asked him.

David cleared his throat. "It's the name given to infiltration of the Labour Party by the extreme Left."

The Prime Minister's face became hard. He lit his cigar. "I need to know about it, David. In detail."

"I understand, Prime Minister." He continued, awkwardly, "Frank tells me there's some chance of political embarrassment in this. For everyone. I'd better say straight that I've been in the Labour party man and boy, and my – wife-to-be is encouraging me to be ambitious there."

The older man was giving a rueful little grin. "They say behind every great man is a great woman, don't they? Go on."

David said it straight. "Doing this won't stop me being an MP, will it?"

"Not as far as I'm concerned," the Prime Minister told him. "In fact, if you're asking if I reward loyalty – of course I do. I only wish there was more loyalty about. Politics is a world of shadows and half-shadows. You never know who to trust."

"Well, you can trust David," Frank said.

The PM nodded slowly, then reached behind him. "Have you seen copies of this before?"

It was the magazine *Forward*.

155

David flicked through it. November, 1965. Alan Hoyle was listed as a contributing editor. The articles were the usual mixture: Vietnam, and the hard Left's view of the trade unions and the Labour representatives in parliament, but there was a surprising readiness to name names and be vicious. He handed the magazine back, surprised and impressed by its new, slick look. "I've seen most issues, right from the beginning in '62. None were like this."

Frank shook the thing. "There's real money behind this, sir – you mark my words."

David sat back. "Is Alan Hoyle really the motivator? He's not much older than I am, and he seems no more dangerous than – oh, a dozen other student agitators. I can't really see post-war Oxford crawling with pro-Communist agents. I know that happened in Cambridge, but that was thirty years ago."

"It happened, though." The Prime Minister and his colleague exchanged glances. David suddenly realized they had some confidential information to go on: he wondered if he could ask what it was. "'Forward' may be some kind of conspiracy, David, and it's certain Hoyle is their leader. We believe he may –" He stopped, his mouth twisting humorously. "But we can't hang a man just on a rumour. Tell me, what's he like?"

The Prime Minister sucked on his cigar as David, after thinking it over very carefully, began to give his analysis.

"Alan Hoyle: very clever, extremely charming when it suits him – ambitious, determined, a Marxist and a revolutionary. He's been East, many times."

The PM sniffed. "But can he lead? Has he patience, get up and go, that kind of thing? You see, we believe the entryists want their own MPs."

"I think he has a lot of hate," David answered soberly, "but that's no handicap. I'm from the industrial North, I spent three years around Oxford, and I have some media connections in London. There's a tide of dissatisfaction in this country, and I think he means to use it to sweep many things away. Parliamentary democracy would be the first."

"Not as long as I'm Prime Minister and party leader," the older man said firmly, but he was looking down at the floor. "So you investigate Forward, David. But I also need complete confidentiality from everybody. You'll report only to Frank here, or myself. We want

156

you to tell us everything you can find out about Alan Hoyle's political connections."

He watched David's considered nod of agreement.

Frank Deacon added sombrely, "For the record, you'll be my researcher, paid out of party funds. And you'll have my gratitude, and the party's. But you must understand this will be a politically dangerous investigation, David. Politically dangerous, perhaps even physically dangerous."

"I understand." Physically dangerous? David tried to look firm.

The Prime Minister leaned forward, eyes shining. "Then you'll do as we ask?"

"As you said yourself in America last month, sir, the hottest parts of hell are reserved for those who're neutral in a moral crisis. I'll do it."

The PM smiled. "Good man."

"It's not how I would have wanted it, though," Frank rumbled.

Then the Prime Minister stood up and began to pace the Persian carpet. "But they're against us, Frank; plotting, plotting. When George Brown asked MI5 for their assistance – simply the names of secret Communists in our movement – Hollis wheedled his way out of compliance . . ."

The Prime Minister's words were meant for the MP, but David had heard enough to shock him. What was happening in this country?

He sat down again after Frank ushered him outside the room. Frank had obviously decided it was essential that he meet the Prime Minister before the MP made his arrangements. It was the sort of courtesy typical of the man. And undoubtedly the Prime Minister had wanted to look him over before proceeding. It was the first time he had met a Prime Minister in person, and David couldn't help but be impressed. He recalled that phrase of C.P. Snow's about the corridors of power.

A secretary appeared, knocked, and then opened the door. His back towards David, he said softly, "I'm sorry to disturb you, Prime Minister, but the White House is on the telephone."

Through the half-open door, David could see the PM standing by an antique armchair. He blinked rapidly at the news and fidgeted, clearly surprised and a little ill at ease. "I'll take it on the secure phone in the Cabinet Room," he said on emerging, and passed David without a word.

* * *

157

It was only five o'clock in Washington, DC, and the President, standing by the French windows of the Oval Office, watched the Washington Monument floodlights coming on.

It was frosty outside and there were no roses left in the rose garden, but inside the air was warm and still, almost soporific. He walked away from the window to sit down in his customary workplace behind a big antique desk, and pressed a button on his intercom. Putting his hands behind his head, he stared broodingly at the huge eighteenth-century fireplace.

George Kenton, one of the White House aides, an efficient and alert New Yorker, came in answer to the call.

"Mr President?"

"In here," said the most powerful man in the world, waving a thumb.

Kenton disliked his boss as a man. This President had bad manners and worse friends, and he was adept at a form of back-door politicking that would never have been seen under Kennedy. Cross him, Kenton knew, and a guy could wind up drinking Thunderbird wine in Battery Park, but the President was not alone among men of power in being remote and intractable. Today, however, his mood was pensive.

As he crossed the floor Kenton saw the memoranda and the Boeing briefings the President had been reading, scattered across the desk. Rough notes for the State of the Union address he would deliver in twelve days' time lay beside them, amended in pencil.

"Listen, Kenton, how do you like this?" The President looked over the text again, and began quietly reciting the proud words. "Our nation is strong, strong enough to fight a brutal and bitter war in Vietnam, strong enough to pursue its goals in the rest of the world, strong enough to build the great society here at home – and strong enough to do it without raising taxes . . ."

"Excellent, Mr President," Kenton said enthusiastically.

But the President sighed, put the papers down and rubbed his eyes. There were more pressing matters to attend to. He looked again at the Boeing briefing, and ran over the deal he had sketched out once more. There had to be a solution. One that tied up the war, the politics and those sons of bitches at Boeing neatly in one tidy package. He crooked a finger.

"What's Boeing's line now, Kenton?"

"They're still waiting for an answer, Mr President," Kenton murmured respectfully. He knew the views the President had expressed on Capitol Hill when still a Senator. "Boeing remain convinced that our leadership in commercial aviation will be lost unless we pursue Mach-3 technology. They figure we have to beat the Russians for the sake of national prestige, and get ahead of the Europeans to capture the commercial market. Lockheed agree, but say it's going to cost more than the original estimates."

"Everything always costs more than the original estimates," the other man said grittily. He put on his steel-framed glasses, and now looked up at his aide. "So they want me to step on the Brits?"

"I think that's the general idea, sir."

"One of the worst beatings we'll ever get is if we have to look up to a Soviet SST, the way we had to look up to the first Sputnik. And by Christ we'll get our guys to the moon first. So you tell them I'll do it," the President said. "And, Kenton, you better get me Downing Street. I guess I'm going to have to tell the PM."

It took Kenton several minutes to set up the call. Then he handed over the telephone and discreetly withdrew, already thinking about how he was going to phrase the memo to Boeing. The President leaned back in his tall swivel chair, holding the phone loosely in his hand.

"Hello, Prime Minister. I have to come back to you about your supersonic passenger plane. Yes, Concorde, Prime Minister – I'm afraid you're going to have to cancel."

There was a silence broken only by indistinct protestations from across the Atlantic.

"I have this problem with Boeing over their SST, you see."

The protests continued and the President's voice took on a cutting edge. Eventually, his calm wore thin. "I don't give a good *god-damn* what you want from de Gaulle. Tell him that if he wants to compete with us over this he won't have anywhere to fly to. U.S. landing rights can be withheld on noise grounds. He hasn't done us any favours over Vietnam."

The President leaned forward, looking at the document entitled *STA-2 Preliminary Appraisal*. As the Prime Minister responded, he listened with lessening interest, knowing already what he would offer the man as a sweetener.

"So I can take it as done, then. I'm under pressure from both Houses on this, and they expect action from me. I need the legislature's approval for a one hundred and twelve billion dollar budget. I mean to get it."

159

He played the tip of a pencil across the blue folder cover, circling the word *Preliminary* over and over. "Now, that means we have some leeway. Back us positively over Vietnam and you could be in for a one quarter billion dollar share of that money. Specifically, I have right here an Air Force appraisal of your Stanton Industries' new *STA-2* low-level strike airplane; you've impressed our boys, and the Pentagon may consider buying. They'll want to know where I stand on it soon."

For a moment, he turned and looked up at the big bald eagle that emblazoned the crest behind him. There would be those who would disagree with foreign supply of strike aircraft, even though it was the British supplying them, but he knew their reasons were more connected with defence stock holdings than concern about foreign dependency. After all, more than half the ejector seats in America's airborne forces were supplied by an English company and no one had complained about that. There were certain parties who needed to be taught that the war wasn't an excuse to get rich quick, but an honest to God crusade against the spread of Communism.

When the President replaced the phone in its cradle he tried to anticipate how the effects of his five-minute conversation would spread out around the world. He scowled, telling himself for the fiftieth time that day that it was a tough world, and his was the toughest job in it.

"Kenton, get me two seltzers and a glass of water," he said, adding to himself as Kenton disappeared, "Talking to that sonofabitch is enough to give any man an ulcer."

David looked up as the Prime Minister returned with a tall man who David supposed was another secretary, and told him with a self-congratulatory smile, "That was the President himself on the telephone. I think I've just got rid of our white elephant, and clinched one of Britain's biggest ever export deals into the bargain: over two hundred and fifty million dollars' worth of STA-2s."

David lowered his eyes, feeling that what he had heard must be a state secret. Then he realized that he had just come into a piece of very valuable commercial information, and he thought immediately of Alex Stanton – that typical Stanton. He remembered what terrible things he and his family had tried to do to Maggie and her father, although it hadn't done more than cause hurt and embarrassment. Things had changed, and 1965 wasn't 1956. This time Will Langton

160

was winning.

Frank came out of the Prime Minister's study some time after eleven o'clock. He looked down at David, his expression unreadable. David had placed his hands on his kneecaps, and a pleasant, non-committal smile on his face.

"Come on," Frank said. "It's about time I gave you a lift back. You're still staying near the Oval?"

"A stone's-throw from the ground," he assured Frank. "But I'll find somewhere permanent, now."

"You understand," Frank said when he was behind the wheel of his Rover, "it might be necessary for you and Megan to live apart, if only for security reasons."

"Apart?"

"I'll tell her," Frank decided, as they passed the neo-Gothic splendours of the Palace of Westminster.

"She won't be pleased," David replied.

Traffic had been light; he remembered crossing Lambeth Bridge before Frank's car turned into Kennington. He got out into bitter cold and waved to Frank as he drove away. The big gasometer loomed over the redbrick rows of flats, the pub. He pulled out his key as the door of an E-type Jaguar opened and somebody stepped out onto the street.

"David," the familiar voice said, "what the hell's been happening?"

David scowled at Alex and decided to tell him, exactly.

It was, *The Times* reminded Alex some days later, the first anniversary of Churchill's death, and he remembered how the huge dockland cranes had bowed when the funeral passed by.

Late January in Knightsbridge, flurries of snow swirling down the empty street from a London sky both grey and turbulent. Occasionally, he saw expensively-dressed people step quickly from their cars into tall, well-heated houses, or go rapidly along the street muffled up in thick coats and scarves. Outside, there was only ice and misery.

For hours now, or perhaps days, Alex Stanton had been seated by the big bow-fronted window of his bedroom, dressed in blue pyjamas and looking out at the street below. He felt very alone here, a thousand miles away from the clear Mediterranean light and china-blue skies of Greece, and a world away from Maggie's liveliness and good humour.

That was still the way he remembered her . . .

It was time to begin again, he told himself, but he had lost interest in everything. After what David had told him he did not fool himself. Maggie was lost to him.

Hugh, too, was preoccupied: there was still a strike crippling their activities in the North East, and Hugh and Beauford had proved unable to settle it – though Hugh had been so secretive it was hard to tell what had been happening . . .

Alex stood up and sighed, thinking he ought to get dressed. Then, with surprise, he saw a familiar maroon Rover heading down the street towards the house. He threw off his pyjama jacket and began to dress, and by the time Cameron Kintyre was at the door he was ready.

Alex led Cameron through the marble-floored main hall to a little drawing room at the rear of the house, which held a Renoir portrait, Second Empire furniture, and overlooked the stark pear trees in the long, snow-mottled rear garden. Frost had smeared the windows, but here a coal fire burned in its cast-iron grate and warmed them with its orange embers.

The small, nattily-dressed Scotsman set down his pigskin briefcase and within minutes had invited Alex to two concerts and a dinner party, his pale green eyes gleaming. Alex had poured them both straight whiskies almost before his friend could speak. Normally, he didn't touch spirits before six, but he had seen that Cameron was behaving with a false, overblown levity that was unusual even for him, though Alex was used to his friend's circumlocutions. Somehow four thousand acres of grouse moor, a tumbledown castle and Cameron's ancient title had done little towards building a self-possessed man.

"Is everything all right, Cameron?"

Cameron's face became suddenly sympathetic. "I was thinking of asking you the same question."

"You'd better spit it out," Alex told him, folding his hands together on his lap.

"It's just that since you came back from Greece no one has seen hide nor hair of you. And look at you, now. Your hair uncombed, no tie; you look like you've just got out of bed."

"I'm fine."

"You're not yourself!"

Alex looked himself up and down. "Then I don't know who I am."

Cameron ignored the joke. "What happened in Greece, Alex? Is it something you want to talk about?"

Alex took a deep breath. "If you must know, Maggie and I have split up – *for good*."

Cameron flushed. "I did know. I'm sorry. And I realize how much she meant to you."

Alex shook his head as if trying to dispel the bitter memories as it all came back to him. "I loved the woman, Cameron. I was going to marry her." He turned away. The pain in him was like a wound that had to be concealed. "Never mind. It was a very romantic episode, and I suppose I allowed my feelings to run away with me." He stood up, staring at the frosted window pane. "It will never happen again. I suppose I had been annoying her, Cameron. I didn't mean to – but, God, I had so much on my mind. Work for the family, or strike out on my own. There was a deal I had a chance to get into which was very profitable, but very dangerous. But I cared for her, I really did. Maybe I should have showed it more."

"So that was the end of it?"

"No. I wrote her a letter, giving her this address, and I've had no reply, Cameron. I couldn't bring myself to ring her parents – that wouldn't have done any good, anyway. Not a Stanton talking to Will Langton."

"I suppose you're quite sure of that."

"I'm not sure of anything any longer. Eventually . . . you remember David Bryant?"

"Of course."

"I traced him. He's living in London, actually; borrowed a Labour MP's flat. We had a bit of a confrontation."

"About Maggie and other things?"

Alex remembered meeting David in the street: their low growling voices, their mutual anger and suspicion. "Apparently my dear cousin Hugh used one of the family contacts in Fleet Street – the press, when our backs were turned, made Maggie into some kind of whore. Bloody terrible, Cameron. And she blames me!" He suddenly smashed his glass in the fireplace. "Well, that settles one thing. I'm not working for Hugh, and I'm not working for his father."

"Hugh was only doing what he thought best."

Alex hardly heard him. Work? He and Ray had still heard nothing from the Turkish connection. The only good news on his horizon was the tip he had received from an apologetic David Bryant – or, beyond him, from 10 Downing Street itself. David blamed himself for the split in Greece, and he had told Alex that President Johnson

163

would buy a huge quantity of Stanton STA-2 strike planes. It was probably a breach of security, but Alex had seen the opportunity immediately. He had risked seventy thousand of his own on buying more Stanton shares, anticipating a large profit as soon as the White House confirmed the STA-2 deal. If the Americans bought, the Stanton Aircraft Division would be back in the big league.

After much heart-searching and a long struggle to repress the rage and anguish he still felt about splitting up with Maggie, he had told Hugh, but Hugh had not been even mildly impressed with the source of STA-2 information, and Alex doubted that he had acted on it.

Cameron fingered the rim of his whisky glass and then emptied it in a gulp. "She's an investigative journalist – isn't that the term?"

Alex shrugged. "She wanted to be." He heard his own words and realized he was talking as if Maggie were dead. To him, in a sense, she was. "She's an ambitious woman. I think she felt trapped with me."

Cameron studied his face. "You know, *I* never much cared for her. I always knew she would hurt you in the end."

Alex was irritated. It was not something he had wanted to discuss. "You're beginning to sound like Grace."

"Your aunt was right." Cameron reached down for his briefcase and hauled it to his lap as if it contained something immensely heavy. He opened it and handed Alex a newspaper with yesterday's date. Inky lettering that soiled his fingers promised articles on the Vietnam war, new careers in social work, and the arms trade . . .

"Page thirteen," Cameron said. "I thought it would be better if you knew what people were saying. And where it was coming from."

"*Dealers in Death*," Alex read the title aloud. Beneath it was the by-line 'Maggie Langton'. He scanned quickly through the article with an increasing cold anger.

"It compares my family to scum selling heroin on the streets of Soho," Alex said slowly, then, quoting, "'. . . Alexander Stanton, the other heir, is a millionaire playboy, hedonistic and immoral . . . living in luxury on profits from Third World arms dealing, on money that should have been spent on the poor people of those countries, not on feeding the addiction of their ruling cliques . . .'" And there were photographs: an aerial view of the Elswick factory, juxtaposed with pot-bellied African children, her picture of him standing on the jetty at Larnaca with the *Nereid* in the background – beside a dead Vietnamese baby. He was surprised just how arrogant the picture made him look.

Alex's jaw flexed. He ripped the newspaper in two, and then into four, then very deliberately laid the quarters onto the glowing coals of the fire.

"Journalism! That's a bloody smear!"

He was sickened, as if he'd been punched in the guts. Was this how Maggie had felt all the time?

"You see! She slept with you, but only to learn your secrets, man!"

"Don't worry," he snapped. "I can see through the bitch, now."

"What are you going to do?"

Alex watched the printed pages curl and brown one at a time, disappearing in a blaze of flame. He looked up at his friend, the anger and pain in his face suddenly undisguised. "She can't publish that and get away with it."

"You volunteered the information. She was under no obligation to keep it to herself. You weren't employing her. No court would condemn it."

"Court? I never said anything about courts. There are other ways."

"Not violence, Alex, *please.*" Then Cameron leaned forward to touch his friend's arm. His voice was lower now, and it barely carried to Alex, but there was an element of disgust in it. "She's hurt you, I know. Traded on your vulnerability. I'm sorry. But it's the way they work, women like that. Believe me, Alex, I've heard it all too often. Stick to your own. At least you'll be treated fairly and decently. Just forget about her. Shortly, it'll all be forgotten."

"Will it?"

The damage to his personal standing would be marginal and short-lived, Alex knew. But that wasn't the point. It was Maggie's betrayal that filled him with bitterness.

Cameron was silent for a moment. He refilled his glass from a cut-glass decanter. Alex waved the whisky away. He'd had more than enough already and felt sick to his stomach. He looked down at the fire and shook his head slowly.

How could she have done it? How could anyone have written that about someone they had professed to love?

"What made her do it, Cameron? What did *I* ever do to her that could make her want to hurt me this much?" For the briefest moment he felt like crying. But he recognized it as weakness and choked it off quickly, hardening his feelings.

Cameron said nothing, and Alex's mind went back to that last moment on the quay at Hydra, but there he met only the fierceness of Maggie's emotions. Loyalty, he thought; loyalty to yesterday's battles.

"I'll make her pay for it, Cameron. I will!" He was standing up and the power of his decision filled the room. If she thought he was like that – then he would become all that, and more.

Alex looked down and saw that Cameron had been watching him, his face registering concern. He wondered then if Cameron Kintyre was really the brother he should have had, the kind of friend Hugh ought to have been.

The Scotsman hesitated, then nodded as if to pledge his loyalty, even his love.

"Whatever I can do, Alex. *Whatever* I can do."

"Thank you, Cameron," he said, stiffly, not doubting his friend.

Maggie stood quite alone at the window. The news had reached her that evening. The strike her father had led had ended in a compromise. An average wage increase; fewer redundancies than the firm's management thought necessary.

In a way, all that terrible sacrifice had all been for nothing. It had cost her Alex's love, she realized now. David had come to her yesterday and tried to explain Alex's point of view, but after that article she had written about him she knew it was too late.

Beyond, in the darkness, Hampstead Heath stretched away towards the east where a gibbous moon rose and was reflected in the still water of the Ponds. The Heath itself was grey and mysterious, and she imagined that she was looking back in time to an age when highwaymen haunted its paths and the rich feared to cross it.

Behind her, the party was in full swing.

Anthony Harvey, her host, was a Bond Street jeweller who believed in filling his huge house with the famous, the intelligent, the beautiful, and the rich. It was his yacht on which she had left Hydra, and his kindness that had seen her safely aboard a London-bound flight at Nice airport.

Since then, she had been working.

Maggie had stepped over to the window to feel the night's coolness on her cheeks, but as she stood there she felt a mood almost like nostalgia coming over her. She told herself it was tiredness, but knew

166

it was something else. It crept up on her when she relaxed, and took her back to Greece, and her months with Alex.

She hated even to think about him now. She had come to realize that they were the inhabitants of different worlds, that they had always been separated by politics, background and social class. As her father had always been sure, it was a chasm too wide to be bridged, and she had been foolish to believe it could be otherwise. Now, by her article, she had declared open war on the Stanton clan.

"There's Rita Tushingham –" somebody said.

Behind her, flashbulbs were going off, splashes of white light that caught the group of partygoers who surrounded Michael Caine. The society magazines would soon be filled with pictures from this evening's gathering. A champagne pyramid came crashing down.

It bothered her that she was being drawn into the seductive coils of the London party circuit, becoming a part of it. It was all so easy and carefree, as intoxicating and addictive as a drug, a fantasy land of drink and talk and famous faces and the gossip that always followed after. While she turned in her pieces to the newspapers, to *Forward* and, lately, *Capital Life*, the new listings magazine for alternative London, it was possible to tell herself that she was working, making contacts, plying her trade, but going to bed smashed at three a.m. and getting up after noon was a lifestyle she knew she couldn't afford for very long.

"Forget-me-not thoughts? Or are you making plans?"

Startled, Maggie turned to look at the man who had spoken to her. He was a slim, good-looking man in his mid-twenties. An American. In the midst of the silks and velvets and flamboyant colours of the party, his beard and choice of army fatigues seemed like a political statement rather than a choice of clothing. The music changed TO the Beatles singing 'We Can Work it Out'.

She shook her head vaguely, not sure if she wanted to talk, though something in his eyes kept her there. He saw she didn't have a drink and offered her his own. "It's sourmash bourbon," he said, as if it ought to be her favourite drink. "From Kentucky. Do you want some?"

"I'd love some," she said, smiling, wondering what kind of success would allow a man to get away with fatigues and a baggy plaid shirt at one of Anthony's exclusive evenings.

The man was still holding his glass out to her. Smiling her thanks, she took it from him.

167

"Let me see." He was looking at her carefully, appraising her, as if he were a fashion designer looking over a new creation. "You come to a lot of these fancy get-togethers, but really you're a serious-minded lady. Am I right?"

He had the softest of accents, with neither the harshness of New York, nor the laziness of the Southern States. It was pleasing to the ear. And what Maggie could have taken as a pick-up line came across instead like a question that needed an answer.

"As a matter of fact, you are right. On both counts."

"That's good, because I've had enough rich man's small-talk for one evening."

"You seem to have something to prove," she told him.

"Is that a bad thing?"

"Well, you're certainly a very direct man."

He looked at her again in that appraising way. "I guess that probably makes two of us, and it seems to me neither of us would want to insult the other's intelligence."

She smiled. "So what is it you want to talk seriously about?"

"You," he said. "And me."

His name was Terry Katz, he was from San Francisco, a news photographer, but he'd made his name in Vietnam, taking big risks in Charlie country in search of striking images. He'd toted his battle-scarred Nikon round Saigon and the paddy-fields of the Mekong delta for almost a year after leaving the Marine Corps. Going almost everywhere south of the DMZ, and flying missions with the air cavalry over Hue, he had been in search of material that would bring the war home to America, and he had succeeded. Time and again he had hit his targets – the front pages of almost every major newspaper in the United States.

Maggie listened to his plans singlehandedly to stop what he said was an unjust war, and knew that she'd met either a visionary or a fool.

Later they moved up into the quiet of the terrace garden, and she learned which it was.

Terry was a good listener, eager to hear about her politics and ambitions. Perhaps it was because he was an American that he seemed unusually open-minded, she thought. She had never known an American well, but she felt she might begin to know this one.

When she asked him again about Vietnam, he touched her arm and told her. "You have to go there to get any idea what this is all about," he said. "It's dirty, squalid, a race war, a doctrinaire war.

168

We shouldn't be there. And one day we're going to regret we ever were."

"How long did you cover the war?" she asked, her head inches from his as they stood close together, leaning on the rail.

"A year and a half, plus my time fighting."

"That's a long time to spend out there."

"Not as long as the nineteen-year-olds who're doing the shooting. It worries me how they programme those kids in boot camp in San Diego, and twelve weeks later they're in 'Nam. Then they can spend two or three years wondering every waking minute if they're going to get picked off by a Cong sniper, or step on a mine, or get stabbed in their sleep by their whores – and then they start taking revenge ..." He looked at his feet and sighed. "One day we'll expect them to come home and just forget all about it, but they won't be able to. No more than I could."

"You're right telling people about this," she said with conviction.

"Bring it on home," he said quietly. "All the way with LBJ. Immortalizing our shame is what I'm really doing. And I don't expect to be loved for it – not by most people."

Terry awed her somewhat. She imagined him on assignment out there, roaring around on a Harley-Davidson, clicking away as the bullets flew, laughing, unarmed in VC territory. It was an impossibly romantic view, and she knew it, but she couldn't help herself. Besides, he smelled nice.

"How long are you going to be in London?"

He slipped an arm round her as if he had been doing it all his life.

"This month at least," he said. "Maybe the next, too. Then I have to get back. I have a crate of negatives to sort."

She half-turned, and put her hand over his on the rail. He was only two or three inches taller than she, but Maggie felt secure next to him, and realized how much she had missed that feeling in the last few weeks.

"Why not sort them out here?" she said.

"I want to produce a book on 'Nam, before it breaks big. I can only do that back home. I think I need the perspective."

"That's a pity," she said, feeling real regret.

"But for the moment I've borrowed a friend's flat while he's away." Maggie looked at him, eyebrows raised. Terry went on, "I'm busy making his furniture smell of chemicals. And wishing there was someone there." He hesitated, then smiled and lowered his head

169

to touch her lips gently with his own. She drew her head back as if offended by what he seemed to be implying.

"I need a writer," he said, quickly correcting her impression. "Someone who can lick my prose into shape, and caption pictures. Someone with experience, and a sympathetic viewpoint."

She looked straight at him. "How about me?"

"Well. You want to work for me?"

"I'm good. We could work together."

"The two of us? That sounds very possible." This time there did seem to be a little mischief in his dark blue eyes. "But let's talk about that over breakfast."

Maggie's work on Terry's project was long and difficult: it was the biggest challenge she had so far taken on. Working late hours, often into the early morning, studying hundreds of pictures and retelling Terry's episodic stories and piecing together his chaotic notes. The historical background had to be right, too.

The work cut her off from normal life, and made her think deeply about the events in that poor, war-punished appendix of a country on the other side of the world.

His photographs were graphic documentaries of what modern weapons could do to flesh and blood. It was impossible to assess them unemotionally, impossible to treat them as mere forensic evidence for the prosecution of a nation's policy, but Maggie tried.

Terry's deadline could not be put back – people were dying every day they worked – so Maggie found herself happy to decline invite after invite. Her producer friend Laurie Cochrane tried to recruit her to the BBC, but she told him over the telephone that she was committed – in every way. This was no time for distractions.

There was only one friend from the old days who made her meet him. He had news to give her of his and Megan's coming marriage and she congratulated him, warmly – the first of her friends . . .

Maggie could not forbear asking about Alex, but David shook his head and toyed with his glass. "He saw me one night, you know. Look, I told him what had happened. He said it wasn't his fault."

She snorted. "A likely story."

"Whatever, Maggie, but I want to tell you that I don't think I'm a bad judge of character, and I believe him."

She said nothing.

170

"I also saw him at a party last week, Maggie, and he gave me a message. 'Tell her that I owe her something, and I always pay my debts.'"

She tried to laugh, but even to her ears it sounded more like a sob.

When she told her parents over the phone about splitting up with Alex, her father couldn't resist the temptation.

"I told you so."

"Oh, Daddy, of course you were right, and I'm sorry about the trouble I caused you. I should have known better."

"There was no trouble," he said, laughing. "The young ones don't have their old man's talent for throwing dirt. There's no substance to Hugh and Alex Stanton. Their attempts to use the papers fooled nobody. I'm a man of standing around here, now, and people know me far, far better than they know them. They forgot that."

"Well, it's over now," Maggie had said, sighing.

Finally, a week ahead of schedule, Terry asked her to go with him and their book to New York. She agreed. First, though, there was something she had to do for old time's sake.

The tiny chapel was tucked into a green fold of the hills, where the road curved and then fell away towards the Welsh coast. Inside the crowded church, in a light which filtered through ancient stained glass, the service was ending.

Outside, the morning was fresh and bright; a good omen. The guests spilled out from the church and began to gather on a small strip of grass beside it. The wedding party posed for the official photographs. The wind was troublesome; from time to time Megan would reach up to hold onto her veil, while David brushed back his sleek black hair. Both bride and groom smiled as they looked into each other's eyes, clearly pleased with the vows they had taken.

The ritual of the photographs complete, the party made their way up the hill to a local hall.

David and his new wife sat in the centre at the top table, looking from face to familiar face, pleased that so many had taken the trouble to come.

Maggie was there, with her new man, a courteous, bearded American in his late twenties, sitting beside her. Even as David looked at her red hair, she smiled across at him, and blew a congratulatory kiss.

Frank Deacon stood up and banged the table with a big hand, demanding silence. He had given the bride away and it fell to him to make the first speech. It was warm and witty, and Frank's Welsh command of public speaking enabled him to make the whole gathering forget their stomachs and direct a tide of goodwill towards the happy couple.

David clasped Megan's hand beneath the table and kept thinking, She's mine for life. Megan's mine for ever.

The thought moved him deeply, much more than he thought it could. Although he was not a religious man in any formal sense, the ceremony had woken something in him that responded to the solemnity, the meaning of the ritual. For ever until death, that was what he had said. He had always thought the words were trite, but now they really applied to him.

Everyone was laughing at Frank's speech. David smiled, although he hadn't heard a word. Megan at his side was beaming and talking to David's father.

Further down the table Bronwen caught his eye. She smiled at him, unblinking, an almost electric gaze that disturbed him because he couldn't look away from it. She forced him to look back at her, and he could do nothing until she released him.

I don't want to remember, he thought. This is my wedding day, mine and Megan's, and the marriage vows are now our vows. Whatever has passed before must be forgotten. He squeezed his wife's hand tenderly and kissed her, but somehow his mood had been blighted.

Later, in the evening, when the speeches were over, all the telegrams read and the slow dancing begun, David walked around thanking everyone. Alan Hoyle had appeared unexpectedly after the last coffee cups had been cleared away, accompanied by a beautiful black girl.

Though he had acknowledged Hoyle distantly, David had avoided him for a while, letting the man circulate and chat freely with whoever he wanted, without the least show of defensiveness.

Hoyle had been invited at Frank Deacon's suggestion, and though Megan had asked him why he could possibly want to invite the man along, David knew he couldn't tell her. He would have to handle Alan very carefully to prevent himself being inadvertently compromised.

Now he crossed the crowded room to welcome Alan warmly, wondering what the man would tell his sponsors now that he, David, was married to Frank Deacon's niece. The more Frank appeared to be making David his protégé, the more Alan would be attracted – so long as David continued to hold out the promise that he was in sympathy with the views of Forward.

"You heard about Maggie running off to Greece with Alex Stanton?" Alan said after he offered David his good wishes and introduced his quiet West African companion.

"Yes, of course," David said, drawing in a breath and looking around. He saw Megan holding hands with her two young cousins, who both looked up at her with delight. It was a hell of a thing, he thought, to have to do this kind of patriotic business on your wedding day.

"But she certainly didn't bring Stanton with her today."

"No," David said. "They split up out there – didn't she tell you?"

"I haven't seen much of her lately. I had business at the Sorbonne. The political situation in France is looking very promising, you see. But don't you worry, I'll get Maggie on my side as soon as I need to."

"You don't have to impress me, Alan."

Hoyle smiled slyly and waved towards Maggie's flame-red hair. "I'm sure she'll be much more useful to the cause away from the Stantons' influence. I mean, she's now with that photographer Terry Katz, isn't she?" Alan said. "Fighting against the U.S. in Vietnam, and this sell-out government – no offence to Frank Deacon, of course. That makes sense. At Oxford she struck me as being, how can I put it . . ." He searched for the right words: "A hard-working girl."

David was non-committal, not sure if Maggie was being criticized. "You must read her articles in *Capital Life*."

"I do. She certainly does her homework." Alan's grin tightened. "And so do I."

David made himself smile back, thinking he should steer the conversation clear of this dangerous ground. Megan's mother came across and offered Alan a choice of egg and cress or red salmon sandwiches. He took two salmon ones, and smiled at her.

"Are you going somewhere else in Wales?" David asked. "You can't have come all this way just to see me get married."

Alan tossed his head. "Oh, I'd have come anyway," he said lightly. Then he leaned forward. "Actually, I am in Wales on business. *A little trip to the docks, David.*"

173

"Oh, really?" David said with interest. "You must tell me about it, back in London."

"Cassandra and I would love you to drop by just as soon as you can."

The black girl showed a row of perfect teeth and glanced at Alan.

"In that case, I'll be in touch."

"Tell Megan to take it easy."

"I'll tell her that," David said as they parted.

David continued to watch as Alan went over to catch Maggie up in animated conversation. Hoyle produced a notebook from his jacket pocket and scribbled something on a page before tearing it out and passing it across.

"Why not look the flat over?" David heard him say. "When you get back to London."

Whatever Alan was doing here, David thought as he considered the precise reasons for the man's visit, he hadn't come only to attend his wedding. That much was obvious. Alan had once told him that to find out what a man really was, it was only necessary to meet his friends, and though Hoyle was probably on his way to meet seamen's union representatives at the Milford Haven oil terminal, something mad him feel flattered by Alan's detour. He felt he had just cleared a major hurdle, and when he turned to seek out Frank Deacon with his eyes he saw Frank already staring back.

There had been a good reason for getting a sizeable cache of capital together.

That had come in the form of an encouraging call Alex had received from Ray Hacker, three weeks ago. Ray had laid the groundwork for selling the STA-2 to the Pentagon, and then, incredibly, he had been sacked abruptly from Stanton Industries last year. There was a financial pay-off, but it was still a dismissal, and it hurt.

But they both had plenty of ideas; they had decided to go into business together. Alex had been given a chance to double their money and, as he said to Ray, the more they had to double the better it would be. There was a risk of loss, of course – and not merely all his money.

The Turks were now ready to deal. If the paperwork could be handled, they would buy a shipload of Stanton Industries arms.

It had cost Alex everything he had left to set up this deal, using up his credibility as well as his cash and much of his time. He suspected

174

the arms would go to the PLO, to be picked up somewhere in the Middle East; maybe a quiet spot like the Lebanon.

It was not a pleasant thought. Using his family contacts in the world of diplomacy, Alex turned up one morning at a Hatton Garden diamond merchants. The office was like a fortress, he noted: a steel front door, bulletproof glass, bars and alarms everywhere. He rang the bell three times and was admitted. A fit, tanned young man, a *sabra* from the Negev, brusquely searched him. Then he was led upstairs, to a darkened room.

Behind a desk sat a craggy-faced man with white hair. He smiled briefly, turning a pair of spectacles over in his hands. There was a desk light shining down at his elbow.

Alex recognized the shadowed face from a French Embassy reception. He shook hands. "I thought you were Mossad."

"Sure, you were right." The Israeli's heavy accent had an American tone. "I won't give you my name: this side of Tel Aviv I only use pseudonyms. Sit down, Mr Stanton. What do you want to talk about that's so secret?"

Alex came around to the other side of the desk, pulled open a drawer to reveal a small cassette-recorder. He clicked it off and removed the tape: "So secret I want my name off the record completely."

The man seemed annoyed Alex had heard the machine working; his brows creased together, but a faintly admiring smile came to his rough face. "All right."

Alex sat down. "I want something for Stanton Industries – some of the U.S. money that comes to you to buy arms. I also want access to the arms Israel exports, subject to Mossad's approval of the end-user."

"That is a lot. You must be offering us the earth, Stanton."

"I'm offering you a chance to clean the most violent faction of the PLO out of everything they make in a year. Listen, they've offered dollars to me and my partner through Turkish intermediaries; they want to buy guns from the Stantons."

"So, good for you, and a problem for me."

"Not if I give you the details of the shipment."

The white eyebrows rose. "You take that risk for us?"

"Then you can hit them, on the high seas. No witnesses. No risks."

The man lit a black cheroot. His eyes glittered.

"You intend to 'give' us the details."

175

"For a favour or two back. That should go without us saying. Either of us."

"So," the Israeli said. "So much terror, which I can stop."

"So, what do you think?"

The old man sucked on the dark cheroot, thoughtfully. "I like your plan."

So did his government, later, back in Tel Aviv.

Alex had been kept busy ever since. It was always difficult to arrange the illicit export of arms, Stanton family connections or not. But he knew he stood to make a fortune, and that Hugh, even though he was a Stanton, would never dare to do anything with so much risk.

If this deal doesn't work out, he thought, I'll be ruined – and so will Ray. Or worse than ruined.

But he smiled as he climbed into his car, glad to be alive in a way he hadn't been since Greece. It's the joy of risk, he thought. He knew now that it was necessary for him to go at life full tilt. Alex ignored the speed limit as he drove through the bright sunlight of the run-down London docklands, but it was past ten o'clock by the time he drew up in an isolated dockside cul-de-sac in front of two lorries, put on the hand-brake and got out.

He looked around, saw nothing suspicious, and walked quickly down the cobbled street towards the dock. The air was hot and Sunday-still. Then somebody stepped out from behind a huge American car.

"Son of a bitch," Ray said, "you're late."

"I know," Alex said, not breaking stride. "I'm sorry."

"I used all my $75,000 pay-off from your cousin on this deal, Alex. And I borrowed. It better not go wrong."

"It won't."

They passed through an opened gate. The bribe for that had been small. Here, the dock water gleamed silver, a huge Victorian expanse like an inland sea, but there were only half a dozen ships within sight.

They found their way to number fourteen berth, but there was only a rusting wall of steel – the hull of the 12,000 ton Turkish freighter, the *Bodrum*. There was no gangway going up from the dockside, and nobody visible on board.

Ray put two fingers in his wide mouth and whistled.

"When they got there," Alex said, "the cupboard was bare . . ."

176

Ray nodded thoughtfully. "You think your cousin Hugh'll take back those two truckloads of arms we bought?"

"Of course – at a substantial discount."

Then somebody appeared on deck and looked down. The sun was behind him, but he was big and a Turk and he was carrying a meat hook as long as his arm.

"Is late," he growled, peering down at them. Then he walked away, the steel hook slung over his shoulder.

It was several minutes before a rickety gangway was pushed down towards them.

Ray had been sitting on an iron mooring bollard. He stood up quickly, not looking at Alex. "Cyprus, then to Syria. It sounds like our guns and ammo are headed for the Mid-East."

"I suppose you're right. They cost somebody a pretty pile of U.S. dollars, though – and we take a goodly slice of the action. As my family used to say round about 1776, 'profit is king'."

Alex led the way, holding on to the rope. He was feeling quietly pleased with himself until he was met by the big Turk who roughly frisked him before letting him step aboard. Afterwards Alex looked dubiously at the man's dirty hands.

"You're late," the man said in guttural English.

Alex grinned. "Saturday night last night."

The seaman stared sourly at his immaculate light suit and fine tan shoes. A knot of deckhands had come to the side; ugly, hard-looking men. The big man growled some words at them, sending them below.

They were conducted through a hatch and into the ship's galley where three or four unshaven seamen lounged around a wooden table. On it were glasses of dark coffee and a great block of mildewed cheese from which one of the hands pared slices with a big-bladed kitchen knife. Cat-like noises came from somewhere in the ship, and with surprise he realized it was the sound of women. The whole place stank of boiled fish and garbage.

Ray Hacker sat at the table, looking put out. He was explaining to a stocky, sullen-looking man who was clearly unimpressed with the proceedings.

"I'm sorry," Ray said shrugging. "There was nothing we could do about that. We had to have half the money up front. You know how it is."

"You double-crossed me. I have to go back to my principal, last week. I say him, give me all the money, in cash."

177

"Good," Alex said. "So you have the other half here."

"He say to me he was almost taken by the Israelis. Maybe it was your fault!"

"No," Ray shook his head. "I guarantee we knew nothing about it."

"You don't do good business!"

Ray levelled a heavy finger at the man. "Hey, Esref, don't tell me about good business."

"You are a thief! In Turkey, we take a thief and –"

The big Turk drew a thumb across his neck in a quick gesture. He was growing angry.

Ray stood up, his sheer bulk impressive. He spoke with cold ferocity. "Your mother."

A huge man holding the kitchen knife stopped chewing on his slice of cheese.

"Gentlemen," Alex said, placatingly. "Please. There's no need for recriminations. Captain, if you're no longer prepared to see the contract through, I'm sure there are plenty of other –" He reached out and the big Turk brought the knife down like lightning towards Alex's hand. The tip bit half an inch into the hardwood tabletop, missing Alex's hand only by passing between his splayed fingers.

"Don't touch!" the Turk shouted. He shot up from his seat.

Alex did likewise. For three seconds he and the Turk stared at each other fiercely, and Alex knew that everything was going wrong.

Then Ray grabbed the knife, wrenched it out of the table and sent it spinning across the galley towards a dartboard that hung on the wall. It stuck in at an oblique angle, splitting the disk and severing the wire overlay.

The seamen in the galley looked at Ray with new respect, and he sat down immediately, saying calmly, "Can we talk some business now, Esref?"

The Turk reluctantly took his seat once more.

As he too sat down, Alex reached inside his jacket very slowly. He pulled out a brown envelope and held onto it tightly. His voice was as clear as ice. "The way I see it, there's a penalty to be paid, on behalf of both Mr Hacker and myself, to you, Captain, as the aggrieved party."

The Turk's eyes glittered as he looked at the envelope. He dismissed his men, who slunk away from the galley, then Alex ripped the end of the envelope off and spilled half a dozen crisp thousand dollar bills onto the table.

178

"Jesus H. Christ, Alex!" Ray growled. "What the hell are you doing?"

Alex waved him silent, and slowly counted out the bills.

"First I check," the Turk said suspiciously, but he was clearly hooked.

Alex slid a single bill across the table. The Turk picked it up, held it to the light looking for the watermark, then wetted a finger and dampened the bill with saliva. He tore a small triangle off the corner of the empty envelope and rubbed it rapidly back and forth across the green side of the bill. When he turned the scrap of paper over it was smeared with green. The Turk smiled, revealing gold fillings.

"Okay," he acknowledged. "Only real dollar makes green like this."

The Turk reached out towards the rest of the money, but Alex grabbed his wrist.

"No! Not yet," he said firmly. "First, you tell me who the shipment is really for."

The Turk pulled away. He looked insulted and angry. He was unused to being crossed. An ugly expression came over his face and he grabbed a handful of air. "Okay. I take your money. I *kill* you!"

Alex smiled. "Captain, you leave England without a cargo and half your money gone and my bet is the buyer will kill *you*. Right?"

Ray sat back, his big frame dwarfing the man opposite. "I guess that puts you in a bind, Esref. Why don't you tell my partner what he wants to know?"

The Turk grimaced. He nodded. "The final delivery is to Syria, in the port of Latakia. That's all I know!"

"So who's it for?"

"You think I care! I know nothing."

"Then who made the deal with you?"

"I don't know any name, who he is!"

"That is a shame." Alex began to gather up the bills.

The Turk scowled. "In Marseilles they call him Candyman, is all I know."

Ray drew a deep breath. "Now, you wouldn't be putting us on, would you?"

"I am Esref Firat!" The Turk's eyes widened at his word being doubted. "I tell you, he is called Candyman. From the big heroin connection to New York. He say these guns to Abu Jihad."

"I'm sure Mr Hacker believes you." Alex put down the money and stood up. "Take it. It's yours. Perhaps now you can give us your principal's money and we'll get the loading completed."

"Now?" The captain seemed reluctant, suddenly.

Alex stood up, smiling. The Turk hurriedly bellowed something in Turkish. One of the crew came back and stood standing in the doorway, arms that were heavy with muscle folded across his chest. He eyed the Englishman and American blankly.

Firat pulled forward a heavy, metalbound case with two padlocks on it. He opened them up with some show of reluctance. Inside, the case was packed with neat bundles of notes. Alex and Ray both checked, this time, then made an exact calculation as the dollars were piled up on their side of the table.

"My figure is", Alex said flatly, "one million, five hundred thousand dollars."

Ray reached forward, grinning, and shook the Turk's hand. "Then we have ourselves a deal."

They went out on deck. Now that they had agreed to the business, it would go ahead immediately.

Alex wanted to get it over quickly, smoothly and with a minimum of fuss because this was the moment of maximum risk, and one for which he could not prepare. The gamble was fixed odds. But it was a sunny Sunday morning, the wharf seemed completely deserted, and he believed in his own good fortune.

Within minutes a big unmarked articulated truck had drawn alongside and half an hour later a series of ribbed steel boxes had been winched into the ship's hold on wooden pallets. Machine-guns, mortars, explosives, ammunition, enough for a small war.

Despite the delay it caused, the Turk insisted on opening one of the first boxes. The steel was bolted and had to be approached with a wrench. Alex watched him lift off the lid and peel back the oil-paper to reveal the barrel of a Stanton MM-55 heavy machine-gun. He ran a cursory eye over it.

"Is good, your guns?"

"Stanton hardware is the best," Alex assured him.

That was undeniable. The Turk drummed his hands on the packing case, then had the box closed up again.

It had taken perhaps an hour in all. The whole operation went unobserved, except by a trio of prostitutes who appeared at the gangway and hobbled off across the quay towards a Greek cargo ship berthed a hundred yards away. Certain kinds of international trade knew no real restrictions, Alex reflected, and had scant regard for national boundaries. It was as simple as that. Everybody would whore if the money was right.

They watched the truck until it disappeared, and in an eerie silence broken only by the distant calls of seagulls, took their leave of the morose crew of the *Bodrum*. As they walked away, Alex's sense of tight anticipation gave way to a warm feeling of satisfaction. Hacker broke it with angry words as soon as they were clear of the dock gates. "You just wasted six grand on the guy you were calling 'Captain' back there!"

"Wrong. I paid him six thousand dollars for a reason."

Ray checked they were out of sight of the ship and then turned on Alex. "You must be crazy. You know this business works on confidentiality! You were asking questions about final destinations. That's a real big no-no. Even asking can get you killed!"

"I wanted to know where the consignment was going, and I had the feeling the Turk would tell us." Alex smiled. He was unperturbed by Ray's words.

"Do you know who that Turk was? Esref Firat is the most murderous son of a bitch this side of Istanbul. The minute he gets into Marseilles he's going to go straight to the Candyman and tell him about all these questions you've been asking. Do you know that the Candyman is a big buyer for the most dangerous faction in the PLO? You're fucking with trouble there."

"Is that a fact?"

"That is a fact!"

"Look, I'm sorry, Ray, but I needed to know where the shipment was going," Alex said.

"What the hell for? We got paid."

Alex grinned; Mossad had paid him, too. "Because what goes where depends on who wants what, and it's important to me to have some idea who's going to use it, and on whom."

Ray slapped his hand against the brick wall, looking big and brutal. "Goddammit! You're not getting scruples, are you?"

"No. I know exactly what I'm doing, believe me. Here, let me see you to your car."

Afterwards, Alex drove west through the deserted City. At Sunday lunch-time, the traffic was nonexistent, and he swept down past St Paul's Cathedral and pulled up at a public phone box. He rang the number he had been given without mentioning his name. "You were right, it does involve Syria. The consignment's going on a Turkish-registered, Turkish-owned vessel called the *Bodrum*. Sailing tonight from London to Latakia. Tell your people good hunting." He hung up and went back to his car, whistling tunelessly.

As he drove away, Alex watched a train rolling slowly across Blackfriars rail bridge, frowning after it as he pondered the question.

"It matters to me who uses Stanton hardware," he said at last, to himself. "And sometimes you can be paid an awful lot of money just to make sure a shipment doesn't arrive. And all the money I get, I have a use for."

The forty thousand pounds his contact with Tel Aviv had provided was already in his Cayman Islands bank account, and the extra Stanton shares he would now buy should give him some real influence over the company. The non-arrival of the shipment of Stanton armaments would cost the Abu Jihad group millions in hard currency, and effectively cut off the Candyman's main source of supply for a year. The Israeli navy would see to that. Then, later, there would perhaps be some paperwork at Lloyds of London, the insurers, on the loss of the *Bodrum*. Nothing more. The only drawbacks Alex could see were the breach of trust he had inflicted on Ray, and the wrath of the Arab terror group upon hearing what had happened to their shipment. The first problem could be smoothed out over a bottle of J&B, but the latter might prove a little more intractable . . .

There was a blast from a nearby car horn. Alex looked up and found that the lights had turned to green – and that he had attracted a little pleasing attention from a pretty girl in a black Mini.

He smiled back at her, and she wound down the window and threw a business card with her name and telephone number into his lap. But before he could respond she'd screeched away.

As an omen, he reflected, it was as good as any. Then the good humour drained out of him as the anger came back. He had money, now, the beginnings of a fortune. Enough to prove some things to Hugh, and to Maggie.

On May Day, 1966, as arranged, David spotted Hoyle on Horse Guards Road close to the head of the lake in St James's Park, and near the back of Downing Street. He walked quickly past the Foreign and Commonwealth Office, past the Home Office and then,

182

just before the Treasury, turned left into the park so that David lost him.

A minute later David made his way down Birdcage Walk, entering the park by a different gate. On this warm spring afternoon the park was crowded with sunbathers and tourists. David felt sure no one could have followed him. He wiped the sweat from his forehead and sat down on a park bench that overlooked the lake.

Two children were flying a kite through the trees behind him, shouting noisily. He opened his newspaper and pretended to peer at it.

Hoyle sat down beside him. He was his usual urbane self, well-dressed and self-confident, though he was cautious enough to have insisted that they met in the park.

"How's life, working for our former Cabinet Minister?"

"Frank is well-connected," David said. "You'd have to be inside the Westminster system to know how good his links are. Officially I'm his researcher, speechwriter. But I think I'm being groomed for stardom."

"I'm sure you are," Hoyle said, faintly astringent. "It must give you an advantage, being married to his niece. Just as long as you remember that you're in with us, now: Forward."

"A more dynamic and modern name than the Levellers."

"That's why I changed it. So, what do you have for me?"

David folded his paper and unobtrusively passed it on.

"Did it have to be the *Daily Telegraph?*" Alan said. "Right wing rag."

"Aren't they all?"

The headlines on the front page ran into an article about a tremendous explosion that had torn a Turkish freighter apart in the Bay of Biscay, sinking her with all hands. The force of the blast had been so great that it had been heard in all the coastal towns of northern Spain. The paper's theory was that the ship had been smuggling explosives.

"Did you get what I wanted?" Alan asked pleasantly, lifting the rolled-up paper.

David hesitated. "Lists of constituencies penetrated by the far Left. It doesn't name many names, Alan, but they seem to think Liverpool and Coventry are the out-of-town centres. Is that really correct?"

Alan brooded, looking out at the fringe of lakeside earth pecked bare by the waterfowl.

"They know too much," he said shortly, then raised his eyes to the sky. "Class struggle is inevitable in our society. As in our eventual victory."

"In a war," David hazarded, "you need allies. Any kind of allies."

Alan's eyes strayed towards the Palace roof where, through the trees, the Royal Standard stirred in the light air.

"Oh, we have allies, all right. Very good friends."

David sucked in his breath. In the royal household? But then there was no guarantee that the man was serious. He had always been a name-dropper, claiming friends in high places.

"I'd like to do more," David said suddenly. He knew he was taking a giant risk.

Alan trained his eyes on David's face, then looked away. "Are you up to it? Getting out there amongst the grass roots of the movement?"

"I'm certain I can, and I want to. But I sometimes get discouraged. It seems there's so little the few of us can do."

"That depends where those few are placed," Alan said. "There's going to be a seamen's strike."

"What?"

"Total shut-down," Hoyle said. He smiled, shading his eyes from the sunshine as an old lady in a fur-collared coat led a nervous Yorkshire terrier past.

David was stunned; he could tell this was not mere boasting. "That's incredible."

"It's a major undertaking, but we must be tightening the screw all the while. And I want you to help."

"Of course," David said earnestly. "When? Where?"

"You're most useful to the organization right where you are at the moment. Forward needs you; we have forty or fifty full-time organizers already, but you're a good source. I like your willingness, but you'll have to meet the others before a decision can be made to widen the scope of your activities. It'll take time. Be patient and trust me."

"I will." David nodded slowly, wondering just how long it would take before he was introduced to 'the others' – and who they might be.

"There's only one minor problem . . ." Alan's voice trailed off. He looked away so that David could no longer see his steel-grey eyes.

"What's that?"

"I can imagine some of our less sophisticated brethren finding it difficult to understand your owning shares. Especially Stanton Industries shares."

David swallowed. Alan's eyes were on him once more, and he had been caught like a rabbit in a car's headlights. "Stanton shares? I don't deny it. If it's good enough for the miners' pension fund, it's good enough for me."

"I don't give a damn about your shares, you understand," Alan assured him. "But if you'll take my advice you'll get rid of them. Remember, when we're in power there'll be a day of reckoning."

"Yes. I see."

After he left Hoyle, David went back to Westminster Hall to collect his briefcase. How could Hoyle have known about the shares? And if he knew about them, how much else did he know?

He went into one of the telephone booths and rang his stockbroker. Still the STA-2 deal hadn't been announced, and the Stanton shares had continued to fall, losing a shilling each since he had borrowed to purchase them. For a moment he considered holding on to the shares and leaving Forward alone instead. Then he had to speak.

"Sell them," he told the man miserably.

"But, Mr Bryant, you stand to lose a substantial amount – "

"Just sell them."

As he put the receiver down he wondered in a mood of suppressed anger how long it would be before the Pentagon confirmed the STA-2 deal formally, and how long it would be before he paid off the £500 loss he had sustained. The idea of his buying his own flat, and Megan perhaps coming up to London to join him, had been set back indefinitely.

David returned to his day's work. As Labour was in power, his nominal post as Frank Deacon's parliamentary researcher gave him perfect flexibility to seem to be about legitimate business almost anywhere he wanted to go. He thought the Department of Trade offices on Victoria Street might make a good start. He would check into the possibility of a seaman's strike and then report to Frank; and, hopefully, there would be something the government could do.

Later, Frank listened carefully in an office he had commandeered in the Privy Council building on Whitehall.

David had done some careful investigating, through intermediaries in the trade union movement and in the press. There *was* a strike brewing, exactly as Hoyle had claimed.

185

"That's not to say", David said carefully, "that Hoyle and his friends have total control over events. But if there's even a chance that British trade could be crippled I think the PM should be told."

Frank stood up. "Let's hope you're wrong, David. I'll tell him and the government will think about taking some precautions. But, tell me, do you really believe this man and the others can cause a strike?"

David shrugged. "It's still an open question."

Frank sighed, suddenly looking old and a little stooped. "It's a hard thing for me to take your questions and turn them into government decisions, David. Maybe you should be in Parliament yourself."

Maybe I should, thought David.

By the end of the month Frank and he had their answer. The National Union of Seamen's leaders ordered a national strike that closed Britain's ports. The strike dragged on through June, causing a devastating financial crisis over and above the country's balance of payments problems. More 'PM MUST GO' banners appeared at demonstrations as the strike began to polarize the Socialist movement as well as the nation.

David saw with concealed despair the self-inflicted damage the nation's economy was sustaining. It meant lost goodwill, lost confidence and lost markets. Frequently those losses were irreversible and created long-term problems. Severe deflation was the only way to avoid devaluation.

The Prime Minister's phrase about the strike being conducted by a "small group of politically motivated men" was taken up by the newspapers, and when David looked at the secret notes he had made he knew that despite Forward's small membership – less than two thousand, Alan Hoyle had told him – the attack was much more dangerous than anyone had yet begun to suspect.

In July, the Prime Minister made another crisis broadcast, introducing general restraints in all areas of the economy, higher taxes and a complete six-month wage freeze. Appealing to the television camera, he said with brutal frankness, "We are under attack. This is *your* country, and *our* country. We must work for it."

David turned off the TV, wishing he had Megan beside him, and wondering despairingly if his own research was influencing anybody in the government at all.

Terry set their airline bags down in the hallway of their fashionable Flood Street flat. "Can we unpack later?"

"Okay, you come and eat. Alan's stocked up . . . and how I've missed real English cheese!" Maggie was delighted to be home.

Terry grinned at her. "I'm not hungry yet, but you go ahead. Give me some of the wine – anything, so long as it's chilled."

"It'll have to be rosé!" she shouted from the kitchen.

Half an hour later he sat at the big pine table watching her eat ravenously. It was as if they'd never been away all summer. Except that now she was bronzed from hours on the La Salle Club's tennis courts, rested, and happier. And her Levis and cheesecloth shirt owed more to the West Coast than to Carnaby Street.

"Happy to be back home?" he asked her.

"America's a *great* place!" she said, her mouth half-full of Guernsey tomato, "but there's no place like home. It's incredible what silly little things you miss!"

She thought back over their trip. The two months in San Francisco, where they'd covered the emergent movement whose members called themselves hippies. Maggie had been filing stories for the East Coast and British magazines on Abbie Hoffman, the Diggers, Alan Ginsberg and the rest: they were inventing a new radical politics that side-stepped traditional left-wing thought. '*This decade will be remembered for its colour –* ' she had written, remembering her own forties childhood of rationing, cloudy skies, black-and-white photos and boiled potatoes.

They'd flown back across country to New York and re-edited their book in two weeks of intense work. Then they sat back in front of the lay-out boards and went through what was now titled *Vietnam Nightmare.*

He had pushed back from the last image, Dr Martin Luther King speaking about the promised land in front of the Lincoln Memorial. Terry had been there, in '63. He quoted solemnly, "The struggle goes on, 'until justice flows like water and righteousness like a stream'."

"Amen to that."

He rubbed his eyes. "What do we have here, Maggie?"

She turned over the last page, still overwhelmed. "We have the book of our time, Terry. Your pictures, my words, the first rock'n'roll war. Vietnam. The struggle for justice."

"Vietnam." He shrugged his shoulders, feeling strangely subdued. The book had somehow become her project. His pictures, but her

her editing, her thoughts. Now, he knew, the public would have to decide which was more memorable.

Maggie was overjoyed. She decided to celebrate, and for another week she exhausted him in a dizzy round of Manhattan's tourist traps by day and lazy Village jazz spots or SoHo warehouse parties by night.

Then the weather had got too humid for Terry, and he had taken her off to the Grand Tetons in Wyoming to walk in the crisp clean air of America, where the jagged bones of the country burst through, but she had dragged him down to Idaho Falls, and to the U.S. Atomic Energy Commission's Reserve in search of stories and secrets.

Maggie had not wanted to admit that she felt a longing to come home, but he had known the signs. After all, he was an expert on exile.

"There's so *much* of this fantastic country still to see," she marvelled.

Terry had laughed. "I'm glad of that, Maggie, because there'll be other trips and other days – won't there?"

Now they were back in quaint, crusty old England, but they hadn't quite lost the flavour of America. Maggie finished eating and went through to the bedroom. Terry followed her, watching the shape of her backside in her tight jeans. She picked up her bundle of mail and lay down on the bed beside him. He squeezed her firm, warm breasts through the thin material of her shirt, but she was preoccupied with her correspondence. Paying him no attention, she pulled one or two letters from the bundle and slit them open with her fingernail. Cheques.

Alan Hoyle had taken care of the bills. One of his friends had been staying in their flat while they were away. It was good to be able to cover his outlay from her own pocket and still have enough for that Austin Healey sports car she'd been promising herself.

She showed Terry various items as he struggled to unbutton her shirt, pushing him away, laughing her excitement over commissions for articles, letters from old friends, another note from Laurie Cochrane . . .

Terry rode the zip of her Levis down, but she knocked his hand away.

"Come on, honey, I'm as horny as . . . What's the matter?"

She rolled off the bed, wrapping the two halves of her shirt tightly around her, and almost ran from the room.

He lay back on the bed a moment, then went after her. He found her in the kitchen, pouring herself a long glass of red wine.

"What is it? Maggie?"

She shook her head and made a grab for the crumpled papers on the table, but he took them out of her hand.

"Don't be stupid," he told her in a wounded tone. "Is it something I shouldn't see?"

There was a grey bond envelope, unstamped. It contained a stack of torn papers. He knew without having to be told that these were Maggie's own letters because they were all in her handwriting, but there was also a big photocopy folded in half – a printed page with barely-discernible photos of starving children and a tank factory. As he opened it he saw a Coutts & Co. cheque stapled to it. It was for £40,000, and signed A.J.F. Stanton.

Terry looked up, baffled by her reaction. Tears were coming to her eyes and she turned away from him.

To him the cheque seemed like great news. There was a further paper underneath. He turned to it, and saw it was an invoice. Beneath Maggie's typewritten name and Chelsea address was a simple explanation for the money.

'For whoring', it read.

2

David looked suspiciously at the cheque lying on the restaurant table.

"Look, Alex, thanks for this meal and everything, but really –" He waved his hand in the air. "Two thousand pounds."

"Take it. The STA-2 tip-off made me much more. I bought four million pounds of Stanton shares through one of my Swiss nominees, because I knew news of the Pentagon's intentions would leak – and did. A 300 million dollar order for the STA-2 means that all the insiders who hear about it want Stanton Industries shares. I've made a fortune. So, please, take the money."

David nodded, and suddenly gave a wry smile. "Not so much a token of your esteem, more a token of things to come?"

Alex reached for the Beaujolais bottle. "Let's say I feel generous with my money. Or call it a delayed wedding present to you and Megan."

"Thank you, Alex. What did you do with your profit?"

"Oh, I don't plan to sell out straightaway. Mostly I've been investing in Stanton Industries shares, getting in and getting out at the right time. I can ride the share price up and then right down again. I'm doing very well."

"Insider dealing."

Alex laughed, suddenly. "You know, Ray couldn't believe that was legal here."

"You really want to make Stanton's take notice, don't you?"

"Yes." Determination flowed out of him. "I want to turn around the company that made my family's fortune."

"I'm even more ambitious," David said. He had never said this aloud before, not even to Alex. "I foresee so many problems here.

190

But in spite of all the incredible pressures, I want to turn around the nation."

"That's dedication, David. But do you realize what I want to do, what you want to do – that it's the same ambition? Or as you used to put it, duty. If you include the shares I inherited but still can't vote I have my holdings in Stanton Industries up to almost five per cent. And with love, knowledge and devotion, those holdings will grow. I want to do a great work in the world, David. Like Abraham Stanton, who armed Washington's armies; like the others whose guns won the Crimean War, and those hard-fought battles in France sixty years later. What we made, David, changing the world."

David was excited. "We'll do it again, Alex."

"Yes. Here, have some more of this wine. Excellent year."

"Thank you," David said, sipping. "It certainly takes the chill off a cold February day."

Alex laughed. Hacker and he had just pushed through a third large arms deal; and the Pentagon would be shipping everything out to Saigon. "Things are hotting up all over, David. Ray and I have gone into business officially. Delaware, one of the U.S. States, has nice loose laws about incorporating and running corporations; so our head office will be there. We're going to *sell*, David. From the Pentagon through the Middle East to Vietnam."

Money equalling success. But there was more to life than that. David was toying with his wineglass. "Listen, I know it's none of my business –"

"Maggie." Alex's face was blank. "Don't blame yourself, David. It was probably inevitable. You know her. You know me. Somebody hits me, I hit back, hard."

"Yes." David sighed. "She told me about that cheque. I suppose it was your intention, Alex, but you certainly hurt her."

Alex raised his glass. "To the hurt."

"I was wondering –"

"Isn't she pleased with that American photographer?"

This was dangerous ground; but David wanted to see his friends happy. "Terry's very likeable, but I don't know how reliable he is. She might get hurt."

Alex nodded. "So there's some justice, after all."

It was now the spring of 1967, and Maggie knew that this was her time.

191

She could hardly remember the last occasion she had thought about Alex, and as for his money, she had put that to very good use and then tried to forget the whole busiess and get on with her life.

Though Maggie had resumed her political interests, she found herself increasingly diverted by the new, chic London that was emerging. She began to write for fashion and style magazines, a couple of them in New York, and dressed up for parties – parties that happened every weekend, and almost every night – in the most outrageous and exotic fashions she could find. Maybe, she thought, it was a reaction to the grey, pinched post-war world of her youth: maybe the Summer of Love was everybody's reaction.

Or maybe there was something else she was trying to forget . . .

Still she remembered last winter when a girlfriend had been so depressed. When they all flew out to Zermatt to open a stylish winter shop at the exclusive Swiss ski resort, she had told Maggie the news.

"I'm pregnant, Maggie."

Maggie congratulated her, thrilled, but that night, lying beside Terry in their Swiss hotel room, she could not help staring at the ceiling and thinking of herself.

She was committed to her ideals, successful at her work, had the right man in her life and an expanding international circle of friends, yet still there was a nagging dissatisfaction deep inside her. What had she become? A wanderer, rootless and powerless, through a world she had left completely untouched and unchanged, for all her cleverness and talk. She had never created anything; never had the child she had secretly thought about . . .

She turned to Terry, but he was snoring gently, suddenly a stranger to her. Even if she did wake him, she knew she couldn't make him understand her, any more than she had been able to make Alex understand. She stared up into the darkness and heard the strange, insistent tones of a continental police siren. Bands of light from the Venetian blinds momentarily flashed blue against the wall above her, and she twisted about again, trying to get comfort from her pillow, but failing. Then, suddenly, she found she was crying.

A long queue of cars moved slowly down the Mall. It was the beginning of summer, and the day was hot. Alex asked the chauffeur to wind down the side window.

Today's event was one of the three royal garden parties held each year, and Alex alone of the Stanton family had been able to attend. The invitation from the Lord Chamberlain with its flowing copperplate writing and regal crest had named Hugh and Hugh's parents also, but his mother and father were in South Africa, and Hugh himself was talking with the U.S. Navy in North Carolina. Duty to Stanton Industries, Alex knew, was the only thing that could have kept his cousin away.

Alex thought about the contrasting lives he and his cousin had come to lead.

Hugh dealt with top-level military delegations, visited embassies and presidential palaces, and represented the biggest single defence contractors outside America. Alex, as a partner in Hacker-Stanton International, the partnership they had formed, bought some of the Armaments Division's output, and he found himself operating at the sharp end, supplying crates of guns and grenades covertly to mercenaries and freedom fighters around the world. It was often dangerous and usually illegal; but what of that?

It's highly profitable, and I've got away with it so far . . .

Alex was deeply tanned from a recent spell in Nigeria, working with the Ibo rebels in the Eastern Region of Biafra. Hugh was to supply the Federal forces. Nigeria's oil money meant there was much to struggle over. Once inside the tall, black, cast-iron railings of the Palace Yard, Alex's thoughts turned to the day's entertainments. The chauffeur dropped him and Alex strolled acknowledging those he knew, stopping for a word here and there, but heading all the time for his favourite spot near the lake.

He settled his grey top hat firmly on his head and walked out towards the lake past big, peppermint-striped marquees that served strawberries and cream, cucumber sandwiches and elegant spiced canapés. He stared across the lake. The water gleamed in the English sun. The thirty-nine-acre garden spoke more eloquently of privilege than any ostentatious display could: the grandeur of the Duke of Buckingham's old Palace still had the power to impress.

Alex watched the rippling water, and was lulled by the muted sound of traffic which carried over the high brick wall. He was hailed by a familiar voice. "Hello, Stanton – pissed already?"

"Hello, Clarence." He smiled pleasantly at the new Lord de Soutey, the eighth of the line. "Not yet."

De Soutey looked around. "Bit of a middle-class hole."

"Compared with Hollingston?"

Clarence gave a mock shudder. "National Trust will end up

taking over the house, I bet. The estate manager wants the park to be turned into a sort of zoo as the only alternative. What a prospect!"

"Death duties, I suppose?"

Clarence shrugged. "Can't see what the Socialists want with our Turners and Rembrandts."

"I expect it's the five million quid they'll fetch at auction."

Clarence snorted. "End up in some ruddy Texas art gallery, the lot of them."

Alex shook his head sadly.

Clarence took his arm, tried to turn him. "Have you met Sarah?"

"Who?"

"My half-sister. She's around somewhere – Father remarried this Swedish woman in his dotage, you know. If he'd been less of a ram he might have lived long enough to see Ted Heath get in, and keep the paintings in the country."

"Versailles is so much more impressive, don't you think?"

Alex turned and looked at the woman who had spoken.

She was tall, willowy and dressed entirely in white: court shoes, a clutch bag of fine Italian leather, a pearl choker, delicate white gold jewellery on her wrists. Her ash blonde hair was caught up inside a broad-brimmed summer hat, and her smile, though curiously remote, was warm and completely captivating. She was an astonishingly beautiful woman.

"Of course it's more impressive," he said, looking at her approvingly. "But I dare say the presence of a monarch counts for something."

She laughed, looking back at the tents and the guests that milled around. "Look at them all. Provincial politicians jockeying for an OBE or a seat in the Lords – wasps buzzing round the honey jar."

"The sort who want to give their medals back because of the Beatles," Alex said, but he was paying little attention to what she said. What she *was* interested him much more. "The French say we British prize recognition above all else – including achievement itself."

"The French may be right. They're certainly correct about English reserve." She smiled at him again. For a moment Alex's grasp of social etiquette failed him. For the first time since his split from Maggie he couldn't put smoothly into words exactly what he wanted to say to

194

a woman. Then, to his own surprise, he said exactly what he was thinking.

"You're very beautiful."

She laughed in unaffected delight.

Clarence shook his head sadly and wandered away. "Can't think what people see in her."

"You shouldn't say that," she told Alex, "You embarassed him. And me."

"Not even when it's true?"

"Especially not when it's true. And you can't possibly know if I'm beautiful or not."

Alex tilted his head questioningly.

"Real beauty can only be seen by the inner eye."

He laughed and let her lead him back to one of the marquees, where, over neat little crustless sandwiches and China tea, they continued their talk.

"Look," he said, starting suddenly, "I really am forgetting my manners. I must introduce myself – I'm Alex Stanton."

She nodded as if in acceptance, and said, "I'm Sarah Amanda de Soutey. You must call me Sarah."

She put out her hand, too high to be shaken. Alex took it, raised her arm as if in a courtly dance, and refused to let go until she began to laugh.

"You're right," she said. "But you're no gentleman. A gentleman would have kissed my hand."

"Ah," Alex corrected, "this is not Versailles."

She looked at his hand for a moment, then took it, holding it firmly but languidly, not relinquishing it. She uncurled his fingers and began to trace the lines of his palm with her finger.

"How happy are you, Alex?"

He regarded her sceptically. "I thought you were supposed to tell me that."

"Do you know some people have a gift?"

"For what?"

Amused, she nodded, as if she saw all his secrets. "You have been crossed in love – I see that in you."

It made him look at her again, impressed, but he covered his feelings with a grin.

"Maybe you're right."

"You didn't think it still showed."

"Does it?"

She touched his chest, where his heart was beating faster. "Alex, you shouldn't try to pretend. You can't. You must trust me – I can see your soul."

A slow smile spread across his face, a grin of pure pleasure, and not the kind of expression he usually chose to show to a woman outside of the bedroom.

"Nineteen sixty-eight will be a great year for you," she said.

"I hope you're right. This year has been a litle mixed." He thought of the deal Ray wanted to set in South East Asia. The prospect of sinking money into a ramshackle airline project that mainly comprised a dozen Boeings mothballed in Arizona had sounded frankly ridiculous – until Ray explained there was a U.S. government connection.

"Yes," she said, straightening his hand once again. "There have been problems, but that's all behind you now. You're a man of ambition. You look to the future, not to the past. I admire that . . ."

Her eyes half closed, and she staggered.

Alex put out a hand to steady her, saw that she was close to fainting, then sat her down. A concerned footman brought a glass of water, and Alex made her drink it.

"I'm all right," she said. Her voice sounded confused and her face had lost all its colour.

"You almost blacked out."

"I seemed to see . . . Just the sun. I'll be all right in a minute."

Alex stayed with her until she had recovered. If this was her second sight, it had its disadvantages.

At four o'clock one of the military bands played the National Anthem. The Queen and Prince Philip, and lesser members of the royal family, appeared at the garden entrance on the north side of the palace. There were presentations from the Duchy of Lancaster, and of Cornwall, and the guests began to form a line that stretched along the terrace, so that the Queen, acompanied by the Lord Chamberlain, and followed by an Equerry and a Lady-in-Waiting, could greet her guests on her way to take tea.

Alex and Sarah were asked by one of the Gentlemen Ushers to step forward, and the Queen chatted briefly with Sarah, while Prince Philip, whose own handicap was five, made a small mention of Alex's polo prowess before the royal couple passed down the line.

"Thank you, sir. I'll tell Hugh you gave us both your good wishes."

To the sounds of a Sir Arthur Sullivan overture, Sarah and Alex walked back towards the trees. She had quite recovered her colour, and seemed now to be in a reminiscent mood.

"I prefer the parties at Holyroodhouse," she said wistfully. "Have you ever been there? There are great thistles planted in tubs, and the High Constables of Edinburgh with plumed hats and batons. Instead of Yeomen, you see Archers in green uniforms. Scotland is so colourful."

Sarah's ice-blue eyes had an unearthly depth. So different from –

He checked himself. No comparisons. Then he raised a glass to her, enjoying the warm sunshine, the excellent champagne, her compelling beauty.

"To the future," he said, and for the moment forgot about the toils of the murky, frightening business Ray Hacker and he were going into.

Frank took off his spectacles, frowning. "What a pity, David."

"It took the Roman Empire centuries to fall."

The newspaper headline said: BRITAIN TO WITHDRAW FROM EAST OF SUEZ.

Frank sighed. "Things change quickly, today. I'm old enough to remember the Russian Czar on his throne in what used to be St Petersburg. That seems like ancient history now."

"Mmm." David straightened his tie, then rested his head on the heel of one hand. "Speaking of Russia, I was wondering if you still had links with our intelligence services."

"My past in Berlin isn't that much of a secret."

"I don't suppose there are too many secrets left here – now that George Blake has run out on a forty-year sentence and turned up in Moscow."

"No." Frank tugged at the loose flesh below his chin. "I hope you're not becoming despondent, David. This is still Great Britain: the third most powerful nation on earth."

"For now."

Frank sat back in the comfortable chair. "Do you have anything more on Hoyle and his crew?"

"Nothing especially exciting. Though I dare say if Alan Hoyle were ever secretly followed, he might lead us to some interesting people."

"That may well be. Followed, eh?"

197

"I hope not," David said, roused. "Listen, what I'm doing has to be strictly confidential – even if you are an old intelligence hand, and to all intents and purposes my father-in-law."

Frank Deacon smiled proudly. "Megan is a fine girl, David. You're a very lucky man."

"I know," he said honestly, reflecting that it had taken him a while to realize it.

It was warm again that afternoon as David walked past the Ministry of Defence and crossed over Whitehall by the Cenotaph. The streets were busy as the great ministries emptied themselves of civil servants. Across the road, the entrance to Downing Street was cluttered with colourfully dressed foreign tourists, marshalling themselves for a photographic session. It was hardly surprising that visitors were attracted here, he thought. Within half a mile of where he stood was the seat of Government, the Treasury, the headquarters of the armed forces, the Anglican heart of Westminster Abbey, the royal palace and the head offices of most of Britain's biggest corporations.

David was used to it now; it was part of his life. He had spent the last three hours in the House of Commons library. Trade and Industry statistics still rattled through his head. He felt now he had mastered his brief, and had begun roughing out Frank Deacon's next speech so that it read like a leading article in *The Times* – it would sound good in the Commons, David thought, when delivered in Frank's simple, authoritative style.

The traffic had slowed, now, and he became half-aware of a black Daimler that seemed to be causing an obstruction a little way along the curb. David watched the back of a number 77 bus as it waited at the stop. He had put in a satisfying day's work, and was about to start convincing himself that a bus-ride home might be more pleasant than the Underground on such a fine day, when his eyes strayed to an *Evening News* billboard. The words made him stop dead: STA-2 – YANKS DECIDE.

"Damn!"

He grabbed a copy from the pile, remembering the money he had lost because of Hoyle. Were the Americans buying, or not?

"That'll be fourpence, sir."

He fumbled for pennies, then found the headline. It read: JET DEAL TO BE SIGNED SOON – STANTON CHAIRMAN 'OVERJOYED'.

His eyes quickly scanned the article, with mounting satisfaction; he might have lost his own money when Hoyle made him sell the shares prematurely, but that sacrifice couldn't be helped and seemed small, now. As long as the STA-2 prototype passed a formal trial, it would be bought. Though the decision had come too late for him to profit by it, it was superb news for the nation and for Stanton's.

"Alex," he said aloud, "you must be delighted! *Three hundred million dollars!*"

Then he considered what else the contract meant: from Bristol to Newcastle upon Tyne there would be highly-paid work guaranteed for thousands of men.

"Excuse me, sir."

David moved aside, still engrossed in his thoughts, but then he realized that the big, stone-faced man beside him was speaking to him.

"What is it?"

"Mr David Bryant?"

"Yes?"

"My name is Detective Sergeant Walker. I must ask you to accompany me, to answer some questions." He flashed open a card with an EIIR stamp and his photograph.

David's mouth pressed shut. He closed his eyes, but opened them again quickly.

"Am I . . . under arrest?" he said uncertainly. All the blood seemed to have run from his head.

"It would be best if you came along with me now, sir."

"Yes. Yes, I suppose it would."

He realized with terror that this had to be connected with Hoyle, and the minor secrets he had been forced to give the man as bait. He wondered if even the Prime Minister could protect him – if he would want to. He faced ruin.

He shivered. He felt as guilty as hell, ill with guilt. He could think only of Megan now, and how she would feel when he was allowed to make that call.

"How did you find out?" he asked, as he felt the big man's hand grip his upper arm and steer him across the pavement. "I suppose it must have been an agent inside F–"

"Just get in the car, sir," the man said stolidly.

David's head bowed as he was led to the Daimler. It had tinted windows; the driver was wearing a fawn mackintosh. The policeman opened the rear door and bent David down to push him into the back, and as the door was shut David looked at the man who shared the rear seat with him.

He was a man with a slightly downturned nose and creased face, dressed in a blue three-piece pin-striped suit and wearing a regimental tie. He was somewhere in his early forties. He took David's hand in a firm grip as the policeman got in the front passenger seat, and the car merged with the rush-hour traffic.

"Forgive me for this, Mr Bryant – David, if you'll permit me – but I thought at this stage it would be best to keep everything off the record."

David sat quite still, white-faced, stunned. He had already decided to cooperate completely.

"Is that possible?" he said. He heard his own voice as if it was someone else talking.

The man chuckled. "It's frightfully cloak and dagger, I know, but one can't be too careful."

David realized then that he had been wrong – entirely, wholly wrong. This was something quite different from his work with Hoyle.

"My name's Peter Carlton," the man said. "I work for MI5, directorate 'F'. We're responsible for countering domestic subversion, and I'm afraid we need more help from you."

With mounting terror, David realized that, no doubt from the best of motives, he had been betrayed. Sickness rose in him. His work with Hoyle was no longer a secret.

"'More' help?"

The grin was carnivorous. "Exactly."

The wake of the nuclear super-carrier CVN-65 curved like a scimitar as she steered into the wind, and on deck a pair of McDonnell F-4 Phantoms readied for take off.

The newly refitted *USS Enterprise* was a seaborne military airbase. She carried ninety jets and helicopters, and more firepower than all the fleets of all the navies before 1945 put together. Hugh Stanton looked down and marvelled at her deck area, a gigantic expanse of tarmacked steel sectioned off with painted lines into lanes, lifts, runways and parking zones. The great square 'island' superstructure threw a shadow across the deck where tiny figures in coloured suits supervised the preparations high above the wrinkled surface of the Irish Sea.

200

He turned to Sir George Leslie, one of the main voices on the Stanton Industries board. "Very impressive indeed. My only regret is that the Royal Navy can't match this."

Leslie grinned. His narrow mouth creased into jowls that made his face square. But his eyebrows, upturned in a perpetual query, had begun to lose their fierceness, and had turned grey like his hair. It was time for him to retire, and Hugh felt the time was fast approaching when the old man would have to be shown the door.

"I don't think there's much doubt about who rules the waves these days, Hugh," he said. "It was good of them to invite us aboard. A pity Alex isn't here."

Hugh looked at Sir George with both respect and irritation. He had a knack of meaning more than he said, and his continual opposition to Lord Beauford's proposals was becoming troublesome to the merchant banker. He wondered how Leslie would react to the stunt he had arranged.

"Yes. He'd be interested to see this sort of thing," Hugh said, waving a finger at the deck. "He's off with that model woman, so he'll miss the show."

"You have something planned?"

"Something of a selling point," Hugh said quietly. He looked at his watch and smiled. "You'll see."

The Admiral, the senior officer present, was their host. He came over to stand with them. His cap was heavy with crusted gold, his grey shirt and trousers workmanlike and more casual than the formal blue of his British counterparts'. Beyond him, still standing apart, were the men most central to the exercise, two American civilians who looked out through the big rectangular windows as two grey jets were catapulted into the air, trailing shimmering exhaust. The planes turned together, gaining height, then wheeled round under full reheat to fly past them.

"The sound of freedom, gentlemen," the Admiral commented with pride as the jets came past, making the enclosed bridge shudder.

Hugh envied the officer's aura of personal assurance. It was something that came only with a lifetime of command and thorough familiarity with his job. He knew better than anyone that the 89,000 ton nuclear ship was his responsibility, and that it had cost the American people $450 million to build, with the technology it carried worth as much again.

201

"Yes," the Admiral said, bracing himself stiffly. "We have to maintain a constant state of alert here, gentlemen. We must be ready for any and every eventuality."

Hugh smiled, and turned to look at his own corporate representatives who were standing beside Royal Air Force senior brass. They were all speaking in low voices, pointing up at the conical stack of electronic countermeasure aerials and 'billboard' SPS 32 and 33 radar scanners that were the eyes and ears of the U.S. Navy's fleet.

Hugh hoped that Pike's boffins knew enough to upset the radars. If so, the Admiral and the two American politicians were in for a shock.

He clasped his hands behind his back and turned to engage the Admiral in a little distracting talk. "Tell me, Admiral, are you expecting difficulties fitting the STA-2 into your operation? In terms of modification, I mean?"

"Every new commission has its teething troubles," he replied, "but I don't forsee any major problems, Mr Stanton. Personally, I'd weld the Eiffel Tower onto the *Enterprise* if I had to. I've seen the specifications, and I want that plane in service with us at any cost. The option to buy ninety-five of your planes is bound to be confirmed – and then doubled, maybe."

The Admiral's principal guest frowned: a Senator who had years of seniority. "That's a dangerous thing to say to a manufacturer, Art. But I think we all have to admit that, from a technical point of view, Stanton Industries' STA-2 is a hell of an airplane."

"There are some things we in Britain still do excellently," Hugh said politely. "Credit where credit is due, even to a rival manufacturer – the Hawker Harrier is a marvellous plane. First vertical take-off and landing jet in the world."

"Though it's not the superfast fighting machine which is our STA-2," Sir George said as soon as he heard the prearranged cue-line. "You must realize our plane is the fastest in the world."

They smiled briefly, having made their point, then Hugh consulted his watch once more. The observing party were aware that the specially modified test aircraft was at this moment flying down from the Stanton airfield at Wharton in Lancashire. What the Admiral and his colleagues did not know was that it would be flying in at zero feet in a surface-hugging configuration and coming in from the south, 'pecking the lobes' of the Americans' radar, and the Stanton people hoped it would evade detection completely.

Hugh moved across the bridge to stand alone at the far windows. He narrowed his eyes at the horizon and for a moment glimpsed a silver speck glinting. Then there was a rising whistle and the shape lifted in a terrifying split-second, skimming over the enormous ship from stem to stern.

Before the rest of the party could focus on it, the plane was gone. Technicians down below had flattened themselves on the deck and stared after it, but there was nothing to see. Only the sound was left behind.

"Jesus Christ!" someone said beside him.

"Gentlemen," Hugh said, elated, "I give you the STA-2!"

Spontaneous applause broke out across the bridge, cowboy whoops from and whistles from the junior officers.

Hugh lowered his voice and spoke to Sir George Leslie. "Three hundred million dollars. At least."

The older man nodded in the direction of the Senator in the dapper grey suit. He was not moving at all.

Hugh remained soft-spoken. "There's something wrong? You think he feels we shamed the U.S. Navy, somehow?"

Sir George shook his head. "Can't be that, man – not if the naval crew is applauding us. It must be something else."

But what could it be? Hugh wondered uneasily.

Later, as they shared the Navy's hospitality in the senior wardroom, Hugh found that the Americans were unstinting in their praise. The stunt had not upset them. It had been a calculated risk, taken to impress them, and it had worked handsomely. They all toasted the aircraft in an atmosphere of magnanimous good humour, but Hugh felt that the senior Pentagon representative and the man from the Armed Services Committee remained less enthusiastic than the military personnel. He moved over to speak to them.

"Senator, I believe the President is going to make an announcement soon about which of the competing firms will win the SST contract in the U.S.," he said.

"That's correct. I'm afraid there's been a good deal of speculation about that. Down in Georgia we're kinda worried that Boeing will get the deal."

"Yes, that would be unwelcome news for Lockheed."

"Yeah, we think the Tri-Star project ought to keep a few people busy. I guess you must feel the same about the engines you're working on."

"Oh, yes, Senator, we have a fine technical facility and first-class engineers; we have several joint ventures with other manufacturers, like Rolls Royce."

The Senator looked at Hugh's gin dubiously. "Your Concorde project still coming along just fine?"

Hugh made an equivocal gesture. "The Prime Minister and the rest of the Cabinet wanted to do away with it the moment they won the '64 election."

"Oh, really?"

Hugh gave a pained smile. "Though Concorde was based on our own 'Stacey' design, the STA-C – my late uncle's project, actually – they've always considered it a Tory project. They call it Macmillan's family affair, and most of the Cabinet have about as much love for it as the Ancient Mariner had for his albatross."

"So why don't they drop it?"

"De Gaulle refuses to let them. Thank God."

"And you think the French will force it through – and make it profitable?"

"No doubt about completing it," Hugh said. "Paris has been absolutely adamant – is there anything wrong, Senator Argyll?"

At the mention of Concorde the Georgia man's face had become intensely thoughtful. He didn't seem to be listening to Hugh's words.

"No, no," he said, looking up. "I think your STA-2 has made a big impression."

Hugh laughed lightly. "Then you think there's the chance of more orders in the future? There's been a lot of speculation about that."

"Speculation? Even the Pentagon leaks, these days. Well, we'll have to consider that very, very carefully, Mr Stanton."

"Of course, but in principle . . . ?"

"There's still a big question mark over the deal as far as we're concerned."

Hugh allowed himself an enquiring smile. He knew full well that General Dynamics was aiming for the same target, and the notoriously 'persuasive' people at Lockheed would stop at nothing to muscle in on the deal, even if that meant bringing their pocket Congressmen and Senators to bear. Rumour had it that even Prince Bernhardt of the Netherlands had been on their payroll, and it was, of course, no coincidence that Georgia's 20,000 Lockheed workers had benefitted from sales worth $1,700 million in the last fiscal year – twice that of General Dynamics of Missouri, whose own Senate representation was, Hugh thought wryly, somewhat less dynamic.

Hugh met the Senator's gaze with an open smile. "I don't want it to sound like conceit, but I believe you'd have to go a long way to better our 'product' – as you call it. We've invested over a hundred million dollars in research and development and producing our first half-dozen prototypes."

Argyll grinned. "Concorde's going to stay in the game and Boeing's going to get the SST? So something is going to have to give." His grey hair glistened at his temples. "Oh, there's nothing much wrong with your airplane, Mr Stanton. But we have to think twice before buying a plane that our enemies know inside out."

Hugh's smile faded. He suddenly felt sick. "I'm sorry?"

"I guess you don't know," Argyll said, clearly enjoying himself now. "I have here a satellite message from the CIA people at Langley. It came in just before you came aboard earlier today. I didn't want to spoil the party, but it contains something that alters the whole ball game."

"I'm sorry, Senator, I really don't follow . . ."

"It seems the spooks have been hard at work. There's an MI5 source called 'Keyhole'; he fingered some English guy who was monitored and linked to an East German called Schaller. Special Branch followed him too and this morning a guy named Pike was arrested at your factory – a *very* senior man, your people say."

"Donald Pike? *Arrested?*"

"He's been giving the Soviets an inside track on your technology for at least five years."

Hugh's face was pale with shock. His eyes searched Argyll's face for some hint that it was all a joke, but he found none.

"I've known Donald Pike for years," Hugh blustered. "He's been one of my father's chief designers since the war. He has one of the highest security clearances there is. He can't have been a spy."

"With respect, Mr Stanton," Argyll said, a toughness strengthening his words, "the one doesn't imply the other at all."

Hugh began frantically calculating the consequences and saw that all of them were disastrous. Pike was their chief designer; he had access to almost everything inside the Division . . . "But we must have an American sale," he said frantically. "We have to produce in large numbers to produce at all. If we don't sell to you we'll have to cancel – and lose the hundred million dollars we've invested!"

The Senator from Georgia looked at him with pity. "I'm very sorry." He took Hugh's gin from his hand and picked up a bottle of the Admiral's Jack Daniels. "I think you'd better have a real drink," he said.

Carlton had come for him again.

David looked out of the car window, with Carlton a jovially threatening presence at his side. David had lost some of his earlier confidence, since Frank, obviously very upset, had admitted yesterday that he had been passing along some information to his contacts in MI5 – mainly to an old friend from his Berlin days called George Hammond.

"But where does that leave me?" David was frantic. "How many people know what I'm really doing? How long before it all leaks out? I could end up dead – literally as well as politically!"

"Nobody knows, hardly half a dozen top people. Listen, I don't want this man Carlton leaning on you; that was never my intention."

"Very well. Then I'll tell him that I have the explicit backing of 10 Downing Street and that he has to leave me alone."

He should have told the MI5 man exactly where to get off when he had first been approached. Three reasons had prevented him from doing so: the suddenness of the approach, his suspicion that Carlton wasn't who he said, and his own desire not to leave Carlton with the wrong impression. For all David knew, Carlton's threats might have been made to test him. After all, if David had been in the Prime Minister's shoes, he probably would have arranged a test of loyalty.

He grimaced. Peter Carlton did not represent the Prime Minister.

The MI5 man was trying again.

"This picture, for instance," he said, handing over a blown-up photograph.

Two heads, two sets of shoulders. A face half turned to the camera, darker, Middle Eastern features seen full-face.

David handed it back. "An Arab, and Alan Hoyle."

Carlton frowned. "The 'Arab' is actually an Iranian; an anti-Shah terrorist called Fahzdi."

"A killer?" David wondered if it was true. "Where did you get the picture?"

"They met in a London hotel," Carlton said, not answering the question. "I think Hoyle himself has terrorist links."

206

"Then why don't you arrest him? Why didn't you pick up this Fahzdi, for instance?"

"It's difficult to obtain enough evidence to satisfy a court," Carlton murmured. "But you could help us: these far Left people are importing terror tactics."

"Look, crime is crime, and politics is something else. I've already explained that I'm helping the Prime Minister and he wants it to remain confidential."

"But you'll consider my offer, surely," Carlton said. His tone was that of a man who thought he knew precisely how David would react.

"I'm always willing to serve my country," David chose to say safely. There had been something about Fahzdi's dark, liquid eyes he found unsettling and memorable. "I'm not a Communist, I'm a Labour Party man. There is a difference, you know."

"Yes," Carlton smiled. "At least, there should be a difference."

David bit back a sharp retort. The man was goading him, trying to make him slip up somehow.

"You work for Frank Deacon. That can only mean one thing."

David returned a stony expression. What did the man mean?

"During the war," Carlton explained as the Daimler accelerated along Piccadilly, "Frank Deacon was in Intelligence – after '45, in Berlin. He was very active then, and he's been busy ever since. So you come to us very highly recommended."

"Let's not play games. Frank hasn't recruited me to work for you."

"No. I recruit my own informers."

David, insulted rather than cowed, maintained his non-reaction. He hoped that Carlton would realize he would co-operate, and that would be the end of this pressure.

Then Carlton went on. "Strange that you maintain a friendship with the Stanton family."

"The entire family?" David asked ironically. Alex was certainly the only Stanton who was more than an acquaintance.

"As you see, I've taken the liberty of having your background looked into."

David felt profound annoyance, though he chose not to show it. "And to what conclusions did that 'liberty' bring you?"

"I'd call it a pretty clean bill of health, politically. You're a Socialist, but I don't think you're the sort of chap who becomes a traitor."

207

"I'm certainly not an upper-class Cambridge homosexual who's spent years rising through the ranks of MI6," David said flatly, irritated by the way Carlton had automatically linked his Socialism with a suspicion of treachery.

"In that case," Carlton said ignoring David's tone, "you'll be prepared to stand by your country."

"Look," David said, more annoyed by Carlton's smoothness now than by his devious game, "I know nothing about what goes on behind the Iron Curtain, I've never been there. I don't know any Russians, and as far as I know I have no Communist Party friends at all."

"Excellent! And I'm glad you said 'as far as I know' because happily I know rather more than you. There are many active Soviet agents inside and outside the Communist Party of Great Britain, and there are some out-and-out Communists who don't appear on even the secret membership lists at CPGB headquarters."

"How do you know that?" David asked. "Did you break in to check – or just lean on somebody to check for you?"

"There are methods," Carlton said coldly. "Necessary ones. Look at some of your own Labour colleagues, for example, even in Parliament . . ."

"It's no crime to be an open Marxist." David almost snarled at him. "I don't suppose your man Philby exactly advertised his true allegiance."

Carlton said superciliously, "Indeed not, but I'm afraid you're confusing us with MI6."

"I'm not confusing you with anything. I know priscisely what you are and exactly how you think. You and your kind are very well known to me, Mr Carlton."

Carlton was unsmiling now. "Very good. But irony, and our undoubted . . . shall we say, *differences*, aside, there *is* a problem. I'm afraid KGB penetration cuts much deeper than the general public believes, and we must all do what we can."

David thought of the confident, secure image of the country's security services created by Ian Fleming novels and the usual Establishment propaganda – and he wondered if it was still another lie, put about to disguise Britain's collapse. "I suppose you would say that, wouldn't you? You know there are some people inside 10 Downing Street who think the security services are plotting against this government."

"That's hardly surprising," Carlton said ambiguously and with an undertone of menace. "But let's not be naïve, now! Don't you understand what's been happening to this country? What do you think happened about the STA-2 details leaked to the Eastern bloc?"

David said nothing but his mind was working furiously. Had this anything to do with him, and the Alan Hoyle connection? It must, he realized.

Carlton continued in more measured tones. "You're not a member of the general public. You work inside Westminster, and have Labour Party connections. You have ambitions to become an MP."

"You really have been checking!" David said fiercely.

"Oh, yes."

"And so you think you can use me. Tell me, what use am I to you?"

Carlton rubbed his chin. "Turn that question round. How is MI5 able to help you? Your future political opponents would have no secrets from you – presuming they're left-wing opponents, naturally."

If that was a joke, David thought it in poor taste. "I'll ask again, Mr Carlton. *What do you want?*"

"I hope you can help me," Carlton said winningly. "Because I think you'll approve of my intentions. I want Alan Hoyle."

"What?" David looked at Carlton hard. "Why?"

"As you have established, Hoyle is a full-time organizer for Forward. He has contacts with the East German and Soviet embassies. People like Franz Schaller."

As soon as Carlton mentioned Schaller's name David understood the true position. His confidential reports on Hoyle really had been getting around: they had followed Hoyle and found Franz Schaller and then a British traitor – Schaller's agent. He blanched, realizing the danger this had plunged him into.

His stomach stirred. "Frank told you *everything* that I've been doing?"

"Never mind the details. Alan Hoyle's an enemy of the state, a Marxist, and I mean to have him. And all the fellow-travellers with him. I want names, David Bryant."

"It isn't a crime to be left-wing! It seems to me that you don't care about Hoyle as a security threat, you just want to use him – and me – to smear my own party. Being Labour doesn't mean you're a traitor. My orders come from the top, the very top, and I've been told to treat

Hoyle and the whole Forward movement as an internal Labour party matter."

"If he is a traitor linked to terrorism, what kind of bloody sense does that make?" Carlton looked grim. "I can give orders, too. And I can pressure you, Bryant. I can go over your past with a fine-tooth comb, and I'm certain I'll find something discreditable there."

There was pain inside him. "Everybody has a secret or two."

"So what's it to be? Will you volunteer, or do I need to force you?"

David took hold of the door handle and cracked the door open just as heavy traffic made the Daimler slow to a crawl. He turned to face Carlton, and said, "I think this conversation has gone far enough. Of course I'm on the side of my country, but I refuse to be blackmailed! In other words, Mr Carlton, I don't want to play your games. Frank will go straight to the Cabinet Office, your superiors, to get you off my back. Find yourself another informer."

He pushed the car door open, stepped out of the slowly moving vehicle, and quickly headed for the steps of Green Park underground station.

Carlton called out after him, "Too late – 'Keyhole'! You're already our informant."

David rang the Knightsbridge flat that night. Alex came to the phone and they made an agreement to meet in a comfortably dowdy pub in Pimlico.

David arrived first and ordered a pint of Guinness.

"Sorry I'm late," Alex said as he came up to the bar. "It's been bedlam."

David tried to shake off his own preoccupations. "The STA-2 cancellation? That must have been disaster for the company."

"Right. Without an American deal we'll have to scrub the whole project." Alex threw back a straight Scotch, then wiped his lips with the back of his hand. A Rolex watch glittered on his wrist.

"How did it happen?"

"Treachery, David, at the heart of the company. I don't know all the names, of course, but we've had police, Special Branch and some hard-faced types from – well, somewhere secret, going through everything, led by a real gung-ho chap called Carlton."

"Carlton? From the security service?"

Alex threw a wide-eyed glance at him, then his expression relaxed into a rueful smile. "I see you are well informed."

"That man is a bastard, Alex."

"So? Maybe he has the right attitude," Alex answered, coldly. "I agree with Carlton. There might have to be wholesale sackings on security grounds inside Stanton's – if we want to keep our government contracts. And the Lord alone knows what the unions will say to that."

"They'll fight you, Alex."

"Langton and his engineers? I suppose so." He rubbed at his eyes. "I went down to Bristol myself, yesterday. They're tooled up for confrontation, David, and we may have to take action against anybody identified as being a security risk. Otherwise . . . we'd made sales of the STA-2 worldwide, but losing the U.S. market has meant cancellation. The Aircraft Division has lost three hundred million dollars."

"And look what it did to the share price."

"A crisis of confidence." Alex toyed with his glass, shaking it. The strong odour of Scotch assailed David's nostrils. Alex threw this one back, too. "This is one time I wouldn't like to be in Hugh's shoes."

"You must have lost a mint of money yourself."

Alex crooked a finger to order another Scotch. When he turned around again, his expression was thoughtful. "Actually, no."

"No?"

"I sold out two weeks ago."

"What? I thought you were building up a slice of your family's company?"

"I still intend to do that. In any event, I inherit my father's percentage when I'm twenty-six. But at the moment Ray and I are still expanding our business. Hacker-Stanton International, registered in Dover, Delaware. You see before you the executive vice-president, otherwise known as the London partner. We're looking at leasing aircraft and, you guessed it, selling arms."

"Arms?" David was taken aback again. "You expect to sell a lot of them?"

"Of course, David. There's a huge market out there. Don't you know there's a war on?"

It was a sweaty, humid morning in downtown Saigon, off Nguyen Ho Boulevard, and Alex had walked all the way to and from the

211

fortified U.S. Embassy. Back in Britain the STA-2 affair had been hushed up; Donald Pike had been reinstated as chief designer, this time under the constant supervision of the security services. Pike, it seemed, could be very useful, now his loyalty was no longer in doubt. The real reason for the cancellation of the STA-2 order had never been revealed to the public.

This was only Alex's second trip to Indo-China, so the crowded noisy streets and the racing olive drab vehicles with their single white stars still interested him. Early yesterday morning he had been flown out of Da Nang with some impressive recommendations for Stanton armaments. If he could turn those into firm orders, Hugh would have to listen to Alex's counsels.

He remembered how, in the Embassy, they had talked about an extra $125 million for Stanton Industries small arms and ammunition, as well as the prearranged airline purchase, and then made it quite clear they were also trying to buy political influence.

"It's getting rough for us all over the world," the man from the U.S. Information Agency had told him. "Look at the politics in your country."

"I know," Alex said regretfully.

"Our presence in 'Nam is costing us blood and a fortune, and it still gets us a bad press almost everywhere!"

Alex had tried to be sympathetic. "My partner and I will sign the deal this afternoon, and I promise you that will give you what you want."

The man with the bristle-haired crewcut stood up to shake hands. "Thank you."

"Thank *you*," Alex said, his own powerful hand matching the other man's. He looked around at their satisfied faces, and the maps of Vietnam that showed nothing but defeat.

They were all fools, getting it all terribly wrong. They thought they could buy devotion, and threaten people into loving them. They could not be more wrong.

He strode quickly into the three-storey building and banged on the desk. "But we try room when you phone us, Mr Stanton, and the door was close then and is close now."

There was a slow-spinning fan above the desk.

"I need the man in a hurry," Alex said impatiently. "We both have to sign some papers. What room is he in?"

212

"Forty-two – up."

He took the stairs quickly and heard giggling behind the brothel door, but there was no answer to his knock.

Alex went outside, and unlocked the boot of the car. He had been to Khe Sanh with the U.S. Marines and he had twice flown over the DMZ as a passenger on B-52 bombing raids. He knew exactly what worked in this country. The boot of the battered Lincoln was full of Stanton guns and Stanton ammunition, and under that was something in a canvas cover they had used on trips into the jungle. Alex grinned.

He passed the desk again, coming in. This time he had something heavy under one arm.

"You see, the door close in forty-two – is *l'amour*, you understand!"

"There are no closed doors in my world."

In the upstairs corridor he had a little audience. Three of the girls, and a man in U.S. Marine uniform, so stoned his eyes pointed in different directions.

Alex banged at the door again, but there was no reply except a faint, feminine giggling. Whistling happily, he pulled the canvas hood off the machine, then jerked at the chainsaw's cord. The motor fired at once, roared, its serrated teeth tearing the air so quickly they were a blur.

"No, no, you must not!" said one of the girls, her face beautiful as a flower. Another put her hand to her mouth and said something about the police.

"You'd better stand back."

Alex started to cut through the door as the girls began screaming. The chainsaw howled; splinters flew past his head, and the air was full of dust. He made three criss-cross slits through the locked door, then kicked his way through after turning off the chainsaw.

The French windows were open onto the balcony. The white-washed room was dominated by a brass bed, larger than usual. Hacker, naked, was sitting up in it, two of the beautiful young whores huddled to his hair-forested chest.

"I told you we had to meet the Embassy guys, Ray. You know I hate to come late when business is involved." He put down the chainsaw.

Ray uncocked the pistol in his right hand, then slapped the pert rump of the girl on his left. "On the other hand, I hate to come early

213

when it's pleasure. Besides," he explained, "I had a couple of things to do."

Later, their contracts signed, they sat in an upstairs bar and looked down on the crowded street as the rain stormed down. It was the monsoon season, so the rain that drummed on the table umbrellas promised a welcome coolness.

"It just gets better," Hacker said quietly, picking up his beer glass and making his own silent salute to Alex and the group of pilots who had assembled at their table.

There was a ripple of assent, and as it died Alex said wistfully, "You know, I like this place. I can see why you want to fight for it. I never thought Vietnam would be like this."

"Maybe, but even if I like to help Uncle Sam, I'm here because the bonuses are good," Maddox, the eldest flier, told him. "No other reason to fly in supplies and CIA case officers."

"For chrissake," one of the others said, "a million dollars a month couldn't make me do it for the other side."

"I want to see you succeed," Alex said.

"I thought you English chappies weren't supposed to be into success?" said Jessop goodhumouredly.

Alex turned to the older man, and said half-seriously, "That's one of the great popular misconceptions. Some of us English chappies want success so badly it hurts. But, of course, it's bad form to show it. Everything must look as if it's absolutely effortless."

"Effortless? Hey, I bet that really demoralizes the opposition!" Jessop said.

Alex smiled quickly. "If you bring it off it does."

"I see where that Empire came from!"

Maddox frowned. "Winning without looking like you're trying? That's great, until you start believing it yourself."

Alex nodded in agreement. "Yes," he said, grinning. "In Ray's words, ten per cent talent, ninety per cent application – I've got that engraved on my heart."

"I should hope so," the Texan said gruffly, but he was grinning too into the rim of his beer glass.

When Alex made to leave, Ray came after him. They walked together to the stairs.

"I suppose you're still seeing that model back in England?"

"Sarah? Yes."

"She's a good-looking woman. You can certainly pick 'em. I saw her picture on the cover of *Vogue* a month or two back."

Alex grinned. "Why, Ray, I didn't know you read *Vogue*."

"Are you planning to marry her?" Ray asked, straight-faced.

Alex grimaced at Ray's gaucherie. This was 1967, after all, not the nineteenth century.

"She has a bachelor place on the King's Road and she wants me to move in with her. Chelsea seems pretty exciting. I think I might rent out my own apartment and do it."

Ray grinned lasciviously. "I've never heard of women bachelors."

Alex nudged Ray off the top step. "What the hell is that supposed to mean?"

Ray turned. His face was serious. "I just hope you know what you're doing. There's not a lot of room for women in this business."

Alex shrugged. "It suits me for the moment."

They pushed through the swing door and into the bar's ground level lavatory. It stank and the sounds of crying children came through the broken shutters from the alley. Ray brushed a hand in front of him as a cloud of flies buzzed up around them.

"This isn't exactly the Ritz."

Alex narrowed his nostrils. "It stinks almost as high as the deal we've just pulled off."

"What?"

"Come on, Ray. You put our money into getting the airline, the whole thing, together, and forgot to tell me who was lined up to buy it."

Ray stood up against the ornate French urinal and laughed. "It's the CIA – and so what?"

"You told me it was Air America!"

"It's the same thing. Biggest goddamned airline in the world as of now, and it's a CIA front. Doesn't that crease you up?"

"I suppose somebody's got to drop rice and ammunition on Laotian hill tribes."

Ray pulled up the zip of his trousers. "Hacker-Stanton International. And there's a million dollars in it for both of us, clear profit. How do you like being worth a million dollars in your own right? I never came close before, and I can tell you I like it a whole lot."

Alex rinsed his hands under a rickety tap. More money meant more influence. "And the guys upstairs are picking up two thousand a month for being shot at?"

"That's business."

A rapid series of explosions, loud and staccato as gun fire rent the alley, Alex jumped away from the window, ducking his head.

"Getting nervy?" Ray said, then he laughed.

Alex pursed his lips, shook his head. Often in Saigon you heard shots, bombs, grenades.

"You should've gotten used to Vietnamese firecrackers by now."

It was almost noon by the time Maggie stirred to the sounds of 'Strawberry Fields Forever'. As she hugged the pillow a little tighter Terry shouted to her.

"I've got your favourite breakfast, honey. Black coffee and peaches."

He came in, grinning, wearing an open-necked denim shirt. The gold chains she had bought him glinted against his chest.

"I think I could eat something else," she said, stretching out languidly like a cat. "You."

He sat down, cross-legged on the bed, and squeezed her ribs as she sat up, squealing.

"It went like a dream this morning," he said. "They want *Vietnam Nightmare* in a German edition now – sixty thousand copies to start with. And you should see what they've been saying in Frisco. There're queues outside the bookstores. Even some poster publishers are looking for rights."

She wriggled up to him, parting her nude thighs around his waist. "Spread the word," she said joyously.

"Amen to that!" he shouted. Then he gave her a sharp look and said, "Our book is doing great. How'd you like to be a tax exile?"

Maggie laughed, setting her head invitingly, then licked her lips until they were wet. Terry's blue eyes drew her. There was a fire in them.

He reached over and pulled out a Mars bar. He unwrapped it and put its tip into her mouth, and when she looked at him she saw he was serious, and remembered the famous story – why not for her too?

She scissored her legs together and caught him.

"Don't go away from me," she said. "Don't – *ever*."

Terry examined the chocolate bar critically. Otis Redding began crooning over Radio Caroline, and the sun gleamed on the Russian icon they'd hung on the wall above the bed. The Madonna's face was pale and aloof. Then he began to give her pleasure, staring into her eyes, knowing that Maggie would love every moment.

They took their afternoon walk down the King's Road to look at the new shops that were opening all along it. The road had become a continuous passing fashion parade.

"Britain really is changing. Where's all the stiff upper lip? The Empire and cold baths?" asked Terry ironically, his long, elegant face crinkled up with good humour.

Maggie suddenly turned to him and embraced him. "I'll tell you what's been happening. The Romans are turning into Italians – and I think it's *great!*"

Terry seized her hand, laughing, and led her away towards the corner coffee bar. "I think it's great too. I love coming here. But something tells me it won't last."

She slowed. "Nothing lasts," she said, shrugging. "But that doesn't stop you enjoying it."

Terry scratched at his unshaven jaw. "I have to go back to Vietnam," he said.

Maggie stumbled over the pavement and Terry pulled her back as someone roared past in a pillarbox-red Jaguar.

"Do you know what?" she said suddenly.

"You're going to tell me."

"I think it's time *I* went to Vietnam."

Alex had returned to England. There had been a hammering in his head: the need to make something of the money he had gained on the premature announcement of the STA-2 sale. He had made a killing by stepping out of the market on the eve of the American cancellation, and won for himself a reputation as an astute operator. Then Hacker had gone back to Fort Worth, set up the airline with more of their money, and they had taken it to Vietnam and developed it as a channel for running operations the CIA did not want to be publicly connected to. When they sold out to Air America in Saigon, they had doubled their stake again, and begun looking for new ventures.

217

Now, one early evening in September, 1967, they were seated at dinner together in London's GPO tower, the technological grey-green cylinder rising six hundred feet above London's streets, waiting impatiently for service in the revolving restaurant that girdled its summit.

The American had promised Alex a celebratory dinner to seal their partnership's success. The modern steel and glass decor seemed to Alex a thoroughly appropriate setting and the lights of London glittered far below like promises.

Hacker spread out a menu and slapped it down. His big, homely face lit up with a grin. "Alex, listen, I want to promise you you won't regret coming in with me."

Alex looked up from the *à la carte* menu. "Two million dollars isn't something I can afford to lose, Ray."

"Damned right! But you won't!" He whistled, then, looking over his shoulder at the crowded room, added loudly, "Jesus, it's hotter 'n a devil's asshole in here."

Alex laughed. "Warmish," he agreed.

"Never hear of air conditioning in this country?"

"Heard of it, yes." Alex beckoned over a waiter. "Lobster salad, I think. Or I could recommend the duck soup, Ray. Sea bass in *vin blanc* vinaigrette. Saddle of lamb . . ."

It was served steaming, savoury, colourful. They began to eat, but Ray only wanted to talk business.

"We need as many of those Arab connections as you can get, Alex."

"I'll be onto that after next Sunday."

Ray spooned up the duck soup. "Pretty good," he said, then looked up disdainfully. "Next Sunday? Aw, come on, Alex."

"A few days of peace and quiet," Alex told him. "Sarah and I are flying to Cannes, St Tropez. Perhaps you'd like to come? I think you'd enjoy it."

"Can't. I have to make some calls, then I want to fly to Dallas. Talk to some people in person."

Alex raised an eyebrow. "I'm glad you're so keen to get to work."

"Hard work's good for the soul."

With a gourmet's anticipation, Alex scooped white flesh from his lobster half-shell and said jocularly, "It certainly does the soul good to meet a man who expresses his gratitude in such a tangible form."

218

Hacker laughed, then fell to seriousness. "I'll tell you something, Alex, you're one hell of a man. And I'll tell you something else –" he waved an encompassing hand over the jewelled lights of London, "this city of yours can be *had* – this entire goddamned world can be had – *if* you have the class and the cash to do it."

Alex sat back at the challenge in Ray's voice.

"I think you ought to go for it," Hacker said. "We only have one life."

"I've got my own ambitions, Ray," Alex said lightly, looking over the lights of the city. "Perhaps all money, though."

Ray dabbed at his lips with a napkin and beckoned back the waiter for more wine.

"Not good enough, Alex. You expect me to be impressed by Stanton Industries. I'm not. It's old time. Why don't you come over to the States with me, and get down to some real work?"

"Just because Hugh made you give up your job doesn't mean Stanton Industries is worthless."

"I had to give it up, sure. But I would have done anyway. They weren't serious – it was just a goddamned game to the SI Board!"

Alex shook his head and gave a big smile. "No, you don't understand. Listen, we were once the biggest arms manufacturer in the world."

"That's not what I mean." Hacker held up his palms, then stabbed one forcefully with an index finger. "Hugh's playing goddamned games, Alex. The family firm is screwed. It isn't industry, it isn't finance, it isn't *commerce.* It makes money – sure – but it doesn't make *wealth.* If it did, you'd be the richest sons of bitches in the world!"

"Fifty years ago we were pretty close."

Lines appeared on Hacker's forehead. "Yeah, and then they invented competition. You ain't on no playing fields now, Alex. I hate to see talent go to waste."

"I still think what I'm about to do is spend a week on the *Nereid* with Sarah," he said adamantly. "I wanted to prove a point to my uncle and Hugh, and now I've proved it."

"That you're your own man? If they can't see that, the hell with them. But you could prove a whole lot more to them."

"If I could get control of Stanton Industries . . . Look, I'm really not that interested in running any other corporation. I don't know if it's my thing."

"You don't know if it's your thing. You sound like a goddamn raggedy-ass hippy." Hacker snorted. "You ever hear of a guy named William Allen?"

Alex reviewed his mental catalogue of names. "No."

"Well, you should. He made history. I met him a few times when I worked for Lockheed. He was born back around 1900 and became lawyer in Seattle before World War Two; that's all, just a lawyer. Then he ends up working for Boeing, and back around 1934 they had him on their board. That man pushed through the B-17 Flying Fortress. Saved this island, and the Free World."

Alex nodded.

"Lean guy, bald, nothing special to look at; but he had intelligence, humour, he could listen and communicate, and he could *decide*. He had the B-47 bomber built, and sold *fourteen hundred* of them to the USAF. In 1950 he and his team came over here to Farnborough Air Show, and he saw the De Havilland Comet. He went back to the States and bettered it.

"I mean, everybody knows Boeing, Alex! The 707, the 727, and now the 747. I guarantee you, its success will match up to its jumbo size. It's going to be one of the all-time greats of aviation history. And all that, Alex, from a guy who was a lawyer in downtown Seattle! Why the hell don't you come back to Dallas with me?"

Alex raised his glass and looked at Ray thoughtfully. "I know what you're saying, Ray, but I have to run my life from here."

"From here? Bullshit!" Hacker lit a cigarette and blew a plume of smoke high in the air. "It's money, Alex, that's what this world runs on. That's what lubricates and powers the machinery."

"I wasn't exactly born into poverty, Ray," Alex said. He liked Hacker, his gusto and intensity. He liked the way he was never afraid to get personal – even when it hurt.

"The trouble with you Brits is that you demoralize and keep down the people who ain't got money. You look down on the people who want to earn it. And the guys who have got it are too godamned complacent to do anything with it."

Alex got the point. "Except for me?"

Hacker suddenly relaxed. "I think my message has got to you."

"And I suppose it's different in the U.S?" he asked lightly.

Hacker's face lit up once more in a broad grin. He pointed a thick finger at Alex. "You're goddamned right it is!"

"What do you want, Ray?"

"Simple. I want you to face facts. Admit that Stanton Industries is finished, that they'll never get over the STA-2 disaster, and that they'll never ever let you in. And then I want you to come with me and start doing business out of Texas and Delaware instead. If you do that, I promise you'll make millions."

Alex smiled. "That's one hell of an offer, Ray."

"Then you'll do it – leave England for good?"

It was a long time before Alex answered.

3

In early August, Maggie and Terry flew to the States. They were on their way to Vietnam again, already thinking of the follow-up to *Vietnam Nightmare*. Maggie had published long extracts from the book in the London magazine *Capital Life* and would do the same for the next photo-book, and she wanted personally to arrange United States' syndication rights in New York before they went on to Saigon.

This went well. In the Fifth Avenue bookstores their work was still selling. She realized Terry and she had touched a nerve.

Then they flew into Vietnam, and the war.

As they drove into Saigon that first day, it was still a terrible place: a steamy, South-East Asian hell. The humidity felt lethal, the temperature had approached a hundred degrees.

There was no night here, only a darkness splashed red and yellow and blue with neon light. The streets were full of prostitutes and pickpockets, and drunken, loud men in uniform, partying to forget. Cars jammed the streets, and youths raced on motor-scooters. There was thunderous rock'n'roll from bars and car horns blared relentlessly. Terry leaned out of the car occasionally and snapped pictures.

A tall GI, happening to see her, grinned and made masturbatory motions at her. She forced herself to ignore it.

"This is a cesspit, isn't it?"

"No," he said. "There's nothing natural about what happens here. The shit stays shit, it fertilizes nothing."

She turned away from a strip joint called *The Pink Pussy*. "What kind of just war can this be?"

Terry shook his head, his Nikon held in both hands. "Forget about the war and people being killed. That's just random, ask anybody;

222

most of the time the wrong people get it. Except for the VC and the top brass, nobody gives a fuck about fighting. The only thing that matters here is the piastre and the dollar – or anything else you can use as currency. And that might be a pack of Kools or Marlboros, or something worse. Smack, maybe, or a virgin girl you can sell to a brothel."

"Oh, Terry, you have to be kidding!"

"Let's get some sleep," he said, touching her arm. "Find a room in the Caravelle, maybe. Tomorrow, I'll show you."

In a hospital she visited next day they found a twelve-year-old girl dying from a venereal disease: infections were so rife here that many strains of disease had become immune to all the usual antibiotics. Maggie held the small, overheated hand. The other children, those who were fit to walk, came up to her with giggles and sweet smiles and tried to go through her pockets. Mostly their eyes were dead.

She didn't say anything, and Terry had to gently shoo them away, though one tiny boy with an artificial leg wrapped his arms round Terry's right knee and burst into tears, refusing to go. A rat skidded across the floor.

"You notice the generals and the generals' wives all have really expensive, imported cars," Terry said quietly.

"Whores live well," Maggie said, blinking back tears. "For a while."

They spent the next steamy six weeks travelling the war-torn country, watching tensely as President Johnson escalated the war. Maggie talked to everybody, Catholic refugees, intellectuals, from the North, shoeshine boys with half-American faces, even brass with the MACV. There were half a million Americans in Vietnam now. The gigantic cost of staying in Vietnam meant that America's liberal approach to domestic problems was becoming impossible to finance; so now the aims of the Kennedy years were all foundering, on the rock of Vietnam.

And all for nothing, Maggie often thought. America couldn't bring any goodness here, give the people anything worth fighting and dying for. All they could bring was their money, thousands of millions of dollars, in the greatest tide of corruption the world had ever seen. She flew to Cam Ranh Bay, the great naval port: but the huge military power there seemed worthless. She remembered how the VC, with the co-operation of local people, had raided Da Nang air base, even though the perimeter was guarded by nine thousand U.S.

Marines. On the road, once, she saw a patrol coming back with a dead Vietnamese tied to the hood like a deer.

"There's a Hacker-Stanton International office in Saigon now," Terry told her, "which is doing lots of business."

"That's despicable," she said. "Alex and Ray! Making money out of blood – and my government's supporting it, you know."

"Then speak out," he told her.

It was strange that there was still so much French, colonial influence on this place. She found that most of the older officials and officers spoke at least a little of the language, and much of the architecture reminded her strangely of provincial France, too. The easy-going, fatalistic attitude of the Buddhists appealed to her.

"No," said one of her contacts from the fortified U.S. Embassy. The three of them had met in a bar, sitting under a whirling fan in a haze of midges and flies. "In June of '66, Saigon had to send in troops and riot police to storm the Buddhist institute. They're not really apolitical or spiritual – they're just pro the North, right?"

"I can't believe it's that simple," she said firmly, wiping sweat from her forehead.

Frank smiled, suddenly. "Oh, I didn't mean it was simple."

Maggie sipped at the harsh rice spirit; it was only the second time she had sampled this Vietnamese drink: at first the bar had refused to provide it. "What about this WHAM business?"

"Winning hearts and minds?" Terry laughed. "No way. The high brass want to have an old-fashioned war, right? Lots of targets and free-fire zones. So they shift people away from the ancestral fields and the ancestral graves, stick 'em in concentration camps and forget them soon as they're behind the wire, and expect the Viets not to mind! It's crazy as well as immoral. God, we have to get out of this shit," Terry said, nervously stroking his camera under the table. "Not us, but the country."

Frank sighed, gesturing for a waiter. "Otherwise we stay here, flailing about with our big fists like we think we're John Wayne."

"Most of the time hitting the wrong guy," Maggie said. She had visited some of the U.S. conscripts in another hospital, infinitely better run and equipped than the Vietnamese one: many of them had been injured in error or through accidents. There had been one young ex-Marine with a burned-away face . . .

It was tragic to watch, and every day more body bags were flown back from South-East Asia. West was meeting East, head-on. In

224

America antiwar protests increased; there were even bombings. The nightmare was getting worse. There was blood and more blood.

Vietnam had shown them even more horrors than before. They were happy to leave.

By the time they returned, London was in a mellow haze. Each daybreak made a sky the colour of smoke. Red and brown leaves crunched like snow as they walked the London parks, arm in arm. On their old haunt, the King's Road, the new philosophy had arrived; she saw fantastic military uniforms, like those on the cover of *Sgt. Pepper*, and heard the bells as hippies passed by in flowing Indian cottons and headbands. East was finally meeting West on a basis of equality, she thought.

But despite feeling that her own stars were in the ascendant, Maggie still couldn't rest.

"I have to speak out," she said to Terry. "I love working on the magazine, on the books, but money isn't everything."

Terry nodded wisely. "You want to talk about 'Nam, don't you?"

She had joined the local Labour party months ago. At the beginning of October she went up to Scarborough as constituency delegate to the Labour Party conference, and was pleased to see the leadership given a rough ride.

She was given her chance to speak, climbing the rostrum barefoot in patched Levis and an open-necked Indian shirt, stating her carefully rehearsed case. It all came back to her – Vietnam, the horror of the war against that provincial-French background of squares and cafés. She described it to them, speaking in a flat, aggrieved tone that was more effective than any rhetoric could be. The paradoxes of America's dreams and fears: the prostitution and corruption, the tortures and street executions, the mass bombing raids, the screaming victims of napalm . . .

"I've seen that horror," she told them. "What's the point? Why can't we stand up here, today, and say from this platform, What is the point of that evil war? As Ho Chi Minh said, 'Vietnam is thousands of miles away from the United States, and the Vietnamese people have never done any harm to the United States', but still they have to be machine-gunned and bombed and burned out of their homes –"

There was a rising murmur: people began standing in the conference hall, many faces enthusiastic, some flushed and angry.

225

"– so that the huge military-industrial complex in America and here, *oh yes, here*, and I could name the firms, can continue to exploit the people and resources of the entire world!"

Angry and overrunning her time, she kept finding the right words until they switched off the microphones, but she showed a clenched fist and many more delegates stood up to cheer her. There was rhythmic handclapping and she raised both arms and brought most of the conference delegates up to their feet.

She left the stage, but it took the Labour authorities – as she called them later, with heavy irony – minutes to restore order. People surrounded her, most to congratulate, some to argue. She found she was hoarse and tired and damp with perspiration, and suddenly wanted to shower and take an hour's rest.

David came up to her when she was leaving the hall. "That was bloody brilliant, Maggie! As good as anything in your book or in *Capital Life!*"

She rubbed at her eyes. "You can tell your friend the Prime Minister he has to listen to us."

"It isn't that simple, Maggie. Suppose we did renounce U.S. policy – what might that mean? The end of NATO? Who knows?"

"NATO," she said scornfully.

"I read your articles, Maggie," he told her gently. "I know what you think. How is the magazine doing?"

"Well, we're a co-operative now; I'm on the committee. It's a bit inefficient sometimes, but I've got the commission to be the eye of *Capital Life* on the world scene." She coughed. "Is Alan here?"

"Alan Hoyle?" David's face shifted a moment. "I don't think so. He prefers to operate behind the scenes."

That evening, in the main conference bar, Maggie talked with Mrs Thornton, a dowdy, middle-aged woman MP.

Maggie's extreme anti-war stance was attacked gently but persuasively by the older woman, and she was moved to say, "Politicians start wars; but ordinary people suffer them. War is never justified as an instrument of international dialogue."

The woman said quietly, "When my name was Lipitz, before I was put in Birkenau-Belsen, I might have agreed with you. But now . . . I know that someone must eventually say 'no', and someone must be brave enough to carry the rifle across the wire."

Maggie looked at the woman's kind face and appealed to her.

226

"Wars start because men, men, are ready to carry the rifle in the first place."

"It's a difficult problem."

"But people are still dying in Vietnam. Now. Today," Maggie said with conviction. "It's dirty, bloody and obscene."

Another MP, a professional in debate, smiled at her. "You must have seen that war is all of those things, Miss Langton. Tell me, how long did you spend in a fox-hole?"

Maggie glared back angrily. "Long enough to know the time for supercilious point-scoring is over."

On the following day, Wednesday, the fourth of October, conference took the vote.

Maggie's motion calling for the country to dissociate itself from U.S. policy in Vietnam was carried.

David read her report in the latest edition of *Capital Life* with delight. Maggie had certainly made an impact at the conference. She had been speaking from the heart, and there were times, he had to admit, when the heart should be heard. He remembered how Megan had told him three months ago now that she was pregnant, and he had been almost overwhelmed by joy.

His own position was delicate, and it was impossible to reveal his true feelings in public. He was living not just one lie, but an overlapping series of lies. Hoyle still had to be shadowed. After his problem with Carlton, David no longer passed on details of his activities with Forward; and he and Alan, naturally, avoided each other's company except in private. They had agreed that David's public association with Forward would be, for the moment at least, minimal.

There was nobody he could be honest with. Not his closest friends, not even his wife.

David sensed he was not the only mole, burrowing away on behalf of Forward. Here in Westminster, under Frank Deacon's guidance, David had grown to understand the complex network of relationships, official and informal, at the heart of the British government. He had begun to think of the day he might be put up as a parliamentary candidate, and given his chance to join the club proper. He knew that such a career could never be based on the duplicity of his relationship with Alan Hoyle. Already having constantly to betray confidences and break trust was making him feel dirty. As an MP it would be morally intolerable as well as criminal. Even though he felt he was doing a vital job, it was a thankless and lonely task, and especially after what Megan had told him, the strain had begun to tell.

"Hostages to fortune," he murmured.

He checked his watch and saw that he was almost late for his appointment with Frank. David stuffed a sheaf of work into his briefcase and prepared to leave. This morning had given him tremendous food for thought. There had been several items of information he had put together, and his knowledge of the foreign exchange markets made him worry.

The catalogue of national ills was long, and still growing. He believed he had identified the next weakness. In 1949, the pound sterling had been pegged at $2.80, but since May it had been under almost intolerable pressure. He knew the Cabinet had been told that the result of EEC entry would be a severe deficit on the balance of payments, and any other disturbance could knock sterling way down against the dollar.

In June, David had woken up to banner headlines: the Arab-Israeli war, which had raged for six days. There were rumours that Stanton Industries in general and Alex Stanton in particular had made a fortune out of that war. It had taken the UN to negotiate a cease-fire, but the Suez canal had remained closed ever since. The results for Britain were serious enough for what the Chancellor Jay had said to make sense. David was now sure that the pound was going to slide, and the only choice the government had was this: it could have a managed decline, or a disastrous, overnight fall. The preference had to be for managed decline, but so far the Labour government had refused to acknowledge reality – in public, at least. He wondered if a proper, State-secret decision about devaluation had been taken in private, but he feared it had not.

He scanned quickly through the latest trade figures. Surely, there could be no doubt about it now? Not when the speculators and foreign banks saw these figures, anyway. He shook his head and turned towards the stairs in a preoccupied mood.

Frank was still in his little office overlooking Whitehall. When David sat down opposite him he suddenly realized how tired Frank looked.

Nevertheless, the Welshman smiled. "Let's have it, David. I need something I can impress the grass roots of this great movement of ours with."

228

"Impress them with horror, Frank; this isn't good news. First, industrial investment here ought to be double its current figure, even at the cost of private expenditure –"

"Cut living standards?"

David put his hands on the desk and leaned forward; his voice became low and fierce. "That's an absolute necessity. Either we do it now, or the international bankers will do it for us. We're losing. We haven't got the tools to do the job. The last three shipbuilding contracts Stanton Industries put in for, one for Greek tankers, two from Hong Kong, all went to a Japanese firm run by someone called Hideki. Our competitors like Germany and Japan are ploughing back the seedcorn of industrial rejuvenation for all they're worth – and they're right. They mean to prevail and they're giving themselves all the right weapons, while we give ourselves nothing!

"Then education has to change, too. We must get more of our best people into industry – send them abroad with foreign languages, excellent products to sell, and *complete* conviction. That's the only way to conquer."

Frank shook his head. "Maybe you should be in the House of Commons, David, telling them straight. Industry here is really doing that badly?"

"It is – and I have the figures to prove it."

Frank hunched over, doodling on his notepad.

"That's something else," David said, hesitantly. "The pound. The foreign exchange markets don't believe the present value can hold."

Frank smiled, grudgingly. "Yes, but as long as the central banks –"

We can't trust foreign governments to spend their own money to prop up our currency. I'm certain of that. I have my own sources in the Treasury; they've convinced me. We need to make plans to let the pound sink to a more sensible level. Will you take that plan to the Cabinet?"

The other man hesitated. "That I'll need to consider, David."

So, David thought, even speaking here as friends, we can't commit ourselves to change. He stood up and looked at his watch.

"If the pound does collapse because of people losing faith, I'm afraid it might cost us a fortune. We do need to plan, Frank. I'll leave you to your considerations."

British industry? David knew that, as much as government or management, the City was to blame. He made his way down to

229

the Circle Line platform, able to envisage the economic danger that lay ahead. It was frustrating to see the solution clearly, and yet lack the power to do anything about it. But things had to start changing now. If it was left until the seventies or eighties, incalculable suffering would have to be inflicted on the nation. Again he considered his chances of being selected as a candidate and at that moment made up his mind to work towards it.

He changed to the Northern Line and stood on the platform feeling sooty tunnel wind blowing through his hair as he considered. With the Suez Canal closed, Britain's import-export trans-shipment costs had risen, making British manufacturers even less competitive in certain key areas of the world. Britain just wasn't *adapting*.

He climbed aboard the tube and unfolded his copy of the *Financial Times*. The two-page spread of closely-printed tabulations absorbed his interest for a few minutes, until he saw something that jolted him and made him think it was just as well he was going to this particular luncheon.

He arrived at Piccadilly Circus, went past the gaudy façades of shops and Shaftesbury Avenue theatres, and turned left into a Soho street.

It was a cold and misty November day; after the superb summer – the newspapers had dubbed it 'The Summer of Love' – the weather, like the economic situation, had taken a turn for the worse.

Alex was waiting for him in a French restaurant; at this time in the afternoon it was not crowded, except for a group of Wardour Street film people who had noisily colonized one corner. As he sat down, Alex congratulated him on Megan's pregnancy, and David was equally polite about the progress of Hacker-Stanton International.

"Ray's the main man in America," Alex said, "and I run the London end. It's going really well, actually."

"Does the taxman know?"

"He knows what he needs to know! There's a lot of my own money at risk in the company."

"How's Harvard?"

"My MBA, you mean? Fine. It's an interesting experience to meet all of the highly-polished corporation men from firms like IBM. We should have more places like Harvard Business School in this country."

David began to voice his economic doubts. "You're right, of course. Have you read the *FT*, Alex? Things are looking gloomy."

"Yes," Alex said, but he was enjoying his food. "Especially for industrial shares."

"And look at the trade balance." David repeated the quotation he had put into Frank Deacon's next speech: "As Charles Dickens put it in *David Copperfield*: 'Annual income twenty pounds, annual expenditure nineteen pounds nineteen and six, result happiness. Annual income twenty pounds, annual expenditure twenty pounds nought and six, result – misery.'"

"It's a crying shame you can't get Parliament to believe that."

David looked at his friend curiously. "I take the *FT* Share Information Service, and I see that Stanton Industries are closer to misery than happiness."

Alex gritted his teeth and admitted, "I'm afraid Hugh seems to be finding the burden of being Chairman of Stanton Industries more onerous than he thought."

David looked at him more closely. There had been a time when he had been thinking of leaving England entirely, and they had argued over it. Eventually, Alex had decided that both his cousin and Sarah needed him. "There's no good news?"

Alex's eyes suddenly flashed with good humour. "Oh, I wouldn't say that. There are still a few people waving blank cheques at us."

David smiled, wondering suddenly what Alan Hoyle would make of the conversation were he to come through the door. "I understand the man who's going to save the Stanton bacon is the extremely ambitious, extremely wealthy, but morally bankrupt Shah of Iran."

Alex seemed surprised. "You didn't read that in the *Financial Times*. How did you find that out? From someone in the Foreign Office?"

David pulled on an earlobe. "I keep my ear to the ground."

"Yes, I'm sure you do," Alex said, looking at him more closely. "In strictest confidence, I may as well tell you – since you probably know already: the Shah intends to take advantage of the Middle East situation. I went with my cousin to the Saadabad Palace, and I now believe he will settle for nothing less than leadership of the Islamic world, if Nasser will just move over."

"After the humiliation inflicted by the Israelis, Nasser must be a broken man," David said.

Alex smiled dangerously; he recalled his father's rage at the time of Suez. "Every cloud has its silver lining."

"Then, short of a revolution in Iran, the Stantons seem to be back in business."

"Exactly – short of a revolution here!"

David laughed. As long as he could watch Alan Hoyle, there would be no revolution on the streets of English cities. "So you took my advice?"

"Right. Straight to Tehran with Hugh; I did some straight talking. I had to twist Hugh's arm, but he agreed to make some necessary modifications to our Mark IX tank. I doubt if he appreciates what I did, though."

"I'm sure he'll appreciate the cheques."

"Ninety million paid cash, and we deliver the tanks and munitions over two years. A gross profit of fifteen per cent – I should hope he's grateful!"

"That much? Maybe you need some kind of coup of your own, entirely your own, to impress him."

"Not a bad idea," Alex mused. "Any suggestions?"

David laughed. There was something attractive about Alex's world, and the staggering amounts of money he had begun to juggle.

"If you're doing business with Iran, you'd better duck next time you see Maggie!"

"But what's the alternative to the Shah? He's doing for Iran what Ataturk did for the Turks, dragging a nation kicking and screaming into the twentieth century. I suppose he is what the Maggie Langtons of this world despise most – bloody hands and ruthless, unsentimental determination. But I hope there'll be no going back on modernization. What does she want to see over there? Mad mullahs in power in Tehran? No, we must back the Shah. He's on our side."

"And we're on his – thanks to money."

"Of course, that's true. Iran has something Turkey never had: oil wealth. That was an important consideration for Hugh. Stanton Industries can get inside Iran in a big way, and I foresee no problems arranging long-term credit for the firm, favourable repayment default clauses and the like. There's all that hard cash too."

"That's a big contract: ninety million," David said. "You agreed to a price in sterling?"

"Of course. It's all in Lord Beauford's bank at this very moment."

David studied his plate, a sudden worry overshadowing his thoughts. "And your cousin has arranged subsidiary contracts in France and Germany, as usual?"

"About a third of the value of the contract. He expects to make a good deal of money."

232

"Your finance – is Hugh going to be dealing in sterling?"

Alex tried hard to judge how much he should say. "What is this? An interrogation?"

David said earnestly, "You're not the only one sitting on priviliged information. I'm not a Fleet Street hack; you can rely on my discretion completely. And after last time, I'm no longer interested in speculation for personal gain."

"Quite."

Alex gave a wry smile. "All right. Yes, we'll be dealing in sterling exclusively. As I said, the ninety million arrived this week. On the strength of it, Hugh has loans arranged in the City – the bulk through Lord Beauford, of course, the remainder through Kintyre Ross. After the huge foul-up over the STA-2 Hugh hopes the Shah will get us back into the big league again. The money will be transferred to the continent soon."

David locked his eyes on Alex's. "Do it immediately," he said simply. "Don't wait."

"What do you mean?"

"Sterling's not what it was. Put the firm's cash into Switzerland or Germany, or the U.S. dollar as soon as you can."

"Hugh isn't very enamoured of my advice . . . What, you expect the pound to be in trouble? And soon?"

"I most certainly do."

They talked less seriously after that. When they finished the meal, David asked, "What's your opinion of James Callaghan?"

Alex shrugged. "Chancellor of the Exchequer? I remember seeing him speak at one of those Guildhall dinners. Man of his word, I think. He says he wants to stand firm against inflation and devaluation. Given those promises, he has my support."

"Then," said David politely, remembering gladly that Alex was picking up the bill for the meal, "I suppose that's all that needs to be said about that."

"Let's hope he beats inflation and keeps the pound steady."

David looked straight at his old friend. "I'm glad you decided to stand by Stanton's and this country, Alex. And don't worry: I'll stand by you. But shift that Stanton money out of sterling just as soon as you can."

As David made his way towards Tottenham Court Road two hippies in Afghan coats stopped him. The girl stuck out her hand.

233

"Hey, man, got any spare cash?"

David swept his dark hair back from his eyes and looked them over. "Ever thought about working for a living?"

"That's a North-East accent," the girl said. "I had a boyfriend from there once."

"Work?" the other said languidly. "It's the curse of the drinking classes."

David dug into his coat pocket and pulled out a handful of silver coins. "Here," he said. "For your knowledge of Oscar Wilde. Where are you headed?"

"California," the girl said.

"Kathmandu," the man contradicted her dreamily, grinning through his beard.

Suddenly David warmed to them.

"I wish I could go with you," he said, "and leave a few of *my* problems behind."

They sat in the Stanton boardroom, the three of them.

"I fail to see any necessity to strip my bank of assets, Alex," Lord Beauford said. "And it can be inconvenient to shift such large sums from currency to currency."

"You get your commission, don't you?" Alex barked.

Hugh, in the chairman's seat, steepled his fingers. "I am inclined to take some cautious notice of Alex's advice."

"For God's sake," Alex said brutally, "what if the pound does take a plunge? Lord Beauford, you have ninety million pounds of Stanton money – virtually our entire liquidity. Think what a loss we might make!"

"The government has made its views about devaluation very clear," the banker said. Clearly the loss of that money to his bank meant more than a possible loss to Stanton Industries.

Alex said desperately, "Even half the money. Please, send it abroad; put it in a dollar account. Let's play a smart game with the money. Or Switzerland; the Swiss franc is one of the strongest currencies in the world. I'd say we could even try the Japanese yen."

"I think not," Beauford said steadily, beaming over his half-moon spectacles.

Hugh moved awkwardly in his chair. "I understand you're very pleased to have our money, Lord Beauford, but –"

234

"Hugh, you and this firm have always had my loyalty. Can you deny that?"

"That's so," Hugh admitted.

"Then I expect the same thing in return. Trust me. And as for you, my dear Alex, you were once a major shareholder in this firm; and in 1970 you will inherit some shares from your father's estate. In the meantime, I am extremely dubious – do take note, Hugh – about your involvement with Stanton Industries and the criticisms you ceaselessly make. You are not one of us."

Alex stood up, fiercely angry. "So much for that. But what about our money?"

Beauford gave an exaggerated sigh, and looked at Hugh. But Hugh had a nifty ability to turn his attention away whenever he wanted.

"Very well." The peer lifted the telephone, dialled. "Ah, my dear Battersby. The Stanton accounts. Take sixty million and convert it into Swiss francs and U.S. dollars. No, not immediately. We don't want to worry the markets."

Battersby? Alex remembered that name. He forced himself to be pleasant to the corpulent peer. "We are grateful."

Beauford's eyes suddenly gleamed. "I understand Hacker-Stanton International has a very large cash flow these days – and makes many transfers from currency to currency."

So he was touting for business? Alex smiled. He stood up and, just before turning away, spoke to the banker. "It certainly does."

It was Thursday evening; a day after the meeting. Alex took a deep breath as he rounded the landing on the fifth floor of the Stanton Industries building, heading towards his borrowed office. He had spoken personally to James Battersby at the bank, who assured him that the transfer of the Stanton funds was well under way. Alex had cross-checked shortly before four, to find that all the Stanton funds were still in sterling. The senior people at Beauford Cleves had already left by then. Annoyed, Alex had spent the rest of the afternoon checking the small print of the Iranian contracts with the S1 legal department. Then he had looked through the rest of the Armaments Division order book. Every contract, and in some cases payment for munitions or tanks was not due to arrive for five or six years, had been arranged in sterling. . . The Embankment lights glinted off the Thames, and rain spangled the window panes as he watched its dark waters for a moment.

235

The night security man, Carrack, trudged up to him and touched his cap.

"Evening, Mr Alex. A cold evening."

Alex nodded. "Six o'clock and the entire place is deserted."

"It always is by this time, sir. Except the cleaners."

"And you, eh, Tom?"

The uniformed man grinned and looked around. "Yes, sir. I love this old building. It's got something to it, if you take my meaning. Like our building on the quayside back in Newcastle."

"I suppose the new offices at Millbank won't have quite the same atmosphere," Alex said kindly.

"All that glass and concrete. I'll be back in Tyneside before the opening, and I can't say I'm sorry."

Alex opened the door to the boardroom. As ever it looked splendid: a glass case of Georgian silver, the highly polished table – Victorian craftsmanship, gleaming under a gigantic chandelier that had once hung in the Winter Palace in St Petersburg. There was the faint smell of lavender furniture wax.

He said goodnight to the nightwatchman and went into the Chairman's suite, gazing at the family portraits and the three big framed blue-prints that hung on the oak-panelled walls. The telephone on Hugh's desk began to ring.

Alex, surprised, went over and lifted the receiver.

"Is Mr Alex there?"

"Speaking. What is it, Evelyn? I thought you left at five-thirty."

"Oh, I'm so glad to find you, sir. There's someone asking for you. He won't give his name. But he says it's very urgent."

Alex sat down in Hugh's chair. He wondered who it could be. "Then you'd better put the call through."

"Is that you, Alex?"

The voice was tinny and distant in the earpiece, but Alex brightened as he recognized its owner. "Well, now –"

"Please!" David Bryant's voice was urgent. "Don't mention my name over the telephone."

Alex looked at his adoptive father's portrait and the old charlatan stared down at him arrogantly. "All right," he said, his stomach tightening. "What is it?"

"I've been in the Treasury this afternoon, Alex. Sterling is going to collapse – I'm sure of it. We've heard the United States' banks are pulling back. By tomorrow night hundreds of millions of dollars will

236

be wiped off the books; the gold reserves have been sliding all week – the pound won't stand it."

Alex knew suddenly what David meant. And he remembered that all the Stanton's liquid assets were still at risk. "*The government are going to devalue the pound?* But they said –"

"There's nothing they can do!"

"*What?*" The British government was powerless; the country was at bay. And the New York banks would already be trading.

"Believe me, Alex."

Alex realized how much David was risking by telling him . . .

"Thank you," he said, already laying plans. "Have you any idea how big the devaluation will be?"

"I don't know exactly, but it can't be far short of fifteen per cent."

Alex said instantly, "That gives us a pound worth two dollars forty. My God, that's make or break on the Iran deal! Our profit on ninety million pounds!"

"I couldn't just sit here and see you ruined." David's voice was hollow. "Stanton Industries took enough of a hammering when the Americans cancelled their order for the STA-2."

"Thank you again. I'll do what I can."

At six-thirty in the evening in London – once the financial capital of the world – the prospect was bleak.

But immediately he put the phone down, Alex tried to contact Hugh. The housekeeper in Knightsbridge suggested he might be at one of his clubs. He was not. Alex rang Craigburn to be told that his uncle and aunt had left for Cannes. He phoned the Carlton Hotel and was told that they'd gone on to Monte Carlo. Rainier's palace confirmed that the *Nereid* had not yet arrived in the principality, and was presumably still en route. Alex knew there would be no time for a radio message and cursed.

He did manage to catch one of the non-executive directors, Lord Gifford Cecil, who told him politely but firmly that Alex's status as a family member and minor shareholder meant nothing, legally – and that he had no interest in Alex's confidential information. "Lord Beauford gives us advice; he's an international banker."

"He certainly is," Alex said, slamming the phone down.

Alex tried to ring the firm's legal and financial staff, but suddenly realized that without official authorization from the directors they were powerless to act. Lord Beauford would ignore any advice from Alex himself, and he knew he couldn't contact the other members of the Board without giving a detailed explanation, and that would take far, far too long – as well as spreading David's confidential news through their interlocking directorships faster than wildfire.

He kept trying until almost nine. Only then did he realize the system here had beaten him. He made two simple calls to New York and Los Angeles to rescue his own money, having already taken Hacker Stanton out of sterling.

It was not a large amount, but the smart money had been moving, too. The pound began its collapse.

Alex left a brutal note for Hugh which he tacked to his office door, and then drove back to the King's Road penthouse.

When he finally got into bed beside Sarah, he found he couldn't sleep. A scratch calculation revealed that this incredible state of affairs had indeed cost Stanton's fifteen per cent of their ninety-odd million – thirteen million pounds. It had reduced the profitable Iranian contract Hugh had just signed to a worthless liability to which the company was now irrevocably committed.

On Friday, everything happened as David had predicted. There was sheer panic on the foreign exchanges, and when business began in Britain the Bank of England spent £250 million trying to prop up the pound – all of it wasted. Lord Beauford's bank did move the Stanton money out of sterling, but it was too late by the time the transfer mechanisms had been arranged. The pound had crashed, exactly as David had predicted.

Saturday he spent pushing his own plans through. The following evening, Sunday, 19th November, 1967, the Prime Minister made his infamous broadcast. In their Chelsea apartment, Alex sat with Sarah and watched the black-and-white image in frustration and anger. It was Britain's great misfortune, he thought, to have such a man in Downing Street at this critical moment in history.

The 14.3% devaluation was necessary, the Prime Minister explained, and he went on to say disingenuously, "That doesn't mean, of course, that the pound here in Britain, in your pocket or purse or in your bank, has been devalued . . ."

Alex was enraged. "Look at that man, Sarah! It's time for a shakeup in this bloody country, starting right from the top!"

But Sarah was in her own world, and she said nothing.

There were eleven directorships at Stanton Industries: his father's seat rarely filled by the old man, except at the Annual General

Meeting; Hugh as chairman, acting as overall managing director; Lord Beauford the watchdog from Beauford Cleves, of which he was chairman, and which had substantial investments in Stanton Industries; and the three Divisions of Aircraft, Shipbuilding and Armaments were each represented on the board by a divisional managing director. Sir George Leslie still ran Shipbuilding, resisting all attempts to dislodge him though he was beyond retirement age, and Armaments was in the charge of a jolly man in late middle-age who had struck Alex as being good on the manufacturing side and out of his depth in everything else. The remaining five seats were occupied by the City knights and lords Alex referred to as 'the stuffed shirts'. Most of them were old enough to remember the First World War, and too many of them, he knew, had attitudes to match.

Alex didn't see his cousin at all during the weekend, and by Monday morning his anger had congealed. He made a point of ringing Hugh at nine, then at nine-thirty, and then at twenty minute intervals until he finally got through at ten past eleven.

"I take it you received my note, Hugh?" he said icily.

"Since it was tacked to the door, I could hardly avoid it."

"It was one way of getting your attention. I've tried just about everything else over the years. Don't you realize what a disaster the pound's collapse has been to us?"

"I am capable of doing simple mental arithmetic, Alex."

"Well?"

"Well, what? I listened to your advice last week, I listened to Lord Beauford's. We did try, didn't we? But it's hard for me to go over his head."

Alex was enraged. "Whose bloody company is this?"

"It isn't my private domain, nor yours. And anyway, what can be done after business hours on Thursday night?"

"Quite a bit, as I proved! I certainly changed my sterling accounts into other currencies. And as for 'after business hours' – for God's sake, isn't it time we Stantons ran a twenty-four hour operation? If I'd had the necessary authority I could have made the transfer through New York or Tokyo."

Hugh was obviously taken aback. "Your association with the company doesn't entitle you to interfere in the running of it."

"It was an emergency! Hugh, what does it have to be for you to consider it money? A chest full of gold sovereigns like what George Washington sent us?"

239

"You're not a director of Stanton's, Alex. Perhaps that's just as well with the piratical attitudes you've learned from Ray Hacker. We prefer tried and tested ways of doing business. Ways that have served us well for generations. I don't like what you're implying. How could I possibly have known you had spies sneaking around Westminster?"

"It was a friend of mine, not a spy. I trust him absolutely!"

"But why should *I* listen to him?"

A flood of anger rose in Alex's throat. "If Stanton's had acted on Thursday night we could have saved 14% of ninety-two million – thirteen million pounds, which was lost just to keep Lord Beauford sweet! And the reason you didn't know was because you couldn't be found. By God, I tried! But nobody knew where you were."

"You couldn't have contacted me in any case. I was travelling to Kintyre's estate in Scotland."

"Hugh, I'm absolutely appalled! Thirteen million!"

"Look, you know I disapprove of Mr Hacker's business philosophy, and I regret your associating with him," Hugh said, using his big brother voice. "If you must, then you must. I do appreciate what you have done, selling so much of the Armaments Division's output to the Shah and to Israel – just don't bring Hacker's hustling methods into Stanton Industries."

Alex's fingers drummed on the edge of the table. "Ray's hustling methods have made us all a good deal of money; and Hacker-Stanton International promises to make us even more. Do I see any sign of gratitude from you?"

He heard Hugh bang the table. "Stanton Industries represents industry, good industry. That earns us our profit, not hustling and spying. Trust me!"

"Damn it, Hugh! We've just lost thirteen million, and worse, the tank factory will be working for the next two years on a fixed-price contract that *loses* money. What if inflation goes up again? We lose even more! As it is, a year's profits have been wiped out completely – *Armaments is going to make a loss*! Try explaining that to our shareholders."

Hugh snorted. "I blame the French."

"What? The French?" Alex said dubiously. "*Arranged* the devaluation?"

"It's de Gaulle's personal crusade to damage us as much as he can. I'm sure of it. And now he can point to the instability of sterling as another reason to keep us out of the EEC. He wants to stab his old

240

ally in the back. If only we'd known he'd do this twenty years ago when we liberated his country."

Alex frowned. "He's simply putting his country's interests first, Hugh. That's the reason he keeps saying '*non*.'"

Hugh grunted. "Shortsightedness!"

"I think not. It's good for the French to carve up Europe to the benefit of German industry and French agriculture. De Gaulle sees Britain as wanting to get in on his act."

"Think what this will do to our imports," Hugh said, reminding Alex irresistibly of his mother.

"Make them 14% more expensive, I shouldn't wonder," he answered.

Hugh sat back, recovering some of his composure. "It's not a laughing matter, Alex."

"I wasn't laughing. But it does occur to me that this opens up a whole new export potential . . . I was thinking –"

Hugh ignored the comment and cut in, "– then to see the PM on the BBC yesterday telling us that the pound in our pockets has not been devalued – it was monstrous! Why can't he admit his policies have failed?"

"Callaghan probably wants to resign," Alex said thoughtfully. "He probably will once his Treasury business is put in order. A shame he's been put in this position, really. I think the man has integrity. I just hope the pound crashing has been a lesson to all of us."

Hugh's mood tempered into conciliation. "Of course dealing abroad is a problem, but the contracts always come in. We'll remain in profit in the coming financial year and beyond, I assure you. What do you expect – bankruptcy? This is a set-back, that's all." Hugh was silent a moment before continuing in a more reasonable tone. "I'm just as annoyed about the way this Socialist government has handled things as you are. Look, when can I see you for lunch?"

"Today." Alex had been hoping to catch his cousin in a good mood. He was sure there was room for one more person on the Stanton Industries Board of Directors. He knew that Lord Beauford was an enemy, opposed to him personally, but also working against the interests of the family firm. He wondered if he could persuade Hugh to share his view.

"What about White's? Shall we say half past twelve?"

"All right."

241

"Splendid! But I shall have to leave by three. I have to contact our suppliers on the Continent this afternoon to talk over this whole unfortunate business."

Maggie read the report in the *New York Times*. On 1st January, 1968, three days ago, the government of North Vietnam had said it would open peace negotiations as soon as the bombing and all other acts of war against it were halted.

If the American editorial was right, the war might soon be over. She sighed, and put the paper down. Outside, snow drifted past the window, swirling along Flood Street. *Vietnam Nightmare* had made them enough money to buy the big house where they had once rented a flat. As Maggie sat cross-legged on the rug in her loose white flannel robe and thought of the Christmas she had just spent with her family back on Tyneside, she smiled. Terry had enjoyed it. He had got on quite well with her father, whose view of Americans had been changed for the better, and even her mother's surprisingly direct questions about marriage hadn't seemed to worry him.

On Boxing Day, they had gone up to the desolately beautiful beaches of Northumberland, and climbed the sand dunes of Druridge Bay, walking miles along the coast, hand in hand. Their return along twisting country roads brought them past the high stone walls of the Craighburn estate, and the gatehouse, where she gunned the engine of the Alfa Romeo and sped by at eighty. Even so, Terry wanted to take a photograph of the estate.

"It's nothing," she told him, "just an old folly from the past."

Terry had looked at her curiously, surprised by the emotion in her voice.

The ring of the telephone brought her back to the present.

"Maggie, I've been trying to get hold of you for three days. Barbara and I have got the finance for the special. It's been approved." It was Laurie Cochrane.

"Laurie, that's wonderful! An hour of peak-time viewing about Vietnam? I'd *love* to do it.'

"No buts?" Laurie said. "You amaze me."

"No buts this time. I'll be over tomorrow. Nine a.m. sharp!"

She was almost dancing as she put the phone down. There was no doubt it paid to hold out. Wait till Terry heard about this, she thought. At last here was the opportunity to make a real statement of truth. TV had the power to bring the war right into the people's living rooms. She sat down at her desk and typed

out: *Fact: 1967 – U.S. personnel assigned, 485,600; casualties, 71,401*
. . .

Three weeks later, the Tet offensive in Vietnam had come and gone. Most of the cities of South Vietnam had been attacked. In Saigon even the grounds of the U.S. Embassy itself had been briefly seized during a suicide attack. Hué, the ancient Imperial capital, had been taken. Terry had left for there immediately. Maggie used some of his images in her documentary.

Tet had been on television screens all over the world as Maggie worked her customary twelve-hour day. Friends in America provided current footage; she scripted the programme herself, knowing there had never been a better time for this film.

As the rough cut began to run, Maggie sat beside the film editor she had specifically requested in Dubbing Theatre One. There was a buzz of expectancy, with thirty people crowding to watch the screen.

Maggie became part of the audience. She flinched in fear, felt outrage and tears, applauded the crippled veteran denouncing Nixon, and knew, again, that the Vietnam war would have to end.

At the finish she stood up, brushing back her hair. "This isn't a final cut, quite, but it's tight and hard-hitting, and carries a potent message. And I'd like to thank Laurie Cochrane here for giving me this opportunity."

Laurie was thoughtful; he said, "I only work here, Maggie."

"I was hoping for more of a reaction, Laurie,"she said, irritated by his near silence as most of the others crowded around to congratulate her, impressed by her nerve as well as her technical ability.

"I'm sure it's extremely powerful," he said. Then, looking at his watch and gathering up hs clipboard and notes he smiled quickly. "Forgot to tell you, but I've got a meeting at two. High level. Must rush."

She called after him, "Surely we're here to make programmes, not to go to bloody meetings!"

There was more discussion, more cups of coffee, then somebody said, "Run it again."

Her own voice, calm and authoritative on the sound-track, narrated the film. She gave the stark facts about escalating U.S. involvement. Then the scene cut to archive footage of black rubber body bags being returned home, to shots of Vietnamese nationals running from their burning houses, to summary street executions, to the self-immolation of Buddhist priests, and back to the U.S.A., as Chicago policemen charged into the crowd for the second time and hand-to-hand fighting broke out. The raggle-taggle army of protesters advanced on the hand-held camera: students in flared jeans or smocks, long hair held back by headbands. The sound of chanting faded up: "*Ho Ho Ho Chi Minh!*"

When the viewing was over, she and the crew went down for more coffee.

"That was the best thing I've ever seen," a young secretary told her. "I cried, you know."

There seemed to be adoration in her eyes; Maggie felt a little embarrasssed.

The editor smiled, pleased to be involved in a project like this. "People will have to take notice of your opinions now."

Maggie sipped from the thick olive-green cup. That was all she wanted.

A messenger came over to invite her to Laurie's office. She stood up quickly. "I plan to get the programme scheduled as soon as I can. Thank you, all of you."

Laurie beamed at her. "A remarkable achievement."

"I'd like to think so."

"A little too strong, though, we thought."

"'We'?" she said. "And what the hell does 'too strong' mean?"

He turned away from his desk. "You'd better take this as an apology. We can't use the film."

Maggie stood up, furious, her hands clenched into fists. "You're cancelling? They've leaned on you! Establishment bastards!"

"Look, I'm sorry," Laurie said. "But don't blame me, I just work here."

"Christ, I bet the guards used to say that at Belsen!"

"You can't seriously compare senior management to –"

"But what about you? Unless you're just their bloody messenger boy!"

He pinched the bridge of his nose and tried to contain his feelings.

"It's censorship," she said. "Blatant!"

"No one stopped you making the film, Maggie," Cochrane offered in his most reasonable voice.

"Nobody stopped me making it, but what good is that if they won't allow it to be shown?"

"That's their prerogative, Maggie."

"To suppress programmes?"

"Look, the BBC has an obligation to . . ."

"Jesus Christ! Laurie, I don't want to hear about the damned charter. You have a duty to inform and educate! We're talking about the freedom of the press!"

"Oh, don't let's get into that again," Laurie said, getting hotter now." "There are standing instructions –"

Maggie cut in. "Don't give me that. The man upstairs is a bureaucrat who takes his orders from above. Someone wants all the unpleasant facts bottled up. I'm going in to see him!"

Laurie tried to block her path.

"You can't do that!" he said, but she had already pushed past him and was marching along the curving corridor.

Twenty minutes later she stepped out of the lift, shaking. At reception she turned left past the glass cabinet in which an array of television awards gleamed in gold and silver. Her film had been judged unsuitable for television screening on the grounds that it was likely to overstep the bounds of public taste. It was to remain in its can, probably for ever. She did not even have a copy of her own to show privately.

An hour-long item on a royal visit to Australia had already been scheduled in its place.

She got home exhausted that afternoon, after an extravagant visit to Harrods Food Hall. Tonight, she had arranged for Peter Watkins and some other film people to come over for dinner, and she wanted to make sure she got it just right.

As she came in Terry met her at the door. "Terry! You're back from 'Nam!"

He only kissed her briefly. His face was grave. He had a telegram in his hand.

"I'm afraid you've had some bad news," he told her tenderly. "It's your mother."

She drove north up the M1, quickly, alone. There had been no reply from her parents' home when she rang, though nothing had been said about hospital in the telegrams. She was worried, even though her mother had always been quietly vigorous – the bedrock of family life, indestructible. What could harm somebody who had never been ill in her life? The windscreen wipers clicked as she drove through a shower somewhere past Nottingham.

It was after dusk when she reached Tyneside. She pulled off the road and found a telephone box, but there was still no reply from home.

Eventually, she drove straight to the hospital that was close to their new house and left her black car outside. The complex of buildings was concrete and plate glass and plastic; soulless and intimidating. It took her a long time to find the enquiry desk, and the nurse by the card-index had no entries today under 'L' for Langton.

Maggie was annoyed, and the strip lighting was dazzling. Then something terrible occurred to her. "So either she's been discharged or –"

Dead? Her mother couldn't be dead. No, please.

The nurse's kindly, harrassed face creased. "I'll look at the individual names on the ward-lists."

There was a footfall behind her, too close. She turned quickly. It was her father. She looked at him.

"It's too late, lass." Then his craggy face crumpled.

Maggie whispered it. "When?"

"Your mother died an hour ago."

He was crying, painful, tearing sobs. It didn't matter that people in the foyer were looking at them. She took her father in her arms and started to cry, too. "Oh, Dad! What can we do now?"

"Alex," the voice on the phone said, "I hate to say I told you so – but I did."

"I'll get onto the Stanton Board yet!" Alex snapped. "Listen, the STA-2 cancellation and this devaluation have really hit the firm. Okay, they're both one-off events, but they add up to a serious loss. I'm going to put it to Hugh that he has a rights issue – puts out more shares which I'll guarantee to take. The only alternative to that is for SI to borrow more, and he wouldn't want to do that."

"Why not?"

"Well, cowboy, that would really give Beauford the power of life and death over our company. Hugh's wily enough not to want that."

"Does Hugh have a choice?" Hacker sighed. "Anyway, I still have a place for you, here at our headquarters in Dover, Delaware."

"And you still have good deals."

"Dead right. Listen, you did really well with the Israelis before the Six-Day War. It was like they owed you something."

Alex laughed. It was true that his old contact in Mossad had introduced him personally to most of the high-ranking Israeli leaders. "You're fishing for information, aren't you? Well, it used to be you who told me how this business works on strict confidentiality."

"Right." Ray's laughed rumbled for a moment. "Listen, the Pentagon want to work off-shore to ship more weapons to the 'Nam theatre. Laos, Cambodia, you know. Shipments off the books. You agree?"

"Of course, Ray. I know it's easy shipping to South East Asia – *and* they pay in U.S. dollars . . ." Alex calculated. "I'll get onto Hugh on Monday; I'm afraid there's no one around at the weekend. A consignment of that size isn't any problem, though. What about the new airline?"

"A dozen pilots, with back-up; nearly all ex-military. The CIA should love them," Ray said. "Only this time I don't want to do anything through Saigon."

"I agree. I was thinking of Phnom Penh."

"We have one of the people you found for us out there, don't we?"

"The Special Forces guy they threw out? That's right. I'll telex him over the weekend, get back to you in person."

"Then I'll see you on Monday night, Alex. Early."

Alex put down the phone, stirred his Earl Grey tea and listened to the commotion on the street. It was a late Sunday afternoon and the strollers were making their way home through Chelsea's civilized streets.

He picked up the revolver from the coffee table, a Stanton .45 calibre 'manstopper', Indian Army issue, manufactured in 1922. He cocked the mechanism. The action was smooth and simple – rather like Hacker-Stanton International's business deals, he thought with a smile. The last two months had seen a number of contracts come in, including a sizeable deal with a mercenary group fighting the MPLA in Angola, but the latest, with a man calling himself 'Mr Soames' they had met in Beirut, had worried him. Alex knew he already had enough enemies in the Middle East.

He looked out of the window, down to where tourists and youths paraded in packs along the street, and suddenly he felt horribly hemmed in. Sarah was away in Fiji, showing her body to some photographer; Hugh was in Lagos again bargaining with Nigerian generals. Even David had taken his wife to Paris for the weekend. He looked around, suddenly annoyed.

This was Sarah's place, and always had been. He was here perhaps half a dozen nights every month; Sarah only a few more.

Sometimes he felt as though he was living inside the pages of a glossy magazine at Sarah's place. Her taste dominated the flat. Since coming to live with her he had felt the decor of the luxuriously appointed penthouse, her domain, to be far too exotic. It wasn't to his taste, and he missed his own comfortable and low-key surroundings. For a moment, he wondered precisely what she was doing, and then decided that he'd rather not know. He loved her. He was too sure of what he felt to question that. But sometimes he did question his own good sense in having fallen in love with someone as erratic and flamboyant as Sarah.

Though he had known her for more than a year now, there were still distances between them. Sarah was aware of that gap, too; and she said she longed to bridge it but could not. Their lives were too separate, kept that way by both their careers, and when they did spend time together they seemed to be incapable of forgetting the rest of the world.

And besides, she was very, very unlike him.

He sighed, wondering if he should make an effort to see more of her. But he had to spend much of his time in America, and she had her own career, too.

The de Soutey fortune was not inconsiderable, founded as it was on the ownership of shipping and publishing interests, yet at times she behaved like a pauper, scolding him for wastefulness. At other times she seemed not to know the value of money. She would spend a thousand pounds on a trinket, and the next day give it away to a charity shop.

She had changed in the months since they had first met, but she was still the most beautiful woman he knew, still a top-flight international model and a favourite with the gossip columnists. She moved in pretentiously artistic circles whose members Alex found almost totally incomprehensible, had learned to ski on one of Ken Russell's movie sets, was invited to studios by François Truffaut, and went shopping with Jane Asher. William Hickey's column had in the past described her as 'a close personal friend' of Mick Jagger. He didn't know whether to believe her when she said she knew the most 'mystical' Beatle intimately, but he wished she'd told him about the

248

affair she'd had with Warren Beatty while he was in Saigon. Instead he'd found out by chance from one of the bitchy queers who hung around the fringes of her world. And there were others she saw, people he didn't approve of, low-lifers and hard, shadowy types who appeared from time to time.

Sarah had begun to worry him. He'd come to realize that her brightness had a dark side.

He heard someone on the steps to their front door, and wondered immediately who had got into the building past the security locks. Alex knew he had enemies . . . He got up and went to the concealed desk drawer where he kept ammunition for his collection of Stanton hand-guns. He pulled out shining brass cartridges and thumbed three into the heavy 45-calibre revolver.

There was a noise at the door; muffled clinkings. Alex stiffened, holding the gun. He turned, the hammer cocked back.

A key jangled in the lock, but it could hardly be Sarah.

Then he heard her call "Hello?"

Delighted, relieved, he locked the gun away and went to greet her.

"Sarah! You're back!" he said, a question hanging in his voice. They squeezed one another and he kissed her.

"A big argument with Jack."

She assumed a look of complete innocence. He knew she meant Jack Slaney, the tyre calendar man whose idea the Fiji trip had been.

"Sarah, you didn't . . ."

She laughed. "He just tried it on once too often, Alex. I had to slap his face."

"And he fired you?"

Straightening up, she said. "No. I fired him."

He loved her in that moment, more than he ever had before. She slipped out of her dress, and kicked off her shoes.

"Be an angel, Alex. Get my robe – the Chinese one."

Obediently, he walked through the apartment, past Japanese screens and hanging plants, to their bedroom with its heavily patterned Afghani rugs. He found the robe, brought it out and held it up for her.

"I want to shower first," she told him.

He followed her to the frosted-glass door and watched her turn the shower on herself. Alex took her extended hand and nibbled at it. Immediately he was sexually excited. She tasted fresh, almost edible.

"I could eat you alive," he said.

When she emerged, her sun-bleached hair was piled up and pinned; a white towel was in her hand. The sight of her firm schoolgirl breasts roused him, then. He wanted to touch her, but she fended him off.

"Not now, Alex. I've got to go somewhere."

"Can't it wait?"

She looked up at him with a suddenly challenging look. "No, it can't wait."

She moved past him, wrapping the robe around her. He followed her into the living room, a little annoyed that her mood had fallen apart again so quickly. He wanted to ask her what was wrong, but knew better.

"No problem," he said lightly.

She bent over the hi-fi and put on Ravi Shankar, then stood back a moment listening to the slow introduction to the *raga*. She swayed, bright-eyed. "India, India, Bombay and Coromandel, Madras, Darjeeling."

He would try to bring round her humour before it turned to coolness again.

"India? Tell me about Fiji."

They had island hopped to uninhabited atolls, gone to Vatukula gold mines and the Blue Lagoon . . . and there had been insects six inches long, and a million other things to tell him about as she combed her hair. He listened as well as he could, then asked her where she was going, casually, as if it was an afterthought.

"I might go to one of Roddie's clubs," she said. "You can come too, if you like. I went to his wedding a couple of years ago. At St James's. David Bailey took the pictures."

"St James's, Piccadilly?" he asked.

She laughed. "No, silly – St James's in Bethnal Green."

"Oh," he said, dismissively. Then, thinking again, "You mean in the *East End*?"

She shot him a glance. "You're such a snob, Alex."

"Can I help it if there are more and more people on the social circuit from unacceptable places?" he said, mocking her. "I mean . . . the East End! You'll be telling me you have friends in Liverpool next."

"Will I?"

He smiled. "Would you mind if I *did* come along?"

"I said you could, didn't I?" She ran her thumbnail down the tines of her comb so that they pinged. "But we'll go somewhere else.

250

Somewhere I can –" She stopped speaking and looked suddenly pale and guilty, like a child.

"What's the matter?"

"Nothing." Sarah looked all about her, not meeting his gaze.

"All right, I'll stay away from 'Roddie'. We'll go somewhere different, anywhere you want."

Outside, Alex handed her into his car and went round to the driver's seat. She was brighter now, almost electric, and he found it hard to know why he had begun, half an hour ago, to dread the thought of their evening out.

He drove up Sloane Street and into Park Lane with the hood down, taking the corner at Marble Arch – where the infamous Tyburn tree had once stood – so quickly that the tyres squealed.

She loved him to drive fast, and she looked out now with bright eyes, at the window displays of the big Oxford Street department stores talking animatedly as they followed Holborn and Newgate Street to Cheapside, in the heart of the Sunday-still City. Sarah waved a hand at a highly ornamented sandstone edifice close to the Bank of England, calling it "Papa's offices". Then she directed him right, and they went over London Bridge itself, into Southwark. Suddenly, they were in south London, in a poorer part of town, where the sky seemed lower and the buildings, some still war-scarred, were more crowded together.

They got out of the car on a sidestreet off the Old Kent Road. Sarah seemed unusually excited as she turned to face him beneath a Victorian streetlight, wearing a look of hungry anticipation.

"Is this right?" Alex asked her dubiously, looking around. There were people hurrying along the street, and to their right was a patch of waste ground, a bombsite left over from the Blitz, another of the wounds of history that no one in this country had tried to heal. She waved a hand airily. Then, as they walked along the cracked pavement together, Alex heard the sound of a jazz trumpet.

"It's just here," Sarah said.

Alex hesitated. Inside the doorway a big man in a ruffled shirt watched them. His nose had been broken pretty conclusively, Alex noted. Surprisingly, he took Sarah's coat, and asked her how she was. His voice had a rough South London tone.

They went through into the main bar and sat down. Alex looked around at a brightly-lit interior that was decorated with garish pink wallpaper. The carpet was a mass of orange and black swirls, and

251

the bar was framed by a tasteless partition of curly wrought iron and patterned glass. People sat at alcove tables, and smoked in groups round a small L-shaped dance-floor.

"I feel like getting drunk," Sarah said.

In response to Alex's order, a bottle of what appeared to be Spanish 'champagne' arrived. A tea towel was wrapped around it obscuring the label, and it sat in a cheap aluminium ice bucket. As the waiter set it down on their table, Sarah got up and excused herself. Then a big man came over and sat in her seat.

"I know you," he said.

Alex looked at him.

The man was heavily built, and the suit he wore was tight on him, as if he was about to burst its seams. His small eyes seemed immobile and lifeless. "I used to run another club, up West."

"Then that's quite possible," Alex said, trying to smile. He put out a hand. "Alex Stanton. How do you do?"

"Very pleased to meet you, Mr Stanton," the man said, expressionlessly. "I'm Roddie. Roddie Fredericks. My friends call me Roddie."

Alex shook the man's strong hand. Ronnie Fredericks. He wondered if it was the man's real name.

"Worrying, you coming here with Sarah," he said glassily.

"I'm sorry?" Alex said.

The man scratched his huge jaw and laughed. "Especially after last time . . ."

He made Alex feel he had to reply. He was about to make a remark when the uninvited conversationalist said, "The last bloke she brought here called me a poofter behind my back. I didn't like that. He won't do it again. But I can see you've got good manners, Mr Stanton."

This time Alex's smile was more than a little forced. Even when the big man laughed at his own comment, it was a humourless, rather cold laugh that chilled Alex. It isn't worth the risk of being smart with this one, he decided. He has a very strange sense of humour, and the physical capacity to indulge it. Whatever else he might be, Alex doubted that he was queer. Alex began to reply when without warning the man snapped his fingers. Alex stopped in mid-sentence.

The young waiter came back to their table.

"Take this gnat's-piss away, Lenny. This is Mr Stanton. Don't you know that?"

The waiter scurried away and returned with a bottle of Dom Perignon. Sarah was still nowhere to be seen. The big man

252

forced the cork out of the bottle and poured Alex a shallow glass full.

"Mr Fredericks, what's your –?"

"Roddie. All my friends call me Roddie."

"Well, Roddie, what's your line of business?" Alex enquired, looking round.

"Business?" the man replied. He lifted his arm, to indicate the club, but the action pulled aside his jacket to reveal a shoulder holster from which the butt of a .45 automatic protruded. "This is my business."

"That's a coincidence," Alex said as pleasantly as he could. All his instincts were telling him there was danger here. "It's my business too."

The man stood up, snapped his fingers. Another man came up. "My driver," Fredericks said. He smiled. "I think I've kept you long enough."

Alex nodded politely and watched the heavy-set man leave. Then he looked around once again for Sarah, this time with growing concern. She had been away over twenty minutes and there was something going on that he did not like. Finally, he looked at his watch, stood up.

The toilets were in a short brightly lit corridor, their doors facing one another. Since he was out of sight, he decided to push the door to the ladies room ajar and shout her name. But before he could do so, the broken-nosed man came out, grinning.

"I think you'd better go back where you came from."

Alex stopped, raised one eyebrow; the man was challenging him. "What do you mean?"

"You 'eard. Or else I'll have to do something about you."

Alex raised both hands. "I don't want any trouble."

"I didn't think your sort would."

Alex smashed him under the jaw, an uppercut that lifted the man onto his toes, hit him twice, quickly, in the midriff and then straight in the face – very hard. The man slumped backwards against the wall, his eyes wide open and dazed, blood trickling between broken teeth.

"Nobody tells me what to do." There was anger in him; a blazing, intestinal rage. "*Nobody*."

Somebody came down the passageway behind him. Alex stood up quickly, light-headed with anger, his knuckles raw. The couple backed away. He had terrified them. He looked down and saw there was blood all over his suit.

253

Then he kicked open the door marked with a female outline.

Inside the brightly-lit powder room he saw something that made him stop dead.

Sarah was standing against the mirror, her back to the tiled washstands. Her purse was beside her and banknotes had spilled out of it. In front of her kneeled a short dark-haired man in a leather jacket, holding tightly to her elbow. She was glowing with pleasure. In the man's other hand was a glass syringe.

The syringe was full of blood.

Alex drove her home.

When they had been thrown out of the night club, Sarah's empty bag tossed after them, he had been white-faced with rage, but there had been nothing further he could do except pull her in beside him in the Jaguar. She had both hands in her hair and her face was tragic. "Alex, you've spoiled everything – they're my friends!"

"Friends!"

A man came up before Alex could roar off noisily into the night. "You, Stanton, you're bloody banned!"

Alex remembered somebody involved with this club was armed; he started the engine, saying nothing.

"You think we over-charged the bint – why don't you call the police?"

The jeering question followed them from the club and spun round in his head all the way back up town. It was a futile question, because the answer was obvious, and painful.

If it came out that Sarah was a heroin addict it would be the end of her. Alex turned the wheel viciously, cornering sharply. He could imagine the pack of tabloid reporters hanging round their door like hyenas if the news got out about Sarah's addiction. Within a week, he knew, they would have stripped away from her whatever self-esteem she still possessed, and then no power on earth, not even his love, would be able to help her.

She started to cry. "If you really loved me you wouldn't spoil things for me! I have to do it, don't you understand!"

"No, I don't understand. Why didn't you tell me? Maybe I could help, even now."

She was sobbing heartrendingly. "You help me? You don't even know me, and you care less – you're only interested in your own business, Alex, guns and money and guns, you bastard, and the only word you know is 'me'!"

"That isn't true!"

"Master of Business Administration! Master! Business!" She jeered at him.

He twisted the wheel. "I'm not like that."

She laughed. "Look in the mirror. Look into your soul."

He wiped his face and found that despite the cool night he was sweating. He doubted if Sarah realized just how much she meant to him. He looked at her and made a promise to himself as he drove past St Paul's. After tonight, it would all be different; he would give her more, give her anything she asked for. Not even Stanton Industries was worth the life of the woman he loved. If she had believed in him more, she might have come to him for help instead of hiding the dark secret of her addiction. For a moment, after he had turned into the King's Road, he closed his eyes.

Maybe, in a way, Sarah's habit was his fault. His fault for not showing her just how much she meant to him. His fault for not spending more time with her. He had been selfish and ambitious and blind, just as he had been with Maggie.

He helped her from the car and put her on the leather sofa. He looked down on her. "Listen," he said, "I'll change. If that's what you really want. And I'll put you in a clinic, get you over this. Do you have any addresses?"

She shook her head, not looking at him.

"But you're going to have to work at this, Sarah. Do you want to?"

This time she nodded, her eyes still averted.

He felt better already. The situation was under control. Pain ignored was pain abolished.

She whispered something he didn't catch. He squatted down in front of her, smiling. "I'm sorry?"

"I thought you were so strong. I thought . . ." She looked at him. He could not read her face. "My body. Not me."

He tried to make a joke of it. "I make love to all of you, don't I? Body and soul."

"You don't understand me at all, do you? And you don't want to."

"Oh," he said brusquely, "you mustn't think like this. You need a good doctor to set you to rights."

She closed her eyes. "I'm tired."

255

He put her to bed, agonizing long and hard about whether he should call a doctor. But she was sleeping peacefully now; she had opened her eyes languidly and smiled at him before lying back like a sleeping princess on the black silk pillows. It was as if for her the horrors of the evening had not really happened. For Alex, it was too real; a nightmare that left him dazed and cold with fatigue. Even in a place so well-policed as London, there were men with guns, drugs outside the law. He remembered stories he had heard about Sarah's other friends. Perhaps a word to his godfather in the Home Office . . . He arranged Sarah's hair tenderly about her head, kissed her forehead, and climbed in beside her.

Things had to change. He had to get things straight with Hugh, finish his time at Harvard Business School, then make it right for Sarah.

When he woke up later that morning, the room was cold. Through the open window the noise of rush hour traffic filtered through his hangover, abrasive like grains of sand in his head. Fractured memories began to coalesce, and he rolled over. The space beside him was empty. He felt panic gripping him.

Then it wasn't just a bad dream.

He called out for her, but there was no reply. He staggered to the bathroom and paused at the door, feeling faint and nauseous. Then he saw the bright blood-red slashes across the bathroom mirror and for a moment thought it really was blood, coagulated, from an addict's syringe. Then he read the words and realized they had been written in lipstick.

"No!" He bit into his knuckle until it bled again, but he knew it was the end. She had gone to India with her troubles and her addiction, and left him behind for good.

She left a last word. *Goodbye.*

Alex realized, numbed, he might as well start packing before moving back to Knightsbridge. He had lost her, and Sarah had lost herself.

4

Maggie put down her coffee cup and tried not to think about Sarah de Soutey and Alex. But it was hard. The scandal surrounding the famous model's death from drugs was in all the papers.

Sarah had died in a squalid commune in Agra called Third Eye, and Alex had vanished, some said to America.

It was a bad business, Maggie thought – the dark side of the self-exploratory, self-indulgent Sixties.

"Let's talk about serious money," she said to the meeting.

There were psychedelic posters on the walls of the crowded *Capital Life* office – modern icons in day-glo paint, Marx, Che Guevara, Hendrix and the rest. She looked down the long cluttered table at her colleagues as they came resentfully to order.

Three days before, she had been with most of them outside the American Embassy building in Grosvenor Square, fighting to get in and drape a North Vietnamese flag over the big gilded eagle that perched on the roof. But as she'd watched the lines of bobbies linking arms, she'd thought of the young people who two months earlier had been shot down in front of Russian tanks in the streets of Prague, and the stark contrast had struck a dissonant chord in her.

"I think the money aspect is secondary, y'know," Moondancer said, giggling. He was the listings editor, and too often completely stoned, and over the last few weeks she had seen more and more errors in his work.

The others – mostly men – looked at him. It was a curious split, Maggie thought. The party people and the party political people. Easy-going, colourful, inefficient; narrow, humourless, intriguing. She sighed. There had to be a way of bringing everything together.

"Listen," she said suddenly, "the advertising income has been steadily dropping since the Christmas rush – it's down fourteen per cent on what it was last year. Like it or not, we need the advertisers, so I suggest we really try to get our act together and present the –"

"Let's raise the cover price," Stella said. She stared at Maggie demurely. "More bread."

Maggie shook her head. "Uh-huh – and sales go down, so in the end, less income. Even worse, Stella, it opens the door to the competition."

Moondancer said, "Why's the talk always about competing, man? Things are just fine."

"Balls," Maggie said. "Don't you understand? Our magazine is on the brink of failure – we have to save it, have to!"

"Hey now, Maggie." Kai, the general manager, wore a striped T-shirt and a ring in his ear and looked like a pirate king. He turned to the others and backed her up in his own smooth, sweet way. "I hate to be so basic as to talk about the bread, but the overdraft's real uncool at the moment. Forty-eight thousand, and those guys at Barclays hate my ass."

"Then again," Maggie went on, "suppose we did want to change our printer, we'd need money to settle our old account with the Holborn people. But there can be a lot of success to be had from publishing if you go at it right."

Maggie stared at her colleagues. The air was fuggy with joss-sticks and dope haze and the pulsating colours of the decor.

"I really don't think we can go on like this," she said harshly. "Every week our wages bill goes up but less is produced – less that's good, anyway. I think our staff ought to be cut by twenty-five per cent, and we really ought to make the effort to change printers. Look, the way we're going, we're heading for bankruptcy!"

Stella raised a finger. "Those guys in the printshop are our friends, Maggie."

Maggie shrugged. "Tell it to Barclays Bank."

Kai scratched his beard. "I don't think there's enough money in *Capital Life* to let us do that, Maggie."

She drew breath and leaned over the cluttered table. "I'll find the money. I'll write off thirty thousand of our debts and I'll make myself reponsible for changing printers. But there's a big 'if' – I want us to switch from being a co-operative to being a limited company."

Stella threw her pencil across the room. "Fuck you, bitch! You just want control!"

Maggie stared back, loathing her. "That's right. I'm sick to death of having responsibility without power, of pouring in hour after hour of unpaid work, and writing off my own money too!"

She pushed her papers back into their cardboard wallet and stood up straight. "I'm through with this crap. This magazine's going to do the business – or be mercy-killed. There is no alternative. If you don't like my offer – get the money yourselves!"

"Oh, I was forgetting." This time Alex's smile was radiant. "Congratulations."

"Thanks. I had to hurry back from a conference in Moscow for the birth."

"Moscow? Not more bloody socialism!" Alex's expression rather than his tone made it a joke. "Have you named the baby yet?"

"Megan's suggestion. Naomi – it means 'the pleasant one'."

"That's a lovely name, David. You must be very proud."

"I am," David answered simply. He remembered beaming down at the tiny, newborn child cradled in his arms, and laughing with joy.

"She's beautiful, love," he told his wife. "So . . ." Words had failed him.

Megan smiled at him, watching him from her hospital bed, and reached out to take the child back from him. The curtains were closed around her bed. "She is, but she's also hungry, so hand her back, will you?"

David had looked at them, mother and daughter, and felt himself blessed. He was a family man now, properly.

Alex lifted his two suitcases, as a large-bottomed American lady went by. Then he put them down, just before check-in, and turned to his old friend. He looked that little bit older, now.

"I just have some business things to work through with Ray."

"I understand." David stretched out his hand; Alex held onto it. "I'm sorry about Sarah. I see why you want to leave for a while. Good luck."

When David got back to the office he shared with Frank, there was some good news from Stanton Industries – Rolls Royce consortium. Lockheed had finally signed them up for the billion-pound contract; the new engines, backed by £400 million of government money, would be put into production.

"Thank God for that," David said.

"The relevant minister managed to squeeze a little more government assistance out of the Treasury bods."

"That's very interesting, Frank," David said. "Identifying the party with advanced technology is the way to go."

David was an invited guest when the Prime Minister recorded his unctuous New Year's address, promising that 1969 would see more social benefits; but the economy was in such straits that it seemed an obviously empty promise and David was impatient. Few people believed the reforms would materialize, and there were those who now seriously doubted his political will.

David was one of them. "Frank, this can't go on."

The older man gave a grim smile. "You and your namesake ought to get together."

"Who? Oh, David Owen, you mean."

"I read that speech you gave to the Tribune group. Impressive grasp of economic detail, David."

"Well, we have to get it right. Next year we stand to import an extra thousand millions pounds sterling of manufactured goods; soon the trade gap will be intolerable. Look at shipbuilding, for example. As recently as 1950 we built almost half the ships launched. And now –". He shook his head.

"Your friends the Stantons have certainly been having problems."

"They'll get worse," David predicted. Hoyle had been using his influence in the unions to make sure of that. Drummond, the local head of the Shipbuilding Division, had tried to close an obsolete yard on Wearside, for which there was no work. The unions had threatened a complete shut-down, and Stanton Industries had retreated; the yard was still open – and the workers still idle.

Frank grimaced suddenly, and bent forward. David got up, concerned. "Are you all right, Frank? You look a little pale."

"Indigestion," Frank said.

"There's a lot happening today I can't swallow either."

It soon became clear to David that the Prime Minister, in spite of the good intentions he claimed, could not prevail: the trade gap was widening. The only thing that remained firm in his policies was the rhetoric. Indeed there were already rumours in the corridors of power that he might be deposed by a Cabinet coup.

David was appalled: efficiency had to come to Britain, but the party was split and ineffective. When the grey eminences of the TUC stepped in and gave a 'solemn and binding undertaking' to reduce strikes, the laughter and derision that greeted the government's climb-down echoed around the nation. David realized that this government, the one for which he had worked so long and so hard, was rapidly becoming a spent force. It was unable to resist the hard Left, and unable to modernize the country. The decline would go on, and in the next pay round the country would be plunged into more hopeless turmoil.

And yet with so much goodwill in the world towards Britain, so much talent and technical know-how in the country, so much wealth and influence still to be found in London, the decline was a paradox. Surely there were others who could see that, others who cared for their country? But nothing was being done, and the internecine rifts between those with power and those who wanted to take it from them were bursting wider. It seemed to David to be criminal negligence taken to the point of treason.

The 2nd March, 1969, would be a big day for the Aircraft Division of Stanton Industries.

Alex flew from Washington, DC back to Europe, and drove down from Paris; he had stayed overnight in the Hotel George V.

He sighed, approaching the outskirts of Toulouse in his rented BMW, thinking of Sarah, who had been so beautiful. Now she was dead, but he was alive and had to go on. He knew that the only cure for unhappiness was devotion to something other than oneself. Lately he had spent much of his time in America, helping to run Hacker-Stanton International. A success today, he hoped, would rekindle his ambition to do something inside Stanton Industries that would surprise the world.

The meeting with the family did not go well.

Almost as many telephoto lenses were pointed at Alex as at either the test pilot, or the sleek white plane in front of the hangar.

"You shouldn't have come," Hugh chided as he pushed his father's wheelchair into the VIP enclosure. He did not seem pleased that his cousin had made the effort to get to Blagnac airport, and his nerves were obviously unsteady. "I mean, you seem to have become an American these days, what with your ancestry and all this Hacker Stanton business."

"Yes, Alex," Grace echoed. "These photographers are such a nuisance."

261

He looked at his family. "Aunt, I couldn't very well miss today – although I expected a warmer welcome."

The family chauffeur shepherded the group through the gate, shielding Alex from as many prying camera lenses as he could with his back. Even so, reporters called out questions.

"Now we have a celebrity in the family," Sir Edward said, trying to raise himself to good cheer. Sardonic humour was the closest he came to joviality these days. The progressive slackening of the muscles following his stroke had given the corner of his mouth a downturn that most people initially interpreted as an expression of disgust. Alex remembered what he was supposed to have done to Maggie's father, all those years before – and what his son had done to Maggie. He turned away, wondering if the Langtons would forgive him, if they saw him now. His uncle still jeered at him, belittling him. "The French press must think you're a person of some importance!"

Alex tried to shrug it off. "Sarah was well known in France. It'll blow over." He knew that there had been pictures of her in the ramshackle commune near the Taj published in *Paris Match* that week. Even though they had been taken months ago, the thought of them tormented him. He would never see her again, and she had been so beautiful.

Watching the press, Alex was reminded of Maggie and her articles about the Stantons. He said harshly, "Look at them trying to turn me into a star. The gun-runner with the junkie girlfriend. Why don't they just leave people alone!"

Grace reached across and squeezed his arm, trying a bleak smile for his benefit, but she was uncomfortably cold after waiting in the March wind, and found it hard to express warmth. He saw Sir Edward try to wink, but he only succeeded in expelling a tear from his eye.

Alex composed his raw-edged emotions as best he could, and turned to the matter in hand: Concorde, and their involvement with Rolls Royce in making the plane fly.

He looked about at their hosts.

A crowd of townspeople lined the roof of the terminal. Toulouse had staked its claim to a piece of aviation history two centuries before when the Montgolfier brothers had ascended in their balloon from its town square. Now, he saw the French test pilot, dressed in his leather jacket, go down the tarmac beside the sleek white aircraft.

He motioned Hugh towards him, and said, jerking a thumb at the runway, "This ought to show the world we mean business, eh?"

262

"It certainly will."

"Maybe – if it all goes well. I understand from Ray that matters are coming to a head in Seattle. Nixon's calling for facts about civil flight faster than sound, and the people on his committee aren't telling him what he wants to hear. They don't think going supersonic will be commercially viable."

"Nonsense!" Hugh said sharply. "Economics is not the difficulty, only that the Boeing people over in Seattle have massive problems with that over-ambitious swing-wing design of theirs!"

Alex raised an eyebrow. "The American public are bridling at the thought of unlimited sums of money being poured into the project."

Hugh's eyelids quivered. "They can afford it even more than we can. A hundred million dollars is nothing on Capitol Hill. Nixon knows they can't cancel the SST before we cancel Concorde without losing face. And we are not going to cancel!"

Alex rubbed his hands together and showed some of his impatience. "Perhaps they're more concerned over making a profit than maintaining face."

Hugh turned away, anxious to withhold from Alex any opportunity to resume his pursuit of their standing argument on the direction Stanton Industries ought to be taking. "The Russians are still building: that alone should keep the U.S. in the hunt. Anyway, our Concorde is still a superb plane."

"But will it *sell*?"

Hugh said nothing, and Alex backed off from a confrontation. Though the Stanton Armaments Division was again in a reasonable state of profitability, the Shipbuilding Division was losing money, and in the aftermath of the STA-2 cancellation, the Aircraft Division was in danger of collapse. Alex could not resist it. He still remembered that day in Oxford when he had read the views of Maggie and David on Stanton Industries. They had predicted disaster. That day had changed his life, given him purpose, and a glimpse of greatness.

"Hugh, what about the engine projects we're working on with Rolls Royce?"

Hugh turned away. "What of it?"

"Ray's contacts in Lockheed say the contract's in trouble."

Hugh turned back suddenly, his features quivering with rage. "Don't you ever say that in public again! What are you trying to do, destroy all confidence in Stanton Industries and Rolls Royce?"

"Of course not," Alex answered toughly. "I'm asking a straight question, in private, and I'd like a straight answer."

Hugh wiped at his lips. "If there are any financial problems, the banks will assist us. Lord Beauford is a good friend."

Alex shook his head. Things had come to this? Charity. He said so.

Hugh would not be moved: Concorde was the way ahead; the Americans were wrong; the STA-2 was an unfortunate piece of bad luck . . . But Alex knew they couldn't live on Hugh's valiant sales of STA-1 variants to the Third World much longer.

Three men approaching caught Alex's eye. An upright figure in a dark overcoat and blue scarf headed towards the Stanton group. He was accompanied by a taller, thinner man, gaunt and grey and inconspicuous, who wore a tweed jacket, and who seemed unwilling to make eye contact. The third was a hard-faced much younger man who followed the second man closely. Together they made an odd couple. Alex recognized the first and raised a hand to acknowledge Peter Carlton, whom he remembered from the security scare at the Bristol engine plant.

"That damned east wind!" Carlton said, looking down the runway balefully. "That's what's been holding us all up for the past two days."

The security man seemed a little troubled; and from Alex's view, his downturned nose seemed even more distorted than usual, adding a sinister element to his appearance.

Hugh moved over to greet him.

"Peter – how are things? Pity it's not our man taking 002 up, eh?"

Carlton looked to the gaunt man, who moved away, still saying nothing. Carlton turned, shook hands with Hugh, then leaned forward to do the same with Alex.

The gaunt man shifted his weight uneasily. He remained detached. There was something curiously uneasy in the atmosphere.

Alex remembered the thin-faced man from his boyhood days as Donald Pike, the designer responsible for the STA-1, and later, the overall concept of the STA-2. He had been with the firm since the Forties, and had been involved in the Concorde project from the beginning.

Alex took a step towards the man, but Carlton put a hand in front of his chest. "I wouldn't."

"No?" Alex did not bother concealing his surprise. What was Carlton shielding? He began to think furiously, recalling that Pike had been taken off the military project at just the time the American deal had gone sour and the project had been terminated. Had there been a security scandal? A cover-up? Carlton had hinted as much when Alex had met him at the Stanton aircraft plant outside Bristol.

Now, Pike was being treated like a pariah. Alex watched the man carefully, and saw fear in his face. What could explain Carlton's curious behaviour towards him? Alex wondered, and then his deliberations were set aside as the aircraft was brought to the end of the runway.

This time, instead of the anticlimax as Concorde braked to a halt on the runway, Turcat opened the throttles.

The noise was stupendous. The magnificent white dart continued to forge down the runway, accelerating. Black exhaust flared from the engines, and blasts of orange light shot into view as it passed them with an immense, crackling roar that made the earth shake. Then the nose-wheel lifted and everyone held their breath, until the main undercarriage followed it up off the runway.

There was sudden, spontaneous cheering. The plane was airborne at last. It was beautiful. They had done it.

Alex breathed it. "Oh, but it's magnificent . . ."

"Olympus engines," Hugh said proudly. "Rolls Royce and Stanton Industries working together – the cream of the British engineering industry."

But Alex had seen the divisional accounts; and he knew how many millions of pounds had been poured into the Concorde project. Boeing had just flown their first 747. Alex had an uneasy feeling he could already tell which plane would be the commercial success.

Within half an hour, the test pilot was standing proudly on the tarmac, embracing the president of Sud Aviation, shaking hands with Hugh and Sir George Edwards of BAC. Alex imagined the eight Pan Am Concordes that would soon be plying the route to North America – if Hugh's predictions were correct. It was a marvellous vision, one that filled him with pride and satisfaction, but it was a vision in which he couldn't fully believe. The costs of Concorde, like its predecessor the Stanton Comet, were more than sky-high, and like his ancestors Alex was very aware of the bottom line: profit, or loss.

He looked across at his uncle, at the lop-sided smile that had broken out down one side of his face, and he knew that this time the tear he saw on his cheek was one of pure emotion.

As the crowds began to disperse, Alex asked Peter Carlton to accompany him. They crossed the smooth tarmac, and Alex made a comment that caused Carlton to look up sharply.

"How long has Donald Pike been *persona non grata*?"

"What did you say?"

"You heard me, Peter. I was wondering what a good investigative journalist might make of this business over Pike – not to mention the links between STA-2 and Concorde."

They were well out of earshot, and Carlton stopped and took out a packet of Senior Service from his pocket, making a cage of his hands as he lit up and sucked on the cigarette.

"You wouldn't really go to the press?"

Alex toughed it out. "Ring up somebody like Maggie Langton? Only if you lie to me, Peter. Now, what's been happening to my uncle's chief designer?"

"I wouldn't give sixpence for the state of that man's soul."

For no reason he could specify Alex immediately thought of his father's plane, the STA-C, breaking up over Long Island. But that had been an accident. "What do you mean, exactly?"

"Donald Pike was caught giving away highly classified design details to the Russians. He's a traitor."

Alex was appalled. "Christ, you mean that's why the Americans cancelled their STA-2 order? That man cost us three hundred million dollars!" Alex stared in disbelief. "Then why . . . ?"

"Why isn't he in Parkhurst Prison? Well, you see, he's still a very talented designer, and a very useful route to Moscow."

"I don't follow."

Carlton sighed. "Traitors can generally be persuaded to turn and turn again. We took him off military hardware right away, of course, but he still talks to the Kremlin about Concorde – if you understand what I mean."

"You mean he's a channel to feed disinformation to Moscow?" Alex's lips curled in disgust. "I've heard a story the Russian TU-144 is, through industrial espionage, based on Concorde."

"We can't keep any secrets in our country any more!" Carlton looked savage for a moment. "But this time all their espionage will pick up is a pack of lies."

266

Alex nodded, all his muscles taut. This was another thing he had been excluded from. "Does my cousin know?"

"Of course, Alex. One more secret that must be painful to keep."

Alex did not feel compassion for anybody involved in this mess. "So Pike will get away with his treachery!"

Carlton's eyes were cold. "He thinks so. You'd be very surprised, Alex, at some of the promises my predecessors made not to prosecute traitors."

"So you promised –"

"I'd promise the earth to a traitor to get him to talk. But it would be an empty promise. Understand?"

Alex nodded. Carlton had made a puppet of Donald Pike; and he would not let Pike escape. "I'd be as ruthless myself. More so."

"I'm sure. I've heard those stories about your involvement in the Middle East." Carlton gave a sweet, disingenuous smile. "As for Pike; if there is a trial, it will be held *in camera*; though you may be interested in the names of his associates . . . And anyway, who is going to believe the word of a self-confessed spy? I didn't promise Pike immunity in front of his lawyer."

"Three hundred million dollars . . . That almost brought the company down, Peter. And that man still draws his salary and stands here among us."

Something Carlton had said surfaced in Alex's memory. Hands clasped behind him, he turned to the other man. "What was that about this traitor's associates?"

Carlton hesitated. "The tip-off came from a source called 'Keyhole'. Mean anything?"

Alex shook his head.

"No, of course not," Carlton said, very much as if something had been confirmed. "Our source named the original Eastern bloc contact as Franz Schaller; but he had diplomatic immunity, and expulsion is a joke to people like that. We think there was an intermediary, though . . . somebody who seems quite close to a good friend of yours."

Alex laughed. "I hardly think we move in the same circles."

"No?" Carlton said, a sudden harshness in his voice. "Then try *this* name on your acquaintances."

Alex raised an eyebrow.

"Alan Hoyle."

"I think I remember –"

"Or David Bryant."

"*What?*" Alex went cold.

"Don't trust that man. I think David Bryant is playing a double game; his heart is really with the other side."

Alex could not believe it, but as he looked hard at Peter Carlton, he was uneasily aware that he would not care to have an enemy like that – and David was far more vulnerable than he was.

There were no papers today. The printers were striking, along with other unions, against the government's anti-strike proposals. Alan Hoyle was very happy, and was hoping the electricians would be next. David sighed, imagining the country plunged into darkness, and went to the florist's.

Every time Megan came up to London he tried to make it an occasion for her. Today he put fresh flowers in the living room and he had two bottles of Chablis cooling in the refrigerator. Picture postcards that friends had sent him brightened the wall beside his IBM electric typewriter – Ayers Rock, Toulouse with Concorde over it, an aerial view of Rio, the bronze mermaid in Copenhagen. One day, they would both go to such places, but for the moment there was work to be done.

The really damning material on Forward was locked securely in a bank vault and updated each week, but his notebook contained cryptic details sensitive enough to warrant locking away. He looked at his watch; it was almost noon. He tidied away his file, and locked the notebook in his desk drawer before leaving for Paddington.

Megan would be here for over a week. They had decided that Naomi could be left with Megan's mother. David's cramped flat, which was also his workplace, wasn't suitable for the child.

Megan arrived on the 12.45 train and came through the ticket barrier in a summer dress, looking as lovely as ever – though a trifle less self-possessed than he remembered her in Fishguard. She looked good as always, but the capital and the provinces of 1969 were certainly different worlds.

David noted her make-up, and the fact that she had her hair styled like Jane Fonda, but as she came smiling towards him David felt a momentary pang of guilt. She couldn't be put off forever with his pep-talks about the price of success. He was sure she would have brought with her half a dozen more adverts from the *Nursing Times* offering positions in the big London hospitals. She embraced him quickly, pecked at his cheek and looked him up and down.

"Well," she said, noting his expensive suit and gold cufflinks, "quite the man about town, aren't you?"

David looked away. "It's a necessary part of the image. If I'm to move up in the Big City, I can't afford to look like riff-raff."

He took her two small leather cases, and she linked arms. "That's a fine thing for Uncle Frank's protégé to say."

"Of course," he said, soothingly, and led her quickly to the Tube entrance. "How's Naomi? How's your mother keeping?"

He had thought of taking her to a West End show, but finally settled for the Swiss Cottage Odeon, and a re-run of *From Russia With Love*. She sat quietly through it as Sean Connery taught several women and numerous Russians and Bulgarians the facts of life, but later over the Peking duck in a Soho restaurant she seemed to be struggling to make him hear her.

"I'm listening," he told her, automatically charming, but behind his smile he wondered if he was lying to his wife.

"If only you would," she said brokenly. "I love you, David. I want to be with you. Is that so hard to understand?"

"Of course it isn't. Megan, I love you. It's simply that I have so much on my mind."

"Your work, you mean?" she said accusingly. "You never talk about it to me."

"Of course I do."

"No, you drop some names from time to time. That's a very different thing."

He still found it difficult to come to terms with her moods and passions, even after three years of marriage. He picked at his dinner without zest and listened with ill-grace, then remembered himself and gave her another bright, artificial smile.

"Did you like the film?"

"Sean Connery's so attractive."

"Strange how people like to believe in James Bond, isn't it?" he said. "It's as though we're clinging to the myth of British Imperialism. We may not have an Empire any more, but we're still there, behind the scenes, discreetly pulling all the strings. Then you look at all the scandals – Philby, Blake, the others –" He shook his head.

"You think about such things often?"

"Yes, and I'm starting to think that it's all an Establishment con-trick. In every way you can measure, this country is going down and down and down."

269

Megan was taken aback by his vehemence. "I think people watch James Bond films for the travel and adventure. Everyone wants a bit of escape now and again."

"Entertainment is more than that," he insisted. "It's mythology. I see the 007 myth as cold war comfort. The real people in state security, our side and theirs, are bastards. They have to be. And I'm starting to think the KGB bastards are the competent ones and they really are going to win."

She looked at him over her egg fried rice. "That's what you really do, isn't it?"

Instantly he closed off. "What do you mean?"

"Is that why you and Uncle Frank don't let me come to London?" she asked. "I heard you tell him in Wales that you had men watching your flat all through March."

David breathed deeply, turning his head from side to side as if her moving was something that was already settled between them. "London's a big and dangerous place, Megan. It's full of people who want to succeed, and if it doesn't make you, it breaks you. If I'm going to make it, I must work. I need time."

"That's what you told me when you wanted to be an actor," she said, barely concealing her reproach. "You've had three years. You can't be a weekend husband forever."

"Lots of MPs do it."

"David, you're not an MP!"

"No. But I've decided I'm going to try to be."

"Then I'll help you. Here in London, if this is where you want to live."

He tried another tack. "During the week I have to work very long hours."

She looked at him, her lips pinched together. "Even with Naomi, I could work in London and earn money, David. I could."

"It's not the money!" Though David felt angry, he couldn't tell her the risks she and their daughter might run if they shared his life here. What if Hoyle and all those dangerous men he controlled ever turned against him, or his family? He did not like the answer he was forced to give. "You know how small the flat is, Megan. There's hardly enough room for me as it is; how could I work with the TV on and Naomi demanding attention?"

"Then we'll move," she said. "We could easily get a bigger place if you were prepared to move a bit further out."

"Without your mother to baby-sit, and you working shifts, we'd see each other even less than we do now. Is that what you want?"

"I don't want what we have now," she said firmly. "You're missing your daughter's childhood."

David was scared that one day his work against Hoyle would backfire; he did not want Megan and his daughter frightened or endangered. "Perhaps you should ask Uncle Frank's opinion."

She put out her hand and touched his knuckles gently. "I already have. But I don't care what he says. I've applied to St Thomas's. I'm tired of waiting, David."

Her brown eyes looked into his, and he turned away from the challenge of her gaze.

The next time she came up to London it was with Naomi under her arm and a suitcase in her hand. "I've got that job at Thomas's Hospital," she said. She had come for good, and none of David's arguments had been able to dissuade her.

They put a deposit on a small terraced house in Shepherd's Bush and moved in a leather three-piece suite and a big rented colour TV set. David borrowed some tools and turned the spare room into an office. He put up shelves and attached stout Banham locks to the doors and windows. By midsummer they'd got back into a routine of sorts, but they both took a break from their cares on one particular night.

Maggie appeared on television, interviewing the new head of the PLO. She had flown to Beirut to do it.

"That's one up for your friend Maggie," Megan said, with a trace of envy. "What do you think will happen to Israel?"

"There'll be more problems, Megan. I only hope some kind of compromise can be cobbled together. That's the only thing which will bring peace to the Middle East – but I suspect the men in power in Moscow at the moment want to de-stabilize the area."

Megan said, apparently guilelessly, 'Maggie looked very sincere and attractive, didn't she?"

"She wants to get into film-making; documentaries to begin with. I can't help thinking this is a bad night for her debut, though."

Megan had changed channels again, pausing to marvel at what the screen brought into their living room. "I suppose you're right. I know what people will be remembering tomorrow morning."

"Look at it," David said. He was openly amazed now.

They were both held by the most astonishing sights ever to pass across a television screen.

Each image transcended the last: an unforgettable picture of Earth seen from space, lovely, liquid blues and hazy browns, oceans and continents with no political boundaries and no hint of man's works. Then the view changed again to the ancient lunar plains on which two human shapes saluted the flag of the United States.

Megan sat beside him, cradling a mug of coffee on her knees. Along with a billion and a half other watchers, they stared at the TV screen, listening to the matter-of-fact technical small talk of Houston.

"I can hardly believe it," she breathed. "It's incredible."

David rubbed the back of his neck. "The work of half a million people, twenty-five billion dollars . . ."

"Oh, but it's worth it," she said.

"I wonder if the people waiting for kidney machines would agree with you," he said suddenly.

She turned to him in annoyance then, unhappy for the spell to be broken. "And there's enough money being spent on atom bombs in this world for a thousand moon landings. Why didn't you think of that?"

"Yes, you're right," he said soberly. "Sorry."

"20th of July, 1969 – a great day for all the world," she told him. "And you can underline that in red in your bloody appointments book if you want."

David watched it all, torn right down the middle. He wanted to share Megan's enthusiasm, and admit the wonder in this supreme moment of history, which would make the name America live forever, but he had to be careful. His job was to say only those things people like Hoyle wanted to hear, and to say them as if he believed them – and that meant saying them in private to Megan.

Her eyes narrowed. "Sometimes I think you get more like that nasty, cynical Alan Hoyle every day."

"Do I?"

"No," she said, considering. "It's like another act. I've come to know you, David Bryant. I'd just like to know why you still put on the act! What's Alan Hoyle to you, anyway?"

She was, in every sense, coming much too close to home.

272

"Supposing –" He found himself wanting to tell her everything.

She wrinkled her nose again. The two astronauts bounced across the sea of dust that had been dead for a billion years. "Supposing what?"

"Supposing I brought down the baby oil – would you let me massage it into you?" His eyes glinted lasciviously. "All over?"

"Well," she murmured, "I certainly might consider it. If you ask me nicely that is."

He stood up. "Nicely."

"You're sure you're not too busy looking at the moon landing?"

"I could always watch the TV over your shoulder."

"And I could always slap your face!"

"I wouldn't do that," he said, grinning. "You might enjoy yourself too much."

Just before nine in the morning, following the instructions he had been given, he sat in Frank's office and dialled. The ringing tone stopped abruptly and Alan Hoyle's cold, suspicious voice asked, "Who is it?"

David suddenly remembered what his job really was. "It's me," he said, not giving his name. For some reason he felt very tense. "You told me to ring."

"I want you up in Manchester this afternoon. Is that possible?"

"It's important?"

"You can take part, directly, in a Forward action. You can earn our trust, David."

David thought it over swiftly, but knew he was committed. Where, exactly, Hoyle would not say, nor what their mission would be. From the excitement in Hoyle's voice David realized that, at last, he was about to penetrate the heart and soul of the Forward movement.

"You'll see something, David, take part in something vital for once. For the revolution!"

"I'm looking forward to it," David lied.

He put the phone down, thinking of Megan, hiding the sick excitment he felt. He knew that he could not continue to live like this much longer.

Frank came in at nine, carrying a rolled-up copy of *The Times*. He looked at his desk-diary, at David's entry for today.

"So. You have to leave later this morning?"

273

David looked up from the heaped papers on his desk. "That's right, Frank. Still chasing Alan Hoyle, you know. This time to Manchester."

"Is there anything new to report on Forward?"

It felt bad to lie to Frank Deacon. It was difficult, too. Nevertheless, David knew he had to do it, and to do it convincingly enough to disarm the astute Welshman until he had all of the evidence he needed – because David had sensed that Frank was thinking of pulling him out. He could not let that happen. Not yet, with no chance of actually getting Hoyle convicted. "Nothing in particular."

"You've met some of their top people, haven't you?"

He cleared a space on his cluttered desk. "Only a couple. They're very cautious, very capable. But Alan Hoyle really is the key. I'm sure of it. Even mentioning his name to the security services led them to Franz Schaller and some other people."

Frank took off his glasses. "My friend – George, I'll call him – has taken a look at Carlton's files. Hoyle spends much of his time underground, you know. He's very good at evading surveillance. Too good, for an amateur."

David nodded solemnly. "I can imagine."

"This is really more than entryism, isn't it?"

David sighed, loosening his tie, and did not answer directly. "It all runs so deep, Frank – Liverpool, Manchester, London, even abroad . . ."

"We're heading for disaster in this country. I find it painful, David. Physically." Deacon looked at him more closely. "What's happening in Manchester?"

"After I've found out, I'll let you know."

"You'll let me know," Frank echoed. He rasped one finger along his jaw. He had lost a lot of weight lately. "David, you've let me know nothing. Not for months. Look, I'm sorry about leaking some names to MI5, but at the time it just seemed to be my duty. How much do you know?"

"Almost nothing we could take to the party hierarchy – or that would hold up in a court of law."

"I don't suppose there'd be much point in taking 'nothing' to the police."

David hadn't been able to stop himself flinching when Frank had mentioned the police. "No point at all. Not yet."

"Surely Special Branch should be informed – even the boys in MI5?"

"One day, of course; as soon as I have hard evidence." Frank had obviously reached a decision. David rushed to speak first. "Please don't pull me out yet, Frank; I honestly feel I'm almost there. I just want a little more time."

"Davey, I appreciate what you've been doing, God knows. But I don't want you to risk any more."

David made a gesture of denial. "I'm no hero. It's just that an investigation like this takes time. There's no real danger. Don't you think I'd say if there was?"

The older man looked through the grimy windows towards Parliament Square. "All the same, the price you've paid –"

"I know Megan was unhappy about our living apart," David cut in. "But it happens. There are all kinds of jobs that would mean separation. Like yours, for example."

"David, that was understandable. She wants what any woman wants." Frank shifted in his seat, and added quietly, "You're a bloody good liar, and I never quite know what you're thinking unless you want me to know, but I can tell from your attitude what you think. You believe Hoyle is dangerous, don't you? That's one of the things that worries me. I'm aware of the risks you're taking. But, look you, if the investigation means that much – you know I can't order you to stop."

"Thanks, Frank. If the police go barging in now, I'll never get any further, and I'm sure there's much more. I feel like I'm about to enter the charmed circle. Forward is a conspiracy, and it's dangerous. It promotes disorder, class conflict, submission to the USSR, even armed insurrection. I have to finish what I started."

"Remember, you're no use to anyone at all in Quarry Bank cemetary."

He nodded. Frank was quite right: if they found out what he was doing they would almost certainly try to silence him. Permanently.

It was raining in Manchester. David got out of the taxi, the second he had taken since leaving the railway station. He shivered in the cold wind. As far as he could tell he had not been followed – not by Forward, not by Carlton's men, not by the police.

"You sure this is right?"

"Certain," David said, pulling out some pound notes to pay the man. He nodded at a used-car lot behind a wire fence: ERNIE'S AUTOS – NOTHING ABOVE £150. "That's what I was told to watch out for."

He crossed the street to shelter under the projecting roof of another ramshackle warehouse, then glanced around.

This area was dominated by one huge building squatting behind high walls. Its windows were all masked by heavy grilles, and a tall brick tower, like the chimney of some monstrous Victorian mill, watched over the grimy run-down streets of the district.

A car door opened and Alan Hoyle loped over to join him, grinning. He was wearing stained overalls marked Canning Transit, one of the front companies Forward had set up. They shook hands quickly, got in the car and Hoyle drove off.

"That must be Strangeways Prison," David said, peering through drenching rain.

"Yes," Alan Hoyle said. "What a monstrous place – and only for the sons of the poor, David. Only for the poor. Where's the justice in that?"

"Justice," David said thoughtfully.

"You brought gloves, like I asked you?"

"Of course. I don't want to leave fingerprints any more than you do. Now, what do you want me to do?"

Hoyle turned down another street of run-down warehousing, then braked sharply. He gestured through the curtain of the rain, towards another vehicle marked with the Canning Transit letters. A Ford van, a large one.

"I want you to go over there, David, open the door, check the load. It's very important to Forward."

"Why does it have to be me?"

Hoyle said, irritably, "Because if you are caught, your political connections will get you off and cover this up – all right?"

David took the keys, and ran the fifty yards, the drenching cold of the rain making him gasp. He stopped at the van and put out a hand to touch the cold, rain-spattered metal. What if there was a bomb here? Could that be possible? He flinched. Or perhaps the police were keeping this van and its load under observation, and Hoyle would simply drive away, laughing, leaving David alone on the scene and guilty.

276

He swore under his breath and unlocked the rear doors, then slid back the driver's door, then the passenger's. In the back were black-painted crates, which looked heavy. That was all. He settled into the passenger seat, sighing. He had had the terrible thought there might have been a murdered body back there.

Hoyle swung into the van, slammed the door shut. He looked around quickly and turned on the engine, which fired at the third try.

"That's a relief," he said. He glanced at David. "I'll prove that I trust you, David. We have here something stolen from Liverpool docks; we've kept the – things hidden for three weeks. The van was left here overnight, under observation. No police, no nothing. The goods are ours, we've got away with it. Now I'm taking them somewhere we can get at them. All right?"

"But why am I here?"

Hoyle drove away, carefully, the windscreen wipers clicking. "The thing is, David, not everybody trusts you. But after this, you'll be incriminated, and you'll be one of us, for good."

David thought that over expressionlessly as Hoyle drove on through the back streets.

Hoyle braked, stopping the van abruptly in front of a pair of decaying gates. Rain had filled the potholes in the road with oily water. Here, David saw, the pavement was not only cracked but shattered from the weight of heavy trucks. This grey and drizzling afternoon had subdued even the Forward committee-man.

David looked on as Hoyle tapped his hands against the steering wheel, whistling tunelessly.

A police car had turned the corner. It slowed as it approached them, stopping under a skein of 25,000 volt cables that hung over the road near a sub-station. Its windscreen wipers flicked spasmodically in the rain. David, frozen, sensed Hoyle sinking down behind the wheel; he reached forward, and David realized he was probably reaching for a gun. Rain drummed harder on the van's roof.

David found it hard to speak. His limbs, too, felt weak. "D'you think they're here for us, Alan?"

"I hope not. For all our sakes."

"What if the police check our plates?"

"Everything's legitimate," Hoyle said confidently. "Except the load."

Then two bedraggled youths wearing colourful woollen hats appeared in front of a transport depot – a Stanton Industries depot, David noticed, appalled.

The youths looked away from the police car and then at one another, walking quickly now down the middle of the road. The police car rolled forward, threatening, but as the boys reached an alley between two warehouses they darted into it, and the police car took off in pursuit.

"Fascists," Hoyle said.

"Worried?"

Hoyle pinched together finger and thumb. "If anything goes wrong, we're *that* close to ten years apiece in a place like Strangeways."

"What?"

"There's been murder involved," Hoyle said suddenly. "What did you think, that I'd operate by sending letters to our so-called left-wing press?"

David met his eyes. Everything he had suspected was true. "No, I didn't think that."

Hoyle's eyes were glowing. "When I took the Levellers away from Bonnington, all those years ago – he didn't drown by accident. *I killed him. And it can't be proved!*"

David felt like shuddering, but he kept his face expressionless. "I should hope it can't be proved. You've got to be careful, Alan, or you'll get us all in trouble."

"Trouble?" Hoyle laughed. "Trouble? This could be where all the trouble starts," he said urgently, "here, today. So take the keys, and start transferring the stuff."

As he sorted through the full key-ring, David was suddenly shaken by the powerful understanding that he was no longer *pretending* to help Forward, he was actually doing it – that since the early morning the act had overwhelmed the actor.

He was as guilty as they were.

He got out quickly. Turning up his collar against the rain he unlocked the gates and swung them back. The rain was coming down in curtains now, heavily enough to flatten his hair and soak through to his shoulders. Hoyle looked up and down the road, then backed the Ford van into the cobbled yard, tight up against the warehouse doors. David shut the yard gates, swearing.

The doors were heavy, corroded iron a century old. They made the van doors seem like tin foil. David dashed the red rust from his gloves as Hoyle flicked on a light. Inside, the loading bay was dry and gloomy. At its rear a glassed-in despatch clerk's office stood dark and unused behind its cobwebbed windows. There were wooden crates and green plastic drums, waist high, with black identification numbers stencilled on them.

Hoyle exploded, *"Don't* go over there!"

"What . . .?"

Hoyle went to where a junction box hung, and thumbed up a row of four red switches. "I should've said. A little surprise for Joe burglar. The whole place is wired up."

"Alarms – I should've realized . . ."

"No, a little deterrent." Hoyle grinned. He took three paces into the room and waved his hand in the air, making contact with a thin wire stretching into the darkness. At one end an eye secured it to a hook and a sheathed cable. There was another at head height and another below the knee.

"Three phase, one phase per wire."

"But that's industrial supply. 440 volts. It's lethal! What if some kid gets in here?"

"Anybody who gets into this place has to be very determined. It wouldn't be some daft kid."

"But even so – if it kills someone, that's manslaughter under British law. You can't protect property at the risk of someone's life."

"The law," Hoyle said indifferently, and turned away.

Together, they carried the crates from the van and stacked them three high. They had been daubed with black tarry paint to obscure the markings on the lid and sides, but the outlines were occasionally just visible as they carried them under the light. Sequences of numbers mostly, but he couldn't make them out, let alone memorize them.

The crates were not large, but they were heavy, and the rope handles allowed them to swing precariously as they were raised, showing the weight distribution to be uneven. David could smell machine oil. Engineering parts, he guessed, being smuggled abroad.

"Buggery," Hoyle said, wiping sweat from his forehead. "I'll get that Thermos of tea, David."

David was panting. "I could do with a break."

279

When Hoyle stepped outside David kneeled in front of the stack of wooden boxes. They had all been painted black, to hide whatever writing had been on them before, but the crates had been stencilled very heavily – and he found his sensitive fingertips could still make out the thickly-painted original letters, which were not always perfectly concealed by the haphazard repainting job somebody had done.

"Stanton Industries," he whispered to himself. Then: "War Department; 1956. Numbers, too." He memorized the designations for half a dozen of the crates. War Department. Guns, therefore – Stanton guns. His suspicions hardened, and as soon as he could do so without Hoyle seeing, he looked around, knowing that he would have to return here, and saw a dirty window with iron bars across the frame, and a bolted catch.

Now he had the consignment numbers he had hard evidence . . .

Hoyle came back, grinning. "Bloody rain. Still, we're warm enough." He looked around as he unscrewed the top of the Thermos. "I like it warm."

David avoided meeting his eyes. He knew he had a chance to finish Hoyle once and for all, as long as the guns were still in this warehouse and as long as he gave evidence against Hoyle in open court.

He would have to risk everything to do that. Everything.

There was the sound of a car stopping outside. Suspicious, Hoyle went to investigate. David saw his chance, jumped up on a crate and slid the window bolt back. Now, he could get in, if necessary. Hoyle returned, and they resumed work.

"What's inside?"

Hoyle smiled, but said nothing.

They finished very soon and locked the warehouse again. Hoyle looked around quickly, but did not notice the tiny window onto the yard.

They went in the van to Manchester's Piccadilly Station where David was to catch the fast train to London. David rubbed his aching hands and asked again about the crates.

"They came over from Liverpool. The next leg of their journey is sometime today or tomorrow. I don't even know the exact time myself."

"But what've we been doing, Alan?" David wondered if he could reach a phone and tip off the police before the guns were moved.

Hoyle hesitated. "When the time comes we must be prepared. It's part of my brief to bring the mechanism to readiness."

David realized Hoyle had to be coerced into an admission. "They're guns, aren't they?"

Hoyle said nothing.

"For use against our own people. . .

"Not the people, David. The army,, the police – when the day comes, we'll need protection. We can't rely on stones and Molotov cocktails when they've got CS gas and guns. The IRA learned that lesson."

David nodded, tensely. He had to be very careful. "I'm not a pacifist, Alan, but this – I can't believe there'll ever be a rising on the streets of England."

"Naturally, I prefer to work within the system and assume power bloodlessly," Hoyle had said, a strange light in his eyes." "But I can already foresee a time when the fortunes of this country will be brought low. Unrest will spread, and someday people will look at the economy and see there's almost nothing left. There'll be massive reorganization, crisis, rage. It will start in the cities, in the poor parts of town, in the ghettoes and slums. That day of wrath will come. That's where the revolution begins, and we have to be ready, David, ready with arms and organizers."

Hoyle drove into the station car park. He bought a platform ticket and gave David his ticket for the six o'clock train to London, Euston – a non-stop service. He accompanied David through the barrier and along the platform, even climbing aboard the train as it waited. David couldn't shake him off, nor could he be seen to be trying.

All the while, Hoyle talked compulsively about 'the day', and about how there were Forward members all over the country pledged to rise. David knew that he must get back into the warhouse. If he could somehow get down those numbers they could be traced to their origins . . .

His thoughts were blasted by a guard's whistle. The train was about to leave and Hoyle had stayed with him to the end. As the carriage began to shudder forward Hoyle stepped down onto the platform. His face was split with a mad grin. He pulled something out of a pocket, and his gloved hand slapped against the palm David had automatically extended. David looked down.

"Jesus!" His fist closed around the cartridge. He looked around quickly. Talk about incriminating evidence. A bullet.

"You keep it," Hoyle said, laughing at his expression. "It's what we give our traitors, like the Irish do. But you're one of us now, see?"

281

David pulled the door shut and judged he had enough time to run down the window for a last word as the train began to move.

"I'll see you in London, then."

"Right – and get me that Foreign Office stuff we talked about."

David smiled. He tried casually to run the window back up, but it jammed. His contact with Hoyle was broken at last, but the train was gathering speed.

A sallow youth in a tattered suede coat and dirty pale blue scarf lounged across the door space at the end of the carriage. He had self-inflicted tattooes across the backs of his hands and beneath his ear.

"Excuse me."

David reached across him and opened the carriage door. The train lurched, slowing for a bend. David leaned out, holding on by one hand. A ringing, shearing noise came up from the tracks as wheel flanges shaved the rails. David steadied himself, then leaned forward.

"What the 'ell!" The youth gawped, standing back.

"Do me a favour – pull the door shut after me, would you, please?" David said. The panic rising in him was tangible. He looked down onto the maze of points that jostled the carriage. The train was picking up speed again, the cold wind coming through the door increased. It had to be now.

"You're not a bloody paratrooper, mate! You can't do that," the youth told him incredulously.

"I've left my wallet in the station bar."

Then he jumped headlong into the darkness.

"Hello, Maggie," Megan said rather coolly into the telephone. "How are you?"

"Fine," Maggie replied. "I hope you can still come over next week for dinner."

"Oh, no problem. I have a reliable babysitter at last."

"Listen, I was wondering if your husband might be around."

"Ought to be, later," Megan answered, picking up Naomi who had started to bawl. "I'll ask him to give you a ring back, should I?"

"If you could: I'd like a couple of thousand words on the Irish situation, quickly. He isn't at home at the moment?"

"No," Megan said. "He's off somewhere with that Alan Hoyle."

"Oh? Talking to a Forward group outside of London?"

"All he told me," Megan said, "was that it's something to do with law and order."

David limped away from the taxi, rubbing at the abrasions on his left cheek. His head still rang. The pain in his leg was agonizing, but still he had to scramble over the brick wall around the Forward storehouse, then, gasping, force himself to shin up the rusting, cast-iron drainpipe. The metal was slick with rain, and it was hard to grip.

Then, fifteen feet above ground, he had to work at the window for long, terrifying minutes. Ancient metal squeaked: one of the panes was cracked, and he would have simply smashed it and let himself in, except that the window-bars were set so closely together. It was quite dark except for an orange streetlight, and hard to see. Only as thoughts of failure began to assail him did the catch come loose allowing him to climb in.

"I hate this," David breathed. "I hate it." He had to check if the arms were still there – to get firm evidence before he called the police in and risked blowing his cover.

He sucked his torn and bloodied finger as the possibilities ran through his mind. What if he blundered into one of the electric wires? What if there were other surprises Hoyle had said nothing about? *What if he was discovered?*

It was useless. He knew that if he was found here by Forward, no excuse on earth would rescue him.

That was a risk he had to take, and suddenly adrenalin pulsed through him. He slipped down inside and shone his penlight around.

The interior was empty. The crates that he and Hoyle had stacked earlier were gone. Then he paused, eyes flickering around, ears straining for any sound. Nothing. The place was empty. He thought of ringing for the police now, but without the guns, what would be the point?

Then he remembered the bullet.

David returned to London late that night, exhausted, his hands sore and his shoulders stiff. He wondered what Alan Hoyle thought of him now. Had he earned his trust? David grimaced. Hoyle had won; he knew he had incriminated himself, and for what?

He had no answer.

283

He sat down in front of the fire, an opened can of lager beside him. He felt shattered, almost ill with tension, but at least he had been able to memorize some of the code numbers on the packing-cases. That, at least, was hard evidence to give, and he had the bullet, too. Perhaps it was time to stop his mission and give his testimony.

The thing that bothered him was Alan Hoyle himself. His monologue had been frightening.

Megan wasn't sympathetic. They went to bed late, and David did not sleep well, wondering whether to finish his Forward mission immediately, or let it run for a few more months. He could not decide, though he seemed to toss and turn for hours.

The ringing of the bedside phone awoke Megan first, and for once she was the quickest to answer it, reaching across David's chest. He flinched, terrified it was something to do with Alan Hoyle. Where was his daughter Naomi?

"Oh my God," Megan said. David came fully awake instantly; he recognized the terror in her voice. "Yes. I understand. I'll be there – or one of us will be there –"

"Megan!" He put the light on. The glare was painful, all-revealing. There were tears in her eyes, and her face, puffy with sleep, looked totally vulnerable. He knew at once it was something very bad. "What is it?"

"Uncle Frank's just been rushed to hospital. I'll have to go there, David. Can you ring my mother?"

He rose to the crisis at once. "Yes, while you dress. You can phone me from the hospital later."

He did not have to ask whether or not it was serious. Would Frank even live to hear his words on Forward? They looked at each other for one long moment, their single thought unspoken, but mutual. If Frank was seriously ill, here at last was the chance for David to come into his inheritance.

David arrived shortly after eight in the morning, with his daughter.

By then, Frank was out of immediate danger, but the perforated ulcer had been life-threatening as well as agonizingly painful. He sat up in bed resting on the heaped pillows, pale as milk and almost incapable of movement. He tried to smile at them as they sat at his bedside, but his expression was ghastly.

284

"David," he said, wheezing slightly, "I can't go on. I'm hurt. I'm hurt."

"I understand," David answered, in a hushed tone. "Listen, you shouldn't make any decisions when you're ill – not even if I'm the beneficiary."

Frank's eyes moved from his niece to the young man he sometimes thought of as his son. "Fishguard," he said. "Home. My seat in Parliament . . . I'd like to see you it come to you."

"I will try," David said calmly, his heart beating so fast the blood made a rushing noise in his ears. "Thank you, Frank."

Megan reached across the invalid and took his hand.

Alan Hoyle tried to contact him twice in the next week, but he did not take the calls. Eleven days after Frank had been rushed to hospital, in a surprisingly ill-tempered meeting of the constituency's general management committee, David was selected as the Labour candidate for the by-election.

In an atmosphere of disagreement and decline the electors of Fishguard and North Pembroke were going to the polls. It was a by-election that the whole country watched anxiously. The contest was in a marginal seat, and it was seen as a major test of the Labour government's popularity.

In his four years around Westminster David had always dealt carefully with Fleet Street and, working for Frank and the party apparatus, he had fostered warm relations with the TV commentators Now he was able to put himself across as an analytical thinker, able to praise his own government's policies straightforwardly and entertainingly, and also come up with alternatives; his studies in history and economics paid off suddenly, earning him the esteem of the public as well as his colleagues. Frank, now well on the way to recovery, was giving him full backing.

Events thrust him forward into the public eye.

"Look at these newspapers, David!" Megan had gone back to Fishguard with him, to canvass. "A 'man to watch' . . . 'the thinking man of the seventies' . . ."

He threw others in front of her. ". . .'linked to Forward' . . . 'under the sheep's clothing of moderation, Mr Bryant is another Marxist wolf about to descend upon the fold' . . ."

She stood up, ready to head for the doorsteps again. "Well, you have the privilege of proving them wrong, David."

Every time David covered the pavements of Fishguard, looking at coloured posters in the windows of houses and shops, the press followed him; he did well, they liked him, and he looked good on television.

Megan, naturally, was working hard for his victory, too, and it sometimes seemed that she was related to half the people on the electoral register.

"I probably am," she told him. "Roots, David, that's what people like around here – that and money in their pockets!" She added that it was wonderful to see his name and earnest-looking face appearing everywhere, and David also got a real kick from it all. He visited schools, factories, pubs and clubs, always with a ready smile, always putting across a platform of optimism and competence.

Four days before polling Frank and he sat down with pictures of the men the other parties had put forward. One was a wily solicitor with slickly plastered hair and a strident voice, and another was a bearded lecturer with leather elbow patches on his jacket and the slow mannerisms of a pipe-smoker.

"Look at them." Frank was scornful. Now that he was headed for retirement, some of his vigour and all his warmth had returned. "You get out and give them a bloody good hiding. You can do it."

At a public meeting, David took Frank's advice and challenged the other candidates to appear with him on television.

They could not refuse. Indeed, for several minutes they could not answer at all. They looked to their local aides and tried to hide their embarrassment as the hall rang with laughter.

David had made his challenge in Welsh.

The following night in London's Lime Grove TV studios, the lights were hot, and he felt faintly ridiculous after the make-up girl had finished – there was more powder on his face than on a baby's bottom, he complained half seriously – but when his turn came he smiled broadly at the stuttering Conservative and accused him of employing circular arguments about the economy.

"That makes you a good Tory, no doubt," he said with an amused expression, "but, you see, when the Labour Party talks of round

286

figures, *we* don't mean multiplying inflation and unemployment by pi."

Soon after that the campaign was over; David had somehow caught the popular mood, and was able to rise high above the hints and allegations about his acting career and his links with Forward.

"Is there some kind of problem over me being a retired actor?" David said in annoyance. "I'm sure if I were an American politician nobody would mind."

His little girl was at her grandmother's house when the result was declared, just before midnight. Naomi had been allowed to stay up as a special treat to watch television, and she sat anxiously uncomprehending in front of the screen – a serious-faced toddler with her mother's dark eyes.

In the crowded municipal hall David waited for the result, head bowed. The candidates' votes were given in alphabetical order, and David came first. His face changed completely as he heard the figure and calculated what it must mean as noise erupted around him.

It meant victory, by the record majority of 2,972 votes. The flashguns went off, Megan held his hand high for him, the other candidates were magnanimous in defeat. Then he kicked off to the victory party with an ecstatic crowd of constituency helpers, family and friends.

I'm in at last, he thought jubilantly; I'm a Member of Parliament, and there's even more to come!

There was a big party afterwards, full of Labour workers and Megan's relatives. The party leader had telephoned his congratulations; there were telegrams from others. David kissed babies and shook hands.

Megan came up with a broad-shouldered young man. "My cousin Peter."

They shook hands. The man had a strong grip, and Army was written all over him, David decided.

"I've got some good news too, love. I've just been promoted to sergeant."

"Then that's something else to celebrate," David told them both, smiling. "I hope you'll have a glass of champagne with us."

At two-thirty in the morning, in the glare of flashing disco lights, Maggie Langton arrived and kissed him warmly. David was elated and thoroughly enjoying his big moment, but he noticed that Maggie, too, was in tremendously good spirits; her eyes flashed and she kept tossing her head so that her long red hair swirled tantalizingly.

"I see I'm not the only one on top of the world tonight. What's *your* good news?"

She had to bawl to be heard above the music. "Look at your television – ITV, eight o'clock next Thursday. I'm presenting a discussion programme about the American involvement in Vietnam."

Early the next morning there was a phone call.

"Alex Stanton," the crisp, low voice said, "calling you from New York. I just wanted to congratulate you, David."

"Thanks," he croaked, "but do you know what time it is?"

"I could tell you what time it is in America, but you wouldn't believe me."

David sat down on the stairs and pulled his dressing gown around him. "The fleshpots, eh?"

"I wouldn't quite say that, though of course I'm not a married man like you . . ."

"Alex, what about our plans – turning around Stanton Industries and then the country? Where have you been?" The absence of his friend suddenly seemed personal.

The ghoulish chuckle came from a million miles away. "In hiding, let's say."

"But did it work out for –?"

"I'm going to try to set up more deals in the Middle East. I hope to get something above 150 million dollars signed, sealed and delivered by the end of the year. It might be enough to get me on the main Board of Directors for Stanton Industries. Then I can start trying to turn the family firm around for good and get it back into the big league. But now that you're an MP I need your help more than ever."

"What do you want me to do?"

"Set up a meeting with the Foreign Secretary, him, me, you. Subject: the Shah. I have had an approach from Tehran, David, but I won't do anything without government backing."

"I'll try to make sure you get it." David was impressed by Alex's determination to force through changes in Stanton Industries, though he knew there was still a high probability of failure; and he had come to think that without major changes in Stanton's much more than its three hundred years of history would be finished. "When somebody comes to write the secret history of our time –"

"Write it? David, we're living it."

David knew he was right.

There was another phone call, at a more normal hour that morning. Alan Hoyle.

"I just wanted to congratulate you myself, David. The first of us to be able to say 'So-and-so, MP' – that's good."

"Yes, thank you," David said cautiously. "Of course, it means I'll be very busy from now on."

"Of course," Hoyle said. "You want office, high office. That's understood. But I hope you won't be turning your back on your old friends."

This was exactly what David had intended. "You have something to suggest?"

"I have another target in mind. Something quite close to you."

"What?" David lowered his voice. "The Cabinet itself? The Prime Minister."

"You'll just have to trust me that it's something important. Cheers."

It was only two days before summer recess when David was able to go up to London with Frank.

It was a marvellous summer day, today. The two men stood on the iron span of Westminster Bridge and admired the view up the river.

"'Earth has not anything to show more fair . . .' That's this city, Frank! In lines composed by Wordsworth on this very spot, 3rd September, 1802."

Frank roared with laughter. "I swear you're touched sometimes!"

"It's a great honour to be called 'touched' by a peer of the realm." David looked kindly at Frank, knowing how much he owed this man.

Frank spread a hand over the silver-grey water, as if he was giving his blessing to the Thames and the history it represented. "I've decided what title I shall take," he said with gravity. "A Welsh name. From the old pit-town of my father and my grandfathers. I shall be Lord Tytryst."

David's approval was clear.

Frank smiled suddenly and looked down at his own strong hands on the bridge; they had blue scars, from his time as a boy at the mine face, long before the war. Frank Deacon was the finest man he had ever met, as well as one of the most conscientious and able. "Tytryst. It means 'House of Sorrow'."

289

They clasped hands solemnly, and David thought how marvellous it was to have tradition and continuity weave the years of a man's life and the generations of his family into one visible fabric.

"You're so lucky to have all that behind you, so that you remember exactly who you are. I never even knew my own grandfathers."

Frank held onto David's hand. "Grandfathers? Does it matter what they were? You should be more concerned to know what their grandson will be – and that's a quote from a man infinitely wiser in the ways of politics than William Wordsworth: Abraham Lincoln."

"I should know better than to trade quotes with you, Frank," David said, smiling. "The Lords' gain is the Other Place's loss."

Frank shrugged. "It's just as well I'm getting out. I tell you, that gang of Leninists you've been investigating will be running the party next."

"I think not."

"You haven't backed away yet, have you?"

"I can't, Frank. I just can't."

"You're an MP, now. Use that as an excuse; turn your back on that man Hoyle."

"Frank, my being in Parliament makes me more valuable to Forward and my job much easier. Hoyle has promised me an introduction to more of the top people in Forward. I must have more names, otherwise everything I've risked will have been for nothing. Hoyle wants me more than ever, now: I've been offered the chance to lead a Forward grouping inside Parliament itself. And besides – he says he has another target, something very close to my heart. You must see that I have to find out what that target is."

"Mark my words, David, and be careful. There are forces abroad in the land that care nothing for parliamentary democracy. There are madmen who dream only of blood." Frank stared into David's face. "There really is a lot more to that Forward story than you ever let on, isn't there?"

David stopped smiling. "I can't talk about that in any detail, Frank. Not yet. Not even to you." He hesitated. "If I should – if there's some mishap, I've left a full record in a safety-deposit box in my bank."

"You expect something like that!"

"No. At least, I don't think so. It's hard to tell how much of what Hoyle tells me is propaganda and exaggeration."

"Alan Hoyle is an evil man."

David spoke the simple truth. "I'll be watching him for a while yet."

"And he doesn't suspect?"

"He sees himself as the irresistible wave of the future; and I'm just so much flotsam and jetsam, tossed upon the tide."

"I hope you don't get swept away," Frank said quietly.

Below, to their right, sooty blocks of stone rose up from the Thames's dark surface; above, the Gothic mass of Sir Charles Barry's architectual masterpiece, the Palace of Westminster, blackened by the smoke of Britain's past greatness, stood proud and erect above the unhappy ferment of the present.

The tall clock tower of Big Ben beckoned them both with its unique carillon, striking out the hours. David looked at his watch.

"Twelve o'clock."

"I'd better be getting along," Frank said. "There's a lot to do."

David laughed energetically. "There certainly is, Frank. There certainly is."

The next day, in a ritual whose roots were in the Middle Ages, David looked across the crowded debating chamber from the bar of the Commons. Pugin's exquisitely carved wooden panels set the tone, and green leather and sparing ornamentation in gilt underlined the sober function of this place; but they were images from another century. The Labour benches, as the government party, were to his left. The Leader of the Opposition and his shadow ministers were seated, a nice metaphor, to the right. It was like a political cartoon, he thought – a caricature of the nation divided.

Then the two most senior Labour members from Wales, escorted him onto the floor of the chamber. They by-passed the Table of the House, and the ornate mace upon it.

Mr Speaker, in his absurd eighteenth-century costume and wig, beamed down as a clerk handed David the oath.

David looked quickly to the gallery where Megan sat with Frank. Maggie, next to them, smiled at him and gave him a quick wave. Nearby, Alex Stanton leaned forward from his bench, ignoring her even though she occasionally turned a glance that was half sultry and half sour in his direction. Maggie was very lovely and as their eyes met she tossed her head in the old familiar gesture and blew him a kiss. Alex flinched. Even at this climatic moment David could feel the tension between his two old friends, that powerful brew of sexuality, personal force, and politics. What was wrong with everybody here? If only this was a nation to bring people like that together instead of making them enemies . . .

David cleared his throat. In his quiet, commanding voice he read the centuries-old words:

"I, David Fulton Bryant, do swear that I will be faithful and bear true allegiance to Her Majesty Queen Elizabeth, her heirs and successors, according to law, so help me God."

Then David signed the folded parchment of the Test Roll, and smiled quickly as the Speaker shook his hand before he turned to the next business of the House.

Even before he reached his thirtieth year, he was here. He knew there was a great deal to do. The stakes could hardly be higher. The economy was grinding itself down into nothing; and every failure was a new opportunity for Forward's Alan Hoyle and all the other fellow-travellers. He imagined, suddenly, earlier Parliaments: free men defying kings, then Pitt and Palmerston and the others shaping the world, and later Churchill thundering against a continent dominated by evil, and he silently promised all the ghosts which haunted this august chamber that he would do his best – because the price of failure was all too obvious.

5

David was summoned from the party conference bar, though he was deep in conversation with Maggie and her father. Maggie had a notebook in front of her, and her father was boisterous as ever, planning how to bring down any government the Tories might form. "Easy. The bloody dustmen come out, and the streets stink. Then the miners and the power-workers strike, and the streets are dark. Your lad wouldn't have a chance."

Langton was accompanied by a man called Sutton, David noted, with a wide-eyed intelligent face, who obviously looked up to Will and was very aware of his daughter.

Will clapped David and the other man on the shoulder with his big hands. "You must get together, lads. An' I tell you, if I had a couple of sons like you, I'd be proud."

David was touched. He did not want to leave, but Hoyle's summons, passed on by a Coventry delegate David had already met, was peremptory.

Then Will turned to the other man and wagged a finger. "Though they do say Satan was proud, Jackie Sutton, and look what happened to him."

It was the end of September, 1969. Alan Hoyle, shirtsleeves rolled up, led him into his darkened hotel room before shaking him by the hand. Since Manchester, and David's by-election success, they had talked quite frequently over the phone, but hardly ever met face to face.

"You're at the party conference this year?"

"I'm right here," Hoyle said. "This is the conference that counts. Sit down."

David slumped into an armchair. The heavy brown curtains were drawn, and the room was hot; the gas fire hissed at them.

"What is it you want, Alan?"

Hoyle hesitated. "You're developing a good cover as a centrist MP in the party, David. Which I appreciate, though Manchester proved whose side you're on."

"It certainly did," David said smoothly. He still had the bullet, a deadly souvenir. "I'm sorry I'm so busy, these days. Especially as you've talked about something important coming up –" He looked at Hoyle expectantly. He had to find out what this secret was before he turned his back on Hoyle and his world forever.

"That'll come later," Hoyle told him brusquely. "I'm thinking about the next few days at the moment."

"Very well, how can I help?"

"You know some of the delegates; you know the parliamentary party. Now, there's a motion coming up tomorrow morning which I want you to start gathering votes against."

"Tonight?" David said dubiously, regretting his fourth glass of Guinness.

"Exactly."

"What motion is it?"

"Resolution 421(b). About Northern Ireland."

David did not move. Was this a trap? "I don't understand. That motion wants us to open negotiations with the IRA and pull out of Ireland entirely. It's a Left motion. You can't want me to *lead* the opposition to it!" Recently Catholics in the Bogside had applauded as army engineers erected barricades to protect them from Protestant extremists.

"Yes I can." Hoyle gave a wide smile, reached over and touched his knee. "I want to see some radicalization, David – and so do my supporters. So I want the army to stay on the streets and go in, hard, every time there is aggro. I want the troubles in Ireland to spill over into the mainland, David. I want the Irish dagger pointing at the heart of London. So do you see why I don't want the government to feel impelled to negotiate a settlement? Or to pull out yet, undefeated?"

"I understand. You can consider 421(b) a dead letter," David said flatly.

Hoyle nodded slowly, then unfastened the collar of his shirt. "Things are hotting up nicely."

It would be hotter in hell, David reflected.

"Oh, by the way. Your friend Stanton."

"Alex Stanton?"

"The same. Keep tabs on him. He's on the list, David. He's on the list."

And you are on mine, Alan Hoyle, David thought.

For weeks, David had heard nothing from Alex Stanton. The Foreign Office had given cautious approval to his plan: no more than that.

David had learned in the pages of the financial press that Hacker-Stanton International was spreading its corporate nets ever wider. Four small companies with strong defence connections had been bought in less than a year; the Delaware corporation was expanding. There were rumours in the gossip-columns and other places that Alex was more estranged from his family than ever, and David had read in a satirical magazine Maggie wrote for that Alex was going to take up American citizenship – sponsored by President Nixon. He did not believe the rumour, quite. But whether Alex Stanton was sunning himself in the Cayman Islands, or signing a deal for gunboats with the Israeli navy, or working at maximizing the company profits from their registered office in Delaware, David couldn't say . . . until one day there was another phone call from some mysterious corner of the world.

"It's me," Alex told him. "A bit more tanned and care-worn since last time. But I wanted to hear from you directly – I know it can't go through official channels . . . The Foreign Minister said 'yes' to you, David? In person?"

"Yes, but only if your scheme stays unofficial."

"And you can come abroad if asked – for five thousand pounds?"

As soon as David confirmed it Alex rang off.

In contrast, ever since the '69 party conference Alan Hoyle had called him twice weekly with news of meetings and 'opportunities' for him to involve himself more closely with Forward. David was getting impatient, having to drive all over the country two or three times a month to show an enthusiastic face at turgid political meetings, knowing these fellow-travellers were of no real importance to Forward's schemes. But in the same week he heard from Alex Stanton, he made another breakthrough.

Since Hoyle had shown him the warehouse full of guns David had opened his mouth to no one, and now his discretion paid dividends. Hoyle took him to a meeting in Coventry at which he was introduced to three of Forward's national executive members, by name. The

295

talk was hard and factual, and David was told that Forward were at last getting ready to make another significant move, this time on the industrial front. They told him, proudly, about the massive engineering company in the Midlands they had bankrupted.

He tried hard to find out what had been targeted this time, but could not.

When he returned home late on Friday, it was to another phone call. This one was from Bronwen, his wife's sister.

"I want to help you celebrate becoming an MP," she told him.

"I've already celebrated," he said firmly. "With Megan. With my wife."

"Look, we both know Megan's gone off to my mother's. Hasn't she? She's bound to be away for the weekend at least."

"So what?" he told her, impatiently. "I don't want you coming over when she isn't here."

"She'll never suspect anything. Trust me, David."

"Look, I'm busy. Important official papers and things." The only paper he had handled all day was the *Sun*, but he didn't want to admit that. "Of course I don't want to be rude, but I honestly have no time."

Bronwen insisted it would be all right, her voice sounding strangely flat, and that they could have fun together.

"That isn't the point, Bronwen. Fun! I'm married, and I'm a father; I don't want to commit adultery in my marriage bed!"

"Don't be such a coward, David. Even if Megan comes back, I've got a perfect right to be there. I'm your sister-in-law, and I was with you first, remember?"

He told her angrily to leave him alone.

An hour later, he was transcribing descriptions of Forward's national committee when he heard the front door to the house open quietly. He jerked upright, suddenly scared, and pushed the notes behind his desk. He stood up with his notebook in his hand, then dropped it as if it was too hot to hold as he heard somebody moving about downstairs, then a faint creaking as someone came up the staircase.

He swallowed, his eyes moving over the room. Was there anything here to use as a weapon?

No, he answered himself. Nothing.

Fear gnawed inside him.

There was a radio playing somewhere in the council estate.

Otherwise, the world was silent. He took a quick breath. It was only then he heard Bronwen's voice. Megan must have lent her a key. He felt weak with relief but, dry-mouthed, could not speak.

She came into his study, her eyes unnaturally wide. She had on a dark blouse, long black leather boots, and a shiny leather skirt which made the eye travel up from her dimpled knees.

"Here I am, my love."

He stared at her. What was the matter with her, and what did she mean, trespassing like this?

She kneeled down, giggling, and began to undress him. One hand fumbled with his shirt buttons, the other was unzipping his flies.

David had never seen her like this before. There was something wrong here. "Bronwen, this is crazy – stop it!" He pushed her away. "Look, you can't stay here. I have to go to Iran soon and Megan –"

Her eyes glittered up at him. "She won't be back till Monday. Trust me, David. We can be alone together. Listen, I've got some of the powder they send out from Bolivia. It's great."

"You've brought drugs into my house!"

Bronwen was like a cat, clawing at him, refusing to see sense, so he pushed her away. Then she was sitting on his desk, taking off her blouse and putting her fingers inside her low-cut brassière. "Look at me, David. Look what I've got to offer. I know all the tricks now. Sex, the best you'll ever have . . . I can lick you till you come, or any other way you want it."

He grabbed her shoulders, shouting at her. "You must be mad! Now you listen, you have to get out of here!"

She kept on coming back until he slapped her hard, but her mad eyes glittered back at him – she had to be high right now – and she put one hand to the flushed cheek where he had slapped her and said, "I can take it, darling."

He bunched up her clothes in one hand, rammed the bundle into her arms, then pushed her downstairs and threw her out onto the street. Rain swept down suddenly, cold. He slammed the front door behind her.

But it was not over yet. She beat her fists on the door and then began shrieking at him out in the street, almost crying with anger and the indignity of the rejection.

"But I'll be back! I'll be back!"

He sat down on the double bed and listened to her and realized he was drenched in perspiration. God, he thought, I must be mad to

297

mess with somebody like her – suppose Megan found out from the neighbours!

He remembered, suddenly, that he had not taken the key from her. There was something else nagging at him, too. He looked around, grim-faced, dreading what he would see. He moaned.

His confidential notebook was missing.

He tried to think straight.

Probably his deliberately obscure notes would mean nothing to Bronwen, but there was at least a chance she would make use of his notebook.

In the wrong hands, it could ruin everything.

His wife returned early the next morning, all smiles, with a bag of household items her mother had been saving to give her.

"Oh, and my sister was supposed to drop in. Did she?"

"Not as far as I know," he said steadily. He had decided there was nothing he could do or say about Bronwen. He could only hope the notebook's details were too cryptic to mean much to her.

Megan sniffed. "I really don't know why I gave her that front door key. She never was very reliable. I don't know, Paris, Melbourne, Delhi. And boasting about all her men and taking drugs at parties. Air hostess indeed."

David went to the Commons the following day, a little later than he had planned. He was still worried about Bronwen stealing his notebook, and about her being on drugs; even without them, she was flamboyantly irresponsible. He did not want her to confront his wife and now he deeply regretted those moments of weakness all those years ago.

He paused only to check his mail before going to the Chief Whip's office in the almost deserted Commons. The whips were responsible for party discipline in general and, more specifically, for making sure the party's MPs would actually be in the Commons at the right time and enter the lobbies to vote for the government – not an easy thing to achieve if the legislation was unpopular.

It was a senior man rather than the chief whip himself. David sat down, crossed his legs.

"So," the man said, smiling quizzically, "you want some time off to go gallivanting abroad?"

"It's approved at a high level," David pointed out. "I hope it won't create any difficulties for you."

"Nay, lad – not with the '66 election giving us a majority of over ninety seats." His satisfaction with the number was plain. "Though when we have the numbers, some of the boys in Parliament feel less inclined to follow party policy – they feel rebellion will be good for them without troubling the Labour government overmuch."

"I've heard the PM say every dog is entitled to one bite," David said quietly.

The man grunted, fiddled with some papers on his desk. "So you've been summoned to Iran."

"By the Minister of the Shahanshah's Court, Assadollah Alam – a former Prime Minister."

"A power behind the throne, you mean." The man pulled at his lower lip. "That amounts to a personal invitation from the Shah. Unusual."

"I wouldn't know."

"You've been to Iran before?"

"No. Speak a little Farsi, but I've never been to Iran or met the Shah."

"I understand you have links with these big munitions people, the Stantons, though."

David shifted in his chair. "More or less."

"Yet you write for the Forward magazine?"

"Sometimes."

"You know how to keep your mouth shut," the whip said, grudgingly respectful. "All right. I dare say this is some kind of cloak-and-dagger operation if the Foreign Office want you abroad. We'll cover for you. You can go. Just let me know the day before you fly to Iran."

"I'll try," David said politely, getting up to go, "but I've been told I might have to leave in a hurry."

David went straight home and told Megan he would be going abroad sometime soon. She talked about taking a few more days off in Wales.

"Whatever you'd like," David said grandly. "I expect to be well paid for my services this time."

She looked at him, her face distinctly judgemental, but said nothing. They went to bed early, but David did not sleep well. Megan heard him muttering to himself in his sleep, something

299

about 'notebook'. When in the morning at some ungodly hour the telephone rang, she turned over under the sheets, trying to shut out the disturbance.

She couldn't get used to the phone calls David took at all hours. Once she heard the ring she was unable to ignore it, and at home late-night calls only ever meant bad news. She listened now to the instant wakefulness in David's voice. He never seemed fully to relax in London; when roused from sleep there was never any grogginess.

"Hello?"

Megan sighed, as the small-talk changed quickly to business.

"Yes, no problem – I was working late anyway," David lied, "after what you said. What's been happening to you, Alex? . . . Yes. But why so soon?" He seemed shocked.

There was a long silence.

"Of course . . . Yes, I understand, and it is a lot of money, Alex." He frowned. "You don't want me to leave directly from my house? What's up, you think somebody's following me? . . . All right. Thanks. Your car can pick me up. Say, Earl's Court Tube. Five-thirty. I'll get a cab there. Good night."

He put the telephone down and turned to Megan.

"Are you awake?"

She grunted into the blanket.

"That was Alex Stanton. He has a chance to pull off something really big. It might be enough to get him onto the Stanton Industries Board of Directors. He's worried about the firm, you know."

"How does that affect you?" Megan mumbled.

"He wants me to go to Iran."

She rolled over. "When?"

"This morning. I told you I'd be off abroad, if you remember. It's only for a few days, and he says he'll pay me five thousand pounds."

Megan digested what he had said and sat up. A look at the clock confirmed it was already ten past two. She reset the alarm for him. Allowing half an hour for the taxi ride to Earl's Court gave them less than three more hours in bed.

"But you haven't heard from him for months."

"I've done him a favour or two. He's just taking the chance to repay me, that's all."

"I only hope you're right. I wonder what Uncle Frank thinks about this idea."

"Don't tell him or anybody, Megan. This is serious business and it has to be confidential – I gave my word."

She shrugged her shoulder away from him. "It sounds like a lot of money for a few days' work."

He didn't tell her about the meetings with the Foreign Office mandarins, nor about the other advice he had given over the years. "Yes," he said thoughtfully. "It does."

He got out of bed, turned on the gas fire and sat down in front of it, looking tired. Now he had to contact Alan Hoyle and cancel his Tuesday appointment, too, and lock away all his confidential papers. Where had he left his notebook? He could not remember. Then it came back to him. Bronwen.

"David, you're a fool to trust that man."

"I very much hope you're wrong, Megan," he said.

The high-powered Rover took him from Earl's Court straight to Heathrow.

"Plane leaves at seven sharp, Mr Bryant," Reid told him, bustling behind him with the luggage. "You don't want to be late."

In the frigid dawn air over the runway, David saw the plane was a Boeing 737 in the Stanton livery of black and gold.

Most of the passengers were, he found, Stanton employees, sent on permanent or short-term contracts to train the Shah's army, air force and navy, and keep the Shah's planes and ships and gigantic arsenals of Stanton arms in good repair.

The men were boisterous. After take-off there were card games, which David joined in. He asked questions about Iran and listened carefully to the answers.

"Bloody hot, bloody dangerous. Y'bugger, have you seen the way they drive? Hand on the horn on the wrong side of the road, expecting everybody else to get out of the way. I've seen some terrible crashes there, terrible. Cars, coaches, lorries, full of women and children and animals as well as grown men. And what do they do after people are hurt? Half the time they just stand around mumbling *Insh'allah*."

"What does that mean?"

"That it's all God's will, Mr Bryant."

A quiet voice told them they would be landing in Tehran in another hour.

301

It seemed to be late afternoon here. David blinked, stepping down from the plane, and realized that by travelling so far east he had lost several hours out of his day. Tehran's air was bitterly cold. An airport bus took him with the others to a terminal, and here David was hustled past gigantic portraits of the imperial family – the Shah, Empress Farah Dibah, the Heir. He showed his passport, had his luggage searched, answered the usual questions, and somewhere along the way he was separated from the Stanton employees.

Then two people came forward out of the crowd in the glass-walled lobby to meet him. He put his bags down.

"I am to be your interpreter. From the government." The woman who spoke was very beautiful, and her accented English made her sound more French than anything. She had on a tailored trouser suit of some dark and glossy cloth David did not recognize, a white shirt, and diamond earrings. She took his hand, her dark-liquid eyes glinting. "I am Zuhreh Bakhash, Mr Bryant. It is an extreme pleasure to meet you."

The man following her had broad shoulders and a drooping moustache. He wore a striped shirt, open-necked, and blue jeans. He spoke English that was basically American, with a few deep vowels that immediately made David think of the North East.

"And my name is – well, call me 'Mikey'. I work for the Stantons, right? I've even been to company premises in Tyneside for training courses. 'Howay the lads'." He smiled, and David shook his hand. He had an even firmer grip than David had anticipated.

"I am a guest in your country," David said to both of them, remembering what he had read about Islamic hospitality.

Zuhreh said, "You will be staying with Major Coombes?"

"Pardon?" He did not know anybody called Coombes. "I'll be staying wherever you put me, happily."

"Major Coombes is the Stanton agent in Iran," Mikey said.

There was a pause as other travellers pushed past, and David looked from one face to the other, not knowing what to say.

"But you are the guest of our government," Zuhreh said sweetly. "We will find you an excellent hotel, therefore. And now, a porter for your luggage."

As soon as she had turned her back Mikey leaned close to David and said softly, "SAVAK."

"What?"

302

For a moment the man's dark eyes flashed fear. "Zuhreh works for our secret police; *Sazaman-e Etelaat va Amniate Kechvar.* You must not trust her."

Outside the airport David saw the modern concrete towers of Tehran were dominated by snow-silvered peaks to the north; the Elburz Mountains, he recalled from a guide-book. Taxis blared horns at other taxis; the sun shone directly into his face for a moment, achingly bright.

Zuhreh led him to a dark Mercedes saloon. They drove him straight to the Royal Tehran Hilton through heavy, noisy traffic that was snarled up in several places, policemen bawling and waving their arms and not being obeyed. Snow swirled down as they got out of the car before going inside the huge modern hotel.

"Enjoy yourself, relax," Mikey boomed. "And tomorrow, we call for you, and show you this land of ours."

"I'm looking forward to it," David said.

The only thing he did before going to bed was ring the British Embassy and tell the ambassador's secretary he had arrived.

They picked him up quite early the next day in the same big, air-conditioned Mercedes limousine. His stay in Iran would start with a tour. In Tehran, they took him to the museums, the Arabian Nights bazaar, and then to the central bank to see the Iranian crown jewels, including the famous Peacock Throne itself.

"Impressive," David acknowledged.

"Iran, the Persia that was, is an empire much older than your British Empire," Zuhreh told him, in a low voice. "On the tomb of Darius it says: 'I am Darius, the great King, King of Kings' – Shahanshah, we would say now – 'King of the lands peopled by all races, for long King of all this great earth, reaching even far away.' He was a great ruler. Like His Imperial Majesty today."

"I can believe it," David said politely.

Tehran, as he found, was a strange mixture of the Islamic past and the twentieth century. There were modern hotels, women dressed exquisitely from Parisian boutiques, fast cars, new Stalin-style public buildings, and rows of spendid plane trees; there were also women wrapped in all-concealing black from head to foot, animals pulling carts, and stinking drainage channels in the streets. When they told him that as recently as 1963 over eighty percent of the population had been illiterate, and he saw for himself the immense gulf between the newly-enriched classes and the poor, he could not help wondering if this whole country had not come too fast too far.

The next day they drove him along the new highways to Qom, the sacred Shi'ite city.

David was impressed by this place. It had gardens, fountains, many more people in traditional dress, and it was warmer than Tehran had been. At dusk, David walked through the crowded, unpaved streets, looking up at the wonderful decorated cupolas of the mosques, and he could not help thinking they were far more lovely, and far more Iranian, than all the Shah's new public works.

One sight stayed with him. A one-legged pedlar was at a street corner, his face grave, sun-browned and bearded under a grey turban, with swathes of bright silk in a dozen different colours slung over his left shoulder. He was playing a crude flute.

David's escort took him to a traditional tea house. It was not crowded, though he noticed the dark looks the men inside it were giving him as Mikey explained that tea, chai, was the national drink of Iran, and given as a sign of hospitality.

The tiny cup placed into his hands was full of bitter, strong black tea. Following Mikey's example he put a sugar cube in his mouth and sucked his tea through that.

"It's so bitter it's bringing tears to my eyes," he said. "Sorry."

"No matter," Zuhreh told him, turning a harsh face to the tables of gesticulating, gossiping men, who now fell silent immediately. "We will go from Qom now."

She crossed the street to buy a newspaper. Leaning on the car David said to the man, "A beautiful city, but I do not feel too welcome here."

Mikey shrugged, and David realized he did not know the man's true, Persian name.

"What do you think of us?"

"Of you personally?" He grinned, but his eyes had become shifty.

"Yes. Your opinion. Not as a Stanton employee nor as an engineer – but as an Iranian. Look, I'm a foreigner, an infidel. I've seen the way poor people especially look at me."

This time Mikey gave him a direct look, with wide eyes. "My father was a farmer, poor to you, rich to most Iranians then. He had trained in theology for a while. What he told me was that in Iran the aghas, the lords, have been foreign so long, and always are out for themselves and never for the people. You must have heard of our famous Koh-i-Noor diamond, the Mountain of Light?"

"That's Persian?"

Pigeons cooed in the trees behind a wall. "Oh, yes. It was taken from us by the Moghuls of India. The British took it from them. It is in London now, in the Crown Jewels. It is Persian but it will never be for Persians. Like our oil, perhaps."

"I don't think –"

Zuhreh came back, annoyed. "I tried to find an up-to-date newspaper from your country, Mr Bryant. Nothing. Let us go." They got into the car and Mikey began playing, quite softly, a cassette of some wailing Middle Eastern music. Zuhreh spoke scornfully. "In Qom they are backward; ignorant mullahs living on yesterday's learning – like medieval theologians, yes, in this year 1970."

Their driver added, "Yet the Eighth Imam, Reza, says 'Whoever visits the shrine at Qom will go to heaven.'"

David settled back in the seat and recalled a name Alex had mentioned. "Didn't one of the ayatollahs come from here? The leader of the troubles in '63 – Khomeini, is that right?"

Before Zuhreh could answer Mikey rapped out quickly, "And Imam Ali said about Qom that out of this city shall come the Twelfth Imam – one who will 'invite all peoples to the truth, from East and West'."

Zuhreh kept turning the conversation towards the Stantons in general, and Alex Stanton in particular, as they drove on towards their next destination. David refused to be drawn, and he could tell from the increasing tension in the car they were not far from putting an end to this tourism and starting on whatever secret business he had been summoned here for.

They stopped this time in Isfahan, the second city of Iran. In a whirlwind two days, based in the Shah Abbas Hotel with its wonderfully decorated lobby, David saw the sights – the city arranged around the huge square with trees and fountains which was called Meidan-i-Shah, with the magnificent royal mosque.

The last night they left the old city to see where the new industries were being built, about ten miles out of town.

It was dark, with only a thin slice of moon to light the desert landscape. The beams from their car headlights bucked up and down on the road, and when they got out, it was cold enough to nip at exposed flesh. David blew on his cold hands, remembering

305

wind-swept nights in his native North East. The sky was black and cloudless; the jewellery of the constellations gleamed. Among the tall, unearthly industrial structures, they saw welding torches at work, flaring like fireworks.

"It is a billion dollar steelworks," Zuhreh said, "being created for us by the Hideki Corporation of Nippon; Japan, that is."

David turned from her to Mikey. "It's incredible. It seems to be a different world from Isfahan and Qom."

"It is," he said, for once sobered. "Iran is different . . . Do you know what is east of us? No? I tell you. North-east, the Dasht-e Kavir, the Great Salt Desert. East, all the way to the south and the Gulf, the Dasht-e Lut, the Great Sand Desert."

"What my country has", Zuhreh said tartly, "is only deserts, history, oil, and the Shah."

"No!" Mikey said. Even in the moonlight David saw his eyes flash. Finally, the lines had been drawn. "We also have our God: Allah."

There was silence for a long time.

Then David said, "When will I be taken back to Tehran, to meet whoever it is I'm supposed to meet?"

"Soon," Zuhreh said. "Very soon."

It sounded like a threat.

Maggie flew into Heathrow early on Friday morning. She had been in Los Angeles for a week.

Terry hugged her in the hallway. "Hey. It's good to have you back."

She kissed him hungrily. "Sorry about the delay. Is the meeting set up?"

"You bet." He grinned at her like a schoolboy. "Come on in."

A man in a grey suit was waiting in the main living room, a glass of water beside him. Maggie smiled briefly at her accountant and then sat down and went through all the figures; a Dali lithograph splashed colour across the Flood Street wall, and the tension grew.

Terry was looking over her shoulder.

"Well?"

"Maggie," the accountant, a trim man from Highgate, gave it to her straight, "you've brought the magazine into profit – into considerable profit. I'd like to congratulate you."

Terry went to get the bottle of champagne out of the fridge.

She was overjoyed. "I'm glad – and I did it without compromises!"

306

Later that morning Maggie returned to her office. Her thoughts ranged to the Far East; she wondered at the high hopes she had had back in 1966, and how they had mostly come to nothing. She was jolted from her reverie by Kai, now her chief editor, who came in with a visitor.

It was Alan Hoyle. She smiled at him and waved him to a chair, then told Kai, "I want to run a big piece on the Misuse of Drugs Bill. And I think there's mileage in the campus demos at Oxford and Warwick over files kept on students' political activity. Can you get someone up there?"

"Okay, I'll put Sally onto that; she turned in two good profiles on Enoch Powell and Eric Stoddard. I'd like to use her again."

"Fine. If she's talented, put more assignments her way."

The office suite was a hive of activity now, rows of neat tables, each with a typewriter or drawing board. They had knocked through the wall into the adjoining room and added much-needed space. It looked cool and efficient now, brightly lit and tidy, though despite the urging of the interior designers, she had put her foot down when it came to giving office space to rubber plants. She looked at Kai's retreating back and stretched her arms. Things were going well; the magazine and its staff were growing up at last – and she was publisher and, with Terry, effectively the owner.

"Well, Alan, you've picked a pretty hectic moment, but what can I do for you?"

Before he could speak, Kai was back at her desk with another visitor, a dark-haired girl she vaguely recognized. Her Welsh accent was enough for Maggie to recollect where she had seen her before. "Of course, Bronwen – David Bryant's sister-in-law. You came with him to the launch. What brings you here?"

Bronwen settled herself demurely on the chair beside Maggie's desk and hung onto a big brown envelope as Alan Hoyle sat beside her and sipped his coffee.

"I read your magazine articles on Sarah de Soutey and that Alex Stanton. They made me think – especially the one about her dying in India, and how he's now an important gun runner."

Alex Stanton. Alex! "Please go on."

"So I was wondering . . ."

Maggie assumed an expression of interest.

307

"Well, did you know that David's been working with this Stanton? Doing work abroad for his gun company?"

"David has?" Maggie's interest suddenly increased by several degrees. Alan turned sharply to look at the Welsh girl, too.

"I was at his flat – just picking up something for my sister, actually – and I happened to read some papers he'd left out." She pulled a notebook from the envelope. "He's gone to the Middle East and he expects to meet that man Stanton. To sell arms, and he doesn't want anybody to know."

Alan raised an eyebrow. "The Mid-East, and secret consignments of arms – now I find that interesting, Maggie." He turned to Bronwen. "You don't happen to know where exactly they're going?"

"To Tehran," she said. "Why?"

"Oh, perhaps I could get a friend or two of mine to meet them."

Maggie's head jerked up. Just for a moment she thought she had heard an unexpected note in Alan's voice; a note both surly and threatening. But his face was as good-natured and open as ever, and she decided she must have been mistaken.

She looked at Bronwen speculatively, weighing her up. This was what she liked.

Bronwen leaned forward. "Well?"

Maggie opened the notebook again, and read the various cryptic entries concerning people referred to as 'H' and 'S'. There was mention, too, of Stanton Industries, and also Hacker-Stanton International. H and S: she wondered if that meant Alan Hoyle and Alex Stanton. She read on, remembering the time Ray Hacker had rendezvoused with the *Nereid* and brought those terrifying Turks on board. So Alex was still making money out of peddling bullets and bombs, she thought acidly. And now David had been drawn into the foul business.

"So you're suggesting I make use of David Bryant's notebook?" Maggie said, looking at Bronwen closely. She flipped through the notebook again, quickly checking dates and entries. The recent notes contained information on various committees and organizations that had dealings with the Middle East; though quite how that tied up with the Shah and his arms-buying she couldn't imagine. Then, terrifyingly, it occurred to her that Alex must have some kind of hold over David . . . She looked from Alan to the Welsh girl. "How much do you want for it?"

308

The question seemed to unsettle her a little. "I don't know – maybe five hundred pounds?"

"Five hundred pounds?"

"Well, say three hundred, then."

Maggie leaned back in her seat. "You'd sell David out that cheaply?"

"What's the matter – it's a good story, isn't it? Labour party leading light, Frank Deacon's heir and brand-new MP, out trying to sell arms in the Middle East with a notorious playboy – isn't that political enough for you? I bet he's in Tehran with Stanton right this minute. You can check up if you don't believe me."

"I'll do that."

"Are you trying to protect the Labour party because you think there's going to be an election soon?"

That was certainly true, and it was astute of Bronwen to have worked it out. "You know David has ambitions to get into government?"

"Yes. And I can tell you other things about David Bryant. Very personal things."

Alan pulled at his lower lip. He was keeping very quiet, Maggie noted. She closed her eyes. So David *was* sleeping with his wife's sister. She had suspected that, even at the wedding. How could David be so reckless? He had already confided to her his ambitions. The damage a scandal could do him at this stage could easily be enough to destroy his plans completely. Maggie decided she had to help him, and she watched as Bronwen straightened herself on the chair.

"How long has this been going on?"

Bronwen shrugged. "Since before he married Megan, actually. You could say she stole him from me. Or tried to."

"And you stopped seeing one another just a few days ago?"

"Maybe."

"I somehow thought that might be the case." Maggie got to her feet, and wandered around the table. "Okay, I'll give you a hundred for it."

Bronwen pulled the envelope back towards her. "I want three hundred!"

Maggie shrugged and dropped the book casually on the table. "A shame. I think it would have made interesting reading: a tawdry scandal based on the viciousness of a spurned lover – that kind of thing."

Hoyle began to reach out towards the notebook, but Bronwen picked it up, scowling. She paused, seemed to think it over and said, "All right. A hundred and fifty might do it."

"Will do it." Maggie took the book back. "Cash or a cheque?"

"I'd better be going," Hoyle said suddenly. He stood up. "Tehran, eh?"

Maggie found herself wishing she had put him out sooner.

There was gunfire in the night in Tehran. All the next day, nobody came to see David at all, and he was driven to ask one of the waiters serving dinner about what he had heard.

"No guns," the man said, stiffening, his voice low. He backed away from the table. "I hear nothing, know nothing."

David could feel fear in the atmosphere.

Early the following morning there was a polite knock at his door at about eight-thirty. He had just finished shaving and he wiped away the foam before bawling, "Come in!"

Alex Stanton stood in the doorway.

"Alex!"

"Indeed it is." He had huddled up in a dark cloak and what was presumably rain had plastered his blond hair down damply. "Let's go out."

"But what about –?"

"Not here, David." He pressed a finger to his lips, then pointed into the corners of the room. Hidden microphones. "I hope you haven't been indiscreet."

"Only when afflicted with diarrhoea."

There was a car and a driver waiting outside: a black Range Rover with gold Stanton insignia, and John Reid at the wheel.

Reid drove carefully, making much use of the mirrors; he had clearly been trained to observe, David realized. There was also a gun, a 9 millimetre Browning automatic, in the glove compartment – the same gun the SAS used, Alex mentioned as he checked it over.

"Languages," Alex said as they drove north through the crowded city. Under the cloak he was wearing a light-coloured suit he said was Italian. "Why are the English so bad at them?"

"I thought you spoke fair Greek and fair French, Alex," David said from the back seat. "Not to mention passable Farsi."

"I can't match you, David," Alex said easily, the flattery unusual for him. "You have a gift."

"That isn't the reason I'm here."

"No, of course not: an MP from the governing party adds weight – but of course nobody actually in government could commit themselves personally, because that would make me official, which I'm not . . . Still, your languages must help. Can't be many MPs with your ability. Funnily enough I saw Hugh with a Japanese phrase-book a while back."

"Japanese?" Then David added hesitantly, wondering if Alex was being sincere or merely flattering: "You know I'm by no means a foreign-policy specialist. Well, except inasmuch as foreign policy is intertwined with foreign trade."

"Oh, you'll do." Alex lounged back as the traffic thickened, folding his hands together behind his head.

When they were through the worst of Tehran's insane traffic, where cars jockeyed with trucks and donkey-carts for possession of the road, Alex suddenly opted to drive. He began to talk compulsively about his real father, the United States, and Stanton Industries.

"Look, Alex, I think the company is heading for serious trouble, too."

Alex was not looking at him, but his hands were tight on the wheel. "I need money to become important to the company, David. I must get it!"

The road went up into the mountains above the city. David disliked the vertigo he felt as the cliffs fell away sheer to his right, and Alex's refusal to queue behind slow buses. Although Alex drove excellently, his impatience while overtaking on upgrade hairpins was quite frightening, even though the Range Rover was a V8 with a three and a half litre engine and built like a little tank.

"I need your complete backing here," Alex said suddenly. "And perhaps afterwards I'd like your opinion on what transpires."

"You'll have it."

"Later I may need your help in London; however this is seen from the viewpoint of the Foreign Office, they must not back out on me."

"I'll do my best." David licked his lips, worried at Alex's serious-ness. He was already in over his head, and the water was getting deeper by the minute. He remembered the bullet in his safe at home. Those guns in Manchester had been supplied by Stanton Industries through Hacker-Stanton. "What are we doing here? Is this for – terrorism, Alex?"

Alex sighed: a non-verbal complaint that he was so little trusted.

"Don't be so damned silly," he said, turning back to the road ahead. "What do you take me for?"

David decided not to answer. Then Alex braked sharply. "John, let's swap places again."

Soon, they began winding up a newly-surfaced stretch of private road that cut through the dusty hills.

David glanced around from the back seat. "Where are we going?"

Alex gave an unpleasant smile and turned the heater up to maximum. "A secret, I'm afraid."

The heat inside the car was making David sweat again. He was intense as he turned to Alex. "Look, tell me where we're going and what you're doing!"

Alex frowned, a crease of annoyance that did not disappear quickly. "Maybe I ought to ask you that."

"What? You invited me here, didn't you? Not the government – you!"

Alex's voice was light but strangely threatening. "I didn't mean here, David."

About half a mile further on, the road ended. A big white house roofed in cool, emerald-green tiles, and surrounded by a high wall also tiled in glassy green, appeared to their left. It had tall wrought-iron gates, and quite an array of aerials and satellite dishes above the roof.

"Stop here, please." Alex reached out to an entryphone box and announced himself. The gates swung open. Inside the compound were lawns that were winter-brown, now, and a pair of dolphin fountains playing into a circular pool.

"I've never liked this place," Reid said. He was wearing a loose jacket with rolled-up sleeves and his heavy forearms rested momentarily on the wheel. "We should have more of our people here and a better alarm system. And higher walls. A good sniper up on those slopes –" He shrugged.

"Next year, maybe." Alex looked and sounded stressed. "For now, stay alert, then. We don't want anything to go wrong."

The housekeeper – an Iranian, David judged – white-haired, his face the colour of hazel-nut shells, came out to meet them. He showed them through the marble-floored entrance, past large glass cases in which David saw a display of modern Stanton small arms as well as jewelled, antique swords from the Middle East. Then a door was opened. The sunlight was excluded from this room by louvre blinds,

312

but when they were flung open onto a vision of Tehran David stood and looked at the view over the gardens, impressed.

"It was owned by a minor royal," Alex said, joining him. "Until last year."

In the cold wintry glare of the afternoon it was a relief to stay inside the warm, exotically decorated rooms, and sit on canvas chairs, sipping tonic water. Reid took another chair, planted it in front of the door and closed it on them. A guard? David wondered. Or something even more sinister? He did not like this atmosphere at all. He spread out his arms, looking around the room and noting the decorative Iranian brassware and wooden carvings, trying to identify their precise origin.

"You're right about this," he said at last, holding the tall glass up to Alex. "Keeps the head clear."

"The touch of quinine – Jesuit bark? Not my usual habit," Alex admitted. He sat down. "You'll find this house keeps Muslim customs, most of the time. It serves Hacker Stanton International here – me, that is, mostly."

"A one-man band." David closed his eyes. He tapped his glass with the inside of his wedding ring thoughtfully. "I just hope you're not overplaying your hand."

Alex leaned over the table to pour himself another tonic water. "Come now, you've known me since, what, '64? We've done each other favours. Would I let you down?"

David did not touch the glass; instead he glared back. It was clear he would have to make the point with brutal frankness.

"You have a nasty habit of turning on the old Etonian charm when you want something. If you can't be honest with me, I can't do you any more favours."

"Not even for five thousand pounds?"

David stood up.

"Not for five hundred thousand pounds. I won't be bought."

Alex put down his glass and looked wounded. "I'm sorry you see it like that."

"And that won't work either." David spread his hands, quick to release the tension. "Alex, I need to know exactly what I'm doing here. And I'm not going to be *handled*."

"Don't you want lunch?"

"Not till this is settled, Alex," he said. "What do you have to say for yourself?"

313

Alex did not seem to be in a good mood. "David, one of the things I'm paying you for is your silence. This is very, *very* important. If it comes off it'll be one of the most significant sales I've closed so far. And 1970, don't forget, is the year I inherit my father's Stanton shares."

David looked at him as he restlessly paced the room. He did not seem too confident at the moment. Then he sat down again and stared at David until David shifted about restlessly and said, "What's the matter?"

Alex's face was both grim and cruel. "As you pointed out, there are certain things to get settled between us."

David looked at his old friend and saw a stranger. Suddenly, he felt threatened. He had to force the words out. "Go on."

"Now, I have reason to believe you work closely – very closely – with a far-Left radical called Hoyle. Alan Hoyle. A man who believes in the workers' state – on the approved East German model."

David gave a tight smile.

Alex stared at him for several seconds. "You don't give anything away at all, do you?"

"My forte."

Alex jumped up, came over, poked a finger at his chest. "*Whose side are you on?*"

David was breathing hard. "Maybe it isn't your side. I mean, you drag me here under false pretences. What if I am really your enemy? What if I think Hoyle and the Eastern bloc are going to win?"

Alex put his hands in his pockets. "David, you know a lot about me and my plans. Much more than my cousin Hugh. More than just about anybody outside of Hacker-Stanton International. If I do end up thinking you're a traitor – here in the Shah's Iran – it wouldn't take much to have you dead in a ditch." Alex's eyes clouded over, as if he was actually planning it. "No, it wouldn't take much at all."

"I'm a traitor? Thanks very much," David said, his sarcasm matching Alex's brutal coldness. "You should know –"

"Now don't talk while I'm interrupting you! Look, what *are* you doing with Hoyle? Is he blackmailing you or something?"

There was a strange ringing noise in David's ears. "It was Carlton who put you onto me, wasn't it?"

"Maybe, maybe not."

David considered for several seconds, thoughts whirling through his mind. Could he trust Alex to stay quiet? And even if he was honest about what he had been doing, would Alex trust him afterwards? David had a sudden vision of being shunned by everybody decent from all points of the political compass: the price of being compromised.

Then he looked Alex straight in the eye.

"Yes, I do shadow Alan Hoyle – and that's just what *he* thinks I am. A shadow puppet, imitating his moves. But that isn't the truth."

"No," Alex said, still not relaxed. "Explain, please."

"I'm following Hoyle and some of the people he leads because I think he's dangerous. And that isn't because he might stand up and preach that the Soviet Union is a workers' paradise. That's his democratic right, and I know the people of our country well enough to know they would never fall for that in a thousand years. No, that isn't the problem. Hoyle's a conspirator, a violent one. He wants to get people he influences into positions of power – in the media, among Labour MPs, and, most of all, trade union leaders. He wants our country, Alex, and I'm trying to stop him."

"God in heaven," Alex said.

"He starts wildcat strikes, he blackmails, he puts his own people into positions of influence and makes use of them. And he has his eye on individuals, Alex, and individual companies. There was a big firm in the Midlands, defence contractors, that went bankrupt recently." He named it. "A firm not unlike Stanton Industries."

Alex rubbed at the end of his nose. "All right, David. I'm convinced. You're taking a hell of a risk, aren't you? I only hope it all works out for you."

David licked dry lips. "Supposing you'd thought I was a traitor, after speaking to me now . . ."

"I can read your mind, David." The blue Stanton eyes glittered. "Oh, no, nothing like that. An assassin's bullet? No." He laughed. "I suppose we'd arrange a road accident, something of that nature. Anyway, Reid will take you back to your hotel now. I hope you'll be okay for a party tonight. And, do believe me, I'm glad I've still found a friend in you."

"There's one question I've still got myself, Alex."

Alex Stanton looked him over. "Ask away."

"Apart from this interrogation . . . why do you want me here?"

Alex laughed, then turned away. "Apart from having to settle accounts? Wait around, David, only a little longer. Then you'll find out."

Major Coombes had been the Stantons' man in Iran for a long time now. His villa in the northern suburb Zargandeh was large and rather untidy, and very traditional. Alex walked through the glowing, heavily scented flowers in the hothouse, where it was warm and humid, then out into the wild garden where it was cool. He paused by the pool to stand there, arms folded, with a line of familiar Tehran plane trees at his back and the tiled house in front of him. The stone walls around the estate were unusually tall, and beneath the vines was barbed wire; the house itself had steel shutters inside and out for the windows and the doors; even the ones which were carved and looked ancient, were reinforced.

"It's a fortress, Major."

The upright man with pepper-and-salt hair and trim moustache admitted as much. "Remember, I've been here since the wild days – the Russian and British invasion in '41. I was here when the Communists' Masses Party was in the Iranian government and also when Mossadeq was Prime Minister and stirring up people against the Brits and the Americans. And I was here when the White Revolution started in '63 and a Tudeh hit squad came to my house with machine-guns and grenades to kill me." He sighed, his fingers flexing along his thighs. "My wife was murdered instead, Alex."

"I heard the story," Alex said. "I'm sorry." He changed the subject deftly. "What was Mossadeq like?"

Coombes's head turned towards him for a moment. "A strange sort of chap; used to try to run the country from his sick-bed – rather like Gandhi, don't you know. And, also like Gandhi, a very clever propagandist. Still, General Zahedi arrested him at the end. Not even clever propaganda beats the bayonet, Alex."

"Maybe," Alex said. "But the world isn't entirely composed of bayonets – in spite of what I say in my sales pitches."

"No." The older man sighed. "This is a wonderful country; but I don't know if I like all the changes that are happening and I love my own country more, Alex."

Alex was scrupulously polite, but firm. "Major, we must face facts. There will be a strategic vacuum in the Gulf and in the Indian Ocean – because Britain cannot afford her imperial rôle any longer. We must do everything in our power to make sure that vacuum is filled by our friends and not our enemies."

"Friends?" Coombes snorted. "The Shah's his own master now."

"That's the way of the world," Alex said steadily. Then he added, "Thanks for being on my side."

"Well, Hugh hasn't forbidden me to help you, you know!"

"Not quite," Alex said. "But – thanks, anyway. I'll remember it. And if I bring this sale off my gratitude will be very tangible indeed."

Coombes shook his head. "To build up the Shah so much . . ."

"Who else can we work with, here?"

"You're right, of course. Most of the traditional, immensely rich noble families wouldn't have his belief in modernization. And the mullahs would be dangerous."

"I agree absolutely. So if the Shah can hold back that tide he's doing the West a great favour."

"But . . . to give everything to the Shahanshah, building him up so much . . ."

"Do you think it can't be done, or it's just ill-advised? I'm afraid the days when the King of Kings was a mere puppet are long gone."

"Unfortunately long gone," Coombes said, delicately. "Is it really possible to be unaligned, Alex? All this 'Third World' nonsense!"

"I hardly think the Shah is neutral, Major. As for his being independent, we must face facts. In the 1950s perhaps there was only Stalin on the one side, and the Anglo-American alliance on the other. It's different now. In foreign policy you can only use the tools to hand."

"Is the Foreign Office really backing you, Alex?"

Alex's blue eyes opened wide. "Now would I lie about that? What do you take me for."

There was a silence. Then Coombes said, "Every time I think of you I remember the old saying: 'Scratch a Stanton, find a pirate.'"

"Hugh's no pirate," Alex said.

The two men began to laugh.

By nine o'clock there were perhaps a hundred guests at the party: mostly men, often in the splendid full-dress uniforms of Iran, and Iraq, and other Middle Eastern countries; there were also attachés from the embassies. Other men were, like Alex, in dinner jackets and black ties, and a few, like a Nigerian import-export millionaire, had chosen national dress. Alex and Major Coombes had waited

317

beside the door of the huge hall to welcome people. Coombes's elder daughter Shirin stood with them as hostess – his wife had been Iranian, Alex recalled, a Bakhtiari from an old noble family.

Finally, the party was in full swing. Doors had been opened onto a floodlit terrace and there were braziers for those who felt the cold. Alex crossed to the buffet tables, his step springy and athletic. The dishes, on gold and silver plates or almost as expensive blue Wedgwood, were by turns Persian and Western, and he found them delicious. A deft waiter appeared.

"Champagne, sir?"

"Excellent idea." Alex accepted a glass, sipped it in a silent toast. Thank God David had not proved to be a traitor. He remembered Donald Pike and he promised himself that, if he ever had the power, that man would pay in blood; treason should never prosper. He exchanged politenesses with a Czech he knew from the embassy, then sipped the champagne again, appreciatively. A fine vintage. Coombes had certainly done him proud, he reflected. There were also Iranian wines, from Shiraz and, a vintage new to him, a red called Sardasht from Azerbaijan. He wondered what Hugh would say, if he ever got word of this. His eye swept over the room. There was a stir as a square man led in a little party of high officials and two beautiful women. Alex went over to greet the Shah's Prime Minister formally, and as he murmered pleasantries, the Iranian lit his pipe, his face cunning but very human and wise.

"And perhaps later –" Alex said, his heart stuttering.

"He will be there, Alex."

"My other guest, even more honoured – if that is possible –?"

"Not to talk money, no, but perhaps he will talk philosophy."

"I understand," Alex said. "Of course I'll be available at His Imperial Majesty's convenience." If he shows up, Alex thought to himself.

He grabbed a handful of green olives and began chewing them one by one, swallowing them stones and all. Then he heard a conversation behind him.

"Ah, Bryant? The MP? Pleased to meet you. Of course, we don't get too many MPs in this part of the world. Especially not Labour MPs – Marxists or Socialists or whatever you call yourselves these days."

Alex turned around slowly, grinning.

"You should already know I'm no friend to Communists – but there's no use pretending to be a reactionary old duffer to me.

318

I know you're no opinionated bumbler. Not if you work with Alex."

Coombes's eyes glinted. "Just disarming a possible opponent in advance, dear boy. Always be underrated by your enemies if you want them to give themselves away. Ah, Alex. Your political friend."

"Well," David said, gesturing around, "this must be the fleshpots, right?"

Alex scratched his jaw and smiled grimly. "Don't relax yet. You realize that if the Soviets were to hear about this meeting, they'd probably try to kill us. I have some plans they won't like at all. Also, they want the Shah out and his schemes destroyed."

David stood up straight at that, thinking carefully, worriedly, about the manifold implications of this dangerous enterprise. "Somebody might shoot at us! Thanks for telling me that at the outset."

"I thought I did. Five thousand pounds must have said something to you."

In David's mind the phrase re-echoed: . . . *they'd probably try to kill us* . . . There was, he found, little comfort in the knowledge that there was no obvious way the Soviet Union's intelligence service could know he was here.

Alex lowered his voice. "There are people high in the Shah's entourage who see Iraq as a prime enemy – not just the military confrontation over the Shatt-al-Arab waterway, where the Tigris and Euphrates flow down together to the Gulf, but because of oil rivalries and the Arab-Persian struggle."

"Is that likely?" David said, surprised. "Surely Iran is much larger and more powerful?"

"Of course, but it isn't that simple," Alex said, edgily. "Not when the USSR *and* Arab oil money both back Iraq. In the late fifties the Iraqi communist movement came close to taking power there. Now I think that General Hasan al-Bakr and Saddam Hussein might well be inclined to throw their forces against Iran – if there was some kind of internal problem here. That's why loyalty and friendships are so important to the Shah. And to me, come to that. In unity there's strength."

"It still sounds like excuses to me. Excuses for arms-dealing, to be candid. Isn't much of what we've been talking about really just a scramble amongst developed nations to stake out their claims – not to develop 'friendships' at all?"

Alex said nothing, and only gave an ironic smile.

319

Others, diplomats without bias, joined in and quietly explained Iranian realities as they perceived them, and David found his own prejudices confirmed. Foreign influences, foreign capital, and foreign armaments meant that the Shah could disregard his people almost entirely. David had several glasses of champagne, listening. Then people began to crowd around him, asking about the government back in Britain and what its plans were. He seemed to be enjoying social success here. David had an interesting time talking to the Iranians. Then, though he was polite about it, he did not stint on his criticisms of the Shah's Iran.

He caught up with Alex after breaking away, champagne glass in his hand. Alex was looking worried.

"What are they doing in this country?"

Alex answered mildly. "What the Shah wills, David."

"But it's all happening too fast! Isn't that obvious – and obvious that you must carry the people with you? Not enough water in Tehran, not enough electricity, and billions of dollars spent on weapons the Iranians are twenty years from being able to maintain! What about the people?"

Alex looked tired, and he kept glancing around at the big room over David's shoulder. "This is the Middle East, David. Asia. This is the land of the warlord and oil and the Koran. There aren't too many comfortable, civilized liberals in this part of the world." He held up a hand. "I know what you're going to say. My esteemed friend the Shahanshah is a dictator. True. There is SAVAK, the internal security agency, everywhere here – even in this household, no doubt. Also true. Nevertheless, what alternative is there? Fifteen years ago getting on for ninety per cent of the population were illiterate. Any mullah ignorant of everything except the Koran could threaten all the Shah has achieved. So, tell me, who is the progressive then?"

"The Shah stands for progress?" David said scornfully.

"Now you're sounding like Maggie. Listen, it's always been like that here! Even in the days of Darius they had spies everywhere – 'The King has many ears and many eyes' is a famous Persian proverb."

"I see. So that makes it right, does it?"

Alex scratched at his head, looking disturbed. "You've been telling other people all this! I just hope to God nobody takes offence, otherwise you might be sleeping it off in Evin prison tonight. Listen, as far as I'm concerned the Shah has the right to protect himself and what he has achieved. Because this is a wonderful country, David. Do you know that 'Paradise' is actually a Persian word?"

David said brusquely, lowering his voice, "The Shah runs a tyranny."

"What do you expect? David, I was hoping you would back me up here."

"I didn't say I would," David replied impatiently. "You're like the Shah: you take consent for granted and if that doesn't work you impose consent by force."

There was rage in Alex's eyes. The Shah had not come, he had lost face; and perhaps the huge deals they had talked over would not happen now. "I believe what I believe, David, and I believe in what I'm doing. I'm not ashamed and I have no moral qualms – and I know this situation far better than you! How could you have our kind of democracy here? Russia shares nine hundred miles of border with Iran and is always attempting subversion. And what the people believe in is not your notion of progress but religion: Islam, Shi'ite Islam. An extremist's religion, obsessed with blood and martyrdom. The Shi'ites have made Ali and all Twelve Imams infallible. Do you really want that kind of fanatic running Iran and exporting *their* bloodstained notions to all the world! David, I thought I could count on your support. I *need* your support – later, you'll see."

"You ask for an awful lot," David said, in the moment before he turned away.

There was something of a stir as a young girl appeared at the head of the stairs that swept down into this banqueting hall. She was wearing a veil across her face, but it took Alex a moment to realize what the fuss was about as he recognized Yunussi, Coombes's younger daughter. The veil had been banned by the first Pahlavi Shah in the twenties. Her eyes glittered at the assembled notables and she swept down the stairs with the arrogant self-possession of a sixteen-year-old girl showing off.

She was also wearing the traditional black woman's dress, the chador, which the Shah's government had always opposed.

The royalist officers, posed in groups, in many cases turned to stare with open anger. Alex stepped forward quickly as Yunussi set foot on the polished floor, took the young girl's hand and raised it to his lips for a kiss. She flushed, there was laughter, and suddenly the moment of tension had dispelled. Alex caught Coombes's eye and flashed a hand sign to show that everything was under control.

321

He came over quietly. "Thanks, Alex. The younger generation."

"It's the same everywhere."

Coombes pulled a pipe out of his mouth, and for a moment his lips pressed together in anguish. "Doesn't she realize what she's doing – representing black reaction and insulting the Shah?"

Then Reid shouldered through a group of English and American businessmen in suits. "Looks like they're coming now, Mr Stanton."

Alex walked quickly to the stairs, turned left onto the balcony overlooking the fountain garden and the main gates. Movement caught his eye – a white Lincoln Continental with jet-black windows approached, preceded by a red Mercedes and followed by another, this one green. Both escort cars were packed with men.

Nothing was being left to chance, Alex thought. He buttoned his dinner jacket formally as the heavily armed men took over the tall gates in the wall and heaved them shut, then spread out around the house. Some carried machine-guns, openly. Thinking better of it, he took his jacket off completely, and instead of going outside to meet the security men he went down to the house doors, seated himself in an armchair and placed his hands in full view.

The Middle East had been the powder keg of world unrest since the middle of the century, and the Shah and SAVAK would be taking no chances.

Alex heard rapid steps on the marble flooring in the lobby, then a man in a cream suit, swarthy and unsmiling, came into the room. He saw Alex, and without any acknowledgement skirted his chair and stood beside it, waving the rest of the SAVAK contingent into the house.

The sound of car doors slamming had roused David so that he came to the balustrade above the main entrance. At the same time, three more Iranians appeared, two in dark suits and sunglasses, and one in a brown safari suit. They then went on into the kitchens as a group. David stood with an expression of mild interest on his face. "They're really going to check for poison?"

"More likely frighten the cooks," Alex said, drily.

As the cream-suited man turned, Alex saw that he was wearing a shoulder holster. "You are Stanton, I think. I recognize you from an English embassy reception." His English was guttural, but passably fluent. "I am Major Omar Ali Mansur."

"Yes," Alex said, rising. "You are in charge of security tonight?"

322

The light-suited man smiled and thrust out a hand. "We have been delayed." He looked around the room carefully, and smiled as Alex shook his hand. "Now, you understand that for a while nobody can leave, and nobody can enter – except for –"

"Of course I understand," Alex said tersely.

The men checked the party thoroughly for about ten minutes. Then Major Mansur clicked his fingers, and an aide brought a walky-talky. Mansur spoke rapidly into it, in Persian. Afterwards he sipped the strong tea Alex had sent for from the kitchen.

Alex seemed to hear something, and looked up.

"No," the Major said. "It is not the helicopter. But when it comes it will land in front of the house, so for some few moments everyone must remain inside."

"I understand," Alex said tersely.

Then Major Coombes appeared in the doorway. "Alex," he said, "they're ready."

Alex gestured with a flat hand, palm up. "Lead on."

He followed Coombes along a corridor into a quiet part of the house, on the top floor. Here they parted, and Alex walked into the room and sat down at the foot of the ornate Turkish table. The painted steel shutters were closed, and an open fire burning some fragrant wood, perhaps cedar, provided more than adequate warmth.

"Gentlemen," Alex said politely, to the two uniformed men and the other in an expensive Western suit who were already seated. "You all know who I am?"

Major-General Azargun sat back, proud in his white uniform that was embellished with a chestful of decorations. He was a broad-shouldered, sour-looking man, intelligent but narrow-minded, and fanatically devoted to the Shah. He had distinguished himself leading the secret Iranian expeditionary force in Oman. Alex respected him and even liked the rough warrior a little. "You know me, Alex." His English was ungainly, but good enough to have got him through Sandhurst twelve years before. "And also my colleague Colonel Azari."

Alex turned to smile politely at the man opposite the general. Azari was a senior man in SAVAK, Alex knew, mainly charged with maintaining relations with the Kurds – a proud nation and a culture unfortunate enough to be without a country of their own, and instead condemned to be an awkward, courageous national minority in both

323

the Soviet Union and Turkey, as well as straddling the mountainous border between Iraq and Iran.

"Colonel Azari," Alex murmured. "So good to see you again."

"A good business, always," he said roughly, giving a gap-toothed grin. He was an overweight man reputed to be a torturer. "You and I, we work well together, yes?"

Alex did not deny it: indeed could not deny it, as Azari had already put millions of dollars worth of contracts his way – personally, which meant that in return Alex had to top up Azari's two numbered Swiss bank accounts.

The third man, darker, with a handsome face and a strong, cleft chin, was peaceably eating a cake of Iranian *soghan*, picking out the pistachio nuts from the caramel. "You know who I am, Mr Stanton?"

Alex narrowed his eyes and searched through his memory for the face. "Not as far as I recall."

"Ah," the man said, disappointed. "It was at your Craigburn, on the night when your cousin and rival was made the heir."

"I certainly remember the night." Alex stuck out his hand. "Pleased to make your acquaintance – and if you tell me it's again, well then you're doubly welcome.'

The man gave a broad grin. General Azargun said, "So, may I present Mr Abd-ul-Mugheri, a businessman we have dealings with. Formerly with Oman, you understand."

Mugheri stood up, reached over the bowls and notepads on the table. Alex took his hand, and drew Mugheri a step closer. His chunky gold rings rubbed against one another as he squeezed Alex's hand.

"So," Alex said, "there is more to be done; is there?"

"First," General Azargun said, "there is another request for help from the Kurdish forces fighting in Iraq, through Barzani's office in Tehran."

"So soon?" Alex said, surprised. There had been full-scale risings of the Kurdish north of Iraq starting in 1961 and continuing. It was an open secret they were supported by the Shah, though never directly. Alex had provided arms for the rebellion for the past four years. "Is that a sign of strength or of weakness?"

"Iraqi weakness," Azari said gruffly, before drinking a glass of vodka. "The Arabs cannot break the Kurds. Even now al-Bakr is negotiating with them in his capital. His people in Baghdad will have to give way – if a little more pressure can be applied."

"Remember, Alex," the General said, "we want an Iraq that is in three, as it ought to be. Kurdish, Sunni, and Shi'ite."

"And also," Alex said politely, "an Iraq that gives way over the Shatt-al-Arab waterway?"

"That, too, of course," the general said with a shrug. "I speak plainly. I am not a politician. And I know I can rely on your discretion."

"The thing is," Azari said, "you have provided arms before, most excellent arms. This time we want to give the Kurds only Russian-type arms – can you do that?"

"Russian guns?" Alex could almost smell the money. "In what quantities?"

"We are thinking of brigade strength actions, Alex."

"So, let me think." Alex went over to the long polished teak display table, taking his notebook with him. "I assume you don't actually mean I have to smuggle weapons out from behind the Iron Curtain?"

Azari seemed disappointed. "Even as a Stanton, you could not do that?"

"Now, let me finish," Alex said, tapping with his pencil. The thought of Vietnam flashed through his mind. They had captured Eastern bloc weapons in abundance, there. And his contacts in Israel; the June War of '67 had left them with huge quantities of Soviet weapons. Then there was the vast Czech works that produced so much in the way of small arms for the Warsaw Pact forces; people he could deal with direct. "We are talking of – how many men?"

"Ten thousand must be armed," General Azargun said at once.

"So, AK-47 automatic rifles and, naturally, ammunition. And suppose I could find some 130mm field guns? Excellent artillery weapons, even better than the U.S. equivalent."

"Is that possible?" the Omani, Mugheri, asked directly.

"As long as the price is right I'm here to make such things possible," Alex said tautly, scribbling on his pad. Even if he could get such heavy guns, there would be so few they would be little more than expensive tokens. But then, Alex reflected, the Shah would not want the Kurdish insurgents to become too powerful ... "There would need to be grenades, grenade-launchers, maybe RPG-7s if I can get them. And mortars, light and reliable and suitable for guerrilla-type operations – I think I could provide up to a hundred 82mm mortars of the M1937 Soviet pattern."

325

"Let us talk figures more precisely," the General said, looking pleased. "You have impressed me, Alex. I did not think you could loot so much from the Soviets."

"Scratch a Stanton, find a pirate," he said quickly, deciding to charter a freighter through a Taiwanese front company to transport the weapons from Saigon to an Iranian port not on the Shatt-al-Arab waterway. "I can get your guns. Not immediately, but I can do it."

"Not immediately?" Azari said at once.

"Four, five months," Alex said. "The guns I buy for you must be serviced and inspected, you see. But as a token of goodwill I can fly in samples of everything except the 130mm heavy artillery by the end of next month, so you can start training your cadres then."

"That is good," Azari said. "Now, let us decide on quantities."

They settled on that. Then they had to talk money. Alex could not quote a final price without checking with Ray Hacker and their Saigon contacts, but in principle at least they could shake hands on the deal at a figure of fifty-five million dollars, trans-shipment costs to be extra.

"Mr Mugheri will charter the freighter," General Azargun said.

"Excellent, so there will be no risk to the government of Iran whatsoever. And Soviet weapons should mean that the Soviet Union gets the blame – or at least that any accusations against His Imperial Majesty's government can be blurred and refuted."

"You have contacts in your news media, contacts which could help us?"

Alex thought of Maggie. "I think not," he said regretfully.

"And soon," General Azargun said, "you may want to think about Oman; the old Sultan, in his palace with all his wives, is – obstructive."

The Omani businessman nodded. "He has exiled me, and his family, and his own son and heir is under house arrest. And you know the prince, because I was with him at Craigburn."

"I'll think about all that," Alex said. Were they talking about a coup? He felt a thrill go through him. "But, again, I'd need the approval of my own government."

"Excellent. Because, beyond simple commercial considerations," the General mentioned in the lightest possible way, "there is the continuing toleration of the British base on the island of Masira – so important after the loss of Aden to the Soviets, Alex Stanton. And do not forget the strategic tanker route so vital to Europe. The Straits of Hormuz are a mere fifty miles wide. And the land now called

326

Saudi Arabia, the little Gulf states like Bahrain and the Emirates, well, they may not always be friendly. Remember what happened when you British lost Aden."

"We must not lose the Gulf for the West," Alex said simply. "I was talking about that only this evening with my colleague Mr Bryant, the government MP."

"Yes. So, you are happy, with our guns which go to the Kurds?"

"No problem," Alex said, spreading his hands as the SAVAK Colonel poured himself another vodka.

"Then we'll go ahead," the General murmured. "Any delay may be dangerous."

"Now, about how payment will reach me. I take it we will use secure intermediaries, as usual?" Alex asked.

Mugheri indicated the General. "This gentleman has made use of me to arrange delivery of the shipment under suitable conditions for our somewhat difficult circumstances. I, myself, am to arrange payment to your Hacker-Stanton International, Mr Alex Stanton."

"And that payment is to be through a third party, of course?"

"A Swiss bank, or whatever channel you find convenient."

"What I'll suggest", Alex said, casting a glance at Azari, just to remind the man Alex had a certain hold over him, "is that we operate via the Swiss. I suggest we employ the Asconia Reich Bank in Zurich for the purpose. The bank's owner is a man in whom Mr Hacker and I have confidence, and the Swiss may be relied upon to keep their heads cool and their mouths shut."

The Omani businessman made a quick gesture. "I know the bank."

Alex was impressed. "I'm so pleased we're all acquainted. Then you have no objection to Asconia?"

Mugheri shrugged. "So long as they don't mind dealing with Valetta."

"Malta?" Alex asked.

"The rent from British bases must be replaced somehow."

"Quite," Alex said. "But to return to the subject of this meeting, I suggest we meet again in about a week when we can settle things absolutely."

"I have a yacht," Mugheri said, "moored in a resort on the Caspian. We could perhaps meet there. It is a poor thing, but my own." He smiled widely for the first time, his teeth flashing gold.

327

"Not for me, thank you," Alex said hastily. "Not the Caspian; there is just cold Russian water between the Iranian shore and – the other side."

"Indeed, yes," General Azargun growled. "I forbid that. No, we can meet at my villa. Next Wednesday, if that is enough time."

They agreed it would be. Mugheri left and Alex, satisfied, got up to go as Azari spat chewing tobacco into the open fire and sauntered away.

"A moment, Alex," the General said.

Alex turned, briefcase clasped in both hands. He was a little surprised as the General closed the door.

"About the – other matters. The long-term plan, about buying into your Western armaments industries direct, through discreet intermediaries."

"You like it?"

"In his majesty's eyes, there is a problem."

Alex felt his blood freeze. "Yes?"

"We have done much business, Alex, but you are a pirate; you boast about it. You are not government, are you? You are not even a true Stanton, because you will never inherit. All you have is your father's name."

At the mention of his father Alex stood bolt upright and anger flared on his face, making even so brave a man as Azargun take a step backward.

"I am my father's heir! Isn't that enough?"

"Regrettably, Alex, it is not. There must be someone more official to vouch for what you have said, or our more serious business cannot be concluded."

Alex stood there for several seconds, staring straight at the man. Only one thing occurred to him, and he knew he was taking a chance.

It was all he could do.

"Very well," he said, disdainfully. Would nobody ever have complete confidence in him? He drew breath and knew he had to play this one to a finish and try to disguise all the disquiet he felt. Blandly, he continued. "So I must prove I am official, or we cannot do that business?"

The Iranian General answered simply. "You must."

6

The roar of the helicopters had died away by the time David Bryant realized what was happening. Even the men who had gone poking through the rooms had not prepared him for this. He saw heads turn to the banqueting room's arched entrance; then the heads bowed.

He finished pushing a canapé into his mouth and realized the champagne had made him a little drunk. The man who appeard in the doorway was not particularly tall but he had an upright bearing, and David remembered that the Shahanshah was the son of a fine soldier. He stayed still for a moment, in evening dress, and turned his gaze slowly among the company. He had a dark, brooding face and rather sad eyes – an impressive if not particularly commanding figure, David thought. Then he was surrounded by a crowd, Coombes and his elder daughter prominent among them. A man even kissed the Shah's hand.

David poured himself a cup of Earl Grey tea. Then a man in a cream suit came up to him.

"You are the Socialist, are you not?"

"Yes, I'm –" David saw the man was wearing a shoulder-holster, and a gun. "I didn't meant to –"

He scowled. "Come, now."

David had to follow him; a Persian chandelier glittered overhead.

The Shah was not in a good mood, it seemed. He was medium tall, a similar size to David.

"Mr Bryant, MP," he said, coldly formal.

Eyes turned to him. Not friendly eyes. "That's correct –" he said, wondering what honorific title to use. Excellency, majesty, what? "Majesty," he finished awkwardly. "I am very glad to be here."

329

"Are you? You seem very critical, for a guest. I had hoped a friend of the Stantons would be more gracious. Especially a friend in Her Majesty's service. Why do you make so many difficulties for us, and come here and criticize our nation? The Communists always make their propaganda to the West – they have a human rights Mafia, working against us." His upper lip curled. "But I do not see their kind protesting about this 'human rights' inside the Soviet Union or China, or in all the countries the Russians have conquered."

"I hope it is not unseemly to speak one's mind," David said steadily. "I meant no offence."

The Shah's dark eyes became hooded. He gestured at David with a cut-glass tumbler in his hand and David saw bullet-scars on his face, from the 1949 assassination attempt. "Always people come here and criticize. And yet we are proud here, and we have reason to be! Look at your country, now. Strike-bound, inefficient, weak. It is being ruined by a lack of discipline. If everybody is for himself there can only be chaos."

"My country has problems," David admitted, realizing he was sounding apologetic: the country that had invaded Persia in 1941 and deposed the Shah's father and, with Stalin's Russia, ruled till after the war, must now have representatives who apologized. "There are problems of adjustment to the twentieth century there, as there may well be here."

A uniformed man came to whisper in the Shah's ear, so he looked away over David's shoulder before speaking again. "Your troubles stem from a lack of will and vision. Perhaps it is all tiredness, after the Great War, World War II. Europe suffered, true. Then there was a fantastic explosion of affluence for Europeans – but only because of science and the exploitation of Third World countries." His English was excellent, with an accent set somewhere between standard upper-class and French. He looked David up and down now. "What is really wrong with you all? Why are you destroying yourselves? With what are you going to replace the old white Christian civilization that you did not create but only inherit?"

"That remains to be seen, Majesty," David admitted sadly.

Then the Shah inclined his head as courtiers surrounded him, and as David bowed he walked away. The man in the cream suit came up to David and took him by the upper arm, his grip strong.

"You must go with these men."

330

There were two of them, grim-faced and stocky. They led David away quickly and he wondered, taking a gulp of air, if he had really offended his hosts so badly.

He was taken along a passageway, up a dark staircase. Electric light blazed across the landing, on rich Persian carpets scattered everywhere and on the two men sitting on chairs, sub-machine-guns slung across their laps. There was a brief conversation and then the door was opened and David was pushed into the room.

Alex was there, standing by a long table where papers and a familiar black briefcase were scattered. The room was shuttered and hot; the fragance of burning wood wafted around. David looked at the other man – an Iranian officer, presumably a very senior one, in full-dress uniform. He had a strong, rough-hewn face and he looked at David appraisingly, then at Alex, who had kept his own features expressionless.

David wondered what mischief they had been plotting here.

"Welcome," the harsh-voiced officer said. "I am General Azargun. I deal with – certain matters inside and outside Iran. You are Mr David Fulton Bryant, the government MP."

David let the inaccuracy pass. "I am."

"You have worked with your Foreign Office and with Mr Stanton, I believe." It was not quite a question.

Alex stepped back two paces, out of the General's line of sight, and his face distorted with tension and David met his eyes for a moment.

Suddenly David found himself lying desperately for Alex. "Of course, I am a very close friend of our Foreign Minister and I have known Mr Stanton since Oxford in England, several years ago, and I have worked with him often – sometimes through Stanton Industries, sometimes through Hacker-Stanton, and often it is personal, him, myself."

Out of the corner of his eye he saw that Alex had smiled and briefly made an 'O' with his right thumb and first finger. Emboldened, riding the current of the moment and a little intoxicated by the Dom Perignon and his brush with the Shah, David continued smoothly. "Naturally, I cannot reveal in detail what Mr Stanton and I have done together, nor can I explain the secret policies in the Middle East of Her Majesty's Government – but I believe you want some kind of affirmation from me?" He cocked his head expectantly.

The General looked faintly puzzled. David's English, formal and slick, had been almost too rapid for him to follow.

"Then, on your honour as an MP, you will vouch that Mr Stanton has your British government, all your armed forces and your big banks and your BBC, on his side?"

"I trust him, we in government trust him – absolutely," David said, aggrieved. "I tell you on my honour as an MP."

The broad-chested Iranian turned. "Very well, Alex," he inclined his head, "so you are not a pirate but have all your British government resources behind you. That is good, very. Then after consideration His Imperial Majesty will put forward the money."

"Excellent!" Alex said, grinning broadly.

"As long as our oil revenues are not interrupted and as long as you obtain your Russian weapons so that we can pass them on to the Kurds."

"Agreed," Alex said tautly. "Now, may I have a word with my colleague in private?"

"Of course, Alex," General Azargun said. "I will be with the Shahanshah."

The door closed. Alex went over and leaned his back against it, folding his arms. David dabbed at his forehead with a handkerchief, rubbing at the sheen of perspiration. They looked at each other. Then, simultaneously, both men began to laugh.

"'On your honour'," Alex quoted.

"– 'as an MP'!" David was still chuckling. "Haven't they heard about English hypocrisy out here?"

"Not recently. Anyway, thank you – for taking the risk of committing yourself."

David was curious, now. "What are you trying to get them to do?"

"It's years away, yet, but one day I'd like some of the Shah's oil wealth to be put directly into industry. Through intermediaries, of course."

"Such as yourself?"

"Such as myself."

"What was that about Russian weapons and the Kurds?"

"Believe me," Alex said with feeling, "you don't need to know the details. But, listen, I'm grateful. Thanks again for your support. I'll remember this." He gave a twisted smile and began to gather up the papers.

David stood up and poured himself a cold tonic water and took it with him to the window where the exterior steel shutters had been closed. He stood by it, apparently gazing out at the chinks of light from the bonfires outside, but really his eyes were focused on the reflection of Alex. The image of Colonel Lawrence came to David, and he remembered the time he and Alex had once found his house in an undistinguished suburban street in Oxford, close to where David had studied. He had found it difficult to believe that so ordinary a place could have produced a man who had effectively redrawn the political boundaries of the Middle East single-handedly . . .

An involuntary thrill passed through him as he thought of the business Alex was transacting in the Middle East. Weapons for the Shah and his proxies, weapons from the United States, Britain, and even the Soviet Union. If it all worked out, Alex would be better off by millions – as well as fortified by the gratitude of someone important at the entrance to the Persian Gulf. How important would that make Alex? David tried to calculate. A friend of the Shah of Iran? Alex would be very, very important.

If all his schemes worked, money would pour into Stanton Industries again – if, that is, Alex gave his old family firm the contracts.

Alex clicked shut the locks on his case. "Can you stay a day or two more? Just till the first money comes in. And perhaps we can discuss working together on some other projects."

"Well," David said, "I believe some of the Conservative MPs have a dozen directorships. I think I could do something with you – especially as you decided not to have me killed."

Alex grinned at him.

They stayed in Major Coombes's villa all the next day, sitting by a telephone and playing chess. At dusk, a meal was brought. "I wonder where that money is," Alex said, thoughtfully. "From oil wealth in Tehran, to Kuwait, to Malta – to a Swiss bank, and to me."

The confirmatory call from Switzerland did not come till late, but they decided to leave anyway. Now that the money was there, why wait?

Outside the villa, David looked up on the way to the parked Range Rover. The sky over Tehran was black and full of familiar stars; he felt tired, but tired in a good way. Working with Alex had made him feel close to his old friend.

He slapped Alex on the back. "Tonight, I feel like your brother!"

Alex smiled, standing there with feet spread wide, like the statue of some famous man. "Brothers in arms."

It was much later that same night when Hoyle took the call from Tehran. The line whistled and crackled, as bad as ever. He had to concentrate as Fahzdi explained in halting, discreetly coded English that the two of them had escaped him. No expression crossed Hoyle's face. There would be other times for Alex Stanton, after all. And if David was still working with him, so much the better – when the day of reckoning came. Hoyle nodded briefly to himself without saying anything. Then he put the phone down. His masters behind the Iron Curtain would not be pleased.

Then he picked the telephone up again, and re-dialled: this time, to a house in Coventry.

"I put some of our people into his house, that's right. No, they didn't find anything. It looks like our friend isn't playing a double game after all, just making some notes for his own use ... a bad habit I'll get him to stop. Oh, just some stupid bitch putting it about and gossiping afterwards. I wanted to be absolutely sure, that's all. Can we use him again? I'd be prepared to, certainly. We still don't have enough MPs in our pocket."

He cradled the phone, gently, and sat staring at the fireplace. Fahzdi would have tried to kill them both. He remembered one night in Oxford, several years back. David, Maggie and he at the Levellers' Club, young people plotting how to change the world. He had spoken to Maggie. "There are always casualties in revolution."

Wait till David got home ...

He smiled, sure all this would have a salutary effect. He would have use for a more cowed David Bryant. When a general strike finally toppled a British government, they would need people in Parliament ready to form an administration more responsive to the needs of the people – as expressed through organizations like Forward. He hoped that day would not be long in coming.

Megan met him at Heathrow, when he flew back from Tehran after his week away.

It was a slightly awkward occasion, he felt as he gave her a quick embarrassed kiss. He had upset her by going away so quickly, but there had been no alternative, and what was Megan's temporary lack of forgiveness when set against his mission? What price the neglect of his wife and child?

On the flight home he had slept and dreamed of the consequences of his actions. Iran and Iraq, and behind them the two superpowers. In two days Alex had materially affected the future of the world, and he had helped. It was a terrifying glimpse of power, the breast-pocket of Adolf Hitler seen through the sight of an assassin's gun . . .

"You spent all the time I was away with your mother?"

"Mmh. Haven't been back to the place since, David." Megan drove, and David sat beside her, feeling nervous about the traffic. Naomi was strapped into a kiddie seat in the back of the car, and she was unusually quiet, as if affected by the tiredness in her father. Megan tried chatting with him, interpreting his exhaustion as coldness. Finally she put a direct question to him.

"David, what exactly were you doing with Alex Stanton?"

The droning engine noise stood between them as the green of the Berkshire countryside sped by on either side. How could he tell her about a world of which she knew so little?

"I was simply helping Alex Stanton arrange a little war on the Iran–Iraq border, Megan dear."

He couldn't say it.

"Alex wanted political advice on some Middle East investments he plans. Large-scale business, you know."

The answer seemed to satisfy her partially and she didn't press him.

As London's grey outskirts filled the horizon David thought again about Alan Hoyle. He was almost sure it was time to deliver his report.

He only hoped his masters would be ready to listen.

Then Megan asked him about the money. He prevaricated, smoothly. "All depends on the outcome. If it comes off it could mean as much as five thousand pounds."

"You told me you'd get five thousand automatically."

"Don't worry," he smiled, knowing the money was already on deposit in one of his bank accounts. It would be used not for him, nor for his family, but to finish his investigation of Forward. "It's a virtual certainty it'll be that amount. It'll take a while to sort out though."

She took his hand for a moment. "And then we can buy a bigger place. Another bedroom and a big garden for Naomi, although I'm getting sick of this horrible gloomy London. And then we can start thinking about a son."

"Yes."

"I'm glad you said yes," she said, glancing at him, "because I think I'm pregnant again."

"Oh, Megan," he told her, enthusiastically, "that's wonderful."

She let go of his hand. "I'm glad I can still say something to get your attention."

He was shocked, and realized how far apart they had drifted. "You don't mean that."

"Of course I do." She changed down a gear, slowing as the smoke-belching diesel in front of her slowed too. "All I ever wanted was a simple, straightforward marriage. Not too much to ask," she said distantly. She said it as if she thought he wasn't listening, as if he never did these days.

When they entered their house they knew at once there was something wrong.

David ran along the narrow hall, alert for some unspecified danger, going straight upstairs to the door of his office; he bent down to look at the door frame. The wood near the lock had been roughly treated, the moulding had splintered away as though a jemmy had been used against it. He fumbled with his key, but the door swung open; the lock had been broken, the room beyond ransacked. He stood with his fists raised. Megan ran up after him. Her face was numb with shock, and she raised a hand to her mouth in anguish at this violation.

"I'll ring the police –"

"No!" He turned around. "Just – I'll see you in a minute, all right?"

Megan went downstairs again, and David checked his desk. The lock had been forced, making a shameful mess of the mahogany surface. All the papers from his private drawer had gone. He looked up, looked around, appalled. They had only been the barest sketches of notes, but his electric typewriter and some other valuables were still here . . .

"Oh, David!"

Downstairs, every drawer in their small living room had been emptied onto the floor. The cushions of each piece of furniture had been slashed and the stuffing pulled out in handfuls. Even the scatter cushions had been turned inside out. Most of David's books had been ripped from their covers, all the cupboards turned out, and a yellow plastic duck of Naomi's had been crushed underfoot.

He followed her again, back up the stairs. Megan looked ill. "I'm terrified, David. This wasn't just a robbery."

"No."

Some vicious intruder had been through their bedroom too, disembowelling the mattresses, slashing Megan's dresses and swiping cosmetics and bottles of perfume onto the floor so that even now the room was heavy with scent. She looked at him, her eyes bright with tears.

"What about the police, then?"

"I'll call them in a minute," he said. "I just wanted to check what was gone before they started poking and prying."

He stood behind her as she knelt over the dress he had bought her in Paris that Easter.

"*Now* do you see why I didn't want you to come to London?"

She looked up at him, aghast at what he had said and the anger in his voice.

"David, what is it you're doing? Who did this to us?"

He turned his face away from his wife. He went downstairs, and picked his way slowly across the devastated kitchen and stood amidst the smashed crockery and upturned drawers. There was water on the tiled floor, making it slick and dangerous.

No matter who had done this, there had been no need to push it so far. A break-in was upsetting enough; this wrecking was terrifying – Megan was right. He thought uselessly about who might have done it, his racing mind conjuring up first Bronwen in a rage, then the hard face of Peter Carlton, then the cold threatening voice of Alan Hoyle ... Or maybe somebody had heard about his dealings with Alex. But his notebook and associated scraps of notes, alone, had been taken, and that was the only fact he had.

"I wish I knew who did it," he told his wife. He had the feeling much of the damage was a result of his row with Bronwen, but she would not have searched so carefully, nor, surely, taken the papers from his desk. Then he remembered that the front door had not been forced opened and that Bronwen had a key. In the smashed mirror in

337

the kitchen he saw his face was chalky white. "Seven years of bad luck
. . ."

So perhaps it was Bronwen. Then somebody else, better organized,
had followed – ruthless, searching everything. What were they trying
to find out?

He spooned coffee powder out of a cracked jar on the floor and
into two cups, trying to avoid the broken glass.

"I'm going to ring 999 now," Megan told him, from the doorway.

He answered in a dead voice, deciding now that he had to finish
his report and hand over the investigation of Forward to somebody
else.

"Yes. You do that. You get the police onto this."

She still hadn't moved and suddenly they were talking about
another issue entirely. "It's really time to bring them in?"

He looked at her, his face expressionless as his voice; he was tired.
"Yes."

Maggie had to go abroad shortly after David returned from his
Tehran adventure, and returned only in the spring. The opinion
polls had begun to favour the Labour government again, and the local
elections sweepingly confirmed the trend. Maggie felt the sudden
optimism in the party, and all the talk was of a June election. Then
the Prime Minister set the date.

She tried twice to return David's notebook, but he was never there.
Election business, Megan told her, and Maggie felt embarrassed to
say anything over the phone since the matter concerned adultery.
Then, on 29 May, 1970, Parliament was prorogued and the campaign
began in earnest, the two parties heading for polling day almost neck
and neck.

Inside their Smith Square headquarters, the Conservatives' Thursday Group planned their tactics well. Maggie knew that people's basic
concern was with the way the economy was being handled, and the
high level of tax provided an issue. The Opposition began to hammer
the government.

Maggie covered the run-up to polling day for a U.S. news agency,
spending some of her time aboard the fifty-seater plane Stanton
Industries had provided for the Opposition.

She left the plane in time to review the television coverage in an
article for her own magazine, and here the balance seemed to favour
the Labour government.

338

The Prime Minister was interviewed in the garden of Number 10, and the rather mild questioning never disturbed his affable manner. The Conservative leader, on the other hand, was given to Robin Day from the BBC's *Panorama* programme, and this interview was a much rougher affair.

Maggie was delighted. It was more important than ever to ensure a Labour government was returned to power. Much of her new readership was in the newly-enfranchised eighteen to twenty-one age group, and in her articles she insisted to them: 'In spite of all our disappointments, there must not be a right-wing government here – even if that means returning a Labour government as spineless and uninspired as the existing one.'

She took a weekend off to fly to Florence with Terry, then returned determined to get in touch with David and return his property.

Megan told her that David would be home around six that night, so she drove over to his street through the rush-hour to give the brown notebook back to him in person. It was actually after seven before she saw David come towards her, swinging his leather case as he stepped between two parked cars.

She tapped his shoulder after getting out of her car. "David?"

He turned around quickly, his face strained and shocked, then relaxed as he recognized her. "Maggie. It's you." There was a pause she did nothing to fill. "I wonder if you'd care to step inside, have some tea or something?"

"No," she said. "I've got a present for you."

He took the envelope, pulled out the notebook.

When he looked up again his face frightened her. "Where did you get this? From Alan Hoyle?"

She found she was trembling, and her voice quavered with emotion. Did she still feel for him? "I bought it off your lover, if you really want to know. For a hundred pounds. Isn't adultery cheap?"

He seemed strangely relieved. "Thank you, Maggie. I won't forget this."

"But David, don't you know that Megan loves you?"

He looked tired, and his usually neat black hair was awry, but he stared back at her and he was not ashamed. "Maggie, I've done many, many things in this life I'm not proud of, but I've paid for them all. I've tried to do my duty, most of the time. I wish you could believe that."

She looked at him for a long time, then her chin dipped. She added, her green eyes glinting with humour, "Though it's astute of you to work that out about Alan."

"What?"

"Oh, he was there when Bronwen tried to sell me the story of your scandal – Labour's newest MP an adulterer with his wife's sister, then going off to Tehran to deal in arms alongside Alexander Stanton."

His face had tightened. He seemed to be looking at some other horizon as things, finally, fell into place for him.

"She said all that, did she?"

Maggie was worried about his reaction. "Yes."

"I suppose Alan wanted to read my notebook."

"Yes," she answered. "But I didn't let him! He asked me, but I told him no. I'm on your side, Davey!"

"Thank God," he said. Then he closed his eyes for a moment. "What do you think of Alan Hoyle, Maggie?"

She wrinkled her nose. "A very able man, I suppose, with an incredible range of contacts. Although there is a certain intellectual ruthlessness in him . . . It impresses some women, but it isn't to my taste . . . Why do you ask?"

"I'd like to give you some advice, Maggie. I'd stay away from him. Alan Hoyle is dangerous."

"Yes, but . . ." She lifted her shoulders in the beginnings of a shrug. "I thought you associated with him – a lot."

"I suppose a lot of people think that, don't they?" He clutched the leather case with his notebook now safely inside, like a shield in front of his chest. The evening sun gleamed on his dark hair as he shook his head. Though the polls all pointed to a Labour victory he did not seem optimistic. "It's probably too late for me, Maggie."

"God," she said, "you know, there've been two or three occasions when he's put me onto stories, or asked me to send journalists to investigate issues . . . You mean he's been using me for some scheme of his?"

"It's much more than a scheme, Maggie," he told her soberly.

He had no proof that Alan Hoyle had sent people to raid his home, but he suspected it. Now that his family had been involved, it was time to speak out and hand over his investigation to the competent authorities, in spite of all the urgent business connected with the election. He began writing his formal report on the Forward movement.

By then, his old friend and sponsor Lord Tytryst, Frank Deacon, was out of active politics entirely. He had given up the little office he used to share with David, and now he spent much of his time in Wales, writing his memoirs, or enjoying the sober debates in the House of Lords. So David rang 10 Downing Street himself, but could not get the Prime Minister. Word eventually came back that he was too busy for a formal meeting, and eventually David met him in a lift in the Commons. He hinted about Forward, and that he was ready to talk; and he mentioned his own worries about the election – his instincts told him not to trust the opinion polls.

The PM looked at him as if he were a stranger, and a dubious one at that.

"I hope you will consider what I've been saying, sir." Then more people crowded in, an all-party group, and David could no longer speak.

It was during the following week that David Bryant was at last summoned in secret to Number 10 to deliver his report on entryism. It was emphasized that there would not be an agenda, nor minutes, nor a formal record of any kind.

David sat in the back of the official car, holding his attaché case on his lap. Everything had been cleared out from the safe in the little Whitehall office; all his papers and his prized notebook had been shredded or burned. There was only his report. Earlier, the mirror had confirmed that he was immaculately groomed, and he felt himself to be a pillar of respectability. What he had in his case, however, proved he had been anything but that.

After speaking to Maggie it became clear that Bronwen had been first. She had gone to Maggie to try to embarrass him. Failing that, she had smashed up their house herself, vindictively, as well as interesting Hoyle in David's other activities. He thought of her now, but only with sadness, even though she had started all this trouble. She had also saved his life by giving the notebook itself to Maggie, because when the thorough professionals from the Forward team had searched the house after her, they had found nothing incriminating. That had been lucky, very lucky, and it had decided him. There was only one avenue, now. He straightened, as the car stopped.

Behind that famous black door, the highest in the land . . .

On this, perhaps his twentieth visit, the Downing Street lobby had a comforting familiarity. He was conducted to a ground floor meeting room, where, unexpectedly and to his great surprise, three people

341

were waiting for him. Frank Deacon was there, but so was the Prime Minister's security advisor, and a third man, quiet and bespectacled and unknown to him.

On the threshold, David looked from man to man, and asked, "Is this *proper*, Frank?"

"You can speak freely here."

David hesitated. He looked along the row of seated men. "My original instructions specified you," he told Frank, "and the PM only. No one else."

Frank told him to sit down. His face was grave.

"The PM is busy with the election." He put out an open hand to the unknown man. "May I introduce Mr Hammond. George Hammond. He's with the – Home Office. A very senior chap. You of course know the PM's security advisor. You can speak openly with all of us."

David felt betrayed. As he had suspected long ago over Carlton, MI5 involvement had been sanctioned over his head and without his knowledge. That meant the stakes had been raised prematurely. They were at least treating the Forward conspiracy as a national problem, though, and not as merely an internal Labour party matter.

He sat down and pulled the report from his briefcase.

Frank reached out a big hand, but David held onto the blue folder and insisted, "This is the original, and it's unique. There are no copies. I've destroyed all my working papers and the rough drafts."

"I'll respect it, David."

"I'm concerned about confidentiality, and I'm starting to worry about my own safety. My home was burgled and ransacked a while ago."

"There's no need to worry too much." Hammond faced him blankly, his heavy-framed glasses making his eyes unreadable. "Let's get to the substance of this meeting."

David saw there was no alternative; he had to speak out. He put it to them bluntly. "Alan Hoyle claims he inherited Forward by – murder. He says that the founder, a don called Bonnington, a crypto-Communist, was drowned. Deliberately."

Frank, Lord Tytryst, looked shocked. "So that's what kind of man Alan Hoyle is!"

"We're just talking hearsay, here," Hammond said crisply. "Perhaps it was mere boasting. It wouldn't stand up in court! You'll have to do better than that, David Bryant."

"I've personally seen what must have been one of their arms caches."

Frank was appalled. "Why didn't you tell me before?"

David hesitated, wondering if he was actually incriminating himself.

"I had to see this through, Frank. I had to find out – not everything, but enough."

Frank said harshly, "So these boys have guns – and Irish links, I suppose?"

"It's even more complicated than that."

The security advisor looked at him quizzically.

Frank Deacon's voice was harsh. "What kind of weapons do they have?"

"It was in that warehouse up in Manchester, Frank, near Strangeways Prison. I helped move Stanton Industries packing cases, lots of them. I noted some of the designation codes, and checked with – someone I know who has access to their Armaments Division records."

"Well?" Hammond barked. "What did you find?"

"It was a stolen consignment of Stanton machine-guns. Stolen in Liverpool."

Hammond said, "To be trans-shipped by Hacker-Stanton International, consigned to Beirut."

"That's right," David said, surprised.

"Those guns were hijacked off the Liverpool docks, David, and the night watchman was murdered."

David swallowed. So Alan Hoyle and his man Jake really had killed.

"I don't remember hearing about that."

"No," Hammond said. "A 'D' notice to kept it out of the press."

"I think that's excellent evidence for my case," David said. "I've seen weapons." He produced the bullet Hoyle had given to him. "As you can see, they're preparing for civil war, and they're not fooling."

He had the attention of the meeting now. The others kept staring at the bullet, as David intended. For an hour, he sat in the glare of a window and spoke. Outside, the June overcast sky was the white of a blind man's eye. Inside, the room was hot and stuffy and civilized, thoroughly English, from the civil service carpet to the robin's egg blue of the walls.

343

He told them how the Forward web had been formed in tight secrecy by disaffected Leftists and revolutionaries all over the country, from Glasgow tenements to communes in Dorset; in back rooms in Liverpool and Leeds and suburban houses off London's North Circular, in the SW1 apartments of influential sympathizers, contacts were being made and plans laid.

"The organization I penetrated is certainly the largest and best-organized of the entryist groups," he said. "It has a complete, extremely secretive structure that covers the mainland. It also has Irish links, strong ones, and I believe it has helped active service units in terrorist acts in Birmingham and London, although I was unable to get details. It numbers at least eleven thousand members – and their number is growing. Some of them are in high places, or they soon will be. They have student leaders, trade union officials – and they want to get first Labour party officers, then MPs like me, and then government ministers."

Frank Deacon was unmistakeably shocked.

"Is this possible?"

"It's very possible, Frank. It also happens to be true. The country is under attack. These people have no faith in parliamentary democracy. In their eyes there's no alternative to armed struggle."

Hammond suddenly spoke up. "We know that an MP with close links with the Labour leadership has taken money from behind the Iron Curtain. In Parliament there are others, we think, perhaps up to Cabinet level."

The PM's man shook his head. "The PM's *explicit* instructions are that there is to be *no* investigation of MPs, or of the Lords, unless he gives formal permission."

Hammond's face became a smooth blank. "Of course, though I must point out that the PM has hardly ever given us such permission."

There was a strained silence. David held onto his report like a lifebelt. *To Cabinet level* . . . Neither the security advisor nor Frank Deacon had made denial. It was true, therefore. The nation had been penetrated almost to the highest level.

It occurred to him, more clearly than the first time, that he was already too late. He wondered what he would do if they buried his report on Forward.

Frank sat back in his chair. "Let's have the rest," he said harshly.

David ran through the history. Forward had both money and organization. It practised political indoctrination, it sent emissaries on trips abroad, and there was even the hint of secret training camps in unspecified foreign locations. Every member was educated to expect and promote struggle, and to expedite the arrival of civil strife. Its key people were taking positions in the trade unions, in government and the civil service, and they were making a special effort to penetrate the BBC, the police, and the armed services.

Frank's face was grim. "Who sits on the national committee?"

"It's self-selecting; a Politburo. Ten members, but they're only ever referred to in the records by letters, A to K excluding I. Apart from Alan Hoyle's, I only know three names, but setting any question of politics aside, I believe I have evidence to link them to arson, assault, and murder."

The three men looked at one another. They were taken aback, but David wondered if they really believed him yet. He continued: "Though they purport to raise their income from a levy on their members, the figures suggest a supplementary source."

"Supplementary?" the security advisor asked.

"An external source."

Hammond instantly sat up. "From where?"

David shook his head. "I don't know. But if you're asking me about my suspicions, I suspect from abroad."

Frank was staring into space, his jaw set. "Gentlemen, I think our duty is clear."

"Take it straight to the PM," the man on his left said.

"I will." Lord Tytryst looked straight at David. "There may be a delay because of the election, but afterwards there'll be expulsions from the party, and Forward will be placed on the Labour party's proscribed list." He looked around. "I know some people say the PM hasn't the stomach for a fight with the hard Left, but this will prove to be different."

"I'm sure," David said politely. "I'll leave the report with you, Frank."

Frank added, "I'll pass on a copy to Mr Hammond, on the understanding that David's name is not connected."

"As you say," Hammond said, rising.

It was a warm day in Downing Street, and a crowd had gathered beyond the barriers. Election fever had begun to raise the political temperature. George Hammond glanced that way before turning to David.

"I don't see what more you can do, without resources and proper training, but I had the impression that you wanted to find out a little more about Mr Hoyle and his activities."

David hesitated. "I've taken many risks to continue this investigation, and I want to see those risks made worthwhile. But I have to confess that I've implicated myself in Hoyle's activities much more than – well, much more than now seems wise."

"But you don't want to back off?"

"No." He hesitated. "I saw Hoyle last week, at his insistence. He told me the next attack he plans is on a target I am personally interested in, and can help him destroy – he thinks."

"And that is?" George Hammond asked, smoothly.

"Stanton Industries."

On the evening of 23 July, almost a month after the election, David was sitting down to dinner with his wife. He had just flown in the day before: an all-party Parliamentary investigation.

"And you liked Japan?" she called, from the kitchen.

"Liked it?" He gave a harsh laugh. "I was impressed, and depressed. They mean to win, Megan. I saw their cities and their factories and shipyards. World War II is being continued by them, but with commercial means. They intend to take on the world, and beat us."

"Well, it'll be up to the Tories to stop them, now."

He sighed. "Yes."

He contemplated the surprise result of the 1970 general election before he began to eat. The Tories had defeated the Labour government, romping home with a majority of 31 seats in Parliament. There had been only a million votes in it, but the electoral system had magnified this absurdly. There was no consensus here; simply two sides promoting the vested interests of their own supporters, not promoting fairness, competition or progress. As ever, the new government would change nothing, and would never deliver, and the public would soon grow disenchanted and install the opposition again, only to have the alternative government fail, too.

It was an adversarial charade that satisfied nobody. David threw his feet up on another kitchen chair and the newspaper fell apart across the tiled floor.

"Left, right – left, right – left, right –"

Megan looked at him as she put the salad bowl down. "I've never had that reaction to my spaghetti Bolognese before."

"Entire praise, Megan." He raised the fork to his lips and sucked at the spaghetti. "It's lovely."

"I hope it won't spoil your appetite, but there's something else in the paper – about somebody you know. It's on the back page."

The headline said: OLD ETONIAN EXPOSES SCANDAL. He read, stunned, that Lord Beauford had publicly praised the assistant director of client relations in his merchant bank for exposing the scandal of tax evasion by some of his millionaire clients after the Inland Revenue had started an investigation. Four low-level employees had been sent to prison for concealing this – "claiming, in suitably cowardly fashion, that Mr Battersby and I were the real culprits in this matter. Of course, we knew nothing of it, and I wish Mr Battersby well in his new career." David shook his head and threw the pages down with the rest. Was there no justice?

Megan sat down and reached for the Parmesan cheese, frowning at the newspaper around his legs; she had always been neat. "What happens to you now, David?"

"A majority trimmed to 915," he remembered, sighing. "It'll be years before I have even a chance of government office, now."

"As long as you don't end up working with that Alex Stanton again."

"Actually, he may be on Stanton Industries' main Board of Directors, soon."

"Quite a coup for him."

"Of course, but I suppose he's something of an expert in coups." David smiled at her. "He inherits control of his father' shares this year, and of course he has money of his own – with more to come. So he gets a non-executive directorship. Then, if he can persuade Hugh, he wants the Armaments Division to run himself. If that comes off, he's going to offer me something in Stanton Industries, in their International Relations department. It's an advisory job, only part time, obviously. I might take it, might not."

There was something else on his mind, too. In a pencilled note hidden inside a Bible on his office bookshelves he had Hammond's extension number at the Curzon Street headquarters. It seemed to him that it was his duty to phone the man soon, and talk business, because there had been no reaction at all to his report on Forward, from Frank or anybody: it was simply 'under consideration', and he had the feeling it would stay that way for ever.

He stabbed a fork hard into the salad. Alan Hoyle was dangerous and had to be stopped. David could not give up trying, in spite of all the risks. Lately, Hoyle had spent more time cultivating David than ever, asking many questions about Stanton Industries and the Stanton family's enemies in the trade union movement and the media. David worried over what he was planning; he feared it might be serious.

Later that evening, David watched impassively as Robert Dougal read the early evening news bulletin. Iraq had blamed the Soviet Union for helping its northern, Kurdish rebels; and the Iraqi government claimed to have captured weapons as proof.

Alex would have the rest of his money, therefore, very soon.

Book Three
1

David drove through the heart of Mayfair, past tall, pretty houses, and then past the shuttered concrete fortress that housed the headquarters of MI5.

By contrast, a few streets away, the London office of Hacker-Stanton International was as discreet and luxurious as a Swiss bank. David got out of his car here, locked it, and walked up the spotless stone stairs as a security camera swivelled to follow him. A metal bell-push was beside a brass plate engraved with the firm's name, and addresses in Dover, Delaware and the Cayman Islands.

Inside, he had to wait in reception as a polite, uniformed man X-rayed his briefcase, as if this was an airport departure point. The pretty, well-groomed blonde girl at the desk picked up a telephone.

"He's here, Mr Stanton. Right on time, as you said."

David realized his punctuality had made him predictable; and he did not like being predictable.

The girl led him up stairs thickly carpeted in red, white and blue and knocked on a heavy door. Alex himself opened it, grinning.

"Good to see you, David. Wendy, could you get us some tea?" Alex turned back to him, fresh-faced and in a good mood. "Never seen my lair before, have you?"

"No." David glanced around. "I see there's money in what you do."

"Yes."

"And some risk?"

Alex hesitated. "You mean the security, do you? Well, you may remember the car bomb last month – an Iraqi blew himself up where

349

South Audley Street and Curzon Street cross. I've reason to believe he was heading here."

"My God."

"Still, I've taken steps. We have contacts with Baghdad, and I don't think we'll be bothered by them for a while. Now –" David was ushered up to a long conference table. Facing him, seated in a leather swivel chair, was another man.

Alex made the introductions quickly. "David Bryant, MP."

The man leaned over and extended his hand. David shook it.

"I've heard a lot about you. Looked forward to this. Ken McCourt."

His lightweight suit and neatly-clipped beard gave him a sharp Californian look; there was nothing of the stodgy Home Counties executive about him, David reflected, but his accent, smooth and mid-Alantic, had something unexpected in it.

David sat down in another chair. "Did I detect a trace of Ulster in your speech?"

"You did," Alex said crisply, "but Ken's been with Ray and me in America for the past couple of years, working on the production side – you'll remember we've been buying defence-linked companies. We took him from Lockheed. I finally picked him because he has spent three years in Tokyo and is fluent in Japanese – the language as well as their business methods."

"I see," David said, the Swedish chair creaking comfortably under him. After his coup in Tehran, Alex was obviously tooling up for something else; perhaps a push into large-scale production.

"Something you probably won't know yet, David. As from next week, I'll be on the Stanton Industries Board of Directors. Non-executive, obviously, but I'll be there."

"Congratulations. It's been long enough coming!"

"I get the voting rights in the Stanton shares my father left me soon. Hugh was – good enough to let me take up my seat in advance." Alex grinned ruefully, his eyes rather shadowed. David could imagine there had been a struggle with Lord Beauford and Hugh. "I remember when Hugh inherited his place; the summer of '63 it would be, after President Kennedy was here. There was a massive celebration at Craigburn for Hugh. There'll be nothing for me as far as Stanton Industries is concerned."

"There's this," David said, opening his case and producing a bottle, which he gave to Alex.

Alex held it up to the sunlight. It was a single malt whisky, pure and golden. "Laphroaig," he said, pleased, "from Islay."

"It's the one," David said. "Now, I'd like to suggest you open it, and we'll drink a toast."

"May I?" McCourt said, opening a glass cabinet and finding some Waterford tumblers. He turned to Alex. "To Stanton Industries, its founders, heirs and successors – to good fortune for it."

They each drank a small glass, ceremonially.

"Now," Alex said, sitting down, "to business. Over some of Wendy's Earl Grey tea, I think. First; David, I want to employ you as a consultant. Personally, not through this company. My project is bringing Stanton Industries safely to the year 2000. I'll need management, staff, unions, government, somehow working together towards that goal. So, any objections?"

"Not in principle," David said, cautiously. "Though you have to remember my position and my public image. As an MP I'm vulnerable to accusations of special interests, and I do have other duties which must take priority."

"I understand exactly," Alex said, softly. "The country and Stanton Industries both have enemies enough. But you're with me?"

David hesitated briefly, then finally committed himself. "Yes."

He remembered toasting Stanton Industries with Alex as he followed Hoyle out of the anonymous terraced house in which they had been staying. The tenant was a retired, embittered railwayman; his knowledge of Marxist theory had been impressive, but there was no generosity in his spirit. The present Tory government already had the worst strike record since 1926. There were those, David knew, who intended to make it even worse. First industry and then the government would be brought down.

"You were with that Alex Stanton?"

"At the beginning of the week, back in London," David said. "Looks like he'll be on their main board soon –"

"I think I heard that. Didn't he give an interview about restoring 'the old glory of the firm' or some such nonsense?"

"He thinks a lot of the company."

"Stanton Industries? It's like this country – vulnerable," Hoyle said softly, shutting the front door behind him. "I think I've proved that to you. The balance sheets, for example."

That had shocked David as they worked over the data last night. Such information could have come only from a very highly placed

351

source indeed – either in the company itself, or in one of their banks' headquarters. He moved with Hoyle to a battered BMC Morris 1100. It was a drizzly November afternoon, already growing dark. The northeasterly wind ate into David through the fabric of his dark blue suit, and he shivered, admiring the taller man's ability to disregard the weather's bite.

"The whole country is vulnerable, Alan. If you'd seen what I saw in Japan – the biggest dry dock in the world, the most efficient factories . . ." He shook his head. "The shoe will pinch, even for America, when Tokyo starts the trade war."

"Fuck America." Hoyle laughed. As soon as he'd settled himself in the driving seat, he drove away quickly.

"Not much of a car," David commented.

"No," Hoyle said, as he picked his way through the Tyneside traffic. "But it does the trick. Like my clothes, you understand."

David knew what Hoyle meant: Lenin too had valued his credibility. Dedication, decent poverty – he had to admit that Hoyle was fashioned after an authentic original. Today the man wore a green rollneck sweater and a pair of neat grey trousers under his nylon anorak – a change from the white shirt, tie and expensive grey suits he usually wore in the capital. He made David feel conspicuous.

"I feel we're getting there, David."

"We ought to be. Unless you should be driving in reverse."

Hoyle was not really listening. "Excitement. Purpose. Like a Provo active service unit, with a three hundred pound bomb in the back."

"When did you do that?"

This comment Hoyle noticed. He laughed. "Ideas are the sharpest weapons, David."

That was true enough.

Hoyle turned on the radio. A disdainful BBC voice that might have been reporting events taking place on another planet told them about the war in Cambodia, mentioning Maggie's recent expulsion from the country. The windscreen wipers ticked away hypnotically as David pulled his black attaché case onto his lap. As he opened it Hoyle glanced in.

"Everything there?"

"I read the Geddes report last week, and then updated the information. I'm abreast of the current state of the shipbuilding business."

Hoyle laughed, his hands light on the wheel. "You're well prepared, then. You'll be asked to deliver a short summary of statistics. I want you to lay 'em on thick."

So far, Hoyle had divulged little else about the meeting except that it was very important, and he had deflected all David's questions in his characteristically cagey way – he had a highly-developed facility for speaking powerfully but saying nothing of substance.

They passed through the suburb of Byker, then followed a big yellow bus down the narrow canyon between Parsons' giant turbine factory and the dismal terrace of houses that fronted it, heading towards Wallsend and the tall yellow cranes of the shipyards.

"I'm looking forward to this," he told Hoyle, then threw in a leading question. "Which of the Stanton yards are we going to?"

"It's an important meeting. We brief the regional command, then we'll decide on precise targets. You'll find there's a great deal of local support. You're from here. That's one of the reasons the Executive of the movement thought you should be involved. And, of course, we may need our own voice to speak in the House of Commons."

"I dare say, but which yard are we visiting?" David remembered that big strike back in '56. That, too, had started in the Shipbuilding Division. Now a new, unpalatable thought occurred to David as he saw which way they were heading.

Hoyle pulled out from the roadside a little way, forcing an overtaking Ford Consul to give up the idea. The driver hit his horn three times in displeasure and dropped back.

Hoyle studied his mirror with annoyance. "Did you see that?" he asked David. "Some people around here take appalling risks."

David had got the message; he agreed to shut up.

There was a high red-brick wall topped off with a rim of broken glass, ornate iron gates with the company crest rusting above, and a security hut to their left. The gateman put his head out and looked them over. He wore a blue serge, police-style tunic and peaked cap. He was old enough to have respect for his uniform, and proud enough to show two wartime medal ribbons sewn on the breast.

Hoyle wound down the window. "Union representatives. Meeting for four-thirty."

The security man consulted a book and tore off a perforated windscreen sticker before waving them through.

David recognized the vast, low outline of the sheds with dismay. This was no shipyard, but a steel rolling mill, where ingots of white hot steel were extruded into sheets. It was antiquated, but still the largest in Britain.

Hoyle drove along its flank, a third of a mile of filth, soiled brick and corrugated iron.

Here David's father had served his time as an apprentice before the industrial accident that had enabled him to become a publican. In those days, twenty-foot high letters had been painted along the shed, proclaiming STANTON INDUSTRIES. Now David saw that decades of northern weather had almost totally obliterated the lettering. Weeds grew in the bicycle racks below, and heaps of rusting scrap cluttered the corners. There was no pride here, that was obvious.

Hoyle parked the car and got out. "Your side locked?" he asked. "You can't be too careful. There are thieving bastards around. Remember the Manchester warehouse?"

David looked up, startled. "What about it?"

"I didn't tell you – some stupid bastard unbolted one of the barred windows, and I think somebody got inside. We could have lost everything."

"Jesus! What about the – stuff?"

Hoyle threw him a hard, judgemental look. "The other team had already taken it straight back to Liverpool. They hid it in a place not connected to Forward at all."

David exhaled loudly. "But somebody broke security. Who did it, Alan?"

Hoyle looked at him again, unblinkingly. "I don't know. And I don't see how we can find out, now. You see, the other boys moved in straight away. Might even have been one of them getting careless or wanting fresh air or something." Hoyle sighed. "You can't take chances with things like that."

"That's a fact." David tried the car door handle and peered around through the drizzle. "I'm surprised you could just book an appointment to get in here," he said.

Hoyle seemed momentarily perplexed. "Why? We're on official union business. What can they do about it?"

David wondered what Will Langton would have said about his union being misused like this. "They've no idea what takes place?"

"It's none of their business, and there's nothing they can do about it. We have fixed agreements with management about provision of union meetings, David. It's a free country, and we take advantage of the fact."

There was a rumble which grew to a massive roar that shook the earth like a gigantic runaway train hurtling through the shed. Then a group of four men dressed in overalls appeared from a door and approached in single file along the wall, sheltering from the rain.

"Comrade Hoyle?" one of them asked.

"I'm Hoyle. Comrade Robinson?"

"That's right."

There followed a dour exchange that did not include David in its compass. After a brief time in which the men looked suspiciously over David's suit and case they all went inside the huge shed, into the world of industry – a world that was like a sermon on Hell made real.

David drew back in alarm from a hissing, white-hot slab of steel as big and as fast as a car that thundered towards him on a bed of powered rollers. He felt the radiant heat burn his face as it went by. The noise of its passing was a physical assault. Further back, huge mechanical hammers crushed burning blocks of metal, and sent sparks flying. The men who worked there wore asbestos suits and face masks, and wielded long tongs and spikes.

"My God!" David shouted to Hoyle. "It's terrifying!"

"You can bet there aren't many Old Etonians earning their living here!"

The group dispersed, leaving them to follow Robinson in a tortuous journey through the shed.

The heat and vibration penetrated David to the bone, as jets of super-heated steam played out of piping in a way that made him think his flesh might at any moment be scalded away. He couldn't help wondering what dreadful stories of industrial accidents circulated in this hellish place. How could men stand to spend eight-hour shifts in here, day in, day out, for year upon year?

Hoyle turned back, looking for a reaction and finding it. He grinned, as though he was enjoying it. High above them a few grimy fluorescent tubes lit the shed, and the caked panes of glass set in the roof admitted a brown blur of light. But the incandescent blocks of metal branded Hoyle's open features with a red glare. He motioned in the direction of the far end of the track. David followed, looking up at the rolling machines. They were grey, huge and squat, a three-high stack of rollers. Vertiginous stairs led up to a precarious catwalk, across the track. They mounted and looked over the rail at glowing, rippling sheets of quarter-inch steel moving along the bed forty feet below, sheets that would probably end up as part of the ships made in the Stanton yards on the Tyne or the Wear.

"They've not spent a bloody penny on this place since the war!" Hoyle shouted. He punched David on the shoulder, making him grasp the railing firmly, then bounced down the iron stair after the reception committee, while David followed more cautiously.

There was no doubt that Hoyle was a capable man, David thought. He had to admire his energy and single-mindedness. It was such a pity he applied it to so negative a cause.

David followed them out of the mill, into a warehouse where a gantry crane stacked tight coils of thin sheet steel like outsize toilet rolls, then past an area of red rusted drums, to a low brick shack built within a corner of the warehouse structure. Robinson led them in. In front of the hanging clipboards and memoranda that covered the walls, four men sat at the long laminate-top table, holding mugs of tea.

Robinson slammed home the bolts on the door, shutting out the noise, then Hoyle sat down on one side of the table, with David to his right. One of the men wore a pair of Stanton overalls, another an Arran sweater, and two, to his surprise, were in dark suits like himself. It was obvious they were pleased to see Hoyle.

"I'd like to introduce David Bryant, comrades," he told them, eyes sparkling. "Our MP – the first of many. He's a public figure so we won't, we can't, disguise his name."

Introductions passed round the table. David sensed the men relax. His own interest heightened: he looked unobtrusively at the men, noting details of their appearance, just in case the names he had been given were *noms de guerre*. Then with a shock he realized the exact nature of the meeting.

He had supposed it was to be a case of the general, armed with the authority of his high command, about to instruct his staff officers, but he saw it was otherwise. These men were all clearly powers in their own right. It was a much more important meeting than he had imagined. It remained for him to find out just why they had come here to Stanton's mill to hold it.

Robinson banged the table with an empty tea mug. "Comrades, I now declare this meeting of the Regional Committee in plenary session."

David's head throbbed as he tried to follow the talk and retain the details. Should he try to alert Alex to what was going on? he wondered,

356

or go straight to George Hammond in the security service? Could he afford to risk compromising himself? And above all, why had he been asked along?

The meeting followed the classic form, except there were no minutes taken and the speed with which they got down to specifics was impressively businesslike. David suspected this was the first time all the members of the local Executive had met together. It seemed that Hoyle had never met Robinson before, though he clearly knew the others. If David was correct, it meant that though this was the biggest meeting Hoyle had yet allowed him to see, now they were willing to discuss business openly in front of him. Perhaps, David speculated, it meant they needed him.

The talk soon turned to local matters.

"I sent young Croft along to the union man at region," the shipyard representative said, bringing David's thoughts sharply back to the discussion. "Langton packed him off, though. He's a hard man."

"Aye, a pity he's not on our side," said another, looking obliquely at David.

"Croft tried some tough talking –"

"Threats, you mean? What happened?" Hoyle said.

"Langton gave him a black eye," the other replied ruefully. "He's an obstacle. He has no interest in political striking, he always clamps down on wildcat action, and he's got a tight hold on his following. All the Tyne and Wear yards look for his say-so."

"He doesn't know about us, does he?" David asked innocently.

"He knows there's a radical faction," Hoyle said harshly. His face creased for a moment. "Put him down for immediate action. We've got to oust him or control him if we're going to get the Stanton strike to last as long as we want."

"But the members are loyal to him."

Hoyle brooked no 'buts'. He stabbed his finger into the table. "Then they must be turned – or he has to be got rid of. We can't have a strike ending in a compromise, Billy; this must be total commitment or it won't work."

"But I know Langton's going to push hard during the current pay round. We could get him to set a high figure for a wage claim – too bloody high for the Stantons to pay. That way we're sure of a good long fight."

One of the others looked up. "Supposing he decides to settle the strike before we want him to?"

"He has to be prevented," Hoyle said. "Understand it plainly. This strike has to go all the way. We have many friends in other unions; they'll back us up. It's been four and a half years since the dock strike, and we need another victory."

The man in the darker suit answered him. "That's what we're here for, Alan. If William Langton gets in our way –" he gave a sudden venomous smile" – we'll give him more than a bit of libel in the papers, won't we?"

"Fine," Hoyle said, and continued. "So, to the specifics. I want to talk about shipbuilding. It's an important division of Stanton Industries, and its fortunes have national and international consequences. Don't forget that British trade depends on ships, and so does the defence of the realm. It's also a part of British industry which is in deep crisis – an Achilles' heel for the Stanton Board of Directors and their backers in the City, as well as the government. I'm going to list their problems, and I want you to regard each of them as opportunities for us. First, there are restrictive labour practices – tight division of labour into watertight compartments between trades."

Hoyle paused and looked from face to face before continuing.

"Secondly, we're all aware of the poor relationships between the labour force and the management in most yards. I don't have to say that this distrust can be very helpful to us. If you can drive a wedge between management and the workforce on any issue at all, do it."

There were nods around the table as he went on.

"Thirdly, management use outdated methods and seem to be utterly uninterested in the long-term success of the company. Since they show no loyalty to the company, they can be easily undermined."

David nodded at that. There was no doubt Hoyle had done his homework. "Nobody loves a loser," he said.

"Fourth, and linked to the last point; ownership and bad policy at board level. There has been long-standing and massive under-investment. If we can demonstrate this neglect clearly and loudly enough, sympathy will inevitably leak away from the fat controllers in the City."

At this point Hoyle turned to David. "Comrade Bryant has been asked to expand on these points."

David took out his notes and began smoothly, "In 1950, this country was still by far the largest builder of ships in the whole world: we had forty per cent of the world total. The decline since then has been catastrophic. By 1968 the UK share was no more than

358

five per cent. Spain, Sweden, Brazil and Japan have all passed us in the league table . . .”

When David had finished the catalogue of facts Hoyle stood up and moved to the blackboard behind him. “There’s no way *anybody* can respect management that allows defeats like that, is there?” Then he drew out the structure of the Stanton empire and pointed to one of the three boxes he had outlined. “Stanton’s weak point now is its Shipbuilding Division. It has an overwhelming burden of debt. If the division fails, because of the way the company is structured, the whole edifice will come tumbling down. The Aircraft and Armaments Divisions will be forced into bankruptcy, with all of the chaos and reorganization that goes with that – and then we can insist on nationalization to settle the strike. Nationalization – with our own union people on the board.”

One of the others looked up. “What if the Stanton family borrow more money to tide them over?”

“Impossible. I happen to know they’ve already mortgaged themselves up to the hilt and beyond. Last week the Finance Director had three refusals from different banks – no more money, under no circumstances.”

“That bad, is it?” one of the men said.

“I’ve – obtained copies of the company balance sheets,” Hoyle said. “They’re still losing money; they have a burden of debt that’s almost insupportable even without a crippling strike. A hike in interest rates would probably finish them. If we pull off this strike, no financial institution will help them out. We’d be talking bankruptcy for certain.”

Robinson said dubiously, “But the Aircraft Division has turned in good profits in the past, so maybe –”

“But only yesterday the Minister for Aviation Supply told the Commons that the government were having to bale out the Stanton – Rolls Royce jet engine project with a further £42 million, making £89 million in all. For a Tory government to do that, the project must be in serious danger of failure. And we all know how important those engines are.”

David knew that the Stanton Aircraft Division was heavily involved in major aircraft engine projects with Rolls Royce, and so already had huge problems of its own. He also knew that there was little prospect of the company surviving damage to its vital subsidiaries. Hoyle’s plans to inflict that damage sounded horrifyingly convincing,

359

and the meeting was listening closely when Hoyle delivered his *coup de grace*.

"The Stanton management are trying to persuade a big Japanese industrialist to enter into a co-production deal on shipbuilding. Nevertheless, it's an ideal opportunity for us. While Stantons concentrate their energies on the Japanese gambit we make no moves – the Japanese must be encouraged and their enthusiasm brought to full pitch. Then we call an all-out strike that will sweep away the supports on which Stanton's have chosen to rely."

"It sounds great – in theory," one of the Forward members said doubtfully.

Hoyle followed up. "That's right. It does require precise timing. We have to know *exactly* where the company stands at each juncture. Move too soon, and we just might allow Stanton Industries to save themselves, too slow and the Japanese become irreversibly committed – and according to David the Japs have financial reserves huge enough to survive even a months-long strike."

The man in the dark suit sat back. "Timing is crucial, agreed. Now, you must have a source inside Stanton's head office?"

Hoyle looked around the table. "Two."

"At a high level?" Robinson asked.

Hoyle gave a smirk. "That would be telling."

"So how are we going to know the right moment?"

"What if I told you one of us here has the confidence of someone at the very heart of Stanton Industries?"

David listened to Hoyle's words with alarm. He began to search his memory for candidates for a highly-placed Stanton mole. Alex, if he were told, might be able to do something about it. There was even George Hammond, inside the security service. He looked to Hoyle, who looked back, smiling, and held out a hand towards him. Then the truth of who Hoyle meant hit him with the force of a steam hammer.

"Someone here has done confidential work for Alex Stanton. Isn't that right, Comrade Bryant?"

He had to acknowledge it. Luckily, Robinson continued. "The government are pushing through their Industrial Relations Bill – making the Prime Minister an open and obvious enemy of the working class. Set up our strike, get industry closed down, get the miners' union on our side –"

David finished it for him, knowing it was all too possible. "And the government falls."

360

The tall house in St John's Wood had been advertised in *The Times* at £39,900. A high price, but Alex decided it was worth it for eight bedrooms, an underground garage, cellars, a huge garden with a conservatory. It was midway between Primrose Hill and the splendours of Regent's Park, and close enough to the zoo to hear the lions roar at night. Alex had bought it cash down and moved in, thinking it would be a fine place from which to conduct his affairs.

As he walked home alone, alongside the old Grand Union Canal, he followed the outer circle in the park past the Zoological Gardens. It was a briskly cold day and the sky had been swept clear of cloud. He looked up at the clear English blue: there were children running about under bare London plane trees, and their ringing voices intruded into his thoughts. No matter; his decision had been made.

Tomorrow, Alex would show his plans to Hugh. Plans that applied the principles of export-led growth to Stanton Industries. Plans that if adopted would at last begin to get the three divisions moving. It was possible: the Japanese had proved it could be done, and the Germans were not far behind – David had shown him the detailed figures at their last meeting just before he went up to Tyneside on some sort of union business.

"That's the competition, Alex."

They had analyzed the competition together. David had used government resources to investigate the Japanese and West German economic miracles.

"It's possible to do that with this country – with Stanton Industries?"

"It's a risk, Alex, but we have to take it. Now you're on the Stanton main board, Hugh will have to take a different attitude . . ."

Alex had replied simply, and sadly. "I used to think of him as my brother, you know."

"Well, I don't have a brother, either," David said sharply. "Now, you're sure to keep a place on the main board?"

"I have the Stanton shares I inherited and others I've bought. My connection to Tehran is absolutely secure. More specifically Gillespie, the present MD of the Armaments Division, is sixty-five; he'll be retiring within a few months. I intend to get his job. I told Hugh I want to be on the Board of Directors and to get control of Armaments and that – if he wants my support – those things are my price. So now that I have voting control of my father's

361

shares, I'm guaranteed a permanent seat on the main board – as a non-executive director at first, but there in the boardroom with the rest."

"You have Hugh's word?"

"Yes." Alex sighed. "Why has he always twisted away when I've asked him for this? There's some secret behind it, David, some reason for Hugh and his father not to trust me. I wish I knew what it was."

"Some secrets are better left alone," David said, with feeling.

Alex was already doing all he could to encourage the board to accept his plans to develop a missile sub-division capable of sustaining growth to the end of the decade, and to change the Aircraft Division into the Aerospace Division. His idea of working with the Ministry of Defence to market British-made weapons systems aggressively in the Far East and South America was beginning to pay dividends. Of course he would need a forward-thinking financier to back him, but using Hacker's method of straight talking and dogged persuasion he felt he could pull it off.

There was much work still to be done in his own area, Alex realized, but nevertheless the magnitude of the company's problems in the Shipbuilding Division repeatedly attracted his thoughts. He hoped Hugh would take his proposals in the spirit in which they had been conceived. There was a crisis coming, and he had to make sure that Stanton Industries survived.

Tonight, unusually, he had absolutely no commitments; he would relax alone.

As soon as he closed the door, he poured himself a tall glass of vermouth and ice, and settled into a critical examination of the living room as a Miles Davis album played.

The room was decorated to his taste in subdued pastels, furnished discreetly in steel-grey leather and tubular chrome; he had decided to throw off the garish, fuzzy thinking of the Sixties, but had he perhaps tended too far towards the cold and clinically modern in his choice? There ought to be warmth here – a house should be a home . . .

As he was by himself he checked the TV guide in the paper, but the doorbell rang immediately he had chosen his evening viewing.

Cameron thrust a bottle of Mouton Cadet into Alex's hand.

"I thought I'd come over and see your new place. Hope you don't mind?"

362

Alex welcomed his old friend and showed him into the living room.

"Do you live here alone?" Cameron asked, and when Alex said he did, he seemed surprised. "It's a big place. You must have plans."

"I always have plans, Cameron."

They had a drink. Cameron smiled quickly. "Are you as rich as people say, Alex?"

"Now that", Alex said, "would be telling. How's your business?"

"Oh, progressing well," Cameron said vaguely. "I hope we might be able to work with Hugh one day, Beauford permitting, I suppose." He picked up a photo album and began to leaf through. "How are your family, Alex?"

"Fine, I believe. I don't see much of them, you know. If nothing else I'm not even in this country all the time."

"A wonderful thing, family." Cameron held up a picture from before the Great War. An eerie sepia image of a young man in a Henley blazer and straw boater, all tall angularity and a patrician face. "At first, I mistook this for a picture of Hugh."

"It's our grandfather. One of the great Stantons, you know. Worked with Lloyd George getting the munitions industry right in 1914–18; and he was even more powerful in World War II. The Japanese shot down his plane somewhere north of Australia."

The evening proceeded pleasantly, until half past nine, when Alex turned on the television to watch a documentary on British industry today.

As Alex turned up the volume, it was to hear a gloomy report: a catalogue of strikes and declining trade, investment and employment was delivered. Then the presenter turned to the camera. "... Significantly, that's the story not only for this country. The United States, France, West Germany and Japan – all are facing this crisis. Can we overcome it in Britain? One man who believes we can is the chairman of Stanton Industries, Hugh Stanton."

Both Alex and Cameron stared at the screen as the camera cut to Hugh, interviewed in front of a tanker building at the Stantons' Wallsend yard.

Hugh's words galvanized Alex: "Stanton Industries is now poised to sign a multi-million pound contract with the Hideki Corporation of Japan. Their representatives will come here to discuss a co-production deal with us later this year. If all goes well, sufficient orders will come from the deal to provide the Tyne and Wear yards with work until the start of the nineteen-eighties."

Though Hugh was impeccably dressed, in a blue pin-stripe suit, white shirt and blue silk tie, he looked ill at ease.

"What the devil is he playing at?" Alex was unable to believe what he had heard.

On TV, Hugh explained: "I'm very pleased with our prospects here. For some months, we have been preparing the ground for these new arrangements, and the chairman of Hideki, Mr Saigo Hideki himself, will fly here in February to sign the memorandum of understanding personally. Just to put the deal in context, the extra investment he has promised is equal to the entire Stanton Industries research and development budget for the next five years."

The interviewer toughened his line. "How would you answer those who say that you're surrendering the initiative and selling out to your rivals?"

Alex's hand tightened on the arm of his chair. He knew the question must have struck an exposed nerve in his cousin.

Hugh assumed a patient expression. "Everyone must understand that we live in an era of peace and prosperity. The days in which ruthless competition across national boundaries characterized trade are over. Ours is an age of internationalism and co-operation. The Japanese in both government and industry agree with us that the path of co-operation is a better way."

"Government and industry is one and the same in Japan!" Alex said angrily. "They'll co-operate, all right – to cut our throats!"

Hugh continued, trying to maintain a front of able sagacity. "I expect that in the years to come this agreement will be seen as a turning point for Stanton Industries."

"No, no, no! It's the wrong philosophy entirely! The Japanese won't tolerate a beggar. You must be their superior before they'll pay you court. To *pretend* to be their equal is fatal." Alex was appalled by what he heard.

End credits rolled over an aerial picture of the Stanton yard to brassy title music. Alex switched off and began to pace back and forth.

"Hugh told me nothing of this!"

"I suppose he's had this in mind for some time," Cameron said, quietly.

Alex burned with indignation. "To my certain knowledge he hasn't ever put it forward at any board meeting. I find out about his decision from watching the *television*, for God's sake! It's absolutely unforgivable!"

Cameron disagreed. "You were very busy with your own concerns. I suppose he felt you had no time to be consulted. Or he wanted to keep it strictly confidential. After all, when all's said and done, it's a divisional matter."

"Confidential! You think I'd go to Fleet Street or our competitors with this! And this is a *major* policy decision, concerning the whole of Stanton Industries, Cameron. It's not going over my head – that would be his prerogative – he's gone behind my back!"

Cameron smiled at the confused metaphor. "Hugh's a capable fellow. Master of figures, you know."

"He's not a bloody accountant, he ought to be a leader!"

"You should give him a little more credit – a little family confidence."

Alex stopped his pacing and cast a deadly look at his friend. "On what grounds? He's headed the firm for five years and done *nothing*! And he's had carte blanche from my uncle to drag the company down any blind and winding alley he chooses."

"You're over-reacting," Cameron said reasonably. "Though I suppose a little jealousy is understandable in the circumstances."

Alex's voice grew strained. He beat his breast emphatically. "I've had to build my own business. I've learned the hard way. In the past year I've been to eleven countries to sell Stanton products in markets they hadn't got near and still Hugh tries to treat me like a schoolboy."

"Selling by what methods, though?"

"Methods the world understands. That's why customers have confidence in me."

Cameron's question was heated. "But what confidence do *you* have in Hugh? You treat him like a *fool* – you know you do – often in public. What do you want him to do? He's always listened to you."

"He's *never* listened to me!"

"A voice crying in the wilderness," Cameron said with a twist of sarcasm. His disagreement with Alex was drawing him into a fight. "You're the sort of man who's convinced he's right whatever happens."

Alex grabbed a fist full of air. "But what if I *am* right? The French, Germans, Japanese – all our competitors – understand today's business world. Like Ray keeps telling me, you've got to get out there and win! Hugh spends all his time with like-minded club members who think the Pax Britannica still exists, that eventually the damned foreigners will see sense and subscribe to the cosy, civilized British way of doing business."

"So everyone has to lie and cheat and claw their way to the top, just because you do?"

"That's the way the world works, now, Cameron. Can't you see that?"

Alex was horribly roused now.

"No," Cameron said flatly. "I think you should behave better and try to treat Hugh better, too."

Alex turned on him. "He sent you, didn't he? He knew I'd hear about this and he's making use of you to sweet-talk me!"

"He isn't making use of me at all," Cameron answered hotly. "I agree with him."

Alex's fists had clenched. "With him. Not with me!"

Cameron stood up in tight silence. "I'm leaving," he said, suddenly. "Hugh's only doing what he thinks best."

"That's not good enough," Alex rasped. "Too much depends on it. In a contract bid there are no prizes for second place."

Cameron snatched up his jacket and put it on, waiting for an apology. It did not come, so he marched out of the room and moments later there was the sound of the front door slamming.

Alex picked up the phone an instant before it rang. It was David.

"Yes," Alex said, "the situation has changed. I think we must meet to discuss it."

David was waiting patiently in the directors' bar on the eighth floor of the Millbank headquarters of Stanton Industries. The board meeting, presumably, had overrun. He flipped through the dossier again, looking at a tough, under-fed Japanese face, the biographical notes about Saigo Hideki and the analysis of his business empire.

It made fascinating reading, and he hoped it would be useful to Alex.

By the time Alex turned up in a crowd of soberly suited men he was over an hour late. David sat watching from a corner table overlooking the Thames, able to tell that Alex's air of good nature was an act.

"Sit down," David said.

"I intend to," Alex answered sharply. He pulled up a chair, sat down, frowning at the other Stanton people in the bar. "I have far more right to be here than you do."

"Well, of course," David said, puzzled at the sharp tone. "I'm only your guest."

"And my friend, I hope." Alex was still staring at the other, far more convivial, drinkers. Hugh was at another table with Lord Beauford. They seemed very self-satisfied, and a crowd of managers circled them.

"Is there something the matter, Alex?"

"There's a lot the matter." Alex paused, not looking at David. "You told me you heard about this Japanese business in advance."

David's chest tightened. "Yes."

"Would you like to tell me how?"

"I can't, Alex. I just can't."

This time Alex met his eyes. "That isn't good enough, David. I think there's a crisis coming. We have to work together on it, or –" He grimaced. "This has to be confidential but, as you know, the firm is in a financial crisis. It's vulnerable."

"Vulnerable," David said, echoing Hoyle. He felt uneasy.

Alex insisted. "Tell me how you know more Stanton secrets than I do."

David thought everything through, knowing he could no longer work against Hoyle on his own. The secrets, pent up in him for so long, could spill again. It was with relief that he said, "All right, I'll risk my life and I'll tell you. Remember Tehran? I told you about Forward."

"Yes." For a moment, there was murder in those Stanton eyes.

"Ever since 1966 I've been shadowing them for the benefit of the Labour movement, MI5 and, I hope, my country. And if you ever breathe one word of that in public I'll be ruined at best and, at worst, dead."

Alex's eyes, which had widened, suddenly closed. "You're still a spy! But what does that have to do with Hugh's plans?"

David swallowed, suddenly half regretting that he had told the truth in spite of an almost overwhelming sense of relief at having confided in Alex. "Forward has an informer in your headquarters. Somebody here."

"Then – is that how you heard about the Japanese involvement before I did? Why didn't you tell me?"

367

"Forward has its sources, too, and I believe Alan Hoyle, Comrade Hoyle, answers to Moscow. And as for not saying anything, the first rule in intelligence is never, never, compromise your sources."

"Never compromise you." Alex nodded, taking it all in. "What happens now?"

"They try to bring you crashing down, Alex; Stanton Industries, then all industries here, then the system itself."

For a long moment, the lights in the bar flickered, then went out. In the abrupt darkness people gasped: and all the lights along the Thames died too.

"Look at that," Alex said. "Darkness everywhere."

Three heartbeats later the subdued lighting in the bar came on again, at a lower level than before. The Stanton headquarters had its own generators, for just such an emergency.

"The power-workers' 'go slow'," David said calmly. "Though they're not Forward-controlled."

"Not yet." Alex gestured with one hand, first at Lord Beauford beaming around his table, then at the extinguished lights of south London. "The split in this country is so wide I'm beginning to wonder if it can be healed at all. And I know plenty of people want that split to get worse."

"I could give you a few names too," David said, and finished his drink.

David decided to spend Christmas, 1970, as a family man. Fishguard was lovely and, as soon as snow fell, the ferry port for Cork and Rosslare became beautiful. Back in June, he had been obliged to watch the new Conservative government taking office, and six months later when he had become a father for the second time, he'd promised Megan that his son would be born in Wales.

"Now we're four," he'd said in the hospital, raising the infant in his arms.

"I hope you're not too disappointed," Megan had joked. "No son for you yet."

"That doesn't matter," he said, smiling down at the new-born baby.

"Let's call her Julie – after Julie Christie."

David had laughed. This was an aspect of Megan he had not seen before.

Now Christmas had come and gone, and Parliament was still in recess. He no longer spoke to Frank about his real mission. The work he did against Forward had passed beyond anything Frank could help him with. Now he had been retained by Alex as a paid economic advisor: a tame MP on the payroll always looked good, Alex said. David's reasons for accepting were as much to do with reassuring Alan Hoyle that his link with the Stanton board was intact, than with any conviction that he could help the ailing company survive.

David wanted time to enjoy his family. He saw how much strain their relationship had suffered from his investigation of Forward, and he had got nothing out of it; nothing to show for all that sweat and danger – nothing to show – yet. So he extended their New Year holiday until the end of the month while Alan Hoyle sunned himself at a political get-together in Havana.

It was striking how different he felt away from the pressures of the capital. He liked his constituency work, helping people and listening to their problem; sometimes being listened to was all they needed. He learned more Welsh, and songs like 'Cwm Rhondda'. Here in Wales there were none of the anxieties that continually assaulted him in London. Here, he was abrasive, less suspicious; more generous and self-confident. Megan loved him again. This was the man she had wanted to marry, the good-natured and intelligent man she had fallen in love with.

Nevertheless, while they were in Wales, David used the phone to keep in touch. He tried not to call when Megan was in the house, and he discouraged people from ringing him back. For the first time in years he felt able to relax.

The film version of *Under Milk Wood* was being shot in Lower Fishguard, and soon the set-designers had turned the town into a picture-book cliché: stone bridges, pink houses, tall Welsh dressers with gleaming plates, Irish rain. Megan was thrilled to see Richard Burton, his wife and Peter O'Toole parading in the streets of her town.

They had Maggie and Terry to stay for a few days in January. Maggie was delighted to see the new baby; she cooed over the cradle, rather to David's surprise.

The two men talked a lot, and David saw the moderating influence this cool and easy-going American was having on Maggie. Terry was a comfortable companion – perhaps he was right for Maggie and her wild excitements. Terry had changed, though. David wondered how much Maggie, with her fierce loyalty, recognized it. He still seemed

369

naturally endowed with a keen sense of right and wrong that hadn't sprung from any religious upbringing, but David thought politics and morality interested him much less these days – although Terry was careful to echo Maggie's opinions politely.

Terry Katz saw through hypocrisy of all kinds with a rather cynical clarity; but in spite of his obsession with Vietnam he seemed essentially low-key. He had contacts in Hollywood, and he was interested in film. David had the impression that money interested him more than it had, too.

Maggie, of course, remained an idealist, but for all that a good woman. And though idealists were better company than cynics, nevertheless, the occasional company of realists would have been even better. David sighed, wondering if Alex was still abroad with his latest girlfriend.

Late one Friday night in the middle of January, during an enjoyable four-way conversation about the film world, the telephone in the hall began its insistent ring. When David went to answer it, the voice at the end of the line immediately upset his peace of mind.

He turned quickly to close the door.

"David," the voice said briskly, "I need your help."

"Oh?"

"Can I see you in London, on Monday?"

"About what?"

"The co-production deal."

David's spirits fell. He knew Alex would press him about everything, his links with Forward, what the Labour party would say and do about a strike at Stanton Industries, what the attitude of the government would be. He made a reluctant noise.

"Don't worry, I'll make it worth your while."

"No, you can't do that, Alex," David said with irony, "but I don't suppose I can turn you down. Monday at eleven suit you?"

"Fine. Come over to Stanton HQ."

As he put down the receiver and returned to the living room, David saw both women looking at him. His wife had sensed, as she always did, the spell of their private world being broken.

"You're going back to London a week early?"

"I need to. Alex still thinks my ideas and his get-up-and-go together are going to save Stanton Industries."

"Is he right?"

David laughed shortly. "He'd better be right."

370

Maggie's expression had become thoughtful. She had heard Alex's name and when David sat down again, offering more wine, she began very gently to manoeuvre the discussion towards shipbuilding.

Shipbuilding, and Stanton Industries, were both very, very close to her father's heart, over and above his job.

They lingered by a computer-equipped office overlooking the Thames in the Stanton Industries headquarters. A sign on the opened door simply read: MD, Armaments Division.

David smiled. "One of these days, eh? Or maybe you should inherit what your father used to run – that Aircraft Division."

"It was called the Aviation Division, then. Afraid there won't be time for the full guided tour today."

David turned his head. "I'ts lucky I packed my overnight case. Where are we going? Washington, DC? Cap in hand to Wall Street? To take tea at Number 10?"

"Somewhere that was mighty when those places had hardly even been thought of – and we're taking the train."

David followed him. "Just as long", he said, "as we aren't riding on the Orient Express."

"I've convinced you both?" Ken McCourt asked.

Alex recapped his pen, and looked at the culmination of two weeks' work. It was the detailed plan to rebuild Stanton Industries. "I can't argue with any of that. That's my money in the company, and the family's future. We can't afford any more blunders."

Ken McCourt, Alex's newly-imported assistant, looked serious. "No. But if we get in now, after a crisis, we can make people change, change utterly. And that's the only thing that will save the firm now."

"Shipbuilding is also employment for seventeen thousand people," David insisted. "If you make a mistake over this, it could be an end to half of those men's livelihoods. And of course, long-term, it may spell disaster."

Outside the compartment, the Durham landscape rolled away gently towards the sea, a landscape dotted with the winding gear and spoil heaps of collieries, and in the distance the triple towers of the great Gothic cathedral of Durham.

"Let me quote this," David told him, wanting to press the point home. "Shipbuilding: the chairman's report for Hawthorne Leslie.

Sir Matthew says, 'the profit from Marine Engineering is somewhat higher than in the previous year'."

"In cash terms only," Alex acknowledged. "In real terms, it shows a decline. Exactly as it is for us. Go on."

"'On 1st January we signed a Technical Assistance and Manufacturing Agreement with the Westinghouse International Company of America'."

"Like Hugh's plan —"

"Let me finish." David tapped the other part of the statement about the direct competitors to the Stanton yards, Swan Hunter. "This is shipbuilding as such. It's a *disaster* – they're taking losses on all their long-term, fixed-price contracts, and it's getting worse."

Alex rubbed at his eyes. "Upper Clyde Shipbuilders look like they're headed for bankruptcy. I don't know. According to Hugh, the Japanese have offered us substantial resources and advice on working methods; a huge sum is involved. He hopes that it'll be enough to tip the balance, and keep Stanton Shipbuilding number one in the UK."

"It's not as simple as that," McCourt said. "Shipbuilding is competing in a world market, against the Japanese and others. If you or he are looking to cross-subsidize the Division from Aircraft or Armaments, you should think again."

David raised his voice to object, but McCourt repeated the point: "Look, Alex, it's no secret that the STA-2 fiasco has cleared out the Aircraft Division, leaving it desperately hanging onto Concorde and the engine development deal you have with Rolls Royce. All throughout January Rolls' shares have fallen from what used to be virtually gilt-edged status to less than ten shillings. So Aircraft is looking for money; it can't help Shipbuilding out. Only Armaments is healthy."

Alex shook his head. "There's nothing like enough in the division at the moment."

"What about the Saudi contracts, or the Shah?"

"The next large payments aren't due from them till the end of the year," Alex admitted.

"So you've no reservoir there either, and Hugh's aware of that. It's easy to see why he's tempted by Japanese money." David thought for a moment. "What about fixing up a big, short-term loan with British money?"

"No," Alex said. "We're already in debt up to our necks. I don't want to drown."

"We have to cut," McCourt said. "You've seen the figures. There is no alternative."

"And you want me to present that reality to Will Langton's engineers, to my party, and to the House of Commons?" David sighed, and looked out of the window. They were already pulling into Newcastle, and had settled so little.

"But the Japanese deal – I'm still convinced it's unnecessary," Alex said. "A big cash injection now could get us through the worst of the current crisis."

David shook his head and delivered the killing blow. "You can't rely on Lord Beauford. I was in the Industry Department last week. He's been fishing in Germany after buyers for unspecified heavy industry assets."

"What?" Alex said. "People to buy Stanton equipment, you mean!"

David pointed back towards London. "He may be one of the powers on the Stanton board, but his first loyalty is obviously to his own merchant bank. Look at the man's record. There's no doubt in my mind that, given the opportunity, he would hive off as many parts of the company as he can."

"You mean to say that if we're driven to him for hard cash, cap in hand, he'd see us split up?"

"Exactly."

"But he's . . . It would be against the national interest!"

David's mouth opened in an ironic grin. "He's a bloody asset stripper. The only interest he has is self-interest. He made his start that way in the Thirties – I've researched the details, I can prove what I say. And it's my guess that he'd do exactly the same to Stanton Industries." David looked appalled. "Just when we should all be standing together!"

Alex shed a look of bitter anger. "Then what are we to do? It seems Hugh had to take the Japanese offer. He was grasping at straws."

"Look, we've both gone through the figures a hundred times, Alex," McCourt reminded him. "The firm's in serious trouble. It's going to take this Japanese deal, or something like it, to save Stanton Industries now."

"I just hate having to postpone what I must do to Armaments. But if the firm has to get through a crisis, and there's no money in the company treasury and we can't borrow . . ." Alex sat back from the papers he'd spread across his lap. His confidence had suffered a severe set-back. "So the poor little maid is forced to marry a Japanese husband because she's destitute?"

"Do you know how the Japanese treat their wives?" David asked.

"Yes." Alex grimaced.

The train slowed, passing out onto the high-level bridge, gliding high across the River Tyne into Newcastle's magnificent Central Station. As they passed through the ticket barrier, David looked up at the big station clock, then his eyes followed the complex of tracks that stretched north to Edinburgh and south across the Tyne to London. In the great days of Victoria, men had come here and created a leviathan out of iron, coal and steam. The railways, perhaps the greatest British invention, had made the country one, but like so much else the system was in decay.

Alex took McCourt aside and told him to get a taxi to the Northumberland Hotel, and find out what he could about the Hideki team's plans. He and David would be coming along shortly, but had a little personal business to attend to first.

"Let's have a drink," Alex said.

David nodded. It had been a comfortable first-class ride on one of the newer, smoother trains, but his mouth was dry. They went into the public bar of the Royal Station Hotel, where Alex insisted on buying him an India pale ale.

They sat down at a small corner table and David closed his eyes. It was now or never, he thought.

"Alex, I don't think the Japanese will go through with the deal."

Alex looked up in surprise.

"Why do you say that?"

"The Japanese fear of strike action. It's one thing they can't hope to gain control over, and if they suspect the unions will hamper their plans for Stantons they'll pull out, and the chance of a rescue will be gone."

Alex was puzzled. "But they surely know the national position: Ford workers claiming parity of up to fifty per cent, the tanker drivers out, the unions up in arms over the Industral Relations Bill – but equally, they know our own industrial relations have been relatively good over the past fifteen years. It's there for all to see. Why should things suddenly change?"

David chewed at his lip and said, "Because there's going to be a massive strike, starting at the Stanton yards."

Alex stared at him. "How do you know?" he asked disbelievingly.

374

David took a deep breath. "Because as you know I'm on the inside of Forward, and I know Maggie and her father. The mass meeting will be announced today. The proposal is for a massive wage increase, or a strike. You won't pay, so there'll be a strike. I guarantee it."

"Surely they won't strike now, David? We'll explain to them that the company's relying on that deal with the Hideki corporation and their members' jobs are relying on it too."

"They've been lied to so often in the past they wouldn't believe you." David smiled grimly, and quoted from a previous Stanton diatribe. "'Marxist bastards', you once called them."

"Treasonous Marxist bastards, that's what I call them now."

David was torn by divided loyalties, and by the disastrous facts of the situation. It felt like a physical pain inside him; his fist clenched round the dimples of his beer glass. The time had come for plain speaking.

"Alex, the company has been mismanaged for years – you say that much yourself. Hugh and his father before him have been paying their City cronies dividends from profits that should have been ploughed back into the business. You might not call it corruption, but what does a name matter when the result's the same? They've come damn near to gutting the whole bloody operation."

Alex looked away, his face now carefully blanked. "Even if that were true, it doesn't justify striking. It's a nursery truism that two wrongs don't make a right."

David imagined the accusations that would be flung at him if ever his duplicity was revealed – accusations of treachery and of double-dealing, not all of them inaccurate. As Alex rose to go back to the bar, he called out, "That's easy to say – when you're a bloody millionaire."

In the ornate, high-ceilinged bar the few patrons, mostly middle-aged businessmen, were grumbling about tax, football and the one-day strikes that were being called across the country to protest against the government's erosion of union priviliges. Some glanced over. He regretted raising his voice.

When Alex returned his expression was like granite. He said, "David, help me break the strike."

"Break –?" David felt frightened. "That's an awful lot to ask."

"I know it is. But if Stanton's goes under, there's much more than one man's career at stake; thousands will lose their jobs. Can I count on your loyalty, David?"

He had to whisper it. "That could destroy me."

"Only you have the connections, David! Nobody else."

"And don't I know it."

"You're a good friend of Maggie's. She respects you, and, more to the point, so does her father. You know this radical Alan Hoyle. You're a Labour MP being groomed for the top. And – you've worked with me."

David folded his arms and grinned sourly. "You bastard! So this is how I earn my wages, is it? It's not just my brains you want, but my political connections, too. Alex Stanton: ever the practical man."

"Somebody in this damned country has to be," Alex replied, equally toughly. Then he leaned forward, hands on the table, to make his appeal. "Look, for whatever reason, Maggie's father hates my family –" he rode David's comment down "– it goes back further than the time Maggie and I spent together in Greece and that '65 strike. There was a trike back in 1956, during the Suez crisis. I understand it all got rather sordid."

"Rather sordid? You mean your uncle used his influence to crush Will Langton brutally by printing lies about him in the press!"

"David, that was years ago."

David was like a barrister summing up his points in court: "But David Bryant is both a friend, and a loyal and well-connected member of the Labour party – which means that now Stanton Industries can use him."

Alex's earnest gaze never wavered. "I showed you everything about the deal. I asked you in to consult. Surely you don't doubt my motives? If you can do something about the strike it will be good for the firm, good for the workers, good for the region. If you're right, the Japanese won't sign should the strike go ahead. What am I asking for that's so wrong?"

"If it lasts a week, they'll pack up their bags and go looking for deals in Hamburg." David sighed, backing off. "I don't think Langton will listen. You know Maggie isn't exactly tractable, and she has all his stubbornness."

Alex looked suddenly older than his years: his blond hair had been closely trimmed, his grey business suit was entirely unobtrusive, and his tie was an anonymous herringbone pattern. He no longer came across as the swashbuckling entrepreneur David had seen at work in Iran. He appeared as an ordinary man suddenly hung about with extraordinarily heavy responsibilities, but his wealth and position were facts David could not ignore.

Alex's voice was almost pleading. "The devaluation business in '67 really rocked us, David, and the STA-2 business was even worse – throwing in millions to design a couple of superb prototypes, and then after the Americans cancelled their order we couldn't even afford to build it! The shares have slipped twenty per cent since then, and we haven't paid a real dividend for two years. Things are stagnant, and we're losing too many of our best people. The heart's going out of Stanton's. As we both know, if Hugh doesn't get Hideki's monogram on that co-production contract it's probably the end. It's that simple."

"No wonder the workers don't trust the owners in this country," David scowled. "It's always been the final argument of the parasitic owning classes: 'If the company fails, I only lose an asset, but you starve. But if you work hard so that the company propers, I and my friends with share certificates in their bank boxes will get fat off the cream. So you can never win, and I can never lose.' It's vile!"

Alex threw him a black look. "I didn't create the system."

David pursed his lips and tried to compose himself. Langton might have argued over it, but Hoyle was acting. And Alex had made the mistake of thinking Langton was his only opponent.

"David," Alex said again, "you have to help me!"

"All right, Alex," he said at last. "I'll try. But if I fail, you're on your own."

377

2

In the house on Flood Street Maggie was going over the proofs of her Cairo interview with Anwar Sadat.

The phone under the Dali rang, and she waved irritable fingers till Terry answered it.

"It's your father," he said, covering the mouthpiece. "Something about taking on the Stantons. You want to speak to him?"

She snatched the phone, her heart racing. "It's happening at last, Dad?"

"Aye. And this time we have them, lass, by the short and curlies."

She imagined his big fist making the familiar clenching gesture. "Starting next week?"

"That's the plan, so I hope you can bring up a film crew and give us some favourable coverage – and bring pencils and your typewriter, too."

"I'll be there, Dad, and I'll do everything I can to help you," she said, her voice quavering. "You reckon the Stantons have money enough to settle your strike?"

"The Stantons – or somebody else at the head of the firm. Jackie Sutton was doing some investigations for me. They can get the money. Their sort always can. But I think they'll fight; and we'll fight back even if they bring old Ted Heath himself against us."

She put the phone down and turned to Terry, but he was leafing through some airline brochures and there was a frown on his face.

He didn't look up. "Don't even ask me, Maggie. I'm going to the West Coast."

She was hurt, suddenly. "This could be long and bloody, Terry. Don't I get your support? And think of the news value, if we do set up a strike that brings down the government."

378

He glanced at her briefly, then stood up and threw down the brochures, and she wondered if in her preoccupation with business matters she was letting him slip away. She remembered suddenly that she had never had the time for the follow-up to *Vietnam Nightmare* she had once promised.

"Your father, you, Alex Stanton? And David, I bet you. No. I never interfere in family business." He was walking away from her, his tread determined.

"Terry, *you* are my family!"

Maggie heard him go up the stairs as she waited for a reply that never came.

If it came off, it was going to be the largest strike Tyneside had known since 1926. Already, nationally, the engineering workers' union had backed the Ford strikers in their claim for parity. That might mean a fifty per cent wage rise – but, as Will Langton explained to the twenty-three thousand men who had crowded into one end of Newcastle United's stadium at St James's Park, it was time Stanton Industries' workers took their share too.

He leaned forward into the microphones. "If that's fair, then our claim has to be fair. Twenty-two per cent, comrades, not a penny less. And if we don't get it, what shall we do?"

"Strike!" they answered him, loudly. "Strike!"

"Comrade Robinson has spoken about the Tories' Industrial Relations Bill. I stand with your local leadership, and I put the region at your disposal. Strike! Strike! Strike! Twenty-two per cent! No surrender!"

The crowd roared back, "No surrender!"

It was cold on the windswept platform. Feedback in the public-address system howled round, making it difficult to understand the speeches, but Maggie stood behind her father and applauded. At their backs the massive grandstands echoed Will Langton's words as the trade union and Labour contingents clapped. On the pitch, and among the mass of workers, vendors threaded their way, selling copies of *Forward* magazine and collecting addresses in their search for new activists. Meanwhile Langton, a powerful public speaker, brought the crowd to a high pitch of enthusiasm. He ended by re-stating their clear objective and getting the approval of the mass meeting: it was to be twenty-two per cent, or the Stanton yards would stay closed.

Maggie clapped as the Labour Lord Mayor of Newcastle stepped

379

forward to speak. She had never been more proud of her father.

Langton stepped down from the scaffold, pulling his raincoat tighter about his chest.

"I thought you were fabulous, Dad!"

He looked at her soberly, as if from a great distance.

"I hope so, lass. This is no time for fence sitting. It's them or us. And you can quote me on that."

She nodded, still happy. "I'll do my best to see the TV people, at least, give us the benefit of any doubts, but you can expect Fleet Street to make a monster of you."

"Bugger Fleet Street."

"I'm with you all the way, Dad – no surrender!" she called after him as his entourage closed around him.

She watched the crowds surging from the ground with fire in their bellies and marvelled at the way her father had brought them to this state of solidarity. What Alan Hoyle had told her was true: shipyard workers' wages *were* falling behind; surely they deserved the very moderate twenty-two per cent they had come to demand.

That evening, she sat with Forward members in a pub in Wallsend, and listened to the arguments raging. As they waited for Alan to join them there was high-spirited talk about the way they had pulled Stanton Industries to the brink. It was the way of the future, they told her. They were hastening the collapse of the Establishment, that non-elected and self-seeking clique of power-brokers who held the real power in the land. Then Socialism would prevail at last.

"Do you think Stanton's will fall?" she asked them.

There were nods around the table.

"And then?"

"And then", one Forward activist said confidently, "the State will be forced to concede true worker ownership of the means of production. Stanton Industries will be ours."

When Alan Hoyle arrived later that evening, he was treated as a celebrity; people stood up and applauded his entrance.

Maggie was astonished to find he had brought David Bryant with him. David seemed equally surprised to see her there, and perhaps a little embarrassed. So Alan Hoyle really did have some kind of hold on David. Her instincts told her to say nothing.

Later, she started to inject questions about the Japanese bid into the discussion.

"I still can't quite figure out what the Japanese are doing here," she told them.

"I think I've worked that one out," David answered. "They've got the supertanker and cargo ship business effectively sewn up, right?"

"True," Hoyle acknowledged.

"Now they want military contracts too."

Maggie agreed it made sense. "They can't build at home; their constitution forbids it. So they need an off-shore capability."

David nodded. "They want to get their hands on technical details. Stanton's naval architecture is internationally well-respected."

"Also true," Maggie acknowledged. "In fact, from Hideki's point of view the deal is perfect. They buy into Stanton's and into military know-how at the same time. Then two or three years later they move the entire warship operation to Singapore, where the labour's cheap. Maybe that's another good reason to strike, Alan?"

"Yes, show Stanton we won't be buggered about," said one of Hoyle's younger supporters.

"Might be a good angle for your publicity," David said thoughtfully. "Keep out foreign owners. But if the yard doesn't get some kind of financial backing, it'll collapse. Workers will be thrown on the dole now. We ought to think about that."

"They won't let that happen," Maggie said firmly. "Like UCS on the Clyde, where the government has given money. The Stantons will go to Parliament or their City friends and scratch the money up when they see there's no alternative. As my dad says, there's always more money – for the rich!"

David lowered his voice, wishing he could have this conversation with her in private. "Suppose they can't – just suppose they're *really* on the point of bankruptcy. What then?"

Alan swiftly made a joke of it. "Just the sort of lies they'll try to feed Maggie's father. You've been reading the *Financial Times* again, David. Dangerous capitalist propaganda – and pernicious too – you'll find yourself believing that stuff if you're not careful."

David laughed, but Maggie was watching his face with interest.

When he went to the bar, she followed unobtrusively. "Look," she said, "what do you think about this strike? Isn't twenty-two per cent fair?"

His face was shuttered. Beer slopped out of the two fistfuls of beer mugs he held. "What does 'fair' mean? It's fair in the context of what other unions are demanding – but the main point is it's economic

381

nonsense, which is a hard fact."

"The government –"

His voice was low, and now he wore a bland smile. "If the government prints money, that means inflation, which ruins any wage-rise anyway. And suppose the big banks and the Tories don't rush in and support Stanton Industries?"

"Of course they will," she said.

He gave a brief, harsh laugh. "You believe every good story has a happy ending, don't you? Check into Stanton Industries' finances yourself."

The idealistic young men planning to bring down the firm were more uplifting company. David did not stay much longer, and if his attitude was going to be so negative she was glad he was no longer there.

Maggie had left her London people to fend for themselves. Loyalty had brought her here, to her father's side. The following day, she rode with him to the big meeting in Gateshead. Because the tanker drivers' strike had hit petrol supplies, they went in the official union car.

Will turned to his daughter. "Today the executive council of the engineering workers are going to make the Ford strike official, opening the way for the transport union to follow. As for us, we now have the Armaments plants out on strike, and most of the Aircraft Division. Now your man David was telling me the Hideki delegation arrives today and will meet the Stantons at the Shipbuilding divisional offices tomorrow." He grinned. "That calls for something special."

Under dark and lowering clouds that drifted eastward across the sky, Maggie saw through the car window evidence of the advance of progress. Working-class suburbs had once marched in terraces down to the river Tyne, and the places she had played as a child had all been swept away, devastated by the bulldozers; square miles had been levelled into a wasteland of brick dust. Only at the boundaries were buildings standing, the signs of now non-existent streets still on their walls.

Will Langton pointed out the Lord Nelson pub. "They might as well knock that down, too."

"Oh, they always leave the churches and the pubs, Dad."

"At least the planners know some things are still sacred!"

He leaned forward, and pointed out a crane that belched fumes and jerked an iron ball against a tottering brick wall. The rest of the row of terraced houses were still standing, but they had been gutted.

"Do you remember?" he asked her. "That's where your Aunty Margaret used to live."

Maggie nodded.

"And over there – that's where me and your mother began proper courting. It was the summer of 1940, after Dunkirk, and me with one leg still in plaster. I don't know what she must have thought."

Maggie's eyes began to swim with tears. "You've never talked about that before."

"Aye," he sighed. "It's all coming down. They've ripped the heart out of Byker. It's just a name, now, and soon there'll be nothing left."

"But there'll be a new town," Maggie enthused. "Council flats with modern conveniences and proper facilities. Everyone will have a bathroom and an indoor toilet, and even a telephone. Homes fit for heroes at last."

He looked at her with a shrewd smile then, a twinkle of his old self. "Don't be so bloody soft."

"It's not soft," she said indignantly, though mindful she was his daughter. "It's what Socialism's been fighting for all these years, isn't it?"

He snorted.

"If you think that, young lady, you've been more affected by that Oxford education than I thought. I bet you've been listening to that Redgrave woman."

"You don't know anything about Vanessa's politics," she said.

"Vanessa, now, is it?" he said haughtily. "I'll ask you this, my lady, can you imagine living in a world filled only with the products of today? Living in modern buildings, having only post-war art and literature and music to listen to? Nylon shirts and fish fingers, plastic spoons and muzak and paper handkerchiefs. It's a cultural wilderness, and a pretty good definition of hell. It's also a pretty accurate description of the lives of most poor people in England."

He looked down at her lap, at his daughter's hands clasped together over a copy of Newcastle's *Evening Chronicle*. Its headline read: STANTON STRIKE – LANGTON SAYS "NO SURRENDER!"

"Progress! I'm not talking about colour televisions or a dozen channels of ITV showing imported soap operas; that isn't *my* favoured vision of the future. And as for hordes of overpaid council bureaucrats

383

ordering the working man to 'improve' himself . . ." Langton's grim face distorted in a mirthless smile. "For God's sake, in the old days using an outdoor toilet was no problem, and everything was always kept clean. What we Socialists always stood for was the right to human dignity. It's worth all your concrete council blocks."

The car turned onto the main road, past the grimy sandstone of a big Victorian building that had been half pulled down.

"That's the Mechanics' Institute," he told her. "Built by men – knocked down by mice. Or should I say *rats*? They want to put up a supermarket in its place. I ask you!"

"You've got to move with the times, Dad," Maggie said ebulliently.

He glanced at her and back at the ruined building. "I get that kind of talk from Annie's husband. He's an insurance man, you know. These young fellers with their soft hands think they know it all. I'll tell you, Maggie, they don't know the half of it. Instant gratification on borrowed money! Where's solidarity, self-sacrifice, courage? Where have all the *men* gone?"

Maggie smiled. "The world's changing, Dad. And changing for the better."

"Rubbish! And it's about time you started to realize it." Her father fixed her with a stern look. "I don't know about all this Vietnam stuff you're concerning yourself with, you ought to be thinking about your home. It's being destroyed just as surely as if Hitler's bombers were still flying over. But everyone seems blind to it – taken in by all this talk of hot and cold running water and indoor toilets. These bloody high-rise slums are going to be disasters, you take it from me."

She looked at him warmly. He had never changed. And he never would.

"At least Sir Edward Stanton and that lot won't be lording it over the area much longer."

"That's what you think, is it?"

"You're going to break him, Dad."

He shook his head. "I don't know if I like to hear you speak like that. I want what's right for my members, that's all."

"But you're going to close them down, you're going to squeeze Stanton's until the pips squeak."

He laughed, slapping his knee. "That sounds like one of those so-and-so's from Forward." Then he grew serious again. "You'd better understand that I'm not fighting Stanton Industries – the firm – except insofar as it benefits my members. I may hate that family, I

384

may want them out of the Stanton management, but I certainly don't want the yards to close down. Unemployment's bad enough round here without that."

"But you said –"

"Twenty-two per cent is what I said, no more, no less. Quote me honestly, lass! And I said it because that's what it takes to get a fair living wage."

She fell silent, thinking about what David Bryant had said last night. Despite herself, she couldn't help thinking that there might be some truth in it, and that what Alan Hoyle wanted was something very different. What she had told her father was true – the world *was* changing, but perhaps he was right, and it wasn't always for the better.

She couldn't help wondering who would win the battle for Stanton Industries, too.

That day in early February, 1971, became a turbulent one.

For hours, storm clouds hung over the Tyne, threatening and black. At about three in the afternoon, the storm broke. Lightning flared north to south across the sky, thunder came rumbling like rumours of war, and the rain swept down in stifling, blinding curtains. Tugs hooted in the river, traffic in the town began to grind to a halt, and the pickets who were camped out in front of factories and shipyards all over the region took shelter.

The Stanton offices stood on the riverfront.

Long ago in the Middle Ages, pilgrims had left from the quays that were once here, travelling to all the great shrines of Christendom. Later, mariners had departed for the Greenland whale fisheries, to take slaves from Africa, and then to ship coal and manufactures to all the world.

Far above, the great green span of the Tyne Bridge, a replica of the one which crosses Sydney harbour, threw its high arch across the river. The buildings that stood below it were old, but still dignified. One in particular seemed grander than the rest, though its sandstone was blackened by pre-war pollution. Above the entrance were cut gilded letters that spelled out STANTON INDUSTRIES – SHIPBUILDING DIVISION.

The rain stopped and the low sun came flooding out over Gateshead. Inside the marble-floored lobby the assembled men watched the weather brighten with relief. Hugh and his father,

Alex, managers and board members, all waited for the Japanese with anticipation.

Sir Edward, sitting in his wheelchair, his hair thinned and eyes watery, waited impatiently. It was hard to envisage him as the progenitor, a hero of D-Day, a self-assured master of both industry and the City. Alex watched him fussing stiffly, wondering that qualities of leadership and determination could boil down in adversity to such cantankerous ill-humour.

As he waited, Alex fumed at the reports of the strike meeting he had read. Twenty-two per cent was well above the 1971 average wage rise of 13%. If this kind of spiral were allowed to continue it would soon reach the realms of insanity. Despite this, two days ago, at a Guildhall banquet for the Overseas Bankers' Club, Chancellor Barber had called the statutory control of pay 'crude, unworkable and unfair'. Alex judged that kind of talk likely only to stoke up inflationary pressures and union militancy still further, and make life impossible for trade union moderates.

He looked down at the cobbled quayside and beat the announcement from the doorman phoning up from the main entrance. "There they are! Exactly on time."

The Japanese delegation in white, rain-beaded limousines drew up in a perfect line outside, and dapper men in blue suits and black-rimmed spectacles stepped out, smiling and looking round.

Alex went down to receive them with the other directors, Hugh, Hugh's father, and the Shipbuilding chief Sir George Leslie. There were journalists outside and inside, and a company photographer also.

Alex murmured to Sir George, a dapper little man in his late sixties, who looked rather unhappy today, "So the new masters are here, eh?"

The knight shrugged. "This was none of my doing. Hugh and the finance people say we're desperate for new money. Simple as that, Alex. Unless you'd like to loan us fifteen or twenty million sterling yourself?"

Alex managed a polite chuckle.

The main doors, made of polished, nineteenth-century teak and twelve feet tall, were ceremoniously drawn back. A riverine stink wafted in faintly from the Tyne.

Then the dozen or so Japanese entered, smiling, and all shook hands with the Stanton men, nodding their heads in small bows. Alex heard them speak American-accented English either directly

386

or through their three interpreters with the men who had received them on their previous, exploratory visit, making comments about the miraculous change in the weather. They seemed quite at ease, courteous and self-effacing. There was none of the nervousness or arrogant behaviour Alex had somehow expected.

"I'd still have preferred this meeting to have taken place at the main yard," he confided to Sir George between preliminary handshakes, "but the pickets have discounted that option."

"Might have been switched to London, I suppose. I heard a whisper the strike committee are planning something."

"Or Craigburn – that's impressive enough, and secure behind those high walls of the estate. If we were going to make something of receiving them, it ought to have been done properly . . ." Alex shook another hand before turning back to Sir George. "They've already toured the yards?"

"Tyne, Wear and Tees – at the beginning of negotiations three months ago."

"Hugh still hasn't had the goodness to tell me the details, you know."

"How's your man McCourt getting on?"

Alex hesitated, then admitted it. "We have a detailed plan for restructuring all of Stanton Industries."

Sir George said dourly, "I don't know if you'll ever have a chance to implement it, Alex."

The door of the final car was opened and the Japanese parted in deference as a square, authoritative man with closely-cropped iron grey hair stepped out onto the wet pavement.

Hugh came forward. "Mr Hideki, how delightful. Please come inside and let me present my father, Sir Edward." He showed Hideki up the steps, his tall figure craning down, one hand on the bannister and the other against the small of his back, both men climbing at Hideki's pace.

Alex took Sir Edward up in the building's Edwardian lift, and as he stood beside the wheelchair, he put a hand on his uncle's shoulder.

To Alex's surprise, he took his nephew's hand and squeezed. "It's good to have you here with us," he said, then lowering his voice in case he was overheard through the open fretwork of the lift, he said, "Hugh will need support, though he'll never ask for it. Be ready to give it to him."

"I will, Uncle. I will."

387

Suddenly, things became clear. I have to stand by Hugh now, Alex thought, because there's no alternative. Either we all hang together – or we all hang separately.

They went into the boardroom through double doors, past massive glass-cased makers' models of the *Mauritania* and HMS *Nelson*. It was a curious division, Alex thought as he looked at the management team. Half the group were hard-handed craftsmen who had worked their way up from apprenticeships begun in the twenties and thirties; a minority were university-educated men. The division's illustrious history dated back to keels laid for the Victorian navy, but now there were debts of over twenty-eight million pounds. In a brutally frank interview Alex had with Dan Drummond, the real head of the division, that had become quite clear. All possible lines of credit were exhausted. In the five yards, on the three great rivers of the North East, a seventeen thousand-strong workforce was maintained, and it was clear that this situation could only be continued if the strike was settled and the deal pushed through. To Alex it seemed they were trying valiantly to shore up a fundamentally decayed edifice. It was frightening to realize the difficulty.

In Japan it had all been different.

Throughout the sixties, while the western nations questioned progress and faltered in their will to move forward, Hideki had been one of the key figures driving Japan up the steep hill. Already they were pushing far ahead of the moss-grown British, and America would be next. Though he was now over seventy, Saigo Hideki was still on target to see the final goal of his life achieved, the day when Japan replaced the United States of America as *ichi-ban* – number one – industrial power in the world.

Informal mixing with the Hideki team had begun as pleasantries were exchanged. Alex forced a smile, painting over his feelings; his forebodings were unsettling him. He made an effort and chatted with the Japanese with gusto, picking at canapés and, more discriminatingly, at a big green fish-shaped plate of *sushi*.

"Alex, I'd like you to meet Mr Hideki." Hugh presented him with a quick gesture of introduction. "Mr Hideki – my cousin, Alex. He's a Stanton director, a shareholder, vice-president of Hacker Stanton International, and is soon, perhaps, to take charge of our Armaments Division."

The old man's eyes glittered. "Arm-am-ents! The old glory of Stanton's."

Alex found himself bowing automatically, though shallowly. Wasn't there some etiquette regarding the depth of a bow? he fleetingly wondered. Better not in future, unless one is certain of the form . . .

"An honour," Alex said.

"Very please to meet you," Hideki said like a memorized formula, and moved on, an intense spirit dressed in a black suit from Bond Street. He had impressive presence – but then Alex had expected no less.

"Remember me, Alex? It's good to see you again, old boy."

Alex half-recognized the voice from his schooldays. He turned and nodded tautly as he placed the man. James Battersby – plumper than he had been in his student days, but every bit as obsequious.

Battersby brushed at his silk tie. "I'm in public relations now, looking after Mr Hideki's visit. This is a marvellous opportunity to see the new trends, the rising nations. Absolutely first-class people the Japanese, and Mr Hideki is a fantastically important man in his own country. Working for him is very rewarding."

Alex glanced down at Battersby's extra large whisky and said drily, "I imagine it would be."

"My father's done some work for you, I believe. He's very highly regarded, of course, an extremely well-connected QC."

Alex scanned the room, looking for escape. He recalled the name. "Yes, I'm sure we employed him two, possibly three years ago. The Inland Revenue queried one of our tax write-offs, as I remember."

He smiled at the thought, and Battersby replied with a gesture of contained modesty. Then Alex stripped his smile away.

"Sir John Battersby, QC, lost our case. And the six hundred thousand pounds that went with it. Excuse me."

From the centre of the room Alex walked to the stairs, then to the big window that overlooked the river. He watched bright sunshine glistening on the filthy waters, and hit the teakwood sill three times with his fist in an attempt to exorcize the apparition. At this moment, James Battersby was about the last person he wanted to meet. The slavish manners of the man disgusted him. Quisling, he thought.

His attention was caught by movement on the bridge. He saw marching across it something that relegated everything else to the background: a huge phalanx of men with red banners, moving towards the Stanton gates.

Battersby was pushed suddenly out of his mind; he stared up at the bridge. The marchers were still streaming forward.

389

Alex opened the window and peered out. Sir George came over, too.

"It looks like a political procession," Alex said, worriedly.

They stood at the window together and watched the head of the crowd approaching along the cobbled quay. Hundreds of people snaked down the street that led to the waterfront. They tailed back right across the bridge into Gateshead.

"The march must be at least a mile long," Sir George said. "How did they arrange it so swiftly? The police can have had no idea . . ."

In the first ranks, escorted by hastily summoned police on foot, and led by a colliery brass band that was playing the *Internationale*, were William Langton and the Lord Mayor.

"– though cowards flinch and traitors sneer, we'll keep the red flag flying here!"

It was spectacular and dignified enough to make Alex recall the days of his childhood when a procession had possessed the power to thrill him. The demonstration came closer. He saw the Edwardian banners of union lodges, blown concave by the wind, were held up across the body of men, and here, below them, the mass of men came to a halt.

He looked at their faces, hungry for that kind of simple purpose. They were proud and determined men from the shipyards, supported by others from factories, foundries and the mines. Alex watched their banners with a sinking heart as they engulfed the building and the delegation's cars, and he turned as Sir George murmured something and William Langton passed out of sight, swallowed by the huge crowd.

Sir George's face was both grim and sad. He had to raise his voice to make himself heard over the brass music. "The finest men on earth, Alex."

Alex pulled the window shut, and stepped back from it. Downstairs they closed the great front doors with a bang.

The crowds along the street continued to cheer. The journalists loved this confrontation, of course. Alex saw the flashbulbs go off, dazzlingly. The crowd closed in, mobbing the corner building. Then the chanting began, reinforced by hand-clapping.

"No surrender! No surrender! No surrender!"

With despair in his heart, Alex Stanton watched the delegates coming out to see the commotion. Some of the Japanese were waving at the mass of workers, smiling, then they seemed suddenly

390

to appreciate the aggressiveness of the hand gestures offered them, gestures from the tribal warfare of the football terraces.

Alex seethed. "This is suicidal. If only they knew it! They're hammering nails into their own coffin lids."

He turned on his heel and went to help his cousin do what Ray Hacker called 'toughing it out'. He had never felt so angry. He knew his face was white with suppressed rage.

For an hour the building remained surrounded, with its occupants imprisoned inside. At one point, the Japanese crowded around their chairman, fiercely anxious for him, as Battersby ran around trying to reassure them. The septuagenarian Hideki boss sat stolidly in one corner, unmoved.

Alex tried to persuade the old man to talk, pointing to a five-foot long, cased model of a destroyer which a Stanton yard had built for the Imperial Navy in 1902. "It performed excellently in the Russo–Japanese war, contributing to the famous Japanese rout of the Czar's fleet."

One of the executives translated the chairman's comment smoothly: "That was the first victory of an Asiatic power over a European, Mr Stanton."

But not the last, eh? Alex pointed to another model. "This is HMS *Surprise* – launched in the early thirties, I believe."

Hideki's eyes suddenly blazed with fury. "You show me this?"

Even Alex was shocked by this fervour, and disconcerted, too. What could this old ship be to the Japanese industrialist? "It's only a model. From before the war. I understand it's made out of -"

Then Battersby reappeared, and interrupted. "The police are driving a wedge through the mob, Mr Hideki. We'll soon be at liberty to leave." He dabbed at his perspiration and vanished from Alex's disapproving gaze.

"These, outside, are your *workers*?" Hideki said with disgust.

"Don't worry, Mr Hideki. They're staging a demonstration against the government's Trade Union proposals, and hope to embarrass us here today, but they have no quarrel with your delegation."

Hideki shook his head, growled. The interpreter said, "In Japan, our society has *wa*, inner harmony. Such things are quite impossible there."

"It's much less serious than it appears," Alex soothed, and the story of the Nissan strike in '53 that had lasted four months came to him, but he said nothing.

391

"Your workers are contaminated by Socialism, Mr Stanton."

Hideki suddenly stood up and led Alex rather than Hugh or Sir Edward onto the carpeted landing.

"Your firm has old glory, many valuable secrets, techniques, contacts. I am interested, understand."

"I understand," Alex said toughly, knowing the ultimatum would come next.

"I can give your company one week to settle this strike," Hideki said crisply. "No longer."

By now, the reinforced police presence had made itself felt. The crowd was persuaded to disperse, and the Japanese delegation stalked down to their limousines.

Upstairs, as caterers began to clear up the remains of the buffet and dismantle the bar, Alex found his cousin. He sat down beside him, recognizing the effect the ultimatum had had on his state of mind. Hugh was sitting dazed, staring into a paper cup that might have been full of tears.

"Alex, we'll never bring the unions to their senses within a week. It's impossible."

Hugh's father waved a stiff hand. There was some of his former briskness in the gesture. "Don't worry. I know how to settle strikes. I'll talk to Langton. I've dealt with him before. Bring me a telephone."

"But father, I –"

"I said, bring me a telephone!"

"I've fixed up a meeting with Hideki," Hoyle told David as he drove up the Great North Road and out of town that night. "I thought he might be interested in the real story of the strike. I bet he was impressed this afternoon – tens of thousands of us, David!"

David shifted uncomfortably. Hoyle had picked him up from his father's pub, and during the journey he had been asking David questions about Stanton Industries. David had been forced to answer all too many of them.

"You know the Japanese have employed somebody we know?"

"You're joking! At Shipbuilding, Divisional HQ?"

"Right," Hoyle said. "It was Battersby – from Oxford, if you remember. I think he was there when I was doing my research degree at Brasenose. I tell you, we have no problems about getting on with him. He knows what it's all about!"

392

David momentarily closed his eyes and said dryly, "Somehow I thought you would see it that way." He forced himself to smile. "But why do you want me along tonight?"

"What's wrong with associating with me, David? Anyway, think of the future. Maybe we'll make you an intermediary officially." He laughed. "'Locally-born MP takes a hand to settle strike . . .' But for now, you can be available for us to question you." A police car passed them in the other direction, its blue light flashing. Hoyle's voice suddenly became harsh. "You're on my side, aren't you? We're just talking, nothing illegal."

David sensed a threat. "Of course, Alan."

"Now, you've done some research about this for Alex Stanton, haven't you? So tell me all about the Japanese, David." Hoyle braked as they came up to some traffic lights; cars queued behind and thin snowflakes drifted through their headlights' beams.

David was used to having people pick his brains, and this seemed harmless enough. He settled back and talked softly, sure of his knowledge. "Hideki's corporation is intensely vigorous. His people have their origins in the dispossessed samurai of the Meiji reform – when the Emperor dismantled the feudal structure by edict." David now knew a great deal about the history of the combine they called 'the octopus' because of its stranglehold on so many sectors of Japan's economy. He said, "They have tentacles everywhere, from heavy engineering to automobiles, airlines to tuna fisheries, paper mills to insurance. And shipping, of course, not to mention shipbuilding."

Hoyle was grinning. "Sounds like the big league, eh?"

"Hideki himself started the business during the First World War, at the age of seventeen, with electrical equipment he had copied from designs in American textbooks. Between the wars, he moved into power plant, then locomotives."

"Then the war came?"

"The annexation of Korea and Manchuria in the thirties provided him with his big opportunity, just as it did for his three friends who started Nissan Motors. Like them, he moved into the military truck market. Then, with all his connections in the army, navy and air force – shipbuilding, submarines and battleships – he did very well, and then the war itself saw a very profitable move into munitions for him. Of course, since the MacArthur Constitution of 1947 there's been no chance of a war industry starting up again. Not that it's made much difference to their expansion: they're making a fortune out of the U.S. involvement in Vietnam, for example."

Hoyle was excited. "It's just got better and better for Hideki, hasn't it?"

"No." David steadied himself as they swung round a roundabout. "In 1945, when American bombers flattened his factories and burned down his shipyards he must have thought it was all over for him."

Hoyle smiled. "It would have finished most people, you mean. Go on, David – you tell a good story."

"But something happened that gave Hideki a real, strong reason to go on: he happened to go to talk with the Navy in Kure. That particular day was 8th August, 1945."

Hoyle whistled. "Wasn't that –?"

"When he went home to Hiroshima, it had been levelled by the atomic bomb."

"My God."

"With his granddaughter, Kiko, as one of the 160,000 casualties – though she didn't die."

"What did Hideki do, then? Was he one of the people who wanted to resist an invasion of the Jap mainland, or what?"

"This is mainly speculation, now, because Hideki doesn't feature in the history books and he never gives interviews. But I suspect that he was left with little but an intense desire to get even with the victors. His only son was killed on the bridge of a Japanese cruiser, and his granddaughter was badly hurt in Hiroshima by the bomb."

"What happened in '45, when the Americans came?"

"That was very hard to find out," David admitted. "There's a lot that's obscure. On the face of it, he's lucky he didn't end up facing a war crimes tribunal, especially since he held military rank himself – not just a ceremonial rank, either. He certainly kept a low profile till the fifties; officially he had no power in his own company. Officially. Rumour says differently, though. He was forced by the American occupation to postpone the reconstruction of his *zaibatsu* until 1952, but from then he's been one of the principals in Japan's economic miracle." David turned his head. "Not a man to cross, I would say."

They pulled off the road into the capacious car park of the Northumberland Hotel. Hideki's party had taken over the entire top floor, and, after they were both body-searched, the old man granted

394

them an audience in his suite. Some of Saigo Hideki's reasons for doing so soon became clear.

Hoyle, uniquely, seemed uneasy. "You know me, I believe, and my associate? I represent Forward, the real power in the union and the strike. This is Mr David Bryant, a Labour MP and – an adviser to me. He is very useful because he knows Stanton Industries well."

Hideki stood up and turned his back. "I like useful men."

"I spoke to your assistant, James Battersby. He was hinting our strike may be of some use to you, if it makes the Stantons more vulnerable."

Hideki turned around. Though the man smiled, it was clear as he called for tea that his memories were sharp, and his personality was intimidating. His eyes turned harder and blacker as he questioned Hoyle, staring at him.

"You are man who recognizes power, Mr Hoyle?"

Hoyle licked his lips. "I am."

"You understand the will-to-power, the desire for revenge?"

This was like some kind of obscene catechism, David thought, but he felt the powerful emotional undercurrent that flowed between the two ruthless men.

"I understand those things perfectly, Mr Hideki."

The old man turned away, to the balcony. "I embrace both power and revenge. Let me tell you this story.

"In the winter of 1932, Mr Hoyle, the Stanton yard launched the last of their 'C' class cruisers, HMS *Surprise*. In the spring eleven years later, that ship sank our own carrier, *Fukuoka*, with all hands. My son, Ito, was a young naval lieutenant on the bridge at the time."

David kept silent, because suddenly it all made terrifying sense. Hideki's words had struck an ominous note; and David feared that this man wanted Stanton Industries and everybody connected with it laid low.

Hideki's hand tapped lightly on the table top, then his smile broadened again, showing massive dental work. "Also, Stanton engineers were part of the team who were sent to Los Alamos, in 1944. Is that not true?"

Hoyle showed surprise over his teacup. "To work on the bomb?"

"They were very fine craftsmen. Very knowledgeable technical people. They were asked to build the special casings of Little Boy and Fat Man. Very sad. Very terrible." When Hideki looked up again, he wore a new and impeccably polite face. "Mr Battersby, please come in."

The Englishman entered from the next room. His eyes were on David as he laid the case down on the table.

Hideki looked around the room. His power filled the room, dominating it. "Everybody leave. I will speak to Mr Hoyle in private when I give him my – gift. I do not want any misunderstandings. Or witnesses."

David was amazed. Since Hideki's desire to acquire the Stanton yards was clearly not simply a business decision, the outcome was much less certain. Perhaps he was turning the screw on Stanton Industries quite deliberately, hoping the strike would serve to bring the cost of his acquisition down. Perhaps he was actually on the point of calling the whole thing off. Perhaps he wanted to destroy –

His staff, four of them, bowed low. Then one turned to David, smiling politely, but the hand that took his upper arm felt like steel pincers.

"You must go," the squat Japanese told him, staring into his eyes from a few inches away.

Battersby had left immediately. They had *him* well-trained, David thought sourly.

Hoyle waved a hand imperiously. "Wait in the car."

David gave an ironic bow, then was escorted out of the room to the thickly-carpeted corridor outside. Other floors, and the other windows and doors along them, gave out sounds of music and talk, light, and warmth. When David reached the ground floor, however, and turned up his collar and walked out into the freezing fog, he could only see one light on the top floor.

In the car, he turned on the engine, radio and heater. What was Hideki doing? he wondered. Simply interrogating Hoyle about the strike and Forward's intentions, or attempting something more?

He rubbed his hands together, trying to warm them, and wondered how long he would have to wait.

Hideki still stood at the window, watching David turn to look up at this lighted room, them slam the car door and start the engine.

"I saw that man with the Stantons."

"That's right. On instructions from Forward, me, he's been doing some work with them."

"You trust that Bryant, Mr Hoyle?"

"I have so much on him that it isn't a question of 'trust' any longer. I could break him in an hour."

Hideki turned around, smiling. "Then that will do; your position is enviable, his position is –" He made a strange gesture with his hands. Then he went up to the table, very light and spry, spun the case half way around, and sprang the catches. Inside were banded wads of banknotes.

Hoyle's face glowed. "How much is there?"

Hideki told him.

"Forty thousand pounds!"

"Please accept this small token, Mr Hoyle."

"For Forward?"

"For the strike. In the hope that it will continue. I do not wish Stanton Industries to recover. The Stantons cannot save themselves, or their company. I intend to take their inheritance, cheaply. Very cheaply. But my intervention is not to be spoken of – ever."

"I understand," Hoyle said, turning up a wad with his thumb. In his underground world, there were many frightening people, but the razor edge of Hideki's will was terrifying him. Hoyle felt as if the floor had tilted towards this ancient, soft-spoken Japanese, and he did not want to meet the other man's eyes.

He was scared of what he knew he would find there.

"You must meet my gaze, Mr Hoyle."

Hoyle knew he was sweating. "I –" His voice had gone drier than bones. He wanted to leave. There was nausea in the pit of his stomach. He could not breathe. Finally, against his will, he looked up.

"You must ask the question, Mr Hoyle."

"Yes." Hoyle wiped at his forehead. "This money you've given me to help bring down Stanton Industries – how far are you willing to go?"

He read the answer, as he had known he would, in Hideki's eyes.

David slipped back into the lobby to make a phone call, but got back to the car in time to hear the evening news on the radio.

Hoyle came back ten minutes later, his face pale and – shocked, David would have described it.

"Drive me, David. Don't say a word otherwise."

David shifted seats and waited until Hoyle was settled in, case on his knees. Then he drove out of the car park past a large Rover that

397

had a tail of tin cans and a scrawl of shaving cream on its back window that said *Just married.*

"Where do I go, Alan?"

"Just drive!"

Hoyle seemed shaken, on edge. David noticed his hands were pressed hard and flat on the case. He tried to remain calm in the car as he drove back towards the city.

"I've got some news that –"

"Just drive, I said!"

David shifted up into fourth. The tension in the car could almost be touched. When David looked at him, Hoyle's face seemed strange. Then he spoke, and David heard the excitement in his laugh. "Lenin was dead right. The rich *will* help the revolution along out of jealousy of one another!"

"Not today."

"Huh?" Hoyle turned his head. "What do you mean?"

"It seems that Sir Edward Stanton has somehow got Langton to agree to settle the strike. It was on the radio. They'll be having the public signing of the new union-management agreement at midday tomorrow. It seems that Langton and Stanton Industries have agreed a compromise settlement. The strike is finished, Alan."

Hoyle's face was suddenly dark, like thunder. "What? Langton can't do that!"

"He still controls most of the delegates on the strike committee."

"No he doesn't!" Hoyle said scornfully. "Listen, you want to know the names of the committee members *I* control? I'll tell you!"

David carefully memorized the names, shocked that even Jackie Sutton, Langton's close friend, was on the side of Forward.

"Langton thinks he's 'settled', does he – some kind of moderates' sell-out, you take it from me! But why didn't you tell me what he was planning?"

"I just found out. Listen, I don't know Maggie – or her father – *that* well, and I don't imagine he confides everything to her. You don't suppose I tell my wife everything I do, do you?"

Hoyle laughed as they stopped at a set of traffic-lights. "No, I certainly don't."

David said nothing.

"Well, we can do a lot with forty thousand pounds. I want to use it. And I'm prepared to go all the way."

* * *

398

Early on the morning of Thursday, the following day, Hideki's team returned to the negotiations. They sat in session all morning, the meeting going on until noon. As a non-executive director, Alex was condemned to wait patiently to hear the progress of the talks until Hugh emerged during a break.

"How's it going?" Alex asked, buttonholing his cousin.

Hugh looked tired, but triumphant. "I think my insistence that the strike is over has brought the Japanese to the brink of signing. Thank God."

"They're really that interested?"

"Alex, they've heard some rumours about our R&D in the Shipbuilding Division – they're talking about paying four or five million pounds just to be cut into that."

"Have they, now?" Alex said thoughtfully. Research and development in Shipbuilding. It meant something to sell, at least. "What does Sir George say?"

Hugh looked at him obliquely. "He's resigning, Alex."

"My God . . ." That did not sound hopeful at all. "What about the sympathy strikes in Armaments and Aircraft?"

"Not solid," Hugh said tiredly. "Not yet. If we settle today we'll settle all of our union trouble."

Alex found that hard to believe, especially since Forward was involved. When Hugh left for the men's washroom, Alex followed him.

"Is nothing sacred, Alex?"

Alex smiled. "Not if it concerns Stanton Industries. And besides, it's nice and quiet in here. Move aside and I'll join you . . ." Alex relieved himself on a glazed wall dated 1892. "Your father's just turned up, you know. He wants his moment of glory at the press conference . . . How d'you think he brought Langton round?"

"Threatened to sell his daughter into white slavery, for all I know! Look, I'm really much too busy to speculate about things like that. Father's brought it off; he did it although we couldn't, so good luck to him! We'll get the full details later. Now, if you'll excuse me, some of us have real work to do here, helping to save our firm from a very serious mishap indeed."

"Aunt Lilith," Alex said, smiling crookedly, "all those years ago . . ."

Hugh towelled his white hands dry. "Sometimes even I can take offence, Alex, and I *do* have a memory."

"Of course," Alex said, following him outside. "It's just that that's the first time you've admitted how serious the situation is."

Hugh's eyes were haunted. "Alex, I've had father to please, Lord Beauford being uncooperative, press speculation, industrial relations problems, ludicrously high taxes, outdated plant, ruthless foreign competition to deal with . . ." He ran out of words, then turned to go.

"But that's the nature of the game, Hugh."

Hugh turned back for one last moment before the beeswaxed doors of the boardroom closed on him. "It isn't *my* game, though."

It was hard to disagree with that, Alex thought.

He went to help lift Sir Edward's wheelchair into the executive dining room, and comfort the invalid with dry sherry and that morning's *Times*.

The article splashed across three columns in the business section, and the staff writer was very complimentary about Sir Edward's 'extremely tough but extremely effective bargaining skills'.

"Look at that, my boy! Fame at last!"

There were people waiting expectantly in one of the large conference rooms on the ground floor. Some of the firm's creditors, and a deputation of bankers; there were also financial journalists, a small group of local notables, and Alex had invited David Bryant.

Outside Stanton's Shipbuilding Division HQ, TV lights flared brightly. Will Langton was followed up the steps by his daughter, a union lawyer, and a crowd of journalists. They were stopped in the wood-panelled hallway, and then ushered into one of the large conference rooms on the ground floor. Will demanded to see Sir Edward, staring pointedly at his watch.

"I was asked here at twelve. This is discourtesy."

It was several minutes before the lift doors were pulled back to reveal the old man's wheelchair. He seemed unperturbed by the commotion as he was wheeled in, and he greeted Langton pleasantly.

Maggie stood by her father, her silk dress immaculate and her face expressionless.

"Now," Sir Edward said, as the photographers took their flash pictures, "I'm glad to be able to announce in front of our Japanese guests there in the back rows that the, ah, recent disagreements within Stanton Industries have been settled amicably. Mr Langton and his union friends have seen fit to accept our revised offer, and therefore will be calling off the strike."

The journalists stood up, wanting to ask their questions. Sir Edward's face glowed with pride under the hot lights, but before he could begin to take questions Langton got to his feet.

"Traitor!" somebody by the door said – a Forward activist with a forged NUJ pass, playing to the TV cameras. "You sell-out bastard, Langton! The workers, united, will *never* be defeated!"

He was hustled out quickly.

Langton loomed over the man in the wheelchair. Sir Edward looked self-satisfied, out of touch, weak. Still, Alex reflected, somehow he had won.

"I am glad to say", his uncle said, a hollow boom, "that justice will be done."

"That it will."

Langton folded his arms. Alex looked carefully at Maggie's father, but there was no weakness there, only an immense, craggy dignity. This man, he suddenly realized, was in the right.

Langton spoke slowly, looking around. "I hope you gentlemen and ladies in the press, you people behind the TV cameras, are recording this carefully."

Alex's instincts were sounding an alarm. The union's solicitor, a square, bespectacled man, was staring carefully at the crowd. Alex stood up suddenly.

"First, I'd like you to listen to this recording my daughter made for me."

Maggie fiddled with something in a case, and then Alex heard his uncle's voice—scratchy and fading, with clicks on the telephone line, but clear and unmistakeable. The audience was murmuring, stirring, standing up too. "Oh, Lantgon, don't be a fool! I'll pay you the money in Switzerland, in the States, anywhere you want – very private and tax-free! Five thousand pounds, Langton! No scruples, now; all you have to do is to deliver the votes of a majority of your strike committee."

Alex suddenly felt sick to his stomach. In a slow-motion dream, he watched Sir Edward's face begin to crumple, as if an ancient, proud mountain range were crumbling into sand in front of him.

His heart went out to his adopted father, in this moment of utter humiliation.

Nobody had moved. Langton's voice was bitter as he held up the reel of tape. "I have here Sir Edward Stanton's offer – I hope everyone heard it, because it's nothing more than a shabby bribe!"

Sir Edward, aghast, began to protest, but his denials were shouted down.

"My daughter recorded everything you said on the telephone, Stanton! Don't bloody lie about it. You've built your life on threats and bribery and it's time you paid. It's time someone beat you at your own game." His hand swept towards the crowd. "You all heard it and I have transcripts here. He offered me money to call off the strike and settle for eight per cent. To betray my membership!"

There was sudden pandemonium and Alex began pushing forward through the crowd.

"But you agreed, Langton. You agreed!"

Will Langton's rage showed. "I don't take bribes, Sir Edward. The strike goes on. Twenty two per cent – and no surrender! No surrender!" He punched the air. Sir Edward's face had crumpled; suddenly he looked old and beaten, and his face was chalk pale.

Alex reached the podium, and Maggie looked down at him, her face blotchy with emotion. Their eyes met for one long, electric moment, and Alex realized, with dazzling clarity, that he still meant very much to her.

The press conference began to break up in confusion. The Langtons both stalked away from the platform and out of the building, followed by many of the press. The others stayed to interrogate Sir Edward.

"Bribery, Sir Edward! What's your reaction to Langton's claim that you've built your career on 'threats and bribery'?"

"Will you be suing him for slander over his accusation?"

There was laughter at that comment; some people began to sit down. Sir Edward's jaw was trembling; he sat in his iron chair hunched up and ancient, great pouches of flesh under his eyes. He looked around the hall as if he had never seen it before.

"Let's have some answers, Sir Edward!"

There was a murmur of ridicule. He still said nothing, his eyes wide and shocked. Then a thread of saliva drooled from a corner of the old man's mouth. There was no laughter now, only a pained embarrassment for everyone.

Then Alex jumped up beside him. He put a hand on his uncle's shoulder, but addressed the crowd.

"On behalf of Stanton Industries I sincerely regret whatever

402

misunderstanding has taken place. My uncle is seriously ill; you are hounding a sick man, and I beg you not to do it." He left a long, deliberate pause, looking around the room. "As for the strike, we can only repeat yet again that we cannot – and I must repeat that, cannot possibly – meet the full twenty-two percent claim for all our manual workers. The money is not there, and I am prepared to open the Shipbuilding Division's books to any firm of accountants nominated by the engineering workers' union to prove it. Did everybody hear me? Full disclosure – print that, please. Full disclosure will prove that I'm telling the truth. I assure you we will make every effort to find an acceptable compromise, but this strike action is putting the future of the entire company at risk."

He wheeled Sir Edward away. Doors shut behind him, but when he looked down at the only father he had known for almost twenty years tears came to his eyes.

The old man was wheezing as they helped him into the dark family car that would take him home to Craigburn, and permanent retirement.

"I'm sorry, Alex. I'm sorry that I thought I could help and instead ruined any possibility of –" He turned his face away, suddenly. Then he held his head in his hands and his shoulders were shaking in spasms. "I betrayed my trust. Alex – your father and I, we should never . . . Forgive me. *Forgive* me."

Something deep inside Alex was shaken by his uncle's complete collapse, but this made his own strength even more necessary, and he sqeezed his adopted father's shoulder. "I don't know about your generation's arguments. But I'm strong enough to forgive."

"If you knew –"

"I must worry about today."

The old man's eyes were bleary and haunted.

"I'll ring Aunt Grace," Alex told him. "You'll be taken care of."

"But the firm! The family!"

"It's in my generation's hands, now. I'll try to be worthy of it. Now you have to go."

The iron gates to the directors' car park were quickly opened, quickly shut. Just before the big Rolls accelerated away some members of the sightseeing crowd booed.

Alex stiffened, then went back inside. He saw Hugh.

"Well?"

403

"The Hideki team have left. There'll be no further negotiations until the strike is settled; and Mr Hideki must fly back to Tokyo within a week."

Hugh was trying to brace himself, but Alex was not impressed, and soon Hugh seemed to deflate wearily. When McCourt asked what he was going to do now, he could say only, "I suppose we'll get by somehow."

"Get by?" Alex said.

Hugh produced a quick, taut smile. "We always have in the past."

"Can't you see, the old days of glory are over?" Alex said. "Uncle's ruined everything. You'll never move Langton now. The Japanese link is broken and the strike is still on. What do you intend to do?"

Hugh twisted his head around; he looked shattered. "There's not much I *can* do."

Alex hesitated, then plunged in. "I can get the men back to work by Monday morning."

Hugh looked up in annoyance. "How? By magic?"

"No, by offering them twenty-two per cent."

Hugh stared along the table and back. "But we haven't got the money to pay it!"

"Yes we have. Twenty-two per cent of nothing is nothing. The redundancy notices could start going out on Friday. Five thousand of them."

"A *third* of the Division's workers?"

"There's no alternative. Thousands more will have to go later, I dare say. If there're no orders because we're too expensive, then we might as well face facts and get out of the shipbuilding game. This isn't a damned charity. We'll have to ask Beauford Cleves to roll over our debts; and I think Kintyre Ross might be usefully approached. Then if we can postpone the Rolls Royce aero engine payments for a few months –"

"Wait a minute –"

Alex fixed his cousin with a firm look. "Hugh, as you say, there's nothing you can do. I suggest you listen to me, and do as I say. Between twenty-five and thirty million would ease our liquidity problems. So long as Rolls Royce can help –"

There was a commotion behind them.

"I wouldn't count on Rolls Royce!"

404

David Bryant was standing in the doorway, his jacked discarded, his waistcoat unbuttoned, his tie slackened. He was breathless as though he had just run upstairs.

Everybody turned to look at him.

"The news has just come through . . ."

"David, what is it?"

"Rolls Royce have just announced it. *They're bankrupt!*"

"Ridiculous!" Then Alex saw that David was deadly serious, and he rememberd the rumours – the huge cost over-runs on the joint engine project. He seemed to shrink back inside himself. "*They've gone bust?* But they're the jewel of British engineering. Half the air forces in the world depend on Rolls Royce engines. All Britain's submarines, Polaris . . . I don't believe it! Heath wouldn't let that happen – would he?"

Hugh looked at David Bryant and saw it was disaster.

"What are we going to do?" he shouted, and the anguished echo rang in the empty room.

3

The police line was thin, blue, unimpressive. Instead of metal crash barriers to hold the crowd away from the gates of the Shipbuilding Division headquarters there was only a single slack rope; luckily, people were still in good humour as they joked and jostled, but the group of journalists standing to one side wondered how long that would last. Not many more days, they decided, shivering. More snow began to fall.

Then there was noise from the ground floor of the building and the Langtons walked out. There was applause, which Maggie's father acknowledged with a chopping gesture and a grim smile. Then his black Ford came out of a side alley and braked. He and his daughter stepped in as people banged on the car's roof and a flurry of sleet came in off the river.

The powerful car took them away from the cobbled quayside, and up to the grand Georgian sweep of Grey Street.

Maggie turned her gaze from shoppers with coloured carrier bags to her father. She felt sickened, but love and duty called her; she reached over to touch her father's shoulder and tried to put exultation into her voice.

"We won that round."

His craggy face quivered. "So many years I spent, dreaming of getting my revenge on him. And look at him now. A man of straw. Nothing." He shuddered.

She felt stiff, unnatural. "We beat him."

"You think I'm the kind of man who enjoys kicking a cripple, Maggie? That was awful – poor, used-up old man, trying so hard to be what he was all those years ago. Failing so ignominiously to protect his own. Shameful to fail!" He shook his head. "In spite of everything he's tried to do to his workers – and to me and mine – he won a medal on D-Day, you know,"

"But he was guilty, Dad."

"Maggie, we're all guilty; that doesn't excuse brutality, selfishness – *ever*. Don't you forget that. Though you'd think the two Stanton lads would have stopped him."

Maggie lit a French cigarette, ignoring the fact that her father wrinkled his nose at her. "Dad, I don't always follow you; certainly you've never made it a rule to follow my advice –"

"No," he said, "but I ask for your opinion, don't I?"

"So you can't really expect Hugh Stanton or Alex to take responsibility, can you?"

"To take responsibility? I don't know, Maggie. When I look at the state of Stanton Industries or the country there's something in me cries out: 'This is wrong! We must do it better! We must stand together, work together to prevail!'" She saw his lower lip curl down. Their car left the city centre, and then crossed a road bridge over the multiple tracks of the railway that led east to the coast and up to Edinburgh. "Did David Bryant ever show you that play he was going to put on in London?"

"No," she said, taken aback. "What's that got to do with anything?"

"It was about one of the early Stantons. The play was done in a way I didn't like – characters talking straight to the audience, historical name-dropping, some bloody crude parallels to the present day – but the story had atmosphere and he was certainly asking all the right questions. What do we owe to ourselves? What do we owe to our country, to our time? What must we do?"

Her father's hoarse voice had a thrilling cadence; but she could not give much of a reply. "I don't know, Dad. I've always been much better at asking questions than giving answers."

He smiled at that, his bushy eyebrows lifting. The driver turned right opposite the gates to Stanton Park and pulled off the road, into the driveway of a redbrick Victorian house with a round tower on one corner. It was his new home – leaded windows, a spiky hedge for privacy, everything strong and old.

"Must have set you back a pretty penny."

"I have a low-interest loan from the union, and some money for the running costs. I do a lot of business out of this house. And don't forget, I'm regional secretary. Next step up is to be president of the union. Two and a half million members, Maggie. And I intend to go that far." He sighed, touched her head for a moment. "Lovely hair, you have, lass. Lovely. And you have your mother's eyes. I only hope that Yank who won't marry you is treating you right."

She pushed out of the black car and slammed the door. "Listen, Dad, I've told you before. Things are different now."

He looked at her, his eyes large and ironic in the failing dusk light. "They are? I hadn't much noticed that, myself. Where is he?"

She turned away. "In Los Angeles, if you must know."

"Film business again, I suppose?" He pursed his lips. He loved his daughter above anything on earth. "Maggie, you've your mother's grand Irish heart in you. It's a pity you don't have my hard head."

She looked over the road, past the traffic. Here the sunset was red and gold, spectacular as it so often was here, and the ruins of a medieval pele tower were stark against the western sky. A park-keeper came by, long gardening tools slung over his shoulder, and she saw the man pause to stare at some new grafitti painted on the large green sign proclaiming *Stanton Park. Hours sunrise – sunset.*

The rest of the words her father read out aloud.

"Presented to the people of this city by Sir Edward Stanton, 14 May, 1956, in memory of his brother Michael Alexander Stanton."

Their driver had gone inside and left the front door open. Maggie suddenly felt cold.

"Let's get in front of the fire, Dad."

Once they were inside, he stopped to speak to the union officials he had in the ground floor strike headquarters. She went straight up the wide stairs to the round, tower room he had moved her old things into – school uniforms and reports, family memorabilia, her battered old books.

She found her first copy of *Lord of the Rings* there. It had been a sixteenth-birthday present, and she turned to the tender handwritten inscription from David Bryant. In pride of place over the old dressing table was an enlarged framed photograph of her Irish grandmother over from Kerry, her father, her mother, her elder sister and, seven years old, Maggie herself, radiantly happy with bucket and spade on the sun-hot golden sands near the Spanish city.

Family. And who did she have, now?

It was enough to break her heart.

The news about Rolls Royce had devastated Alex and Hugh. That collapse was almost certain to bring down Stanton Industries, too.

Last November Rolls Royce had been given a huge injection of cash from the government and the commercial banks: if that hundred million pounds had not saved them, then Stanton Industries was probably beyond rescue. Hugh had gone off to speak to Beauford Cleves in London, but he had not held out much hope.

Alex agreed. "The firm's taken a knock-out punch, we're on the canvas – and the count is nine."

"I'll do what I can," Hugh said. He was trembling. "But we absolutely must have £20 million pounds – or we go under."

"Then try to get it in a loan."

"I'll probably need to go to London in person."

"Do that. I can take charge here."

It had seemed natural to Alex to take command. After he had had Sir Edward escorted away in a Craigburn-bound car, Alex ordered a meeting of all the local senior managers from Armaments as well as Shipbuilding, in the large hall where the press conference had been held.

Immaculate in his dark Savile Row suit, tall, he pounded up the steps to the stage and then turned to survey the roomful of stricken men: Stanton Industries executives, some of them of thirty years' standing.

David moved towards his old friend, as Alex and he sensed the hostility in so many faces: and who could blame them?

Alex said quietly, "I'd better tell you the situation. Shipbuilding is in deep, deep trouble, which goes beyond the strike. The Rolls Royce crash has temporarily damaged Aircraft. Armaments is in healthy profit still, but that's only one Division. There are debts of £40 million hanging over us; and we need half that again merely to carry on. So all I can promise any of you is a bloody struggle for survival. But it's a struggle I intend to win, and I'd like as many of you as possible to stand by the old firm and by this family."

The senior yard manager stalked out of the ranks, twisting his grey tie off his neck so that the shirt button ripped away. There was grief as well as anger in Dan Drummond's face. "Stand by the likes of you, Stanton? And bloody Hugh? We've had enough thick and idle bosses' sons in this part of the world! Stand by you! I come here for wages, Alex Stanton, and can you promise me them?"

Alex stood there. His face was like cast iron, hard, implacable and gleaming. He had not moved. "I told you, Drummond. This is a risk

– but I and my family are taking it too. There'll be no more lies; no more promises that the Stantons can't keep."

The yard manager had tears in his eyes, but he was not ashamed. "To think of all the years we've stood for you lot! Bloody public school bastards. I've lied to good men and cheated them, Alex Stanton, to keep the likes of your uncle safe. You know we *used* to build ships around here? The finest ships that ever there were! We used to make tanks and guns that we sent all the way around the world, *and now you and yours have ruined all that forever!*"

Everybody stopped dead; the emotional tensions were like palpable forces, rending and tearing.

"Don't you have any loyalty, Mr Drummond?"

"Loyalty has to be earned, Stanton – and there'll be no 'Mr' from me today. Our loyalty isn't a bloody inheritance! What've you and yours done to earn it, lately?"

Alex stared at Drummond, as the other men stirred. It really could end here: everything could be at an end – no more shipyards, no more huge factories, no more superb Stanton engines leaving the production lines for jet fighters and Concorde. The jobs of thousands of men and the savings of hundreds of investors were at risk, and suddenly the disaster was like an unbearable, crushing weight.

For the first time, Alex moved – quickly and decisively, and his voice was crisp. He came to the edge of the stage. "I've been preparing for this day for five years. I've fought against the Board's mismanagement, and you all know it. I fought and I lost, but I have my contingency plans even for a situation like this. Now, if any of you want to pick up your redundancy money, you can do that tomorrow and you can go. If any of you want to stay, then stay – but in that case you're staying to fight!"

Alex held his breath as the slow, anguished exodus from the huge room began.

Nearly a third of the men chose to leave; and then he stepped down from the platform and gently escorted one old man who had remained to the door.

Drummond was one of the last to leave. He looked Alex up and down.

"Follow a Stanton? A Stanton? I won't follow some idiot without the brains to find his own arse in the dark!"

"Goodbye," Alex said coldly as the man stalked out and slammed the huge door. So much for Dan Drummond. Then he said to them all, "I'd like you senior people to be at your desks tomorrow morning and through the weekend preparing cost-cutting schemes. Go through the books in detail, because I need to know *exactly* what's profitable and what isn't if I'm to save anything from this disaster – and, yes, I know it means working on a Sunday . . . and, no, I can't promise you when you'll be paid. That's the way it is. Identify the dead wood we must cut, and I'll ring through to all of you by four tomorrow afternoon, but in the meantime Mr McCourt here speaks with my authority. I may as well tell you that Sir George Leslie has resigned and that the Head of Division for Armaments will be retiring – so for those of you with energy and ambition there's plenty of room at the top. I'm ringing now for a small team of people from head office in London, too. For the moment that's all."

They left very quietly, though their faces seemed determined. But Alex could tell they had no faith.

Then Hugh came back in, carrying a silver tray with teacups. For some reason, perhaps because his cousin was here and the atmosphere had changed, he seemed to be relieved. "Everybody has to muck in together, what? Help us through the crisis, like in the war."

Alex handed a cup and saucer to David and sipped his own tea thoughtfully. "No luck with Beauford Cleves or the others?"

"None," Hugh said, his face long. "One merchant banker told me that now Rolls Royce has gone, he sees our stock as 'a highly speculative purchase'."

"I see." Alex laughed shortly. "From blue chip to bankruptcy in one easy lesson."

Hugh clattered his cup down. "You think the lesson was easy, do you?"

Alex put a hand on his shoulder. "No recriminations, Hugh; not here and not now. I give you my word."

"Naturally, I tried to speak to Lord Beauford . . ."

David looked up. He had never liked the peer, nor his business methods. "He agreed to help?"

"I didn't even manage to speak to him. First he was 'in conference' with the IMF people over from New York; now he is 'on his way to Geneva by the late plane'. I don't think we can expect much from him – certainly not the £20 million we need by the end of next week."

"Five working days from tomorrow?" David said, obviously shocked. "Is that possible?"

"I'm still working on a rescue plan," Alex said instantly. "Make sure all our contacts know we aren't about to roll over and die, Hugh."

"Thank God," Hugh said, closing his eyes. "If we can settle the strike, the Japanese will –"

"David and I are getting together on that," Alex told him. "You know he's a good friend of Will's, apart from their party political contacts. But settling the strike won't give us that £20 million, especially with Rolls Royce gone. I think we're going to need government action; we must press our friends in Parliament hard – and use the press."

David nodded. He looked cool-headed, now. "I'm due back in London on Monday. I'll go straight to the Commons and start lobbying the Labour members; if the government acts – and I have to stress *if* – I can guarantee all-party backing for a rescue plan."

The corners of Alex's mouth turned down. "There's something else. You see Maggie more often than Will. I'd like you to – tell her the truth about the firm. I hope she's got some respect for facts, at least. You can point out that the only way the Stantons will go will be through bankruptcy, and if that happens, dozens of small firms and tens of thousands of workers will pay the price."

David felt uneasy, but was obliged to agree. "So I fix the Langtons for you."

"Tell them the truth. That's all I ask, David." Alex suddenly turned to Hugh. "What can we do to get the government on our side? Who do you dine with in the Cabinet, Hugh?"

Hugh looked uneasy; he held the teacup with both hands, tilting it and looking down. "Father used to take care of that kind of thing, didn't he? Father's always been the public, ceremonial face of Stanton Industries."

"Should he have been?" David said bluntly. "Today's exhibition will have done the standing of the firm no good at all."

Hugh's nostrils flared, but rather than confront anybody directly he turned away to discharge his anger. "Who are you, David Bryant? Sir Edward Stanton is –"

Alex interrupted him. He stared at Hugh. "I see David as my brother. What's more, he's quite right, and my uncle is past tense – he *was*, Hugh, he *was*. He's resigned as non-executive deputy chairman and he will never have official standing again. And besides, was he putting across the right image for us – and can you be honest, Hugh?"

Hugh's mouth opened weakly, then suddenly closed. "No." His eyes were glistening, but he spoke firmly. "Father was yesterday's man. I must also admit my error over politics. We need to be heard in the House of Commons; we *must* be heard in government."

Alex agreed. "Exactly. And don't mistake me, Hugh. For the last twenty years, you and I have been like brothers, with one head of the family. I love and respect your father, too – but out of that love and respect I want to do now what he would have done in his heyday!"

"It can be done," David said, excited; he had already decided how to go about lobbying the relevant MPs. "The government can be moved. Look at their actions to help Rolls Royce last year, reluctant or not! £89 million from the Treasury; and an arranged £18 million from the banks."

Hugh looked unhappy. David knew he had lost faith; he did not believe. Probably Alex sensed it, too, because he leaned forward to speak more softly.

"Take tonight off, Hugh. Look after your father. David and I will join you at Craigburn later, but don't wait up."

David said nothing. After Hugh had left, Alex turned to his old friend and showed his teeth.

"Well, it looks irrevocable, now. Hugh will have to go along with me, and we can forget about the other non-executive members of the Board. None of them will defy a Stanton. I'm in charge, David. At long last."

It was strange, but David did not now remember how many hours had gone by since the disaster of the press announcement and the Japanese walk-out – but suddenly he was aware that it was night and there were ships' riding lights out there on the river, red and green in the dark, and on the far, darkened bank of the Tyne streetlights glimmered like a mirage. Time itself seemed compressed and foreshortened. They went up the grand stairs together, to the eerie echoes of the cavernous, unlit Stanton Divisional boardroom, and he felt cold.

A secretary came in, wearing her long overcoat because of the cold. "Your reply from Switzerland, Mr Stanton."

Alex glanced at it, then crammed the paper into a pocket.

413

"It can be done, David."

David waited before he asked about Alex's plans; but after listening to Alex speak he felt much better. "I am hopeful, Alex. The firm, and the nation, has got itself into a mess, but there is still a chance to come through; there'll be blood and tears and sweat, but hope will be enough to live on, for a little while. What do we do?"

"The strike," Alex said, ruminating, his hands behind his back. "And this Japanese interest."

He had not answered David's question.

"Did you see the way Maggie looked at you, at the press conference?"

Alex turned so that the single desk light shone away from his face. "No."

"Neither did I." David scratched at his eyes. "In fact, she didn't look at you at all."

"Well, now . . ." Alex stopped speaking; then he made his face into a mask. "Interesting comment, David. Yes, I suppose I do mean something to her still. Lucky you're so observant."

"Speaking of being observant, what did the telex say?"

"It's from somebody Hacker-Stanton and I myself as an individual have dealt with in the Swiss banking system."

"But what did it say? Good news?"

Alex tapped a pocket. He was grim-faced. "No."

David rubbed his hands together. There was no central heating in this old building. He felt very isolated, and wondered if Alex felt the same. The pickets were still outside, trying to cut them off from the world. Inside, only an emergency night staff remained, and they did not trespass on this meeting. But now that they were alone David could suddenly feel the horror Alex felt. Alex Stanton was on the edge of disaster, and he knew it. David watched him turn from the river to stare at the portraits of his ancestors; six different generations. From the chimneybreast hung the double portrait in oils of Samuel Stanton and his son Albert Edward looking down on today from the world of 1868. Those faces had seen the yards on the Tyne, Wear and Tees rise to their turn-of-the-century greatness, when over 35,000 men had been employed on Tyneside alone. They had looked upon the even more titanic efforts made to win victory in 1914–18. Albert Edward Stanton, Alex's grandfather, had helped Churchill take charge and then administered much of the nation's armaments and shipbuilding efforts in World War II. Those men

414

had seen greatness, and David wondered dispiritedly what they would have thought of today – would they really see Alex as someone they would be proud to have as their inheritor? But that didn't matter, David realized, jarringly. For good or ill, Alex and he, today, now, were all there was to defend Stanton Industries. There was every likelihood that the Stantons' history was about to finish here – unless Alex had a plan brilliant enough to save them all from the industrial wreckage of Britain.

Everything seemed to pivot around Alex now, and David was beginning to worry that his friend might not be capable of victory. In this room full of daunting history, what David heard – when it eventually came – shook him.

"This may be Judgment Day for Stanton Industries, David: only the few will be saved, and the condemned will be thrown down from on high into hell . . ."

"*Dies Irae*," David said softly.

For a time neither man spoke. Alex was thinking deeply, with the worry lines on his brow cast into deep shadow by the single light.

It was a complicated plan, then.

David was desperate to hear the details of the rescue, so he sat down on the edge of the boardroom table as Alex picked up a phone and began to dial.

"All right, Alex, let's have it."

Alex stopped dialling, his left forefinger poised over the old-fashioned Post Office dial. Now he looked tired and irritable, caught in mid-action.

"Let's have what?"

"I thought you needed me to help you, for God's sake! That means I need to know what your contingency plan is – you know, what you promised the men."

Suddenly Alex relaxed and gave David a bright, wide smile that seemed strangely out of place in the huge nineteenth-century boardroom with its polished antiques and its lovingly preserved historical aura. Then David suddenly remembered that his mother had been American; and seeing the smile, he relaxed too.

"Thank you, David. I was beginning to think I hadn't brought it off, but if I can convince even you –"

David was remembering that he had had virtually no sleep for thirty-six hours. He rubbed at his closed, sore eyes, partly because he was beginning to get angry – or perhaps this was all Alex's way of saying that he didn't trust anybody and intended to do it all on his own . . . He opened his eyes again.

"Brought *what* off, Alex? What is your plan?"

Alex said drily, "David, isn't it obvious that there isn't a plan yet? I'm fighting for the life of the company, and if we're to get out of this, we'll get out of it partly because people have confidence in us; that's why I lied. I'm buying time, David, and the only cost is words."

David's hands twitched. It had been a lie! But if there was no plan of salvation . . .

Alex continued. "I must find the money, David. You must help beat Forward and settle that strike."

"That'll take a miracle."

"Don't you believe in miracles, David? Because I do." He finally placed his call. "No, I don't know what time it is there, but I must speak to him. Tell him it's Mr Stanton from England and I *need* him; he knows what loyalty is, and he'll understand." There was a wait of a minute, then Alex's voice suddenly changed. "Tell Mr Hacker he can reach me through this number at any time; because we're in a crisis I'm having the phone manned overnight. Tell him to make plans to come to Britain, and to bring his chequebook." He put the phone down, his eyes looking somewhere else – looking to the United States, David speculated.

David asked, "A mystery godfather?"

There was an edge to his voice, now. "Nothing mysterious about Ray; but he'd better call back quickly. I need help, and so does the firm."

David had listened carefully to the tone, holding his hands together. This time there were no lies; the situation was desperate.

Alex stood up and extinguished the light. The coloured darkness outside and the river noises swept in. "Hungry? Let me take you to that French place down on the quayside, David."

David smiled suddenly. "Stanton Industries will pay, I presume?"

"Why not?" Alex said lightly. He stood up, reached out for his Burberry, which he had thrown over the back of another chair. "If we go bankrupt, we go bankrupt for over £40 million – not for the cost of our supper."

To David's surprise, Alex was very good company for the rest of the night; they talked about the government as well as finance, and

416

David told Alex for the first time about his ambitions to get into government. To finish things off after their excellent late supper they went to a casino. Though David lost twenty pounds, Alex won twice that playing roulette. They had actually made a profit on their evening.

It was a long ride out to Craigburn, though, and the night suddenly seemed vast and very cold.

"Why are you telling me this, Mr Drummond?" Will Langton said suspiciously into the telephone in his office at home.

"Why do you think? I hate those useless bastards, just like you do. Anything would be better than them. But you're not just up against Hugh Stanton and his father, now."

Will gestured, and his daughter and Robinson, the second most powerful member of the strike committee, came to listen. "More than Hugh, more than his old man. What d'you mean?"

"The other one – Alex, the one they call the Yank – he's there, running things with some people up from head office. And what's more he's been ringing up people in America, looking for their help."

"Has he, indeed!" Will covered the mouthpiece. "Alex Stanton's in Shipbuilding headquarters, running things with Hugh, trying to get buggers with open chequebooks over from the States." He stared at Robinson, at his daughter, then spoke to Drummond again. "So, he's joined the family at last, has he?"

"Right. And I'll tell you that unscrupulous bastard means to win."

"Thanks," Will said. "If you hear anything more, I'd appreciate knowing." He put the phone down.

"Well," Robinson said, harshly. "Young Alex has joined the Stantons, has he?"

"That's a surprise," Maggie said hollowly. "He's never really been accepted by them, you know."

Robinson stood up, stretched till his joints cracked. "Maybe we can stop him being accepted even now. I'll have words with Alan Hoyle about that. And you, Maggie." He turned a dark gaze to her. "You used to know him of old, didn't you?"

"Quite well," she said.

It was Sunday; three days since the Rolls Royce crash.

417

Maggie was to see her father off to the crucial late-night meeting. He came crashing down the stairs. "Maggie!"

Without being asked, she straightened his tie, brushed off his lapels.

"There's still some production going on at their factories – managers and strike· breakers and such – but if I can get the drivers to back us, the Stantons are finished. They won't be able to move a damn thing in or out of their factories, bought and paid for or not." His eyes gleamed, and he seemed even more broad-shouldered than usual. He turned back to her on the doorstep. "Don't you wait up, our Maggie."

She waved until the car was out of sight. Then she went to bed and read one of her schoolgirl diaries. It was strangely depressing reading sweet gushing words from another, more idealistic world – 1962.

She lay awake for some time, thinking that boys and pop music meant so little now, hoping that Terry might ring from Los Angeles, but there were no messages from the contemporary world for her.

Maggie got out of her unyielding bed at seven, to find her father already had the three phones in use – and had them in use twenty-four hours a day. There was a postal strike, so nothing could be done by letter.

She wondered if her father had won his case at the meeting, but did not want to disturb him now to find out. She wandered through the few rooms left unlocked. Two people still slept on camp beds in the corner of the office. The entire ground floor of the house had been turned into strike headquarters. She saw copies of *Forward* and *Socialist Worker*, and frowned. Yesterday her father had had a little spare time and so, pleased, he had showed her the system. In a bank of locked card-index files his staff maintained a list of union members' names as well as large files of other supporters – all prepared to lend their time or money, or their muscle on the picket line. Later last night, over a beer before he left to meet the transport drivers, he had told her that he had other, private files he kept in a concealed safe cemented into the floor of his cellar.

He had looked at her proudly, a powerful, self-disciplined man. "This battle is going to be my D-Day, not Dunkirk. Whatever the tactics, whatever the cost, we are going to win, and the Stantons are going to lose."

418

By nine, there were over twenty people in her father's house, union staff, supporters, and others.

Maggie cooked breakfast and took it up to her father's first-floor office, where he was already phoning Members of Parliament.

"Thanks," he said. He blinked, red-eyed but grinning. "After last night I feel as rough as bullets –"

"Did you do it?"

"Oh, aye, I got the transport drivers' support."

"So the Stantons can't shift *anything*?"

"No," he said brutally. "It's the end for Sir Edward this time. I hear there are already moves in the City and in Westminster to get the man and his family out of the firm completely. Including your precious bloody Alex."

"He isn't my Alex, Dad."

He grunted. "So you say now."

Maggie was thoughtful as she laid out the blue china plates. So Stanton Industries had run out of money and goodwill. Alex would never be able to lord it in the boardroom, now – and it served him right.

She sat down to watch her father eat.

"What time did you get in, Dad?"

He shrugged his powerful shoulders and began to demolish the eggs and bacon and fried bread. "Long after midnight. Have you got the daily papers?"

She passed them over one by one, and leafed through herself. She read a word-for-word account of what Alex had said and done after she and her father had left, and she suddenly found herself blushing. Alex had spoken with such dignity that she felt ashamed.

"Looks like the government's getting involved," Maggie said, looking up from another paper. "Back-bench Tories are accusing the PM of 'weakness'. They want to send in the army to break the strike."

He shook his head, bacon speared on his fork. "The bloody army, indeed."

After her father had taken the edge off his appetite he turned to the most old-fashioned of the Tory dailies: there was a large gap where the second-page editorial would have been. He beamed at her and thumbed the blank area.

"The print unions did that. Killed Stanton Industries' propaganda stone dead – our people in London were tipped off by a friendly

419

journalist. Old Sir Edward had got his cronies to denounce me in the papers – again. God, the man has learned nothing. He thinks it's still 1956!"

"Or 1856." She smiled. "Now it's *our* turn to use our influence in Fleet Street."

"That's right, our Maggie. Thanks for what you can do."

She pretended to take offence. "So that's why I'm here, is it?"

"No, course not. I trust you. Absolutely. There's those on the strike committee I'd trust about as far as I could throw them. Like comrade Robinson, for example. He's after my job and he thinks I don't know it."

"He'll never have the respect you've got. And with the Stanton's scalp hanging on your belt . . ."

"Aye," Will said, scratching his unshaved jaw thoughtfully. "Let's hope we can settle quickly. Twenty percent'd do me, unofficially." He looked at her.

"How unofficially?"

He rattled the newspaper. "Let's say I wouldn't mind if that figure appeared in the press."

She grinned. "Twenty percent it is."

The traffic on the road opposite was light; she glanced outside, to see that the stark trees in Stanton Park were rolling under the swirling north-easterly wind. Snow gleamed in the park.

Langton stood up, threw down the paper, and to his daughter he was as determined and inexorable as the force of gravity. "But this time the Stantons go down."

"That's the best news I could have, Dad. I hate them!"

He raised one eyebrow ironically. "Then you'd better watch yourself, lass – they say that love and hate are just two sides of the same coin."

It was almost two weeks since the beginning of the strike, two weeks that had cost Stanton Industries perhaps £25 million in lost production, and that much again in lost orders and credibility. Hugh Stanton did not understand why the papers and TV seemed so unsympathetic. It was almost as if the Stantons had hidden enemies, showing themselves only through the slanders and inactivity of third parties.

Hugh was met outside the Houses of Parliament, in the public garden south of the old craggy and smoke-stained buildings. It was a bitingly cold day, and the wind that whirled a sprinkling of snow off the Thames was icy.

The member for Newcastle strode over quickly; he was an old-school Tory, with a high colour in his face and a brisk, impatient attitude. "The government are pushing through their Bill to salvage Rolls Royce at four." He spoke tersely; Hugh could tell he was not liked by this man. "What do you think your losses are?"

"Over Rolls Royce alone? Well, there's our large stake in the joint engine project, although of course we aren't directly bound by that loss-making contract with Lockheed ... Then there are straightforward trade losses; money owing to us by the Rolls people that can hardly be repaid, now. I estimate it's cost us over £20 million. Then there's the terrible damage being done to us over the engineering workers' strike and their absurd claim for twenty-two per cent –"

"Your problem," the man said. He turned away, so that Hugh had to hurry to follow. "I'll take you to the Strangers' Bar, then to the public gallery."

"Is there any advance news?" Hugh asked, a little breathlessly.

The man stopped and gave a humourless smile. "You mean, will the government bail out Rolls Royce *and* Stanton Industries?"

Hugh's lips twitched expectantly.

"I haven't a notion. But if your own bankers won't help you stave off bankruptcy, why should the government step in?"

Lord Beauford sat by a single telephone in his City office. He had the papers all prepared; within twenty-four hours he could loan £20 million to Stanton Industries and, at a suitably astronomical rate of interest, help bail them out. While he waited, he read through some interesting background material on Maggie Langton and her father until, shortly after five, the phone rang.

He picked it up. It was a good friend, an MP since 1945. Beauford listened carefully. He had no intention of helping the Stanton family, unless the government stepped in. "For Stanton Industries, then . . . I see."

Maggie was called downstairs to the phone. "Terry?"

The voice was as soft, but there was an awful hubbub in the background. "No, afraid not. It's David. I'm still in London – catching a train at King's Cross, as a matter of fact. I thought

421

you'd want to know, and your father. I was in Parliament today for the second reading of the Purchase Bill for Rolls Royce – they're going to push it through the committee stage and third reading tonight. I said something about Rolls Royce's suppliers, meaning Stanton Industries, but the Solicitor General just got the debate bogged down in legal technicalities. It doesn't look too hopeful from *anybody's* point of view, actually. No specific mention at all of Stanton Industries; so no money."

"I see," she said. She cupped the mouthpiece with her left hand and lowered her voice. "In other words, to continue the strike risks bankrupting the business, and the government won't rescue the entire firm whatever happens?"

"That appears to be the position. That's the risk – twenty-two per cent and no surrender could mean bankruptcy, or anything – including a take-over by Hideki and an asset-stripping operation."

"God, I hope Alex Stanton hasn't told you to work on me."

"Maggie," David said crisply, "what he asked me to do is what I'd be doing anyway – which is telling you the truth. I don't want you to fool yourself that if you put enough pressure on Stanton Industries the City or the government is going to rush to bail them out."

"Well, I'll leave a message for my father," she said tiredly, "but goodness knows what he'll do now. There doesn't seem to be much room left for compromise, not with these Forward people trying to run the strike."

"*Forward* are taking over the strike committee?" There was a strange tension in his voice.

"Trying to. Robinson's one of them, isn't he?"

David could not resist it. "Of course, but you've supported Forward yourself."

"But now they want my father out, David!" She made an effort, quietened. "Anyway, when it comes to Forward – you can talk."

There was a long pause. "What are you going to do tonight? I should be back by ten."

"I'm expecting Terry to call me – he's flown to Honolulu for the weekend. If he doesn't, I'll be gloriously drunk long before ten," she told him sourly.

There was no movement; the strike went through till the weekend. The press had estimated, accurately, that it was costing Stanton Industries twelve million pounds every week it lasted. Then one of their suppliers summoned them to the High Court to sue them for monies owed; others joined in the law-case, quick to strip the Stanton carcass while there was flesh on the bones. Maggie heard a rumour that the suppliers had been under pressure from a City bank, but nothing could be proved.

The court gave Stanton's until 22 February, a Monday, to pay off £10 million. On the Stock Exchange, as business closed for the weekend, Stanton Industries shares dived.

Early on Monday morning, responding to Alex's phone call, Ray Hacker flew in from Texas.

First class on Pan Am was as comfortable as ever and there were no problems with customs or immigration, so Ray picked up his bags, whistling, and bulled his way to the head of the queue for a taxi.

"Terrible," he said to the dismal English morning. England? If anything, it felt like more than the 10,000 miles from Dallas to London.

In the back of the black cab he read the day's *Times*. The government was in trouble, Rolls Royce had already gone down, taking several associated companies with it – and it looked like Stanton Industries would follow. Next Monday was one deadline he had noted. Ever since Alex had called he had been observing the situation from the other side of the Atlantic, and it did not make pretty viewing.

But in spite of the forty million pounds the firm owed, in spite of the brutal, weeks-old strike, he still had the kind of loyalty to Alex Stanton that money alone can never buy.

I must be crazy, he thought. Then he laughed.

That night he assembled the team from Hacker-Stanton, in a Kensington hotel Alex had recommended. Ken McCourt was there, too, looking unaccustomedly perturbed.

"Let me check, Ray. You, a couple of – of physical guys, and a Japanese interpreter?"

Ray glanced around. "Right."

"What about our electronics expert? Where is he?"

"I'm right here," said the scarred man with the half-Japanese face. "Electronics, bugging, no problem. I was CIA. And I speak fluent Japanese as well as three other Asian languages."

The next day, at mid-morning, they left to catch the train from King's Cross.

423

It was late afternoon by the time they arrived: they got out at Durham, posing as tourists. Then Hacker had them driven from Wearside to Tyneside in an inconspicuous hired Ford. As always, he was being cautious – taking the measure of the situation himself.

"I've got my rooms booked, right under where the Jap delegation are staying, so you can do whatever is necessary there soon as we get in."

His temporary address amused the others: "– as long as the other side don't suspect."

"I don't see why the Tokyo people should," Ray told them, turning up the BBC news on the radio. "They probably think they're dealing with English gentlemen."

The drive took an hour; Hacker was unimpressed by the bumpy, bending English roads still half covered with dirty snow, and he was not much moved by the two murky rivers. He saw abandoned NCB coalmines with huge slagheaps beside them, and a vast steelworks much of which was nineteenth century. For ten minute they stopped opposite the huge and delapidated Stanton shipyards in Wallsend with their rows of pickets at the gates. In the twilight he saw a plume of fire from the coke-works somewhere on the southern shore.

And he had seen the faces of the people who lived here.

From a kiosk overlooking the mouth of the Tyne he bought a local paper from a woman who rubbed her chapped red hands together and complained about the cold.

The headlines were stark. STANTON STRIKE: FIVE IN HOSPITAL AFTER VIOLENT SCENES. LOCAL MP DEMANDS GOVERNMENT INTERVENTION.

Maggie, too, had put staff on the case after what David had told her. Was Stanton Industries really tottering and, if it was true, was that what she wanted?

She made an excuse to leave the house and use a public telephone, because she did not want her father to suspect that she was asking these searching questions. All she still wanted was to discover the world was black and white and to be on the side of right. She put on her old Afghan coat and refused to do the one thing her father asked – to take one of his burly assistants with her, in case of any trouble.

It was night. There was fresh snow in the streets and the cold was making her nose run. She talked for no more than five minutes.

She asked her questions about Stanton Industries and listened carefully to the answers her researchers had come up with, then she slammed the handset down in the phone box, and stared at her own ghost-faint reflection in the dirtied glass panes. She had not liked the information her own news desk had given her. What do I tell my father now? she thought frantically. What do I tell him?

In the house again a secretary came up. "Oh, there was somebody on the phone for you, Maggie."

"Oh?"

"Terry, he said his name was."

Maggie took off her fur coat and tried to make her smile polite. "Can I have a quick word with my father?"

Langton had to leave a meeting to speak to her. He was in shirt-sleeves, sweaty and irritable. "Christ, the Coventry and Liverpool delegates want to turn this into a political national strike – and they say they can get backing in the mineworkers' union . . ."

"You don't want that?"

"Another general strike? No," he said flatly. Then he lowered his voice. "This is still a straight money issue as far as I'm concerned. Neither the bloody Communists nor Forward are taking over *my* fight – they can start one of their own if they're so confident of winning!"

Maggie looked at his harrassed face and suddenly realized what was happening. "They're turning the screws on you, aren't they?"

He nodded. "Forward is showing its heavy hand. God knows where their money comes from but they're able to pay to keep their activists on the picket-line and at strike meetings; if money won't do their talking, they use this." He showed her a huge, scarred fist. "It's all getting very, very serious, Maggie. Five in hospital after last night's trouble, and the firm must be down by twenty million pounds since the strike began –"

"More like thirty million, I hear," she said automatically, then covered her mouth.

He looked hard at her, his eyes wild and angry. Then he smiled. "Correct. It's been over two weeks now, so thirty million pounds is about right, lass. But where did you get that figure from?"

She stared at him, then lowered her voice. "Why did you give me a wrong figure?"

He shrugged. "You've been checking independently."

"Well, now you know."

425

"Yes," he said, strong and dignified. "Now I know. What do you think?"

"I'm making comparisons with Rolls Royce. My people in London have been taking soundings. If they and Stanton's have to bail out of the engine deal with Lockheed – and Lockheed has its own financial problems, God knows – that'll mean cutting half the 80,000 Rolls jobs. Even if the company is eventually re-floated, they'll cut maybe a third of the factories, a third of the jobs. I'm scared of that happening here! What would it do to Tyneside and Wearside if the Stanton businesses did collapse!"

Will nodded, then looked back over his shoulder. "Nothing good. You may be right. I've decided to take up Stanton's offer and look at their books."

"Tomorrow. I know that already, Dad. I have my own sources, don't forget!"

"But what *I* don't know is whether or not you're still on my side."

She put her hands up to her face. "Dad, I'll never never never let you down, but I'm scared we're getting in over our heads. The Japanese, even some of the people in Forward . . . I know Stanton Industries are on the rocks, but what makes you think the government or the banks will bail them out? What if they just bankrupt Stanton Industries like they did Rolls Royce? What about that – every one of their yards and factories shut down and tens of thousands of people joining the unemployment queue?"

Her father said nothing but his face had turned grey. "Maggie, what makes you think I can stop it?"

"Hey!" One of the delegates had left the conference room. It was a man Maggie recognized from her evenings with Alan Hoyle – Robinson, a powerful man with a blotchy, sour face. "Will, let's issue that statement asking for our comrades in other unions to support us – even if we have to go over the elected leaders' heads."

Maggie looked at him, her lower lip curling. "Is that democratic?"

Like most of his kind, he was a sexist; she could tell as soon as he looked at her in cold contempt. "*Democracy?* I want to win."

"Will, Will!" A young man from the union's regional office came pounding up the stairs, a slip of paper in his hand. "I've just heard – the Stantons are trying to use scab lorries to get through our pickets at the Dewsbury depot over the county line in Yorkshire, and the police are backing them!"

426

Will flushed. "Right, call out the bloody troops. Get our lads into action, a mass picket. We close that place down even if I have to put ten thousand pickets around it!"

Maggie helped phone union offices and sympathizers. They were to rendezvous at the big storage depot where Stanton Industries distributed its armaments – and she would be there, too, with her news photographer and a tape recorder.

Her father gave her a statement to release to the press, demanding that the police stop protecting stike-breakers, otherwise there would be a bloody battle in the streets and, when people were hurt, it would all be the fault of Stanton Industries. She rang her contacts, wanting to get the union's point of view on the record – and as many film crews and journalists on the spot as possible.

More people arrived at her father's house while she was doing that, shouting, some carrying furled-up banners and others holding bottles of beer. A convoy of cars left Newcastle soon after, heading south through the freeze-up. Maggie went with them.

Alex looked at the main gates. He had chosen Dewsbury carefully, mainly because it dealt with armaments. There were thousands of tons of arms and explosives here, and the depot itself, for reasons of security, was built like a prison. High brick walls surrounded it. There were pickets massed beyond the tall gates, but most of the employees here had come in; many of them were formerly with the armed forces.

The secret government machinery had finally been put into operation. There was now a North-East control centre set up in an office in police headquarters, under the authority of George Hammond, the section head in MI5, with Carlton in charge of it. Alex and he had flown down together from Tyneside in a Stanton Industries helicopter.

"Look at this place, Alex!" Carlton stormed. They had seen the ring of pickets from the air. "Military supplies blockaded! If it was up to me I'll say frankly that I'd bring in the army immediately."

He turned to Alex. "I'm having many of the principals in this little drama kept under observation. There'll be a mistake, sooner or later. Those bastards from Forward will over-reach themselves – then the law will move in."

"And millions of trade unionists will strike to get them out of jail," Alex pointed out, "unless your case is cast-iron. We must be realistic. Is that really the way to handle things?"

Carlton flushed. "It's a damn sight more civilized than the way this matter would be handled in the Soviet Union."

Alex laughed, then stood up. "I can't deny that." He turned to the police officer in charge. "Listen, chief superintendent – won't you let me do it my way? I have contracts to fulfil."

The senior policeman was holding his helmet. He obviously disliked working against the picket-line, and the involvement of MI5. "That may be, Mr Stanton, but it's my responsibility to maintain the Queen's peace. There are already thousands of pickets out there, and I have barely a thousand officers."

Alex turned back from the window. "They have no bloody right to close down this place! They're breaking the law! I call what they're doing intimidation."

"So do I," Carlton said; he wore his old regimental tie and his face was flushed with excitement. "This isn't a trade dispute any more, it's more like civil war."

The policeman frowned. "What can we do? Arrest five thousand people for obstruction?"

"I want those lorries out," Carlton said sharply.

Alex did not like the way the meeting was going. "Look, Chief Superintendent, I understand your position – but I'd still like to do this my way."

The chanting from outside grew stronger, clearer. A sea of heads was closing in on the gates: the blue uniforms of the police were a line clearly buckling under the pressure.

"No surrender!" There was a faint chorus of handclaps. "No surrender!"

"I have my orders, sir. We'll get those lorries out. But I'm afraid I'm the man in charge."

"But your way is dangerous. Why don't you let me do it my way?"

"Mr Stanton –"

Alex put his hands to his head. "This is all so crazy. I'm simply trying, like the hauliers, to go about my lawful business. I want to move my goods and those trucks are going to leave. The Prime Minister's office is behind me."

The man, in his fifties, looked at Alex with distaste. "I've given you the benefit of my opinion, Mr Stanton. I'm the man with the experience and I'm the man in charge."

"We could have a riot out here if you press ahead." Alex put his coffee cup down. He was in shirtsleeves, looking out at the grey sky.

"If this was summer," he said quietly, "there'd probably be thousands of them out there. And where would your police be then? If we're going to have riots in this country we should have riot squads to cope with them."

"Exactly," Carlton said. "I can tell you both now straight from the Cabinet Office that the government are very, very worried about this situation."

Alex looked up from his large-scale map of the depot and surrounding streets. "I know something about covert operations. Listen, why don't we arrange a diversion at the front gates, then I'll send the first half-dozen lorries out in convoy by one of the back roads."

"I'll keep the Queen's highway open," the policeman said.

The police were pushed back towards the high walls of the depot. Maggie was only three or four rows behind the first pickets, her tape-recorder slung at her waist and her long red hair hidden inside a headscarf. A BBC film crew were somewhere behind her. The hot crush of panting male bodies was tremendous and she found it hard to breathe; the pressure was starting to frighten her. Nevertheless, this tape would be the best radio she had ever heard – if she could persuade one of her contacts to put it on the air.

"I'm standing outside the gates of the Stanton Industries depot in Dewsbury, North Yorkshire," she said into the hand-held microphone. "The pickets are determined to close the place. Feelings are running very high." The mass in front of her pushed the police line back further. "Watch out," she said, "or you'll crush them to death against the gates!"

A head turned beside her. "Fuck the police."

There was shouting, swearing, and she saw the first truncheons begin to rise and fall and men cry out with pain. Then bottles and half-bricks flew over her head, landing among the police.

Then the factory's hooter blew, three long notes. She saw the big gates begin to open and she gabbled again.

"That noise is obviously a signal. I can see the gates begin to open. The pickets are enraged; there are pitched battles as the pickets try to close in while the police fight brutally to clear the road ... Of course, any lorries coming from this part of Stanton Industries could be loaded with explosives. Will Langton, the union's regional secretary, has described this attempt to break the strike as 'madness' – oof – and, I quote, 'the police should be ashamed to go up against the working man like this'."

An arm smacked her across the face. There was panicked shouting somewhere off to the right. She was suddenly scared by the realization that there were thousands of people behind her, and no way to retreat. She gave a brief, hysterical laugh.

Robinson was beside her as a movement in the crowd lifted her clear off her feet. He was bawling about Forward and smashing the state. The pressure suddenly reversed, and somebody stumbled beside her and went down. People yelled, clearing a space to heave the picket back to his feet.

"I can see the first lorry coming through, now. A couple of policemen's helmets go flying . . . the lorry is revving its engine, though it's only coming forward at a crawl. Oh, a brick has just smashed the windscreen. Now it's moving forward far more swiftly, two pickets holding on to its side, smashing at the side-window . . . there's another lorry behind, but people have got through the police line . . . fighting all around now."

Then there was a single scream, heard clearly across the hubbub. For a moment the two sides disengaged, stopped fighting as more sleet swirled down.

Then there was a confusion of shouts.

"Get an ambulance! Our lads have been run over!"

"They're bloody dead!"

"Kill the scabs!"

Maggie pushed to the front as enraged pickets smashed at the first lorry, which had come to a complete halt. There were two bodies by the side of the road. The police had regrouped, but only to retreat, the bowed head of the lorry driver in the middle of a number of them.

She saw her father, standing, white-faced, with some other familiar faces. One of the Scottish Forward people came over, breathless, blood running down his head.

"Will, there's two of our lads dead down there, and there's rioting broke out around the depot."

"Let's go," Robinson said, shaking a fist. "Burn those lorries!"

Somebody produced a cigarette-lighter; others, matches. The overturned lorry began to burn. Robinson was smiling, and suddenly Maggie remembered that this was an arms depot.

430

"Run!" she said, waving her arms. "There's guns and ammunition here!"

The two lorries exploded about five minutes later, not violently enough for them to have been carrying explosives. There was a big ironic cheer from the mob of pickets. The police had retreated.

"A damp squib," Robinson said, and Maggie realized that he was disappointed.

The disorder grew worse. Bricks flew at the depot walls, and all local roads were blocked.

Then a youth in an NCB jacket came running round a corner. "More of the miners are joining in. They say the Chief Constable has asked for reinforcements!"

Robinson roared, "That's great! Now, Will, let's start stirring things in Newcastle, too – stretch the police force until it snaps and the Tories have to call out the troops. And we'll take them on, too!"

Maggie listened to the horror, hardly believing it – even though she had heard it planned out in detail a dozen times or more.

Everything Alan Hoyle had predicted was happening.

4

Alex had sent the first trucks out empty, not expecting them to get through in spite of assurances from the Chief Superintendent. It gave him no satisfaction being proved right, especially after he learned about the ambulances and the two men declared dead. The rioting after the deaths meant that Stanton Industries' production had to close down completely, as employees' safety could no longer be guaranteed, and he knew the Stantons, once again, would become mythologized as villains. In spite of the angry phone call he had made Hugh put through to 10 Downing Street, the government could, or would, do nothing more. Hugh, a clean hands and consensus man, was not optimistic.

Alex flew back to Newcastle early that evening by helicopter, cursing, wishing he had defied the system and got the Armaments trucks out in the way he had wanted.

The evening papers and the nine o'clock news on television were full of Stanton business. Maggie's tape was broadcast over a still photograph of the blanket-covered bodies; there was film of the riot. Alex stared at the screen as the newsreader announced the death-sentence calmly. Almost everybody left in the shipyards and factories was to be sent home, because of the disorders. Production would cease.

It seemed to be the end, and the firm's people, tearful or resigned, would know it.

In his commandeered top-floor office in the Shipbuilding head-quarters, Alex sat down with David early the next morning. Frost still spangled most of the window, though he had lit the gas fire himself half an hour ago. He ordered a pot of Earl Grey and fresh coffee immediately.

"Blood," he said grimly as David warmed his hands. "Our own blood, shed by our own people. That's what we've been brought to in this nation."

"There can't be much hope now, can there?" David asked him, gently. "I've tried, but I can't offer anything more from Parliament."

"The government won't help. I realize that now." Alex's chest heaved. Then the secretary came in with a silver tray. He thanked her, giving his old dazzling smile, then poured. "Every hour, I've been able to feel Stanton Industries dying. Fewer of our phones are answered, fewer of our employees risk coming to work, less and less business is transacted. Every hour of every day."

David came over to the desk that had been polished until you could see your face in it. "Why have you done all this? You could have been an American, and you're already rich. You didn't have to do anything for your family's concern."

Alex snorted, undid his striped tied and flung it off. "Are we so different? Would you run away? Look at what you've been doing over Forward – and that must have been dangerous and thankless. Why did you do it?"

David spread his hands. "There was nobody else."

"Exactly." Alex stood up suddenly, and went to a plan press in one corner of the office. He opened a drawer, and pulled out a huge blueprint which he turned to hold up to the grey morning light. David saw the sleek lines of a jet airliner, and that the date in a lower corner was February, 1952. "From the old Aviation Division, misfiled. This is the forerunner to Concorde. My family's STA-C. Look at the sweep of those wings!"

David looked over his shoulder, as Alex comforted himself with past achievements. "It looks superb."

Alex folded it, reverently. "My father Michael Stanton died in that."

"The Long Island disaster?"

"Yes." Alex turned away, replaced the twenty-year-old blueprint. He stood up again, dusting off his palms. "The body was never found. That was what I'd call a sacrifice. There is a memorial, though: pure white marble like the Taj Mahal."

"I've seen it." David wiped his forehead. "With Maggie, years and years ago. We were trespassers on the Craigburn estate."

"I used to stand by that white marble and feel the grooves where the words had been carved and think about my father and the family

433

firm. I always knew I would be here, one day, if I really wanted it."

David nodded slowly. "You've never told me that before."

"I've never told anybody before. But I used to argue with Hugh. 'This will be my firm!' he'd tell me. 'Why?' 'Because it's *my* right to inherit it!'" He turned to David, a savage light in his eyes. "You are aware the other directors, the government – that they're all backing off? It's down to the Stanton family to save Stanton Industries. Hugh and I are the last of the line, and – we could turn against each other even now."

"If you did that," David said steadily, "that really would be the end for Stanton Industries."

Alex laughed. "I'm entirely aware of that. I just hope Hugh is."

David finished his tea. "You asked me over if you remember."

"Indeed." Alex rummaged through some papers, then handed over a thin folder. "The accounts for the Shipbuilding Division: accountants' figures, absolutely guaranteed. I'd like the strike committee to see them."

"Of course." David took the blue folder, opened it up and glanced inside. "I'll give it to Will."

In this fifth week of the postal strike, the flow of letters had ceased completely, and only vital documents came through by courier; it was rumoured that the power-workers and telephone staff would strike next.

David's Labour colleagues in the House of Commons, at his request, would make another representation that afternoon, but the Heath government would again refuse to intervene in the Stanton Industries strike. It had already been made clear, off the record, that the Stanton family were not regarded as adequate stewards of the company's best interests.

It seemed to be only a matter of time, now.

Europe was grinding to a halt. Massive drifts of Siberian snow had suddenly swirled out of the black eastern sky; the temperature had plunged far below zero, forcing traffic off the roads and railway tracks all over Europe and grounding planes in airports. In Sweden, a public service employees' strike had closed down railways, social services, schools, the law courts. In Britain the president of Langton's engineers, spoke with the authority of the Trades Union Congress;

the TUC was set to break the law by defying the Industrial Relations Bill, and there were unruly marches throughout the country to 'kill the Bill'.

Maggie was on Wearside early, to attend the double funeral with her father. She was still shocked, shocked by the violence here and by the latest headlines she had read – this time South Vietnam had invaded Laos. As far as she knew, Terry had been unable to interest a film studio in his Vietnam notions. She thought about him as she listened to the funeral service.

Maggie nudged her father, who sat stiffly by her in a dark, formal suit in the freezing church.

"Look at those two wreaths over there. From Stanton Industries."

He grunted, looking dour and old. "It's a small enough token of respect."

She sat among the scented masses of flowers and the tall, lighted candles in the cold church, murmuring her responses. Forward had its agents even in the house of God; she heard them preach non-compromise, hard action, no surrender. It was despairing to see all this hatred, but she could not forgive Stanton Industries, either. After the coffins were paraded outdoors, before they were slid into the two long black hearses, she saw the gold and white Stanton wreaths torn from the coffins and trampled underfoot by the angry mourners there in the street in front of photographers.

Robinson appeared on a special, high noon edition of the BBC television news, shaking his fist at the interviewer and promising more violence.

Maggie, looking at him, believed it. And standing behind Robinson, in a blue duffle-coat, she saw Alan Hoyle.

David turned from the news bulletin to the tinted fifth-floor window, wondering what would happen to his North East, now that the last of his initiatives in Parliament had failed. He was worried that Alex might do something desperate to try to end the strike, and the fact that the Japanese had somehow begun to sponsor the activists of Forward verged on the terrifying.

It was as if the entire nation was heading for disaster with the speed and momentum of an express train.

A restrained voice said, "That was our friend Mr Hoyle in the background, wasn't it?"

435

"Of course it was, and his minder Jake was there, the murderer; with the cap. And Hoyle was smiling. He knows he's winning." David turned round. "George," he said to the middle-aged man behind the desk, "Alan Hoyle has to be stopped."

"We agree," Carlton said. "The question is, how? I mean, just look at what he's done already."

The press-cuttings were spread across the desk in police headquarters on Tyneside. They told the disastrous story of the strike. Lost markets abroad, more bankruptcies in British industry, the pound sliding down and down towards worthlessness, tens of thousands of jobs at risk.

David pointed out one sober article. "If all these jobs are lost when Stanton Industries is destroyed, Forward could take power inside the Labour party, and perhaps take power inside the next Labour government, too. And surely no one here has any illusions at all about what would mean?"

Hammond looked up as Carlton turned off the television with a snap of the switch. In the light of the single lamp that shone down from beside his shoulder, his bespectacled face was grave. "I take your point, but I fail to see how my powers can help you. I have absolutely no influence within that strike committee; and only its members can ensure a compromise now."

David squared his shoulders. "Perhaps I'll have to speak to them myself, or at least to Will Langton."

This time Carlton's expression was full of respect. "You'd risk exposure to save Stanton Industries?"

"People have died for less." David glanced at a clipping; a Reuters article from Tokyo. "There's nothing to be done with them, is there?"

"The Hideki people? Myself, or the security services, acting against the Japanese –" Hammond shook his head slowly, so that the light glinted across his glasses and David could no longer see his eyes.

"We must do something. Listen, if Forward find out I've been working against them," David said, "I might be killed. I know it. Even worse, I have a family."

"David, I'm not at all complacent about what's happening, but it very rarely comes to blood on the streets in this country."

"But it already has, and it will again unless it's all stopped now. Bonnington is dead. That nightwatchman, his brains smashed out in

436

Liverpool. Two dead here on the picket-line. I foresee worse. These are madmen, dreaming of blood."

The police were represented by a chief inspector from the Special Branch. "It's been put to me," he said hesitantly, "that we ought to pick up Alan Hoyle and this man Jake and sweat them about the Liverpool murder and the dockside hijacking."

"I'd go for that," Carlton said. "I'll interrogate them myself."

"Then can I get a warrant? My Chief Constable is quite insistent about –"

There was a click as Hammond took off his glasses and put them on the desk. "That must be a last resort. Hoyle at least will be a fanatic, and trained . . . What about this man Robinson? We have witnesses to other minor crimes at least, threats of violence, that girl he bribed at Shipbuilding headquarters."

"Just give me this Jake," Carlton said. "He'll sing for me."

David turned back to the window and looked down the city street as the talk continued, glimpsing the river beyond the rooftops. He was trying frantically to plan ahead.

He looked at his watch. It was almost one o'clock, and everything that Hoyle had planned was coming to pass. He lowered his head and looked at Hammond, hoping that the security services could do something: but there was no sense of optimism in this room.

Finally, he spoke. "Look, George, can I take this file of press-cuttings your researchers sent up?"

Hammond's expression was more unreadable than ever. "Of course." He looked at David expectantly.

Finally, with reluctance, David spoke again. "I'll go to see Will and tell him."

"A bloody trade unionist?" Carlton barked. "Tell him what?"

"The truth," David said.

It was snowing again as David drove down towards the park and Will Langton's house. He had left it till seven, hoping he could speak to Will alone: he whistled tunelessly through his teeth as he parked the car, hoping he would not give himself away, knowing that this might be necessary.

He had spoken to his wife earlier, but he'd told her nothing about what he was proposing to do.

The door was opened by a familiar face: a stocky man, a trade unionist – Langton's friend Jackie Sutton.

"Oh, hello again," David said, smiling quickly. "Will's here?"

"In the kitchen," the other man replied, "having a cup of tea with Maggie. I'll take your coat and send you through."

There were still people here; some Forward supporters, too. As they passed an open door, David saw Robinson sitting inside with Jake.

Maggie and her father were sitting around the table over a pot of tea and discussing the next day's newspapers, speculating about what line they would take on the strike. David sat down in the warm room full of the familiar smells of tea brewing, old fried food, Maggie's perfume. Jackie Sutton lingered in the doorway.

"I just thought I'd tell you, I spoke to Alex Stanton today. He was really down about everything," David began.

Will squinted at him. "And the other one, the chairman?"

"Kissing arses in London," David said crudely. "Excuse my French, Maggie. I doubt if he likes the taste, and I'm almost certain it won't do him any good."

"It's good news," Will said. "By God they'll have to settle, soon."

David checked their expressions unobtrusively: Maggie was looking harsh, Will grim, and only Sutton seemed happy about the news. He caught Will's eye.

"I wonder, perhaps I could have a word – the Parliamentary Labour Party."

"Of course," Will said. He stood up. "I'll take you upstairs, leave the kitchen to the young ones."

"Oh, I've got some phone calls to make," Maggie said.

David followed Will upstairs. He had decided he had to take the risk of a direct approach, for the good of everybody.

"Fancy a drink?" Langton had opened a cold bottle of brown ale. It had come straight from the fridge; moisture hung on it like pearls. He drank from it slowly, tilting the famous shape so that the beer ran into his mouth. Then he wiped his lips, looking thoughtful. David sipped from a half-pint glass.

"Two things, Will. First, Alex Stanton gave me the company accounts for Stanton Industries. I also have some cuttings from newspapers and magazines about the effects of the strike. I think you should look at them. I also want to tell you what Alan Hoyle is." David explained, holding no secrets back from Langton – Hoyle's history and his ambitions were laid bare. "And I believe there's an East German–Moscow link, too."

438

Langton's eyes glinted. "Moscow? That's pure speculation. But the rest was your experience, wasn't it?"

"Yes."

"In other words, lad, you're a spy."

"That's right, Will," David told him, "and if Hoyle ever gets to hear abut this, I'm dead."

Langton stood up, and looked thoughtfully at the younger man's slight figure, slumped wearily in a chair. "It's nothing I hadn't suspected about that Forward inner circle, Davey. They're ruthless bastards, and I never believed the movement was limited just to publishing a magazine ... Remember, I was in Spain during the civil war: I've seen my name on a Stalinist death-list. But ... Alan Hoyle a murderer."

"Hoyle or Jake, his minder." David blinked slowly. "You should read the accounts, you know."

Langton put on his spectacles and frowned at the figures, the conclusions. He whistled, softly. "This is all true?"

"Some of it's on file; the financial returns, tax, records at Companies House. Check with the accountants who signed the report. The Stantons have told them to speak freely."

"Now, I'm not an accountant, David," Will exhaled, tapped the end of his nose, "but it looks to me like the Shipbuilding Division at least is bankrupt."

"Very close to it."

Will shook his head, irritably, tossed the papers away. "I wish you hadn't shown me that. It'll be hard to demand twenty-two per cent now."

"Something has to give, Will. Listen, there's no point in fighting the battles of 1871 instead of 1971 – the honest workman and the top-hatted capitalist are things of the past. That just isn't the war we have to fight now. If you can't settle with the Stantons, the only alternatives – the *only* alternatives – are bankruptcy, or an asset-stripping operation by this Japanese firm or the London bankers."

Will gritted his teeth. "I have to make peace with the Stantons!"

"What alternative is there? This isn't a left-wing paradise we're living in; it's the real world. And Alex Stanton is ruthless, competitive, very experienced in international business, with a Master's in Business Administration from Harvard and excellent international contacts – and Hugh Stanton to restrain him."

"But he's a bastard. I remember Maggie –"

439

"What do you expect? 'Nice guys come last', they say! If British industry comes last . . . we're finished."

Will said nothing for a long time as he finished his beer. Then he said, "It won't be down to me alone. I'll show the figures to the rest of my committee, but you should leak them as well. Get them into the press so the lads on the picket line know there's no more money."

"Maggie can do that, if you tell her to," David said firmly. "Then you'll help me – and settle that strike for a compromise figure?"

The base of the bottle slammed onto the table. "It may be too late for that, Davey. This is a battle, and men have died. Besides, the strike committee has to make that decision, not me – and that's split between people like me, prepared to compromise, and the far Left."

David swallowed, then reached for the other bottle of brown ale. "If it's really too late, Will, then God help us all!"

"God help us indeed, because nobody else will."

"Who's behind you on the committee?"

"After we see and talk over this accountants' report?" Will grimaced, mussing up his grey hair. "I don't know if I'll carry a majority with me even then. See, Robinson will never compromise – and he'll say the Stantons killed two pickets and there's blood on their hands."

"They didn't, though." David looked up suddenly. "Listen, Will, I have an idea." He explained quickly. "Won't that give you your majority, all fair and square and democratic?"

Langton sat forward over the table, listening carefully. He looked thoughtful, but said nothing after David finished. There was the sound of thunder somewhere.

Then Langton answered. "It sounds a bit unprincipled, David."

"Yes." David paused. "You don't like it?'

Langton stood up and reached for his hand. "Like the notion? I love it." He laughed. "If Hoyle isn't there, if Robinson isn't there . . . I'll get Jackie to sound out some of the people leaning to the Left now, who might change."

"I'm sorry," David said, "I know you love him like a son. But Jackie's in the pocket of Alan Hoyle."

"What?"

"He was in East Germany last year with Hoyle. I have proof – photos, documents. He's Forward, Will. Forward, body and soul."

After reading abut the funeral, Alex turned to the business section of his newspaper, hoping to find some good news. But the headline that greeted him read *Bankruptcies Rise to Highest Level for Ten Years*. Rolls Royce shares had slumped from 126 to 17½. Alex dialled Hugh in London.

"Hugh, any news?"

There was silence for a moment, before Hugh's voice came down the line. "I'm not – completely unhopeful about Lord Beauford."

"I hope he isn't just leading you on. Try everybody."

"His bank must be our best hope, Alex, given our long history of co-operation."

Alex gave a harsh laugh. "I don't like him, and vice-versa. And I wouldn't rely on history too much." He paused. "I'm trying to re-open negotiations with Langton."

"Good! Bring him round at any cost."

"The cost I was thinking of – well, remember McCourt's figures? I think we could settle for up to twenty per cent, if we cut costs immediately afterwards."

"I'll agree the figure: twenty per cent. Anything to get production started. How's it going otherwise?"

Alex thought a moment. The head office staff here on the quayside had to run a gauntlet every day; facing threats, and sometimes thrown bricks and promises of even more serious violence. It was an intolerable situation on every level, and Alex knew in despair that he could not keep the company afloat much longer.

"I'm still fighting," he said toughly. "I've asked Ray first to try and raise money on our shares in Hacker-Stanton, then to get some contracts signed abroad. Money for Stanton Industries, Hugh."

Hugh sounded strained. "This won't be forgotten, Alex."

The buzzer on his desk went immediately after the conversation. His secretary opened the door. McCourt came in and sat down.

"Morning, Alex."

"Morning."

"Let's get to work."

They opened their discussion paper again; they had gone through all the figures for the three Divisions, and come up with methods to slash costs by almost a fifth.

"Thank you," Alex said to McCourt, after they had finished. The huge, brooding portrait of Abraham Stanton looked over their shoulders as they sat there with graphs and balance sheets, working through the afternoon as snow frosted the huge windows with their

441

view of the sombre Tyne. "I wonder if Hugh is doing any good in London. He's trying to get more money out of Lord Beauford."

"There's a note here about demarcation; we must remember that if we ever do negotiate with the union. Training everybody in the yard to do every job, no waiting around for a tradesman from another union – that's how the Japanese do it, according to David." They worked on, finalizing every detail. Then Alex, sighing, closed the file. "I don't know now if I'll ever be able to make use of those plans, unless we settle." He glanced across at McCourt's glum face. "By now David will have passed Langton the real financial facts."

"So Langton knows we couldn't give twenty-two per cent to everybody?"

"Yes." Alex suggested it hesitantly. "Could I talk directly to Langton, do you think?"

"Not a chance." McCourt shuffled through the reports. "The man refuses our phone calls, and he is always accompanied by his people, or he's in the union car with a union driver."

Alex stood up, stretched. "If only there was some way of getting him to re-open direct negotiations."

McCourt tidied papers into the safe. "Am I needed here any more, or should I go back to London?"

"I'd like you to go and baby-sit the Armaments Division. Ray Hacker will try to get a foreign bank to loan us money against Hacker-Stanton security – money we can put to helping S1. The banks here seem dead set against us."

"Have you any idea why they should have turned against us?"

Alex shrugged. "I could hazard a guess."

McCourt hesitated in the doorway, looking back at Alex, a solitary figure beneath the great portrait of Abraham Stanton. "There's something about that picture and you ... something about the eyes."

Alex spun around in his swivel chair, and shook his head. "Evil old bastard, isn't he? Still, he had his moment on the stage of history, and he played his part for all it was worth; and he won."

"You can't say more than that about the best of us."

"If I can sit here in a year's time and say that much about me, I'll be happy enough, Ken."

"If ..."

The phone rang as McCourt left. David passed on a rumour he had heard that Forward were now going to take direct action, using terror tactics, after the approved international model. "The word came straight from friend Hoyle. Until you end the strike I'd double-check your security on all your plants – and on yourself."

"It's not that easy," Alex said, "but I'll try. Maybe the police can do more."

To make this particular call, Alex left his red E-type behind. It was too conspicuous, and over the last three or four days he had been aware that there was somebody trying to follow him; and he did not like it at all.

He drove out of the snow-swept city alone, under a grey, weeping sky. David was going to London again for one last try; he had a touching faith in democratic government, and he had said he intended to make a direct, non-party appeal to Parliament. After the treatment Hugh had suffered, Alex was not hopeful about anything to do with Westminster.

He left his borrowed car in an out of the way corner of the tree-screened car park, then strolled into the foyer, brushing off snow from his long leather coat.

It seemed strange to enter Hideki's hotel – though of course there was an excellent reason for Ray to be here. Alex grinned, thinking of it.

After the lift doors opened on the expanse of rich red carpeting he went up to the numbered door and knocked on it. A heavy voice shouted out. "Come on in!"

Alex walked into the luxurious suite.

The big Texan turned, scratching his belly with one hand and holding a bourbon on the rocks with the other. He was wearing dark trousers and a check Western shirt. "Alex."

Alex grinned. "It's been a while, cowboy, but thanks for coming."

Then they were banging each other on the back and shouting.

"My cousin's been to London, cap in hand, asking for money from the government or the banks. But I don't want to have to take it. I want to make it work myself, Ray – without compromises! Do you believe me?"

Hacker sat down on the blue-leather Chesterfield. It creaked under his weight as he waved a big hand at the bourbon bottle. "I know that you'll give these strikers, City people and Tokyo tycoons a damn hard fight, you old son of a bitch!" His eyes glittered. "I'll help you, Alex. Nobody scares me. But I – hell, I've done some real checking, like you

443

asked me. CIA and State and everything. That Tokyo guy is *seriously* tough. Not to mention lucky, and rich."

Alex poured himself a drink. "How tough?"

"First, tough in building up that business over half a century now – then lucky that old Doug MacArthur didn't haul him in front of that War Crimes Tribunal in post-war Tokyo."

"I heard that, too, and I *know* he's damned rich. The industrial empire he runs is far larger than Stanton Industries – and we aren't small-scale. I was hoping for sales of over £650 million for the three Stanton Divisions this year. That's near enough two billion dollars."

"Two billion dollars, mostly linked to Armaments and Aircraft – the only areas Japan is weak in. I see why they're here, Alex. And why they want the biggest 'in' to Stanton Industries they can get." Hacker swallowed the last of his drink, got up, leaned over the balcony rail and spat out the two ice-cubes. It was a cold day out there, but he didn't seem bothered. He remained with his elbows resting on the rail, his back to the luxurious room. "I think he's going to play hardball, Alex. Like you done asked me, I brought some of our best people over, but you and me and your half-assed City of London put together aren't going to outbid him, if it comes to that."

Alex shook his head, still sprawled on the Chesterfield. "I don't think he's going to bid for Stanton Industries fair and outright. The family trusts still control over a third of the firm; I have several percent myself – so he knows he'd be hard put to buy a majority share, and even then we'd never be off his back."

"Then he either wants a few parts of you – like your heart and brains and balls, maybe –"

Alex's face flashed agreement and he finished the sentence: "– Or he'll hold on while Rolls Royce goes down and this strike continues and try to push us into bankruptcy. Then he'll get *everything*, cheap."

"He does business good then. Rough, but good. For him."

"I know," Alex said. "And we've already seen the colour of his money."

Hacker came back in and poured himself another bourbon, turning his back. "That so?"

Alex smiled and stretched his legs. He felt sure he could tell what Ray was thinking, just from his voice. "Hugh was shown a certified cheque for $25 million."

"Jesus!" Hacker turned around, bear-like. "That was just his money to impress? Alex, how much might you need?"

444

"In dollars? I'd need more than $45 million just to keep Stanton Industries from going under."

"I'm not that cash-liquid, Alex, never have been . . . Even if it came to buying you out."

"I'm not asking for that!"

"Not yet."

"Not yet, anyway. I like being part of Hacker-Stanton – and we've done some damn good business in the past."

Hacker was looking straight at him, unblinking, holding the drink so that it was almost but not quite spilling onto the Persian rug. The atmosphere between them grew heavy. "How much can you and your old-money family raise?"

"Less than half of what we need."

"Then it looks bad for you, Alex. And for your family."

"I don't intend to lose this one, Ray."

Hacker's lips compressed for a moment. "What do you want me to do?"

"Try some of the European banks we've done business with, see if you can borrow against our stakes in Hacker Stanton International."

"'Our' stakes. That's a hell of a lot to ask, Alex!"

"I know it is," he said curtly. "But if we get into Stanton Industries cheap, we'll make millions. Then chase up every possible order we might get in the Middle East, Tehran to Tel Aviv, with the usual commission. But we must have cash in hand to keep things rolling. Thing is, I'm looking ahead. Ever the optimist. I want to see off Hideki and gain what they call 'face'; someday, I'd like to go to Japan and do business there. That's the oyster I'd really like to crack."

Hacker gave a slow nod. "You really think they're going to be that big, do you?"

"Yes. I've had that friend of mine, David Bryant, use government sources to check into what the Japanese are doing there. It isn't just limited to a few lines. Except for armaments, planes and the oil business, they do everything – ships, steel, electronics, consumer goods like watches and cameras, their motorcycles are wiping out the British industry and *you'll* be next. One of the architects of all that has taken over the top floor of this hotel and intends to take over a whole lot more."

Hacker glanced at the ceiling, then put his bourbon down and backed away. "You trying to scare me? I thought that's what I was trying to do to you."

445

"No," Alex said steadily as he poured himself another drink. "I'm just telling you that I've seen the very worst, and I'm still here."

There was a long pause as Ray collected his drink and stepped outside. Alex joined the other man on the fourth-floor balcony. They looked out, their breath steaming in the cold air. The grounds of the hotel, the car parking and outbuildings and the big new covered swimming pool, spread out for two hundred yards, and most of the snow had been swept up. Then, grey-green and strange and ancient, the woods of Northumberland clawed at the smoke-grey wintry sky.

"It's an old country," Ray said, shaking his head.

Alex finished the bourbon. "It is that."

"You could maybe try going straight to Langton, man to man. He probably hates Forward more than you; they must threaten his position every working day. And he must have the figures about your company now."

"I can't get to him," Alex said. "My only line of communications is through David, and he hasn't said much lately. Well, I suppose between Maggie's father and me, he sees both sides of the question . . . Anyway, old man Langton is never alone, he won't speak to me on the phone, even when he's in his car he has a union driver with him."

"You could try and convince Maggie."

"I could," Alex said, steadily. He had been trying. "Tell me, Ray, what's really on your mind?"

Ray was still not meeting his eyes. "Alex, I was never that impressed by your family firm, by your uncle and cousin – or your country. I don't think they have the right stuff. I need to know this, now. Today, how far *are* you prepared to go?"

Alex tried to make light of it. "Don't you know how serious I am from the kind of people I asked you to put into your team?"

"But will you use them, Alex?" Ray asked, low. "Will you use them so that you win? I need to know. Or else I'll take all my people and get back on the plane!"

"Ask me again how far I'll go."

"How far?"

Alex spoke slowly. "All the way, cowboy."

Just one floor up, another arrangement was being made. Hoyle had returned to talk to Hideki.

For a long time, the elderly Japanese had been staring south-west. His home was the land of the rising sun; this country belonged to

446

a setting sun. Hoyle's attempts to bargain had not moved him; nor the man's pleas. The towers of the city were still visible below the red-gold sunset haze, he noted, pleased by the beauty of the effect. It took the sun a long time to set here. The river and the industrial belt around it was out of sight, though he was mindful of it, and its history.

So little a time to rise to such greatness and then to fall.

Hoyle, perspiring, repeated the same point. On the level of character there was nothing about this man that Hideki did not know.

"More money is absolutely necessary. I have people to pay off, and we have to support the strikers."

Hideki frowned, gestured with one hand. "For what purpose?" his interpreter asked, and Hoyle explained quickly.

Hideki listened carefully as his interpreter repeated the English phrases in crisp contemporary Japanese – the language of the business samurai, not of the *haiku*.

He answered himself in his creaking, accurate English. "Your plans sound – effective. I authorize further $50,000 US, so to be paid through our nominees in Switzerland to the Forward account there." He turned around. His rheumatism pained him, but he overrode the tearing, grinding pains. "That strike must last, Mr Hoyle. There must be the gravest damage done to Stanton Industries. I do not give cash – the blood of my company – for nothing. Understand, you are making a personal commitment to me, if you accept my money."

"I'd take thirty pieces of silver," Hoyle said, not lowering his head.

Fluently, Hideki's interpreter explained the reference.

The old man nodded his head, and dismissed the traitor; the blood money would be given to him, and that was all Hoyle wanted.

Hideki turned back to the view. He watched Hoyle get into the car, then drive away.

An executive asked him, "Is it really safe to speak here, Hideki-san?"

He cracked a smile, though he did not turn around, and he made his voice harsh. "Of course! The Stanton family do not have the initiative to find interpreters who speak our language, let alone use eavesdropping devices here."

"Then we will stay until they are in our hands?"

Hideki had become quiet; he spoke like a man in a trance. "It is my destiny to secure for us again the means of war."

447

There was more, but he did not speak it aloud though it was always with him. There was his son to be avenged. The Atlantic allies had involved Stanton Industries in their Manhattan Project – to make the A-bombs they had dropped on Hiroshima and then Nagasaki, that had caused the final dishonour of defeat and surrender, that ultimate shame the people of Japan would have to slave forever to expunge.

He clapped his hands together, and they sent in his English servant.

"I have thought, Mr Battersby, about the proposals of your old *oyabun*, Lord Beauford."

Battersby's pink face beamed. "Yes?"

"Armaments, I will have; military shipbuilding, yes, we share. He is to have the Aircraft Division, for selling. Everything we do not want, after we take over the company, we close down. Tell the Lord Beauford that."

"I'm sure he will find it very satisfactory," Battersby replied.

Maggie had come back late in the morning, after spending the night with her sister and her husband. She had to admit that there was something warm about their family life and she loved their children. They had eaten curry and drunk several bottles of wine later, and she could not help wondering if this was real happiness: family, roots, children.

Her sister's husband finally asked her straight out. "I read in the paper that Stanton Industries is almost finished."

"So they say." Maggie did not want to talk about this at all.

He sighed. "I suppose this strike'll kill off the firm. But you realize, don't you, that there're lots of other firms and jobs round here that are dependent on them?"

Her sister Annie had deftly changed the subject.

Nevertheless, Maggie had been thinking ever since. The 20% compromise figure had been placed in several newspapers, and so far the strikers on the front line had not opposed it. There was a chance, maybe, that all parties could compromise . . . because she was beginning to think more and more that the alternative was not a victory for trade unionism, Socialism, and the working man, but disaster.

Because of the postal strike, there was no ordinary mail. Everything had to be sent by courier. In the delivery from London was a strange, rambling airmail letter from Terry. It had been sent from San Francisco and it was not affectionate. Terry said she was selfish, and he blamed her for not being in L.A. with him. Maggie tore it up, upset, in the privacy of her tower bedroom.

The rest of her correspondence was to do with the magazine. It did not interest her, somehow. London was like L.A. – a long, long way from home. Nevertheless, she picked up the phone and called Kai up. The strikes and the economic situation were damaging her magazine, too. They chatted on gloomily for a while, and he raised the issue of Stanton Industries. She found herself saying, "Actually, I'd like you to ring up the Stanton PR department in London and arrange an interview for me."

"No problem, Maggie."

"Make it as soon as possible – oh, and I'd like to speak to the future head of their Armaments Division."

"Right," he said, and she could hear him scribbling it down. "To see Alex Stanton, as soon as possible."

"What? Alex said as McCourt covered the phone's mouthpiece, and the red dusk faded. "Maggie wants to set up a meeting with *me*?"

"That's right. It's her magazine calling. What should I say to them? I mean, if you could get her to write an article giving our point of view that would be a real coup for you."

"It certainly would." Alex glanced at one of his files containing notes on Maggie's movements from the firm of private detectives shadowing all those involved in the dispute on the union side. Last night, she'd been with her sister's family. "Just fob them off, for the moment. Say I'll be in touch later."

"It's her managing editor in person."

"Later, tell him."

"There's nothing I can tell this man about you and Maggie?"

"Not a thing. Not yet." He put the phone down. For no reason he could define he felt better than he had done for days. "Tonight," he said, "I'll be in that safe house, incommunicado. No calls at all, unless it's a major emergency."

McCourt was smiling at him.

Maggie dressed down for an evening out in her old student clothes, a red plastic mac, baggy Italian sweater, loose on a tight black t-shirt, and frayed jeans that had been shrink-dried on her years ago. They still fitted. She took a bus into town, sitting on the top deck right at the front, as she had done as a child. She started to smoke a

French cigarette, soothed by the familiar accents of her childhood all around her. She fingered her bent CND badge thoughtfully and wondered what she should say to her father – tell him to compromise, immediately, before it was too late?

It was a dilemma that caused her almost physical pain, this uncertainty as to which was the right side: Alex, or her father. Her father, or . . . Alex. All the remembered joy and pain came back, swirling through her mind again and again.

She sighed. It was probably just as well Alex hadn't replied to her overture about an interview.

She got off by the mighty stone portico of the Central Station, but there was nobody here to meet her. Maggie headed east along Neville Street, going past the old Lit. and Phil. building; Joseph Swan, the Stephensons, others, had given demonstrations there, in the time of her great-grandfather. She had no conscious idea where she was going, but as always she walked briskly to get there. The sound of a motor bike's gravelly engine rent the air.

She crossed St Nicholas Street opposite the old gatehouse of the castle, and slipped under the massive, blackened iron railway bridge. Trains rumbled threateningly just overhead. They had demolished much of the medieval city to get these railways built, she recalled. There was no such thing as progress without a price.

Then, in almost total darkness, she turned left and reachd her first destination: a grime-blackened wall of massive carved stone: the keep of the Norman castle – a soaring, brutal part of the structure that had given her city its name. In the year 1082 the Norman conquerors had ordered it to be raised; that and other castles had dominated the north utterly, until the coming of industry. She lingered there, then went to the pretty gatehouse, looking down at the cobbled street called Amen Corner; there were fine redbrick and stone buildings there, lit up by the tall streetlights.

She went back past the keep, and quickly down an ancient stone stairway that led from the Bridge Hotel to the waterfront near the hydraulic Swing Bridge. The river's cold breath was salty. She heard footsteps behind her and turned her head as she momentarily stopped by the Red House, but only a courting couple seemed to have followed her. Streetlamps made yellow balloons of light as she followed the bend of the river under the huge metal arch of the Tyne Bridge.

Maggie walked up to the imposing Georgian building. There were still lights on in upper-storey offices. Over the huge, closed doors

450

carved, Latinate letters told her that this was STANTON INDUSTIRES: SHIPBUILDING DIVISION.

She buttoned her scarlet mac up to the collar as damp blew in off the river, and stayed there thinking for a long time, her eyes on that name again: Stanton, Stanton. She wondered if Alex was inside.

It got dark early in February, but the night was not her enemy. Streetlights came on in bursts of illumination that she saw spread, haphazardly, from street to street on both sides of the Tyne. Houses, thousands of ordinary, decent people in them, the people of home. This was her home, and in spirit at least she would never leave it. The smell of salt and iron came from the flood tide and the sound of a train; somewhere on the river a ship was hooting.

A police car stopped near her, and she began to walk quickly away. She went back to the old stone steps and began to climb them; the grit laid here crunched under her feet. There was the sound of a motorcyle somewhere, echoing up the steps, revving up, then accelerating away. A crazy kid, she thought, her mind irresistibly drawn to her first boyfriend. Danny, young Danny. He was dead now.

At the top of the crooked steps she stopped, panting slightly, in front of the cobblestoned area between the Bridge Hotel and the stone castle. Music came down to her from a half-open window in the pub's upper storey, a man's baritone voice, double bass, an accordion, guitar.

> "There were three men came out of the west,
> Their fortunes for to find . . ."

There was only a single light high on the castle keep, though behind her, as she turned up the collar of her mac, the windows of the Bridge Hotel were glowing. The one light was so high on the stark, indistinctly black keep she had to strain to look up. The cruel song continued. She really felt she was in the presence of stones laid down eight centuries before; stones laid here in blood, thirty generations ago, to cow and terrify. A horned moon looked down, its light gleaming off the roofs of parked cars and the rounded, glistening cobblestones.

Maggie peered about her, but there did not seem to be anybody out here in the moonlight. Then she suddenly became aware of the music that came down from above, the brutal, ancient lyrics sifting through her mind with the ease of old memories.

451

> "They hi-red men with sharp pitchforks
> To pierce him through the heart . . ."

There was a chill within her, and the cars that hissed by on the High Level Bridge seemed to come from another world. Her chest felt tight and she could not stop herself from feeling lonely and afraid. The wind that came off the river breathed ice. It felt cold and strange here, and dream-like, as if time itself had somehow been twisted back on itself.

Maggie felt unutterably sad. Then she heard the motocycle again, roaring, as if it was coming up here. She made herself step round a red Ford transit van, sure there would be nothing of the past there.

She stopped dead.

In front of her was an unmoving figure in studded black motorcycle leathers. It leaned back on a Norton 750, the same bike Danny Robson had died on. For a moment, it was all eerie.

> "They rode him around and around the field . . ."

Maggie went forward slowly, one hand outstretched, as if this was a ghost and she feared to meet it. "Danny? Danny Robson?"

The full-face helmet turned; blankly threatening, like a medieval knight's. The song overhead continued inexorably.

> "They hi-red men with crabtree sticks
> Who cut him skin from bone . . ."

The leather gauntleted hands went up to the helmet and began to remove it.

"Danny, is that you?" Even to her, her voice was rising up towards panic. "Oh, Danny! *Danny*!"

> ". . . served him far worse than that,
> For they ground him between two stones."

The helmet came off completely, and swung in one hand as the other tousled the familiar blond hair.

"I hope I haven't changed that much."

452

Maggie put both hands to her mouth. It was Alex Stanton.

Smiling slightly, he began to move towards her.

It was a kind of million-pound poker game – all the time the bids were getting higher, but nobody was quite certain what was in the pot waiting to be won, or what might be lost.

But the pot was Stanton Industries, and Hugh knew that to stay in the game at all he had to come up with money by Monday. Money? he thought. Millions of pounds, a fortune . . . and I have only these last few days.

The restaurant was quiet, decorated in subdued English browns. Lord Beauford dabbed at his lips with the white napkin, belched politely, and beamed across the wreckage of his meal at Hugh Stanton.

"I love eating, Hugh. Especially fine oysters like these."

Hugh smiled back more tentatively. He felt achingly unsure of his ground. He looked round quickly at the restaurant: dark and discreet, brass lamps and hunting prints hung on the walls, and the only sounds were the quiet, upper-class voices of men from the other discreet booths.

If the City of London was going to cut your throat, Hugh had to acknowledge, it would do so with impeccable good manners, and the public spilling of blood would be minimal. He sipped at his Romanée Conti again, and then pressed the peer. "I've always thought of you as a kind of uncle."

Beauford must have misheard him. "A *kind* uncle? I have my own shareholders to think of, Hugh."

"Of course, but you've been so very helpful to me and to Stanton Industries in the past, I am hoping you can be helpful again in this dire hour."

"In the past," Beauford said, as if the words were distasteful. "Hugh, you must understand; I am willing to help you, and Stanton's, but there are all these rumours going about!"

"I can't help that talk – and Alex and I only wish we could find its source!"

Beauford looked away quickly. "You've had no success?"

"None, in tracing the rumour-mongers." Hugh tried to smile as Beauford switched his interest back with a big, avuncular grin. "But you've already lent us £20 million; you've seen our order-books – except for the Shipbuilding Division, they are still full. Look at

453

the rest of British industry: in comparison with much of it, we are strong."

"Then why do you come to me, Hugh, and ask me to allow you to increase the firms's debts – when it's common knowledge that this strike has brought Stanton Industries to the verge of bankruptcy?"

Hugh found he was perspiring. He swallowed, his collar painfully tight for a moment, like hands around his throat. Beauford had to help; and he had to convince the man who had dealt with them so often in the past – and unless Lord Beauford was a consummate liar, Hugh felt sure he was inclined to assist Stanton Industries, as long as he could justify it financially to the board of his own merchant bank.

"Our problems are temporary and hardly unique to us – look at Rolls Royce!"

Beauford pursed his lips; his pouched cheeks flattened. "Is that supposed to encourage me to risk money on you?"

Hugh realized he had made a mistake. He backed away hastily. "Of course, Stanton's have the problem of the new aero-engine too, but it's a far smaller part of our business than it was of Rolls Royce's."

"And besides," Lord Beauford said politely, "it isn't just a question of my faith in you; of course that's never been in question."

Hugh's heart lifted. "Then you'll –"

"There's also the question of your brash young cousin."

Hugh said nothing.

"Use your authority over him, Hugh; he doesn't know his place, and he's full of mad ideas – always has been. Wasn't he to blame for those two deaths and all the bad publicity? Terrible publicity. You must stop him."

Hugh was almost dripping perspiration; he felt sour heat rising from his body. "The courts have given us a final deadline: we must find £10 million by Monday, 22 February. Then there are our running costs. Unless I come up with perhaps £20 million to tide us over, I hardly imagine I'll be Chairman of the Board for much longer."

"It's not an impossible sum," Beauford said carelessly. "If we were to lend it to Stanton's with the requisite amount of publicity, I think the way your firm is seen would be changed utterly – for the better. Your shares are at rock bottom. Your cousin is regarded as too much of a maverick for my Board members to risk money on any company he's involved with. If, say, Alex Stanton was dismissed from his position in the company, I would invest several million pounds in buying your shares very cheaply. You could do that, too. Borrow

454

from me to do it if necessary. Then the new loan of £20 million could be pushed through within a couple of days, but your company could announce it immediately. The shares would rise – by at least a third, I calculate. We would both make millions."

Hugh knew he had done it; saved Stanton Industries from going under – but the price asked was the betrayal of Alex and the loss of his own integrity.

"Thank you," Hugh said weakly, playing for time. He was frightened, but he concealed it. The foundations of his world were suddenly quaking. He had always thought – been brought up to think – that Beauford and his sort were the finest Englishmen to be found.

Lord Beauford lit a large cigar. "I've recognized the potential in Stanton Industries for a long time now."

"It's good of you to say so," Hugh said calmly. Did he have to sack his own cousin to satisfy this man? Alex, who had risked so much to keep SI going, was to be the sacrifice demanded. Was there really no alternative? Loyalty to the family, or loyalty to the company? Which was more important?

He thought frantically. The money was a necessity, there was no more time to obtain it; and he could find no one else to assist Stanton Industries. Therefore he had to go with Beauford. There was no alternative that he could see in all this wintry wasteland of despoiled hope, broken promises and financial disaster.

Hugh wondered sullenly who he would send to demand Alex's resignation, but then found an iron-hard determination in himself that surprised him. In the name of the family, he promised himself one thing. If Alex had to go, he would tell him so himself. He sighed, hating the thought. All their disagreements seemed unimportant, now. They had been fighting together to try and save the company and he realized now he had enjoyed it.

Beauford had been examining Hugh's face as different expressions flickered across it.

"I'm sure young Alex will find something to occupy his time," Beauford said. He smiled.

He liked his plan. Hugh would be forced to dismiss his cousin Alex. Alex, Beauford had come to think, was a very independent young man, with powerful connections in America and elsewhere. He might even, just possibly, be able to keep Stanton Industries in the hands of the Stantons if he was to remain on the Board, and that, Beauford had decided, would never do.

455

Beauford had other ideas. His Swiss nominee had already bought Stanton shares, very cheaply. As soon as the strike was ended one way or another, the Stanton Board would announce the new £20 million loan: Hugh would be their spokesman. The shares Beauford had already bought at the bottom of the market would soar in price.

Immediately after Hugh's announcement he would sell them, and all his Stanton Industries holdings, and make quite, quite certain that no extra money was lent to Stanton Industries, by Beauford Cleves or anyone else.

He would make a fortune, and the firm would inevitably go under. Beauford Cleves would come up with some plausible explanation for reneging on the deal which would ensure their reputation remained inviolate.

Lord Beauford had excellent contacts, and he had a shrewd idea which firm of liquidators would be appointed after Stanton Industries was bankrupted. He had already made a gentleman's agreement with Saigo Hideki to buy up the parts of Stanton Industries he could make highly profitable by a quick asset-stripping operation, and nobody would stop him – except, perhaps, Alex Stanton, if he was still in the employ of Stanton Industries.

It was a legal way of printing money, he reflected as he beamed at Hugh. As long as you were ruthless enough, you could not fail.

Hugh spoke with surprising firmness. "To suspend Alex from the Board of Directors I'll need another director's authorization. Naturally, I expect that written authorization to be yours."

"Oh, you'll have it, of course. Because I'm sure you'll give me every satisfaction, Hugh."

"Maggie? The weekend starts here."

He was so good-looking she felt weak, but tried to hide it. "You remember that, do you?"

He gave the familiar, thrilling smile. "Your favourite programme – I wouldn't forget that, Maggie. It hasn't been that long."

"It's been long enough," she said, accusingly, biting out the words.

"That was then, this is now. Please don't blame me alone for the past." As always, his gentleness surprised her. Memories came back in a warm flood: Greece in the summer sunshine, Oxford in the autumn mist. "Because I'm not the only one in the dock – am I?"

She admitted it, shivering more from emotion than the cold. "No."

"How have you been?"

Snow swirled past the lamp, casting strange shadows on the pavement. "My mother died, you know."

He came forward and hugged her quickly. "I feel for you, Maggie. My father, my mother – remember?"

"Thanks," she said, looking straight into his eyes.

They held each other for a long time, his zips and buckles hard against her body, then Alex stepped back. "Let me look at you, Maggie."

Under the streetlight she looked tired, and pale, but her beauty – he remembered the long red hair, the eyelashes, the green, sensual eyes he had so much admired – had not faded. Maggie was strangely glad she had not dressed up for this evening, and instead looked like the student Alex had once known, so long ago. "I'm still the same, Alex."

"Now that you appear on TV and run that London magazine?"

Maggie said it again, so that he would understand. "I'm still the same."

"Fine." He laughed, raised his hands. "Where do we go from here?"

She took charge. "Let me take you to one of my old haunts so we can talk properly."

They ended up in the Red House, perched on high stools in the stone-flagged back bar that was supposed to be centuries old. The dark bar was beginning to get crowded; there was a haze of cigarette smoke, loud talk, and rock music. Alex, in a studded leather jacket and massive knee-length boots, shrugged through the crowd to buy the first drinks. He sat down and glanced ironically at Maggie's clothes. "In disguise tonight, are we?"

"I'm looking for a few old ghosts. It seemed appropriate to dress the part."

He raised his glass of beer, and she saw the tip of one finger was scarred. He had a brutal self-confidence, even more than before. "Am I a ghost to you, Maggie?"

"Oh, no," she said breathily. "You're very much alive. Isn't this wonderful! And to think that the Japanese are employing *Battersby*!"

The statement seemed to strike him as incongruous, too. He began to laugh with her. "I suppose he's exactly what they want, if you think about it. Do you reckon they're going to start production here?"

"Foreign capitalists."

457

"They're the best capitalists in the world – at the moment."

Their lively debate warmed her. They gesticulated, laughed. She was no longer cold. Stanton Industries, his family, her family, all here for centuries. It seemed to Maggie for a fleeting moment that they could get together over the strike, settle it, and save Stanton Industries and all its tens of thousands of jobs.

"How are things inside the firm, Alex?"

"Not good," he said, cautiously. He had bought a bottle of the local brown ale and he put both hands around it. "That's no secret. I was hoping Hugh would stand with me, but . . . I sometimes think he's hiding something."

"About your father?" Her nose wrinkled. "Why don't you go straight to Hugh and say that to his face? It might bring matters to a head, and you might find out the truth."

"If there's any truth to be found out," he said wryly.

"What's going to happen, Alex?"

"To Stanton's? I really don't want to close down Shipbuilding, Maggie. Look in the headquarters building sometime, see the museum – it's ongoing history, and it should make all of us very, very proud."

"You're that close to a shut-down?"

"Yes."

"Do you need money?"

"I need millions to keep the firm going." He looked at her measuringly. "How's your dad, running that strike? Still want to bring us low?"

"I don't think so. About your uncle –" She shook her head. "Neither of us wanted that. Not really."

"It was shaming. For everybody." Alex sighed, made a cradle of his hands. "I'd better warn you, a couple of papers have dug up that business about you and me in Greece. It's nothing to do with me, in case you ask."

"Old gossip columns," she said. "It seems so long ago."

"You never married Terry?"

She shook her head and looked into her drink; in the Bloody Mary ice cubes were melting into nothing. "No, I never did. No children. Has there been . . . anybody for you?"

"Not like you, Maggie." He looked sad for a moment. "I suppose you heard about Sarah. She died of a heroin overdose in a miserable hippie shack in India. The Sixties killed her, Maggie."

458

"I suppose you're right. Look at everything! Vietnam, the Bomb, starvation and disasters."

He said kindly, "You used to think you were going to change the world, didn't you?

"Yes. Justice and mercy, and righteousness like a stream. But I think we did change things, a little," Maggie answered. "There's more colour, more freedom – and no turning back."

He stared at her challengingly. "This country can't live on colour and freedom alone."

"No," Maggie said, doubtfully, and knew her beautiful self-belief had been spoiled. "I suppose that's right. Maybe it was all wrong and self-deluding from the beginning. That's what you believe, isn't it? I think things started to turn sour in '68 – both Martin Luther King and Bobby Kennedy shot down, remember?"

He was looking at her, listening with an intensity she found disturbing.

"It's so good to be with you again, Maggie."

Maggie suddenly felt both drunk and cheerful. She lit another French cigarette after offering one to him, though he still didn't smoke. There were roots in people; there was still family, loyalty, right and wrong – nothing had really been lost.

"Likewise."

The people here were younger than she: the same age she had been, when she was coming here regularly. Maggie stood up. A man in a long blue denim coat smiled at her but she ignored him. "It's time for me to go, Alex. I'm tired of everything." She was trembling suddenly.

His voice was low, soothing. "Come with me, Maggie. If only for a cup of coffee."

Maggie could not help responding; she smiled. "Just coffee."

Alex blew her a kiss across the table, and whistled one chorus of a familiar tune. The song had always been a favourite of hers since childhood. She swayed to the remembered beat, tapping a toe on the wooden floor.

> "If I had another penny, I would have another gill,
> And I would make the piper play
> 'The Bonnie Lass of Byker Hill'.
>
> "Byker Hill and Walker Shore –
> Collier lads forevermore!"

459

He laughed. "Very nice. Bonnie lass." Then, to her surprise, he recited the next verse for her.

> "My Ginny she is never here,
> My Ginny she is never here,
> And when I call out, 'Where's my supper?'
> She orders up another pint of beer!"

They had another pint of beer, for the sake of old times and new.

Once outside, she began shivering suddenly. Alex walked away quickly and kick-started his motorcycle, then twisted the throttle so the roar became ear-splitting. He stared at her. Then he shouted. "Let me take you for a ride."

It was like the old days all over again. She walked forward stiffly. "Fine."

Climbing on behind him, she put her arms around his waist as she had done all those years ago with Danny. The engine's note moved up towards the shrill, and she felt as if she were melting inside. Exhaust fumes made her cough. She leaned her cheek on the black leather of Alex's shoulder. He let the clutch out quickly – and the bike almost took off.

The Norton 750 engine was as powerful as a small car's and it was roaring as he threw the bike over, left, left again as soon as they were on the Swing Bridge. She was yelling as the speed raced up. He took the bike down through the cobbled back streets on the Gateshead side. There were few cars here, though she thought she saw headlights behind. Alex rode the machine superbly, his gloved hands light and his head always turning to the mirrors.

Maggie was laughing, now that the danger had passed and she was confident about his skill. She pressed her face against his helmet, her long hair flying. "You really still are the crazy bastard David says you are."

"I'm still what you knew, Maggie," he shouted back at her over the roar of the bike. "That was me, the real me! I'm still the same!"

They crossed back to the north side of the river at Scotswood. After they left the bridge behind, he took her across to the western part of the city. Clouds had covered the sky, and occasionally their back wheel slipped – more frost, she presumed. The cold was certainly biting at her now.

She no longer cared where they were, because all the old anger had started to boil up again. She had been kidnapped, she thought.

460

It was freezing on this motorbike. She had no idea where they were going, and she knew Alex Stanton must want something from her or her family. Like her father's integrity.

But she knew that all the Stantons' money put together could not buy a moment of her father's time nor an ounce of his respect.

They ended up in a tree-lined street of ordinary semi-detached houses. Pre-war redbrick, she guessed. He slowed. Her teeth were chattering and she had to hold him tightly, but the cold did not seem to affect him at all. The engine throbbed as they went up a short, steep private road. Maggie looked up, gasped, as she saw the overwhelming sails of the windmill huge against the starry sky. The house had been converted from a local landmark. There were no lights in the windows. They turned straight into an empty, open garage. Alex kicked down the side-stand, pulled the bike over, and switched off the engine.

The abrupt silence was shocking as a blow. Maggie coughed, got awkwardly off the passenger seat and stood looking around at do-it-yourself tools and car spares. She was stiff and aching; the roar of the powerful engine still echoed in her head and she felt a little dazed.

Alex switched on an electric light and bent down to clang the garage door shut.

Maggie blinked, dazzled.

"I don't think anybody could have followed me here," he said, conclusively. "One of my friends owns this place. Very nice architecture, with a heated swimming-pool. Perhaps we can use that tomorrow." He looked at her carefully. She lowered her eyes, flushing. "Let's go inside."

She found herself following him all the way up the stairs, her hand on the rail. The carpet was thick and soft and the house was tropically warm because its central heating was turned up high. She felt hot, suddenly, flushed.

They stopped at the head of the stairs. The walls were roughly plastered stone; some of the windmill's huge machinery had been preserved inside the restored room. Alex slowly pulled down the huge zip on his black leather jacket, his handsome face under the tangle of blond hair serious and a little fuller than it had been.

"I'd like you to do one thing for me, Maggie."

She said nothing.

He took her by the arm and guided her to the telephone, and dialled a number. He listened, then said, "Will Langton, please."

461

She stared at him as he held the phone out to her.

She found herself taking it, and speaking, though there was a catch in her voice. "Dad, please don't be angry, but I've been talking to Alex Stanton. Maybe it's time you talked to him yourself."

There was a long pause. Alex's hand tightened painfully around her upper arm. His breath rasped in his throat. Then her father said gruffly, "You'd better put him on."

"Mr Langton," Alex said calmly, "I know this may be an imposition, but I think we need to speak to one another. If I ring you early tomorrow morning, will you be prepared to talk to me?"

She heard him say, surprised, "I'll talk. I don't say you and me'll ever agree, but I'll talk. In good faith. And . . ." His voice cracked for a moment. "Just take good care of my daughter, that's all!"

Alex said quietly, "I've never hurt her intentionally and I never will. Thanks for giving me your time. Good night."

He put the phone down. Triumph blazed out of his face.

Maggie said sharply, "This isn't the only reason I'm here, is it? So you can speak to my dad?"

His mouth twitched. "Why do you do it?"

"What?"

"Why do you look at all the people who think nothing of you and want to think the very best of them, while when somebody loves you like I do you always want to think the worst of them? I'm glad you're here, Maggie. God, you don't know what it's been like without you."

She was going to make a blisteringly sarcastic reply – the words formed inside her head – but what her lips said was different.

"Alex, Alex."

He opened the door to the bedroom.

"No!" She was shaking so much she could hardly speak. She started to cry, but her body betrayed her, and told her that these tears were tears of joy. "No, I won't! I *can't*! I hate you, Alex Stanton, I hate you!"

There was no joy on his face, only burning anger. He struck her across the mouth.

"Then let's make hate."

"Bastard!" She hit him back.

He glared into her eyes. "Bitch."

They stripped quickly, throwing their clothes aside. He was hard and ready for her immediately. She felt heat come from his body and she realized that she was trembling violently in his arms.

They kissed, then he pushed her away. She fell onto the bed. He jumped after her and quickly spread her thighs, his hand slipping into her.

"I want you, Maggie."

She was licking at his face, tasting him, wanting more.

What he did to her on top of that bed was closer to rape than to making love.

Nevertheless, when he spasmed into her for the third time, Maggie still held his shoulders tightly, her nails digging in and drawing blood, and before she lost herself in the heat and blinding light of another orgasm she knew her own face wore the same snarling expression of lust and hatred as his.

Nevertheless, she was more than satisfied.

They had made hate, and she loved it, loved it, loved it.

5

Alex turned his collar up as a cold wind whistled through the cast-iron struts of Byker Bridge, dawn breaking behind him. He stamped his feet, rubbed his frozen hands together, his breath a pale plume in front of him. Langton was late. He wondered if his opponent would turn up at all. He sighed, and looked down at the little river flowing towards the the old distillery and run-down warehouses before it all merged into the riverside industrial area, and beyond there was the steel-grey Tyne.

"Bloody cold," he said, as he saw a familiar face out of the corner of his eye.

"Aye. Where's my Maggie?"

"Safe," Alex said.

"Safe in your bed?"

"We were close before, you know; and she's all grown up, now." Alex paused. "What did you think, that I'd kidnapped her?"

"I wouldn't put it past you, Stanton. Except for the bad publicity." Will's face was hard, giving away nothing.

Alex nodded, recognizing that quality in himself. "You must know what she means to me – I see all that's worthwhile in her, just as you do."

Langton, grudgingly, gave a brief nod.

"Let's take a walk," Alex said. They got off the bridge and walked towards the Tyne. "Well," he continued, "not to waste your time – how would twenty per cent suit you?"

"It'd suit me well; if Hugh Stanton made the figure official."

Alex turned around. "No problem. Are you happy with it, though?"

The older man snorted derision. "You'd be surprised how little of all this has looked good to me. I'm not a wrecker, young Stanton."

"Not so young," Alex said automatically. "And I realize you don't control your committee. So, I say again – twenty per cent?"

He put his hand out.

"I'll try," Langton said, and shook the hand of his enemy.

In the room downstairs students were conjugating Russian verbs, their chanting voices loud.

"I think I might have a way", Alan Hoyle said to Robinson, "to get Alex Stanton out of his family's firm for good."

Robinson's look of harassment turned to pleasure. "Just as well. It isn't working out like we'd thought, is it? Even though we put in all that money and muscle."

Hoyle sat bolt upright, flushing. "Like 'we' thought? *You* have to answer for our comrades' loyalty, Robinson."

"Aye. I do." The blotchy-faced man slurped at his tea, not meeting Hoyle's vivid eyes.

Jackie Sutton sat in one corner of the room, frowning at both of them. "Why is Alex Stanton so dangerous?"

"Because", Hoyle said, "he has financial backing of his own, he's tough and he's clever, and he's reasonable. If anybody can save Stanton Industries from going down, it's him."

Robinson clenched a fist. "Bloody Alex Stanton has to be got at, then! Just like Will Langton!"

"Well, why didn't you order it then? You had two of the lads following Stanton!"

Robinson stood up. "And you know what happened to them! Their car was pushed off the road by a bloody ten-ton Stanton truck – and very apologetic the driver was, too."

Only Sutton had remained calm, his eyes flicking from one Forward man to the other. He knew Robinson wanted Will's job and hoped to become national leader of the union: but Jackie had his own ambitions. "How will you finish the Stantons, comrade Hoyle?"

"Loyalty is a precious thing, comrade." Hoyle laughed. "One of the Stantons' people once told me something of great interest to Mr Alex Stanton. Donald Pike, it was, their aircraft designer. If I can find some means of putting it to Alex Stanton, I don't think he'll feel very much loyalty to Sir Edward and Hugh and their firm. More likely he'd want to tear Stanton Industries down as badly as we do."

"That sounds like one hell of a secret," Robinson told him.

"It's literally a matter of life and death."

* * *

465

Maggie stirred to the sound of birdsong. Tree branches tapped at the huge windowpane, as her eyes slowly opened. Even though the curtains were still closed the room was full of sunshine. It was late in the morning, and there must be a window open, since she could smell a wet, fresh odour that reminded her of spring. She loved it as she wriggled in the pool of human warmth in the bed.

Then she came fully awake, clutching the sweat-damp sheet to bare breasts, putting the back of one hand on her forehead. She ached all over. One side of her face was sore, and the worst pain of all came from her scraped-raw knee where the motorbike had gone past an alley wall in Gateshead – the sheet had stuck to the wound where her blood had dried. She sat up in the double bed, suddenly conscious of the fact that she was naked. Her clothes were scattered over a chair by the dressing table, out of reach.

Was Alex in the house? If he was, what could she say to him?

She was terrified that he would think she had been a whore: drunk, cheap, available. But it hadn't been like that. It had been overwhelming, animal lust – something that he had shared. In Alex she knew she had found understanding and love, and an electric sexuality. What else was there to look for?

Maggie dressed quickly, her hands awkward, her movements clumsy, and she found she had lost one of the turquoise earrings Terry had given her last year. Terry. Maggie admitted to herself for the first time that for Terry it had always been different. For him, there had always been other beds, other women. Perhaps he had only ever wanted what he called fun.

She slipped quietly into the bathroom, a stranger in this strange house, and undressed behind the bolted door. The chrome shower hissed steam and piping-hot water at her. She flung her hair back, her red mouth open. It was too hot but it felt cleansing, and so she stayed in the spray, gritting her teeth and running her hands down her bouncing breasts, ribs, thighs. She reached for the shampoo outside the plastic shower curtain, then massaged it deep into her scalp, her nails digging in painfully. Steam curled up from the hot water beating at her body.

Maggie felt angry; angry with herself, the world, and most of all with Alex Stanton. He meant so much to her that she was scared to trust him, and what she felt was so intense she could hardly cope with it, or acknowledge it even to herself.

Maggie stepped out of the shower and dabbed at her wet, naked body half-heartedly with a towel. She brushed her teeth until the gums bled. She disliked having to put on yesterday's clothes, but she had nothing else to wear.

She crept down the spiral staircase, seeing the Bogart and Chaplin posters that hung alongside on the windmill wall but thinking only of the coming confrontation. No one answered her questioning shout.

Alex had gone. Sighing, she realized that the confrontation could be postponed.

In the brown-tiled, sunny kitchen there was coffee bubbling away and a selection of breakfast cereals. The shadows of the stilled sails were short now, as noon approached. Maggie called out for Alex again, but there was still no answer, and it occurred to her for the first time that he might not be coming back.

She poured herself a black coffee and had some muesli, tapping her spoon on the bowl; the Swiss cereal melted slowly into the milk, and she added a spoonful of raspberry jam. She sipped the hot coffee, her wet hair tied up in a towel, and listened to the silence in the house and to the sounds of children playing in the street down the hill. Everyday houses, everyday folk.

She could not help wondering if it would have been like this if she had ever married someone ordinary, and if that ordinary marriage and life would have been good or bad. She knuckled her eyes. Was it really too late for all that?

On the kitchen table was a list in Alex's brutally readable handwriting, and she picked it up automatically.

> $15 million?
> Crédit Lyonnais
> Lazard Frères et Cie
> Banque Nationale de Paris
> Crédit Industriel et Commercial de Paris
> Lombard Odier & Cie
> Credit Suisse

The list continued.

They were all banks in France or Switzerland, but he had pencilled through every name. Except the last – perhaps they had agreed to help! She glanced at her gold wristwatch. Ten-thirty – enough time to ring up somebody with each bank and ask for assistance . . . Enough time, she thought suddenly, to speak to her father.

When the front door slammed shut she gave a guilty start and got up from the table as if she had been caught spying, but Alex said nothing when he came in and put down two pints of milk and that morning's papers.

He smiled, clean-shaven and dressed in rather formal clothes. She sat down at the table, her mind blank. "Want another coffee?" He looked over her shoulder and for a moment she was terrified he was going to kiss her. "Black? I usually take milk and sugar with mine."

Maggie shook her head. Somehow Alex had taken control of this situation.

Alex sat down with her, as if he had done it every morning for years, opened his *Financial Times* and turned to an inside page. He thumbed a headline there. STANTON INDUSTRIES: SUPPORT FROM AN UNEXPECTED QUARTER?

"Looks like you people in the press are finally on the case."

Stanton Industries? Its boardroom seemed a suitable distance from the bedroom here. She took the bait. "What do you mean?"

"Hacker Stanton International have agreed to back us – to the tune of $15 million, for openers. I've started to trawl the banks I've done business with before to find the rest of the money we need to tide us over. It'll not be easy, but I think I can do it. Effectively it's a US–European combination, set up to resist the Japanese thrust into our industry."

Her mouth opened. "You can save your company?"

"I hope to God! I met your dad. We shook hands on a settlement. If I can just hold everything together for a few more days, I have some people with money who'll –" Alex stopped talking.

Maggie still recognized a good story. "Why do you expect these people to help you? You must have called in all the favours you have owing to you by now."

Alex had decided to trust her, it seemed. "I've something to sell, of course. Here, let me show you these patents."

He opened a black attaché case and pulled out two slim files. She saw the official stamp of the Patent Office and memorized the file designations, then dipped casually into the contents. The science meant nothing to her – one of the patents seemed to be about some kind of industrial paint – but Alex was smiling paternally at the folders. The patents had been taken out in the name of Stanton Industries (Shipbuilding Division) Ltd.

"Engines and industrial paint?"

"Two breakthroughs. The paint is superb: it virtually never wears out, and it's almost friction-free. Excellent for ships. If I put my own

468

marketing skills to work, I'll sweep the world. Inside ten years it'll be the only kind of paint used on ship's hulls – and it belongs to Stanton Industries lock, stock and barrel!"

His blue eyes had lit up, and she looked away quickly. She did not want him to see what she thought of his avarice and ambition. He was ignoring the most important thing of all – their future, or lack of it.

Sparrows fought in the garden, and she stood up to see the golden sunlight that poured in through the suburban trees.

"That's really good news. What do you think the patents are worth?"

"Bare minimum, when I sell? I'd say 20, 25 million, US – for each patent. I have a German consortium interested at that price. They'll make much more in the long run, of course, but I need the money immediately. With that money and a new bank's backing, I'll stand off the Japanese." He blew out his cheeks. "Hideki's main interest is getting into the arms market, including warships, and also aircraft."

"How do you know that?"

Alex's voice was flat, feral. "Never mind how I know. I just make it my business to be well-informed."

Maggie pursed her lips, and watched a black cat stalk a pigeon through the neat grass of the garden. The cat's tail flicked, and she felt sure she could see a glint of cruelty in its eyes. Then it pounced, quick as thought, swiping with one clawed paw – but the bird escaped, its blue-grey featheres gleaming for an instant as it whirled up into flight.

"Wouldn't this Hideki be most interested in the patents? After all, he's come thousands of miles, chasing after your technology."

"I don't want to make Stanton Industries any more attractive to him than it already is. He turned up here waving twenty-five million dollar cheques around – he's big league, all right."

Did she love Alex? Did he really love her? Maggie was desperate to know the answer, but kept strict control on herself and let the professional side of her speak. "That and the Hacker Stanton money will let you beat my father."

She heard his barking laughter. "Maggie, I *admire* your father. I only wish there were more people like him in Stanton Industries and in the government. I'm happy to compromise – as long as he is, and he's told me he is."

469

"And you trust him?"

"I told you," Alex said impatiently, his eyes red and tired, "thanks to you we met face to face and shook hands on it." He shook his head as if to clear it. "Sorry. A bit tired."

Thanks to her. Finally, last night made complete sense to Maggie. She shut her eyes and concentrated everything in her will on keeping her voice steady. "That was the real purpose of meeting me, wasn't it? Getting to my father?"

"Oh, no," he said, and she recognized the voice of the man of the world. "I'm here, aren't I? I want more, Maggie. I really enjoyed myself last night. You're bloody marvellous in bed, Maggie. Best exercise I've had for weeks! I've never known a woman like you."

She found her teeth were grinding together and her eyes were stinging. That was an insult, not a compliment. She took a breath, then another, but could not stop herself from feeling that she was drowning; there was no space and no air in this room they shared. "If you can afford to resist the strike, what about the Japanese?"

"That's a different story," Alex admitted. "They mean to have something from the company; they won't go until they've tasted blood, I'm convinced of it. I only thank God Hideki doesn't know how important the patents are."

She opened her eyes. The patents. "I see. But you know, don't you, that my father will never stop fighting you?"

Behind her back he laughed. "I certainly don't! This morning we opened discussions, off the record – I think we'll settle on something like a twenty per cent increase, perhaps a little more."

She could tell it was true. She felt the blood, the betrayal and the anger, throb below her temples. Even her own father . . .

"Maggie," Alex said gently, and now he touched her shoulder, "you mustn't take these things so personally."

She repeated the lesson in a tone the dead might use. "I mustn't take these things so personally."

"Anyway, I need to get back to town right away, so I can't give you a lift home. Do you want to take a note to your father, from me confirming our arrangements, or can you remember what I said? Tell him that we must compromise –"

Take a note to her father? Was he deliberately treating her like a schoolgirl? Maggie leaned her forehead on the cold glass and told

470

herself that she would die before she allowed Alex Stanton to see her tears.

He was whistling as he left, though he still seemed exhausted, and after the front door slammed shut she heard the sound of a car engine, revving up quickly, then fading away down the quiet, suburban street.

She made more coffee, her hands shaking, trying to be calm, picking up the morning paper although the print swam in front of her eyes. Perhaps she was over-reacting. Stanton Industries was very important to Alex, and he had a great deal on his mind . . .

Suddenly her shell of calm snapped and she turned around, wailing, screaming, tears flowing. She had been abused, raped; she realized it now. She had to stop Alex making further use of her family. She knew her father had wanted her back to the North East because she was family, the only one he could trust absolutely, and she had betrayed his trust with Alex Stanton.

Alex had already seen Will Langton, and if her father gave his word he would do anything to settle the strike.

The phone was in her hand: she dialled home.

"Sorry, Maggie," Jackie Sutton told her. "Your dad's gone off by himself and he's not back yet. Something confidential."

Maggie choked back a single sob then flicked through the thick telephone book with suddenly clumsy fingers and made one call. Gathering up the patents she ran outside, standing in the cold under the stark trees. She shook with cold and rage until the taxi that would take her back to her father's house turned up.

She remembered what Alex had said, and she remembered Greece, and she remembered her father's agony over everything that had happened in 1956. She looked at the patents, knowing she could mortally hurt Stanton Industries and hurt Alex Stanton into the bargain.

She had taken it personally.

Maggie knocked on the door numbered 366. The man who opened it was tall and plump, with a pink complexion. He smiled as she handed over the folders, looking quickly at the Patent Office stamps.

"Alex Stanton says these patents together are worth more than $40 million – enough to get Stanton Industries out of its present crisis. But he could be *made* to sell them for much less, couldn't he? Or better still, stopped!"

"If Mr Hideki likes them." Battersby nodded and tucked the folders under one arm. "You see, if a good QC saw these patents, any sale could be held up for weeks ... I'll pass these documents on to my principals immediately."

Maggie remained in the doorway, dressed all in white. She was made up immaculately, her fiery hair piled up strikingly on her head; French perfume ghosted around her, subtle as music. She smiled, but not pleasantly. "He's also asked a foreign bank to help him. A Swiss bank, I think."

"Indeed? No doubt we can put a stop to that."

"I hope so. Because I want to help destroy that man."

Battersby inclined his head. "Dear Alex. And, may I ask, how can you be sure these patents are really valuable? How did you get them from him?"

She did not lower her gaze. "I stole them – after I slept with him, of course."

Afterwards, back in the city, Alex had driven through the picket line so quickly that two of the men had to jump out of the way. The rest stood beside the brazier warming their hands, jeering. It was just past seven, but as Alex crossed the marble floor by the reception desk the uniformed commissionaire beckoned him over.

"Excuse me, Mr Alex."

Alex turned. "Carrack? How are you? Makes a change, this, from London."

The ground floor was still deserted. One of the back rooms held the few night staff, but that was down the corridor close to the Edwardian lift. Carrack seemed uneasy, fumbling, unlike his usual self. He reached beneath the desk and handed something up. "I got this, from a cousin in America. I thought you might like to see it. I hope you won't tell Mr Hugh, sir."

It was a photograph of three cheerful young men, in the RAF uniforms of thirty years previously; the Battle of Britain. They had smooth, self-confident faces, and seemed strikingly young – too young to be in the King's uniform and risking their lives.

Alex glanced at the names. "I had the notion your name was Tom."

"Clive Carrack was my cousin, sir. He just died in America."

Alex turned the photograph over again. It was dated 14 August, 1940, and inscribed *To Clive and Colin – Michael Stanton*. Alex looked at the man, moved.

472

"Your father's the tall man on the left. His wife, your mother, took the picture. The next day, Clive told me, the Luftwaffe sent over 1,500 planes. We sent our boys up to meet them, sir. Colin didn't come back."

Alex handed back the picture. "This is the first time I've ever spoken to anybody in Stanton Industries who knew my father in the war."

"I only met him a couple of times, sir." Carrack lowered his voice. "They were all got rid of, sir. My cousin in 1951, and after your father was gone, most of the other Aviation people except for Pike, who'd been to Peenemunde – the V2 and the V1, sir . . ."

Alex nodded. Pike, the traitor, with a gaping flaw in his character . . . "Got rid of? What do you mean?"

Carrack didn't answer directly. "You know I've been with this firm almost all my life. I should have a good pension coming. Anyway, I've got my cousin's papers, sir. From America. Old diaries, and a report he wrote about the STA-C – and afterwards there was a show down between your father and your uncle and Pike, the designer, and my cousin, sir. My cousin was got rid of. Pike stayed. Pike stayed, and they say Sir Edward paid off some big gambling debts for him."

"You mean Sir Edward was buying his silence, don't you?"

There was no reply from the former flight sergeant.

"Tell me, what was my father like then?"

Carrack looked back into the past; three decades away and more. "He'd be about your age when I first met him, sir. A little younger, maybe. He had the heart of a lion, sir, but he was a gentleman. He loved this company and this country, and if you were his friend he would stand by you no matter what."

"He's dead, but I hope I can live up to that," Alex said soberly. He felt strange, as if a great weight had been lifted from him. Somebody in the family firm, at last, had acknowledged his father's existence, and the contribution he had made. "You guard the door here?"

The man straightened. "That's right, sir."

"Good," Alex said. "I hope I can see you again very soon. Privately. I'd like to hear about the old days."

"I draw a lot of night duty at the moment," Carrack said. "I'd be the only one on duty, mostly, if it wasn't for the strike. But I'd be happy to talk, sir, and tell you anything you wanted to know, and give you my cousin's papers. He's dead now and he was got rid of even though he must have been right."

473

Alex heard the subtle stresses the man put into his words. "There's something I should hear about?" he asked. The memory of Ray ringing up after he raided the archives and found some of the STA-C material was gone came back to him – and then, not much later, Hacker was gone from the firm, too. "Your cousin must have been the Carrack whose report about the STA-C was taken out of the company records."

"Wouldn't know about the records, sir." The main doors opened and one of the Shipbuilding engineers entered. Carrack touched fingers to the brim of his cap, then looked away. He spoke out of the side of his mouth. "23rd April in 1954."

Something icy touched Alex's spine. "The day my father died? You mean it wasn't quite an accident."

"I have some things to give you sir. Concerning the crash." Carrack turned away, his last words so faint Alex could hardly distinguish them. "Not when. How."

Alex went up to his office and stood at the window for a long time, his overcoat on, the fire unlit. A great sadness had welled up in him. He could not imagine that his uncle could have deliberately caused the airliner to crash, and Hugh had only been a boy then, but still the thought nagged at him.

A day of work on the salvation of Stanton Industries did not seem so attractive now. His secretary came in as he was lighting the gas fire. He tossed the dead match into a wastepaper basket, stood up, feeling unsteady on his feet.

"Just leave me alone till twelve," Alex said hoarsely. "Right? No calls at all. Nothing."

He went to the drinks cabinet, poured three fingers of single malt whisky, emptied the glass in three convulsive swallows, then crashed out on the couch. He did not have good dreams.

His secretary woke him at twelve, with a cup of coffee.

"How do you feel now?"

"Rested, a little." He considered. "Not good, though." Then he smiled. "But getting better. Now I'll give you a list of people to get on the phone for me, starting with Hugh. But first, can you show the yard staff in?"

He felt good now. Excited, knowing he was making the right moves. Early in the afternoon Ray Hacker rang up from Bonn. It confirmed the good news; the bank they used in Germany had just signed the agreement to give them a line of credit up to $25 million, against their stakes in Hacker-Stanton Internationl. "And you can use that money to help Stanton Industries, Alex."

"Thank God," Alex said. He had stood up automatically, he was so high on adrenalin. Now he could see the river flowing, four storeys down – history, streaming darkly by, and polluted enough to kill. "Tell them I'll need to draw on $15 million immediately. That might be enough to give us air to breathe till nearly the end of the month . . ."

"How's it going over there?"

Alex had already spoken to Maggie's father twice, and David had gone over to the union office in the city centre to help establish a tentative understanding.

"I'm seeing the first signs of daylight. But I'll feel better when your man gives me his next report on Hideki. I've left several clues so I hope he can turn his attention to a Swiss bank, next. It should take him a long time. The Swiss are very secretive about money."

Ray sounded puzzled. "But we're not using Switzerland."

"No," Alex said, "but I hope to fool Hideki into thinking we are."

"If you bring this off," Ray said, "you'll live for ever."

"If I succeed, I'll deserve to. So, the very best of luck when you go to Iran. My very best wishes to His Imperial Majesty. You should be assured of a good reception. Major Coombes will meet you at the airport." Alex put the phone down, smiling. Then he made a call to Stanton Industries' bank; he wanted that $15 million on line immediately.

Lastly, he rang up the largest of the three suppliers who were suing Stanton Industries.

"Extend that 22nd February deadline, and I'll set six million pounds against our debts to you."

The MD grumbled. "I'd really have to stick my neck out to do that. My board are sick of waiting, and we have our own cash-flow problems."

"But I've $15 million to turn into pounds and give to you. If you agree to wait, the others won't carry on with their law-suit against us."

"No." There was a long pause. "I'm under pressure from the City; they don't like the Stantons, there."

"Is that pressure coming from a bank?"

"It might be," the man said cautiously.

"A bank like Beauford Cleves – I mean, you deal with them too, don't you?"

The man laughed shortly. "If, and I stress if, Lord Beauford should have advised me to get my money out of Stanton Industries before you go bankrupt, that's no disservice – to *my* company."

Alex thought frantically. It was almost certain that Beauford had acted against the Stantons, although he couldn't prove it – yet. "If I can get that six million pounds paid into court by tomorrow, do I have your word that you'll withdraw the suit?"

Alex's hand closed hard on the telephone. This was the crucial question. He had to have a little more time.

Finally the man answered. "If you assure me in writing you have a new source of financial support *and* the money is in the court's hands by the close of business tomorrow, I'll pull out of the legal action completely –"

"Thank you," Alex said. We might be safe, he thought.

But the man's next words dashed his hopes again. "– just as soon as you settle the strike."

"That's a hard condition."

"Right, it is. Hard, but fair."

"Thanks for taking the risk," Alex said. So he had to terminate the strike, and quickly. "And you have my word that you won't regret it."

He hung up, wondering how much time had gone by. There was a slight noise behind him and he turned around in Hugh's leather swivel chair.

The man in the dark suit had a scarred face, and he was Japanese. He looked dangerous; squat, muscular, very light on his feet, and he came quickly towards Alex, reaching inside his jacket.

Alex stood up slowly to meet his fate.

"Well?"

"Some good news, some bad news," the man said.

"Your eavesdropping devices still work?"

"Sure. And I've had a chance to listen to the tapes, now. First, they don't suspect Hacker-Stanton's boys have been listening to them. Second, Hideki may be prepared to pull out. Third, he wants something. Some patents he had copies of from Langton's daughter."

476

"What?" Alex sat down, and swallowed. From Maggie, this morning. "They're prepared to buy, though?"

"Oh, sure. But they'll beat your price down."

His throat was dry. "They just have to give me enough to keep the firm afloat. They *have to*."

The man departed as silently as he had come. In the tall office Alex kept thinking of his dead father and mother as well as the strike. After all these years, memories of the crash on Long Island came back to him. He could not get the images out of his mind, and he was about to pick up the phone to try and find his cousin in their London headquarters when the door to his left opened.

It was Hugh Stanton himself, looking unusually grave. By his side was another dark-suited man. Alex, turning away from the windows with their view of dark sky and darker water, recognized one of the head office legal staff. They had not knocked.

Alex stood up and ushered them both to seats. They sat down, grim-faced for the coming confrontation.

"How did it go with Beauford, Hugh?"

His cousin seemed cagey. "Some good news, some bad."

"I told you that fat – banker doesn't want to help us."

"I don't see it as helping 'us'. I put the firm first."

"You think I don't?" Hugh and the other man exchanged glances. In the half-lit room the century-old blueprints and photographs seemed suddenly much more real than the trivial world of today. Alex felt cold. "There's something on your mind, Hugh."

"I am still the chairman of this company."

Alex sensed Hugh's hostility. "Am I denying that?"

Hugh's lower lip was protruding, but the Stanton stubbornness was in his long, angular face. "I think you're denying my position, yes. Of course you're a family member, Alex, both my father's adopted son and the blood son of his only brother – but on the Stanton Board of Directors your legal authority is only that of any other director."

Alex stirred, tension crawling up from the pit of his stomach. His fists clenched. "So where are the others? The directors who did the work are mostly gone. The only people left now are you and me and LeBlanc and the stuffed shirts down in London."

"That still comprises the Stanton board, Alex. The Board! Not an individual, no matter what your surname is!"

Alex showed his teeth. "Have you come to dismiss me, Hugh?"

477

There was a long silence before Hugh spoke. "I must do what I think best."

Alex's eyes opened wide. "Think what I've done for the firm, Hugh. I can make Stanton Industries great again, if you'll only let me!"

"But I need straight answers, Alex. You owe me that much."

Alex stood, staring directly at Hugh. Equally serious, the cousins faced one another down. "Ask. And then I'll expect some answers from you."

Hugh hesitated, glancing first at the company solicitor and afterwards turning back to Alex. Then he said, "I want to know where I stand with you. I must know – *must know* – if I have your loyalty."

Alex turned to the third man. "It's Mr Dalton, isn't it? My father sometimes mentioned you. If you could wait outside."

Without even a glance at Hugh, the man left, his shoes hissing through the deep-pile amber carpet. The door closed quietly.

Alex was angry. "You have a written notice suspending me, haven't you? Countersigned by, I would guess, Lord Beauford."

Hugh nodded, dignified in the leather armchair, with his hands folded in his lap.

Alex drew breath, his heart beginning to pound. Had Hugh become so jealous that he would turn against his only blood relation on the board – and do it in this moment of supreme crisis for Stanton Industries? Has Hugh actually decided? he asked himself. Is this when the knife goes in and turns in the wound? He felt a hot glow of rage build up. He felt the impulse to seize Hugh and smash him against the wall. His fists clenched as all the anger of a lifetime flooded him.

Then he looked at Hugh, sitting in front of him so grey and distinguished and, he had to admit, decent.

"What do you want, Hugh? If I have moved in over your head, it's only because there's been a power-vacuum in the company ever since your father's stroke."

Hugh jumped up. "You think I'm incapable of everything except *inheriting*, don't you? This goes back for bloody years! Just because you could play cricket and get a few girlfriends, you think I'm a decorative good-for-nothing, whereas *you*, you –" he stopped talking.

"Whereas I feel I've sweated blood and risked my life and earned my position. Yes, that is what I feel, Hugh. But if you take the side of Beauford against the family now, can't you see that you'll destroy us

478

both? I'm almost there, Hugh! The firm might not fail after all. Don't I deserve your gratitude?"

"I deserve something, too."

"I know that!" Alex barked. Both men were sweating now. "Do you really think I want to take the chairmanship from you, now of all times?"

"So I deserve control! You admit it."

Alex shook his head. "No. You don't *deserve* control. But no more do I. If that's disloyalty, then I'm disloyal, Hugh. But who will you swap me for – Lord Beauford?"

Hugh's face twisted, but it was more with desperation than anger. "You mean you're against me?"

"Hugh! It isn't personal. We must, we *must*, have the very best people we can get taking executive decisions. We give work to tens of thousands of families; we are a prime industry in this region. We arm many of the people who defend this nation with their lives. I can't let them down by accepting anything less than the best. You're my cousin, Hugh. I love you dearly. But I love Stanton Industries and everything it represents more. Can't you respect that in me, at least?"

Hugh sat down suddenly and covered his face, but when he looked up again, he was giving a twisted smile.

"An excellent speech, Alex. I never knew you had it in you."

"I've been practising with David," Alex said drily. He looked at Hugh and suddenly they were exchanging wry smiles. Alex touched his cousin's shoulder, wordlessly.

"Stanton Industries . . . Well, you'd better know about the ultimatum Lord Beauford has given me. For whatever reason, he wants you out. If I sack you, he says he'll help the firm."

"*Sack me!*" Alex tried to calm himself. "Is the aid Beauford offers important enough?"

"Vital." Hugh licked his lips. "Enough money to get us out of this trough."

"In that case," Alex said, "tell him anything you want, anything at all – *as long as you have his promise to help our family firm in writing.*" He let the pause grow long. "Do you?"

"No." Hugh grinned ruefully, as Sir Edward used to. "It's all becoming clearer to me, even as we talk. He doesn't want to help us at all, does he?"

"He wants to help himself."

"What do you suggest we do, then?"

479

"I suggest we hang together, Hugh. Otherwise, most assuredly, we'll hang separately. But I'm not promising anything except this: I'll do everything, make any sacrifice of myself and other people, to make this company, this region, this nation great again."

Hugh looked at him oddly. "You really mean it, don't you?"

"Every word." Alex drew breath, remembering Maggie's advice. "But I want something from you now."

"And what is that?"

"The truth, Hugh. The truth you've been concealing so long. Why did you want me out of the firm, and what has that to do with how my father died?"

Hugh had gone pale; there was sweat on his forehead. Now, at last, he did not look away. "That is the price?"

So there was a secret. "Yes, that's the price."

Hugh said nothing for a full minute. "Very well, Alex, I'll tell you what I know. And then you can decide what you'll do."

Alex suddenly felt shaky. He sat down, too. "I'm listening," he said, surprised at the roughness in his voice. He had braced himself, knowing this was going to hurt.

"My father and your father were rivals, all through the forties and fifties. Do you know that?"

"Yes."

"Your father wanted to make our company international, and move into high technology all over the world." Hugh stared at him for a long time. "Perhaps he was right, Alex. And I bet he would have liked Hacker, just as you do."

"What happened? Why did he die, Hugh?"

"That plane, the STA-C, had a design flaw. I don't know the details – but Donald Pike might even have been told to build something into the specifications. At the very least Pike had a good idea what the problem was."

Alex lips ground together. "Pike, the traitor!"

"He said nothing; as my father told him to. You may remember that many things your friend Ray went looking for, years ago now, were missing out of the STA-C files. One of the things missing was a report by a young flight engineer. I think he was called Carrack. He predicted, correctly, that a long flight like the one over the Atlantic would eventually lead to a catastrophe." Hugh held up his hand. "I don't say that's what my father expected, let alone wanted. A simple refusal by the American federal aviation authorities to licence the plane

480

would have done, been enough to stop your father taking control of the firm. Anyway, you know the rest. I don't suppose either of us will ever forget, will we?"

"No," Alex said softly, sickened. "23rd April, 1954. The STA-C disintegrated over the Long Island shore. And my father and my mother were killed."

"I'm sorry, Alex," Hugh said awkwardly. "I really am. It's haunted me for years, ever since I began to suspect, back when you were at Oxford."

"That's why – ?" Alex coughed. "That's why Ray was got rid of?"

"It's part of the reason. I only discovered the facts when my father told me what had happened when he was recovering from his stroke. And I can only say how sorry I am – how the truth has haunted me." Hugh looked at him, and Alex turned away from the compassion he saw in Hugh's eyes. "So that's what my father did, Alex. And I'm his son."

Alex stood up and came over to Hugh. "Yes," he said, "you are."

Hugh stopped himself from flinching back. "I was a boy, then. I swear to you, though it should be obvious, that I had nothing to do with what happened over Long Island."

"I'll get Pike," Alex said savagely. "As soon as this is over I'll tell Carlton that Pike has to stand trial and go down for twenty years without being exchanged, or I'll tell the world about his treachery – and that the Russians stole details of Concorde."

"I understand how you feel," Hugh said. "If you need to know more about the STA-C you will have to ask my father."

Alex's face was haunted. "For the first time in my life maybe there's one piece of truth I don't want to know."

"What about now," Hugh asked, "today? Can we still work together, Alex?"

"For the good of Stanton Industries," Alex said, "I'd make deals with the Devil himself."

"Right." Hugh took off his jacket. "I'll tell our legal friend he won't be needed, and I'll tell Lord Beauford nothing. Let's get to work."

"I'll get the figures from my secretary," Alex said. Then he went back to his desk and picked up the white telephone, dialled a number. "First . . . Ah, Will Langton, please. My name is Alex Stanton."

The other phone rang. Alex held onto two telephones, one white, one black. He spoke into the black telephone. "Somebody wants me? Won't give his name or any details?" Hugh raised an eyebrow. "If he won't give his name, see if you can find out what he wants."

"I don't think it's another journalist," the switchboard girl said, but Alex was already speaking into the white telephone.

"I'm very glad you have that attitude, Mr Langton. The chairman, my cousin, is right here; he will make the offer of twenty per cent official right now – and you'll recommend acceptance? Excellent. Yes, I understand your position. You can't answer for the rest of the committee, but you'll do your best. You've called a formal meeting of your strike committee and so it'll be decided tomorrow afternoon – one way or another? Right." He paused, then bent his head towards the other phone, turning his mouth to it. Maybe this was something to do with Maggie. A wave of anticipation rose up in him. "Put him through. Say I'll be listening." Then he put on a smile and spoke to Will Langton again, concentrating on the man's words.

Hugh unobtrusively took the black phone from his hand. "Hugh Stanton. You had a confidential message for – Hello?" He frowned, as Alan Hoyle hung up on him.

Alex said very slowly, "Listen, I was wondering, if your daughter is there, perhaps I could speak to her . . ."

Hugh saw his face, which had momentarily been hopeful, suddenly fall.

"She won't come to the phone. I see. And she won't say why not? Yes. I – suppose I have to say I understand." He gave a quick, twisted smile, put the phone down gently. Then he spat out one word. "*Whore!*"

He sat behind the desk, trembling. Hugh realized how much Maggie meant to him, even after all these years.

"I'm sorry about that," Hugh said honestly. "I really am."

Alex looked up, his eyes far away. "You know, reconciling myself to you, and maybe even to your father . . . seeing a bit of daylight in our crisis at last . . . I was just hoping it might have come right with Maggie. That's all. Just a hope."

This time Hugh put a hand on his shoulder.

"I wonder who that other voice belonged to, Alex."

Alex shook his head. There was more noise from the corridor below them, typewriters, doors slamming. Most of their staff had been summoned here in preparation for a counter-attack. They would speak to the public tomorrow.

482

"It doesn't matter now." Alex thought again about his father and mother. Sir Edward would have to tell him the truth. And if it did amount to murder? Alex, put the problem into a compartment in his mind, and resumed work, not knowing if he would still be on the side of Stanton Industries next day.

Next morning, Jake picked David up in an old Ford car and drove him straight to meet Hoyle.

When Hoyle spoke, his tone was cold. "I was hoping to get Alex Stanton – neutralized." He was thinking aloud. "Hasn't happened. We haven't beaten the Stantons yet, but this strike is still a great chance for us, David. Wreck Stanton Industries, wreck part of British industry, especially defence industry, throw thousands of men out of work, teach them to hate their ex-employers, their spineless union leaders, that gutless Labour party . . . You can do a great deal with hatred, Davey."

"I know you can," David said, adding silently: Nothing good, though.

"Even Maggie Langton was saying it again in the union office. That Alex Stanton has a lot of far-right contacts; he's dealt with Saigon, South Africa; he's a thoroughly evil, unforgiving man . . . If the strike lasts, him and his kind will be out!"

The two Stantons looked over the material for the planned publicity campaign on behalf of Stanton Industries. There was a long row of tables, display boards and cases.

"The riches of Stanton history," Alex said proudly. "I want people to realize what they'll be losing, if we go down."

They walked by together. Stanton cannonballs, salvaged from the shattered timbers of a Spanish galleon that had beached itself off the North-East coast, after the Armada sent to conquer England had been beaten. Steel Stanton cutlasses, engraved, lethal, also from 1588.

Alex waved a hand over the next table. "Letters from Cromwell, and elegant Stanton firearms. They had gunsmiths, then!"

"Look at that workmanship," Hugh marvelled. Then he turned to Alex. "You got this idea from David, didn't you?"

"Indeed. He's the chap into history and PR, you know."

Then there was India, beginning with a roped-off area filled by the light cannon Clive had used, and tables with brightly-coloured native documents. Next to it, a display board held an eighteenth-century map; Canada, ceded to Britain by the Treaty of Paris, 1763. A Stanton had organized the guns for that victory.

Other tables showed artefacts from the Crimean War, World Wars I and II, Korea.

But the central table carried relics of the Revolution: the fledgling United States against Great Britain.

"I'd forgotten that," Alex admitted, pointing. "Of course, that's a copy; the original was burned back in Oxford."

George Washington's letter acknowledged that the help of the Stantons in arming his men had been crucial. The American colonies had had many friends in Britain, and Abraham Stanton had risked the family's entire future to help them.

"It just shows what an indomitable spirit will do," Hugh said.

"Let's go upstairs," Alex answered. "I need to see what money will do, too."

He had something else to show his cousin there. Journalists from various newspapers invited to the morning conference came over, too. Alex spread out the papers.

"Impressive," the man from *The Times* acknowledged. "You hope for television coverage, too?"

"All over the world," Alex said.

"This will be expensive," Hugh added, "but we believe it will be worth it, to buy the interest of the man in the street – the voter, you see."

The BBC's industry correspondent scribbled in a notebook. "You think your share price will stop collapsing?"

"I am so confident of that," Alex said, "that I've already given my brokers in both Wall Street and the City instructions to buy. I'm using everything I have readily available in the way of capital, and you may quote this figure: two and three-quarter million pounds."

There was a murmur of surprise from the sober-suited men who had begun to crowd around and look over the advertising that said proudly: STANTON INDUSTRIES – STYLE AS WELL AS SUBSTANCE. If Alex Stanton was risking serious money, perhaps his family concern would really be great again. Alex looked around quickly. The atmosphere was changing. For the first time he sensed real optimism here.

* * *

484

Hugh was delayed, speaking to some more journalists from London. When he went up to the fourth floor, there was a telex on his desk and another man in the room with Alex.

Alex waved the message. "Remember, I told you I was able to raise some money out of my interest in Hacker-Stanton. I've used it to quietly terminate the legal action against us. If we can do something about our strike we won't have to worry about Monday, 22nd February any longer."

"God," Hugh said, "you might save us all yet!"

Alex laughed. "I'd better. It's money, Hugh. Everything I've sweated and worked for."

Hugh slapped his shoulder, a surprising gesture for such a reserved man. "It's both noted and appreciated, Alex."

"Of course, it'll take much more than the money I'm putting in – but there's more to come."

"More? Out of your own pocket again?"

"No, from Hideki." Alex gave a rueful grin. "I – have inadvertently interested him in buying a couple of things from us."

Hugh's eyebrows went up; he played up to Alex, deliberately comical. "Mmh-mmh, as they say! But you're certain it isn't a trick of some kind, a tactic to delay us?"

"Very good, Hugh," Alex said. "You're becoming suspicious. Is it a trick?" He laughed, abruptly. Maggie must have been really annoyed. "His money is real enough."

"You seem very sure."

"I am." Alex turned around in his chair to smile at the man unconcernedly smoking a cigar on the other side of the room by the tall windows. "Hacker-Stanton don't mess around, and we employ lots of talent. I've had Hideki's hotel suite bugged, and translations done from the Japanese – by Ray's head of security."

The Japanese dipped his head, his tough, scarred face turning to the two cousins. "My name is Yamaguchi. At your service."

Alex grinned, looking much more relaxed and confident. "This time we know exactly what they're doing, but they're only guessing about us. It looks as if we can forgt Beauford's kind offer for the moment. I'm sure he'd be asking a sky-high price, anyway. Luckily, we're almost back in the driving seat again."

"What about the strike?"

Alex shuffled papers on his desk. "I've read the cost-cutting proposals our management made. McCourt has given them his okay;

485

so has the Board's Financial Secretary. I think we can offer twenty per cent to the union – then after the men have returned we can make the first cuts. Langton and his union people have looked at our books, so they know it's necessary."

Hugh said softly, "Twenty per cent . . . But even at that price, can Langton deliver his members?"

"That remains to be seen," Alex admitted.

6

Early in the morning Alex drove up through the Northumberland countryside, following the Alnwick road towards Craigburn. He had not slept well. There was too much on his mind: his parents, the strike, the future of Stanton Industries – and Maggie.

He did not know how to confront Sir Edward. Uncertainty, rare for him, seemed to sit low in his stomach. Just after eight o'clock he tuned to a radio newscast, to hear: "– and two men were were arrested early today outside the Stanton Industries Shipbuilding headquarters on Tyneside. When their car was searched a crate of petrol bombs was found. Formal charges are expected this afternoon. When asked for a comment about this, as well as the rumour that the Stanton's strike will end in a compromise, Will Langton said –"

There was a squawk of static. Alex raised a wan smile, left his car outside the Craigburn estate, and scrambled over the wall.

He fell softly into a knee-deep snow drift and headed towards the sunrise, towards the house itself. He was following the advice of Sun Tzu and Napoleon; always surprise an enemy. Here the snow was still crisp underfoot; white sparkled everywhere, and the frigid air had a clean, pure taste.

He realized he had missed Craigburn. He circled the house, going through the undergrowth so he would not be observed, and letting himself into the mansion by a rear door. A housemaid spoiled his entrance by dropping a tray of used breakfast crockery on the quarry-tiled floor. Alex pulled his finger out of an open marmalade pot, licked it.

"Morning," he said, dripping. "Sir Edward in the library, is he?"

The girl nodded, struck dumb by surprise.

487

Alex took the back stairs, rapped on the oak door. There was no reply. He called out softly, "It's Alex."

Sir Edward was huddled in his wheelchair, a rug over his knees. He was staring blankly at a book of colourful Bewick illustrations of the birds of the North.

Alex felt like an avenging angel and, at the same time, like a trespasser. He sat down at the table and crossed his legs, though his trousers were soaked and uncomfortable from his walk through the snow.

The old man did not react to him. He traced the shape of a wing with one forefinger, leaning over to concentrate.

"Uncle Edward," Alex said, coldly, but there was no response. "Edward Stanton!"

"Eh?" His uncle turned, cupped an ear. There was no sign of recognition for several seconds. Then he smiled. "Michael! How was America? How's the plane?" His voice was the old, strong baritone of Alex's childhood, and for a moment the old man's grey-blue Stanton eyes flashed.

This time Alex spoke gently. "Uncle, why did my mother and father die? I must know."

Sir Edward sat back from the open book, and his brow furrowed. "Young Alex, my boy. My adopted son. How is Oxford?"

"I left Oxford many years ago," Alex said politely. "I'm on the Board of Directors of Stanton Industries now, and we're in the middle of a crippling strike; the worst crisis we've faced in my time. Don't you remember at all?"

"Of course. Fetch me a telephone. The Suez crisis, and our workmen have downed tools!"

Alex shook his head, sad to see this wreck of a man. "No, Uncle, it's 1971. Think back, please, to the time even before Suez. To 1954, Long Island. When the *Stacey* crashed."

"Ah, yes." There was flash of the old cunning in Sir Edward's eyes, just for a moment. "I suppose you've come to ask about Pike."

Alex, the careful interrogator, said instantly, "He is guilty?"

"Very well. If you must know. It's true."

"True! You mean –"

Sir Edward gave several loud, wheezing coughs. "Yes, I did protect him. The STA-C, it was so close to my brother's heart, and Pike had worked so hard for us. After the crash, what point would there have been in looking for scapegoats? I'd lost a brother, a lovely

488

sister-in-law, and the firm had been hit so hard ... Had to keep up appearances, confidence in Pike, in the STA-1 and 2, the military planes ..." His eyes glazed over, and he stopped speaking.

Donald Pike.

"I think I understand, Uncle." Alex stood up, tried to smile. It was obvious that Hugh, his father and uncle had all been duped by Pike. He turned to go.

There was a shout behind him. "Michael!"

Alex turned, shaken, and looked back at the shivering, half-senile old man. "I have to go. I have to go to work – for the firm."

"Michael?"

"Goodbye."

Alex trudged away from the house. For the first time in years, he was going to visit the family graves.

Thoughts rattled about in his head as he strode on, unusually hesitant as he pushed through the bare black branches that sprang back into place behind him, as if he had never passed this way at all. They were terrible thoughts. He whistled, tunelessly. The old man was only a shell of his former self, and had hardly been able to meet his eyes. Alex tasted anguish. Was his adopted father truly guilty? He could not bring himself to believe that his real father's death had been more murder than accident. It would remain another Stanton family secret. If anyone was to blame, he thought, it must be Donald Pike.

Birds followed him, circling, but he had no food for them. For a long time, hands in his pockets, he stood staring at his father's memorial. White marble, in the white snow. He read off the date aloud.

"23rd April, 1954. New York." He looked up at the sky, not knowing what to do, and wondered what his father would have done, if he had lived to see this crisis in the family. Would there even have been a crisis if Michael had lived? Alex thought back over his own life. With Maggie beside him, many things might have been very different; but it was too late for second thoughts now.

He moved away. The cold air had settled in his lungs, and he coughed as he brushed away snow with his bare hands. This last gravestone, nearly two centuries old, was mildewed, cracked and massive, and he lingered beside it for many minutes.

"Abraham Stanton." He kneeled in the snow to read the inscription. "*God forgive me.*"

489

Alex left by the front gates, walking quickly to his red E-type, not looking back.

Inside the house, standing at the window behind a half-drawn curtain, Sir Edward Stanton was leaning on his stick and sipping hot coffee topped up with whisky. As he heard the sound of Alex's car start up, and listened as the noise receded into the distance, he smiled.

"You still have a few tricks to learn, young man. How else could I make sure you joined us with the right kind of adventurer's heart? Someone had to save the firm. Someone."

He knew now it would never be his own son. He thought back to Michael Stanton, blaming not Donald Pike, but himself. But he did not look at Alex and feel guilt; he felt admiration now, and a great, sad pride in family. In a strange way, he reflected, thinking once more of his brother, after all these years justice had perhaps been done.

He hoped Alex would win, as he deserved.

Police barriers were put up around the union's office. In another hour, the delegates would assemble there to vote on Stanton Industries' final offer.

The committee were still arguing.

Hoyle banged his fist on the table. "Robbo; who authorized them? Bloody fools! Lurking about under the eyes of the police, their car-boot full of petrol bombs!"

"Nobody authorized them, comrade. It was wildcat action."

Hoyle's face was screwed up with rage. They all knew this was the worst kind of publicity possible, and the fear was that the two men, when interrogated, would implicate the Forward high command.

As he sat with the activists in their hotel and watched the ITV news, images flickered through David's mind. He saw Forward's slogans on the banners the men on the TV screen were holding and he heard the angry shouting as they shook their fists and chanted Forward's line on the "sell-out". He gave a grim smile. They had guessed what Langton would be proposing. Their demonstration looked impressive, but he knew there were only a couple of hundred activists in the stage-managed display. The strike had involved tens of thousands of workers. Hoyle cheered himself up as he watched.

"Listen to them," Hoyle said, leaning forward from the edge of his seat and tapping his shoe to the beat of the voices. "No surrender!"

490

David glanced down at the tapping toe. The carpet was worn and faded, the cheap furniture rickety and scarred by cigarette burns. It was a hot and overcrowded room, a setting made to inspire envy and hatred.

David spread his hands, his wedding ring glinting. "Alan, we have three delegates, Langton has four; aren't the others out of the eleven still uncommitted? It looks to me as if surrender or compromise is very much on the cards."

"Stanton Industries is going to go down!" Hoyle turned his head. "Isn't that so, Comrade Robinson?"

The other man ground out his fifth cigarette in a saucer. Several dog-ends were already dissolving in the grey tea. David grimaced at the disgusting sight and hoped his intestines had more resistance. He had been drinking that tea all morning.

"Right," Robinson said, determined, but nervous. He had been chain-smoking for an hour. "I'll get the strike committee deadlocked, at least – then we can get our rank-and-file people to apply *their* pressure. You've done a great job of fundraising, Comrade Hoyle."

Hoyle looked arrogant. "I scoured the earth to get that money. Our friends abroad paid; now the Stantons will pay – in the hardest currency there is."

"A great job," Robinson repeated, though he looked sour. "Our own people haven't suffered too much. They can make the others struggle on. There'll be no surrender today."

David squirmed in his chair. "Isn't the democratic mandate –"

"I don't bugger about with notions like that, Bryant. I act to bring about a workers' state. If smashing Stanton Industries is part of that, then so be it. There's nothing like a little suffering to radicalize people – and nothing like a little comfort to make them self-satisfied."

David stood up in his expensive blue suit. "I resent that. Everything I've got, I've earned, and I've been in this struggle for a long time, too – ask Alan!"

Robinson lit another cheap cigarette and then exhaled the smoke slowly. It curled to the stained ceiling, then expired. The eyes that turned on David then were full of hatred and contempt. "I'm no bloody lah-di-dah student, and I haven't been corrupted by the poison of parliamentarianism. There's only one road to the revolution, and that road leads through blood."

The Manchester man, Jake, dipped his head. "I agree."

491

"This is my country," David said. He remembered Jake was supposed to have killed the watchman in Liverpool, and perhaps others. But he would no longer be cowed. "*Our* country. I want my people to have a say in it – that's all."

"This is the bosses' country, not ours," the big man said. Jake walked over to the curtains of the room and drew them closed, then moved over to stand by the door. His shotgun was inside a leather case standing in a corner. "I wonder", he said, not to anybody in particular, "if somebody grassed our lads."

David reached for the whisky bottle again and gave himself a large refill, tossing in the last of the diminished ice-cubes. The tension in this cramped, smoke-filled room was terrible. He had a headache, and no certainty that his side would win. Langton was very persuasive, and he had the great gift of inspiring trust and loyalty, but David did not underestimate Alan Hoyle.

Robinson opened the door. "I'll be downstairs in the bar, just in case I'm needed before we leave." He looked David up and down and shook his head.

The door slammed. Forward and its two out of town delegates had taken all the rooms here on the top floor. David was suspicious of the hotel; its clientèle seemed to consist of trade union officials and scrupulously polite East European students, and the ground floor reception area had posters advertising cheap holidays on the Black Sea. The manager was a gruff Pole. David felt he was on alien territory here, and alone.

Hoyle suddenly spoke, pointing a finger at David. "Get on your knees."

David's head jerked round. "What?"

"You heard me."

Then the man from Manchester kicked him from behind, hard around the ankles, and pushed his shoulders down. He cuffed the back of David's head and then moved to stand in front of him, holding the shotgun and breathing hard.

"I have this problem," Hoyle said musingly. He stared sourly into his own glass of whisky. "Jake."

The Manchester man aimed the gun, grinning.

David looked straight into the barrel of the shotgun. Further along it, he saw a hand, and a finger that went through the trigger-guard. There was a distorted face above it, one eye closed, the other eye gleaming.

492

"There's a spy in the inner circle, David."

Nausea crawled up from David's stomach. He tasted its acid at the back of his throat. "The lads with the petrol bombs? I didn't even know about –"

"*Somebody* told Langton exactly who our men on the strike committee are. Including the one man he was supposed to think of as his friend; dear Jackie Sutton. Langton shouldn't've changed towards him, should he? Gave away the fact there must be a traitor. I know it must be you."

David tried to mumble something negative. He wanted to say something about phone-taps, investigating jounalists, but his mouth wouldn't work.

Hoyle spoke quietly. "I want you to admit it. Then I want the names of the other people you've been using, and the names of the people you report to."

David shook his head, unable to trust his voice. His eyes began stinging as his sweat ran into them.

Flat, remote, Hoyle's monotone continued. "Of course, you think I wouldn't dare do it here, even if you don't tell me what I need to know. But you're a Judas, David – and like all traitors, a coward. I'm not. I have the courage to destroy you, David, the courage to destroy *everything*. Don't you ever doubt that."

David's reply was small and hoarse, "Alan, I'm on your side – when you succeed, I want to be *there*. I'm not your enemy."

Hoyle was looking at him strangely; his fists were clenched, his eyes wide open. David suddenly realized that the story about Liverpool docks was no tall tale; Hoyle and Jake had committed murder together.

"Everybody in the world who is not my friend is my enemy! Everybody!"

Jake said, "Open your mouth."

"What?"

The cold metal gun-barrel slid between David's teeth. His vision suddenly blurred; his heart stuttered. He was choking, and still the round metal mouth pressed deeper into his throat. He gagged on its size, its taste of cordite, grease and metal.

Hoyle crouched down and looked into David's eyes. "I'm waiting – but not for long. The names!"

The most terrifying thought was this: it might not be quick and clean when the man pressed the trigger and blew out the back of his throat. It could be bloody and slow. David shut his eyes. He would live for minutes, threshing about on the floor . . .

He opened his eyes again. Hoyle stared into them. "One last chance. Confess, or die." Hoyle licked his lips. "I'm under so much pressure, David. I have to be sure."

David gurgled at him, his eyes bulging.

"Pull the gun back."

The gun-barrel jerked out of his mouth, then poked under his chin, tilting his head back painfully. David spoke quickly, frantically, the words spilling out of him. "Alan, it can't be me! I've been with you in so much, you could destroy me with a single word. Do you think I would have risked all that if I was secretly against you?"

He was seeing the plaster ceiling by the time Hoyle spoke again, and the mouth of the gun dug into his throat. It frightened him most of all that he could not see their faces.

"Then use your influence, David. Prove you're with us. Tell Langton over the phone that the strike has to continue."

"Anything," he said quickly. The gun was taken away, then he stood up and made it, shakily, to the table. He pulled the phone to him and dialled the number of the union office. Is it a test? he wondered. Or did they really intend to kill him if he failed to pressure Langton?

It took several minutes, but he finally put the phone down. His hand was a little steadier. He tried to tell himself he was no longer afraid. "I think you'll have to take me on trust, Alan. Langton is refusing to come to the phone; the strike committee is going into session on time."

In a moment, Hoyle had his overcoat in one hand and his case in the other. The other man grinned, pointed the gun at David.

David choked off his scream. "Jake!"

The large man from Manchester pulled the trigger.

Nothing happened.

"Empty," he said. "This time."

David exhaled a rush of breath.

Hoyle looked around impatiently. He had experienced the release of violence, even if only in fantasy, and his mind was obviously on something else now. "Enough playing around. Let's go."

The line from Los Angeles seemed faint, and the conversation to come from another plane of existence altogether. Terry had become a stranger. Everything that worried Maggie – her father, Stanton

494

Industries, her hurt over Alex – could not be communicated to him, and his easy-going, self-indulgent charm failed to work its usual magic. Though he said he was going to see her very, very soon, she put the phone down in a mood of despair.

Maggie could hear the chanting out on the street. "No surrender! No surrender! No surrender!"

Then her father came to the open door of the little cubbyhole. It was afternoon in the union headquarters in the city. "The Stantons have arrived, Maggie. I've got their word; twenty per cent. I'll recommend a settlement on that basis and I hope I'll get the committee to follow me."

Her back was still turned. "If they don't?"

"They have to follow me, Maggie. I have to win against Forward. Otherwise we push on and drive Stanton's into bankruptcy, and no one wins – we all lose."

She turned on him with tears in her eyes, her long red hair flying free. "Dad, you *can't* back down now! You have to bring them down! They're –" She struggled to find a word.

He looked at her worriedly. "Love, whatever happened between that Stanton lad and you, I can't bear it in mind when I conduct negotiations. This strike has to be settled, by compromise."

The bitterness welled up. "But you always warned me they're bad! Forward are right!"

Will rubbed her head gently, as he had done when she was small. He loved her, but he had his duty. "Maggie, this particular fight is unholy. Peace must come."

He turned to go. In the doorway he paused and swivelled round. "I'm opening the meeting now, and the Forward delegates still aren't here: Robinson and that man up from Bristol."

Maggie raised her head and said miserably, "Maybe they won't come. I suppose they want to keep their hands clean if you do settle."

He shook his head. "They will make their presence felt. I have no doubt of that. The idea of civilized compromise – it's all dirty words to them. They won't give up easily."

His words gave her hope. "So the strike might continue to a finish?"

Langton's nostrils flared. "The finish is here, and now."

David looked out into the street. He felt like a prisoner, and perhaps he was. He wondered if Carlton would risk taking the action they

495

had talked about, because if the authorities neglected to act now, he knew Forward could win their battle. This business about the crate of petrol bombs would surely be enough of an excuse for Carlton to move.

East of the city centre and Langton's union office, they trooped out of the little Jesmond hotel into a deserted cul-de-sac; nobody had been told where they were staying. David knew the men of Forward wanted to manipulate the press, not be investigated by it. It was warmer today, and there was the occasional burst of clear winter sunshine.

Hoyle sniffed the air. "I suppose we'd better get over there and take Langton's committee away from him."

They stepped into the waiting minibus. Hoyle went first, then the Manchester man, then Robinson and the slow-spoken Bristol delegate he controlled. David sat down, his hands between his knees, saying nothing. Forward were determined; and he knew what Langton did not, that three of the undecided delegates had been threatened into compliance. Langton would lose his vote and the far Left would take over his committee.

"No more nominees," Hoyle said. "It's time for direct action. One victory, and the workers follow us."

"We have the will to do it, we will do it," David said. "I predict today will be a turning-point for the whole Forward movement."

"You'd bloody better hope you're right," Hoyle said.

Robinson drove towards the end of the street, grinding up into second, and slowed, prior to turning right, and the atmosphere changed as sunlight poured over their faces.

Then two large cars swerved across their path, blocking the street. An unmarked van reversed sharply across the road behind them.

"Christ!" Robinson said as he braked so hard some of his fellow travellers were thrown to the floor.

Men rushed to surround the minibus, and one man pulled back the driver's door and seized the ignition keys. "Police! Special Branch," he told them, "and you're all nicked."

Robinson's face was livid as he turned to David. "I bet this is your doing! I've never bloody trusted you. If it is, you're dead. Your wife is dead. Your children are dead."

David forced words through a dry throat. "I'm innocent. Alan, I'm on your side. I'll prove it!"

There was an ocean of bitterness in Hoyle. "How?" His eyes

gleamed like tiny flames as he turned to David again. "If you're the traitor you'll burn for this. I'll get revenge."

The police, grinning, began to manhandle them out into the street. A bored, loud voice recited the words of the post-arrest caution. Then one of them, a square-faced man in his mid-forties, presumably senior, said, "We've had reports of intimidation, threats, conspiracy to commit arson – and murder."

"You'll never prove none of that!" Robinson barked. "Show me your witnesses! The buggers will withdraw; they'll never dare face the likes of us in open court!"

"We'll see, sonny."

Robinson was pushed up the steps into the large, unmarked police van. David was next.

"Hang on there!"

He was stopped before he was inside. One of the Branch men flourished the long leather case Jake had taken with him from the hotel, then, carefully, using finger and thumb only, pulled out the gleaming butt.

"A shotgun. What's this for?"

Jake answered, sneering. "What d'you think? For shooting."

"You must be the lad they call Jake ... with the record." The policeman let the gun slide back into its case. "For shooting what? And mind your mouth, this time."

"Weasels," the man said, looking sidelong at David.

"Oh, Jake's shot a few of them in his time," Hoyle said venomously, staring at David, too, "and I dare say a few more in the future."

The policeman shook his head. "Take them away and caution them again before you take their statements."

"There'll be no statements from us!" Hoyle snapped. "We know our democratic rights! Isn't that so, lads?"

"Not a word from me," said Jake, who had smashed out a nightwatchman's brains on the dock at Liverpool.

David heard the metal doors of the van slam shut behind him. Then he was handcuffed and shoved into the wire cage. The others mostly turned their backs on him, but not before a boot stamped down viciously against his instep.

Pain was not a worry – but Hoyle was, and his promises of revenge. Everything had gone badly wrong, and now Megan and the two girls were under threat. David stood there, caged, cold metal tight around his wrists, and terror began to well up in him until it was all he could

497

be conscious of, a terror more powerful even than love. He thought of Megan, who had always loved him. What was going to happen now?

Hugh came stalking up, straightening his tie. "We should leave now."

His eyes said the rest. If the strike was not settled, Stanton Industries was finished. Alex met his gaze. Had this man's father once had murder in his heart? Hugh lingered, faintly puzzled by Alex's hesitation. Alex reached a decision.

The two cousins left together, in the black Stanton Rolls.

Langton has his shirtsleeves rolled up. He stared around; he had been here for a long time. In the union office they sat at a large rectangular table. Used teacups and full ashtrays were everywhere, and briefing documents lay in scattered heaps. The discussion had been long and acrimonious; he knew things could still go either way.

"No surrender!" one of the Forward-controlled delegates said.

"Shut your mouth, Matthews, and listen for once." Langton was speaking, standing up; energy and determination flowed out of him; his jaw was set solid as a rock. "I have seen the audited figures; so have you. They don't lie, man! Under the circumstances I consider the Stantons are generous to offer twenty per cent; I am happy to recommend acceptace of that figure. There is also the question of the new working practices Stanton Industries have asked for. I am willing to concede items one, three, four, five and seven on their list. It's become clear to me lately that our industries – and they're really the people's industries, not the bosses' – must be able to compete." His voice was as powerful as his personality. "I therefore move we suspend any further discussion and vote on my proposal to accept twenty per cent and terminate the strike!"

"But what about Robbo and the other –"

"If some of the Forward delegates boycott this meeting, that's no concern of ours. We have a quorum, don't we? We can take a democratic decision now, by open vote in the committee. So let's do it and settle the matter now! I'll call the roll."

"I object to voting at this time!" Matthews said harshly, white-faced.

"Waiting for instructions from Forward?"

"No! But I still object!"

His objection was voted down, but by a surprisingly narrow margin. It was still terribly close. There were nine delegates here, and the vote was five to four against postponing a decision. Jackie Sutton had voted with Langton. Will wondered if the man knew what he thought of him now; he hoped not.

Sutton said, "Are you sure you want to take that vote, Will?"

Langton remained standing. "And why not? We've just agreed."

"You still want my vote?"

"No, lad," Will said gently, knowing Jackie was in the hands of Forward. "I don't want your vote in my pocket at all. I just ask you to be a man about it. Follow your conscience."

Sutton was perspiring. "I'm saying nowt."

"Is that an abstention?" Matthews said at once, triumphant.

If it was, Will knew he had lost – and he would continue to lose for certain if Robinson and the man up from Bristol arrived. He took a deep breath. "Jackie, I'm asking you again."

Jackie Sutton pushed back from the table, his eyes bright. "So, Will, I'm good enough for you to come crawling to me now – but I've never been good enough for your darling daughter, have I?"

Will realized the man in front of him had been in love with Maggie for years, and many things at last became clear. He nailed Sutton with his gaze. "Nobody's good enough for my Maggie. But what's that got to do with anything? If you bloody like her, man, go off and court her. It's up to her – and you. Now, Jackie, I'll ask you last." Will made eye-contact with everybody. "No more postponements; and we must all choose sides. This is an epoch-making judgement. Together, now, we can save Stanton Industries and everything it represents – or we can send it down to destruction and our own fellow-workers onto the dole queues. Now, comrades, where do you stand?"

He went round the table, asking them in turn. Jackie was white-faced. Matthews turned on him. "Are you going to cross Hoyle? You must be mad!"

Jackie Sutton looked at him. "Maybe I'm mad." He stared at Will. "D'you want my vote, then?"

"If you want to give it me. You're a free man, Jackie Sutton. Remember that," Will said. "But don't vote because of me, vote because it's right. Remember, the measure of a man isn't in whether he wins or he loses – it's in how he fights."

Then he voted and Jackie Sutton voted, and together they passed judgement on Stanton Industries' new offer and, by implication, three hundred and ninety years of history.

* * *

499

Alex tried to conceal his impatience. He hated being dependent on other people, especially when events were as important as this. He knew from David that the extreme Left had come to dominate the committee running the strike.

Will Langton himself opened the door to the side office. His craggy face was grave, but Hugh and his cousin automatically stood up in his presence, a sincere mark of respect.

"Well?" Alex demanded.

Langton looked around. "Only two members of the main board?"

"You have both Stantons: what more do you want?"

Hugh said hoarsely, "What about our proposals? Will the men go back to work as we've asked?"

Langton's eyes twinkled. "If we sign the new agreement, can everybody go back to work on Monday? No victimization?"

"You've signed it, haven't you?" Alex shook his hand firmly.

Hugh was overjoyed. "Fetch me a pen, somebody. Work starts again on Monday, without recriminations. You have my word on it."

After the agreements were signed, Alex picked up his Burberry, and was about to leave when Langton came up to him again. The burly older man shuffled about; it was the first time Alex had seen his family's oldest enemy and newest friend look less than determined.

"Mr Langton?"

"Will, lad. Will." His shoulders straightened. "I fought you and yours to the best of my ability, and I'd do it again if I had to."

"I understand you. Exactly."

"Aye. Well, I'd like another word. A private word."

"Fine, though I'm in a bit of a hurry."

The older man hesitated. Then his light eyes glinted and he said it straight. "You know, years ago, when you took my daughter off to Greece . . ."

"I loved her." Alex spoke calmly. "Don't make any mistake about that. And you can tell her so."

Will fumbled at the papers, unused to talking like this. "I love my daughter, you know. Above anything on this earth."

Alex was tired, but he straightened his back and he looked Will Langton in the eye. "I know what Maggie is worth."

Langton's lips twisted, but he forced the words out, not sure at all that he was doing the right thing. "You've annoyed her, somehow. As a woman, do you understand? Aye, you have. But I love her, Alex

500

Stanton. And I know she isn't happy with her life as it stands, man, not happy."

Alex understood. The two men left the building together. There was a florist's opposite. Their eyes met.

"Maggie's still staying at your place?"

"Where else would my daughter be!"

Alex glanced at his Rolex, then at the masses of colourful flowers in the window display. "I won't be long," he said.

After driving about aimlessly for over an hour, Maggie stopped her black BMW on the seafront at Tynemouth. The North Sea was flat, grey, calm, but she remembered the storms she had seen there. Then she started the engine and began the drive back to her father's house. She had nowhere else to go.

There were no demonstrators in front of it; no journalists to waylay her. It was over, then.

She ran up the stairs to her tower bedroom as one of her father's assistants shouted something about a delivery.

She opened the door on Eden. There were flowers everywhere, red, gold, purple. Maggie gaped, then put both hands to her mouth, awed by these fragrant explosions of soft, thrusting colour. She began to touch the pollen-drowned blooms, roses, orchids, carnations, forgetting her hurt. The air smelled wonderfully fragrant here, and suddenly the sunshine flooded in through a break in the clouds.

Someone had put flowers on the windowsills, on the floor, on her bed, on her dressing table – it looked like the entire stock of a florist's. Who could have sent them?

In the largest bouquet she found a signed card.

Then she heard the shouting from downstairs. "The strike's over! Everybody's back to work on Monday morning – their wages up by twenty per cent!"

She looked down at the expensive cream-coloured card. It was inscribed in Alex's handwriting. "'I always pay my debts'," she said aloud, dreamily. "'Love, Alex.'"

He had won everything. Maggie stood motionless, and knew that she could no longer deny her destiny.

Suddenly someone slipped his arms around her slim waist, and she knew who it must be. She closed her eyes as she felt the two hands come up to cup her breasts. Instantly, she wanted him: she itched to make her one demand and she didn't care about anything else except the narrow bed in front of her and the sweetness and excitement it would bring.

She turned around.

"Terry! What are you doing here? I thought you were –"

He took off his tinted sunglasses. There was the light of excitement in his eyes, and the golden sheen of California on his skin. "I'm here seeing you. My surprise. You see, I didn't ring from L.A. at all." He looked at the flowers. "It's lucky I turned up in time to beat off all my rivals, isn't it?"

She let him take her in his arms and kiss her.

It took the Stantons almost an hour to get from the city centre to the Northumberland Hotel. Battersby's telephone call had been pressing.

They had beaten the strike, but they had not yet beaten bankruptcy. Monday's deadline had been averted, but their debts were still huge and the company's treasury was almost empty.

The Stantons were shown into Hideki's suite. He was seated behind a large antique desk, holding a heavy gold pen in his hand. There were no chairs for them.

The Japanese looked up and spoke in his own tongue. His interpreter said smoothly, "Mr Hideki congratulates you over this matter of the strike. He had thought you were close to an abject surrender."

Alex remembered what the listening microphones had told him: Hideki had come here to fight with the gloves off. "You never surrender in Japan, I suppose?"

Hideki's head jerked around. "*Iye!*"

"I seem to remember 1945 –"

"Enough, Alex." Hugh tugged at his sleeve. "It's rude to point." He turned to the Japanese party. "I understand from Mr Battersby that you no longer feel able to go ahead with the co-production deal."

"*No*," Hideki said, this time in English.

Then Battersby said, smoothly, "Of course, Mr Hideki does have other interests in Stanton Industries. He knows you are desperately short of cash, and has heard the courts here have ordered you to pay over a huge sum by Monday or face bankruptcy."

Alex shook his head, though this information was already out of date. "Whose side are you on, man?"

Hideki said something crisply in short sentences, and his interpreter added, "Is there not a company in England, now sadly fallen far, far from its previous greatness, that once had the motto 'Profit is king'? I admire."

Alex looked at Hideki and suddenly bowed. The old man smiled, as Alex had known he would. He realized with a thrill that even the great Saigo Hideki could be taken for a ride.

This time, the old man spoke in English. "I have present, for Al-ex Stanton, and for Mr Hugh. Here." He clapped his hands. Two cardboard boxes were brought and placed on the desk.

Alex went forward, and opened the box. Inside was thick straw, padding surrounding something fragile. He pushed his fingers through it, then pulled out a wonderful, hand-painted ceramic bowl: the lucent oranges and blues glowed. It was perfect, a glorious piece. But he knew that the Japanese often gave presents not from generosity, nor to show gratitude, but to create an obligation.

"Thank you," he said simply, his mind still full of suspicion.

Hideki was glowing with pleasure, perhaps moved by the painted bowl's beauty, perhaps by the prospect of the business to come. "Rosanjin," Hideki said crisply, giving a gap-toothed smile. "1883–1959."

Alex replaced the delicate bowl inside the box.

"Now, I have wish to buy from you. Two patents."

Alex's jaw dropped. He looked stunned. "What?"

The old man touched two folders.

"Maggie –" Alex said, in cold fury.

The interpreter followed the old man's rapid Japanese. "That does not matter now. Stanton Industries is in desperate need of cash."

"Twenty-five million," Alex said firmly. "U.S. dollars. Each. I can sell them to the Germans for that price, and I have the written authority of the Board to do so."

"Ten," said Hideki. "For both."

"Those bloody patents are worth –"

"Nothing, to anybody, tied up in legal action. I can pick up phone now and a lawyer will have an injunction within the hour. You will be able to sell them to nobody, and you *must* have the money they represent, and that soon."

Alex stared at him, knowing he was right and there was nothing to say.

Hugh said awkwardly, "At least fifteen . . ."

"Fifteen?" Hideki was smiling, toying with them as well as the gold pen.

"Nothing less," Alex said. "Or you can fight us, all the way. Not so easy, from as far away as Japan. And I think the publicity, in America also, would be unpleasant for you."

"For sake of good business," Hideki said, "I will go so high. Now, you must sign. Both, please."

Alex picked up the contract and the certified cheque for $15 million. He had to admire Hideki's nerve. "You're very sure you'll win, aren't you?"

"As always," Hideki said softly, the windows behind him full of the west's red sunset. "Very confident, we win. Now, you will both sign."

The two Stantons signed, the elder first. Hideki let them keep the gold pen.

Alex slipped the cheque into an inside pocket; and he seemed unduly cheerful as they drove away in the dark family Rolls. He had the money in the Stanton account within half an hour – as soon as it was telexed through from Tokyo. He took out several thousand pounds in cash and signed for it as miscellaneous expenses. Then he turned to his cousin, flicking through the thick wad of notes.

Hugh looked middle-aged and sombre in his dark suit. "Don't tell me what you'll do with the money," he said. "Bribery and corruption are criminal offences; you break the Queen's peace, Alex."

"As always," Alex told him. He was laughing, his teeth gleaming. "I'm using this cash to throw a party as well. There really wouldn't be much peace for the Queen, if she turned up. Stanton Industries is back, and it's Saturday night tomorrow . . . Now all I need to do is find a jazz band, and get David out of jail."

The blue-uniformed man was a chief inspector, Scots-born; his bushy brows signalled distaste for his forced involvement with strikes, Special Branch, and rumours of covert action under the influence of foreign powers. He shook his head. "I don't understand all this, Mr Bryant. In my book crime's crime, plain and simple. But what Mr Carlton's made us do . . . Moscow, the Middle East. Guns going to the Irish, and none of it can be proved in a court. None of it!"

David was exhausted: he had been allowed to listen secretly to some of the interrogations. The Forward people were not obliged to say anything, and so far they had mostly exercised their rights. "Carlton was sure Hoyle and his thug Jake would crack."

"Well, they haven't," the policeman said, staring at him curiously. "Not so far."

David could read his mind; for an MP, the man was thinking, David was in strange company. He had been taken away with the others mainly so they would believe David was still, in the eyes of the authorities, Forward. But grilling the Forward men overnight might work. Robinson had been linked to the men with the petrol bombs, but so far Hoyle and Jake had avoided blame for anything. David knew that Carlton would try later to use Liverpool against them; and Carlton believed they would crack then, and start denouncing each other.

David was not so sure.

The policeman frowned as he dialled the number and then handed over the telephone.

A voice spoke out of Wales. "Hello?"

"It's me," David said. His voice was breaking. "Megan, I'm still on Tyneside. I can't come back yet. I must see this through. I must."

He heard her crying. Perhaps she had heard he had been arrested with Hoyle and the others. "Where are you?"

"In a police station. Safe. I'm not in trouble. But the crisis has come."

"That Alan Hoyle!"

"You were right about him. You were right about everything. But things have turned dangerous. The police are driving over to the house. I want you to take the children and go with them somewhere. A hotel, a relation, anywhere."

There was a long silence.

"Megan?"

Her voice was appalled. "You've risked even that? Naomi and Julie . . . your own flesh and blood, David."

"It isn't what I wanted," he choked. "But please go. I hope it'll soon be over." He heard the door to the conference room open and he looked up, to see George Hammond in a pinstripe suit. "I have to go, Megan."

"David! Do you have to? Can't you come home?"

"I must," he said, "otherwise all of the struggle and risk will have been for nothing. I'll be in touch by ringing your mother. I'll tell you all about it then, and I'll join you as soon as I possibly can. Goodbye."

505

As Hammond sat down awkwardly, David looked at his watch. It was one in the morning on Saturday; very early. The strike was over, and Stanton Industries had money from Tokyo in the bank. Maybe, just maybe, it was all over.

Hammond opened his briefcase, closed it, opened it again. "You were right about Alan Hoyle and Forward, David. We both know that. But it seems it can't be made a criminal matter."

David closed his eyes. "You don't think they'll confess, do you?"

Hammond looked apologetic. "I have some bad news. Writs have been issued, political pressure applied. Forward has friends in some surprisingly high places."

"Oh, no." David shook his head in disbelief. "What did they say?"

"We have sweated all seven of them, we cut corners and put them in the high-security wing of Durham jail, a couple of them have made admissions about some very minor matters, we might possibly mount a prosecution against Robinson – but the ones who count, Hoyle, and that brute from Manchester, have said absolutely nothing."

"You mean you're letting them go?"

"I'm very much afraid I have to."

David was devastated. Could he convince Hoyle somebody else had betrayed him? If not . . . "*You're* afraid?" he said.

Hammond looked sympathetic.

Then David squared his shoulders. "Very well. I'd hoped to avoid this, but – I'll go into court myself. Get one of your legal people: I'll make my statement now."

Hammond fingered his tie and spoke very gently. "I would not advise that. And I've already taken Queen Counsel's advice. It's all hearsay, not evidence, David."

"But Manchester –"

Hammond was remorseless. "Some crates, allegedly with markings – or so you claim to the court. What was in them? Do you know for certain? Can you *prove* it?"

"I see," David said miserably. And the bullet he still had was meaningless, on its own. "And the murder on Liverpool docks?"

"Hoyle has an alibi, or so he says. And, of course, he has no responsibility to explain his movements to us – he'd just spring a new defence on us in court."

He lowered his head. "So it was all for nothing, was it?"

"No, certainly not. Hoyle and the others know the finger of suspicion is pointing at them – they'll never know in the future if

506

they're being followed, if their telephone is being tapped, if their homes and offices are bugged. What would be more likely to keep anyone on the straight and narrow? Besides, failing to bring down Stanton's today is a serious loss of prestige. And, you never know, Hoyle and his friend Jake must look at each other and know that, given one word out of place, the other person could be responsible for a murder charge and a life sentence."

Hoyle and his companion had watched the dark street for over an hour, since they had parked outside the gates.

Nothing had moved since midnight; and now the calendars would show it was Sunday. They had been bailed and released late on Saturday evening.

"To think those Stanton bastards had parties, while I was slopping out in 'E' wing in Durham Jail." Hoyle frowned. He had called in every favour he had owing to him, and there were plenty of them; a QC flew up from London with a writ of *habeas corpus* from the High Court. At the same time he had used every threat he could, and there were far more of them than favours owing. He had been released along with Jake, but Robinson and others were still in the hands of the police. Hoyle knew they had nothing to admit that could endanger him, though he knew the damage to Forward might well be terminal.

Only Jake could link him to a capital offence: and for high treason, Alan Hoyle remembered, the authorities could still hang you.

That was one reason they had made very, very sure they could not be followed.

The Manchester man looked at the side of the tall building, towards the cast iron railings that protected the directors' car park; the iron motifs with the letters SI in their curlicues. There were still no lights, no cars. "Let's give it another ten minutes, then go for it." He leaned back over the seat and pulled at the three-gallon can of liquid. It hadn't leaked.

There was only the wreckage of celebration in the narrow back street that curved up from the cobbled quayside behind high, blank walls. There was bunting in dirty coils, and stacked by the bins were empty beer and wine bottles left over from the Saturday afternoon festivities the Stantons had hosted after the strike had been settled. Occasionally a prowling cat howled.

"The Stantons must think they've won."

"They have won," Hoyle said. "But it'll cost them. I hear that the McCourt cost-cutting plans are all in a top-floor office here – they'll be part of the Stantons' loss."

"Somebody grassed us, Comrade Hoyle."

Hoyle looked up at the tall Stanton Industries building. The windows were unlit, and except for the nightwatchman sitting behind the twelve-foot doors, the offices would be empty. "I suppose you're right."

"What about that Bryant?"

Hoyle considered, again. The strike committee looked on David as somebody who, having got on in life, would come to despise his roots: Hoyle knew that was not true. And as for self-satisfaction, a back-bencher in Parliament was powerless, annoyingly powerless, in Opposition even more than in government. "I don't think so. No. He was quite convincing, wasn't he? He would have to have been fooling me for years."

"S'pose so. After all, he did help us with the guns and everything; you must have a lot on him." Jake gave a gruff laugh. "Like you and me. Like that bloke dead on the docks at the 'pool."

"Just like you and me," Hoyle said, his voice flat and dead. "You could have me put away for murder, but of course you'd never betray me." He swept a hand forward, changing the subject. "See, now that the strike is over, no police."

"You know everything, comrade."

Hoyle got out, and quietly closed his unlocked driver's door. He had leather gloves on. "Let's go. There's only one person on duty."

Jake left the heavy can by the car, and strolled around the corner up to the twelve-foot Stanton doors. He rang the all-night bell four times, in the prearranged code one of their sources had described to them. Hoyle saw him disappear inside. Then the door closed and it was dark again.

Hoyle listened to the dark lapping of the river Tyne, the distant murmur of traffic on the five bridges.

In three or four minutes the other man came out again, absently wiping off a foot-long iron bar with a soiled handkerchief. There was no light over the door, and no lights inside now. Hoyle heaved up the petrol and they both entered the building, pushing the two tall doors shut behind them.

"Right, you can hump that now," Hoyle said, putting on the low-wattage nightlight. "I'm paying you enough for it."

"I thought it was them Japs paying."

"As long as you get your money after all this, what do you care?"

The bulky man laughed. He had not shaved since prison; there were dark shadows on his face even in this half-light. "I always had a *yen* to earn big money."

"Let's get busy," Hoyle said, glancing briefly at the bound figure behind the reception desk. "He's tied up well, is he?"

"He'll stay here and he'll fry," Jake said. "What's his name?"

"Carrack," Hoyle said absently. There was a moaning through the gag and blindfold. Hoyle kicked him brutally in the face, then turned back to the Manchester man. "Let's lock this bloke up, in harm's way."

They left a trail of blood as they dragged the dead weight into one of the rooms off the main ground-floor corridor. Hoyle left Carrack there, then stood up, dusting off his hands automatically, even though they were gloved.

"I want a thorough job done, but it won't take long. Fire will go up the central stairwell like lightning."

"You've done this before?"

"You're dead right. In Oxford; a long time ago. But this time I'm going to finish the job."

He produced a match, lit two stubs of candles and dripped wax onto the marble floor to fix them there, then blew out the candles. Jake had flinched back.

"Bloody creepy," the other man said. "I could see the flames, like, reflected in your eyes."

"That comes later," Hoyle told him smoothly.

They went to the far end of the ground-floor corridor and spilled petrol all along it and under the doors of offices. The raw reek irritated their throats, and they both coughed constantly. Hoyle left pools of liquid at the foot of the grand stairs and by the ornate Edwardian lift. Then he took a ball of twine from his pocket, rolled it in petrol, and then thumbtacked one end into the drenched carpet and ran off a length past a door marked 'Personnel'. Then he kneeled, cut the candles midway and wound the petrol-soaked twine around the wicks where he had cut into the wax. Jake stared. "I don't like fire."

Hoyle, still on his knees, was giving a death's head grin. He made a motion with finger and thumb then stood up, pushing at his dark hair. "Ten minutes, would you say, after I light the candles? I used two. One of them at least is bound to work."

Hoyle opened up the personnel records room with his stolen pass-key. The other man followed, humming to himself, as Hoyle put the light on. Filing cabinets in civil service grey lined the walls and a line of desks occupied the centre of the room. Three medium-sized safes, probably too old to be fireproof, were set against the far wall. He checked the door. It was a stout one, with a good lock. The window onto the back alley was small and barred. Everything looked secure.

Hoyle turned around in one smooth, trained motion, and smashed a length of lead pipe across the back of the other man's neck.

Jake crashed down at once, stunned but not dead. Hoyle did not want him dead yet. He leaned over him and smashed both wrists. The man made the mistake of screaming, so Hoyle turned him over and struck him three times across the face. There was blood everwhere, and broken teeth coughed out in a spasm from above the shattered, loose-hanging jaw. The eyes, hollowed by terror, stared up at Hoyle.

Hoyle laughed at him. "I don't want you walking away from this one, Jake. Here."

Hoyle lashed at his knees. The sound of bones pulverizing was very satisfactory. This time, Jake only whimpered, his chest heaving spasmodically. Hoyle was breathing hard when he stood up.

"You didn't really think you'd live to collect all that money, did you?" He shook his head, standing by the door. "And besides, you know too much. When we took those machine-guns off the dock at Liverpool it was murder."

The man stared up at him, not believing. The shattered jaw made him gape.

Hoyle pulled at the metal door handle as the other man began wriggling towards him, mewling helplessly and trailing blood. There was stark terror in the room.

Hoyle smiled. "I'll see you in hell."

The door slammed and then the key turned in it. He went to light the candles.

Alex drove by the river towards the quayside building. "There's a man I want you to meet, David, who knows something about my father and how he died." There was a sudden, heavy threat in his words. "I want to know the truth too."

Wind swirled by; he had taken the hood down passing through Byker and the night was still icy cold.

David was urgent and appealing. "Alex, that was twenty years ago! Don't unbury yesterday's horror."

The Tyne glittered, and the red E-type had passed the Customs House with its royal coat-of-arms over the door before Alex replied. "I've tried to forgive, them, I really have, but it's so hard. That was my father!"

"For God's sake," David asked, "what do you want? Revenge and bloody hands? Would you like to live the way your adopted father has had to? There must be forgiveness."

Alex turned to look at him. David was a good man: he had great generosity of spirit. "Maybe," Alex said, his tone much lighter now.

He had to brake sharply as a car pulled out in front of them and spun onto the quayside, speeding along beside the river and the few moored ships.

David stuck his head out. "You drunken bastard! No bloody lights!"

Alex stopped the engine, pulled out the keys. "I'd feel so much better if . . . There's no memory of my father in the firm. No portraits, nothing. It's as if he never existed."

"Today is what counts," David said, softly. "Today, and getting the future right."

"Let me show you McCourt's detailed proposals," he told David, glancing up at the huge dark span of the Tyne Bridge; "and I also have an excellent twelve-year-old malt whisky up in my office."

He unlocked the tall, carved main doors. The smell of petrol hit them immediately. They exchanged glances, knowing what this must mean. David whispered, "Do you think they're still here?"

There was a sudden noise from behind one of the doors on the right.

David pointed at the reception desk. "Look."

A smear of sticky blood came from behind it, and trailed along the corridor. Together they followed it across the marble floor up to a door below the stairs. Alex pushed at it, but it was locked. There was another scuffling sound in the office.

Alex did not hesitate. Rather than waste time looking for the master keys, he kicked the cupboard door in.

Carrack was on his back, threshing like a stranded fish, red blood running down from his scalp wound. David gagged.

"Tom!" Alex said. "Christ! Let's get him out!"

511

They took the gag off, first. Carrack gargled, coughed, then said, "They're going to burn the place down!"

David sat back on his heels. He thought of Alan Hoyle. "Who?"

"A big lad, Mr Bryant, really big. With an accent – Manchester, maybe, some place like that."

"*Who was with him?*"

"I dunno, sir. Some bloke."

So Hoyle would escape this, too.

The first of the candles Hoyle had left burned down to the petrol, and the entire length of the corridor in front of them exploded into flame. Heat struck out; the yellow fire sucked in air noisily, then went tearing up the huge stairs. Immediately, there was an inferno.

Alex lifted Carrack up, propping him against the wall. He had been tied so tightly he could not walk and he was dazed.

David looked at the low wall of flames outside the office. Heat blasted over them. "We're going to have to run for it!"

"Yes." Alex licked his lips. Smoke curled everywhere; the temperature had already soared. "You take Tom's left arm. Ready . . . *run*."

Flames closed in over their heads. The corridor lights suddenly fused, but they staggered on till they reached the reception desk. The fire was being sucked the other way, up the stairwell, and they were away from the worst of it now.

They got Carrack out of the building, though the grey-haired man was a heavy weight. Alex had an arm around his chest, and helped him stagger forward, down the stone steps, till he could sit down on the kerb, wheezing, holding a blood-soaked handkerchief to his head. His hands had felt very cold, and David realized the man must be in shock.

Alex was doubled over in a coughing fit, so David beat him to the phone box by the gate and dialled 999. The heat built up terrifyingly as he waited for the operator to answer. He flinched away from the yellow glow of the fire, sweating.

"Yes? Which service do you –?"

"The fire brigade. I'm ringing from the Stanton Industries building down on the quayside. Send every fireman you can – the whole building's alight! This is a major incident!" Then he remembered how the uniformed nightwatchman had been battered. "The police and ambulance too –"

David ran back to shut the main doors again, to deprive the fire of as much oxygen as possible, then leaned on the doors for a moment, feeling his heart pound. The Tyne glittered, reflecting the lights on the other shore. A car crept by and stopped. David looked around wildly. He could see Carrack, but Alex had vanished. Had he risked the fire again for some reason? It was cold and he heard nothing except the rising inhalation of the fire. Then he saw Alex, now supporting Tom Carrack, moving across the yard. He remembered the head wound and wondered if Carrack was dying.

As David glanced up at the building flames appeared behind the door at the top of the iron fire-escape stairs that led up from the empty car park. He ran around to that side of the building through the unlocked gates, in case there was anything else he could do.

Fire was brightening behind many of the ground- and first-floor windows. It roared, consuming one hundred and seventy years of history; hand-printed maps, model steamships, oil paintings of Stantons and their works going back to the years long before Trafalgar.

Heat and fumes spilled out of the tall building, choking him as tricks of the wind swirled, and the beginnings of a pillar of fire was visible in the dark mirror of the river.

David bent over, coughing, hearing the first, distant clanging of the approaching fire engines.

Then he heard something close by, from the alleyway. He jogged back in front of the grand facade; smoke was now curling up from below the doors.

There was something smashing through the glass of the tiny, barred window to one side. It had a gaping, bloody hole where there should have been a mouth, and behind it the burning room was already full of choking smoke.

"H – help!" it said in a cracked, weakened scream.

David recognized him, suddenly. It was Jake, the man who had taken Hoyle's orders to kill the traitor in Forward. David looked into eyes full of horror. The fire leapt forward into the room and swirled up from the floor. The man's trousers ignited and he screamed again as he flapped uselessly at the flames with his smashed wrists. There was a sudden, sickening stink of burning clothes and hair.

"Help me, Bryant! *Help me!*"

Jake was burning to death in front of him. More windows detonated and the fire roared ravenously, deafeningly. Inside, something exploded in an ear-shattering boom, rocking the entire Stanton building. Flying glass scythed down. David ducked, hearing it land on the

513

cobbled quayside like a tinkling hail. The temperature around him soared.

The man whirled away from the wall of flames, shrieking, pulling himself up to the window with a forearm hooked through the lowest bar. His hair was now on fire and David saw it curl up and crisp. Jake put out his hand for an instant and David automatically reached into the flames to take it.

His strength became manic. He heaved one of the Victorian bars clear out of the crumbling mortar and flung it behind him. The heat was in his lungs like acid.

The man howled as the fire took him around the waist, his free hand beating helplessly at the flames all over his body.

David was screaming himself as he tore at the other bars, uselessly, until the skin on his hands ripped and he was bleeding. There was shouting from somewhere in the smoke behind him. "David! Where are you?"

The man staggered back to the window, eyes white and wide in a blackened face only inches from David's. "Hoyle! *Hoyle!*"

Then the fire engulfed him completely. Its oven heat blasted David in the face and burned his own hair; he was choking. The fire's roar was deafening and only it could continue to live in the room. Its light filled David's vision, blindingly, as he continued to heave at the bars with his scorched hands.

Alex had to pull him away.

Carrack was taken away in the first ambulance. David and Alex watched for another half-hour, as the fierce heat rose high in the night sky, shaking the stars. By the end, several hundred spectators crowded the quayside, behind the two police cars and the four red engines that flashed blue light and sprayed up water from the hoses. Alex stared at the wreckage. Water glistened everywhere now, ankle-deep and cold, and as the flying sparks and scraps of blazing wreckage fell into it they heard an irregular, satisfying hiss. Together, they stood watching, saying nothing, until the fire was out and the building was a charred, soaked ruin of its former proud self. But it was still standing.

Later the same day, a long convoy of limousines left the city and took the Ponteland Road, heading for the regional airport.

In the last car – the black family Rolls Royce – the Stanton cousins sat with David Bryant. David's hands were bandaged, and much of his

514

hair had been sheared away in the infirmary earlier that morning. He was talking into the radiophone.

"A great notion, Megan, though not very practical as yet."

"You're really speaking to me from the back of a Rolls?"

"Oh, yes." He laughed, shortly. "You're all right? You should be, we should be."

"Because that Alan Hoyle has gone?"

"Rumour says that Hoyle's flown out to the Middle East on a fake passport. But he's gone, and most of his cronies are still in custody."

Megan's voice was cracking with emotion. "I heard about you on the news first thing today. You really had to go into the fire to save that man Carrack? You must be very brave, both of you."

"We had to do it," David said soberly. "The one who died . . . it wasn't very pretty." He shut his eyes for a moment. "I should be able to see you by Tuesday night, okay? But I'm a bit singed around the edges. Not a pretty sight."

"You'll always be a pretty sight to me," she said, "because I love you. All right. Take care till Tuesday."

Alex stretched. "Thanks for getting those Forward bastards out of our hair, David."

David smiled tiredly. "Special Branch sweated them for sixteen hours straight; not one of them cracked. But I had a hell of a time, that first night. Hoyle threatened my family . . . He thought I had betrayed him."

Alex jerked upright. "My God, Megan and the kids!"

"I think it's all right, now. When we were in prison, before they took me away, I told him I'd use my influence in the Home Office to get him and the others off the hook – proving that I was really on his side all along."

"Did you?"

"I didn't need to. His friends had him released. Though of course I told Hoyle I did. To prove my loyalty, you understand." David lifted his shoulders; his voice, not surprisingly, was still a smoky rasp. "Alex, there's no evidence against them that could withstand a decent barrister, in spite of George Hammond – Carlton's section head in MI5 – making every effort. Still, the strike is finished, Forward have lost ground in industry. Their man is dead, and Hoyle has vanished. I think the authorities are rather pleased with the way things turned out, except for the murder and your fire."

515

"So am I, David," Alex told him. "So am I. And we'll build the Shipbuilding headquarters up again, never fear."

Hugh shook his head. "There was insurance for that. Think of the loss we have taken on those patents, though."

Alex lounged back and began to laugh as they drove on through the grey, snow-fringed, sleeping fields of northern England. "I assure you, the loss is acceptable to us."

Hugh peered at him, hands on his knees. Then he too began to laugh. "They are worthless?"

"No," Alex told him, "but you might say I talked up their value, and as soon as the Japanese do some serious checking . . . I had to pay a high price myself to buy them; but I paid because it was necessary for the firm. Anyway, I've reason to believe those patents will be obsolete; both the paint and the engine improvements, inside of two years. Hideki'll have to hurry to get his money back. If he hadn't been so greedy, and if he'd checked them out thoroughly, he'd never have paid over all that money."

The cars drew up in the car park behind the main row of terminal buildings. The delegation left their fleet of limousines. The Stantons followed them. A white Boeing 727 in JAL livery was parked in front of the four-storey central building.

They strolled over to see the Japanese off, as they queued to mount the mobile steps up to the plane in a dignified procession. Hideki himself was in the first group, and did not look back.

"To Tokyo," David said admiringly. "To *saké* and *sushi* bars, and the fastest-growing industries in the entire world."

The jet engines began to roar. The plane taxied towards the main runway.

"I will keep that bowl Hideki gave me," Alex said. He straightened, as the plane began to accelerate, and felt the last of the tension leave his body. "I wonder what he meant by it."

"Oh, I think I know," Hugh said. "A mark of respect, Alex, for you and me and the firm. In spite of everything, we survived."

"He taught me so much," Alex said. "I intend to take Stanton Industries to Tokyo, if I can. I'd love to do business there."

David shook his head.

The three of them had turned to go back to the Rolls when a portly, pink-faced man came jogging up to them.

"Battersby!" David spat.

"There's no need to adopt that tone of voice, David. *I* thought we

516

were friends. The thing is, apparently Mr Hideki won't be doing quite the business here he was expecting . . ." He spread his hands and gave a sick, quisling smile.

"And he's dispensed with your services," Alex finished. "And serve you right."

Battersby turned to David and gave him a sly, unattractive look. "Playing with fire, eh?"

"Playing with fire in every sense," David admitted.

"Since I have no money, I was wondering –"

"No," David said firmly.

Battersby's lips twisted with petulance. He came forward. "But I can make you do anything I want! After all, in Oxford –"

"That's what you think, is it?" David punched him in the face.

Battersby sat down, hard, in a puddle. His limbs sprawled out and he rocked backwards. David saw blood coming from his nose; the man wiped at it clumsily, clearly shocked by David's unexpected violence. Colour flooded his face.

"No," David snapped. He had earned the right to be free. "No blackmail this time, or in the future. I'm not scared of you any more."

The three men towered over Battersby, then turned away to head for the Rolls. Alex threw a last piece of contemptuous advice over his shoulder.

"Try *walking* back to London."

Back in their temporary Newcastle upon Tyne office there was a telex from Ray Hacker waiting for them, sent from Tehran.

MAJOR COOMBES VERY HOSPITABLE. THANK HIM FOR ME. NOW EATING CAVIARE ON THE SHORES OF THE CASPIAN SEA AND DECIDING HOW TO BEAT THE TAXMAN. INCIDENTALLY, JUST SOLD SHAH A HALF-DOZEN OF YOUR HYDROFOIL MISSILE BOATS – A NICE $32 MILLION PRESENT. SHAH INTENDS TO MAKE PERSIAN GULF PERSIAN. AM OFF TO SAUDI TOMORROW TO SEE HOW SAUDI ROYALS WILL REACT. I EXPECT THEY'LL WAVE CHEQUEBOOKS AT ME. BEST OF LUCK SAVING THE FIRM. RAY.

Late on Monday afternoon, Maggie got out of the black BMW with her photographer. It was raining, and the line of men shuffled forward only slowly.

517

"Let's start here."

The unemployment office had dropped everything else to take the thousands of newly redundant Stanton employees, victims of the cutbacks in Alex's plan, onto its books, but it would not be enough; they would have to wait weeks for benefit – after the long strike, that meant that families would go hungry, as though it was a hundred years before and not 1971.

Some of the faces were angry. Some despaired, she saw. There was a BBC television crew here, too, taking pictures.

She parted her wet red hair and stepped under the eaves of the building to do her interviewing. The men crowded around the beautiful woman holding a microphone; Will Langton's daughter.

"It's the end, love. It's the end of history around here. The only future is the dole queue."

"I'm fifty-five. I'll never work again."

"My son had an apprenticeship with Stantons lined up! What's to become of him now?"

"The people in London – the politicians and the union leaders and the businessmen?" This man was angry. "They don't give a damn."

Maggie wondered if that was true. Nevertheless, she closed her notebook with decision. "Somebody always gives a damn; they must. I'll make them."

It was the only promise she could keep. To care, and perhaps to make others care. She stood there in the rain as it fell heavier and heavier, big solemn drops coming down like tears. Ships had been built on Wearside since the fourteenth century: now that was almost over. The country had been fighting a war and, almost unawares, had lost the first series of battles. Here were some of the casualties, she thought. The line did not seem to move. Somebody was playing a mouth-organ, mournful and slow – an old Irish air she remembered her mother used to sing. She imagined Alex and David celebrating this, but after years of decline and mismanagement, what was there to celebrate?

Only the headline in the local paper that an old, old friend of her father's came up to show her.

'STANTON INDUSTRIES WILL SURVIVE,' SAYS ALEX STANTON.

Alex stood, arms folded, by the huge window with its view of the Thames. His face was implacable. "I want three things, Hugh."

David watched, knowing that Hugh had no alternative now.

518

Hugh looked pale, but he managed to give a single, stately nod. "The chairmanship, and what else?"

Alex raised a hand. "No."

"More? I can't give you more –"

"I want something done for Tom Carrack and for the family of his cousin Clive; we dismissed the other Carrack with no reference after he was honest about the flaws Donald Pike built into the STA -C. I've already been to visit Carrack himself. I want the firm to compensate him handsomely, and no arguments over the money: that man almost died for Stanton Industries."

"Consider it done," Hugh said crisply. "What is the second thing?"

"My father . . ." Alex became dangerously mild. "I think it's time I knew all about him. Especially how he died. I must have that satisfaction. Will you let me ransack the firm for memories of him, Hugh?"

Hugh's mouth had turned down. "There will be no secrets from you," he said. "You have my word."

"Good. And I want my father's portrait in the boardroom here. Because I want Michael Alexander Stanton restored to his place in the family history."

Hugh sat down, looking decisive and dignified. "That will be done. But what do you intend to do, now?"

Alex relaxed. "In return, I promise this – I will leave my father dead. I know I can't bring him back. Now, the family must stand together."

"Yes."

David was curious. "What's the third thing, Alex?"

Alex stared at Hugh, implacably. "I want Donald Pike dismissed and prosecuted for treason."

"But I can't –"

"No, you can't take him down to the Old Bailey yourself; no more can I. But you can sack the man and tell Carlton that unless Pike is arrested and charged – *we'll tell the papers everything.*" He took a deep breath. "Agreed?"

"Agreed."

"That's all I want, Hugh. And Armaments and a seat on the Board."

"Very good," Hugh said. Then he gave a tired grin. "More than good." He began to laugh. "We've won, you know. *Won!*" Then the chairman's phone rang in the echoing, panelled boardroom. Hugh picked it up. He covered the mouthpiece and smiled. "It's Lord Beauford, Alex. It seems he finds himself able to loan us £20 million."

"The man is the soul of generosity," Alex said.

"Well?"

"Tell him to take a flying leap into his own rear orifice!"

"I'll do that, in my own way." Hugh spoke into the telephone in his most urbane manner. "Naturally, I am most grateful for this offer; I know exactly in what spirit to receive it. It is not, however, a convenient moment to discuss . . . Oh, you'll ring again tomorrow morning? Of course I'll speak to you then, at nine precisely, unless I don't." He put the phone down, smiling.

"I see you're not so pleased as Hugh and I." Alex sat down on the edge of the huge boardroom table, looking at David's drawn face.

"All those redundancies," David said, his dark eyes haunted. "I've helped close down a large part of our region's heritage. I've been part of giving four thousand men their marching orders. For what, Alex? Can you tell me that?"

Then Hugh was on his feet. "I can answer that, David," he said haltingly. He licked his lips. Figures he could master, but any kind of emotion did not come easily to him. "We have done this so that Stanton Industries *and everything it represents* stays in the hands of people who *care*. I've had my differences with Alex before, God knows, but I've learned one thing from all this trouble. He and I, and you, management and men, region and region – everybody in this nation has to stand together. Otherwise we fall.

"But I have nothing to promise except more struggle. Lord Beauford, Hideki, even Alan Hoyle, they are still around, and Stanton Industries and all of us are still caught between a rock and a hard place – but that's what life is about, and I want to live, and I also want the firm and the country to live."

David laughed, and he swung his feet up onto the long table. "But I can't deny it, I feel great. Think of what we did! We saw off Forward; we saw off Beauford and his City cronies; and best of all we saw off Saigo Hideki all the way back to Tokyo!"

They were laughing in unison – the warm, rich laughter that only the victorious deserve.

David sat back in the chair, hearing the river traffic on the Thames below them. "Is it over?"

"Oh, no," Alex said. "Hideki will be back. The shark has scented blood. He has a taste for it." He bared his teeth and looked at them both. "But so have we . . . Come on, I'll take you both out. I intend to celebrate this victory again and again, in the style it deserves."

David looked around at the boardroom portraits of earlier Stantons, raised to conquer. These men had seen Czars and Prime Ministers, Kings and Presidents, come and go. They had known their own disasters and triumphs, and laughed with their own friends after earlier victories. His bandaged fingers clumsy, David began to gather up his papers, still looking up at the row of determined faces.

He said it aloud, feeling certain they would approve. "Stanton Industries *will* survive."